Purchased

with a donation by

Betty and Hardy
Sanders

THE
NOVELLAS OF
JOHN O'HARA

THE
NOVELLAS OF
JOHN O'HARA

THE MODERN LIBRARY

NEW YORK

1995 Modern Library Edition
Biographical note copyright © 1994 by Random House, Inc.
Copyright © 1960, 1962, 1963, 1966, 1968 by John O'Hara
Copyright renewed 1988, 1990, 1991, 1994 by Wylie O'Hara Doughty

"The Girl on the Baggage Truck," "Imagine Kissing Pete," and "We're Friends Again"
are from *Sermons and Soda-Water,* originally published in 1960 by Random House, Inc.
"Pat Collins" is from *The Cape Cod Lighter,* originally published in 1962 by Random
House, Inc. "Ninety Minutes Away" is from *The Hat on the Bed,* originally published in
1963 by Random House, Inc. "Natica Jackson," "Andrea," "James Francis and the
Star," and "The Skeletons" are from *Waiting for Winter,* originally published by Random
House, Inc. in 1966. "A Few Trips and Some Poetry" is from *And Other Stories,* originally
published by Random House, Inc. in 1968.

Jacket photograph by Ann Zane Shanks

Printed on recycled, acid-free paper

Library of Congress Cataloging-in-Publication Data
O'Hara, John, 1905–1970.
The novellas of John O'Hara.—Modern Library ed.
p.   cm.
ISBN 0-679-60167-8
1. United States—Social life and customs—20th century—Fiction.
PS3529.H29A6 1995
813'.54—dc20   95-6795

Manufactured in the United States of America

2   4   6   8   9   7   5   3   1

JOHN O'HARA

John O'Hara was born in Pottsville, Pennsylvania, on January 31, 1905, the eldest of eight children. Even though his father, Patrick Henry O'Hara, was a prominent and relatively wealthy surgeon, the town's elaborate caste system pegged him as "the Irish doctor." Indeed John O'Hara, an Irish-Catholic outsider in WASP-dominated Pottsville, was a rebellious adolescent: he was thrown out of several boarding schools, and a drunken spree prevented his graduation as valedictorian from Niagara Preparatory School in 1924. The following year, O'Hara's world changed completely when his father's death plunged the family into poverty. Gone forever were the young man's hopes of attending Yale; instead he continued working as a cub reporter for the *Pottsville Journal* until chronic lateness (and frequent debilitating hangovers) eventually cost him his job.

Determined to escape Pottsville, O'Hara shipped out as a steward on a liner to Europe in 1927. (At various times in his youth he had found employment working as a soda jerk, running an amusement park, and reading gas meters.) Upon his return he hitchhiked to Chicago; finally in 1928 O'Hara headed for New York City, where he covered everything from sports to religion on a succession of newspapers and magazines, including the *Herald Tribune,* the *Morning Telegraph,* and *Time.* In addition, he worked briefly as a press agent in the publicity department of RKO-Radio Pictures. A lone distinction marked O'Hara's early hand-to-mouth years in New York: in May 1928 he placed his first piece with *The New Yorker,* beginning an association that would continue stormily for four decades. (O'Hara produced more than four hundred short stories in his lifetime and later took great pride in having published more fiction in *The New Yorker* than any other author.) An ill-fated, two-year marriage to Helen ("Pet") Petit, a young Wellesley-educated actress from a well-to-do Episcopalian family, ended in divorce in 1933. This, followed by a wretched stint as managing editor of a magazine in Pittsburgh, left him in near-suicidal despair. Finally resolving to concentrate only on fiction, O'Hara sequestered himself in a Manhattan hotel to write a series of integrated short stories that became, instead, *Appointment in Samarra*. An instant success when it was published by Harcourt, Brace in 1934, O'Hara's first novel was praised by Ernest Hemingway, F. Scott Fitzgerald, and Dorothy Parker. As John Updike has observed: "*Appointment in Samarra* is, among other things, an Irishman's revenge on the Protestants who had snubbed him, a book in which O'Hara had taken his own advice to his fellow Pottsville scribe Walter Farquhar: 'If you're going to get out of that God awful town, for God's sake write something that will *make* you get out of it. Write something that automatically will sever your connection with the town, that will help you get rid of the bitterness you must have stored up against all those patronizing cheap bastards.' "

The success of *Appointment in Samarra* made O'Hara attractive to Paramount Studios as a screenwriter, and he began the first of a sequence of jobs with major Hollywood film companies that continued into the 1950s. *Butterfield 8,* another popular novel, followed quickly in 1935, along with *The Doctor's Son and Other Stories,* his first collection of short fiction. Yet the 1930s remained a restless time for O'Hara until in 1937 he married Belle Wylie, the daughter of a socially prominent Manhattan physician descended from an old Southern family; thus began the writer's lifelong connection with the Episcopalian enclave of Quogue, Long Island, where the Wylies maintained a summer residence. (The couple's only child, their daughter, Wylie, was born in 1945.) Although O'Hara's next novel, *Hope of Heaven* (1938), was a failure, he quickly rebounded with *Files on Parade* (1939), a volume of short fiction that solidified his reputation as a master of *The New Yorker* short story. *Pal Joey,* his 1940 collection of epistolary tales about a New York nightclub entertainer, served as the basis of the Rodgers and Hart hit Broadway musical, for which O'Hara supplied the libretto. Two more volumes of stories—*Pipe Night* (1945) and *Hellbox* (1947)—ensued before he returned to longer fiction.

A Rage to Live (1949), O'Hara's first "Pennsylvania novel" since *Appointment in Samarra,* was a bona-fide bestseller, yet its success carried a price. A devastating review of the book in *The New Yorker* by Brendan Gill caused O'Hara to sever ties with the magazine— and abandon writing stories—for more than a decade. During the 1950s he published two minor novellas—*The Farmers Hotel* (1951) and *A Family Party* (1956)—as well as two major novels: *Ten North Frederick* (1955) won the National Book Award, and *From the Terrace* (1958), which O'Hara regarded as his major achievement as a writer, was a blockbuster bestseller. Although devastated by his wife's death in 1954, O'Hara married Katharine ("Sister") Barnes Bryan the following year and soon moved to the countryside near Princeton, New Jersey.

In 1960 O'Hara returned to *The New Yorker* with the novella-length story "Imagine Kissing Pete," which became part of the trilogy *Sermons and Soda-Water* (1960). Over the next ten years, O'Hara's output of short fiction was prodigious and established him as one of the finest short-story writers of modern times. Six popular collections of his new stories appeared: *Assembly* (1961), *The Cape Cod Lighter* (1962), *The Hat on the Bed* (1963), *The Horse Knows the Way* (1964), *Waiting for Winter* (1966), and *And Other Stories* (1968). Many critics felt that the mainspring of O'Hara's genius was his unerring precision in capturing the speech and the milieux of his characters, whether the setting was Pennsylvania, Hollywood, or New York. "The work of no other writer," Lionel Trilling once wrote, "tells us so precisely, and with such a sense of the importance of communication, how people look and how they want to look, where they buy their clothes and where they wish they could buy their clothes, how they speak and how they think they ought to speak." Less memorable, however, were O'Hara's novels written during the 1960s: *Ourselves to Know* (1960), *The Big Laugh* (1962), *Elizabeth Appleton* (1963), *The Lockwood Concern* (1965), *The Instrument* (1967), and *Lovey Childs: A Philadelphian's Story* (1969). When John O'Hara died on April 11, 1970, he left behind some fifty unpublished stories that were brought out posthumously in two volumes: *The Time Element and Other Stories* (1972) and *Good Samaritan and Other Stories* (1974). Likewise, *The Ewings,* the novel O'Hara finished shortly before his death, came out in 1972.

CONTENTS

SERMONS AND SODA-WATER

◆

FOREWORD

I am perfectly well aware that each of these three novellas could have been made into a full-length, 350-page-or-more, novel, and since the question is bound to come up, I shall try to answer it in advance: why did I choose the shorter form? The first, and probably the best, answer is that I wrote them this way because I wanted to. It is the answer that other authors will understand. However, I had reasons other than that. The form is one I like in spite of its unpopularity. Edith Wharton, Thomas Mann, Ernest Hemingway, Carl Van Vechten, David Garnett and James Hilton are among the few who have used the form successfully, but how few they are when you consider how many full-length novels are published in any one year, and the authors I have mentioned cover roughly fifty years. The resistance to the novella form comes from the non-professional public, the men and women who want their money's worth when they buy a book, and whose first test of a book is its avoirdupois. I don't quarrel with that right; the buyer of a book may set up any test or standard, or none at all. It is, of course, too bad that he must miss some good writing through the hefting test. I trust—but not too confidently—that a vast number of people will forget to weigh these small volumes.

I have another reason for publishing these stories in the novella form: I want to get it all down on paper while I can. I am now fifty-five years old and I have lived with as well as in the Twentieth Century from its earliest days. The United States in this Century is what I know, and it is my business to write about it to the best of my ability, with the sometimes special knowledge I have. The Twenties,

3

the Thirties, and the Forties are already history, but I cannot be content to leave their story in the hands of the historians and the editors of picture books. I want to record the way people talked and thought and felt, and to do it with complete honesty and variety. I have done that in these three novellas, within, of course, the limits of my own observations. I have written these novellas from memory, with a minimum of research, which is one reason why the novella is the right form. I am working on a big novel that will take two years' research—reading, correspondence, travel—but it is my practice to be writing while I am doing research, and by the time I am ready to start writing the longer book, I may well have written two shorter ones. It will take me two years to *write* the longer book, and at fifty-five I have no right to waste time. Two years' research could mean a lot of wasted time while I wait for answers to letters and go on trips and yield to reading distractions that have nothing to do with the material I need for my longer, longest novel. That one *will* pass the hefting test, if it comes to pass.

I dedicate these books to my wife, Katharine Barnes O'Hara, and to my daughter, Wylie Delaney O'Hara, who sustain me.

JOHN O'HARA

Spring 1960
Princeton, New Jersey

THE GIRL
ON THE BAGGAGE TRUCK

♦

When I was first starting out in New York I wrote quite a few obituaries of men who were presumably in good health, but who were no longer young. It was the custom on the paper where I worked that a reporter who had no other assignment was given this task, which most reporters found a chore but that I rather enjoyed. The assistant day city editor would tell you to prepare an obit on some reasonably prominent citizen, you would go to the office library and get out the folder of the citizen's clippings, and for the remainder of the afternoon you would read the clippings and appropriate reference books, and reconstruct a life from the available facts, keeping it down to forty lines or whatever length the subject's prominence had earned. It was good experience. One time I had to look up Jack Smedley, one of the richest oil men in the United States, and I discovered that his folder was so slim that you could have mailed it for the price of a two-cent stamp; while a Bronx politician of almost the same name had six bulging folders that cluttered up my desk. Later, when the two men died, the rich man was a Page One story all over the world, and the Bronx politician got thirty lines halfway down the column on the obituary page. You got what in more recent times was called a sense of values.

It was through an advance obituary assignment that I first learned that Thomas Rodney Hunterden was born in my home town. I had never known that, and my ignorance was certainly shared by most of my fellow townsmen. The baseball players, concert singers, vaudeville performers, Grade B Wall Street figures, clergymen, army officers, gangsters, and other minor celebrities who were natives or onetime residents of the town were always claimed with varying degrees of civic pride. The people in my home town not only remembered its former residents; they also clung to the memory of the famous visitors to the place—Theodore Roosevelt, John Philip Sousa, Colonel William F. Cody, Ruth St. Denis and Ted Shawn, Ignacy Paderewski, Harry Houdini, DeWolf Hopper, E. H. Sothern and Julia Marlowe, the Borax 20-Mule Team, a stuffed whale on exhibition in a railway coach, the dirigible *Shenandoah,* two reigning Imperial Potentates of the Ancient Arabic Order of the Nobles of the Mystic Shrine, James J. Corbett, Arthur Guy Empey, Leopold Stokowski and the Philadelphia Orchestra, Paul Whiteman and His Orchestra, Billy Sunday, Dr. Frank Buchman, Dr. Russell H. Conwell, and William Jennings Bryan, to name a few who had passed through or over the town. The people of my town were as quick with reminiscences of a suffragan bishop who lived in New England as they were with stories about a whoremaster who operated in Atlantic City, and it just was not in character for them to forget Thomas Rodney Hunterden.

The next time I was home on vacation I had a beer with an old-time newspaper man who knew everything about everybody. "Claude, did you ever hear of Thomas R. Hunterden?" I asked.

"Thomas Rodney Hunterden, d, *e,* n? Sure. Why?"

"Did you ever know him?"

"How would I know *him?"*

"Because he was born in Gibbsville, and he's about your age."

Claude shook his head. "He wasn't born in Gibbsville. I'd know it if he was," said Claude quietly.

"I could take some money away from you on that," I said.

"I'll bet you a new hat."

"No, no bet. I *know."*

It was afternoon, and the public library was open till nine in the evening, so we had a few more beers and then went to look up Thomas R. Hunterden in *Who's Who in America.* My friend Claude

Emerson, who was half Pilgrim stock and half Pennsylvania Dutch, was so miserable at being caught in an error that we went back to the speakeasy and drank more beer, but he was not so talkative. Several weeks after I returned to New York a note came from Claude.

Dear Jim:
If Thomas R. Hunterden claims to have been born in Gibbsville, the man is a liar. I spent an entire day at the Court House in among the birth and tax records. No one named Hunterden was ever born in Lantenengo County since records have been kept, nor has anyone paid taxes under that name. You have aroused my curiosity. Wish I could track this down. If you get the opportunity to interview Hunterden, would be much obliged to hear what you learn.
Yours sincerely,
Claude Emerson

The opportunity to interview Thomas R. Hunterden was a long time coming. I was fired from the paper and it was several months before I got a job as a press agent for a movie company. My interest in Hunterden was non-existent until one morning when I was at Grand Central Terminal, meeting the Twentieth Century Limited. Charlotte Sears, who was one of my employer's not-quite-top stars, was coming in on the Century, and I was there to handle the reporters and photographers. There were three photographers and a reporter from the *Morning Telegraph,* and we were a little group down on the platform, conspicuous only because the photographers had their cameras out and camera cases hanging from their shoulders. The fellow from the New York Central press department came to me with the information that the car in which Charlotte had a drawing-room would be at a point farther up the platform, and our group accordingly moved on.

I noticed casually that a tall gentleman in a Chesterfield and carrying a silver-mounted walking stick was standing at approximately the point toward which we were headed. He paid no attention to our group until he saw the cameras, then there was no mistaking his reaction for anything but panic. He saw the cameras, he put a yellow-gloved hand to his face, and he quickly walked—almost ran—past us and up the ramp and out of sight. I vaguely recognized him as a man whose photographs I had seen but whom I had not seen in person. In a minute or two the Century pulled in and I had other things to think about than a man who did not want his picture taken. I had my job to do.

I reintroduced myself to Charlotte Sears, whom I had met on previous occasions, and we posed her sitting on a baggage truck with her legs crossed and an inch or two of silk-stockinged thigh showing. The little man from the *Telegraph* asked her the usual questions about the purpose of her visit, the future of talking pictures, the rumored romance with an actor who everyone in the industry knew was a drug addict and a homosexual, and the chance of her doing a stage play. The photographers and reporter finished their jobs and Chottie Sears and I were alone. "I have a limousine to take you to the hotel," I said.

"I think I'm being met," she said.

"I'm afraid not," I said, guessing. "I think the photographers frightened him away."

"Mr. Hunterden? Oh, Lord, of course," she said. "But he *was* here?" I immediately identified Hunterden as the man with the cane.

"Yes, he was here," I said. "But as soon as he saw those cameras . . ."

"Of course. I should have warned him. All right, Jim, will you take me to the hotel? Have you had your breakfast?"

"I had a cup of coffee," I said.

"That's all I've had. Have breakfast with me."

On our way to the hotel I told her about the interviews we had scheduled for her and the public appearances she was expected to make. "I hope you haven't booked me for any evening engagements," she said. "If you have, that's your hard luck."

"A charity ball," I said. "At the Astor."

She shook her head. "Nothing in the evening. Tell Joe Finston I have other plans."

"*You* tell him."

"All right, I'll tell him. And believe me, when Finston knows who the plans are with, he won't raise any objections. Well, *you* know. You saw him at the station. To think how close he came to getting his picture in the papers. That was a narrow escape. I should have warned him. Do you know him, I mean personally?"

"No, I've never met him."

"He hates reporters and those people. He has a positive aversion to them. Are you married, Jim?"

"No."

"I know you weren't the last time I was here, but things happen fast in this life. Why I asked is, while I'm in town will you do the honors? Take me out and so forth?"

"That's no hardship, and it's what I'm paid for anyway."

"The only trouble is, you'll have to sort of stand by. I won't know when I'll need you."

"I could guess that," I said.

She took a bath while breakfast was on the way to her suite and I was disposing of the telephone calls from high school interviewers, jewelry salesmen and furriers. "No call from that certain party?" she said.

"Not unless he was pretending to be from New Utrecht High," I said. "Or maybe he was the man just in from Amsterdam. I don't know his voice."

"You don't have to know his voice," she said. "The manner gives him away. He's used to giving orders."

"So I'd infer, although I have nothing to do with the stock market. Eat your breakfast. It's a cold and wintry day."

"I wish he'd call, damn it."

"He will. Have some coffee."

"What do you know about his wife?"

"Mrs. Thomas Rodney Hunterden, a name on the society pages. A doer of good works, I gather. That's all. I could look her up if you want me to."

"No, I just thought you might have some information offhand."

"I don't get around in those circles," I said.

"You and me both," said Chottie. "The way I was brought up, anybody that finished high school is in society."

"Oh, come on," I said.

"Really," she said. "I can do simple arithmetic and I read a lot, but that's the extent of my culture. And travel. It's a good thing I liked to travel or I'd have been bored to death by the time I was twelve. But I liked it. Split weeks in Shamokin and Gibbsville, P A."

"Be careful. That's where I come from."

"Shamokin?" she said. "The Majestic Theatre."

"No, Gibbsville."

"The Globe. I played the Globe in vaudeville, twice, and I did a split week in Gibbsville with a road company of *The Last of Mrs. Cheyney.* You didn't happen to catch me in that, did you?"

"I'd left there by then," I said. I do not know why I refrained from mentioning Gibbsville as the birthplace of her Mr. Hunterden. I think it was because she was upset about the photographers at Grand Central and nervous about the telephone call that had not yet come.

"I was young for the part," she said. "But I was glad to get the job. I had to get out of New York. I don't mean I had to because I was forced to or anything like that, but there was a young polo player in love with me. A strong infatuation, call it. He was a nice kid, but a kid. His parents made life very difficult for me."

"Threatened you?"

"Anything but. They belonged to the school that thinks a young man ought to sow his wild oats, and I was his wild oats. Tame wild oats. I didn't have a bad reputation, and they sort of approved of me as Junior's girl friend, just as long as I didn't show any signs of wanting to marry him. Oh, I visited them and I went for a cruise on their yacht. But then I began to ask myself, what was I? What was I getting out of it? I was a combination of nursemaid and mistress. It was a dandy arrangement—for them and for Junior. Then I began to get sore. I hate being a chump. Other girls I knew would have taken him for plenty. They figured I was just too nice to be that kind of a girl. So I got out of New York."

"But why? There's something missing here."

"Because I was beginning to get a little stuck on the kid and there was no future in it. I wasn't in love with him, but he had charm and I wasn't going out with anyone else, so I began to get stuck on him. But two weeks on the road and he was nothing to me, nothing." She had a sip of coffee. "When I'm on the road I'm a great sightseer. I go for walks. Other people on the bill, or in the company, they travel all over the country, thousands of miles, and all they ever see is the inside of one theatre after another. All they ever read is *Billboard* and *Zit's*. Maybe the *Racing Form* and the *Christian Science Monitor*. But they never read the local papers, or books or magazines. Some of them don't even bother to read their notices, because half the time the hick critics are on the take from the local theatre manager. Those that aren't, they pan everything. We got one notice on *Mrs. Cheyney* that didn't even know Freddie Lonsdale was an Englishman. What a business!" The telephone rang. It was Joe Finston, welcoming the star to New York and inquiring whether she was being well taken care of.

She hung up. "Joe Finston. That heel. Last year he'd have been here in person, but the grosses are down on my last two pictures, so he uses the telephone. This call was to soften me up. He'll be nice to me because he wants to talk me out of my contract, but fat chance he has. I have three more years to go, raises every year automatically. The only way I'll let him out of the contract is if he pays me one hundred per cent of what the contract calls for."

"You know what he'll do, don't you?"

"Sure. Put me in one stinker after another till I holler for help. But it won't work with me. I'll be on the set and made up at six o'clock every morning. I'll go on location to Patagonia. I know all the tricks. Stills that make me look fifty years old. But I worked a lot harder for sixty dollars a week than I do now for six thousand. Finston doesn't know that. Finston isn't show business. He's a picture-business nephew. He doesn't realize that it would be cheaper to settle the contract for a hundred per cent on the dollar now than put me in four or five stinkers."

"Would you settle now?"

"Did he tell you to ask me that?"

"No."

"Then I'll tell you, yes. I'd settle now, this minute. Do you know how much I have coming to me on the contract? Only $1,488,000. That's forty weeks left of this year, and three more years with raises. If you figure interest, that's over a million and a half. I won't get it. He won't settle. But he'd be much smarter if he did, because if you put a star in a stinker you have a bigger stinker than if you had no star."

"You said it. Would you quit the movies if you got all that money at once?"

"Nobody ever quits the movies, Jim. They go into enforced retirement. The talkies killed off those that couldn't read lines or had voices that wouldn't record. But they didn't quit. A queen doesn't—what's the word?"

"Abdicate?"

"Abdicate. And that's the way you're treated while you're a star. Like a queen. Bring in those grosses, and you're treated like royalty. Begin to slip a little, and choose the nearest exit. But that isn't abdicating. That's escaping from the angry mob. I'll do what others have done. I'll take the money and come back here and wait for a good play. The difference is, if you have a flop on Broadway, it doesn't count against you the next time out. And if I happen to get a hit on Broadway, the next time I go to Hollywood I'll start at ten thousand! And maybe Joe Finston will be the one who pays it. Wouldn't that be nice?"

"It sure would." I got up and looked at the scrambled eggs that were being kept warm over an alcohol burner. "You sure you won't have some solid food?"

"All right," she said.

I started to dish out the eggs and the telephone rang. "You want me to go in the other room?" I asked.

"I'll go."

We both guessed it was Hunterden, and we were right. She went to the bedroom and was gone about fifteen minutes. When she came back she was calm and self-possessed. Whatever had been said on the telephone, her composure was now that of a star. I dished out the eggs again and she ate a big breakfast, speaking very little. "I was hungry," she said. "I want to go to the theatre every night I'm in town. Will you arrange for the tickets? I may not *get* there every night, but when I can't, you take some friend of yours. Here." She handed me a $100 bill.

"What's this for? I'll get the tickets from a scalper and have them put on your hotel bill."

"Your expenses."

"I put in an expense account at the office."

"I'm trying to give you a little present, you idiot," she said.

"Oh. Well, thanks. I can use it. Thanks very much."

"I should thank you. You got me through a difficult two hours. Imagine what I'd have been like, missing him at the station and then sitting here fidgeting."

"You go for this guy in a great big way, don't you?"

"I guess I do. Why else would I give a darn? Why else would I keep all my evenings free?"

All this was thirty years ago, as remote-seeming to many people today as the Gay Nineties had seemed to me. New York now is as different from New York then as New York then was from London. The one pervasive factor in all our lives was Prohibition, which made lawbreakers of us all and gave a subtly conspiratorial, arcane touch to the simple act of dining out. Even that was phony, for there were only a few speakeasies which you could not talk your way into, where you had to be known. Indeed, it is harder to get a table at the best restaurants today than it was to gain admittance to the illegal cafés of those days. The other pervading factor, whose influence has been exaggerated in retrospect, was the national greed, the easy dollar in the stock market. But Prohibition, with the speakeasy, and the stock market, with the lucky dollar, facilitated romances like that between Charlotte Sears and Thomas R. Hunterden. Men like Hunterden have always had mistresses like Chottie Sears, but the speakeasy made it all so much simpler and the stock market paid the bills.

In the beginning I mentioned an oil millionaire whose newspaper clippings failed to fill a single folder. That was not true of Thomas R. Hunterden. His record filled three or four folders, and when I visited the library of the newspaper from which I had been fired, and checked what I had read, I now noticed that not a single clipping was dated prior to 1917. According to the other information available, Hunterden was in his early forties when the United States entered the war. His age had kept him out of the army draft, but there was no mention of any war activity whatever, either in his clippings or in the standard reference books of the period. In his brief *Who's Who* sketch he stated that he was born in Gibbsville, Pa., on April 2, 1876, and educated in "public schools" but did not say where; and there was no mention of his parents, a most unusual oversight if it was an oversight. The next item stated that he married Alice Longstreet in 1919. If there were any children they were not mentioned. After that followed a list of corporations of which he was board chairman: American Industrial Corporation, British-American Transportation, Throhu Petroleum, Omega Development, and Omega Holding. He then listed his clubs: the New York Yacht, the Bankers, and several golf and yacht clubs in Florida and South America. The only address he gave was his office on Lower Broadway. The Social Register provided one additional bit of information: Alice Longstreet was not her maiden name. She had been married to a man named Longstreet and her maiden name was Alice Boyd.

I then looked up all the Longstreet clippings and I found what I wanted. In 1918 Forrest Longstreet committed suicide by jumping from a window in his office in the financial district. Surviving were his wife, the former Alice Boyd, and two daughters. Longstreet had been quite a fellow. In the clippings he was often described as the sportsman-financier, prominent clubman, big-game hunter, aeronaut, foxhunter, and so on. He had played football at Harvard and had once set a record for driving his racing car from Rome to Paris. The newspaper photographs of him showed a handsome man with thick black hair and eyebrows, a black moustache, and white even teeth. The pictures confirmed my guess that he had been a wild man. It was not a particularly shrewd guess; the clippings gave the clues. Sporting accidents, expeditions into Africa, a suit for breach of promise, a swimming race from the Battery to Bedloe's Island. I was too young and too deep in the Pennsylvania mountains to have heard of Longstreet, but now he interested me as much as Hunterden, and I knew that in finding out about the one I would be learning about the other.

I had a speakeasy friend named Charley Ellis, who was my age and who was my principal connection with New York society, as I was his with the Broadway-theatre-newspaper world. Charley had a job that he did not take very seriously, and he was easily persuaded to have me to lunch at his club.

"Why the sudden interest in old Forrest Longstreet?" he asked, when I began to question him. "Not that he was so very old. I guess he'd be about fifty-five or -six if he'd lived. He was a friend of my old man's."

"Did you know him yourself?"

"Oh, sure. He used to take me for rides in his car. He had a car called a Blitzen-Benz. We'd go like hell out the Vanderbilt Parkway and on the way back he'd give me cigarettes. Now that I think of it, I guess he was my godfather. Yes, he was."

"Why did he do the dry dive?"

"What's this for? You're not going to put it in the paper, are you?"

"What paper? I don't work for a paper any more."

"No, but you might again. This has to be under the hat."

"It will be."

"Well, Forrie Longstreet was mixed up in some very suspicious stock promotion, and when he killed himself his family gave out the story that he did it for the insurance. The insurance was supposed to pay back his friends that went in on the stock deal. Actually, they were paid back by other members of his family. He blew all his own money, but the Longstreets still had plenty and they came through. My old man collected something, I know."

"What about his wife?"

"What about her?"

"Well, how did he leave her fixed?"

"Oh. Well, it didn't really matter, I guess. She married a fellow called Hunterden, supposed to be in the chips."

"Which one don't you like? Hunterden, or Longstreet's widow? You're holding out on me."

"I know I am, Jim. I don't know what you want this information for, and I liked Forrie Longstreet. Let him rest in peace."

"I think Hunterden is a phony. I know he is, in some things, and I want to find out how much of a phony. I have no intention of writing an exposé, or giving it to the papers, but I've had my curiosity aroused. He's having an affair with Charlotte Sears, and I like her. It's none of my business. She's a big girl now and not a great friend of mine, but she's on the up-and-up. I did a little digging on Hunterden and I happened to come across Longstreet's name."

"Charlotte Sears is much too good for him, but as you say, if she's having an affair with him, what business of ours is it to interfere?"

"Not interfere, but be ready when the roof caves in. She trusts me, and she's a good egg. Would you like to meet her? I'm taking her to the theatre tonight. Meet us at Tony's, twelve o'clock."

"I've met her. She was going around with Junior Williamson a couple of years ago. Not that she'd remember me, but I'd like to see her again."

We said no more about Forrest Longstreet or Thomas Hunterden. Late that night Charlotte Sears and I went to Tony's, a speakeasy that was a meeting place for theatrical and literary people, and Charley Ellis joined us. He was too polite to remind her that they had met in the past, but she remembered him and he was pleased. "What's Junior up to these days?" she asked.

"Oh, he's talking about going into politics."

"Is that his idea, or his wife's?"

"His, I guess. He doesn't know what to do with himself."

"I guess when you have as much money as he has, it gets to be a problem. You don't feel like making any more money, and if you're in love with your wife, you don't go on the make. At least not yet. But he will. There isn't much there, you know. This may sound like sour grapes, but Junior's a mama's boy."

"That's no secret," said Charley Ellis.

"Maybe not, but it's the secret of his charm."

"How could it be?"

"A man wouldn't understand that, Mr. Ellis. As soon as a girl discovers that Junior's a mama's boy, every girl thinks she's going to be the real mama."

"A strange way to look at it."

"You're talking to somebody that learned it through experience. Oh, well, he was a nice kid and I guess he always will be. The women will vote for him. Once. What's he going to run for? Governor?"

"He hasn't said, but I doubt if he'd run for governor."

She laughed. "I could defeat him."

"You'd run against him?"

"Hell, no. I'd support him. The minute I opened my mouth the Democrats would thank me for saving them the trouble. Can you imagine the horror at Republican headquarters if I came out for Junior?"

"You should have been a politician," said Charley.

"Should have been? I am, every day of my life. Ask Jim. In our business Al Smith wouldn't last a minute. By the way, Jim, Joe Finston is taking me to lunch tomorrow, apropos of nothing at all."

Two acting couples invited themselves to our table and in a little while we all went to the Central Park Casino. Before saying good-night Charley Ellis asked me to meet him for lunch the next day, and I said I would be glad to.

"That was fun last night," said Charley Ellis, at lunch.

"Yes, we didn't get home till after seven. We went to Harlem."

"I have to go through the motions of holding down my job," he said. "She's a good egg, Charlotte Sears. Confusing, though. I kept thinking she was still carrying the torch for Junior Williamson."

"Maybe she is."

"She's wasting her time. I didn't want to say anything, but Junior has his next wife all picked out already. Sears is right. There isn't much there. I like Sears."

"Yes, I can tell you do. Why don't you grab her away from Hunterden?"

"Somebody ought to. Hunterden is bad business."

"Take her away from him. She liked you. She said so."

He smiled. "She said so to me while I was dancing with her. As a matter of fact, Jim, and very much *entre nous,* I'm seeing her to-night."

"Good work," I said. "Fast work, too."

"Well, I thought it was worth a try. Maybe she just wants to talk about Junior, but we'll get on other subjects."

"I'm sure you will. I wonder what she plans to tell Hunterden," I said. "You know, I never got the feeling that she was in love with Hunterden as much as she was afraid of him."

"He's bad business. And you want to hear about Forrie Long-street. He didn't kill himself over money."

"You more or less implied there was another reason."

"It was his wife. Forrie was a wild man. Cars and airplanes and all that. But he was crazy about Aunt Alice. We weren't related, but when I was a kid I called her Aunt Alice. Absolutely devoted to her, Forrie was. And apparently she was in love with him till this Hunterden guy came along. Hunterden went to Forrie with a business proposition that looked like easy money, just for the use of Forrie's name, and that's how Hunterden met Alice. Forrie lost his dough, his good name, and his wife, all to the same guy. My old man told me Alice didn't even wait six months before she married Hunterden. But I guess she's paying for it."

"How so?"

"Everybody dropped her like a hotcake. My mother wouldn't have her in the house, even before she married Hunterden. My mother of course was one of those that knew what was going on between Alice and Hunterden, and I gather she had a talk with her, but Alice wouldn't listen. You think you come from a small town, but what you may not realize is that there's a very small town right here in New York, composed of people like my mother and father. They never see anyone outside their own group and have no desire to, and believe me, the gate was closed on Alice Longstreet. The portcullis is lowered and the bridge over the moat has been raised, permanently."

"I see her name in the paper all the time."

"Yes, and you should hear my mother on the subject. 'Alice still doing public penance, I see.' That's what Mother says about Alice and her charities."

"How do the boys downtown feel about Hunterden?"

"Depends on what boys you're talking about. My old man and his friends give him the cut direct, and any time they hear he's in anything, they stay out of it."

"How did he get in all those clubs?"

"There's a funny thing about clubs. If the right people put you up, a lot of members hesitate to blackball you. The members figure that a man's sponsors must have their own good reasons for putting him up, and the members are inclined to respect those reasons, even in a case like Hunterden's. And there are some clubs he'll never get in."

"This one, for instance?"

"Oh, hell, this isn't what it used to be. I mean it isn't as hard to get in. There was a time when all the members knew each other. Now as

I look around I don't even know all the guys my own age. This is where Forrie Longstreet used to hang out. I'll take you upstairs and show you some pictures of him."

"I've seen some. He was a dashing figure."

"In everything he did. He belonged in another age, when all gentlemen carried swords."

"I don't know, Charley. In Walpole's time fellows like Longstreet got into debt and had to do business with guys like Hunterden."

"So they did, but the Hunterdens never met the Longstreets' wives."

"I wonder."

"Well, maybe they did," said Charley Ellis. "You *like* to think things were better long ago."

"Better for whom?" I said. "Two hundred years ago I wouldn't be sitting here with you."

"If you say that, you know more about your family two hundred years ago than I do about mine. I'm not an ancestry snob, Jim. Maybe you are, but I'm not. My objection to Hunterden isn't based on who his grandfather was. Neither was my father's or mother's. It's what Hunterden himself was. And is. I consider Charlotte Sears more of a lady for dropping Junior Williamson than I do Alice Longstreet for marrying Hunterden. When I was in prep school I remember seeing pictures of Charlotte Sears, before she had a reputation as a movie actress. Around the same time Alice, Aunt Alice Longstreet, was a beautiful lady who was a friend of my mother's. But now Charlotte Sears is the beautiful lady, and Alice Hunterden is a social climber, trying to climb back. And having hard going."

"Very instructive conversation," I said. "And that isn't sarcasm."

"A little sarcasm. You know, Jim, people from your side of town, they choose to think that all the snobbery is concentrated in people like my mother and father. But all my father and mother want to do is see their friends and mind their own business. That's the way they like to live, and since they can afford it, that's the way they do live. And incidentally, money has very little to do with it. I know damn well my old man has friends that don't make as much money as you do. But they *are* his *friends*. Whereas, on Broadway, and the Hollywood people, a big star doesn't want to be seen with anyone that isn't just as big a star or a little bigger. And among those people there's nothing worse than a has-been. With my father and mother there is no such thing as a has-been." He smiled to himself.

"What?" I said.

"I said to the old man this morning that I'd been out with Charlotte Sears last night. 'Tell me about her,' he said. 'What's she like?' He's never met her, but he's seen her movies and plays, and he was really interested. But he doesn't want to know her any better, and neither would my mother. That isn't snobbishness, but you might think it is, and I guess Charlotte would too. You're the snob of us two."

"Why do you say that? It may be true," I said.

"One night when you took me to that place called Dave's Blue Room."

"I remember," I said.

"We sat down at a table, a booth, and you knew everybody there. They all said hello to you and they gave me the cold stare till you introduced me. 'Charley Ellis, of the *Daily News.*' Then they relaxed."

"Why was I a snob? Maybe they were, but why was I?"

"Because you were embarrassed in your own crowd, to be seen with somebody that wasn't a member of the crowd. You had to explain who I was. If you hadn't been a snob, you'd have just introduced me as Charley Ellis, or even Charley Ellis, customer's man at Willetts & Ellis."

"You're right," I said.

"Well, Charley Ellis, customer's man, has to make a few phone calls, but if you'd like to hang around for a while I'll play you some pool."

"Thanks, but I'm going up to see La Sears. She has a fan-magazine interview at four o'clock. Any message for her?"

"Just that I'm looking forward to seeing her tonight."

Chottie's maid let me in and I had a half-hour wait before Chottie turned up. It was immediately apparent that her luncheon with Joe Finston had not gone well. "Do you know a good cheap gangster that's looking for a night's work?" she said.

"I know several. Your candidate's Finston?"

"Who else? He offered me a picture that's been turned down by everybody on the lot, and of course when I said no, he said he was going to offer it to me by registered letter, and then if I turned it down he'd put me on suspension."

"That's what you pay an agent for."

"I know, but my agent is on the Coast and this little maneuver is all Finston's, in New York. Oh, I'll figure out something, but this heel, this nephew, Finston, he's doing all he can to spoil my visit. He wants to get out of the contract and then show his uncles what a smart boy he is. To show you how cheap he is, he said if he wanted to, he could legally notify me in New York, today, and if I refused to do the picture, I'd not only go on suspension. I'd even have to pay all my expenses while I'm here."

"Well, from what I know of him, he'd do it."

"Jim, you stay out of it. I know you're on my side, but I don't want you to lose your job on account of me."

"Finston won't fire me, not right away. He wants to get some personal publicity in the New York papers and he's convinced I'm the one that can get it for him. Chottie, I haven't been with the company very long, and you have, but I know something you may not know."

"What's that?"

"Finston has his eye on the Coast. He'd do anything to get in the production end. But his uncles don't want any part of him out there. They don't even like it when he takes trips out there. Don't forget, it's his mother that's a Rosenbaum, not his father. The Rosenbaum brothers want to keep Joe Finston here in the home office, as far away from production as he can get."

"I knew some of this, but not all. I didn't know he was trying to get into production."

"Oh, yes. When he was in college he wanted to be a writer. He told me that himself. He wants to fire all the writers on the Coast and get all new ones. Also directors. He thinks he knows about directing."

"He couldn't direct a blind man across the street."

"I'm sure of it. Well, if I were you, I'd stall him till you go back. Let him say or do anything he pleases. Then when you get back to the Coast, go see Morris Rosenbaum and tell him you understand Finston is getting ready to take over production. If he recovers from his stroke, you tell him you heard a lot of rumors to that effect while you were here. In fact, you say to Morris you got that impression because Finston wanted you to star in this turkey and tried to talk you into it all the time you were in New York."

"I think I'll marry you, Jim."

"Just the way I am? I ought to go out and buy a few things. And you have a date tonight with a friend of mine."

"Well, he asked me. And you didn't."

"I didn't, because it's my job to take you out, and I do it on company money. I don't mean anything to you, Chottie, so don't pretend I do."

"Truthfully, you never did before, but this trip—I don't know. I never knew you before. I'll break the date with Ellis?"

"Oh, no. You keep the date with Ellis."

"Will you meet us later?"

"No."

"Well then, don't be jealous of Ellis. Jealous of Ellis! Well listen to the girl."

I decided to catch her off balance. "Where is Hunterden?"

"Hunterden? Why?"

"Okay, it's none of my business."

"No, it isn't," she said haughtily, so haughtily that I guessed something had gone wrong.

"Sorry I mentioned it," I said. "Now about this dame that's coming to interview you. She's new, but watch her. She's meek and mild, and asks innocuous questions, but she's out to make a score and we've had a little trouble with her. She doesn't write the usual fan-magazine slop."

"Everybody's out to make a score, in one way or another. I wish I had six children and lived in Chillicothe. Any Chillicothe, just so it wasn't New York or Hollywood."

"You've seen all those towns, but you never lived in them, and you never could."

"Don't be hard on me, Jim. I don't know where I'm at. If you want to know the truth, I'm scared."

"Of what?"

"Hunterden. Ellis. Finston. Junior Williamson. Oh, *he* phoned. He saw in the paper I was in town, and he quote just called up to chat unquote. So don't you add to my troubles, please. On the train East I had everything all worked out so neatly. Hunterden would meet me and we'd see each other and maybe get a few things settled. But he ran away from the photographers. And then I met your friend Ellis and I liked him, but he's on the make. Not that I blame him, but here I go with Junior again, only this time his name is Ellis. And I'm scared of Finston. He has a mean little face and I don't think it's going to be easy to fight him." She stopped. "I'm ashamed of myself, Jim. I tried flirting with him, but he wasn't having any. Ashamed and scared. An ugly little man like that ought to be easy to handle, but he just looked at me like I was another man. No, not like another man. He wouldn't have the guts to look at another man with such contempt. Do you know what he said? I can hardly repeat it."

"Don't if you don't want to."

"There we were in the middle of Sardi's and I was trying to use my feminine wiles, hating it but acting. And he said, 'Any time you want to put your clothes back on, let's talk contract.' "

"Did you have any answer to that?"

"Yes, I said I hoped he got a good look because the only way he ever would would be in his imagination. That's when I wished I could mention Hunterden's name, but how can I? I haven't seen

Hunterden since I've been in New York. If you were a woman you'd know what I'm going through with Finston and Hunterden. Slapped in my famous teeth by a little horror I wouldn't even step on, and given the absent treatment by a big shot. And what's in between? An ex-college boy on the make, your friend Ellis. Don't be hard on me, Jim. I'm scared."

"I'll get you out of this interview."

"Can you? I couldn't face a tough dame this afternoon."

"You go downstairs and wait in the limousine. I'll wait till she gets here and tell her you're launching a battleship, or something. I'll get rid of her. I suggest you go for a drive through the Park and come back in about an hour."

"I don't want to be alone," she said. "Please, Jim. You get rid of her and then come down and go for a drive with me."

"Well then, park the car up Fifth Avenue and I'll join you as soon as I can."

I was not in love with Chottie and I never could be. She was a public person and I had already observed that a public person could only be in love with another public person; in Chottie's case another star, a famous young heir, a mysterious but nonetheless public figure like Hunterden. And yet as I made my way to the limousine, and as we drove through the Park and over to Riverside Drive, I wanted to protect her, to keep her from injury, to shield her from roughness. In the Park she reached over and took my hand.

"What are you thinking about, Jim?"

"You."

"I thought so," she said. She did not go on, and neither did I. If I told her that I wanted to protect her, I would be taking away her strongest protection, which was her belief in her own toughness. I saw her clearly as something gay and fragile that could be hurt and even destroyed, but she was as proud of her independent spirit as she was of her beauty and talent. I let her think whatever she was thinking, and for the remainder of the ride she encouraged me to talk about myself and jobs I had had. Back at the hotel entrance she said, before getting out of the car: "Do you want to keep the car?"

"You mean, don't come up," I said.

"That's what I mean. Don't come up. This would be a very bad time to start anything, if we ever are."

"And if we don't now, we probably never will," I said.

"Probably," she said. "I'll give you a wonderful kiss and you'll always know we could have."

"If you give me a wonderful kiss, we will," I said.

"Yes, I guess so. Then no kiss, but when you get old and think back on your girls, I give you permission to include me. We just as good as. Thank you, Jim."

She left me, and I found that the factual part of my mind was busy wondering how old she was. Until that moment she had been among those actresses whose beauty and fame, while they last, make them impervious to questions as to their real names and real ages. But we had come very close to making love, and she herself had been the one to mention age. It was on her mind, and now it was on mine. Until then I would have accepted any age under thirty as a true one for her. With some sense of treacherous guilt I told the driver to take me to my newspaper alma mater, and I passed the next two hours in the files.

Allowing for margins of error, I found that she was no less than thirty-five, and quite possibly thirty-eight. Shows and plays she had been in, the kinds of roles she had played, established her age within those three years. My first thought when I considered her age was that at the time that I was begging my father to buy me an air rifle, Charlotte Sears had her name in lights in Herald Square.

In the morning I was at my desk, doing my routine chores that consisted of making up small items for the movie news columns, and I was summoned to Joe Finston's office. I went upstairs and waited to be admitted.

"Hello, Jim," he said. "Sit down. Two things. First, I'd like you to look this over and see if there's a story in it. It's about me when I was managing a theatre out in Rockaway. It has some amusing stuff in it about how I started in the industry. Don't read it now. I just sort of batted it out because I thought it'd be kind of amusing. The other matter is this Sears dame. We're getting ready to give her the old heave-ho. The key cities are howling bloody murder over her last two pictures and I got nothing but telegrams from all over the country. 'Don't give us any more Sears pictures,' is what they unanimously agree. I don't know what those production guys can be thinking of. I think some of them get softening of the brain from that California sunshine. I can tell you, from my experience as an exhibitor, this dame is costing us. You should see what her last two or three did, the grosses."

"Well, two costume pictures in a row," I said.

"Costume pictures are all right if they make money, but they don't with her in them. What I want you to do, I don't want this dame to have a line, not a line, as long as she's in New York. Cancel all interviews and don't give out any releases on her. I don't care if she climbs the Statue of Liberty, marries the Prince of Wales, she gets no publicity through this office. If you want to plant it that she's on the way out, the gossip writers are all friends of yours."

"Whatever you say, Joe. But I can't ask the gossip writers for any more favors just now. They're laying off the Hunterden story."

"What Hunterden story? Thomas R. Hunterden?"

"Yes, and Sears."

"Our Sears? Charlotte Sears and Hunterden? I don't know about that story. You have to enlighten me."

"Well, now you've got *me* confused. I thought she was all set here because she's Hunterden's girl friend."

"The first I knew about it," said Finston. "Where did you hear it from?"

"I didn't *hear* it. He was there to meet her at the station, the day she came in. And he called her up while I was with her at the hotel. He's married, but I don't know why the gossip writers don't hint at it."

"You saw him at the station?"

"Did I? You should have seen him scatter when he saw those photographers."

"You positively couldn't be mistaken?"

"Not a chance. Thomas R. Hunterden was born in my home town. Gibbsville, P A. Look him up."

"Does she admit it, Sears? I mean about being his girl friend?"

"Oh, sure. She has nothing to lose."

Finston removed his glasses and chewed on the tortoise shell. "Then it's true, eh?"

"What?"

"Well, you hear things and half the time you don't pay any attention, the rumors and gossip you hear." He was trying to lie his way out of his ignorance of the Hunterden-Sears affair, and doing it so badly that I was almost embarrassed for him. He looked at his watch, and I knew he was reckoning the time on the Pacific Coast. "Tell you what you do, Jim, you read that material I gave you and let me know what you think of it. I'll let you know later about the Sears publicity. I still want to think it over a while longer."

"Whatever you say, Joe," I went out, and I stood a moment to light a cigarette near his secretary's desk. Finston's voice came through the intercom.

"Get me Mr. Morrie in Hollywood," he said. "Home, if he isn't at the studio."

I could have been quietly noble about what I had done for Chottie Sears, but she needed some good news and I had it for her. It amused her, too, that I had accidentally but quite truthfully been able to make use of the two men who were giving her the most trouble, to play them against each other without telling a lie. "You know who would have enjoyed this was my grandfather, Pat Somerville," she said. "Did you ever hear of Pat Somerville? An old-time song-and-dance man. And playwright. He wrote dozens of plays and acted in many of them. A good Mick, like yourself, and it was always a feast or a famine for him and my grandmother. Unfortunately it was all famine by the time I came along, and I never got the benefit of any of the feast. But my mother had a lot of wonderful stories about him. One day they'd be putting on the ritz with servants and horses, and the next day men would come and start moving the furniture out of the house." She paused and studied a diamond ring she was wearing. "My mother used to tell me those stories, but she had more spunk than I have. My father—they had an act together—lit out and left her stranded in Pittsburgh without a nickel and she never heard from him again. He took all their money and her diamond ring. In those days show people used to put their money in diamonds when they were working, and of course hock them when there was a long layoff. They boarded me in a house in Brooklyn in those days, so I could go to school. She got back to New York and partnered up with another man and went out again doing the same act. All she said to me was that my father was taken sick with consumption and in a sanitarium. Being a show-business kid, I'd often heard of that. TB was very common among show people, and I guess I cried a little but my father had never been much to me. Or me to him. My mother'd make him come to see me in Brooklyn when they'd lay off during the summer, but he never tried to pretend that I didn't bore him. And the three of us never lived together after I was about eight years old. I was taking violin lessons and it used to drive him crazy when I'd practice, so they always lived in a hotel and I went on boarding in Brooklyn.

"Finally, when I finished eighth grade my mother and her partner got Willard K. Frobisher to write them a new act that I could be in. Songs, dances and witty sayings, and me on my fiddle doing a toe dance. Damn near ruined my legs, that toe-work. Thank God I gave *that* up in time."

"What was the name of the act? Did your mother marry her new partner?"

"The original name of the act was Dowd and Somerville. My real name is Catherine Dowd. Then the new act was Snow and Somerville *introducing* Charlotte Sears. Sears was the name of a face powder my mother used, and Charlotte—just a fancier name than Catherine, and there were thirty-five thousand Kitties, so I became Charlotte Sears. Society people ask me if I have relations in Boston, and out in the sticks they ask me how's Mr. Roebuck. But I was named after a face powder and a famous empress. Who went nuts, didn't she?"

"Yes, I think so."

"Well, I can sympathize with her, the last couple of days. But I feel better now, temporarily," she said. "Anyway, Jim, the story of my life isn't very interesting, but I left out what I really started to tell you. I don't want to be poor. *I* don't want to be stranded in Pittsburgh. I haven't got as much spunk as my mother. Not that I *am* poor. When I began earning my own living at fifteen, I saved something out of every week's pay. I never missed a week. Never. No matter where I was, I'd go to the post office and send back a money order, even if it was only two or three dollars. There was a bank here that show people used to use for that. So I'm not poor. But it isn't only the money. It's something else. All the years I've been in show business, every new job paid me more money than the last one. I've never taken a cut, and I've never taken a job that didn't pay me more than I'd been getting. That's why I'll fight Finston. It isn't only Finston I'm fighting. It's—oh, hell, you know what it is. Do I have to say it?"

"No."

"Do you know the picture I turned down? Do you know the story?"

"No, I haven't seen the script."

"I play the mother of a seventeen-year-old girl. That is, I would if I took the picture. I could very easily have a daughter seventeen, but I'm not going to let fifty million people see me playing a mother to a seventeen-year-old girl that everybody knows is twenty-two. Jean Raleigh. I'm not going to play Jean Raleigh's mother, because then the public will think I must be over forty, and I'm not. I may not have ten years to go before I'm forty, but I'm not there yet. And regardless of how old I am, your friend Ellis doesn't think I'm so old. And Junior Williamson called again today. He won't take no for an answer, that one. You know, it's almost as if he were taking advantage of me."

"How so?"

"This way. He's very anxious to see me and I've told him absolutely no. But he's not going to give up. He told me so. Well, last night Ellis took me to that speakeasy on 49th Street, Jack and Charlie's. I'd never been there before, and who should be there but Mr. Thomas R. Hunterden? He was with two other men."

"Did you speak to him?"

"No. But he kept looking at me and at Ellis, and he didn't like it a bit that I was with Ellis. Ellis and I had a quick dinner and left to go to the theatre and Hunterden was still there with the two men. Well, what I'm getting at is, what if I showed up there again tonight, this time with Junior Williamson? Or tomorrow night? Or every night?"

"Why hasn't Hunterden got in touch with you?"

She did not immediately answer me. "You risked your job for me, so I'll tell you," she said. "But this is between you and me and nobody else."

"All right," I said.

"The reason he hasn't *seen* me is because he can't. He's in the middle of the biggest deal he ever made. One of the men he was with last night was an Englishman, and the other one I guess was a Turk. He wore a fez, so I guess he was a Turk. Hunterden told me yesterday that there were some men in town that he was going to have to be with until they left. In fact, he said he wasn't going to let them out of his sight. I thought he was lying, but I guess those were the men."

"Sounds like it," I said. "Then he still loves you?"

"Love? Hunterden would choke on that word. A man like Hunterden doesn't think about love, although I shouldn't complain. It's a long time since I've said it and meant it. Jim, maybe you'll be famous some day and then you'll understand certain things."

"What would I be famous for?"

"Writing, maybe. You have something, or I wouldn't be attracted to you. Politics, maybe. Or you might be head of a studio."

"Well, what is it that I'll understand that I don't understand now?"

"Two people like Hunterden and me. We're very much alike. I don't know anything about him—that is, the kind of things I told you about myself. I've only known him less than a year. He came out to the Coast and I met him and I fell for him. Not love. And not just sex. I didn't even know who he was, but naturally he had to be *somebody,* to be invited to Morrie Rosenbaum's to dinner. I guessed that much about him. I didn't sit near him at dinner, but after dinner he sat with me and the first thing he asked me took me completely by surprise. He said, 'Miss Sears, if you owned the Rosenbaum Studio, what other company would you like to merge with?' I said I wouldn't merge with any, not if merging meant equal partnership. I said I'd go into competition with one particular studio and drive them out of business, and then buy them out cheap. 'How would you do that?' he said. And I told him I'd steal their biggest stars and best directors. He asked me how I'd do that and I said if he'd give me the Rosenbaum Studio and plenty of money I'd show him how. Well, he wanted to know how I'd go about getting a certain star. I won't tell you her name. Miss Smith. How would I go about getting Miss Smith, who was under contract to a certain other studio? I said in that particular case I wouldn't go after Miss Smith herself, I'd go after a certain cameraman. It isn't so much that he's one of the famous cameramen, but if Miss Smith ever made a picture without him, she'd soon find out that fifty per cent of her success in pictures is due to him. She'd see herself photographed by someone else, and she'd follow the cameraman as soon as she could.

" 'Very interesting,' he said. Then he wanted to know who I'd keep if I suddenly got control of the company, and I said in other words he wanted to know who I'd fire. 'Not quite,' he said. So I told him I'd keep Morrie Rosenbaum, because he was more interested in making pictures than in the stock market.

"Then he made his first personal remark. He said, 'You know, Miss Sears, there's enough for everybody in this business, but if you and I had known each other ten years ago, we could have had most of it.'

"And I said, 'Well, Mr. Huntington, let's take what's left.' I thought his name was Huntington.

" 'No,' he said. 'Let's take our share, and then look into other possibilities, and see what we have ten years from *now.*' That particular moment was when Ruth Rosenbaum decided everybody ought to play poker. It was all right. I won about two thousand dollars, but I didn't see Hunterden alone till four or five days later. A Sunday noon. He came to my house unannounced, without calling up in advance. He came down to the pool, where I was reading the Sunday papers, and he said, 'Am I too late for breakfast, or too early for lunch?' He stayed till Tuesday afternoon, and then he had to go back to New York. Incidentally, Wednesday or Thursday of that week I saw in the trade papers that Guy Smallwood had just signed a new contract with the Rosenbaum Studio. He was the cameraman. You can guess who the star was."

"Oh, sure. She's with us now."

"And getting a picture I wanted to do."

"But I'm surprised that Morrie Rosenbaum didn't know about you and Hunterden."

"We never went out together in Hollywood, and the few times we went to speakeasies in New York, other people were along with us. Hunterden has a deadhead that works for him, and if anybody saw the four of us out together they wouldn't know whether I was with Hunterden or his straight man."

"You started to tell me you and Hunterden are very much alike, then you got sidetracked."

"We are. If I were a man I'd be the same way with Charlotte Sears as he is. I understand where I fit into his life and where I don't. In fact, I don't have to be a man to understand all this. If I were on the crest of the wave, I might be treating Hunterden the way he's treating me. But I'm not on the crest of the wave. I have things worrying me, and when that happens I'm not as sure of myself. No spunk. I'm best at figuring things out when the heat's not on me. Hunterden has this big business proposition bothering him, and he doesn't want to be bothered with a woman too till it's all settled." She smiled. "I wish you were just a moron. Then you could make love to me and I could forget about Hunterden. But if you were a moron I wouldn't want you to make love to me."

"I'm very close to making love to you right this minute."

"I know, and it's exciting. But we better not, Jim."

"If it means so little, why not? Who'd know?"

"I would. The next man that I let make love to me—you don't know what I'm like. I try to run your life, I'm jealous."

"You're not with Hunterden."

"No, because I'm afraid of him. There ought to be another word for love, for people like Hunterden and me. Attraction. Respect. Success. I'm successful, a star. He respects that in me and we're attracted to each other. I know he's a big shot, a star in his own line. So there's a strong attraction that leads to sex. Well, I won't knock sex. I've had affairs that were nothing else and I've stayed up all night waiting for that phone to ring, just like anybody else. But with Hunterden—if I'd refused him on the sexual side, he wouldn't have bothered with me any more, but sleeping with me wasn't all he wanted. I suppose you might say I'm like one of his businesses, but I'm more than that to him and yet it isn't love.

"I don't know about love, anyway, Jim. I've been in love, all the symptoms. Happiness and thrills and desperation. Once I had them change my bookings so I could be on the bill with a magician I was in love with. Oh, he was a bad man, too."

"Did he want to saw you in half?"

"You think you're joking, but he gave me a beating one Saturday night in Baltimore that I never thought I'd make the Monday matinée in Philly. I had to wear black tulle over my arms and shoulders, and I had a mouse under my eye that I had to have leeches for. I was doing a single and up to the last minute I wasn't sure I could go on. But then I saw him grinning at me and I said to myself, 'You so-and-so, you go out there and wow them, and that'll show him.' I did, too, although I was half dead."

"No spunk, eh?" I said.

"Oh, I'll fight. By no spunk I mean I don't have the endurance that my mother had. The long pull, as they say down in Wall Street."

"I think you underestimate yourself all around," I said.

"Not to hear me talk about what a success I am," she said. "Well, a week from now and I'll be getting off the train at Pasadena, with a lot of new clothes and probably a whole trunkful of new headaches. I have two more days in New York."

"How do you figure that?"

"I'm going away for the weekend. To Long Island," she said. She waited for me to say something, but I remained silent. "You won't ask me where?"

"It's none of my business," I said. I could not keep the huffiness out of my tone, and she laughed.

"I like to tease you," she said.

"In more ways than one," I said.

"Oh, now that's not fair. I didn't tease you the other way, and I could have."

"You didn't do so well with Finston," I said, knowing as I said it that it was a cruel and vicious thing to say; but I had no control over, no knowledge of the depth of, the frustration I felt.

She looked at me very calmly. "After that remark you can't stay here any longer," she, the movie queen, said.

I got my hat and coat out of the foyer closet and went down the hall and pushed the button for the elevator. I put on my coat and watched the indicator as the elevator climbed and then began its descent. It was two or three stories above me when I heard her voice. "Jim? Come on back."

I went back and she was holding the door open for me. She closed it behind me and stood leaning against it. We looked at each other and then as naturally as we breathed we embraced, and I kissed her. She reached back her hand and turned the deadlatch. "It's what you want, isn't it?" she said.

"Very much," I said.

"Then I do too," she said.

I had seen, as a hundred million others had seen, the outlines of her body many times, but the extraordinary beauty of it as I saw her in the next few minutes was beyond my past imaginings. There was no bad disposition or sorrow in her love-making; she was pleased and she was happy to be pleasing. I think she was glad to be friends again, to heal the hurt I had inflicted on her and to do so by an ultimate generous act of her own, without waiting for me to express my regret, without pausing to forgive.

I was young, not inexperienced, but young, and my experience counted for little in this new lesson. I was learning for the first time that a woman could be gracious in a calculated act of love, that she could deny the pleasure to many who wanted it, who even wanted to trade love for it, but that she could make a present of pleasure and of the honor of her trust without asking for promises or tokens. Both of us knew that this would not happen again, and that her earlier warning to the next man who might make love to her did not now apply. I had enjoyed what she gave, she had enjoyed the giving. She lit a cigarette for me and asked me if I wanted to sleep, and as she sat on the edge of the bed she seemed reluctant to get dressed again.

"Don't you want to go to sleep?" I said.

"Oh, no. But you can. I'll let you sleep for a half an hour." She took my cigarette and inhaled once, then put it out in the ash tray. "I'll remember this when you're famous," she said.

"I'll have you to the White House," I said.

She shook her head. "No, this is just between us, you and me. You did a lot for me out of niceness, and I couldn't let you think I was a teaser."

"I didn't think that."

"You might have. You did. You thought I was teasing you about the weekend, and I guess I was. Yes, I was. I didn't think I was, but I was. Don't be stubborn, Jim. Ask me where I'm going."

"Where are you?"

"The Williamsons'."

"The father and mother's?"

"No, Junior's house. His wife invited me."

"I didn't know you knew her."

"I don't. At least I've never met her. Have you met her?"

"Hell, no. Or him either. I don't know those people. I only know Ellis through a speakeasy that's open in the morning."

"From something Ellis told me, Junior's wife is quite desperate. And she's pretty clever, too. Junior has his next wife picked out, according to Ellis, and the present one I *think* would like me to break that up. She knows I had an affair with Junior, and I guess she thinks the next Mrs. Williamson won't like it a bit if I show up again. You're not listening. Go to sleep."

"I heard every word you said," I said, and then I dozed off.

It was dark and the traffic sounds of early evening in New York—the beep horns, the protesting second speeds of the buses, and the cab starters' whistles—brought me back to consciousness. Charlotte Sears in negligee and panties, was sitting at her dressing-table. "You rejoining the party?" she said.

"Where's your maid?"

"She'll be here in a little while. I couldn't hide anything from her, so I don't try. I had your suit pressed."

"Have I got a date with you tonight?"

"Well, I have theatre tickets and I have no other date."

"Fine."

"You can do me a great favor, if you will. Have you got a car?"

"No."

"Well, will you hire one and drive me out to the Williamsons' tomorrow afternoon?"

"Sure."

"She offered to send a car for me, but I want to do it my way. If I feel like getting the hell out of there, will you come out and rescue me?"

"Of course."

"Hunterden phoned while you were asleep."

"I thought I heard you talking."

"You didn't hear a thing. You were really out. Anyway, he wants to see me Sunday night, in town, so even if I don't call you before then, will you come out and get me Sunday afternoon?"

"Sure."

"Finston has lost," she said.

"Good work. Did you find that out from Hunterden?"

"I sure did. Morrie called Hunterden from the Coast and said he had good news for him. The Studio was giving me the lead in *Rhapsody on Broadway,* a musical that I'm dying to do. Morrie giggled and said he just thought Hunterden would like to know. Hunterden was taken completely by surprise, but he wasn't annoyed. In fact he was pleased. But the man that really swung the whole thing—little old you."

"Great," I said. "Tomorrow I'll watch Mr. Finston crawl."

"I'm going to do something worse. I'm not going to answer the phone when he rings. I'll let him hang for a week. But doesn't that please you, how it worked out?"

"It certainly does."

"And yesterday I was down at the bottom of the bottomless pit. Do you like champagne?"

"Not much."

"But let's have some tonight, even if we don't drink it all."

"Company money," I said.

"What kind of a car would you like? I mean to own?"

"Don't buy me a car, Chottie. It'd be a waste of money."

"All right, then, not a car, but I'm going to give you something. You wouldn't wear a diamond ring, would you?"

"No."

"How about a trip to Europe?"

"Well, it would be fun to go as a passenger. I've been to Europe, but I worked my way."

"The *Ile de France?* Would you like that?"

"Who wouldn't?"

"You decide when you want to go, and the boat, and I'll pay your fare both ways and all your hotel and travel expenses for a month. Can you get a leave of absence?"

"I don't know, but it won't make the slightest difference. I'll just go."

"Just tell me when, and the trip is yours."

"Thank you."

We had dinner at Jack and Charlie's. It was a small room, low-ceilinged, and no table would seat more than six comfortably, but it was the best speakeasy in New York; the food was excellent, and there were many rumors to explain the high quality of the liquor, the recurring one being that certain highly placed financiers had got Andrew Mellon to allow the Bermuda rumrunners to slip through the Coast Guard patrols. Everything was expensive, and I seldom went there when I was not spending company money.

"Over in the corner, the table that's hidden by the bar," said Charlotte Sears.

"Who?" I said.

"Hunterden and the Turk and the Englishman. Now he sees me." She bowed. "Might as well speak to him if Morrie knows about us. He's coming over."

Thomas Rodney Hunterden, expensively tailored in a black suit and wearing a black silk necktie with a smoked pearl stickpin, shook hands with Chottie. "How do you do, Miss Sears," he said.

"Hello, Mr. Hunterden. I saw you here last night but you didn't recognize me. Will you join us? This is Mr. Malloy, of our publicity department."

"Could I sit with you for a minute?" He included me in the question, but he did not wait for my answer.

"I've seen you before, haven't I, Mr. Malloy?"

"Well, I get around," I said.

"What part of the country do you come from?" he said.

"I come from a place called Gibbsville, Pennsylvania."

"Oh, yes. In the coal regions."

"Oh, you've heard of it?"

"I was born there, but I left when I was very young."

"You two were born in the same town?" said Chottie.

"But I persuaded my parents to take me away when I was two years old," he said. It was not very funny, but it was a remark that put me in my place. "I saw your picture in the paper, Miss Sears. Will you be in town long?"

"Leaving for the Coast Monday."

"Well, I hope we run across each other again. Nice to see you. I have a very good friend in your organization, Mr. Malloy. Remember me to him if you see him."

"Who's that, and I will?"

"Morrie Rosenbaum. Have to get back to my friends." He rejoined the Turk and the Englishman.

"Dying to know who you were," said Chottie.

"And to make sure I didn't get any ideas. He has a very good friend in my organization."

She patted my knee. "Don't let him annoy you. After all, two hours ago."

"What do you think kept me from telling him to go to hell?"

"Me."

"True," I said.

"You can be as independent as you please, but I can't."

"But you are."

"No, I'm not. I cheated with you, Jim, but he's my big moment. He always will be. We didn't find a word to use instead of love, but whatever it is, that describes it. And it's the same with him. He had to know who you were."

"Why not call it love, Chottie? Nobody's going to fine you for misusing the word."

"You get over love. I won't get over this."

"Then you're worse than in love."

"Oh, I know that. That's what I've been trying to tell you."

"I'm a very unimportant guy," I said. "He didn't have to threaten me by telling me what good pals he is with M. R."

"He shouldn't have done that, but he couldn't help it. And don't forget, Jim. His instinctive jealousy was right. Where were you and I two hours ago? The man is no fool."

"I never thought of it that way."

"The same instinct that made him pick me out at Ruth and Morrie's dinner party. He said to me one time, the secret of his success was to find out everything he could about, well, about a business. Get all the facts, and then play his hunches, even when the facts seemed to lead in another direction. Just now he followed a hunch. Maybe I was sitting too close to you, or enjoying myself too much. But he had a hunch, and he was right. Although he'll never know he was right."

"Yes, but maybe he'd be jealous of anybody."

"He wasn't jealous of Ellis. There goes that rhyme again. He saw me with Ellis, but he didn't come to the table. He had no hunch about Ellis, and he did about you. Give him credit." She paused. "Also, I don't like to say this, but watch your step. I'm going to lie to him when he asks me about you, but he may not believe me, although he'll pretend he does. And he might make up some other excuse to have you fired."

"Oh, he wouldn't do that to another Gibbsville boy," I said.

Abruptly Hunterden rose and came over to our table again. "Have you and Mr. Malloy been to the Florence Club, the Chez Florence? I'm taking my friends there later if you'd care to join us. About two o'clock? It doesn't start till late, or is that no news to Mr. Malloy?"

"I've been there quite a few times," I said.

"Miss Sears?"

"All right, fine," she said.

"I see you're just finishing dinner, so I infer you're going to the theatre. Two o'clock, then? Splendid." He went back to his table.

"Well, that was pretty smart," I said.

"Why?"

"Don't you get it? We go to the theatre and we get out after eleven, probably go some place for a drink, meet him at two, and stay under his watchful eye till four or five. The whole evening taken care of, in case I get any ideas. That was damned smart. And at five o'clock tomorrow morning, or whenever, he'll deposit me right at my door, in his beautiful big Rolls-Royce."

"How do you know he has a Rolls?"

"There's one parked outside, so I guess it's his."

"It is. I recognized the chauffeur."

I had failed to anticipate the degree of Hunterden's strategy. At the Florence Club he and his companions were with three show girls from Mr. Ziegfeld's production. The Turk did not drink, but the Englishman and I drank a lot, while Hunterden nursed a highball until about half-past four. Hunterden then made his excuses and departed with Chottie, and the Turk, the Englishman, and I were left with the show girls and Hunterden's Rolls. The girl who got me was sore as hell, as she might well have been, to have had such an unprofitable evening, but at least I got four hours' sleep before going to the office.

I telephoned Chottie. "Do you still want me to drive you out to Long Island?"

"Why? You're not running out on me, are you?"

I laughed. "You're a fine one to be talking about running out. Is everything okay?"

"Blissful," she said, and she meant it. "Will you call for me around five-thirty?"

"Yes. What am I supposed to be, I mean am I your brother or cousin? In case I have to act a part at Mrs. Williamson's."

"You be a devoted admirer that likes to do things for me. That's real type-casting."

"It's a part I like to play, Chottie," I said. I liked this woman in a way and to a degree that probably only another man would understand, although it was a woman—she herself—who had come closest to putting it into words when she declared that you get over love, but you don't get over "this."

I drew some expense money and went up to Columbus Circle and picked out a second-hand Duesenberg S-J, which was on sale for $18,000. It was a phaeton with a tonneau windshield. "I want to hire it for the weekend," I said.

"Not a chance," the salesman said.

"Don't be so hasty," I said. "I want to hire it, and I don't want to pay you a nickel." I introduced myself and told the man that I was squiring Miss Charlotte Sears around Long Island society, and if he didn't want the publicity, I'd just as soon give it to another car. He said he'd have to talk to the manager.

"Get me a picture I can blow up and put in my window, and the car is yours," the manager said. "With Miss Sears at the wheel, of course."

"Of course," I said.

I then got my coonskin coat out of hock and Charlotte Sears and devoted friend drove out to the Williamsons' in style. The Williamson butler was not impressed, but Mrs. Williamson was. "What a beautiful car," she said. "Did you drive from California?"

"It isn't my car," said Chottie.

"It's yours, Mr. Malloy?"

"For the time being," I said.

"I've never driven one," said Mrs. Williamson, wistfully. "Are you in a terrible hurry? Couldn't the three of us . . . ?"

The butler removed Chottie's luggage and we went for a ride out the North Country Road. Polly Williamson took the wheel, and she was a good driver. On the stretch past the Hutton place she hit ninety m.p.h., and after we turned around she took the same stretch at slightly more than a hundred. Her delight was simple and disarming. "I've never done that before in my life. What a wonderful car. Thank you, Mr. Malloy." She herself was simple and disarming, unlike the person I had expected her to be. She was not pretty by the standards of the three girls I had seen the night before; but she had a good figure and legs, and if her hands had not been strong we would have landed in a ditch. The Duesenberg was not a woman's car, and I guessed that Polly Williamson was accustomed to handling big Irish hunters.

She was wearing a checked suit and was hatless, and her blond hair was in disarray from the spin. When we got out of the car at her house she patted the door and smiled. "Can you come in and have a drink?" she said.

"Thanks, but I have to be on my way," I said.

"I hope I didn't make you late. If you're going to be in the neighborhood why don't you come in Sunday afternoon? Don't call or anything, just come if you can."

I almost hated to leave, and Polly Williamson, by her unexpected friendliness, had made me feel I was welcome to stay. She was in her middle twenties, the age of most of the girls I was taking out at that period of my life. She had two small children, and I knew that she was having trouble with her husband. But where I had been led to expect a neurotic, jealous woman, I could see only a young wife who was making an effort to save her marriage by resorting to the kind of intrigue that I was sure was new to her. I do not wish to imply that I saw her as a simple, suburban housewife; the butler wore silver-buttoned livery; the Junior Williamsons' house was only the second largest on the estate, perhaps a quarter-mile distant from the main house whose chimneys and roofs we could see above the trees on a hilltop; and while we were saying goodbye a toothless little man in breeches and buttoned canvas puttees rode past us on a lathery gelding, leading another horse with the stirrup irons tucked up, on his way to the stables. The little man tipped his cap to Polly Williamson. "Just back, Peter?" she said.

"Yes ma'am, just these five or ten minutes," he said, without halting.

"My husband and a friend of his," said Polly Williamson. "They must have stopped in at the big house, but you sure you can't wait to meet them?"

"Afraid not, but thanks very much, and Chottie, see you Sunday if not before?"

Chottie Sears was grinning at me and my not well-hidden admiration of her hostess. "I hope you can make it Sunday," she said.

"I'll try," I said, and put the Duesenberg in gear. I had plans for the weekend; I was not going to waste the Duesenberg; but I drove away reluctantly. I suppose that at that period I was about as fancy-free as it is possible for a man to be, which in my case, however, meant also that I was ready to fall in love with almost any attractive girl. There was an element of pity in my admiration of Polly Wil-

liamson, and that element nullified what would otherwise have been
the awesome effect of her possessions.

I took the Port Washington ferry and spent Friday and Saturday
nights with friends in Connecticut. At noon on Sunday, while we
were having breakfast, I was called to the telephone. It was, of
course, Chottie Sears. "Duty calls," she said.

"How's it going?" I said.

"Not so good. Can you get here around five? They're having
some people in and I have to stay for that, but I want to be ready to
go any time. I'll be packed and everything, so we can leave here
before eight. You don't have to play any part. Polly Williamson
knows who you are. We've gotten to be friends. Her whole plan collapsed last night after dinner. Junior got plastered and he and his
lady friend disappeared about eleven and never came back. We'll see
how things are at lunch, but as of now this marriage is a fiasco, and
for her sake I'm sorry. She wanted to make it go, but he's a silly,
spoiled brat. Wait till you see what took him away from Polly."

The other guests had not arrived when I got to the Williamsons'
house, and without prior information I could not have guessed that
all was not serene. Junior Williamson, dressed for town in a blue
suit, black shoes, and stiff collar, pretended to me that I had cost
him money he could not afford. "My wife wants a Duesenberg just
like yours," he said.

"She can have mine, because it isn't mine. I rented it," I said.

"Isn't it a new car?"

"No, it's second-hand. They want eighteen thousand for it."

"That's quite a come-down from the original price, isn't it? Don't
they sell for over twenty thousand?"

"Around twenty-two, I think," I said.

"That's a lot of money. I'm in favor of renting cars. I always do
when I go abroad."

"Yes, but if people like you don't buy those cars, they'll stop
making them," I said.

"No, not really. There'll always be guys like Thomas R. Hunterden to buy them. You know, Thomas R. Hunterden, the holding-company guy?"

"He's coming here this afternoon," said Polly Williamson.

"That's what made me think of him," said Williamson. "Somebody told me he kept a Rolls in New York, one in London, and one in Paris. And they're not rented."

"Well, I suppose a fellow like that can make sixty thousand dollars in one day," I said.

"Easily, but think of the upkeep. My father and I together, I think there are about eighteen cars on this place, with the two small trucks. A ton-and-a-half Dodge truck and a Ford. That may seem like a lot, but we have a full-time mechanic, an absolute genius with cars, and we get a good discount on gasoline and oil, quantity buying. It probably doesn't cost us as much to keep a Pierce-Arrow going as it does some fellow that has one Chevrolet. And I'll bet you—no. I was going to exaggerate. I was about to say we could run our whole garage on what a fellow like Hunterden spends for three cars in three cities. I was thinking about three chauffeurs, garage bills, and so forth. I suppose the actual outlay is less for Hunterden, but our cars are always in use. That's where the big difference is. Every car on this place is in actual use. My mother, my father. My wife. Taking one of the children to school. Servants to church. Marketing. Actually, if we had room in the garage, my father was thinking of buying a horse van *as an economy.* He gets awfully tired of paying a fellow in Roslyn every month for vanning. Five dollars a head, just from here to Meadow Brook."

The fascinating thing about Williamson's monologue was his taking for granted that I shared his problem: I was in his house, I had his highball in my hand, and I therefore was a sympathetic listener. I had once experienced the same blind, uncomplimentary acceptance when I was sent to interview a Princeton professor who had won a prize for some scholarly research in Sanskrit. Both Williamson and the professor assumed, without the courtesy of inquiring into my interests and my ignorance, that their language was also mine. Williamson had paid no attention to my remark that I was renting a second-hand car, other than to assume that my reason for renting a second-hand car would be the same as his for hiring cars in Europe. If his wife had not been present I would have made a burlesque of his father's persecution by the Roslyn horse-vanner, but I did not want to add to her troubles. I also did not want to kid this humorless man into giving me a punch in the nose. He glowed with health and strength; in the downward turn of the corners of his eyes there were warnings of a bad temper, and he had the meaty hands of a former oarsman. Four—six—eight years of rowing gives them a good fist that they keep all their lives.

Williamson was ready to change the subject, and did. "It's been awfully nice having Chottie here again," he said. "Chottie, you mustn't ignore us the way you've been doing."

"Hollywood isn't exactly around the corner, Junior," said Chottie Sears.

"I know, but don't you have to come to New York a lot?" he said.

"Not often enough," said Chottie.

"Why can't they make their pictures just as well in New York? I read an article not so long ago, about making movies over in Long Island City. Ever since the talkies they have to film everything inside a studio, it said. So the California sunshine isn't an advantage any more."

"Real estate," said Chottie. "The picture companies have a lot of money tied up in real estate."

"California bores me," said Williamson. "That everlasting sunshine."

"Go there during the rainy season," said Chottie.

"The what? I didn't know it ever rained there. But I suppose it must sometime."

I was beginning to understand Williamson and his attraction for women. In ten minutes he had proved to me that he was one of the stupidest men I had ever met, but the society girl and the movie queen watched every move he made and attended every trivial word. He would take a sip of his drink, and they would watch the elevation of the glass, the lowering of it, and then their gaze would go back on his face. His wife had hardly spoken a word since my arrival, and I noticed for the first time a phenomenon of her attentiveness: when Williamson was speaking, she would look at his mouth, and her lips would move in a barely discernible, unconscious forming of his words. Polly Williamson was a rich girl in her own right, from a family as rich as the Williamsons, and was therefore not dazzled as Chottie Sears might be by the Williamson fortune. In an otherwise masculine face Williamson had a feminine, cupid's-bow mouth, and I now recalled Chottie's remark about his being a mama's boy. He was indeed a mama's boy, with the mouth of a pubert and the appetites of a man; the brainless cruelty of a child, and the strength to arouse in a woman an urgent need to give him pleasure. With the addition of my own observations I agreed with Chottie's epithet. Williamson also had a rather musical voice, not at all unpleasant, and he spoke in the accent of his class. He would pronounce third and bird as though they rhymed with an r-less beard. Polly Williamson's pronunciations were identical with his and her voice was nicely modulated, so that in the present company the Williamsons' accent and voices were harmonious, while Chottie Sears, deep-voiced and with a smoothed-over Brooklyn enunciation, and I, with a harsh voice and an Eastern Pennsylvania twang, were two soloists against a duet. Our voices, our accents, and we ourselves were out of place in this house, in this room. I cannot say whether I became conscious of our vocal sounds first and of Polly Williamson's silent lip-moving second or that the order of observation was reversed. But my more vivid recollection is of Polly Williamson's lips. Chottie Sears, experienced in turning on and simulating facial expressions, gave no indication of her thoughts while Williamson boldly dismissed the telephone calls he had been making since Chottie's arrival in New York. He correctly assumed that she would play his game in spite of his having shown a preference for another woman the night before.

Williamson was a study of an arrogant aristocrat at work. He represented strength and vitality, three or four generations of careful breeding (with some rather distinguished citizens in his blood lines), and great wealth. He had begun to serve on many boards of trustees that governed the policies of philanthropies and cultural activity of the city and the nation, which had been preceded by his earlier participation in polo and fox-hunting committees and his support of Yale athletics. I had no doubt that he sincerely believed that a seat in the House, to be followed by a seat in the Senate, a Cabinet office and an ambassadorship in London or Paris, all would and should be his. As these things raced through my mind I looked over at Polly Williamson and wanted to tell her that her marriage was safe temporarily: Williamson would not ask for a divorce until his maiden political campaign was over. But I also would have had to tell her that in the event of his defeat (which I regarded as certain), the marriage was finished.

At that point we were joined by a tall, handsome woman of about twenty-eight. I looked at Chottie Sears, who gave me a quick pair of nods, and glanced from the newcomer to Williamson. This, she was telling me, would be the next Mrs. Williamson. Her name, as she was introduced, was Mrs. Underwood; her first name, as she was greeted by the Williamsons, was Eunice.

Eunice Underwood was actually not very tall and not very handsome, but she had chic in abundance. She wore a small black hat with a rhinestone pin on the left side, and as she entered the room she slipped off her mink coat and handed it to a maid, revealing a black satin dress, of which the fringed skirt was cut on the bias. The dress had long, close-fitting sleeves that came down over her wrists. She wore sheer black stockings and black suede shoes that had rhinestone buckles that matched the ornament on her hat. From a platinum chain around her neck hung a large diamond. Two words came to mind: the word dramatic, and the word mistress. I suppose the first word made her costume a success, even though I would not tell her so; and I suppose the second word was in my mind before I saw her, although I might have had the same verbal association without advance preparation. She was black, white, and sleek. Her hard, high little breasts pointed forward against the shiny satin. I had seen breasts like them on an expensive whore: all nipple and little flesh.

She went up to our hostess and said "Hello, Polly," but did not kiss her or shake hands.

"Hello, Eunice," said Polly Williamson.

"Hel*lo*, there," said Junior Williamson, exuberantly.

She reached out and smoothed down his necktie. "Hello," she said. "Hello, Miss Sears." She then was silent while I was being introduced, but she looked at me and my ready-made suit during the utterance of our names, and I was out of her life before she said "Howja do." She immediately turned away from me and handed Williamson an ivory cigarette holder into which he fitted a cigarette from his own case. I suspected that she had made him change to her brand, since there was no discussion over that. She put the holder in her mouth and Williamson lit the cigarette.

"Have you got crowds more people coming, Polly?" she said.

"Between thirty and forty."

"Oh, well, that's not so bad. I'll be able to find a place to sit with only that many."

"Wouldn't some nice gentleman give you a seat?" said Chottie Sears. Polly Williamson suppressed a smile.

"They're not as polite here as I'm sure they must be in Hollywood," said Eunice Underwood. "That reminds me, not that I've seen many films, but I don't think I've ever seen anyone sitting down in one. They're all so busy shooting at each other or throwing pie in each other's faces."

"A lot of them do sit down, though," said Chottie Sears. "There's a trick to it. We call them prat-falls."

"Do you know where your prat is, Eunice?" said Williamson, laughing.

"I can imagine. Where did *you* learn where it is? From Miss Sears?"

Williamson laughed again.

"Steady, girl," said Chottie Sears.

"You two," said Williamson, laughing. "I swear."

A group of six men and women now entered. Three of the men and one of the women were slightly tight, and Eunice Underwood slowly moved away to a chair in a far corner of the room. "Hey, Eunice," said one of the men.

"Stay where you are, Billy. Don't come over and bother me. You spray people when you're plastered."

"We could do with a little spraying around here," said the woman who was tight, and whom I took to be Billy's wife. A maid brought in a trayful of drinks which apparently had been ordered by the new guests on arrival. The butler stood in the doorway and watched the drinks being served, and then disappeared. Almost immediately another group of six arrived and among them was Charley Ellis.

"Have you been here all weekend?" he said.

"No, I just got here a little while ago," I said.

"I hear there was a bit of a *crise* last night. I thought you might be able to tell me about it."

"Can't tell you a thing," I said. "I was on the other side of Long Island Sound."

"I'll be back after I've said hello," he said. He left me and kissed Polly Williamson and shook hands with Chottie Sears.

Eunice Underwood called to him: "Charles, come here and sit with me a minute."

"I'll sit with you," said one of the other men.

"I didn't ask you, I asked Mr. Charles Ellis."

"I'm giving you your last chance," said the man.

"Is that a threat or a promise?" said Eunice Underwood. "Polly, if I were you I'd tell McDonald to dilute the drinks."

"Oh, I don't think so, Eunice," said Polly Williamson.

"Well, in that case I'm going to have to get tight in self-defense. Junior, get me a martini in a champagne glass, please."

"How'd it be if I got you champagne in a martini glass?" said Williamson, laughing.

"Oh, don't be the life of the party," said Eunice.

Charley Ellis rejoined me. "Where is *Mister* Underwood?" I asked. "Or isn't there any?"

"Eunice's husband? He's feeding the fishes. He got drowned in Bermuda a couple of years ago."

"Oh, that's why she's all in black?"

"No, I don't think that has anything to do with it. She didn't waste many tears on him. Not that he would have on her."

"Has she got a lot of dough?"

"Well, she has enough. But let's just say that if she hooks Junior she'll change her scale of living, not downward."

"Where is she from? She wasn't one of this crowd originally, was she?"

"No, she's from Brooklyn. Her father was a minister."

"Oh, she wants to be a nun," I said.

"I hadn't heard *that*," said Charley. "But I'm told she's tried everything else, and believe me, if she doesn't get Junior she's going to have to change her scene of operations."

"Not very popular?"

"Well, not with the women. Decidedly not with the women. Most of these people have known each other all their lives. Some of them were engaged to be married and married somebody else, but it's a closed corporation, and Eunice, the complete outsider, married Buddy Underwood and played it straight for a while. But she was in too much of a hurry. You can't hurry these people. They've been together too long."

"What was she in a hurry to do?"

"Oh, I suppose get rid of Buddy and make a better marriage. If she'd stuck by Buddy, who wasn't much good, she'd have gotten ahead faster. But instead she went after the men. She's a good rider, and she used that, and she's quite a good tennis player."

"She doesn't look the athletic type."

"She is, though. Don't let that slinky get-up fool you. She rides sidesaddle, and in a top hat and skirt she's even more impressive than she is today. Plenty of guts, too. And knows she's hated. Junior is sort of her last chance, and she knows that. If she doesn't land him, she knows she'll have to clear out. She gets invited everywhere because nobody wants to snub the next Mrs. Junior Williamson, but this is the ninth inning, two out, nobody on base, and she's at bat. A scratch single isn't going to do it for her. She has to knock one out of the ball park."

"Why is she after you?"

"After me? She isn't after me. Polly's my cousin, and Eunice would like to line up a few of Polly's relations on her side. She isn't after anybody but Junior, and everybody in this room knows it. That's why I asked you about last night. If she had an open spat with Polly, that would cook her goose for fair, because Junior doesn't want to be hurried. Don't forget, old Mr. Williamson and Mrs. Williamson are still very much alive. Junior takes Eunice to their house every chance he gets, but the old boy and Mrs. Williamson like Polly and they're crazy about those grandchildren."

"Why would Thomas R. Hunterden be invited here this afternoon?"

"I didn't know he was. That'll be a new face, and you don't see many of them in this house. He'd never be asked to the big house, so I guess Junior invited him."

"Why not Polly?"

"Well, anything's possible. Let's see if Alice comes with him. If she does, then it just means that Alice and one of her hospitals has been working on Junior and one of his hospitals. I don't know. You see anybody you'd like to make a play for?"

"Yes. Your cousin."

He shook his head. "No. Anything's possible, but I wouldn't like to see you make a play for Polly now. If a son of a bitch like Hunterden wants to, that's different. But not a friend of mine. If on the other hand she ever gets a divorce from Junior, I'll be as helpful as I can."

"Thanks," I said. "I could go for her."

"I think she's about the best we have to offer, and I'd like to see her shake loose from Junior, but she isn't ready to give up. See anybody else?"

"The blonde in the blue tweed suit."

"Mary Day? Can be had. The coast is absolutely clear, there. Billy's forever on the make for Eunice and it makes Mary sore as a wet hen. Hey, Mary."

The girl called Mary Day sauntered over.

"Here's a friend of mine that thinks you're pretty darn attractive."

"Why shouldn't he? I think he is, too. And a stranger in our midst. Where are you from?"

"He's a Pennsylvania boy," said Charley Ellis.

"Oh, God. Another Biddle?"

"No, I'm one of the anthracite Malloys."

"Oh, Scranton. I was in a wedding there once and I never saw people drink so much—except here, of course. But somehow it shocked me to see out-of-town people do it. Maybe you were at the wedding. It was—"

"I'm not from Scranton. I'm from Gibbsville."

"Oh, Gibbsville. Well, I know a girl that lives *there.* Caroline Walker, married to somebody called English. I spent one god-awful year at Bryn Mawr and she was one of the few bright spots. How is she?"

"Well, I saw her the last time I was home. She was looking well."

"She invited me to her wedding and I invited her to mine. End of correspondence, but I liked her. She was very nice to me. You give her my love when you see her. Mary Patterson. Can you remember that?"

"Mary Patterson. Sure. I'll remember."

"Are you visiting Charley? I didn't see you at lunch, did I?"

"I'm squiring Charlotte Sears."

"Oh, I want to hear all about her. Is it true that she's going to break up this thing between Junior and Eunice? I *may* have had one too many cocktails, don't you think? I shouldn't drink on Sunday. He who drinks on the Sabbath will live to fight some more. What did you say your name was?"

"James Malloy."

"It won't stick. I've forgotten it already," she said. She was sitting on a sofa between Charley Ellis and me, holding her cocktail glass in both hands. "What did you say it was again? Spell it."

"M, a, l, l, o, y."

"Mallory."

"No, there's no r in it."

"Like oysters."

"Yes. I'm out of season."

"I don't think you are. I think you're very much *in* season, and if you want to know the truth, so am I. You wouldn't like to take me out of here, would you, Mr. Mallory?"

"Where would you like to go?"

"I don't know. I'm open to suggestion."

"I'd love to take you anywhere, if we can be back here by eight o'clock."

"Oh, I don't think we would be. I really don't think we would. In other words, you're spoken for?"

"Not exactly spoken for, but I'm here to drive Miss Sears back to New York."

"Too bad. Or maybe not. Now this old gossip won't have any sleuth. Except that he did hear me proposition you."

"Am I the old gossip?" said Charley Ellis.

"What is sleuth?"

"I thought you were a friend of Caroline's. Sleuth is gossip. An old Bryn Mawr word for gossip. Talk-gossip. But Charley Ellis is a talker-gossip. If you want to know anything about anybody here, ask Charley. Isn't that right, Charley?"

"Just about," said Charley Ellis, not at all offended.

"*But*—if you want to know everything about *Charley,* you have to ask *me.* That's right, too, isn't it, Charley?"

"Just about."

"Ask him something about me," said Mary Day.

"Anything at all?" I said.

"Anything."

"All right," I said. "Has she had her appendix out?"

She laughed. "Go ahead answer him. I want to see what you say.
You're in a spot. You don't know whether to be chivalrous or truthful. Go on, Charley, answer his question."

"You answered it for me," said Charley. "I didn't have to say a
word—and I still haven't. So stop calling me a gossip, Mary. You
get a few too many drinks in you and talk too much, and then you
accuse other people of gossiping."

Mary Day turned to me. "Ask me whether *he's* had *his* appendix
out? The answer is yes. And have you had yours out, Mr. Mallory?"

"You're not going to find out as easily as that."

"Well said, Jim," said Charley.

"Has Charlotte Sears had hers out?" said Mary Day. *"Why, look
at him! He's blushing!* I took him completely by surprise."

"I wouldn't know," I said.

"Oh, come on, it's too late. You got as red as a beet. Why, Mr.
Mallory. And you're the one that started this whole thing about ap-
pendixes. That's rich."

"You jump to conclusions, Mrs. Day," I said.

She was staring at Chottie Sears, who was sitting between two
men, laughing with them and enjoying their admiration. "Some
women just have it, that's all," said Mary Day. "I wonder if she ever
got tight over some damn man." She got to her feet and slowly,
rather shyly, joined Chottie and her admirers.

"She's a swell girl till she drinks, and then—bang! No inhibitions.
Says anything that comes into her head, no matter who gets hurt in
the process." He was trying, I knew, to avoid the topic of Chottie
Sears and me, but he believed Mary Day had made a discovery and
he was resentful of it. He had his masculine pride, and I was his successful, deceitful rival.

"Well, as she herself said, she oughtn't to drink on Sunday," I
said.

"Or between Sundays. She does most of her damage on Sunday,
because there are more people around. But Sunday isn't the only
time she drinks too much. She's another of those girls around here

that set their caps for Junior, and who got him? Her best friend, Polly. I know what fixed that, too. Mary gave up everybody else for Junior, wouldn't even let people cut in at dances. No dates with anyone else, and behaving like an engaged girl, although Junior was going his merry way. And as against that possessiveness, there in the background, so to speak, was Polly Smithfield, the logical one, waiting to be asked. And she got asked and Mary didn't. That was some wedding. Mary the maid of honor instead of the bride, eyes red going up the aisle. Tight as a tick at the reception, and eloped with Billy Day the next week. She was back here and settled down before Polly and Junior got back from their wedding trip."

"Day isn't so much, is he?"

"He never used to be, but Junior has helped him along and he's doing very well. He has a seat on the Stock Exchange that I understand Junior put up the money for, and downtown Billy's known as Junior's man. Considering what he would have been without Junior's help, that's nice going.

"You know, when you have forty or fifty million behind you, that money does double service. Triple. Quadruple. For instance, McDonald isn't just a butler. He's Junior Williamson's butler, with forty million behind him. Junior Williamson's tailor isn't just a tailor. He has a forty-million-dollar customer. And downtown, Billy Day is Junior's man and that much closer to the money, even if he never gets his hands on it. I could probably get Junior's business. Polly's my cousin. But I think Polly wants Billy to have it, and in any case I wouldn't want to be known as Junior's man. Or anybody else's. When my father dies . . ." He cut himself off.

"What?"

He shook his head. "Don't know you well enough, Jim," he said, with finality. "If I talk about it, I won't do it."

"You wouldn't tell me if I guessed, would you?"

"No, but I'd be interested to hear your guess."

"You want to write," I said.

"Well, it's an interesting guess," said Charley Ellis.

"You're probably not kidding your father one bit."

"Probably not. But time is on his side. The longer he lives, the better the chances that I'll give up any crazy ideas I have."

"Why don't you just up and go?"

"The time to do that was when I graduated from college, and never to have gone downtown at all. That was *my* mistake and where the old man was clever. Hell, look at the guys in this room. At least half of them wish they were doing something else. I could tell you about most of them. Eddie Patterson wishes he could be a guide in Canada. Mike Bell should have been a vet. He studied it at Cornell, but now he's a big trader in oil stocks."

"I always wanted to be something else, too," I said.

"You did? What?"

"A millionaire."

Charley smiled. "Do you mean a million a year, or a million all told?"

"I wasn't greedy. At least, not till you said a million a year."

"There are both kinds of millionaire in this room. See if you can tell them apart."

"I guess I couldn't."

"No, I don't think you could, just by looking. Mike Bell probably has a million-dollar income, and Billy Day probably has around a million capital."

"But why does a guy like Bell give up what he wants to do when he has all that money?"

"It's the system, my boy. Or what I call the system, and you know the old saying. 'Don't buck the system or you're liable to gum the works.' Mike went to St. Mark's and then his father allowed him to go to Cornell and study animal husbandry. Then when he graduated, Mr. Bell told Mike he needed him downtown, just about the way my old man did me. You start going downtown, you get a lowly job as a runner or something, and you want to earn a promotion to prove that you could do it if you wanted to. So you earn that promotion and they give you some responsibility, which you have to fulfill. Pride. Meanwhile you're having a very pleasant time. You have lunch with your friends, go to parties, come out here weekends, get married, start having children. You're in the system. You're part of it. And what you wanted to be, or do, that becomes your hobby. In Mike's case, he's an amateur vet. You see, Jim, the best of these guys would have been good at something else. The others, let's not worry about them. They're the Billy Days."

"And what about the Junior Williamsons?"

"How many are there? Not more than half a dozen. Let's not worry about them, either. They're the royalty, and the others are the nobility, the peerage."

"Where are the commoners?"

"Well, there aren't any, not in this group. Not really *in* this group. Eunice is one, and the only way she'll be anything else is by becoming Junior's wife."

"What if I married Polly Williamson?" I said.

"Well, you wouldn't marry her unless you were in love with her and she was in love with you, and we'd know that. You'd get credit for marrying her in spite of her dough and not because of it. But you could never look at another woman, not even flirt a little. You couldn't start spending her money on yourself. You'd have to get something to do that her money wouldn't help you with. *And* if Polly had an affair with another guy, you'd take the rap. It would all come back to your marrying her for her money. And I wouldn't be surprised if that's why Polly wants to save her marriage. She's a very intelligent girl, and she knows there aren't many Junior Williamsons around."

"This is all based on the assumption that I'd give a damn what people said about me."

"Of course it is."

"Well, I don't."

"Well you damn soon would, my friend," he said. "Where are you and Polly going to live? Here? Then you'd be surrounded by Polly's friends. Gibbsville, Pennsylvania? I'll bet your friends would be tougher on you than Long Island. You may think you wouldn't give a damn about Polly's friends or your friends, but people is what people have to live with. And if you're surrounded by hostile people, your friends or Polly's or strangers, your marriage wouldn't last. Oh, just coming in. A perfect example of the commoner."

"I resent that," I said.

"No you don't," said Charley Ellis.

The newcomer was Thomas Rodney Hunterden, dressed for the Scottish moors in August in a tweed jacket and matching plus-threes, tab garters, and fringed-tongue brogues. "Lord Plushbottom," I said. There were others in the room similarly dressed, but the stiffness had not gone out of Hunterden's suit and shoes, nor out of him.

"New York Yacht Club tie," said Charley.

Hunterden made straight for Polly Williamson.

"No Alice," said Charley.

Most of the men showed that they had met Hunterden or recognized his name, but the only woman who greeted him with any informality was Chottie Sears. To my astonishment Junior Williamson took Hunterden's arm and steered him among the men and women, taking care of the introductions. "Mr. Ellis, and Mr. Malloy," said Williamson.

"Mr. Ellis," said Hunterden. "Mr. Malloy, I've had the pleasure. Did you get home safely the other night, Malloy?"

"Yes, did you?"

His quick anger was beautifully controlled. "Quite safely."

"Hunterden, what will you drink?" said Williamson.

"Sherry, please."

Williamson nodded to McDonald. "Damned sensible, I must say. I ought to stick to sherry. I hate the damn stuff," said Williamson.

"Do you? I don't. I like a glass of sherry at this time of day," said Hunterden.

"I don't even like it in soup. I come of a long line of whiskey drinkers, myself," said Williamson. He again took Hunterden's arm, and said: "Well, have you thought that over?" He piloted Hunterden away from everyone else and the two men sat off by themselves, engaged in private conversation. If I was curious, I was no more so than the other men in the room, who were curious and baffled.

"Be interesting to watch the stock ticker tomorrow morning," said Charley Ellis. "I predict a steady rise in Omega Development. That's one of Hunterden's companies. It'll go up a couple of points between opening bell and twelve-thirty. It'll remain steady while these boys are exchanging information at lunch, and then it'll begin to drop off a little because nobody's going to be able to find out a damn thing and the timid ones will take a quick profit. Would you like to make a few dollars, Jim? I'll put in an order for you first thing in the morning, and sell out at twelve noon."

"Do you know how much money I have in the bank?"

"None, the way you say it."

"None."

"Well, I'd lend you some but not to play the market on a tip I gave you."

"Thanks very much, Charley," I said. "I've never been in the stock market, so I didn't lose anything when the crash came."

"Well, that put you on even terms with a lot of guys that had been in it," he said. "At least we found out that Hunterden isn't here on Polly's invitation, and frankly I'm relieved."

"So am I," I said. "They're still gabbing away, Williamson and Hunterden."

"I'm going to see what I can find out from Polly," he said. "Very little, I'm sure, but I'll have a try at it."

The party had grown in size, but there was no individual or group that I felt would welcome my presence, so I waited alone while Charley Ellis spoke to his cousin. She laughed at something he said and shook her head, shrugged her shoulders. Then she stopped smiling and looked over at me and was confused to see me looking at her. Charley Ellis rejoined me.

"Couldn't get a thing out of her," he said.

"I know. So you changed the subject and told her I liked her."

"Yes," he said.

"But she didn't want to sit with us."

"That's exactly right. Can you read lips?"

"No. I almost wish you hadn't said anything about me."

"Would you like to hear what she said? It was nice," he said.

"Sure, of course I would."

"She said she met you at exactly the wrong time. From that I infer that any other time would have been the right time."

"Excuse me," I said. On an impulse I got up and went to Polly Williamson, who was talking with a man and woman. "May I see you a minute, please?"

We stood alone. "Charley told me what you said."

She nodded quickly.

"I have to tell you this. It may be the wrong time, Mrs. Williamson, and it may not last, and I know I'll never see you again. But I love you, and whenever I think of you I'll love you."

She turned away. "I know, I know. Thank you for saying it. It was dear of you."

I left her then and went back to Charley. "You see," he said. "I couldn't have done that."

"You don't know what I did."

"Yes, I do, Jim. You told her you love her."

"Yes, God damn it, I did."

"Did she thank you? If she didn't, I do, for her."

"Yes, she thanked me. Mrs. Williamson." I laughed. "I don't know her well enough to call her Polly, but I had to tell her I love her. How did you know what I was saying?"

"What else would take possession of a man so completely? What else would you have to say to her that was so urgent? And—what else could make her look the way she did when she was first married to Junior? Oh, that was a damn nice thing to do, to make her feel love again. The existence of it, the urgency of it, and the niceness. How long since any two people in this room had a moment like that? Or ever will? You know who I wish *I* could say that to, don't you? You must know."

"No, I don't," I said.

"To *her!* To Polly! I've never loved anybody but my first cousin, and I never will. But it isn't because we're first cousins that I haven't told her so."

"Why haven't you?"

"Well, yes, it is because we're first cousins. Closer than friends. Different from brother and sister. But she'd be shocked and frightened if she ever knew what it really is. It happens, and it works out, but when I was eighteen and she was fourteen I was ashamed because she was so young. And then when we got older she fell in love with Junior. So I've never told her. But now you see why I understand how you feel. You can't have her either." He smiled. "It seems to me we have a lot in common. I haven't slept with Chottie Sears, and you haven't slept with Mary Day, and I'd like to sleep with Chottie and you'd like to sleep with Mary. And neither of us will ever get anywhere with Polly. I've got drunk with friends of mine on less excuse than that. Shall we just quietly start putting it away, beginning with two double Scotches?"

"I'll have a double Scotch with you, but I have an eighteen-thousand-dollar car and a two-million-dollar movie queen to deliver safely. If you're going to be in New York tonight, I'll meet you anywhere you say."

"I think this would be a good night to get drunk. Don't you? How about if I go in with you and Chottie?"

"That would be fine. We drop her at the hotel, put the car in the garage, and start out at Dan's." I stood up. "I'll go over and speak to our friend."

Chottie made room for me beside her on the sofa. "Are you about ready to go?" she said.

"Entirely up to you," I said. "You don't mind if Charley Ellis rides in with us, do you?"

"Not a bit. Love to have him. How soon will you be ready to go?"

"I'm ready whenever you are. I've had all I want of this party, and if I stay much longer I'll only get too plastered to drive."

"You're not plastered now, are you? That's a big drink you have, Jim. And I noticed you jumping up and down and whispering things to Polly. Tell me if you're tight, because I'm scared to death to drive with anybody's had too much."

"No, I'm not tight. But in another hour I might be."

"You don't seem tight, but . . ."

"But what?"

"Well—just suddenly springing to your feet and taking Polly off to one side. You were like a wild man. What made you do that? Whatever you said, it had a big effect on her. First I thought she was going to cry, and then instead of that she turned all smiles. And you hardly know her."

"I told her her slip was showing."

"But it isn't. No, you didn't tell her any such thing. You sure you're not tight?"

"I'm not tight, and I won't take any more till I deliver you at the hotel." I placed my glass on the table in front of us, and she crooked her finger at Hunterden. He said something to Williamson and then came over to Chottie.

"Did you signal me?" said Hunterden.

She made sure that no one was listening, and said: "Can I drive in with you?"

It was obviously an interference with his schedule. "I understood this fellow was to take you in."

"She thinks this fellow is stewed," I said. "Where do you get that this-fellow stuff, Hunterden?"

"Jim," said Chottie. "Please?"

"Hunterden, you're a phony. You don't even tell the truth about where you were born. Where *were* you born, anyway? Not Gibbsville, P A. I know that much. And don't this-fellow me. Nobody ever heard of you in Gibbsville and your name isn't even in the Court House records."

"There's no doubt about it. He is stewed," said Hunterden. "You drive in with me and I'll take care of this nobody tomorrow. One phone call, Malloy."

"Save your crooked nickel. I won't show up at the God damn office." I now knew I was tight; I had not known it before.

"Was your father a doctor?" said Hunterden.

"Yes, my father was a doctor."

"I thought so. I didn't like *him,* either."

"But I'll bet you never told him. If you had, you wouldn't be here."

He turned to Chottie. "This fellow is trying to create a scene, and I don't want a scene here, now."

"Well let's not have one. Take me out of here and stop arguing," she said. "Jim, I don't think I'll ever forgive you for this. You're just impossible. I don't know what ever came over you all of a sudden."

"I'm not used to good booze," I said.

"Come on," said Hunterden. He put his hand under her elbow and they went to speak to Polly Williamson. She turned and said something to McDonald, and I guess he got her luggage from upstairs. Charley Ellis came and sat with me.

"What was that all about?" he said.

"I told him off, and it was damn unsatisfactory. I didn't tell him half the things I wanted to."

"Are you plastered?"

"I didn't think so, but I guess I am."

"Can you drive?"

"Oh, I think I can drive. I'm not that kind of tight. I just want to tell people off, and I'd like to give that Hunterden a crack in the jaw."

"He's twice your age and you have fifteen pounds on him. Don't do that. Don't spoil Polly's miserable party."

"I won't."

"There's something brewing between Junior and Hunterden, and you could spoil it and Junior would blame Polly."

"Oh, I realize that."

"We'll give them a chance to leave, and then you and I can go. I'll drive."

"All right."

He studied my face. "What came over you?"

"What ever possessed me? I'm like Mrs. Day. I shouldn't drink on Sunday, I guess."

Thirty years later I remember most of that spring as well as I do some things that happened a month ago. In this morning's paper they treated Charlotte Sears rather well. She did not make Page One, but they gave her two-column top heads in the *Trib* and the *Times,* called her an "early Academy Award winner" who had come out of retirement in 1958 to win a nomination for best supporting actress as the mother superior in the Joseph S. Finston production, *Benediction at Dawn.* She was described as the last member of a theatrical family that had been prominent in vaudeville during the Nineteenth Century, who had become an outstanding success in the so-called drawing-room comedies of the Twenties and Thirties. Her career, it said, was abruptly terminated in 1930, when an automobile in which she was riding was struck by a train at a grade crossing in Roslyn, Long Island, and she received facial injuries that disfigured her and forced her into a long retirement. In the same accident, Thomas R. Hunterden, in whose car Miss Sears was riding, was fatally injured. Hunterden, a stock promoter (it said), was facing indictment on six counts of fraudulent conversion and other charges. His tangled financial affairs resulted in court action over a period of three years, and his manipulations were instrumental in bringing about the creation of the Securities Exchange Act of 1934. Hunterden, a native of Gibbsville, Pa., was a somewhat mysterious, publicity-shy figure who had made a fortune through speculations during the First World War. Later he sought to gain control of motion picture companies and at the time of his death he had failed in a last-minute attempt to enlist the financial support of a syndicate headed by Ethridge B. Williamson, Jr. During the investigation of Hunterden's financial affairs Miss Sears was questioned by the district attorney in an effort to locate securities worth more than $2,000,000 which could not be accounted for, but no charges were made against her . . .

I remembered that. I went to the hospital every afternoon and read the morning and afternoon papers to her. I would sit by the window so that I could see the print; she would not allow the electric light to be turned on. There were dressings on her nose and chin, and her arm was in a cast.

She had other visitors besides me. Polly Williamson came in at least twice a week. Morrie Rosenbaum made a special trip from the Coast to tell her not to worry. She could have had more visitors, but we three were the only ones she wanted to see. When Morrie Rosenbaum heard that she was going to be questioned about the missing bonds, he telephoned me from Hollywood. "Mally," he said (at $125 a week I did not rate a correct pronunciation), "Miss Sears don't have none of them hot bonds. I stake my life on it. So I got her a lawyer. Not my lawyer. I got her Percy Goodfellow. You know who *he* is? Lawyer to the biggest firms in Wall Street. Bishops he has for clients. The very picture of integrity and a God damn shrewd man. I told him I want him there every minute they're asking her questions."

"Yes sir," I said.

"Oh, why am I telling you? Because you go to hospital and tell her she don't see no district attorney without Goodfellow being there every single minute. You understand? She can't talk to me over the phone, you understand, so you give her my instructions. You tell that little lady we don't want her worrying about a thing. Mally?"

"Yes sir?"

"Tell her love from Ruthie and Morrie. Ruthie is Mrs. Rosenbaum, my wife." He then hung up.

I was never there when Polly Williamson came to see her, but I always knew when she had been there, and not only by the flowers that she continued to bring on every visit. She would stay only ten minutes—a total of twenty minutes a week—but Chottie would always have something to say about her. "It took me a couple of weeks before I got over something," said Chottie.

"What was that?"

"Wishing she wouldn't come. I didn't want her coming here because she felt guilty, because if I hadn't gone to her place this never would of happened. I didn't want you coming for that reason, either. But with you—well, maybe you had another reason."

"I did blame myself," I said. "It was the first thing I thought of when I read about it. If I hadn't got drunk—"

"I know. But you had a man-and-woman reason for coming. I'm in your memory-book. And you're in mine, too, Jim."

"I hope so."

"But Polly doesn't blame herself. I don't think she ever did. She comes here because the night before it happened, when Junior went off with that Underwood dame, Polly knew I was mad as hell at Junior being so insulting. So crude. He was crude. But now when Polly comes to see me, she only stays ten minutes, but she always makes me feel that if she were here instead of me, she'd want me to visit her. Do you see what I mean? She'd *want* me to come. And I've never had another girl that was that kind of a friend. Even if I look like Lon Chaney when I get out of here, it won't all be a total loss."

Another time she said: "Polly was here earlier this afternoon. She came today instead of tomorrow because Etty, the boy, has to go and have his tonsils out tomorrow, poor kid. A wonderful mother, that Polly. But am I glad I don't have children. If I'd of married any of those hambo boy friends of mine—present company excepted— I'd of wanted children. But if I had a son or a daughter waiting for me to get out of here, I just couldn't face them. The first time they'd see me with my face all banged up. I read something one time about Helen of Troy, if she had a nose that was different by a fraction of an inch, it would have changed the history of the world. Well, mine's going to be different, but it sure as hell isn't going to change the history of the world."

My reading to her was usually confined to the theatrical and movie news and reviews, book reviews, the gossip columns, the principal news stories, and occasionally the sail-and-arrive items on the society pages. "Ah, Eunice Underwood sailed yesterday in the *Ile de France,* to be gone a year," I said.

"No matter how I look when I get out of here, I'll have a better figure than she ever had," she said. "I had a lovely figure."

"And still have."

"I wonder what I'll do about that? Oh, I guess I'll find somebody."

She was depressed.

"They're all the same from the top row in the balcony," she said. "They're all the same with a bag over their heads. I saw a comedy bit in a two-reeler one time. The comic, I forget who it was, he sees this girl in a one-piece bathing suit, great figure, and he follows her up the beach and tries to pick her up. Then when she turns around she has a face like Bull Montana. The comic did a Bobby Vernon grando and ran. I don't think it's as funny now as I did when I saw it. Now don't give me false encouragement."

"How do you know I was going to give you any?"

"Because I can see you, even if you can't see me. And you were going to say something encouraging. Don't. They're gonna do what they can, the doctors. I'll have a different nose, and they've got this wire in my jaw. I'll be able to put make-up over the scar in my cheek. I was thinking of changing my name and starting out playing character bits, but everybody'd know it was me. That'd be too good a story for you boys in publicity."

"It would get around, even if we laid off."

"Yes, and the last thing I want is stuff about brave little Charlotte Sears. If I have to be brave I don't want to be brave in public."

"You have spunk, just like your mother."

"That's one satisfaction. I'm beginning to get over my inferiority complex about her. But I'm only—well, I'm under forty, and I hope and pray I find a good man. God protect me from gigolos. God keep me from paying a man to sleep with me."

She in her wisdom had thought it all out, the danger she faced that had been my secret worry for her. We both knew actresses who kept gigolos, and we knew that the gigolos laughed at them and that some of the actresses even made cruel jokes at themselves.

"You have plenty of money," I said. "Look around and get something to do."

"Don't think I haven't thought about that. I could be an agent. I know this business cold, and I have the contacts. A lot of things I *could* do, like being a script girl. Wardrobe. But I was a star, and I don't need the money. I've been trying to think what I could do out of show business entirely. I wish I'd gone to high school, then I could go to college and study to be a doctor. I guess I'll get over that as soon as I get out of here, but it was one idea I had. Open a shop, but I'd soon get tired of that. Interior decorator. Doesn't interest me."

"Charity work," I suggested.

"No, I'm too accustomed to making my own living. I have to do something I'll be paid for, even if it isn't much at first. By the way, Jim. You're still going to take that trip to Europe."

"No."

"Yes. I didn't mention it before because I needed you here. But in another three or four weeks I'll be going back to the Coast."

"I don't want to go to Europe. As soon as you leave I'm quitting Rosenbaums'. I start a new job the first of August. Second-string dramatic critic. It's a job I want. Pretty good pay, and time to start writing a novel."

"Morrie's paying my bills here, you know, so it isn't a question of money."

"Be honest, Chottie."

"Well, I'll tell you. Morrie is paying all my bills and I'm letting him do that. He really wants to, and I want him to. It makes him feel good, he and Ruthie. But of course I'm through at the Studio. I'm going to sell my house and have that money for capital. The money I've invested will keep me the rest of my life, not in luxury, but comfortably. I'll get a little house out in the Brentwood section for me and my maid, and I'll live quietly out there. Morrie told me I'd never have to worry about money, and he's one that keeps his word. Well, if he gives me as much every year as I have been getting every week, finances won't worry me. Morrie says he'll figure out a way to keep me on the payroll. Story department, most likely. He knows I'm a great reader, and if I give them one story idea a year, like suggesting a magazine serial they ought to buy, I'll be earning my pay."

"You certainly will."

"There's one thing I've always been interested in and it's why I always used to go for walks. Remember me telling you I used to go for those long walks when I was on the road? You know, in most towns I played, if you walk steadily for fifteen-twenty minutes, you're out of the business section and you start getting in the residential."

"It's only about a hundred-yard dash where I come from."

"Yes, it varies with the size of the town. But when you get out of the built-up section, you come to the thing that interested me the most. Hold on to your seat."

"I'm holding on."

"Flowers. I love flowers. I used to ask the stagehands who had the best gardens in every town I went to. The wise-guys used to ask me if I meant beer gardens. Sometimes I'd take the trolley to look at a garden, if it was too far out to walk. If there was a real famous one, big, I'd even take a taxi. I have over a hundred books on flowers and gardening. You know, Polly Williamson I discovered knows a lot about flowers, but I have to admit, I know more. You know, most flowers have at least two names. Different names in different countries, like larkspur for delphinium, bachelor's button for cornflower. That's in addition to the Latin names. I never got as far as Latin, so I don't know many Latin names, but I guess I've learned about fifty, the more common flowers. Our California flowers—" She halted. "That's enough of that. When I start talking about our California flowers. Do you know who loved flowers?"

"Who?"

"Loved flowers, and had a great knowledge of them. Tom Hunterden. A discovery we both made by accident. One day he was at my house and he got up and walked over slowly toward one of my rose bushes. 'What's the matter?' I said. 'Do you see a snake?' Up where my house is we get rattlers. 'No,' he said. 'This is a hybrid tea rose, and I've been thinking of putting them in at home.' We didn't spend *all* our time talking about picture business, Jim. Even if you didn't like him, he was a fascinating man."

"Why were you afraid of him? You told me once you were."

"I wasn't afraid of him. But he inspired fear in me. It wasn't only the fear of losing him. It was just fear, Jim. A lot of times just thinking about him would make me afraid of something, I didn't know what. He believed in hunches himself, and hunches are nothing but intuition. I had the same thing after I got to know him. Not hunches. But intuitive fear."

"A premonition?"

"Yes, I guess it was, considering what happened. When I came to New York this last time, when he didn't meet me at the station, I was upset but I was relieved. I thought maybe he and I were through and I'd get over this fear I had. I was glad to make love with you, because that showed me that I wasn't hypnotized by Hunterden. But I guess maybe I was hypnotized by him, if you remember later that night. By the way, did you sleep with that show girl?"

"No."

"She was a real gold-digger. She was a Ziegfeld edition of Eunice Underwood. That's one thing nobody could ever say about me. Will you write to me, answer my letters if I write to you?"

By agreement I did not see her off when she left the hospital, and I did not know the condition of her face. She took the less fashionable trains, and had reservations under fictitious names. Ruth Rosenbaum met her in Los Angeles and helped her to find the house in Brentwood that she bought as Catherine Dowd. With make-up to cover the scar, she did not look too awful unless you remembered the original, but in the new house she had no photographs of herself before the accident, and she was gradually trying to get used to the new face and the old name. All this I learned in her occasional, chatty letters, which came less frequently as time went on. Brentwood was not fancy enough for the movie stars who were buying and building in Beverly Hills, although Greta Garbo lived not far from Chottie's house. "She vants to be alone and so do I," wrote

Chottie, "but I really am. I went shopping in Santa Monica and nobody recognized me. I have not got up nerve enough to shop in Beverly but I will."

Then one day, about a year after the accident, she wrote that she had bought a greenhouse, which she was calling Dowd & Company, and her letters became few and far between. We exchanged Christmas cards, but I stopped hearing from her until 1934, when my novel was published and she sent me some California reviews. She had bought a copy of the book but had not had a chance to read it but would read it before I got to California, which she knew would be as soon as she had read that I had signed with Paramount.

I drove out to have dinner at her house and I realized on the way that I had never seen her face after the accident. I found her house with some difficulty. The place was surrounded by an eight-foot hedge that gave her complete privacy, and since I knew I was to be the only guest for dinner, I parked my car in the short driveway and rang the front doorbell.

She opened it herself, swung it wide and stood smiling.

"Would you have recognized me?" she said.

"Not immediately, not unless you spoke." I kissed her and she hugged me.

"You don't have to be careful what you say. I'm all right. It's so good to see you again. You're older, and more attractive that way. You've been married and divorced, and you've written a fine book, and what kind of a deal did you make at Paramount?"

"One of those seven-year option things. I signed the first contract they offered me because I wanted to get out of New York. How is Dowd & Company?"

"Doing very well. It was tough in the beginning, but I survived the first year, and the second year I just about broke even on the business, and now there's a lot of real-estate activity in this section and that means business for us."

"Us? You have a partner?"

"You'll meet him." She nodded without looking at me. "I found somebody."

"That's the best news, Chottie."

She nodded again. "Yes. I did the other, though. What I was afraid I'd do, out of loneliness and desperation. He wasn't a gigolo with patent-leather hair. He was a young writer, very unsuccessful *and,* I found out, not very talented. I had a hard time getting rid of him."

"How did you?"

"I gave him money to go to Mexico."

"That doesn't always work."

"Not if you have no one else, but now I have someone else."

"Tell me about him."

"Oh, I will. He's married, of course. Separated from his wife. He's fifty, has two grown children that live with her, down in Whittier. That's on the other side of Los Angeles. He's a landscape architect and that's how I met him."

"And what of the future?"

"His wife won't give him a divorce till the daughter gets married, but that will be in June, when she finishes college. Then we have over a year to wait, but what's a year? The wife is as anxious to get out of it as he is, but not before the girl is married off. He has a room over in Santa Monica. Most of his work is around here. Brentwood Heights. Beverly. Bel-Air. He isn't really my partner yet, but I don't know what I'd do without him. I couldn't."

We had a good dinner, starting, as Californians do, with a salad, and we talked without pause until nine-thirty, when the doorbell rang. "That's Lou. On the dot. By the way, he knows about you and our one matinée, so don't mind if he sizes you up."

Louis Grafmiller was a stocky, sunburned man with close-cropped iron-gray hair. "Hello, Catherine," he said, and kissed her on the lips. He shook hands with me and it was a firm handshake.

"Glad to know you, Mr. Malloy," he said. "This girl is always singing your praises."

"Well, she's just finished singing some of yours," I said.

"Have a drink, Lou?"

"Oh, a glass of wine, maybe. Some of that Chianti? You just get in from the East?"

"Monday."

"Your first visit to California, Catherine said."

"Yes, I'd never been west of the Mississippi before."

"It's a big country, and a good country. People don't realize how big or how good. They ought to get around more and see what they have before they turn it over to the Communists. I know I didn't vote to take it away from Wall Street just to hand it over to those other bastards."

I had a quick revelation of what he would do to Chottie's gigolo writer if he ever showed up again. She was well protected now.

"I understand your book is a big success. Do you know Ernest Hemingway?"

"No."

"I like his kind of writing. Catherine gave me your book but I haven't started it yet."

"Are you going to write another, Jim?" said Chottie.

"Yes, when I go back. I don't think I'll stay out here past the first option."

"Don't you like California?" he smiled.

"Not yet. I don't dislike it yet, either. But I'll never be a Californian."

"That's what I said twenty-five years ago, but I'm still here. There are only two states that have everything. California, and Pennsylvania."

"I'm from Pennsylvania."

"I know. So am I. Pittsburgh. You're from the other end of the state. I have cousins in Reading."

Now slowly I was conscious of Chottie's changed face as she listened to our conversation; it was very right that her face should be different when she herself was so different as well. Her face, her name, and the domesticity were all new to me. I was still very fond of what I could remember, but when I left her house she shook hands with me, did not kiss me, and we were both reconciled to the finality of the farewell. Grafmiller walked with me to my car and gave me directions for getting back to Hollywood, and I could not help thinking that he had likewise directed Chottie, but not in the way I was headed. We did not bother to shake hands. Neither of us regarded the introduction as a true meeting, and we paid this silent respect to our harmless mutual animosity.

I never heard from her after that night, although I often went to Hollywood to work on movie scripts. Once on an impulse I looked up Grafmiller in the telephone book and his address was the same as the house where I had met him, hers. Then I heard somewhere that he had died, but the information came long after his death and I did not write to Chottie. She was swallowed up in the anonymity of former movie stars living in Los Angeles—the easiest way for a former movie star to become obscure—until Joe Finston put her in *Benediction at Dawn.* In today's obituaries there is mention of Louis Grafmiller, but not a word about their greenhouse, and for some reason or other that pleased me. On the same page there was an obituary of a man who had once won the 500 mile race at Indianapolis but who died while playing shuffleboard at St. Petersburg, Florida.

I close this reminiscence with one more fact. Thomas Rodney Hunterden was born Thomas Robert Huntzinger in Gibbsville, Pa. I have no idea why he disliked my father, and I am long past caring.

IMAGINE KISSING PETE

♦

To those who knew the bride and groom, the marriage of Bobbie
Hammersmith and Pete McCrea was the surprise of the year.
As late as April of '29 Bobbie was still engaged to a fellow who
lived in Greenwich, Connecticut, and she had told friends that the
wedding would take place in September. But the engagement was
broken and in a matter of weeks the invitations went out for her
June wedding to Pete. One of the most frequently uttered comments
was that Bobbie was not giving herself much opportunity to change
her mind again. The comment was doubly cruel, since it carried the
implication that if she gave herself time to think, Pete McCrea
would not be her ideal choice. It was not only that she was marrying
Pete on the rebound; she seemed to be going out of her way to find
someone who was so unlike her other beaus that the contrast was
unavoidable. And it was.

I was working in New York and Pete wrote to ask me to be an
usher. Pete and I had grown up together, played together as children, and gone to dancing school and to the same parties. But we
had never been close friends and when Pete and I went away to our
separate prep schools and, later, Pete to Princeton and I to work, we
drifted into that relationship of young men who had known each
other all their lives without creating anything that was enduring or
warm. As a matter of fact, I had never in my life received a written
communication from Pete McCrea, and his handwriting on the envelope was new to me, as mine in my reply was to him. He men-

77

tioned who the best man and the other ushers would be—all Gibbsville boys—and this somewhat pathetic commentary on his four
years in prep school and four years in college made an appeal to
home town and boyhood loyalty that I could not reject. I had some
extra days coming to me at the office, and so I told Pete I would be
honored to be one of his ushers. My next step was to talk to a Gibbsville girl who lived in New York, a friend of Bobbie Hammersmith's. I took her to dinner at an Italian speakeasy where my credit
was good, and she gave me what information she had. She was to be
a bridesmaid.

"Bobbie isn't saying a word," said Kitty Clark. "That is, nothing
about the inner turmoil. Nothing *intime.* Whatever happened happened the last time she was in New York, four or five weeks ago. All
she'd tell me was that Johnny White was impossible. Impossible.
Well, he'd been very possible all last summer and fall."

"What kind of a guy was he?" I asked.

"Oh—*attractive,*" she said. "Sort of wild, I guess, but not a roué.
Maybe he is a roué, but I'd say more just wild. I honestly don't
know a thing about it, but it wouldn't surprise me if Bobbie was
ready to settle down, and he wasn't. She was probably more in love
with him than he was with her."

"I doubt that. She wouldn't turn around and marry Pete if she
were still in love with this White guy."

"Oh, *wouldn't* she? Oh, are you ever wrong there. If she wanted to
thumb her nose at Johnny, I can't think of a better way. Poor Pete.
You know *Pete.* Ichabod McCrea. Remember when Mrs. McCrea
made us stop calling him Ichabod? Lord and Taylor! She went to see
my mother and I guess all the other mothers and said it just had to
stop. Bad enough calling her little Angus by such a common nickname as Pete. But calling a boy Ichabod. I don't suppose Pete ever
knew his mother went around like that."

"Yes he did. It embarrassed him. It always embarrassed him
when Mrs. McCrea did those things."

"Yes, she was uncanny. I can remember when I was going to have
a party, practically before I'd made out the list Mrs. McCrea would

call Mother to be sure Pete wasn't left out. Not that I never would have left him out. We all always had the same kids to our parties. But Mrs. McCrea wasn't leaving anything to chance. I'm dying to hear what she has to say about this marriage. I'll bet she doesn't like it, but I'll bet she's in fear and trembling in case Bobbie changes her mind again. Ichabod McCrea and Bobbie Hammersmith. Beauty and the beast. And actually he's not even a beast. It would be better if he were. She's the third of our old bunch to get married, but much as I hate to say it, I'll bet she'll be the first to get a divorce. Imagine *kissing* Pete, let alone any of the rest of it."

The wedding was on a Saturday afternoon; four o'clock in Trinity Church, and the reception at the country club. It had been two years since I last saw Bobbie Hammersmith and she was now twenty-two, but she could have passed for much more than that. She was the only girl in her crowd who had not bobbed her hair, which was jet-black and which she always wore with plaited buns over the ears. Except in the summer her skin was like Chinese white and it was always easy to pick her out first in group photographs; her eyes large dark dots, quite far apart, and her lips small but prominent in the whiteness of her face beneath the two small dots of her nose. In summer, with a tan, she reminded many non-operagoers of Carmen. She was a striking beauty, although it took two years' absence from her for me to realize it. In the theatre they have an expression, "walked through the part," which means that an actress played a role without giving it much of herself. Bobbie walked through the part of bride-to-be. A great deal of social activity was concentrated in the three days—Thursday, Friday, and Saturday—up to and including the wedding reception; but Bobbie walked through the part. Today, thirty years later, it would be assumed that she had been taking tranquilizers, but this was 1929.

Barbara Hammersmith had never been anything but a pretty child; if she had ever been homely it must have been when she was a small baby, when I was not bothering to look at her. We—Pete McCrea and the other boys—were two, three, four years older than Bobbie, but when she was fifteen or sixteen she began to pass among us, from boy to boy, trying one and then another, causing several fist fights, and half promising but never delivering anything more than the "soul kisses" that were all we really expected. By the time she was eighteen she had been in and out of love with all of us with the solitary exception of Pete McCrea. When she broke off with a boy, she would also make up with the girl he had temporarily deserted for Bobbie, and all the girls came to understand that every boy in the crowd had to go through a love affair with her. Consequently Bobbie was popular; the boys remembered her kisses, the girls forgave her because the boys had been returned virtually intact. We used the word hectic a lot in those days; Kitty Clark explained the short duration of Bobbie's love affairs by observing that being in love with Bobbie was too hectic for most boys. It was also true that it was not hectic enough. The boys agreed that Bobbie was a hot little number, but none of us could claim that she was not a virgin. At eighteen Bobbie entered a personal middle age, and for the big social occasions her beaus came from out-of-town. She was also busy at the college proms and football games, as far west as Ann Arbor, as far north as Brunswick, Maine. I was working on the Gibbsville paper during some of those years, the only boy in our crowd who was not away at college, and I remember Ann Arbor because Bobbie went there wearing a Delta Tau Delta pin and came back wearing the somewhat larger Psi U. "Now don't you say anything in front of Mother," she said. "She thinks they're both the same."

We played auction bridge, the social occupation in towns like ours, and Bobbie and I were assimilated into an older crowd: the younger married set and the youngest of the couples who were in their thirties. We played for prizes—flasks, cigarette lighters, vanity cases, cartons of cigarettes—and there was a party at someone's house every week. The hostess of the evening usually asked me to stop for Bobbie, and I saw her often. Her father and mother would be reading the evening paper and sewing when I arrived to pick up Bobbie. Philip Hammersmith was not a native of Gibbsville, but he had lived there long enough to have gone to the Mexican Border in

1916 with the Gibbsville company of mounted engineers, and he had gone to France with them, returning as a first lieutenant and with the Croix de Guerre with palm. He was one of the best golfers in the club, and everyone said he was making money hand-over-fist as an independent coal operator. He wore steel-rim glasses and he had almost completely gray hair, cut short. He inspired trust and confidence. He was slow-moving, taller than six feet, and always thought before speaking. His wife, a Gibbsville girl, was related, as she said, to half the town; a lively little woman who took her husband's arm even if they were walking only two doors away. I always used to feel that whatever he may have wanted out of life, yet unattained or unattainable, she had just what she wanted: a good husband, a nice home, and a pretty daughter who would not long remain unmarried. At home in the evening, and whenever I saw him on the street, Mr. Hammersmith was wearing a dark-gray worsted suit, cut loose and with a soft roll to the lapel; black knit four-in-hand necktie; white shirt; heavy gray woolen socks, and thick-soled brogues. This costume, completely unadorned—he wore a wrist watch—was what he always wore except for formal occasions, and the year-to-year sameness of his attire constituted his only known eccentricity. He was on the board of the second most conservative bank, the trustees of Gibbsville Hospital, the armory board, the Y.M.C.A., and the Gibbsville and Lantenengo country clubs. Nevertheless I sensed that that was not all there was to Philip Hammersmith, that the care he put into the creation of the general picture of himself—hard work, quiet clothes, thoughtful manner, conventional associations—was done with a purpose that was not necessarily sinister but was extraordinarily private. It delighted me to discover, one night while waiting for Bobbie, that he knew more about what was going on than most of us suspected he would know. "Jimmy, you know Ed Charney, of course," he said.

I knew Ed Charney, the principal bootlegger in the area. "Yes, I know him pretty well," I said.

"Then do you happen to know if there's any truth to what I heard? I heard that his wife is threatening to divorce him."

"I doubt it. They're Catholics."

"Do you know her?"

"Yes. I went to Sisters' school with her."

"Oh, then maybe you can tell me something else. I've heard that she's the real brains of those two."

"She quit school after eighth grade, so I don't know about that. I don't remember her being particularly bright. She's about my age but she was two grades behind me."

"I see. And you think their religion will keep them from getting a divorce?"

"Yes, I do. I don't often see Ed at Mass, but I know he carries rosary beads. And she's at the eleven o'clock Mass every Sunday, all dolled up."

This conversation was explained when Repeal came and with it public knowledge that Ed Charney had been quietly buying bank stock, one of several moves he had made in the direction of respectability. But the chief interest to me at the time Mr. Hammersmith and I talked was in the fact that he knew anything at all about the Charneys. It was so unlike him even to mention Ed Charney's name.

To get back to the weekend of Bobbie Hammersmith's wedding: it was throughout that weekend that I first saw Bobbie have what we called that faraway look, that another generation called Cloud 90. If you happened to catch her at the right moment, you would see her smiling up at Pete in a way that must have been reassuring to Mrs. McCrea and to Mrs. Hammersmith, but I also caught her at several wrong moments and I saw something I had never seen before: a resemblance to her father that was a subtler thing than the mere duplication of such features as mouth, nose, and set of the eyes. It was almost the same thing I have mentioned in describing Philip Hammersmith; the wish yet unattained or unattainable. However, the pre-nuptial parties and the wedding and reception went off without a hitch, or so I believed until the day after the wedding.

Kitty Clark and I were on the same train going back to New York and I made some comment about the exceptional sobriety of the ushers and how everything had gone according to plan. "Amazing, considering," said Kitty.

"Considering what?"

"That there was almost no wedding at all," she said. "You must promise word of honor, Jimmy, or I won't tell you."

"I promise. Word of honor."

"Well, after Mrs. McCrea's very-dull-I-must-say luncheon, when we all left to go to Bobbie's? A little after two o'clock?"

"Yes."

"Bobbie asked me if I'd go across the street to our house and put in a long-distance call to Johnny White. I said I couldn't do that, and what on earth was she thinking of. And Bobbie said, 'You're my oldest and best friend. The least you can do is make this one last effort, to keep me from ruining my life.' So I gave in and I dashed over to our house and called Johnny. He was out and they didn't know where he could be reached or what time he was coming home. So I left my name. *My* name, not Bobbie's. Six o'clock, at the reception, I was dancing with—I was dancing with *you*."

"When the waiter said you were wanted on the phone."

"It was Johnny. He'd been sailing and just got in. I made up some story about why I'd called him, but he didn't swallow it. '*You* didn't call me,' he said. '*Bobbie* did.' Well of course I wouldn't admit that. By that time she was married, and if her life was already ruined it would be a darned sight more ruined if I let him talk to her. Which he wanted to do. Then he tried to pump me. Where were they going on their wedding trip? I said nobody knew, which was a barefaced lie. I knew they were going to Bermuda. Known it since Thursday. But I wouldn't tell Johnny . . . I don't like him a bit after yesterday. I'd thought he was attractive, and he *is,* but he's got a mean streak that I never knew before. Feature this, if you will. When he realized I wasn't going to get Bobbie to come to the phone, or give him any information, he said, 'Well, no use wasting a long-distance call. What are you doing next weekend? How about coming out here?'

'I'm not that hard up,' I said, and banged down the receiver. I hope I shattered his eardrum."

I saw Pete and Bobbie McCrea when I went home the following Christmas. They were living in a small house on Twin Oaks Road, a recent real-estate development that had been instantly successful with the sons and daughters of the big two- and three-servant mansions. They were not going to any of the holiday dances; Bobbie was expecting a baby in April or early May.

"You're not losing any time," I said.

"I don't want to lose any time," said Bobbie. "I want to have a lot of children. Pete's an only child and so am I, and we don't think it's fair, if you can afford to have more."

"If we can afford it. The way that stock market is going, we'll be lucky to pay for this one," said Pete.

"Oh, don't start on that, Pete. That's all Father talks about," said Bobbie. "My father *was* hit pretty hard, but I wish he didn't have to keep talking about it all the time. Everybody's in the same boat."

"No they're not. *We're* on a *raft*."

"I asked you, please, Pete. Jimmy didn't come here to listen to our financial woes. Do you see much of Kitty? I've owed her a letter for ages."

"No, I haven't seen her since last summer, we went out a few times," I said.

"Kitty went to New York to try to rope in a millionaire. She isn't going to waste her time on Jim."

"That's not what she went to New York for at all. And as far as wasting her time on Jim, Jim may not want to waste his time on her." She smiled. "Have you got a girl, Jim?"

"Not really."

"Wise. Very wise," said Pete McCrea.

"I don't know how wise. It's just that I have a hell of a hard time supporting myself, without trying to support a wife, too," I said.

"Why I understood you were selling articles to magazines, and going around with all the big shots."

"I've had four jobs in two years, and the jobs didn't last very long. If things get any tougher I may have to come back here. At least I'll have a place to sleep and something to eat."

"But I see your name in magazines," said Pete. "I don't always read your articles, but they must pay you well."

"They don't. At least I can't live on the magazine pieces without a steady job. Excuse me, Bobbie. Now you're getting *my* financial woes."

"She'll listen to yours. It's mine she doesn't want to hear about."

"That's because I know about ours. I'm never allowed to forget them," said Bobbie. "Are you going to all the parties?"

"Yes, stag. I have to bum rides. I haven't got a car."

"We resigned from the club," said Pete.

"Well we didn't *have* to do that," said Bobbie. "Father was going to give it to us for a Christmas present. And you have your job."

"We'll see how much longer I have it. Is that the last of the gin?"

"Yes."

Pete rose. "I'll be back."

"Don't buy any more for me," I said.

"You flatter yourself," he said. "I wasn't only getting it for you." He put on his hat and coat. "No funny business while I'm gone. I remember you two."

He kept a silly grin on his face while saying the ugly things, but the grin was not genuine and the ugly things were.

"I don't know what's the matter with him," said Bobbie. "Oh, I do, but why talk about it?"

"He's only kidding."

"You know better than that. He says worse things, much worse, and I'm only hoping they don't get back to Father. Father has enough on his mind. I thought if I had this baby right away it would—you know—give Pete confidence. But it's had just the opposite effect. He says it isn't his child. *Isn't his child!* Oh, I married him out of spite. I'm sure Kitty must have told you that. But it *is* his child, I swear it, Jim. It couldn't be anybody else's."

"I guess it's the old inferiority complex," I said.

"The first month we were married—Pete was a virgin—and I

admit it, I wasn't. I stayed with two boys before I was married. But I was certainly not pregnant when I married Pete, and the first few weeks he was loving and sweet, and grateful. But then something happened to him, and he made a pass at I-won't-say-who. It was more than a pass. It was quite a serious thing. I might as well tell you. It was Phyllis. We were all at a picnic at the Dam and several people got pretty tight, Pete among them. And there's no other word for it, he tried to rape Phyllis. Tore her bathing suit and slapped her and did other things. She got away from him and ran back to the cottage without anyone seeing her. Luckily Joe didn't see her or I'm sure he'd have killed Pete. You know, Joe's strong as an ox and terribly jealous. I found out about it from Phyllis herself. She came here the next day and told me. She said she wasn't going to say anything to Joe, but that we mustn't invite her to our house and she wasn't going to invite us to hers."

"I'm certainly glad Joe didn't hear about it. He would do something drastic," I said. "But didn't he notice that you two weren't going to his house, and they to yours? It's a pretty small group."

She looked at me steadily. "We haven't been going anywhere. My excuse is that I'm pregnant, but the truth is, we're not being asked. It didn't end with Phyllis, Jim. One night at a dinner party Mary Lander just slapped his face, in front of everybody. Everybody laughed and thought Pete must have said something, but it wasn't something he'd said. He'd taken her hand and put it—you know. This is *Pete! Ichabod!* Did you ever know any of this about him?"

"You mean have I heard any of this? No."

"No, I didn't mean that. I meant, did he go around making passes and I never happened to hear about it?"

"No. When we'd talk dirty he'd say, 'Why don't you fellows get your minds above your belts?' "

"I wish your father were still alive. I'd go see him and try to get some advice. I wouldn't think of going to Dr. English."

"Well, you're not the one that needs a doctor. Could you get Pete to go to one? He's a patient of Dr. English's, isn't he?"

"Yes, but so is Mrs. McCrea, and Pete would never confide in Dr. English."

"Or anyone else at this stage, I guess," I said. "I'm not much help, am I?"

"Oh, I didn't expect you to have a solution. You know, Jim, I wish you would come back to Gibbsville. Other girls in our crowd have often said it was nice to have you to talk to. Of course you were a very bad boy, too, but a lot of us miss you."

"That's nice to hear, Bobbie. Thank you. I may be back, if I don't soon make a go of it in New York. I won't have any choice."

During that Christmas visit I heard other stories about Pete McCrea. In general they were told as plain gossip, but two or three times there was a hint of a lack of sympathy for Bobbie. "She knew what she was doing . . . she made her bed . . ." And while there was no lack of righteous indignation over Pete's behavior, he had changed in six months from a semi-comic figure to an unpleasant man, but a man nevertheless. In half a year he had lost most of his old friends; they all said, "You've never seen such a change come over anybody in all your life," but when they remembered to call him Ichabod it was only to emphasize the change.

Bobbie's baby was born in April, but lived only a few weeks. "She was determined to have that baby," Kitty Clark told me. "She had to prove to Pete that it was anyway *conceived* after she married him. But it must have taken all her strength to hold on to it that long. All her strength *and* the baby's. Now would be a good time for her to divorce him. She can't go on like that."

But there was no divorce, and Bobbie was pregnant again when I saw her at Christmas, 1930. They no longer lived in the Twin Oaks Road house, and her father and mother had given up their house on Lantenengo Street. The Hammersmiths were living in an apartment on Market Street, and Bobbie and Pete were living with Mrs. McCrea. "Temporarily, till Pete decides whether to take this job in Tulsa, Oklahoma," said Bobbie.

"Who do you think you're kidding?" said Pete. "It isn't a question of me deciding. It's a cousin of mine deciding if he'll take me on. And why the hell should he?"

"Well, you've had several years' banking experience," she said.

"Yes. And if I was so good, why did the bank let me go? Jim knows all this. What else have you heard about us, Jim? Did you hear Bobbie was divorcing me?"

"It doesn't look that way from here," I said.

"You mean because she's pregnant? That's elementary biology, and God knows you're acquainted with the facts of life. But if you want to be polite, all right. Pretend you didn't hear she was getting a divorce. You might as well pretend Mr. and Mrs. Hammersmith are still living on Lantenengo Street. If they were, Bobbie'd have got her divorce."

"Everybody tells me what I *was* going to do or *am* going to do," said Bobbie. "Nobody ever consults me."

"I suppose that's a crack at my mother."

"Oh, for Christ's sake, Pete, lay off, at least while I'm here," I said.

"Why? You like to think of yourself as an old friend of the family, so you might as well get a true picture. When you get married, if you ever do, I'll come and see you, and maybe your wife will cry on my shoulder." He got up and left the house.

"Well, it's just like a year ago," said Bobbie. "When you came to call on us last Christmas?"

"Where will he go now?"

"Oh, there are several places where he can charge drinks. They all think Mrs. McCrea has plenty of money, but they're due for a rude awakening. She's living on capital, but she's not going to sell any bonds to pay his liquor bills."

"Then maybe *he's* due for a rude awakening."

"Any awakening would be better than the last three months, since the bank fired him. He sits here all day long, then after Mrs. McCrea goes to bed he goes to one of his speakeasies." She sat up straighter. "He has a lady friend. Or have you heard?"

"No."

"Yes. He graduated from making passes at all my friends. He had to. We were never invited anywhere. Yes, he has a girl friend. Do you remember Muriel Nierhaus?"

"The chiropractor's wife. Sure. Big fat Muriel Minzer till she married Nierhaus, then we used to say he gave her some adjustments. Where is Nierhaus?"

"Oh, he's opened several offices. Very prosperous. He divorced her but she gets alimony. She's Pete's girl friend. Muriel Minzer is *Angus McCrea's* girl friend."

"You don't seem too displeased," I said.

"Would you be, if you were in my position?"

"I guess I know what you mean. But—well, nothing."

"But why don't I get a divorce?" She shook her head. "A spite marriage is a terrible thing to do to anybody. If I hadn't deliberately selected Pete out of all the boys I knew, he'd have gone on till Mrs. McCrea picked out somebody for him, and it would almost have had to be the female counterpart of Pete. A girl like—oh—Florence. Florence Temple."

"Florence Temple, with her cello. Exactly right."

"But I did that awful thing to Pete, and the first few weeks of marriage were just too much for him. He went haywire. I'd slept with two boys before I was married, so it wasn't as much of a shock to me. But Pete almost wore me out. And such adoration, I can't tell you. Then when we came back from Bermuda he began to see all the other girls he'd known all his life, and he'd ask me about them. It was as though he'd never seen them before, in a way. In other ways, it was as though he'd just been waiting all his life to start ripping their clothes off. He was dangerous, Jim. He really was. I could almost tell who would be next by the questions he'd ask. Before we'd go to a party, he'd say 'Who's going to be there tonight?' And I'd say I thought the usual crowd. Then he'd rattle off the list of names of our friends, and leave out one name. That was supposed to fool me, but it didn't for long. The name he left out, that girl was almost sure to be in for a bad time."

"And now it's all concentrated on Muriel Minzer?"

"As far as I know."

"Well, that's a break for you, *and* the other girls. Did you ever talk to him about the passes he made at the others?"

"Oh, how could we avoid it? Whoever it was, she was always 'that little whore.' "

"Did he ever get anywhere with any of them?"

She nodded. "One, but I won't tell you who. There was one girl that didn't stop him, and when that happened he wanted me to sleep with her husband."

"Swap, eh?"

"Yes. But I said I wasn't interested. Pete wanted to know why not? Why wouldn't I? And I almost told him. The boy was one of the two boys I'd stayed with before I was married—oh, when I was seventeen. And he never told anybody and neither have I, or ever will."

"You mean one of our old crowd actually did get somewhere with you, Bobbie?"

"One did. But don't try to guess. It won't do you any good to guess, because I'd never, never tell."

"Well, whichever one it was, he's the best liar I ever knew. And I guess the nicest guy in our whole crowd. You know, Bobbie, the whole damn bunch are going to get credit now for being as honorable as one guy."

"You were all nice, even if you all did talk too much. If it had been you, you would have lied, too."

"No, I don't think I would have."

"You lied about Kitty. Ha ha ha. You didn't know I knew about you and Kitty. I knew it the next day. The very next day. If you don't believe me, I'll tell you where it happened and how it happened, and all about it. That was the great bond we had in common. You and Kitty, and I and this other boy."

"Then Kitty's a gentleman, because she never told me a word about you."

"I kissed every boy in our crowd except Pete, and I necked, heavy-necked two, as you well know, and stayed with one."

"The question is, did you stay with the other one that you heavy-necked with?"

"You'll never know, Jim, and please don't try to find out."

"I won't, but I won't be able to stop theorizing," I said.

We knew everything, everything there was to know. We were so far removed from the technical innocence of eighteen, sixteen, nineteen. I was a man of the world, and Bobbie was indeed a woman, who had borne a child and lived with a husband who had come the most recently to the knowledge we had acquired, but was already the most intricately involved in the complications of sex. We—Bobbie and I—could discuss him and still remain outside the problems of Pete McCrea. We could almost remain outside our own problems. We knew so much, and since what we knew seemed to be all there was to know, we were shockproof. We had come to our maturity and our knowledgeability during the long decade of cynicism that was usually dismissed as "a cynical disregard of the law of the land," but that was something else, something deeper. The law had been passed with a "noble" but nevertheless cynical disregard of men's right to drink. It was a law that had been imposed on some who took pleasure in drinking by some who did not. And when the law was an instant failure, it was not admitted to be a failure by those who had imposed it. They fought to retain the law in spite of its immediate failure and its proliferating corruption, and they fought as hard as they would have for a law that had been an immediate success. They gained no recruits to their own way; they had only deserters, who were not brave deserters but furtive ones; there was no honest mutiny but only grumbling and small disobediences. And we grew up listening to the grumbling, watching the small disobediences; laughing along when the grumbling was intentionally funny, imitating the small disobediences in other ways besides the customs of drinking. It was not only a cynical disregard for a law of the land; the law was eventually changed. Prohibition, the zealots' attempt to force total abstinence on a temperate nation, made liars of a hundred million men and cheats of their children; the West Point cadets who cheated in examinations, the basketball players who connived with gamblers, the thousands of uncaught cheats in the high schools and colleges. We had grown up and away from our earlier esteem of God and country and valor, and had matured at a moment when riches were vanishing for reasons that we could not understand. We were the losing, not the lost, generation. We could not blame Pete McCrea's troubles—and Bobbie's—on the Southern Baptists and the Northern Methodists. Since we knew everything, we knew that Pete's sudden release from twenty years of frustrations had turned him loose in a world filled with women. But Bobbie and I sat there in her mother-in-law's house, breaking several laws of possession, purchase, transportation and consumption of liquor, and with great calmness discussing the destruction of two lives—one of them hers—and the loss of her father's fortune, the depletion of her mother-in-law's, the allure of a chiropractor's divorcée, and our own promiscuity. We knew everything, but we were incapable of recognizing the meaning of our complacency.

I was wearing my dinner jacket, and someone was going to pick me up and take me to a dinner dance at the club. "Who's stopping for you?" said Bobbie.

"It depends. Either Joe or Frank. Depends on whether they go in Joe's car or Frank's. I'm to be ready when they blow their horn."

"Do me a favor, Jim. Make them come in. Pretend you don't hear the horn."

"If it's Joe, he's liable to drive off without me. You know Joe if he's had a few too many."

In a few minutes there was a blast of a two-tone horn, repeated. "That's Joe's car," said Bobbie. "You'd better go." She went to the hall with me and I kissed her cheek. The front door swung open and it was Joe Whipple.

"Hello, Bobbie," he said.

"Hello, Joe. Won't you all come in? Haven't you got time for one drink?" She was trying not to sound suppliant, but Joe was not deceived.

"Just you and Jim here?" he said.

"Yes. Pete went out a little while ago."

"I'll see what the others say," said Joe. He left to speak to the three in the sedan, and obviously he was not immediately persuasive, but they came in with him. They would not let Bobbie take their coats, but they were nice to her and with the first sips of our drinks we were all six almost back in the days when Bobbie Hammersmith's house was where so many of our parties started from. Then we heard the front door thumping shut and Pete McCrea looked in.

There were sounds of hello, but he stared at us over his horn-rims and said to Bobbie: "You didn't have to invite me, but you could have told me." He turned and again the front door thumped.

"Get dressed and come with us," said Joe Whipple.

"I can't do that," said Bobbie.

"She can't, Joe," said Phyllis Whipple. "That would only make more trouble."

"What trouble? She's going to have to sit here alone till he comes home. She might as well be with us," said Joe.

"Anyway, I haven't got a dress that fits," said Bobbie. "But thanks for asking me."

"I won't have you sitting here—"

"Now don't make matters worse, Joe, for heaven's sake," said his wife.

"I could lend you a dress, Bobbie, but I think Phyllis is right," said Mary Lander. "Whatever *you* want to do."

"*Want* to do! That's not the question," said Bobbie. "Go on before I change my mind. Thanks, everybody. Frank, you haven't said a word."

"Nothing much for me to say," said Frank Lander. But as far as I was concerned he, and Bobbie herself, had said more than anyone else. I caught her looking at me quickly.

"Well, all right, then," said Joe. "I'm outnumbered. Or outpersuaded or something."

I was the last to say goodbye, and I whispered to Bobbie: "Frank, eh?"

"You're only guessing," she said. "Goodnight, Jim." Whatever they would be after we left, her eyes were brighter than they had been in years. She had very nearly gone to a party, and for a minute or two she had been part of it.

I sat in the back seat with Phyllis Whipple and Frank Lander. "If you'd had any sense you'd know there'd be a letdown," said Phyllis.

"Oh, drop it," said Joe.

"It might have been worth it, though, Phyllis," said Mary Lander. "How long is it since she's seen anybody but that old battle-ax, Mrs. McCrea? God, I hate to think what it must be like, living in that house with Mrs. McCrea."

"I'm sure it would have been a *lot* easier if Bobbie'd come with us," said Phyllis. "That would have fixed things just right with Mrs. McCrea. She's just the type that wants Bobbie to go out and have a good time. Especially without Pete. You forget how the old lady used to call up all the mothers as soon as she heard there was a party planned. What Joe did was cruel because it was so downright stupid. Thoughtless. Like getting her all excited and then leaving her hung up."

"You've had too much to drink," said Joe.

"*I* have?"

"Yes, you don't say things like that in front of a bachelor," said Joe.

"Who's—oh, Jim? It is to laugh. Did I shock you, Jim?"

"Not a bit. I didn't know what you meant. Did you say something risqué?"

"My husband thinks I did."

"Went right over my head," I said. "I'm innocent about such things."

"So's your old man," said Joe.

"Do you think she should have come with us, Frank?" I said.

"Why ask me? No. I'm with Phyllis. What's the percentage for Bobbie? You saw that son of a bitch in the doorway, and you know damn well when he gets home from Muriel Nierhaus's, he's going to raise hell with Bobbie."

"Then Bobbie had nothing to lose," said Joe. "If Pete's going to raise hell with her, anyway, she might as well have come with us."

"How does he raise hell with her?" I said.

No one said anything.

"Do you know, Phyllis?" I said.

"What?" said Phyllis.

"Oh, come on. You heard me," I said. "Mary?"

"I'm sure I don't know."

"Oh, nuts," I said.

"Go ahead, tell him," said Frank Lander.

"Nobody ever knew for sure," said Phyllis, quietly.

"That's not true. Caroline English, for one. She knew for sure."

Phyllis spoke: "A few weeks before Bobbie had her baby she rang Caroline's doorbell in the middle of the night and asked Caroline if she could stay there. Naturally Caroline said yes, and she saw that Bobbie had nothing but a coat over her nightgown and had bruises all over her arms and shoulders. Julian was away, a lucky break because he'd have gone over and had a fight with Pete. As it was, Caroline made Bobbie have Dr. English come out and have a look at her, and nothing more was said. I mean, it was kept secret from everybody, especially Mr. Hammersmith. But the story got out somehow. Not widespread, but we all heard about it."

"We don't want it to get back to Mr. Hammersmith," said Mary Lander.

"He knows," said Frank Lander.

"You keep saying that, but I don't believe he does," said Mary.

"I don't either," said Joe Whipple. "Pete wouldn't be alive today if Phil Hammersmith knew."

"That's where I think you're wrong," said Phyllis. "Mr. Hammersmith might want to kill Pete, but killing him is another matter. And what earthly good would it do? The Hammersmiths have lost every penny, so I'm told, and at least with Pete still alive, Mrs. McCrea supports Bobbie. Barely. But they have food and a roof over their heads."

"Phil Hammersmith knows the whole damn story, you can bet anything on that. And it's why he's an old man all of a sudden. Have you seen him this trip, Jim?" said Frank Lander.

"I haven't seen him since the wedding."

"Oh, well—" said Mary.

"You won't—" said Joe.

"You won't recognize him," said Frank Lander. "He's bent over—"

"They say he's had a stroke," said Phyllis Whipple.

"And on top of everything else he got a lot of people sore at him by selling his bank stock to Ed Charney," said Joe. "Well, not a lot of people, but some that could have helped him. My old man, to name one. And I don't think that was so hot. Phil Hammersmith was a carpetbagger himself, and damn lucky to be in the bank. Then to sell his stock to a lousy stinking bootlegger . . . You should hear Harry Reilly on the subject."

"I don't want to hear Harry Reilly on any subject," said Frank Lander. "Cheap Irish Mick."

"I don't like him any better than you do, Frank, but call him something else," I said.

"I'm sorry, Jim. I didn't mean that," said Frank Lander.

"No. It just slipped out," I said.

"I apologize," said Frank Lander.

"Oh, all right."

"Don't be sensitive, Jim," said Mary.

"Stay out of it, Mary," said Frank Lander.

"*Everybody* calm down," said Joe. "Everybody knows that Harry Reilly is a cheap Irish Mick, and nobody knows it better than Jim, an Irish Mick but not a cheap one. So shut the hell up, everybody."

"Another country heard from," said Phyllis.

"Now *you,* for Christ's sake," said Joe. "Who has the quart?"

"I have my quart," said Frank Lander.

"I have mine," I said.

"I asked who has mine. Phyllis?"

"When we get to the club, time enough," said Phyllis.

"Hand it over," said Joe.

"Three quarts of whiskey between five people. I'd like to know how we're going to get home tonight," said Mary Lander.

"Drunk as a monkey, if you really want to know," said Joe. "Tight as a nun's."

"Well, at least we're off the subject of Bobbie and Pete," said Phyllis.

"I'm not. I was coming back to it. Phyllis. The quart," said Joe.

"No," said Phyllis.

"Here," I said. "And remember where it came from." I handed him my bottle.

Joe took a swig in the corner of his mouth, swerving the car only slightly. "Thanks," he said, and returned the bottle. "Now, Mary, if you'll light me a cigarette like a dear little second cousin."

"Once removed," said Mary Lander.

"Once removed, and therefore related to Bobbie through her mother."

"No, *you* are but I'm not," said Mary Lander.

"Well, you're in it some way, through me. Now for the benefit of those who are not related to Bobbie or Mrs. Hammersmith, or Mary or me. Permit me to give you a little family history that will enlighten you on several points."

"Is this going to be about Mr. Hammersmith?" said Phyllis. "I don't think you'd better tell that."

"You're related only by marriage, so kindly keep your trap shut. If I want to tell it, I can."

"Everybody remember that I asked him not to," said Phyllis.

"Don't tell it, Joe, whatever it is," said Mary Lander.

"Yeah, what's the percentage?" said Frank Lander. "They have enough trouble without digging up past history."

"Oh, you're so noble, Lander," said Joe. "You fool nobody."

"If you're going to tell the story, go ahead, but stop insulting Frank," said Mary Lander.

"We'll be at the club before he gets started," said Phyllis.

"Then we'll sit there till I finish. Anyway, it doesn't take that long. So, to begin at the beginning. Phil Hammersmith. Phil Hammersmith came here before the war, just out of Lehigh."

"You're not even telling it right," said Phyllis.

"Phyllis is right. I'm screwing up my own story. Well, I'll begin again. Phil Hammersmith graduated from Lehigh, then a few years *later* he came to Gibbsville."

"That's better," said Phyllis.

"The local Lehigh contingent all knew him. He'd played lacrosse and he was a Sigma Nu around the time Mr. Chew was there. So he already had friends in Gibbsville."

"Now you're on the right track," said Phyllis.

"Thank you, love," said Joe.

"Where was he from originally?" I asked.

"Don't ask questions, Jim. It only throws me. He was from some place in New Jersey. So anyway he arrived in Gibbsville and got a job with the Coal & Iron Company. He was a civil engineer, and he had the job when he arrived. That is, he didn't come here looking for a job. He was hired before he got here."

"You've made that plain," said Phyllis.

"Well, it's important," said Joe.

"Yes, but you don't have to say the same thing over and over again," said Phyllis.

"Yes I do. Anyway, apparently the Coal & Iron people hired him on the strength of his record at Lehigh, plus asking a few questions of the local Lehigh contingent, that knew him, *plus* a very good recommendation he'd had from some firm in Bethlehem. Where he'd worked after getting out of college. But after he'd been here a while, and was getting along all right at the Coal & Iron, one day a construction engineer from New York arrived to talk business at the C. & I. Building. They took him down-cellar to the drafting-room and who should he see but Phil Hammersmith. But apparently Phil didn't see him. Well, the New York guy was a real wet smack, because he tattled on Phil.

"Old Mr. Duncan was general superintendent then and he sent

for Phil. Was it true that Phil had once worked in South America, and if so, why hadn't he mentioned it when he applied for a job? Phil gave him the obvious answer. 'Because if I had, you wouldn't have hired me.' 'Not necessarily,' said Mr. Duncan. 'We might have accepted your explanation.' 'You say that now, but I tried telling the truth and I couldn't get a job.' 'Well, tell me the truth now,' said Mr. Duncan. 'All right,' said Phil. So he told Mr. Duncan what had happened.

"He was working in South America. Peru, I think. Or maybe Bolivia. In the jungle. And the one thing they didn't want the natives, the Indians, to get hold of was firearms. But one night he caught a native carrying an armful of rifles from the shanty, and when Phil yelled at him, the native ran, and Phil shot him. Killed him. The next day one of the other engineers was found with his throat cut. And the day after that the native chief came and called on the head man of the construction outfit. Either the Indians thought they'd killed the man that had killed their boy, or they didn't much care. But the chief told the white boss that the next time an Indian was killed, two white men would be killed. And not just killed. Tortured. Well, there were four or maybe five engineers, including Phil and the boss. The only white men in an area as big as Pennsylvania, and I guess they weighed their chances and being mathematicians, the odds didn't look so hot. So they quit. No hero stuff. They just quit. Except Phil. He was fired. The boss blamed Phil for everything and in his report to the New York office he put in a lot of stuff that just about fixed Phil for good. The boss, of course, was the same man that spotted Phil at the C. & I. drafting-room."

"You told it very well," said Phyllis.

"So any time you think of Phil Hammersmith killing Pete McCrea, it wouldn't be the first time," said Joe.

"And the war," I said. "He probably killed a few Germans."

"On the other hand, he never got over blaming himself for the other engineer's getting his throat cut," said Joe. "This is all the straight dope. Mr. Duncan to my old man."

We were used to engineers, their travels and adventures in far-off places, but engineers came and went and only a few became fixtures in our life. Phil Hammersmith's story was all new to Mary and Frank and me, and in the cold moonlight, as we sat in a heated automobile in a snow-covered parking area of a Pennsylvania country club, Joe Whipple had taken us to a dark South American jungle, given us a touch of fear, and in a few minutes covered Phil Hammersmith in mystery and then removed the mystery.

"Tell us more about Mr. Hammersmith," said Mary Lander.

Mary Lander. I had not had time to realize the inference that must accompany my guess that Frank Lander was the only boy in our crowd who had stayed with Bobbie. Mary Lander was the only girl who had not fought off Pete McCrea. She was the last girl I would have suspected of staying with Pete, and yet the one that surprised me the least. She had always been the girl our mothers liked us to take out, a kind of mothers' ideal for their sons, and possibly even for themselves. Mary Morgan Lander was the third generation of a family that had always been in the grocery business, the only store in the county that sold caviar and English biscuits and Sportsmen's Bracer chocolate, as well as the most expensive domestic items of fruit, vegetables, and tinned goods. Her brother Llewellyn Morgan still scooped out dried prunes and operated the rotary ham slicer, but no one seriously believed that all the Morgan money came from the store. Lew Morgan taught Sunday School in the Methodist Episcopal Church and played basketball at the Y.M.C.A., but he had been to Blair Academy and Princeton, and his father had owned one of the first Pierce-Arrows in Gibbsville. Mary had been unfairly judged a teaser, in previous years. She was not a teaser, but a girl who would kiss a boy and allow him to wander all over her body so long as he did not touch bare skin. Nothing surprised me about Mary. It was in character for her to have slapped Pete McCrea at a dinner party, and then to have let him stay with her and to have discussed with him a swap of husbands and wives. No casual dirty remark ever passed unnoticed by Mary; when someone made a slip we would all turn to see how Mary was taking it, and without fail she had heard it, understood it, and taken a pious attitude. But in our crowd she was the one person most conscious of sex and scatology. She was the only one of whom I would say she had a dirty mind, but I kept that observation to myself along with my theory that she hated Frank Lander. My theory, based on no information whatever, was that marriage and Frank Lander had not been enough for her and that Pete McCrea had become attractive to her because he was so awful.

"There's no more to tell," said Joe Whipple. We got out of the car and Mary took Joe's arm, and her evening was predictable: fathers and uncles and older brothers would cut in on her, and older women would comment as they always did that Mary Lander was *such* a sensible girl, *so* considerate of her elders, a *wonderful* wife to Frank. And we of her own age would dance with her because under cover of the dancing crowd Mary would wrap both legs around our right legs with a promise that had fooled us for years. Quiet little Mary Lander, climbing up a boy's leg but never forgetting to smile her Dr. Lyons smile at old Mrs. Ginyan and old Mr. Heff. And yet through some mental process that I did not take time to scrutinize, I was less annoyed with Mary than I had been since we were children. I was determined not to dance with her, and I did not, but my special knowledge about her and Pete McCrea reduced her power to allure. Bobbie had married Pete McCrea and she was still attractive in spite of it; but Mary's seductiveness vanished with the revelation that she had picked Pete as her lover, if only for once, twice, or how many times. I had never laughed at Mary before, but now she was the fool, not we, not I.

I got quite plastered at the dance, and so did a lot of other people. On the way home we sang a little—"Body and Soul" was the song, but Phyllis was the only one who could sing the middle part truly—and Frank Lander tried to tell about an incident in the smoking-room, where Julian English apparently had thrown a drink in Harry Reilly's face. It did not seem worth making a fuss about, and Frank never finished his story. Mary Lander attacked me: "You never danced with me, not once," she said.

"I didn't?"

"No, you didn't, and you know you didn't," she said. "And you always do."

"Well, this time I guess I didn't."

"Well, *why* didn't you?"

"Because he didn't want to," said Frank Lander. "You're making a fool of yourself. I should think you'd have more pride."

"Yeah, why don't you have more pride, Mary?" said Joe Whipple. "You'd think it was an honor to dance with this Malloy guy."

"It is," I said.

"That's it. You're getting so conceited," said Mary. "Well, I'm sure I didn't have to sit any out."

"Then why all the fuss?" said Frank Lander.

"Such popularity must be deserved," I said, quoting an advertising slogan.

"Whose? Mary's or yours?" said Phyllis.

"Well, I was thinking of Mary's, but now that you mention it . . ." I said.

"How many times did he dance with *you,* Phyllis?" said Joe.

"Three or four," said Phyllis.

"In that case, Frank, Jim has insulted your wife. I don't see any other way out of it. You have to at least slap his face. Shall I stop the car?"

"My little trouble-maker," said Phyllis.

"Come on, let's have a fight," said Joe. "Go ahead, Frank. Give him a punch in the nose."

"Yeah, like you did at the Dam, Frank," I said.

"Oh, God. I remember that awful night," said Phyllis. "What did you fight over?"

"Bobbie," I said.

"Bobbie was the cause of *more* fights," said Mary Lander.

"Well, we don't need her to fight over now. We have you," said Joe. "Your honor's been attacked and your husband wants to defend it. The same as I would if Malloy hadn't danced with *my* wife. It's a good thing you danced with Phyllis, Malloy, or you and I'd get out of this car and start slugging."

"Why did you fight over Bobbie? I don't remember that," said Mary.

"Because she came to the picnic with Jim and then went off necking with Frank," said Phyllis. "I remember the whole thing."

"Stop *talking* about fighting and let's *fight*," said Joe.

"All right, stop the car," I said.

"Now you're talking," said Joe.

"Don't be ridiculous," said Phyllis.

"Oh, shut up," said Joe. He pulled up on the side of the road. "I'll referee." He got out of the car, and so did Frank and I and Phyllis. "All right, put up your dukes." We did so, moved around a bit in the snow and slush. "Go on, mix it," said Joe, whereupon Frank rushed me and hit me on the left cheek. All blows were directed at the head, since all three of us were armored in coonskin coats. "That was a good one, Frank. Now go get him, Jim." I swung my right hand and caught Frank's left eye, and at that moment we were all splashed by slush, taken completely by surprise as Phyllis, whom we had forgotten, drove the car away.

"That bitch!" said Joe. He ran to the car and got hold of a door handle but she increased her speed and he fell in the snow. "God damn that bitch, I should have known she was up to something. Now what? Let's try to bum a ride." The fight, such as it was, was over, and we tried to flag down cars on their way home from the dance. We recognized many of them, but not one would stop.

"Well, thanks to you, we've got a nice three-mile walk to Swedish Haven," said Frank Lander.

"Oh, she'll be back," said Joe.

"I'll bet you five bucks she's not," I said.

"Well, I won't bet, but I'll be damned if I'm going to walk three miles. I'm just going to wait till we can bum a ride."

"If you don't keep moving you'll freeze," said Frank.

"We're nearer the club than we are Swedish Haven. Let's go back there," I said.

"And have my old man see me?" said Joe.

"Your old man went home hours ago," I said.

"Well, somebody'll see me," said Joe.

"Listen, half the club's seen you already, and they wouldn't even stop," I said.

"Who has a cigarette?" said Joe.

"Don't give him one," said Frank.

"I have no intention of giving him one," I said. "Let's go back to the club. My feet are soaking wet."

"So are mine," said Frank. We were wearing pumps, and our feet had been wet since we got out of the car.

"That damn Phyllis, she knows I just got over a cold," said Joe.

"Maybe that's why she did it," I said. "It'd serve you right if you got pneumonia."

We began to walk in the middle of the road, in the direction of the clubhouse, which we could see, warm and comfortable on top of a distant plateau. "That old place never looked so good," said Joe. "Let's spend the night there."

"The rooms are all taken. The orchestra's staying there," I said.

We walked about a mile, our feet getting sorer at every step, and the combination of exhaustion and the amount we had had to drink made even grumbling an effort. Then a Dodge touring car, becurtained, stopped about fifty yards from us and a spotlight was turned on each of our faces. A man in a short overcoat and fur-lined cap came toward us. He was a State Highway patrolman. "What happened to you fellows?" he said. "You have a wreck?"

"I married one," said Joe.

"Oh, a weisscrackah," said the patrolman, a Pennsylvania Dutchman. "Where's your car?"

"We got out to take a leak and my wife drove off with it," said Joe.

"You from the dance at the gulf club?"

"Yes," said Joe. "How about giving us a lift?"

"Let me see you' driwah's license," said the cop.

Joe took out his billfold and handed over the license. "So? From Lantenengo Street yet? All right, get in. Whereabouts you want to go to?"

"The country club," said Joe.

"The hell with that," said Frank. "Let's go on to Gibbsville."

"This aint no taxi service," said the cop. "And I aint taking you to no Gippsfille. I'm on my way to my substation. Swedish Haven. You can phone there for a taxi. Privileged characters, you think you are. A bunch of drunks, you ask me."

I had to go back to New York on the morning train and the events of the next few days, so far as they concerned Joe and Phyllis Whipple and Frank and Mary Lander, were obscured by the suicide, a day or two later, of Julian English, the man who had thrown a drink at Harry Reilly. The domestic crisis of the Whipples and the Landers and even the McCreas seemed very unimportant. And yet when I heard about English, who had not been getting along with his wife, I wondered about my own friends, people my own age but not so very much younger than Julian and Caroline English. English had danced with Phyllis and Mary that night, and now he was dead. I knew very little about the causes of the difficulties between him and Caroline, but they could have been no worse than the problems that existed in Bobbie's marriage and that threatened the marriage of Frank and Mary Lander. I was shocked and saddened by the English suicide; he was an attractive man whose shortcomings seemed out of proportion to the magnitude of killing himself. He had not been a friend of mine, only an acquaintance with whom I had had many drinks and played some golf; but friends of mine, my closest friends in the world, boys-now-men like myself, were at the beginning of the same kind of life and doing the same kind of thing that for Julian English ended in a sealed-up garage with a motor running. I hated what I thought those next few days and weeks. There is nothing young about killing oneself, no matter when it happens, and I hated this being deprived of the sweetness of youth. And that was what it was, that was what was happening to us. I, and I think the others, had looked upon our squabbles as unpleasant incidents but belonging to our youth. Now they were plainly recognizable as symptoms of life without youth, without youth's excuses or youth's recoverability. I wanted to love someone, and during the next year or two I confused the desperate need for love with love itself. I had put a hopeless love out of my life; but that is not part of this story, except to state it and thus to show that I knew what I was looking for.

2.

When you have grown up with someone it is much easier to fill in gaps of five years, ten years, in which you do not see him, than to supply those early years in the life of a friend you meet in maturity. I do not know why this is so, unless it is a mere matter of insufficient time. With the friends of later life you may exchange boyhood stories that seem worth telling, but boyhood is not all stories. It is mostly not stories, but day-to-day, unepisodic living. And most of us are too polite to burden our later-life friends with unexciting anecdotes about people they will never meet. (Likewise we hope they will not burden us.) But it is easy to bring old friends up to date in your mental dossiers by the addition of a few vital facts. Have they stayed married? Have they had many more children? Have they made money or lost it? Usually the basic facts will do, and then you tell yourself that Joe Whipple is still Joe Whipple, plus two sons, a new house, a hundred thousand dollars, forty pounds, bifocals, fat in the neck, and a new concern for the state of the nation.

Such additions I made to my friends' dossiers as I heard about them from time to time; by letters from them, conversations with my mother, an occasional newspaper clipping. I received these facts with joy for the happy news, sorrow for the sad, and immediately went about my business, which was far removed from any business of theirs. I seldom went back to Gibbsville during the Thirties—mine and the century's—and when I did I stayed only long enough to stand at a grave, to toast a bride, to spend a few minutes beside a sickbed. In my brief encounters with my old friends I got no information about Bobbie and Pete McCrea, and only after I had returned to New York or California would I remember that I had intended to inquire about them.

There is, of course, some significance in the fact that no one volunteered information about Bobbie and Pete. It was that they had disappeared. They continued to live in Gibbsville, but in parts of the town that were out of the way for their old friends. There is no town so small that that cannot happen, and Gibbsville, a third-class city, was large enough to have all the grades of poverty and wealth and the many half grades in between, in which $10 a month in the husband's income could make a difference in the kind and location of the house in which he lived. No one had volunteered any information about Bobbie and Pete, and I had not remembered to inquire. In five years I had had no new facts about them, none whatever, and their disappearance from my ken might have continued but for a broken shoelace.

I was in Gibbsville for a funeral, and the year was 1938. I had broken a shoelace, it was evening and the stores were closed, and I was about to drive back to New York. The only place open that might have shoelaces was a poolroom that in my youth had had a two-chair bootblack stand. The poolroom was in a shabby section near the railroad stations and a couple of cheap hotels, four or five saloons, an automobile tire agency, a barber shop, and a quick-lunch counter. I opened the poolroom door, saw that the bootblack's chairs were still there, and said to the man behind the cigar counter: "Have you got any shoelaces?"

"Sorry I can't help you, Jim," said the man. He was wearing an eyeshade, but as soon as he spoke I recognized Pete McCrea.

"Pete, for God's sake," I said. We shook hands.

"I thought you might be in town for the funeral," he said. "I should have gone, too, I guess, but I decided I wouldn't. It was nice of you to make the trip."

"Well, you know. He was a friend of my father's. Do you own this place?"

"I run it. I have a silent partner, Bill Charney. You remember Ed

Charney? His younger brother. I don't know where to send you to get a shoelace."

"The hell with the shoelace. How's Bobbie?"

"Oh, Bobbie's fine. *You* know. A lot of changes, but this is better than nothing. Why don't you call her up? She'd love to hear from you. We're living out on Mill Street, but we have a phone. Call her up and say hello. The number is 3385-J. If you have time maybe you could go see her. I have to stay here till I close up at one o'clock, but she's home."

"What number on Mill Street? You call her up and tell her I'm coming? Is that all right?"

"Hell, yes."

Someone thumped the butt of a cue on the floor and called out: "Rack 'em up, Pete?"

"I have to be here. You go out and I'll call her up," he said. "Keep your shirt on," he said to the pool player, then, to me: "It's 402 Mill Street, across from the open hearth, second house from the corner. I guess I won't see you again, but I'm glad we had a minute. You're looking very well." I could not force a comment on his appearance. His nose was red and larger, his eyes watery, the dewlaps sagging, and he was wearing a blue denim work shirt with a dirty leather bow tie.

"Think I could get in the Ivy Club if I went back to Princeton?" he said. "I didn't make it the first time around, but now I'm a big shot. So long, Jim. Nice to've seen you."

The open hearth had long since gone the way of all the mill equipment; the mill itself had been inactive for years, and as a residential area the mill section was only about a grade and a half above the poorest Negro slums. But in front of most of the houses in the McCreas' row there were cared-for plots; there always had been, even when the mill was running and the air was full of smoke and acid. It was an Irish and Polish neighborhood, but knowledge of that fact did not keep me from locking all the doors of my car. The residents of the neighborhood would not have touched my father's car, but this was not his car and I was not he.

The door of Number 402 opened as soon as I closed my car door. Bobbie waited for me to lock up and when I got to the porch, she said: *"Jim.* Jim, Jim, Jim. How nice. I'm so glad to see you." She quickly closed the door behind me and then kissed me. "Give me a real kiss and a real hug. I didn't dare while the door was open." I kissed her and held her for a moment and then she said: "Hey, I guess we'd better cut this out."

"Yes," I said. "It's nice, though."

"Haven't done that since we were—God!" She stood away and looked at me. "You could lose some weight, but you're not so bad. How about a bottle of beer? Or would you rather have some cheap whiskey?"

"What are you drinking?"

"Cheap whiskey, but I'm used to it," she said.

"Let's both have some cheap whiskey," I said.

"Straight? With water? Or how?"

"Oh, a small slug of whiskey and a large slug of water in it. I'm driving back to New York tonight."

She went to the kitchen and prepared the drinks. I recognized some of the furniture from the Hammersmith and McCrea houses. "Brought together by a shoestring," she said. "Here's to it. How do I look?"

"If you want my frank and candid opinion, good enough to go right upstairs and make up for the time we lost. Pete won't be home till one o'clock."

"If then," she said. "Don't think I wouldn't, but it's too soon after my baby. Didn't Pete tell you I finally produced a healthy son?"

"No."

"You'll hear him in a little while. We have a daughter, two years old, and now a son. Angus McCrea, Junior. Seven pounds two ounces at birth."

"Good for you," I said.

"Not so damn good for me, but it's over, and he's healthy."

"And what about your mother and father?" I said.

"Oh, poor Jim. You didn't know? Obviously you didn't, and you're going to be so sorry you asked. Daddy committed suicide two years ago. He shot himself. And Mother's in Swedish Haven." Swedish Haven was local lore for the insane asylum. "I'm sorry I had to tell you."

"God, why won't they lay off you?" I said.

"Who is they? Oh, you mean just—life?"

"Yes."

"I don't know, Jim," she said. "I've had about as much as I can stand, or so I keep telling myself. But I must be awfully tough, because there's always something else, and I go right on. Will you let me complain for just a minute, and then I'll stop? The only one of the old crowd I ever see is Phyllis. She comes out and never forgets to bring a bottle, so we get tight together. But some things we don't discuss, Phyllis and I. Pete is a closed subject."

"What's he up to?"

"Oh, he has his women. I don't even know who they are any more, and couldn't care less. Just as long as he doesn't catch a disease. I told him that, so he's been careful about it." She sat up straight. "I haven't been the soul of purity, either, but it's Pete's son. Both children are Pete's. But I haven't been withering on the vine."

"Why should you?"

"That's what *I* said. Why should I have nothing? Nothing? The children are mine, and I love them, but I need more than that, Jim. Children don't love you back. All they do is depend on you to feed them and wash them and all the rest of it. But after they're in bed for the night—I never know whether Pete will be home at two o'clock or not at all. So I've had two tawdry romances, I guess you'd call them. Not you, but Mrs. McCrea would."

"Where is dear Mrs. McCrea?"

"She's living in Jenkintown, with an old maid sister. Thank heaven they can't afford carfare, so I'm spared that."

"Who are your gentlemen friends?"

"Well, the first was when we were living on the East Side. A gentleman by the name of Bill Charney. Yes, Ed's brother and Pete's partner. I was crazy about him. Not for one single minute in love with him, but I never even thought about love with him. He wanted to marry me, too, but I was a nasty little snob. I *couldn't* marry Bill Charney, Jim. I just couldn't. So he married a nice little Irish girl and they're living on Lantenengo Street in the house that used to belong to old Mr. Duncan. And I'm holding court on Mill Street, thirty dollars a month rent."

"Do you want some money?"

"Will you give me two hundred dollars?"

"More than that, if you want it."

"No, I'd just like to have two hundred dollars to hide, to keep in case of emergency."

"In case of emergency, you can always send me a telegram in care of my publisher." I gave her $200.

"Thank you. Now I have some money. For the last five or six years I haven't had any money of my own. You don't care how I spend this, do you?"

"As long as you spend it on yourself."

"I've gotten so stingy I probably won't spend any of it. But this is wonderful. Now I can read the ads and say to myself I could have some expensive lingerie. I think I will get a permanent, next month."

"Is that when you'll be back in circulation again?"

"Good guess. Yes, about a month," she said. "But not the same man. I didn't tell you about the second one. You don't know him. He came here after you left Gibbsville. His name is McCormick and he went to Princeton with Pete. They sat next to each other in a lot of classes, McC, McC, and he was sent here to do some kind of an advertising survey and ran into Pete. They'd never been exactly what you'd call pals, but they *knew* each other and Mac took one look and sized up the situation and—well, I thought, why not? He wasn't as exciting as Mr. Charney, but at one time I would have married him. *If* he'd asked me. He doesn't live here any more."

"But you've got the next one picked out?"

"No, but I know there will be a next one. Why lie to myself? And why lie to you? I don't think I ever have."

"Do you ever see Frank?"

"Frank? Frank Lander? What made you think of him?"

"Bobbie," I said.

"Oh, of course. That was a guess of yours, a long time ago," she said. "No, I never see Frank." She was smoking a cigarette, and sitting erect with her elbow on the arm of her chair, holding the cigarette high and with style. If her next words had been "Jeeves, have the black Rolls brought round at four o'clock" she would not have been more naturally grand. But her next words were: "I haven't even thought about Frank. There was another boy, Johnny White, the one I was engaged to. *Engaged to.* That close to spending the rest of my life with him—or at least part of it. But because he wanted me to go away with him before we were married, I broke the engagement and married Pete."

"Is that all it was? That he wanted you to go away with him?"

"That's really all it was. I got huffy and said he couldn't really love me if he wanted to take that risk. Not that we hadn't been taking risks, but a pre-marital trip, that was something else again. My five men, Jim. Frank. Johnny. Bill and Mac. And Pete."

"Why didn't you and Frank ever get engaged?"

"I wonder. I *have* thought about *that,* so I was wrong when I said I never think of Frank. But Frank in the old days, not Frank now. What may have happened was that Frank was the only boy I'd gone all the way with, and then I got scared because I didn't want to give up the fun, popularity, good times. Jim, I have a confession to make. About you."

"Oh?"

"I told Frank I'd stayed with you. He wouldn't believe he was my first and he kept harping on it, so I really got rid of Frank by telling him you were the first."

"Why me?"

"Because the first time I ever stayed with Frank, or anybody, it was at a picnic at the Dam, and I'd gone to the picnic with you. So you were the logical one."

"Did you tell him that night?"

"No. Later. Days later. But you had a fight with him that night, and the fight made it all the more convincing."

"Well, thanks, little pal," I said.

"Oh, you don't care, do you?"

"No, not really."

"You had Kitty, after all," she said. "Do you ever see Kitty?"

"No. Kitty lives in Cedarhurst and they keep to themselves, Cedarhurst people."

"What was your wife like?"

"She was nice. Pretty. Wanted to be an actress. I still see her once in a while. I like her, and always will, but if ever there were two people that shouldn't have got married . . ."

"I can name two others," said Bobbie.

"You and Pete. But you've stuck to him."

"Don't be polite. I'm stuck with him. Can you imagine what Pete would be like if I left him?"

"Well, to be brutally frank, what's he like anyway? You don't have to go on paying for a dirty trick the rest of your life."

"It wasn't just a dirty trick. It would have been a dirty trick if I'd walked out on him the day we were getting married. But I went through with it, and that made it more than a dirty trick. I *should have* walked out on him, the day we got married. I even tried. And he'd have recovered—then. Don't forget, Pete McCrea was used to dirty tricks being played on him, and he might have got over it if I'd left him at the church. But once I'd married him, he became a different person, took himself much more seriously, and so did everyone else. They began to dislike him, but that was better than being laughed at." She sipped her drink.

"Well, who did it? I did. Your little pal," she said. "How about some more cheap whiskey?"

"No thanks, but you go ahead," I said.

"The first time I ever knew there *was* a Mill Street was the day we rented this house," she said, as she poured herself a drink. "I'd never been out this way before."

"You couldn't have lived here when the mill was operating. The noise and the smoke."

"I can live anywhere," she said. "So can anyone else. And don't be too surprised if you find us back on Lantenengo. Do you know the big thing nowadays? Slot machines and the numbers racket. Pete wants to get into The Numbers, but he hasn't decided how to go about it. Bill Charney is the kingpin in the county, although not the real head. It's run by a syndicate in Jersey City."

"Don't let him do it, Bobbie," I said. "Really don't."

"Why not? He's practically in it already. He has slot machines in the poolroom, and that's where people call up to find out what number won today. He might as well be in it."

"No."

"It's the only way Pete will ever have any money, and if he ever gets his hands on some money, maybe he'll divorce me. Then I could take the children and go away somewhere. California."

"That's a different story. If you're planning it that way. But stay out of The Numbers if you ever have any idea of remaining respectable. You can't just go in for a few years and then quit."

"Respectable? Do you think my son's going to be able to get into Princeton? His father is the proprietor of a poolroom, and they're going to know that when Angus gets older. Pete will never be anything else. He's found his niche. But if I took the children to California they might have a chance. And *I* might have a chance, before it's too late. It's our only hope, Jim. Phyllis agrees with me."

I realized that I would be arguing against a hope and a dream, and if she had that much left, and only that much, I had no right to argue. She very nearly followed my thinking. "It's what I live on, Jim," she said. "That—and this." She held up her glass. "And a little admiration. A little—admiration. Phyllis wants to give me a trip to New York. Would you take us to '21' and those places?"

"Sure."

"Could you get someone for Phyllis?"

"I think so. Sure. Joe wouldn't go on this trip?"

"And give up a chance to be with Mary Lander?"

"So now it's Joe and Mary?"

"Oh, that's old hat in Gibbsville. They don't even pretend other-wise."

"And Frank? What about him?"

"Frank is the forgotten man. If there were any justice he ought to pair off with Phyllis, but they don't like each other. Phyllis calls Frank a wishy-washy namby-pamby, and Frank calls Phyllis a drunken trouble-maker. We've all grown up, Jim. Oh, haven't we just? Joe doesn't like Phyllis to visit me because Mary says all we do is gossip. Although how she'd know *what* we do . . ."

"They were all at the funeral, and I thought what a dull, stuffy little group they've become," I said.

"But that's what they are," said Bobbie. "Very stuffy and very dull. What else is there for them to do? If I were still back there with them I'd be just as bad. Maybe worse. In a way, you know, Pete McCrea has turned out to be the most interesting man in our old crowd, present company excepted. Joe was a very handsome young man and so was Frank, and their families had lots of money and all the rest of it. But you saw Joe and Frank today. I haven't seen them lately, but Joe looks like a professional wrestler and I remember how hairy he was, all over his chest and back and his arms and legs. And Frank just the opposite, skin like a girl's and slender, but now we could almost call *him* Ichabod. He looks like a cranky school-teacher, and his glasses make him look like an owl. Mary, of course, beautifully dressed I'm sure, and not looking a day older."

"Several days older, but damn good-looking," I said.

A baby cried and Bobbie made no move. "That's my daughter. Teething. Now she'll wake up my son and you're in for a lot of howling." The son began to cry, and Bobbie excused herself. She came back in a few minutes with the infant in her arms. "It's against my rules to pick them up, but I wanted to show him to you. Isn't he an ugly little creature? The answer is yes." She took him away and returned with the daughter. "She's begun to have a face."

"Yes, I can see that. Your face, for which she can be thankful."

"Yes, I wouldn't want a girl to look like Pete. It doesn't matter so much with a boy." She took the girl away and when she rejoined me she refilled her glass.

"Are you sorry you didn't have children?" she said.

"Not the way it turned out, I'm not," I said.

"These two haven't had much of a start in life, the poor little things. They haven't even been christened. Do you know why? There was nobody we could ask to be their godfathers." Her eyes filled with tears. "That was when I really saw what we'd come to."

"Bobbie, I've got a four-hour drive ahead of me, so I think I'd better get started."

"Four hours to New York? In that car?"

"I'm going to stop and have a sandwich halfway."

"I could give you a sandwich and make some coffee."

"I don't want it now, thanks."

We looked at each other. "I'd like to show how much I appreciate your coming out to see me," she said. "But it's probably just as well I can't. But I'll be all right in New York, Jim. That is, if I ever get there. I won't believe that, either, till I'm on the train."

If she came to New York I did not know about it, and during the war years Bobbie and her problems receded from my interest. I heard that Pete was working in a defense plant, from which I inferred that he had not made the grade in the numbers racket. Frank Lander was in the Navy, Joe Whipple in the War Production Board, and by the time the war was over I discovered that so many other people and things had taken the place of Gibbsville in my thoughts that I had almost no active curiosity about the friends of my youth. I had even had a turnover in my New York friendships. I had married again, I was working hard, and most of my social life originated with my wife's friends. I was making, for me, quite a lot of money, and I was a middle-aged man whose physician had made some honest, unequivocal remarks about my life expectancy. It took a little time and one illness to make me realize that if I wanted to see my child grow to maturity, I had to retire from night life. It was not nearly so difficult as I had always anticipated it would be.

After I became reconciled to middle age and the quieter life I made another discovery: that the sweetness of my early youth was a persistent and enduring thing, so long as I kept it at the distance of years. Moments would come back to me, of love and excitement and music and laughter that filled my breast as they had thirty years earlier. It was not nostalgia, which only means homesickness, nor was it a wish to be living that excitement again. It was a splendid contentment with the knowledge that once I had felt those things so deeply and well that the throbbing urging of George Gershwin's "Do It Again" could evoke the original sensation and the pictures that went with it: a tea dance at the club and a girl in a long black satin dress and my furious jealousy of a fellow who wore a yellow foulard tie. I wanted none of it ever again, but all I had I wanted to keep. I could remember precisely the tone in which her brother had said to her: "Are you coming or aren't you?" and the sounds of his galoshes after she said: "I'm going home with Mr. Malloy." They were the things I knew before we knew everything, and, I suppose, before we began to learn. There was always a girl, and nearly always there was music; if the Gershwin tune belonged to that girl, a Romberg tune belonged to another and "When Hearts Are Young" became a personal anthem, enduringly sweet and safe from all harm, among the protected memories. In middle age I was proud to have lived according to my emotions at the right time, and content to live that way vicariously and at a distance. I had missed almost nothing, escaped very little, and at fifty I had begun to devote my energy and time to the last, simple but big task of putting it all down as well as I knew how.

In the midst of putting it all down, as novels and short stories and plays, I would sometimes think of Bobbie McCrea and the dinginess of her history. But as the reader will presently learn, the "they"—life—that had once made me cry out in anger, were not through with her yet. (Of course "they" are never through with anyone while he still lives, and we are not concerned here with the laws of compensation that seem to test us, giving us just enough strength to carry us in another trial.) I like to think that Bobbie got enough pleasure out of a pair of nylons, a permanent wave, a bottle of Phyllis Whipple's whiskey, to recharge the brightness in her. As we again take up her story I promise the reader a happy ending, if only because I want it that way. It happens also to be the true ending. . . .

Pete McCrea did not lose his job at the end of the war. His Princeton degree helped there. He had gone into the plant, which specialized in aluminum extrusion, as a manual laborer, but his IBM card revealed that he had taken psychology courses in college, and he was transferred to Personnel. It seemed an odd choice, but it is not hard to imagine that Pete was better fitted by his experience as a poolroom proprietor than as a two-year student of psychology. At least he spoke both languages, he liked the work, and in 1945 he was not bumped by a returning veteran.

Fair Grounds, the town in which the plant was situated, was only three miles from Gibbsville. For nearly a hundred years it had been the trading center for the Pennsylvania Dutch farmers in the area, and its attractions had been Becker's general store, the Fair Grounds Bank, the freight office of the Reading Railway, the Fair Grounds Hotel, and five Protestant churches. Clerks at Becker's and at the bank and the Reading, and bartenders at the hotel and the pastors of the churches, all had to speak Pennsylvania Dutch. English was desirable but not a requirement. The town was kept scrubbed, dusted and painted, and until the erection of the aluminum plant, jobs and trades were kept in the same families. An engineman's son worked as waterboy until he was old enough to take the examinations for brakeman; a master mechanic would give his boy calipers for Christmas. There were men and women in Fair Grounds who visited Gibbsville only to serve on juries or to undergo surgery at the Gibbsville Hospital. There were some men and women who had never been to Gibbsville at all and regarded Gibbsville as some Gibbsville citizens regarded Paris, France. That was the pre-aluminum Fair Grounds.

To this town in 1941 went Pete and Bobbie McCrea. They rented a house no larger than the house on Mill Street but cleaner and in better repair. Their landlord and his wife went to live with his mother-in-law, and collected the $50 legally frozen monthly rent and

$50 side payment for the use of the radio and the gas stove. But in spite of under-the-table and black-market prices Peter and Bobbie McCrea were financially better off than they had been since their marriage, and nylons at black-market prices were preferable to the no nylons she had had on Mill Street. The job, and the fact that he continued to hold it, restored some respectability to Pete, and they discussed rejoining the club. "Don't try it, I warn you," said Phyllis Whipple. "The club isn't run by your friends any more. Now it's been taken over by people that couldn't have got in ten years ago."

"Well, we'd have needed all our old friends to go to bat for us, and I guess some would think twice about it," said Pete. "So we'll do our drinking at the Tavern."

The Dan Patch Tavern, which was a new name for the renovated Fair Grounds Hotel bar, was busy all day and all night, and it was one of the places where Pete could take pleasure in his revived respectability. It was also one of the places where Bobbie could count on getting that little admiration that she needed to live on. On the day of Pearl Harbor she was only thirty-four years old and at the time of the Japanese surrender she was only thirty-eight. She was accorded admiration in abundance. Some afternoons just before the shift changed she would walk the three blocks to the Tavern and wait for Pete. The bartender on duty would say "Hi, Bobbie," and bring her currently favorite drink to her booth. Sometimes there would be four men sitting with her when Pete arrived from the plant; she was never alone for long. If one man tried to persuade her to leave, and became annoyingly insistent, the bartenders came to her rescue. The bartenders and the proprietor knew that in her way Bobbie was as profitable as the juke box. She was an attraction. She was a good-looking broad who was not a whore or a falling-down lush, and all her drinks were paid for. She was the Tavern's favorite customer, male or female, and if she had given the matter any thought she could have been declared in. All she wanted in return was a steady supply of Camels and protection from being mauled. The owner of the Tavern, Rudy Schau, was the only one who was aware that Bobbie and Pete had once lived on Lantenengo Street in

Gibbsville, but far from being impressed by their background, he had a German opinion of aristocrats who had lost standing. He was actively suspicious of Bobbie in the beginning, but in time he came to accept her as a wife whose independence he could not condone and a good-looking woman whose morals he had not been able to condemn. And she was good for business. Beer business was good, but at Bobbie's table nobody drank beer, and the real profit was in the hard stuff.

In the Fair Grounds of the pre-aluminum days Bobbie would have had few women friends. No decent woman would have gone to a saloon every day—or any day. She most likely would have received warnings from the Ku Klux Klan, which was concerned with personal conduct in a town that had only a dozen Catholic families, no Negroes and no Jews. But when the aluminum plant (which was called simply The Aluminum or The Loomy) went into war production the population of Fair Grounds immediately doubled and the solid Protestant character of the town was changed in a month. Eight hundred new people came to town and they lived in apartments in a town where there were no apartments: in rooms in private houses, in garages and old stables, in rented rooms and haylofts out in the farming area. The newcomers wasted no time with complaints of double-rent, inadequate heating, holes in the roof, insufficient sanitation. The town was no longer scrubbed, dusted or painted, and thousands of man-hours were lost while a new shift waited for the old to vacate parking space in the streets of the town. Bobbie and Pete were among the lucky early ones: they had a house. That fact of itself gave Bobbie some distinction. The house had two rooms and kitchen on the first floor, three rooms and bath on the second, and it had a cellar and an attic. In the identical houses on both sides there were a total of four families and six roomers. As a member of Personnel it was one of Pete's duties to find housing for workers, but Bobbie would have no roomers. "The money wouldn't do us much good, so let's live like human beings," she said.

"You mean there's nothing to buy with the money," said Pete. "But we could save it."

"If we had it, we'd spend it. You've never saved a cent in your life and neither have I. If you're thinking of the children's education, buy some more war bonds and have it taken out of your pay. But I'm not going to share my bathroom with a lot of dirty men. I'd have to do all the extra work, not you."

"You could make a lot of money doing their laundry. Fifty cents a shirt."

"Are you serious?"

"No."

"It's a good thing you're not, because I could tell you how else I could make a lot more money."

"Yes, a lot more," said Pete.

"Well, then, keep your ideas to yourself. I won't have boarders and I won't do laundry for fifty cents a shirt. That's final."

And so Bobbie had her house, she got the admiration she needed, and she achieved a moderate popularity among the women of her neighborhood by little friendly acts that came spontaneously out of her friendly nature. There was a dinginess to the new phase: the house was not much, the men who admired her and the women who welcomed her help were the ill-advantaged, the cheap, the vulgar, and sometimes the evil. But the next step down from Mill Street would have been hopeless degradation, and the next step up, Fair Grounds, was at least up. She was envied for her dingy house, and when Pete called her the Queen of the Klondike she was not altogether displeased. There was envy in the epithet, and in the envy was the first sign of respect he had shown her in ten years. He had never suspected her of an affair with Mac McCormick, and if he had suspected her during her infatuation with Bill Charney he had been afraid to make an accusation; afraid to anticipate his own feelings in the event that Charney would give him a job in The Numbers. When Charney brought in a Pole from Detroit for the job Pete had wanted, Pete accepted $1,000 for his share of the poolroom and felt only grateful relief. Charney did not always buy out his partners, and Pete refused to wonder if the money and the easy dissolution of the partnership had been paid for by Bobbie. It was not a question he wanted to raise, and when the war in Europe created jobs at Fair Grounds he believed that his luck had begun to change.

Whatever the state of Pete's luck, the pace of his marriage had begun to change. The pace of his marriage—and not his alone—was set by the time he spent at home and what he did during that time. For ten years he had spent little more time at home than was necessary for sleeping and eating. He could not sit still in the same room with Bobbie, and even after the children were born he did not like to have her present during the times he would play with them. He would arrive in a hurry to have his supper, and in a short time he would get out of the house, to be with a girl, to go back to work at the poolroom. He was most conscious of time when he was near Bobbie; everywhere else he moved slowly, spoke deliberately, answered hesitantly. But after the move to Fair Grounds he spent more time in the house, with the children, with Bobbie. He would sit in the front room, doing paper work from the plant, while Bobbie sewed. At the Tavern he would say to Bobbie: "It's time we were getting home." He no longer darted in and out of the house and ate his meals rapidly and in silence.

He had a new girl. Martha—"Martie"—Klinger was a typist at the plant, a Fair Grounds woman whose husband was in the Coast Guard at Lewes, Delaware. She was Bobbie's age and likewise had two children. She retained a young prettiness in the now round face and her figure had not quite reached the stage of plumpness. Sometimes when she moved an arm the flesh of her breast seemed to go all the way up to her neckline, and she had been one of the inspirations for a plant memo to women employees, suggesting that tight sweaters and tight slacks were out of place in wartime industry. Pete brought her to the Tavern one day after work, and she never took her eyes off Bobbie. She looked up and down, up and down, with her mouth half open as though she were listening to Bobbie through her lips. She showed no animosity of a defensive nature and was not openly possessive of Pete, but Bobbie knew on sight that she was Pete's new girl. After several sessions at the Tavern Bobbie could tell which of the men had already slept with Martie and which of them were likely to again. It was impossible to be jealous of Martie, but it was just as impossible not to feel superior to her. Pete, the somewhat changed Pete, kept up the absurd pretense that Martie was just a girl from the plant whom he happened to bring along for a drink, and there was no unpleasantness until one evening Martie said: "Jesus, I gotta go or I won't get any supper."

"Come on back to our house and have supper with us," said Pete. "That's okay by you, isn't it, Bobbie?"

"No, it isn't," said Bobbie.

"Rudy'll give us a steak and we can cook it at home," said Pete.

"I said no," said Bobbie, and offered no explanation.

"I'll see you all tomorrow," said Martie. "Goodnight, people."

"Why wouldn't you let her come home with us? I could have got a steak from Rudy. And Martie's a hell of a good cook."

"When we can afford a cook I may hire her," said Bobbie.

"Oh, that's what it is. The old snob department."

"That's exactly what it is."

"We're not in any position—"

"*You're* not."

"*We're* not. If I can't have my friends to my house," he said, but did not know how to finish.

"It's funny that she's the first one you ever asked. Don't forget what I told you about having boarders, and fifty cents a shirt. You keep your damn Marties out of my house. If you don't, I'll get a job and you'll be just another boarder yourself."

"Oh, why are you making such a stink about Martie?"

"Come *off* it, Pete, for heaven's *sake.*"

The next statement, he knew, would have to be a stupidly transparent lie or an admission, so he made no statement. If there had to be a showdown he preferred to avert it until the woman in question was someone more entertaining than Martie Klinger. And he liked the status quo.

They both liked the status quo. They had hated each other, their house, the dinginess of their existence on Mill Street. When the fire whistle blew it was within the hearing of Mill Street and of Lantenengo Street; rain from the same shower fell on Mill Street and on Lantenengo Street; Mill Street and Lantenengo Street read the same Gibbsville newspaper at the same time every evening. And the items of their proximity only made the nearness worse, the remoteness of Mill Street from Lantenengo more vexatious. But Fair Grounds was a new town, where they had gone knowing literally nobody. They had spending money, a desirable house, the respectability of a white-collar job, and the restored confidence in a superiority to their neighbors that they had not allowed themselves to feel on Mill Street. In the Dan Patch Tavern they would let things slip out that would have been meaningless on Mill Street, where their neighbors' daily concern was a loaf of bread and a bottle of milk. "Pete, did you know Jimmy Stewart, the movie actor?" "No, he was several classes behind me, but he was in my club." "Bobbie, what's it like on one of them yachts?" "I've only been on one, but it was fun while it lasted." They could talk now about past pleasures and luxuries without being contradicted by their surroundings, and their new friends at the Tavern had no knowledge of the decade of dinginess that lay between that past and this present. If their new friends also guessed that Pete McCrea was carrying on with Martie Klinger, that very fact made Bobbie more credibly and genuinely the woman who had once cruised in a yacht. They would have approved Bobbie's reason for not wanting Martie Klinger as a guest at supper, as they would have fiercely resented Pete's reference to Bobbie as the Queen of the Klondike. Unintentionally they were creating a symbol of order that they wanted in their lives as much as Bobbie needed admiration, and if the symbol and the admiration were slightly ersatz, what, in war years, was not?

There was no one among the Tavern friends whom Bobbie desired to make love with. "I'd give a week's pay to get in bed with you, Bobbie," said one of them.

"Fifty-two weeks' pay, did you say?" said Bobbie.

"No dame is worth fifty-two weeks' pay," said the man, a foreman named Dick Hartenstein.

"Oh, I don't know. In fifty-two weeks you make what?"

"A little over nine thousand. Nine gees, about."

"A lot of women can get that, Dick. I've heard of women getting a diamond necklace for just one night, and they cost a lot more than nine thousand dollars."

"Well, I tell you, Bobbie, if I ever hit the crap game for nine gees I'd seriously consider it, but not a year's pay that I worked for."

"You're not romantic enough for me. Sorry."

"Supposing I did hit the crap game and put nine gees on the table in front of you? Would you and me go to bed?"

"No."

"No, I guess not. If I asked you a question would you give me a truthful answer? No. You wouldn't."

"Why should I?"

"Yeah, why should you? I was gonna ask you, what does it take to get you in bed with a guy?"

"I'm a married woman."

"I skipped all that part, Bobbie. You'd go, if it was the right guy."

"You could get to be an awful nuisance, Dick. You're not far from it right this minute."

"I apologize."

"In fact, why don't you take your drink and stand at the bar?"

"What are you sore at? You get propositioned all the time."

"Yes, but you're too persistent, and you're a bore. The others don't keep asking questions when I tell them no. Go on, now, or I'll tell Rudy to keep you out of here."

"You know what you are?"

"Rudy! Will you come here, please?" she called. "All right, Dick. What am I? Say it in front of Rudy."

Rudy Schau made his way around from the bar. "What can I do for you, Bobbie?"

"I think Dick is getting ready to call me a nasty name."

"He won't," said Rudy Schau. He had the build of a man who had handled beer kegs all his life and he was now ready to squeeze the wind out of Hartenstein. "Apolochise to Bobbie and get the hell outa my place. And don't forget you got a forty-dollar tab here. You won't get a drink nowheres else in tahn.''

"I'll pay my God damn tab," said Hartenstein.

"That you owe me. Bobbie you owe an apolochy.''

"I apologize," said Hartenstein. He was immediately clipped behind the ear, and sunk to the floor.

"I never like that son of a bitch," said Rudy Schau. He looked down at the unconscious Hartenstein and very deliberately kicked him in the ribs.

"Oh, *don't,* Rudy," said Bobbie. "*Please* don't.''

Others in the bar, which was now half filled, stood waiting for Rudy's next kick, and some of them looked at each other and then at Rudy, and they were ready to rush him. Bobbie stood up quickly. "Don't, Rudy," she said.

"All right. I learned him. Joe, throw the son of a bitch out," said Rudy. Then suddenly he wheeled and grabbed a man by the belt and lifted him off the floor, holding him tight against his body with one hand and making a hammer of his other hand. "You, you son of a bitch, you was gonna go after me, you was, yeah? Well, go ahead. Let's see you, you son of a bitch. You son of a bitch, I break you in pieces." He let go and the man retreated out of range of Rudy's fist. "Pay your bill and don't come back. Don't ever show your face in my place again. And any other son of a bitch was gonna gang me. You gonna gang Rudy, hey? I kill any two of you." Two of the men picked Hartenstein off the floor before the bartender got to him. "Them two, they paid up, Joe?"

"In the clear, Rudy," said the bartender.

"You two. Don't come back," said Rudy.

"Don't worry. We won't," they said.

Rudy stood at Bobbie's table. "Okay if I sit down with you, Bobbie?"

"Of course," said Bobbie.

"Joe, a beer, please, hey? Bobbie, you ready?"

"Not yet, thanks," she said.

Rudy mopped his forehead with a handkerchief. "You don't

have to take it from these bums," said Rudy. "Any time any them get fresh, you tell me. You're what keeps this place decent, Bobbie. I know. As soon as you go home it's a pigpen. I get sick of hearing them, some of the women as bad as the men. Draft-dotchers. Essengial industry! Draft-dotchers. A bunch of 4-F draft-dotchers. I like to hear what your Daddy would say about them."

"Did you know him, my father?"

"Know him? I was in his platoon. Second platoon, C Company. I went over with him and come back with him. Phil Hammersmith."

"I never knew that."

Rudy chuckled. "Sure. Some of these 4-F draft-dotchers from outa town, they think I'm a Nazi because I never learn to speak good English, but my Daddy didn't speak no English at all and he was born out in the Walley. My old woman says put my dischartch papers up over the back-bar. I say what for? So's to make the good impression on a bunch of draft-dotchers? Corporal Rudolph W. Schau. Your Daddy was a good man and a good soldier."

"Why didn't you ever tell me you knew him?"

"Oh, I don't know, Bobbie. I wasn't gonna tell you now, but I did. It don't pay to be a talker in my business. A listener, not a talker."

"You didn't approve of me, did you?"

"I'm a saloonkeeper. A person comes to my—"

"You didn't approve of me. Don't dodge the issue."

"Well, your Daddy wouldn't of liked you coming to a saloon that often. But times change, and you're better off here than the other joints."

"I hope you don't *mind* my coming here."

"Listen, you come here as much as you want."

"Try and stop me," she said, smiling.

Pete joined them. "What happened to Dick Hartenstein?" he said.

"The same as will happen to anybody gets fresh with your wife," said Rudy, and got up and left them.

"There could be a hell of a stink about this. Rudy could lose his license if the Company wanted to press the point."

"Well, you just see that he doesn't," said Bobbie.

"Maybe it isn't such a good idea, your coming here so often."

"Maybe. On the other hand, maybe it's a wonderful idea. I happen to think it's a wonderful idea, so I'm going to keep on coming. If *you* want to go to one of the other places, that's all right. But I like Rudy's. I like it better than ever, now."

No action was taken against Rudy Schau, and Bobbie visited the Tavern as frequently as ever. Hartenstein was an unpopular foreman and the women said he got what had been coming to him for a long time. Bobbie's friends were pleased that their new symbol had such a forthright defender. It was even said that Bobbie had saved Hartenstein from a worse beating, a rumor that added to the respect she was given by the men and the women.

The McCrea children were not being brought up according to Lantenengo Street standards. On the three or four afternoons a week that Bobbie went to the Tavern she would take her son and daughter to a neighbor's yard. On the other afternoons the neighbors' children would play in her yard. During bad weather and the worst of the winter the McCreas' house was in more frequent service as a nursery, since some of the neighbors were living in one- or two-room apartments. But none of the children, the McCreas' or the neighbors', had individual supervision. Children who had learned to walk were separated from those who were still crawling, on the proven theory that the crawling children were still defenseless against the whimsical cruelties of the older ones. Otherwise there was no distinction, and all the children were toughened early in life, as most of their parents had been. "I guess it's all right," Pete once said to Bobbie. "But I hate to think what they'll be like when they get older. Little gangsters."

"Well, that was never your trouble, God knows," said Bobbie. "And I'm no shining example of having a nannie take care of me. Do you remember my nannie?"

"Vaguely."

" 'Let's go and see the horsies,' she'd say. And we'd go to Mr. Duncan's stable and I'd come home covered with scratches from the stable cat. And I guess Patrick was covered with scratches from my nannie. Affectionate scratches, of course. Do you remember Mr. Duncan's Patrick?"

"Sure."

"He must have been quite a man. Phyllis used to go there with her nannie, too. But the cat liked Phyllis."

"I'm not suggesting that we have a nannie."

"No. You're suggesting that I stay away from the Tavern."

"In the afternoon."

"The afternoon is the only time the mothers will watch each other's children, except in rare cases. Our kids are all right. I'm with them all day most of the time, and we're home every evening, seven nights a week."

"What else is there to do?"

"Well, for instance once a month we could go to a movie."

"Where? Gibbsville?"

"Yes. Two gallons of gas at the most."

"Are you getting the itch to move back to Gibbsville?"

"Not at all. Are you?"

"Hell, no."

"We could get some high school kid to watch the children. I'd just like to have a change once in a while."

"All right. The next time there's something good at the Globe."

Their first trip to the Globe was their last. They saw no one they knew in the theatre or in the bar of the John Gibb Hotel, and when they came home the high school kid was naked in bed with a man Pete recognized from the plant. "Get out of here," said Pete.

"Is she your kid, McCrea?"

"No, she's not my kid. But did you ever hear of statutory rape?"

"Rape? This kid? I had to wait downstairs, for God's sake. She took on three other guys tonight. Ten bucks a crack."

The girl put on her clothes in sullen silence. She never spoke except to say to the man: "Do you have a room some place?"

"Well," said Pete, when they had gone. "Where did you get her from? The Junior League?"

"If you'd stared at her any more you'd have had to pay ten dollars too."

"For sixteen she had quite a shape."

"She won't have it much longer."

"You got an eyeful, too, don't pretend you didn't."

"Well, at least she won't get pregnant that way. And she *will* get *rich*," said Bobbie.

Pete laughed. "It was really quite funny. Where *did* you get her?"

"If you want her name and telephone number, I have it downstairs. I got her through one of the neighbors. She certainly got the word around quickly enough, where she'd be. There's the doorbell. Another customer?"

Pete went downstairs and informed the stranger at the door that he had the wrong address.

"Another customer, and I think he had two guys with him in the car. Seventy dollars she was going to make tonight. I guess I'm supposed to report this at the plant. We have a sort of a V-D file of known prostitutes. We sic the law on them before they infect the whole outfit, and I'll bet this little character—"

"Good heavens, yes. I must burn everything. Bed linen. Towels. Why that little bitch. Now I'm getting sore." She collected the linen and took it downstairs and to the trash burner in the yard. When she returned Pete was in bed, staring at the ceiling. "I'm going to sleep in the other room," she said.

"What's the matter?"

"I didn't like that tonight. I don't want to sleep with you."

"Oh, all right then, go to hell," said Pete.

She made up one of the beds in the adjoining room. He came and sat on the edge of her bed in the dark. "Go away, Pete," she said.

"Why?"

"Oh, all right, I'll *tell* you why. Tonight made me think of the time you wanted to exchange with Mary and Frank. That's all I've been able to think of."

"That's all passed, Bobbie. I'm not like that any more."

"You would have got in bed with that girl. I saw you."

"Then I'll tell you something. You would have got in bed with that man. I saw you, too. You were excited."

"How could I help being excited, to suddenly come upon something like that. But I was disgusted, too. And still am. Please go away and let me try to get some sleep."

She did not sleep until first light, and when the alarm clock sounded she prepared his and the children's breakfasts. She was tired and nervous throughout the day. She could not go to the Tavern because it was her turn to watch neighbors' children, and Pete telephoned and said bluntly that he would not be home for supper, offering no excuse. He got home after eleven that night, slightly drunk and with lipstick on his neck.

"Who was it? Martie?" said Bobbie.

"What difference does it make who it was? I've been trying to give up other women, but you're no help."

"I have no patience with that kind of an excuse. It's easy enough to blame me. Remember, Pete, I can pick up a man just as easily as you can make a date with Martie."

"I know you can, and you probably will."

It was the last year of the war, and she had remained faithful to Pete throughout the life of their son Angus. A week later she resumed her affair with Bill Charney. "You never forgot me," he said. "I never forgot you, either, Bobbie. I heard about you and Pete living in Fair Grounds. You know a couple times I took my car and dro' past your house to see which one it was. I didn't know, maybe you'd be sitting out on the front porch and if you saw me, you know. Maybe we just say hello and pass the time of day. But I didn't think no such thing, to tell you the God's honest truth. I got nothing against my wife, only she makes me weary. The house and the kids, she got me going to Mass every Sunday, all like that. But I ain't built that way, Bobbie. I'm the next thing to a hood, and you got that side of you, too. I'll make you any price you say, the other jerks you slept with, they never saw that side of you. You know, you hear a lot about love, Bobbie, but I guess I came closer to it with you than any other woman I ever knew. I never forgot you any more than you ever forgot me. It's what they call a mutual attraction. Like you know one person has it for another person."

"I know."

"I don't see how we stood it as long as we did. Be honest, now, didn't you often wish it was me instead of some other guy?"

"Yes."

"All right, I'll be honest with you. Many's the time in bed with my wife I used to say to myself, 'Peggy, you oughta take lessons from Bobbie McCrea.' But who can give lessons, huh? If you don't have the mutual attraction, you're nothin'. How do you think I look?" He slapped his belly. "You know I weigh the same as I used to weigh? You look good. You put on a little. What? Maybe six pounds?"

"Seven or eight."

"But you got it distributed. In another year Peggy's gonna weigh a hundred and fifty pounds, and I told her, I said either she took some of that off or I'd get another girl. Her heighth, you know. She can't get away with that much weight. I eat everything, but I do a lot of walking and standing. I guess I use up a lot of excess energy. Feel them muscles. Punch me in the belly. I got no fat on me anywhere, Bobbie. For my age I'm a perfect physical specimen. I could get any amount of insurance if I got out of The Numbers. But nobody's gonna knock me off so why do I want insurance? I may even give up The Numbers one of these days. I got a couple of things lined up, strictly, strictly legitimate, and when my kids are ready to go away to school, I may just give up The Numbers. For a price, naturally."

"That brings up a point."

"You need money? How much do you want? It's yours. I *mean* like ten, fifteen gees."

"No, no money. But everybody knows you now. Where can we meet?"

"What's the matter with here? I told you, I own this hotel."

"But I can't just come and go. People know me, too. I have an idea, though."

"What?"

"Buy a motel."

"Buy a motel. You know, that thought crossed me a year ago, but you know what I found out? They don't make money. You'd think they would, but those that come out ahead, you be surprised how little they make."

"There's one near Swedish Haven. It's only about a mile from my house."

"We want a big bed, not them twin beds. I tell you what I could do. I could rent one of the units by the month and move my own furniture in. How would that suit you?"

"I'd like it better if you owned the place."

"Blackmail? Is that what you're thinking about? Who'd blackmail me, Bobbie? Or my girl? I'm still a hood in the eyes of some people."

There was no set arrangement for their meetings. Bill Charney postponed the purchase of the motel until she understood he had no intention of buying it or of making any other arrangement that implied permanence. At first she resented his procrastination, but she discovered that she preferred his way; he would telephone her, she would telephone him whenever desire became urgent, and sometimes they would be together within an hour of the telephone call. They spaced out their meetings so that each one produced novelty and excitement, and a year passed and another and Bobbie passed the afternoon of her fortieth birthday with him.

It was characteristic of their relationship that she did not tell him it was her birthday. He always spoke of his wife and children and his business enterprises, but he did not notice that she never spoke of her home life. He was a completely egocentric man, equally admiring of his star sapphire ring on his strong short-fingered hand and of her slender waist, which in his egocentricity became his possession. Inevitably, because of the nature of his businesses, he had a reputation for being close-mouthed, but alone with Bobbie he talked freely. "You know, Bobbie, I laid a friend of yours?"

"Was it fun?"

"Aren't you gonna ask me who?"

"You'll tell me."

"At least I guess she's a friend of yours. Mary Lander."

"She used to be a friend of mine. I haven't seen her in years."

"Yeah. While her husband was in the service. Frank."

"You're so busy, with all your women."

"There's seven days in the week, honey, and it don't take up too much of your time. This didn't last very long, anyway. Five, maybe six times I slept with her. I took her to New York twice, that is I met her there. The other times in her house. You know, she's a neighbor of mine."

"And very neighborly."

"Yeah, that's how it started. She come to my house to collect for something, some war drive, and Peggy said I took care of all them things so when I got home I made out a cheque and took it over to the Landers' and inside of fifteen minutes—less than that—we were necking all over the parlor. Hell, I knew the minute she opened the door—"

"One of those mutual attractions?"

"Yeah, sure. I gave her the cheque and she said, 'I don't know how to thank you,' and I said if she had a couple minutes I'd show her how. 'Oh, Mr. Charney,' but she didn't tell me to get out, so I knew I was in."

"What ever broke up this romance?"

"Her. She had some guy in Washington, D. C., she was thinking of marrying, and when I finally got it out of her who the guy was, I powdered out. Joe Whipple. I gotta do business with Joe. We got a home-loan proposition that we're ready to go with any day, and this was three years ago when Joe and I were just talking about it, what they call the talking stage."

"So you're the one that broke it off, not Mary."

"If a guy's looking at you across a desk and thinking you're laying his girl, you stand to get a screwing from that guy. Not that I don't trust Joe, because I do."

"Do you trust Mary?"

"I wondered about that, if she'd blab to Joe. A dame like Mary Lander, is she gonna tell the guy she's thinking of marrying that she's been laying a hood like me? No. By the way, she's queer. She told me she'd go for a girl."

"I'm surprised she hasn't already."

"Maybe she has. I couldn't find out. I always try to find out."

"You never asked me."

"I knew you wouldn't. But a dame like Mary, as soon as she opened the door I knew I was in, but then the next thing is you find out what else she'll go for. In her case, the works, as long as it isn't gonna get around. I guess I always figured her right. I have to figure all angles, men *and* women. That's where my brother Ed was stupid. I used to say to him, find out what kind of a broad a guy goes for before you declare him in. Ed used to say all he had to do was play a game of cards with a guy. But according to my theory, everybody goes into a card game prepared. Both eyes open. But not a guy going after a broad. You find out more from broads, like take for instance Mary. Now I know Frank is married to a dame that is screwing his best friend, laid a hood like me, and will go for a girl. You think I'd ever depend on Frank Lander? No. And Joe Whipple. Married to a lush, and sleeping with his best friend's wife, Mary."

"Then you wouldn't depend on Joe, either?"

"Yes, I would. Women don't bother him. He don't care if his wife is a lush, he'll get his nooky from his best friend's wife, he *isn't* going to marry her because that was three-four years ago, and he's tough about everybody. His wife, his dame, his best friend, *and* the United States government. Because I tell you something, if we ever get going on the home-loan proposition, don't think Joe didn't use his job in Washington every chance he got. The partnership is gonna be me and Joe Whipple, because he's just as tough as I am. And one fine day he'll fall over dead from not taking care of himself, and I'll be the main guy. You know the only thing I don't like about you,

Bobbie, is the booze. If you'd lay off the sauce for a year I'd get rid of Peggy, and you and I could get married. But booze is women's weakness like women are men's weakness."

"Men are women's weakness."

"No, you're wrong. Men don't make women talk, men don't make women lose their looks, and women can give up men for a hell of a long time, but a female lush is the worst kind of a lush."

"Am I a lush?"

"You have a couple drinks every day, don't you?"

"Yes."

"Then you're on the way. Maybe you only take three-four drinks a day now, but five years from now three or four drinks will get you stewed, so you'll be stewed every day. That's a lush. Peggy eats like a God damn pig, but if she ever started drinking, I'd kick her out. Fortunately her old man died with the D.T.'s, so she's afraid of it."

"Would you mind getting me a nice double Scotch with a little water?"

"Why should I mind?" He grinned from back molar to back molar. "When you got a little load on, you forget home and mother." He got her the drink, she took it in her right hand and slowly poured it down his furry chest. He jumped when the icy drink touched him.

"Thank you so much," she said. "Been a very pleasant afternoon, but the party's over."

"You sore at me?"

"Yes, I am. I don't like being called a lush, and I certainly don't like you to think I'd make a good substitute for Peggy."

"You *are* sore."

"Yes."

The children did not know it was her birthday, but when Pete came home he handed her two parcels. "For me?" she said.

"Not very much imagination, but I didn't have a chance to go to Gibbsville," he said.

One package contained half a dozen nylons, the other a bottle of Chanel Number 5. "Thank you. Just what I wanted. I really did."

He suddenly began to cry, and rushed out of the room.

"Why is Daddy crying?" said their daughter.

"Because it's my birthday and he did a very sweet thing."

"Why should he cry?" said their son. He was nine years old, the daughter eleven.

"Because he's sentimental," said the daughter.

"And it's a very nice thing to be," said Bobbie.

"Aren't you going to go to him?"

"Not quite yet. In a minute. Angus, will you go down to the drug store and get a quart of ice cream? Here's a dollar, and you and your sister may keep the change, divided."

"What flavor?" said the boy.

"Vanilla and strawberry, or whatever else they have."

Pete returned. "Kids gone to bed?"

"I sent them for some ice cream."

"Did they see me bawling?"

"Yes, and I think it did them good. Marjorie understood it. Angus was a little mystified. But it was good for both of them."

"Marjorie understood it? Did you?"

"She said it was because you were sentimental."

He shook his head. "I don't know if you'd call it sentimental. I just couldn't help thinking you were forty years old. Forty. You forty. Bobbie Hammersmith. And all we've been through, and what I've done to you. I know why you married me, Bobbie, but why did you stick it out?"

"Because I married you."

"Yes. Because you married Ichabod. You know, I wasn't in love with you when we were first married. You thought I was, but I wasn't. It was wonderful, being in bed with you and watching you walking around without any clothes on. Taking a bath. But it was too much for me and that's what started me making passes at everybody. And underneath it all I knew damn well why you married me and I hated you. You were making a fool of me and I kept waiting for you to say this farce was over. If you had, I'd have killed you."

"And I guess rightly."

"And all the later stuff. Running a poolroom and living on Mill Street. I blamed all of that on you. But things are better now since we moved here. Aren't they?"

"Yes, much better, as far as the way we live—"

"That's all I meant. If we didn't have Lantenengo Street and Princeton and those things to look back on, this wouldn't be a bad life for two ordinary people."

"It's not bad," she said.

"It's still pretty bad, but that's because we once had it better. Here's what I want to say. Any time you want to walk out on me, I won't make any fuss. You can have the children, and I won't fight about it. That's my birthday present to you, before it's too late. And I have no plans for myself. I'm not trying to get out of this marriage, but you're forty now and you're entitled to whatever is left."

"Thank you, Pete. I have nobody that wants to marry me."

"Well, maybe not. But you may have, sometime. I love you now, Bobbie, and I never used to. I guess you can't love anybody else while you have no self-respect. When the war was over I was sure I'd get the bounce at the plant, but they like me there, they've kept me on, and that one promotion. We'll never be back on Lantenengo Street, but I think I can count on a job here maybe the rest of my life. In a couple of years we can move to a nicer house."

"I'd rather buy this and fix it up a little. It's a better-built house than the ones they're putting up over on Fair Grounds Heights."

"Well, I'm glad you like it too," he said. "The other thing, that we hardly ever talk about. In fact never talk about. Only fight about sometimes. I'll try, Bobbie. I've been trying."

"I know you have."

"Well—how about you trying, too?"

"I did."

"But not lately. I'm not going to ask you who or when or any of that, but why is it you're faithful to me while I'm chasing after other women, and then when I'm faithful to you, you have somebody else? You're forty now and I'm forty-four. Let's see how long we can go without cheating?"

"You don't mean put a time limit on it, or put up a trophy, like an endurance contest? That's the way it sounds. We both have bad habits, Pete."

"Yes, and I'm the worst. But break it off, Bobbie, whoever it is. Will you please? If it's somebody you're not going to marry, and that's what you said, I've—well, it's a long time since I've cheated, and I like it much better this way. Will you stop seeing this other guy?"

"All right. As a matter of fact I *have* stopped, but don't ask me how long ago."

"I won't ask you anything. And if you fall in love with somebody and want to marry him—"

"And he wants to marry me."

"And he wants to marry you, I'll bow out." He leaned down and kissed her cheek. "I know you better than you think I do, Bobbie."

"That's an irritating statement to make to any woman."

"I guess it is, but not the way I meant it."

Now that is as far as I need go in the story of Pete and Bobbie McCrea. I promised a happy ending, which I shall come to in a moment. We have left Pete and Bobbie in 1947, on Bobbie's fortieth birthday. During the next thirteen years I saw them twice. On one occasion my wife and I spent the night with them in their house in Fair Grounds, which was painted, scrubbed and dusted like the Fair Grounds houses of old. My wife went to bed early, and Pete and Bobbie and I talked until past midnight, and then Pete retired and Bobbie and I continued our conversation until three in the morning. Twice she emptied our ash trays of cigarette butts, and we drank a drip-flask of coffee. It seemed to me that she was so thorough in her description of their life because she felt that the dinginess would vanish if she once succeeded in exposing it. But as we were leaving in the morning I was not so sure that it had vanished. My wife said to me: "Did she get it all out of her system?"

"Get what out of her system?"

"I don't know, but I don't think she did, entirely."

"That would be asking too much," I said. "But I guess she's happy."

"Content, but not happy," said my wife. "But the children are what interested me. The girl is going to be attractive in a few more years, but that boy! You didn't talk to him, but do you know about him? He's fourteen, and he's already passed his senior mathematics. He's *finished* the work that the high school seniors are supposed to be taking. The principal is trying to arrange correspondence courses for him. He's the brightest student they ever had in Fair Grounds High School, ever, and all the scientific men at the aluminum plant know about him. And he's a good-looking boy, too."

"Bobbie didn't tell me any of this."

"And I'll bet I know why. He's their future. With you she wanted to get rid of the past. She adores this boy, adores him. That part's almost terrifying."

"Not to me," I said. "It's the best thing that could have happened to her, and to Pete. The only thing that's terrifying is that they could have ruined it. And believe me, they could have."

In 1960, then, I saw Pete and Bobbie again. They invited me, of all their old friends, to go with them to the Princeton commencement. Angus McCrea, Junior, led his class, was awarded the mathematics prize, the physics prize, the Eubank Prize for scholarship, and some other honors that I am sure are listed in the program. I could not read the program because I was crying most of the time. Pete would lean forward in his chair, listening to the things that were being said about his son, but in an attitude that would have been more suitable to a man who was listening to a pronouncement of sentence. Bobbie sat erect and smiling, but every once in a while I could hear her whisper, "Oh, God. Oh, God."

There, I guess, is our happy ending.

WE'RE FRIENDS AGAIN

♦

I know of no quiet quite like that of a men's club at about half past nine on a summer Sunday evening. The stillness is a denial of the meaning and purpose of a club, and as you go from empty room to empty room and hear nothing but the ticking of clocks and your own heel taps on the rugless floor, you think of the membership present and past; the charming, dull, distinguished, vulgar, jolly, bibulous men who have selected this place and its company as a refuge from all other places and all other company. For that is what a club is, and to be alone in it is wrong. And at half past nine on a summer Sunday evening you are quite likely to be alone. The old men who live there have retired for the night, sure that if they die before morning they will be discovered by a chambermaid, and that if they survive this night they will have another day in which their loneliness will be broken by the lunch crowd, the cocktail crowd, and the presence of a few men in the diningroom in the evening. But on a summer Sunday evening the old men are better off in their rooms, with their personal possessions, their framed photographs and trophies of accomplishment and favorite books. The lounge, the library, the billiard and card rooms have a deathly emptiness on summer Sunday evenings, and the old men need no additional reminder of emptiness or death.

It is always dark in my club at half past nine in the evening, and darker than ever on Sunday in summer, when only the fewest possible lights are left burning. If you go to the bar the bartender slowly

141

folds his newspaper, which he has been reading by the light from the back-bar, takes off his glasses, says "Good evening," and unconsciously looks up at the clock to see how much longer he must stay. Downstairs another club servant is sitting at the telephone switchboard. There is the spitting buzz of an incoming call and he says, "'Devening, St. James Club? . . . No sir, he isn't . . . No sir, no message for you . . . Mr. Crankshaw went to bed about an hour ago. Orders not to disturb him, sir . . . You're welcome. Goodnight." The switchboard buzzes, the loudest, the only noise in the club, until the man pulls out the plug and the weight pulls the cord back into place, and then it is quiet again.

I had been a member of the St. James for about ten years, but I could not recall ever having been there on a Sunday until this night a year or so ago. I was summoned on the golf course by an urgent message to call the New York operator, which I did immediately. "Jim, I'm sorry to louse up your golf, but can you get a train in to New York? I don't advise driving. The traffic is terrible."

"There's a train that will get me to Penn Station about eight-thirty," I said. "But what's this all about?"

The man I was speaking to was Charles Ellis, one of my best friends.

"Charley? What's it all *about?*" I repeated.

"Nancy died this afternoon. She had a stroke after lunch."

"Oh, no. Charley, I can't tell you—"

"I know, and thanks. Are you still a member at the St. James?"

"Yes, why?"

"Will you meet me there? I'll tell you why when I see you."

"Of course. What time will you get there?"

"As soon after eight-thirty as I can."

For a little while the stillness of the club was a relief from the noise and unpleasantness of the train, which was filled with men and women and children who had presumably been enjoying themselves under the Long Island sun but were now beginning to suffer from it, and if not from the damage to their skin, from the debilitating effects of too much picnic food and canned beer. At Jamaica there was an angry scramble as we changed trains, and all the way from Jamaica to Penn Station five men fought over some fishing tackle on the car platform while three young men with thick thatches and blue jeans tormented two pansies in imitation Italian silk suits.

The bartender gave me some cold cuts and bread and cheese and made me some instant coffee. "How late do you work, Fred?" I said.

"Sundays I'm off at ten," he said, looking at the clock for the fifth or sixth time. "Don't seem worth the while, does it?"

"I'm expecting a friend, he's not a member."

"Then if I was you I'd make sure Roland knows about it. He's just as liable to fall asleep. You know, asleep at the switchboard? You heard the old saying, asleep at the switch. That fellow can go to sleep with his eyes open."

"I've already spoken to him," I said. I wandered about in the lounge and the library, not to be out of earshot when Charley Ellis arrived. As all the clocks in the club struck ten Fred came to me, dressed for the street, and said: "Can I get you anything before I go?"

"Can you let me have a bottle of Scotch?"

"I can do that, and a bowl of ice. You want soda, Mr. Malloy?"

"Just the Scotch and the ice, thanks."

"About the only place you can drink it is in your room, if you want water with it. I have to close up the bar."

"It's all right if we sit here, isn't it?"

"Jesus, if you *want* to," said Fred.

At that moment Charles Ellis arrived, escorted by Roland.

"Oh, it's Mr. Ellis," said Fred. "Remember me? Fred, from the Racquet Club?"

"Yes, hello, Fred. Is this where you are now?"

"Six and a half years," said Fred.

"Thanks very much, Fred," I said. "Goodnight."

"I'll bring you the bottle," said Fred.

"I don't want a drink, if that's what you mean," said Charles Ellis. "Unless *you've* fallen off the wagon."

"Then never mind, thanks, Fred. Goodnight."

Fred left, and I switched on some lights in the lounge.

"You saddled with that bore?" said Charley.

"I don't see much of him," I said.

"I'm sorry I'm so late. I got here as soon as I could. I called this number but it didn't answer."

"That's all right. I guess Roland had the buzzer turned off."

"Hell of an imposition, taking you away from golf and so forth. How is Kay?"

"Very distressed, naturally. She said to give you her love."

"I almost asked her to come in with you."

"She almost came," I said. "But she has her grandchildren coming tomorrow."

He was silent, obviously wondering where to begin.

"Take your time," I said.

He looked up at me and smiled. "Thanks." He reached over and patted my knee. "Thanks for everything, Jim."

"Well, what the hell?"

"First, why did I want to see you here? Because I didn't want to ask you to come to the apartment, and I didn't want to go to the Racquet Club."

"I figured something like that."

"How did it happen, and all that? Nancy and I were spending the weekend at her uncle's. We went out to dinner last night, and when we came home she said she had a headache, so I gave her some aspirin. This morning she still had the headache and I asked her if she wanted me to send for a doctor, but she didn't. She said she hadn't slept very well, and I probably should have called the doctor, but I didn't. Then there were four guests for lunch and I didn't have a chance to speak to her. In fact the last thing I said to her was before lunch, I told her that if she didn't feel better after lunch, she should make her excuses and lie down. And that's what she did. She excused herself, shook her head to me not to follow her, and about twenty minutes later the maid came and told us she was dead. Found her lying on the bathroom floor. I can't believe it. I can't be devoid of feeling, but I just can't believe it."

"Did the doctor give you anything?"

"You mean sedative? Tranquilizers? No, I haven't needed anything. I guess I must be in some sort of shock."

"Where are the children?"

"Well, of course Mike is in Germany, still in the Army. And I finally located Janey about an hour ago, at a house in Surrey where she's spending the weekend. She's been abroad all summer. She's flying home tomorrow and Mike has applied for leave. The Army or the Red Cross or somebody will fly him home in time for the funeral." He paused.

"Wednesday morning at eleven o'clock. Church of the Epiphany, on York Avenue. I decided Wednesday so that Mike could be here, in case there's any hitch." He looked about him. "You couldn't ask for a gloomier place than this, could you?"

"No, it's certainly appropriate."

"Well, what do I do now, Jim? You've been through it."

"Yes, I've been through it. The answer is, you're going to be so damn busy with details the next few weeks that you won't have too much time to know what hit you. You're going to find out how really nice people can be. Maybe you haven't thought about that lately, but you're going to find out. You're also going to find out that some people are shits. Real shits. I'll give you the two worst. The old friend that won't make any effort at all except maybe to send you a telegram, if that. You'll be shocked by that, so you ought to be prepared for it. I mean very close friends, guys and women you grew up with that just won't come near you. Then there's the second type, just as bad. He'll write you a letter in a week or two, and it'll be all about himself. How sad *he* is, how well he knew Nancy, how much he appreciated her, and rather strongly implying that *you* didn't know her true worth as well as he did. You'll read one of those letters and reread it, and if you do what I did, you'll throw it in the wastebasket. But the next time you see the son of a bitch, he'll say, 'Hey, Ellis, I wrote you a letter. Didn't you ever get it?' So be prepared for those two. But against them, the nice people. The *kind* people, Charley, sometimes where you'd least expect it. A guy that I thought was about as cold a fish as there is in the world, he turned out to have more real heart than almost anybody. In my book he can never do another wrong thing. The third group I haven't mentioned. The lushes. But they're obvious and you can either put up with them or brush them off. The only advice I can give you—keep busy. Don't take any more time off from your work than you absolutely have to."

"And when will it really hit me?"

"I don't know when, but I know how. Suddenly, and for no apparent reason. When your guard is down. You'll be in the subway, or walking along the street, not any favorite street full of memories, but any anonymous street. Or in a cab. And the whole God damn thing will come down on you and you'll be weeping before you know it. That's where nobody can help you, because it's unpredictable and you'll be alone. It'll only happen when you're relaxed and defenseless. But you're not relaxed, really. It's just that you're weak, *been* weakened without realizing what it's taken out of you. Emotional exhaustion, I guess it is. Then there are two other things, but I won't talk about them now. They may not happen to you, and I've told you enough."

"Thanks, Jim."

"Charley, you know what let's do? Let's go for a walk. We won't run into anybody."

"Yes. Nothing against your club, but I think I've had it here."

So the two of us went for a not too brisk walk, down Fifth Avenue, up Fifth Avenue, and to the door of Charley's apartment house. The doorman saluted him and said: "Sorry fur yur trouble, Mr. Ellis. A foine lovely woman, none foiner."

I happened, and only happened, to be looking at Charley as the doorman spoke. He nodded at the doorman but did not speak. I took his arm and led him to the elevator. "Mr. Ellis's apartment," I said, and frowned the elevator man into silence. He understood.

We got off at Charley's floor, the only apartment on that floor, and he went to the livingroom and sat down and wept without covering his face. I stayed in the foyer. Five minutes passed and then he said: "Okay, Jim. I'm okay now. What can I give you? Ginger ale? Coke? Glass of milk?"

"A ginger ale."

"It hit me sooner than we expected," he said. "Do you know what it was? Or what I think it was? It was the doorman saying nice things, and he didn't really know her at all. He's only been here a few weeks. He doesn't know either of us very well. Why don't you stay here tonight, instead of going back to that God damn dreary place?"

"I will if you'll go to bed. And don't worry, you'll sleep."

"Will I?"

"Yes, you'll sleep tonight. Twenty blocks to a mile, we walked damn near four miles, I make it. Take a lukewarm tub and hit the sack. I'll read for a while and I'll be in Mike's room. Goodnight, Charley."

"Goodnight, Jim. Thanks again."

One afternoon in 1937 I was having breakfast in my apartment in East Fifty-fifth Street. I had worked the night before until dawn, as was my custom, and I was smoking my third cigarette and starting on my second quart of coffee when the house phone rang. Charley Ellis was in the vestibule. I let him in and he shook his head at me in my pajamas, unshaven, and with the coffee and newspapers beside my chair. "La Vie de Bohème," he said.

"That's right," I said. "Come on out, Mimi, and stop that damn coughing."

Charley looked at me with genuine alarm. "You haven't got a dame here, have you? I'm sorry if—"

"No dame."

"I don't want to interrupt anything."

"I wouldn't have let you in," I said. "But I've just been reading about you, so maybe I would have. Curiosity. Who is Nancy Preswell?"

"Oh, you saw that, did you? Well, she's the wife of a guy named Jack Preswell."

"All right, who is *Jack* Preswell?" I said. "Besides being the husband of a girl named Nancy Preswell."

"Well, you've met him. With me. Do you remember a guy that we went to the ball game with a couple of years ago?"

"I do indeed. I remember everything about him but his name. A very handsome guy, a little on the short side. Boyish-looking. And now I know who she is because I've seen them together, but I never could remember his name. Not that it mattered. He didn't remember me at all, but she's quite a beauty. Not *quite* a beauty. She *is* a beauty. And you're the home-wrecker."

"According to Maury Paul I am, if you believe what he writes."

"He's often right, you know," I said. "He had me in his column one time with a woman I'd never met, but I met her a year or so later and he turned out to be a very good prophet. So it's only your word against his."

"I didn't come here to be insulted," he said, taking a chair.

"Well, what did you come here for? I haven't seen or heard from you in God knows how long." It always took a little while for Charley Ellis to get started on personal matters, and if I didn't talk a lot or kid him, he would sometimes go away without saying what he had intended to say. "Now I understand *why,* of course, but I gather Mrs. Preswell hasn't even gone to Reno yet."

"If you'll lay off this heavy-handed joshing, I guess you'd call it, I'd like to talk seriously for a minute."

"All right. Have a cup of coffee, or do you want a drink? If you want a drink, you know where it is."

"I don't want anything but your respectful attention and maybe some sound advice. What I really want is someone to talk to, to talk things out with."

Charley Ellis was about thirty-three years old then, and not a young thirty-three. He had stayed single because he had been in love with his first cousin, a lovely girl who was the wife of Junior Williamson, Ethridge B. Williamson, Junior; he had wanted to write, and instead had gone to work for his father's firm, Willetts & Ellis. His father knew about the second frustration, but I was now more convinced than ever that I was the only person to whom Charley had confided both.

"You may be right, you know," he said. "I probably am the home-wrecker. At least a good case could be made out against me. Nancy and Jack never have got along very well, and made no secret of the fact. But I guess I'm the first one that shall we say took advantage of the situation. They had a couple of trial separations but they always went back together until I happened to come into the picture during the last one."

"But you're not blaming yourself or anything like that, I hope."

"Not one bit. That's a form of boasting, or so it always seemed to me."

"And to me, too. That's why I'm glad you're not doing the *mea culpa* act."

"Oh, hell no. I didn't create the situation," he said.

"Do you know who did?"

"Yes, I do," said Charley. "Franklin D. Roosevelt, your great pal."

"Yeah. The inventor of bubonic plague and the common cold, and now the louser-up of the Preswell marriage. You've been spending too much time at Willetts & Ellis. You ought to come up for air."

"You were bound to say something like that, but it happens to be a fact. Preswell was one of the bright young boys that went to Washington five years ago, and that didn't sit too well with Nancy or her family. Then two years ago Preswell himself saw the light and got out, but he'd made a lot of enemies while he was defending Roosevelt, and he came back to New York hating everybody. He said to me one time, 'They call me a traitor to my class, like the Glamor Boy himself, but my class has been a traitor to me.' He used to go around telling everybody that they ought to be grateful to him, that he and Roosevelt were holding the line for the American system. But then when he quit, he was just as violent against Roosevelt as anybody, but nobody would listen. He'd been so God damn arrogant when he was *with* Roosevelt, said a lot of personal things, so nobody cared whose side he was on. And of course he began to take it out on Nancy."

"What does this gentleman do for a living?"

"He *was* with Carson, Cass & Devereux, but they don't want him back. That's just the point. Nobody wants him."

"Was he a good lawyer?"

"Well, *Harvard Law Review,* assistant editor, I think. I don't really know how good a lawyer he was. With a firm like Carson, Cass, you don't get any of the big stuff till you've been there quite a while. He has nothing to worry about financially. His father left him very well fixed and Nancy has money of her own. Her father was, or *is,* Alexander McMinnies, Delaware Zinc."

"Oh, that old crook."

"Why do you say that? You don't know whether he's a crook or a philanthropist."

"He could be both, but even if he is your girl's father, Charley, you know damn well what he is. I'll bet the boys at Carson, Cass have sat up many a night trying to keep him out of prison."

"And succeeded, in spite of Roosevelt and Homer S. Cummings."

"Those things take time," I said.

"Get your facts right. Mr. McMinnies won in the Supreme Court. Unless you were looking forward to the day when Franklin D. decides to abolish the courts and all the rest of that stuff. Which is coming, I have very little doubt."

"You don't really think that, but you have proved beyond a doubt that Roosevelt loused up Preswell's marriage. Aren't you grateful?"

"You're a tricky bastard."

"It's so easy with you guys. You have a monomania about Roosevelt."

"Monophobia."

"No, wise guy. Monophobia means fear of being alone. So much for you and your four years at the Porcellian."

"I could correct you on that four years, but I hate to spoil your good time."

"All right, we're even," I said. "What's on your mind, Charley?"

"Yes, we can't even have a casual conversation without getting into politics," he said. "Can we forget about politics?"

"Sure, I like to rib you, but what's on your mind? Nancy Preswell, obviously."

He was smoking a cigarette, and rubbing the ashes from the glowing end into the ash tray as they formed, turning the cigarette in his fingers. And not looking at *me*. "Jim, I read a short story of yours a few months ago. Nancy read it, too. She liked it, and she said she'd like to meet you. It was that story about two people at a skiing place."

"Oh, yes. 'Telemark.' "

"That's the one," he said. "They agree to get married even though they weren't in love. Was that based on your own experience—if you don't mind my asking?"

"No. I was in love when I got married, we both were. But it didn't last. No, that story was invention on my part. Well, not all invention. What is? When I was in Florida two years ago I saw this couple always together and always talking so earnestly, so seriously, and I began to wonder what they were talking about. So I thought about them, forgot them, and remembered them again and changed the locale to a skiing place, and that was the story."

"Nancy liked the story, but she didn't agree with you. You seemed to imply that they *should* have gotten married."

"Yes, I believe that, and they did."

"That's what Nancy didn't agree with. She said they were both willing to face the fact that they weren't in love, but where they were dishonest was in thinking they could make a go of it without being in love."

"I didn't imply that they'd make a go of it," I said. "But it seemed to me they had a chance. Which is as much as any two people have."

"I didn't get that, and neither did Nancy. We both thought you were practically saying that this was as good a start as two people could have."

"So far, so good, but that's *all* I implied."

"Do you think they *really* had a chance? Nancy says no. That marriage hasn't any chance without love, and not too much of a chance with it."

"Well, what do you think? How do you feel about it?"

"I wasn't ready for that question."

"I know damn well you weren't, Charley, and that's what's eating you. It may also be what's eating Nancy. Does she know you were in love with Polly Williamson?"

"Never. You're the only one that knows that. But here I am, thirty-three, Jim. Why can't I get rid of something that never *was* anything?"

"Go to Polly and tell her that you've always been in love with her, and can't be in love with anyone else."

"I'm afraid to," he said, and smiled. "Maybe I'm afraid she'll say she feels the same way, and divorce Junior."

"Well, that's not true. She doesn't feel the same way, or you'd have found out before this. But if you admit to yourself that you're afraid, then I think you don't really love Polly as much as you think you do, or like to think you do. I was in love with Polly for one afternoon, and I told her so. I meant it, every word of it. But every now and then I see her with Williamson and I thank God she had some sense. A girl with less sense might conceivably have divorced Williamson and married me, and how long would that have lasted? Polly is Williamson's wife, prick though he may be. And if she wants Williamson, she certainly doesn't want me, and probably not you. Has Polly ever stepped out on her own?"

"I think she did, with a guy from Boston. An older guy. I don't think you'd even know his name. A widower, about forty-five. Not a playboy type at all. Very serious-minded. Just right for Polly. You know, Polly has her limitations when it comes to a sense of humor, the lighter side. She was born here, but her father and mother both came from Boston and she's always been more of a Boston type than New York. Flowers and music and the children. But she does her own work in the garden, and she often goes to concerts by herself. What I'm saying is, no *chi-chi*. She's a good athlete, but there again it isn't what you might call public sport. The contest is always between her and the game itself, and the things she's best at are games like golf or trap-shooting. Skiing. Figure-skating. Polly damn near doesn't need anyone else to enjoy herself. And God knows she never needed me." He paused. "Did you ever hear her play the piano?"

"No."

"She's good. You know, Chopin. Rachmaninoff. Tschaikovsky."

"Charley, I just discovered something about you," I said.

"What?"

"*You're* a Bostonian."

"Maybe."

"The admiring way you talk about Polly, and of course you're a first cousin. Isn't it practically a tradition in Boston that you fall in love with your first cousin?"

"It's been known to happen, but I assure you, it had nothing to do with my falling in love with Polly."

"Do you mind if I take issue with you on that point? I have a theory that it had a *lot* to do with your falling in love with Polly, and that your present love affair, with Nancy, is your New York side."

He laughed. "Oh, God. How facile, and how stupid . . . I take back stupid, but you're wrong."

"Why am I wrong? You haven't given the theory any thought. And I have, while listening to you. You'd better give it some thought, and decide whether you want to be a New Yorker or a Bostonian."

"Or you might be wrong and I won't have to make the choice."

"Yes, but don't reject my theory out of hand. You're a loner. You wanted to be a writer. You're conventional, as witness working in the family firm against your will, but doing very well I understand. And you were talking about yourself as much as you were about Polly."

"Not at all. I was a great team-sport guy. Football in school, and rowing in college."

"Rowing. The obvious joke. Did you ever meet that Saltonstall fellow that rowed Number 5?"

"I know the joke, and it was never very funny to us. A Yale joke. Or more likely Princeton." He seemed to ignore me for a moment. He sat staring at his outstretched foot, his elbow on the arm of his chair, his cheek resting on the two first fingers of his left hand while the other two fingers were curled under the palm. "And yet, you may have a point," he said, judicially. "You just may have a point. Dr. Jekyll and Mr. Hyde. Larry Lowell and Jimmy Walker. Waldo Emerson and Walter Winchell. This conversation may be the turning point of my whole life, and I'll owe it all to you, you analytical son of a bitch."

"That's the thanks I get. Watery compliments."

He rose. "Gotta go," he said.

"How come you're uptown at this hour?"

"I took the afternoon off," he said. "I have a perfectly legitimate reason for being uptown, but I know your nasty mind. Will you be in town next week? How about dinner Tuesday?"

"Tuesday, no. Wednesday, yes."

"All right, Wednesday. Shall we pick you up here? I'd like Nancy to see the squalor you live in."

"Others have found it to have a certain Old World charm," I said. "All right, Mimi. You can come out now."

"Listen, don't have any Mimi here Wednesday, will you, please?"

"That's why I said Wednesday instead of Tuesday."

"Degrading. And not even very instructive," he said.

"Not if you don't want to learn."

My apartment was actually a comfortable, fairly expensively furnished two rooms and bath, which was cleaned daily by a colored woman who worked full-time elsewhere in the building. But Charley Ellis's first remark when he arrived with Nancy Preswell was: "Why, look, he's had the place all spruced up. Is all this new?"

"All goes back to Sloane's in the morning," I said. "How do you do, Mrs. Preswell?"

"Wait a minute. You haven't been introduced," said Charley. "You could have put me in a hell of a spot. What if this hadn't been Mrs. Preswell?" He was in high good humor, determined to make this a pleasant evening.

"I often wish I weren't," she said, without bitterness, but as her first words to me they were an indication that she knew Charley confided in me. "By the way, how do you do?"

"I've often seen you. Well, pretty often," I said.

"And always pretty," said Charley.

I looked at him and then at her: "You've done wonders with this guy. I hardly recognize the old clod." My remark pleased her, and she smiled affectionately at Charley. "Gallantry, yet," I said.

"It was always there," said Charley. "It just took the right person to bring it out."

"I like your apartment, Mr. Malloy. Is this where you do all your writing?"

"Most of it. Practically all of it."

"Oh, you type your stories?" she said, looking at my typewriter. "But don't you write them in longhand first?"

"No. I don't even write letters in longhand."

"Love letters?"

"I type them," I said.

"And mimeographs them," said Charley. "Shall we have a free drink here, saving me two and a quarter?"

"The market closed firm, but have you ever noticed that Charley hates to part with a buck?"

"No, that's not fair," said Nancy Preswell.

"Or true. What's the name of that friend of yours, that writes the Broadway stories?"

"Mark Hellinger?"

"Hellinger. Right. I thought he was going to have a stroke that night when I paid a check at '21.' "

"I very nearly had one myself."

"No, now that isn't fair," said Nancy Preswell.

"I'm softening him up for later," I said.

We had some drinks and conversation, during which Nancy slowly walked around, looking at my bookshelves and pictures. "I gather you don't like anything very modern," she said.

"Not in this room. Some abstract paintings in the bathroom."

"May I see your bedroom?"

"Believe me, that's the best offer he's had today," said Charley.

"A four-poster," she said.

"Early Wanamaker," I said. "*Circa* 1930."

"All you need is a rag rug and a cat curled up on it. I like it. That's not your father, is it?"

"My grandfather. Practically everything in this room is a copy of stuff I remember from when I was a kid. I depended entirely on their taste."

"But you bought it all yourself, so it's your taste, too," said Nancy Preswell. "Very interesting, and very revealing, considering what some of the critics say about your writings."

"What does it reveal to you?" I said.

"That basically you're very conventional."

"I could have told you that," I said.

"Yes, but I probably wouldn't have believed you if I hadn't seen your apartment."

"I think I ought to tell you, though. I went through an all-modernistic phase when I lived in the Village."

"Why are you for Roosevelt?" she said.

"No! Not tonight, please," said Charley.

"You shouldn't be, you know," she persisted.

"Shall we not argue about it? I'm for him, and you're not, and that's where we'd be if we argued till tomorrow morning," I said.

"Except that I think I could convince you. You don't know my husband, do you? I know you've met him, but you've never talked with him about Roosevelt."

"When was *he* most convincing?" I said. "When he was with him, or against him?"

"He was never in the least convincing when he was for him. And he's not very convincing now. But as a writer you should be able to disregard a lot of things he says and go beneath the surface. Then you'd see what a man like Roosevelt can do to an idealist. And my husband *was* an idealist."

"Don't look at me. I'm not saying a word," said Charley.

"I do look at you, for corroboration. Jack *was* an idealist. You may not have liked him, but you have to admit that."

"Yes, he was," said Charley.

"And so were you. But Jack did something about it. You played it safe."

"Jim is wondering why I'm not taking this big. The reason is we've had it out before," said Charley.

"Many times," said Nancy Preswell. "And probably will again."

"But not tonight, shall we?" said Charley Ellis.

"I hate Mr. Roosevelt," she said. "And I can't stand it when a writer that I think is good is *for* him. I'm one of those people that think he ought to be assassinated, and I just hope somebody else does it, not my poor, drunken, disillusioned husband."

"Is he liable to, your husband?" I said.

"I don't suppose there's any real danger of it. But it's what he thinks of day and night. I don't want you to think I love my husband. I haven't for years. But Jack Preswell was an idealist, and Roosevelt turned him into a fanatic."

"He might have been a fanatical idealist."

"*He was!* Four years ago, that's what he was. But there's nothing left now but the fanaticism. Don't you see that, Mr. Malloy? Mr. Roosevelt took away his ideals."

"How are you on ideals, Mrs. Preswell?"

"If that's supposed to be a crusher, it isn't . . . I have a few, but they're not in any danger from—that awful man. Now I've said enough, and you probably don't want to have dinner with us."

"Yes, I would. You're a very attractive girl."

"As long as I don't say what I think? That's insulting, and now I'm not sure *I* want to have dinner with *you*."

There was a silence, broken by Charley: "Well, what shall we do? Toss a coin? Heads we dine together, tails we separate."

"I'll agree to an armistice if Mr. Malloy will."

"All right," I said. "Let's go. Maybe if we have a change of scenery . . ."

"I promise I'll be just as stupid as you want me to be," said Nancy Preswell.

There was not another word about politics all evening, and at eleven o'clock we took a taxi to a theatre where I was to meet an actress friend of mine, Julianna Moore, the female heavy in an English mystery play. Julie was about thirty, a girl who had been prematurely starred after one early success, and had never again found the right play. Her father was a history professor at Yale, and Julie was a well-educated girl whom I had first known in our Greenwich Village days. We had been lovers then, briefly, but now she was a friend of my ex-wife's and the mistress of a scenic designer.

Nancy Preswell began with compliments to Julie, ticking off six plays in which Julie had appeared.

"You must go to the theatre all the time, to have seen some of those sad little turkeys," said Julie.

"I go a lot," said Nancy.

"Did you ever do any acting?"

"*Did* I? 'Shall I speak ill of him that is my husband? / Ah, poor my lord, what tongue shall smooth thy name . . .'"

"'When I, thy three-hours wife, have mangled it?' Where and when did you do Juliet?" said Julie.

"At Foxcroft."

"I'll bet you were a very pretty Juliet," said Julie.

"Thank you. If I was, that says it all. I was cured."

"Well, I was the kind of ham that never was cured, if you don't mind a very small joke . . . I always thought it would have been fun to go to Foxcroft. All that riding and drilling."

"Where *did* you go?"

"A Sacred Heart school in Noroton, Connecticut, then two years at Vassar."

"Where did you go to school, Charley," I said.

"I don't know. Where did you?" he said.

"Oh, a Sacred Heart school in Noroton, Connecticut. Then two years at Foxcroft," I said.

"Too tarribly fonny, jost too tarribly fonny," said Julie.

"That's her Mickey Rooney imitation. Now do Lionel Barrymore," I said.

"Too tarribly fonny, jost too tarribly fonny," said Julie.

"Isn't she good?" I said. "Now do Katharine Hepburn."

"Who?" said Julie.

"She's run out of imitations," I said.

We went to "21," the 18 Club, LaRue, and El Morocco. We all had had a lot to drink, and Julie, who had played two performances that day, had soon caught up with the rest of us by drinking double Scotches. "Now the big question is, the all-important question—*is,*" said Julie.

"What is the big question, Julie dear?" said Nancy.

"Ah, you like me, don't you? I like you, too," said Julie. "I like Charley, too. And I used to like Jim, didn't I, Jim?"

"Used to, but not any more."

"Correct. Jim is a rat. Aren't you, Jim?"

"Of course he's a rat," said Nancy. "He's a Franklin D. Roosevelt rat."

"I'm a Franklin D. Roosevelt rat. You be careful what you say," said Julie.

"The hell with that. What was the big question?" said Charley.

"*My* big question?" said Julie.

"Yes," said Charley.

"I didn't know I had one. Oh, yes. The big *question. Is.* Do we go to Harlem and I can't go on tomorrow night and I give my understudy a break. *Or. Or.* Do I go home to my trundle bed—and you stay out of it, Jim. You're a rat. I mean stay out of my trundle.

Nevermore, quoth the raven. Well, what did my understudy ever do for me? So I guess we better go home. Right?"

"Yeah. I haven't got an understudy," said Charley. He signaled for the check.

"Jim, why are you such a rat? If you weren't such a rat. But that's what you are, a rat," said Julie.

"Pretend I'm not a rat."

"How can I pretend a thing like that? I'm the most promising thirty-year-old ingénue there is, but I can't pretend you're not a rat. Because that's what you are. Your ex-wife is my best friend, so what else are you but a rat? Isn't that logical, Jim? Do you remember Bank Street? That was before you were a rat."

"No, I was a rat then, Julie."

"No. No, you weren't. If you were a rat then, you wouldn't be one now. That's logical."

"But he's not a bad rat," said Nancy.

"Oh, there you're wrong. If he was a good little rat I'd take him home with me. But I don't want a rat in my house."

"Then you come to my house," I said.

"All right," said Julie. "That solves everything. I don't know *why* I didn't think of that before. Remember Bank Street, Jim?"

"Sure."

She stood up. *"Good*night, Nancy. *Good*night, Charley." On her feet she became dignified, the star. She held her mink so that it showed her to best advantage and to the captains who said, "Goodnight, Miss Moore," she nodded and smiled. In the taxi she was ready to be kissed. "Ah, Jim, what a Christ-awful life, isn't it? You won't tell Ken, will you?"

"No. I won't tell anybody."

"Just don't tell Ken. I don't want him to think I care that much. He's giving me a bad time. Kiss me, Jim. Tell me I'm nicer than Nancy."

"You're much nicer than Nancy. Or anybody else."

She smiled. "You're a rat, Jim, but you're a nice old rat. It's all right if I call you a rat, isn't it? Who the hell is she to say you aren't a bad rat? She's not in our game, is she?"

"No."

"We don't have to let her in our game. But *he* does, the poor son of a bitch."

When she saw my bedroom she said: "Good Lord, Jim, I feel pregnant already. That's where Grandpa and Grandma begat. Isn't it? I hope *we* don't beget."

I was still asleep when she left, and on my desk there was a note from her:

Dear Rat:
You didn't use to snore on Bank Street. Am going home to finish my sleep. It is eight-fifteen and you seem good for many more hours. I had a lovely time and have the hangover to prove it. Want to be home in case K. calls as he said he would. In any case we are better off than Nancy and Charles. Are they headed for trouble! ! !
Love,
J.

P.S.: The well-appointed bachelor's apartment has a supply of extra toothbrushes. My mouth tastes like the inside of the motorman's glove. Ugh! ! !
J.

The motorman's glove. Passé collegiate slang of the previous decade, when the word whereupon was stuck into every sentence and uzza-mattera-fact and wet-smack and swell caught on and held on. I read Julie's note a couple of times, and "the motorman's glove" brought to mind two lines from *Don Juan* that had seemed strangely out of character for Byron:

Let us have wine and women, mirth and laughter,
Sermons and soda-water the day after.

The mirth and laughter, the wine and women were not out of character, but there was something very vulgar about Byron's taking soda-water for a hangover as I took Eno's fruit salts. An aristocrat, more than a century dead, and a man I disliked as cordially as if he were still alive. But he had said it all, more than a hundred years ago. I made a note to buy a copy of *Don Juan* and send it, with that passage marked, to Julie. At that moment, though, I was trying to figure out what she meant by Nancy and Charley, headed for trouble. There was trouble already, and more to come.

I waited until four o'clock and then telephoned Julie. "It's the rat," I said. "How are you feeling?"

"I'll live. I'll be able to go on tonight. Actually, I'm feeling much better than I have any right to, considering the amount I drank. I went home and took a bath and fiddled around till Ken called—"

"He called, did he?"

"Yes. There isn't going to be anything in the columns about you and me, is there?"

"My guess is a qualified no. If we went out again tonight there would be, but—"

"But we're not going out again tonight," she said. "I don't have to tell you that last night was a lapse."

"You don't have to, but you did," I said.

"Now don't get huffy," she said. "It wouldn't have happened with anyone else, and it wouldn't have happened with you if it hadn't been for the old days on Bank Street."

"I know that, Julie, and I'm not even calling you for another date. I want to know what you meant by—I have your note here—Nancy and Charley headed for trouble. Was something said? Did something happen that I missed?"

"Oh, God, I have to think. It seems to me I wrote that ages ago. And it was only this morning. Is it important? I could call you back?"

"Not important."

"*I* know. I know what it was. Is Nancy's husband a man named Jack Preswell?"

"Yes."

"Well, he was at Morocco last night. Standing at the bar all alone and just staring at us. Staring, staring, staring. I used to know him when I was a prom-trotter, back in the paleolithic age."

"How did you happen to see him and we didn't?"

"Because I was facing that way and you weren't," she said. "Maybe I should have said something. Maybe I did."

"No, you didn't."

"I don't think I did. No, I guess I didn't, because now I remember thinking that I wasn't positively sure it was he. But when you and I left I caught a glimpse of him, and it was. If anybody was tighter than we were, he was. His eyes were just barely open, and he was holding himself up by the elbows. I'll bet he didn't last another ten minutes."

"Well, just about," I said.

"What do you mean?"

"Have you seen the early editions of the afternoon papers?"

"No. I don't get the afternoon papers here."

"Preswell was hit by a taxi at 54th and Lexington. Fractured his skull and died before the ambulance got there. According to the cops he just missed being hit by a northbound cab, and then walked in front of a southbound. Four or five witnesses said the hack driver was not at fault, which is another way of saying Preswell was blind drunk."

"Well, I guess I could almost swear to that, but I'm glad I don't have to. I won't, will I?"

"Not a chance. He wasn't with us, and none of us ever spoke to him. The *Times* and the *Trib* will print the bare facts and people can draw their own conclusions. The *News* and the *Mirror* will play it up tonight, but it's only a one-day story. However, there is one tabloid angle. If the *Mirror* or the *News* finds out that Nancy was in Morocco with Charley—well, they could do something with that."

"And would you and I get in the papers?"

"Well, if I were the city editor of the *News* or the *Mirror,* and a prominent actress and an obscure author—"

"Oh, Lord. And I told Ken I went straight home from the theatre. Jim, you know a lot of those press people . . ."

"Julie, if they find out, your picture's going to be in the tabloids. I couldn't prevent that."

"And they *are* going to find out, aren't they?"

"The only straight answer is yes. You spoke to a lot of people as we were leaving. Waiter captains. People at the tables. If you can think of a story to tell Ken, I'll back you up. But maybe the best thing is to tell him the truth, up to a certain point."

"He'll supply the rest, after that certain point. He knows about Bank Street."

"That was eight years ago. Can't you have an evening out with an old friend?"

"Would you believe that line?"

"No," I said. "But I have a very suspicious nature."

"You're a blind man trusting a boy scout compared to Ken. He didn't believe me when I told him I went straight home from the theatre. But in the absence of proof—now he's got his proof."

"Well, then have a date with me tonight. Make the son of a bitch good and jealous."

"I'm almost tempted. When will we know about the *News* and the *Mirror?*"

"Oh, around nine o'clock tonight."

"You'll see them when they come out, before I can. If they mention me, will you stop for me at the theatre? That isn't much of an offer, Jim, but for old time's sake?"

"And if you're not mentioned, you have a date with Ken?"

"Yes," she said.

"All right. You understand, of course, this is something I wouldn't do for just anybody, take second best."

"I understand exactly why you're doing it, and so do you," she said.

"I detect the sound of *double entendre.*"

"Well, that's how I meant it. You're being nice, but you also know that nice little rats get a piece of candy. And don't make the obvious remark about piece of what. Seriously, Jim, I can count on you, can't I?"

"I would say that you are one of the few that can always count on me, Julie. For whatever that's worth."

"Right now, a great deal."

"Well, I wish you luck, even though I'll be the loser in the deal."

"You didn't lose anything last night. And I may have lost a husband. He was talking that way today."

"Do you want to marry him?"

"Yes, I do. Very much. Too much. So much that all he ever sees is my phony indifference. Too smart for my own good, I am. Jim, ought I to call Nancy Preswell, or write her a note?"

"A note would be better, I think."

"Yes, I do, too."

"I've been calling Charley all afternoon, and nobody knows where he is. But he'll be around when he wants to see me."

"It's a hateful thing for me to say, but in a way he's stuck, isn't he?"

"He wants to be."

"He's still stuck," said Julie.

At about eleven-twenty I was standing with the backstage doorman, who was saying goodnight to the actors and actresses as they left the theatre. "Miss Moore's always one of the last to leave," he said. "We us'ally break about five to eleven, but tonight she's later than us'al. I told her you was here. I told her myself."

"That's all right," I said.

"She dresses with Miss Van, one flight up. I'll just go tell her you're here."

"No. No thanks. Don't hurry her," I said.

"She's us'ally one of the last out, but I don't know what's keeping her tonight."

"Making herself look pretty," I said.

"She's a good little actress. You know, they had to change the curtain calls so she could take a bow by herself."

There were footsteps on the winding iron stairway, the cautious, high-heeled footsteps of all actresses descending all backstage stairways, but these were made by Julie. She did not make any sign of recognition of me but took my arm. "Goodnight, Mike," she said.

"Goodnight, Miss Moore. See you tomorrow. Have a good time," said the doorman.

"Let's go where we won't see anybody. Have you got the papers? I don't mind being seen with you, Jim, but I don't want to be seen crying. As soon as Mike said 'Mr. Malloy,' I knew. Tomorrow the press agent will thank me for the publicity break. Irony."

I took her to a small bar in the New Yorker Hotel, and she read the *News* and the *Mirror*. The *Mirror* had quite a vicious little story by a man named Walter Herbert, describing the gay foursome and the solitary man at the bar of El Morocco, and leaving the unmistakable inference that Jack Preswell had stumbled out into the night and thrown himself in front of a taxi. The *News*, in a story that had two by-lines, flatly said that Preswell had gone to the night club in an attempt to effect a reconciliation with his wife, who was constantly in the company of Charles Ellis, multi-millionaire stockbroker and former Harvard oarsman, and onetime close friend of the dead man. The *Mirror* ran a one-column cut of Julie, an old photograph from the White Studios; the *News* had a more recent picture of her in the décolleté costume she wore in the play. There was a wedding picture of Preswell and Nancy in the *News*, which also came up with a manly picture of Charley Ellis in shorts, shirt, and socks, holding an oar. There was no picture of me, and in both papers the textual mention of Julie and me was almost identical: Julie was the beautiful young actress, I was the sensational young novelist.

"Were we as gay as they say we were? I guess we were," said Julie.

"The implication is, that's what happens to society people when they mix with people like you and me."

"Exactly. They only got what they deserved. By the way, what did they get, besides a little notoriety? I'm beginning to feel sorry for Preswell. I lose a possible husband, but it must hurt to be hit by a taxi, even if you do die right away."

"You're taking it very well," I said.

"I thought Ken might show up, if only to demand an explanation. He loves to demand explanations. Have you talked to Ellis?"

"No. I'd like to know if there's anything in that *News* story, about Preswell and the reconciliation. I doubt it, and nobody will sue, but either the *News* has a very good rewrite man or they may have something. If it's something dreamed up by the rewrite man he ought to get a bonus, because he's taken a not very good story and dramatized the whole scene at Morocco."

"Thank goodness for one thing. They left my father and mother out of it," she said. "Poor Daddy. He groans. He comes to see me in all my plays, and then takes me to one side and asks if it's absolutely necessary to wear such low-cut dresses, or do I always *have* to be unfaithful to my husband? He told Thornton Wilder I'd have been just right for the girl in *Our Town.* Can you imagine how I'd have had to hunch over to play a fourteen-year-old?"

We were silent for a moment and then suddenly she said: "Oh, the hell with it. Let's go to '21'?"

"I'll take you to '21,' but no night clubs."

"I want to go to El Morocco and the Stork Club."

"No, you can't do it."

"I'm not in mourning."

"I used to be a press agent, Julie. If you want to thumb your nose at Ken, okay. But if you go to El Morocco tonight, you're asking for the worst kind of publicity. Capitalizing on those stories in the *News* and *Mirror.* You're better than that."

"Oh, the hell I am."

"Well, you used to be."

"The hell with what I used to be. I was a star, too, but now I'm just a sexy walk-on. And a quick lay, for somebody that calls me up after eight years. Why *did* you take me out last night?"

"Because you're a lady, and so is Nancy."

"Oh, it was Nancy you were trying to impress? I wish I'd known *that*."

"I have no desire to impress Nancy. I merely thought you'd get along with her and she with you."

"Why? Because she did Juliet at Foxcroft?"

"Oh, balls, Julie."

"Would you say that to Nancy?"

"If she annoyed me as much as you do, yes, I would. If you'll shut up for a minute, I'll tell you something. I don't like Nancy. I think she's a bitch. But I like Charley."

"Why do you like Charley? He's not your type. As soon as you make a little money you want to join the Racquet Club and all the rest of that crap. That apartment, for God's sake! And those guns. You're not Ernest Hemingway. Would you know how to fire a gun?"

"If I had one right now I'd show you."

"When did you get to be such pals with Charley Ellis?"

"I was hoping you'd get around to that. I knew him before I knew you, before I ever wrote anything. As to the armament, the shotguns belonged to my old man, including one that he gave me when I was fourteen. I do admit I bought the rifle four years ago. As to the apartment—well, you liked it last night. If you want to feel guilty about it, go ahead. But you said yourself it was a damned sight more comfortable than that studio couch on Bank Street. What do you want to do? Do you want to go to '21' and have something to eat, or shall I take you home?" I looked at my watch.

"It isn't too late to get another girl, is it?"

"That's exactly what I was thinking."

"Some girl from one of the night clubs?"

"Yes."

"I thought they only went out with musicians and gangsters."

"That's what you thought, and you go on thinking it. Do you want to go to '21'?"

"How late can you get one of those girls?"

"Two-thirty, if I'm lucky."

"You mean if you call up now and make the date?"

"Yes."

"You're a big liar, Jim. They have a two o'clock show that lasts an hour, so you can call this girl any time between now and two o'clock, and you won't meet her till after three. I know the whole routine. A boy in our play is married to one of them."

"The girl I had in mind isn't a show girl and she isn't in the line. She does a specialty."

She put her chin in her hand and her elbow on the table, in mock close attention. "*Tell* me about her specialty, Jim. Is it something I should learn? Or does one have to be double-jointed?"

"You want to go to '21'?"

"I'm dying to go to '21'," she said.

"Well, why didn't you say so?"

"Because you're such a grump, and I had to get a lot of things out of my system."

We used each other for a couple of weeks in a synthetic romance that served well in place of the real thing; and we were conscientious about maintaining the rules and customs of the genuine. We saw only each other and formed habits: the same taxi driver from the theatre, the same tables in restaurants, exchanges of small presents and courtesies; and we spoke of the wonder of our second chance at love. It was easy to love Julie. After the first few days and nights she seemed to have put aside her disappointment as easily as I was overcoming my chronic loneliness. We slept at my apartment nearly every night, and when she stayed at hers we would talk on the telephone until there was nothing more to say. We worried about each other: I, when the closing notice was put up at her theatre, and she when a story of mine was rejected. A couple of weeks became a couple of months and our romance was duly noted in the gossip columns: we were sizzling, we were hunting a preacher. "Would you ever go back to the Church?" she said, when it was printed that we were going to marry.

"I doubt it. Would you?"

"If Daddy wanted me to get married in the Church, I would."

"We've never talked about this."

"You mean about marriage?"

"*Or* the Church. Do you want to talk about marriage?"

"Yes, I have a few things I want to say. I love you, Jim, and you love me. But we ought to wait a long time before we do anything about getting married. If I'm married in the Church I'm going to stick to it."

"You wouldn't have with Ken."

"No, but he never was a Catholic. If I married you, in the Church, I'd want a nuptial Mass and you'd have to go to confession and the works. With a Protestant—Ken—I couldn't have had a nuptial Mass and I'd have been half-hearted about the whole thing. But marrying you would be like going back to the Church automatically. I consider you a Catholic."

"Do you consider yourself a Catholic?"

"Yes. I never go to Mass, and I haven't made my Easter duty since I was nineteen, but it's got me. I'm a Catholic."

"It's gone from me, Julie. The priests have ruined it for me."

"They've almost ruined it for me, but not quite. I don't listen to the priests. I can't tell that in confession, but that's why I stay away. Well, one of the reasons. I don't believe that going to bed with you is a sin."

"The priests do."

"Let them. They'll never be told unless I marry a Catholic and go to confession. That's why I say we ought to wait a long time. I'm thinking of myself. If I marry a Catholic, I'll be a Catholic. If I don't I'll be whatever I am. A non-practicing member of the faithful. I'll never be anything else."

"Well, neither will I. But I'm a heretic on too many counts, and the priests aren't going to accept me on my terms. It wouldn't be the Church if they did. It would be a new organization called the Malloyists."

"I'll be a Malloyist until we get married."

"There's one thing, Julie. If you get pregnant, what?"

"If I get pregnant, I'll ask you to marry me. I've had two abortions, but the father wasn't a Catholic. It was Ken. I paid for the abortions myself and never told him I was pregnant. I didn't want to have a baby. I wanted to be a star. But if I ever get pregnant by you, I'll tell you, and I hope you'll marry me."

"I will."

"However, I've been very, very careful except for that first night."

I have never been sure what that conversation did to us. I have often thought that we were all right so long as we felt a future together without getting down to plans, without putting conditional restrictions on ourselves, without specifying matters of time or event. It is also quite possible that the affection and passion that we identified as love was affection and passion and tenderness, but whatever sweetness we could add to the relationship, we could not add love, which is never superimposed. In any event, Julie stayed away one night and did not answer her telephone, and the next day I was having my coffee and she let herself in.

"Hello," I said.

"I'm sorry, Jim."

"I suppose you came to get your things," I said. I took a sip of coffee and lit a cigarette.

"Not only to get my things."

"You know, the awful thing is, you look so God damn—oh, nuts." She was wearing a blue linen dress that was as plain as a Chinese sheath, but there was more underneath that dress than Chinese girls have, and I was never to have it again. Someone else had been having it only hours ago.

"All right," I said. "Get your things."

"Aren't you going to let me say thank-you for what we had?"

"Yes, and I thank you, Julie. But I can't be nice about last night and all this morning." I took another sip of coffee and another drag on my cigarette, and she put her hand to her face and walked swiftly out of the room. I waited a while, then got up and went to the bedroom. She was lying face down on my unmade bed and she was crying.

"You'll wrinkle your dress," I said.

"The hell with my dress," she said, and slowly turned and sat up. "Jim." She held out her arms.

"Oh, no," I said.

"I couldn't help it. He came to the theatre."

"Oh, hell, I don't want to hear about that."

"I promised him I wouldn't see you again, but I had to come here."

"No you didn't, Julie. I could have sent you your things. It would have been much better if you'd just sent me a telegram."

"Put your arms around me."

"Oh, now that isn't like you. What the hell do you think I am? I've had about two hours' sleep. I'm on the ragged edge, but you don't have to do that to me."

She stood up and slipped her dress over her head, and took off her underclothes. "Can I make up for last night?" she said. "I'll never see you again. Will you put your arms around me now?"

"I wish I could say no, but I wanted you the minute I saw you."

"I know. That's why you wouldn't look at me, isn't it?"

"Yes."

She was smiling, and she could well afford to, with the pride she had in her breasts. "How do you want to remember me? I'll be whatever you want."

"What is this, a performance?"

"Of course. A farewell performance. Command, too. You don't want me as a virgin, do you?"

"No."

"No, that would take too much imagination on *your* part. But I could be one if that's what you want. But you don't. You'd much rather remember me as a slut, wouldn't you?"

"Not a slut, Julie. But not a virgin. Virgins aren't very expert."

"You'd rather remember me as an expert. A whore. Then you'll be able to forget me and you won't have to forgive me. All right."

She knew things I had never told her and there was no love in the love-making, but when she was dressed again and had her bag packed she stood in the bedroom doorway. "Jim?"

"What?"

"I'm not like that," she said. "Don't remember me that way, please?"

"I hope I don't remember you at all."

"I love him. I'm going to marry him."

"You do that, Julie."

"Haven't you got one nice thing to say before I go?"

I thought of some cruel things and I must have smiled at the thought of them, because she began to smile too. But I shook my head and she shrugged her shoulders and turned and left. The hall door closed and I looked at it, and then I saw that the key was being pushed under it. Twenty-three crowded years later I still remember the angle of that key as it lay on the dark-green carpet. My passion was spent, but I was not calm of mind; by accident the key was pointed toward me, and I thought of the swords at a court-martial. I was being resentenced to the old frenetic loneliness that none of us would admit to, but that governed our habits and our lives.

In that state of mind I made a block rejection of a thousand men and women whom I did not want to see, and reduced my friendships to the five or ten, the three or five, and finally the only person I felt like talking to. And that was how I got back in the lives of Charley Ellis and Nancy McMinnies Preswell Ellis.

They had been married about a month, and I was not sure they would be back from their wedding trip, but I got Charley at his office and he said he had started work again that week. He would stop in and have a drink on his way home.

"Gosh, the last time I was in this apartment—" he said, and it was not necessary to go on.

"You ended up getting married, and I damn near did myself."

"To Julia Murphy?"

"Close. Julianna Moore. In fact, your coming here rounds out a circle, for me. She ditched me today."

"Are you low on account of it?"

"Yes, so tell me about you and Nancy. I saw the announcement of your wedding, in the papers."

"That's all there was. We didn't send out any others."

"You lose a lot of loot that way," I said.

"I know, but there were other considerations. We wanted people to forget us in a hurry, so Nancy's mother sent short announcements to the *Tribune* and the *Sun*. You can imagine we'd had our fill of the newspapers when Preswell was killed."

"I don't have to imagine. It was the start of my romance, the one that just ended." I told him what had happened, a recital which I managed to keep down to about fifteen minutes. I lied a little at the end: "So this morning she called me up and said she'd gone back to her friend Mr. Kenneth Kenworthy."

"Well, you might say our last meeting here did end in two marriages," said Charley.

"If he marries her. He's been married three times and if she marries him she's going to have to support herself. He has big alimony to pay. I hope they do get married. Selfishly. I don't want any more synthetic romances. They're just as wearing as the real thing, and as Sam Hoffenstein says, what do you get yet?"

"Everything, if it turns out all right. You remember Nancy and her theory that nobody should get married without love, the real thing? That story of yours we talked about—'Telemark'?"

"Yes."

"Well, to be blunt about it, I really forced Nancy to marry me. All that notoriety—I put it to her that if she didn't marry me, *I'd* look like a shitheel. So on that basis—"

"Oh, come on."

"It's true. That's why she took the chance. But what was true then isn't true now. I want you to be the twenty-fifth to know. We're having a child."

"She never had any by Preswell?"

"No, and she wanted one, but his chemistry was all wrong. We expect ours in March or April."

"Congratulations."

"Thank you. Needless to say, I'm an altogether different person."

"You mean you have morning sickness?"

"I mean just the opposite. I'm practically on the wagon, for one thing, and for the first time in my life I'm thinking about someone besides myself. Get married, Malloy, and have a baby right away."

"I *like* to think about myself," I said.

"That's bullshit, and it's a pose. All this crazy life you lead, I think you're about the lonesomest son of a bitch I know."

I bowed my head and wept. "You shouldn't have said that," I said. "I wish you'd go."

"I'm sorry, Jim. I'll go. But why don't you drop in after dinner if you feel like it?"

"Thanks," I said, and he left.

He had taken me completely unawares. His new happiness and my new misery and all that the day had taken out of me made me susceptible of even the slightest touch of pity or kindness. I stopped bawling after two minutes, and then I began again, but during the second attack I succumbed to brain fag and fell asleep. I slept about three hours and was awakened by the telephone.

"This is Nancy Ellis. I hope you're coming up, we're expecting you. I'll bet you haven't had your dinner. Tell me the truth?"

"As a matter of fact, I was asleep."

"Well, how about some lamb chops? Do you like them black on the outside and pink on the inside? And have you any pet aversions in the vegetable line?"

"Brussels sprouts. But do you mean to say you haven't had your dinner?"

"We've had ours, but I can cook. Half an hour?"

It was a pleasant suburban evening in a triplex apartment in East Seventy-first Street, with one of the most beautiful women in New York cooking my supper and serving it; and it was apparent from their avoidance of all intimate topics that they had decided how they would treat me. At ten-thirty Nancy went to bed, at eleven Charley went in to see how she was, and at eleven-thirty I said goodnight. I went home and slept for ten hours. Had it not been for Nancy and Charley Ellis I would have gone on a ten-day drunk. But during those ten days I met a fine girl, and in December of that year we were married and we stayed married for sixteen years, until she died. As the Irish would say, she died on me, and it was the only unkind thing she ever did to anyone.

The way things tie up, one with another, is likely to go unnoticed unless a lawyer or a writer calls our attention to it. And sometimes both the writer and the lawyer have some difficulty in holding things together. But if they are men of purpose they can manage, and fortunately for writers they are not governed by rules of evidence or the whims of the court. The whim of the reader is all that need concern a writer, and even that should not concern him unduly; Byron, Scott, Milton and Shakespeare, who have been quoted in this chronicle, are past caring what use I make of their words, and at the appointed time I shall join them and the other millions of writers who have said their little say and then become forever silent—and in the public domain. I shall join them with all due respect, but at the first sign of a patronizing manner I shall say: "My dear sir, when you were drinking it up at the Mermaid Tavern, did you ever have the potman bring a telephone to your table?"

I belonged to the era of the telephone at the tavern table, and the thirty-foot extension cord that enabled the tycoon to talk and walk, and to buy and sell and connive and seduce at long distances. It is an era already gone, and I may live to see the new one, in which extrasensory perception combines with transistors, enabling the tycoon to dispense with the old-fashioned cord and *think* his way into new power and new beds. I may see the new era, but I won't belong to it. The writer of those days to come will be able to tune in on the voice of Lincoln at Gettysburg and hear the clanking of pewter mugs at the Mermaid, but he will never know the feeling of accomplishment that comes with the successful changing of a typewriter ribbon. A writer belongs to his time, and mine is past. In the days or years that remain to me, I shall entertain myself in contemplation of my time and be fascinated by the way things tie up, one with another.

I was in Boston for the tryout of a play I had written, and Charley Ellis's father had sent me a guest card to his club. "The old man said to tell you to keep your ears open and be sure and bring back any risqué stories you hear."

"At the Somerset Club?"

"The best. Where those old boys get them, I don't know, but that's where they tell them."

I used the introduction only once, when I went for a walk to get away from my play and everyone concerned with it. I stood at the window and looked out at the Beacon Street traffic, read a newspaper, and wandered to a small room to write a note to Mr. Ellis. There was only one other man in the room, and he looked up and half nodded as I came in, then resumed his letter-writing. A few minutes later there was a small angry spatter and I saw that a book of matches had exploded in the man's hand. "*Son* of a *bitch!*" he said.

His left hand was burned and he stared at it with loathing.

"Put some butter on it," I said.

"What?"

"I said, put some butter on it."

"I've heard of tea, but never butter."

"You can put butter on right away, but you have to wait for the water to boil before you have tea."

"What's it supposed to do?"

"Never mind that now. Just put it on. I've used it. It works."

He got up and disappeared. He came back in about ten minutes. "You know, it feels much better. I'd never heard of butter, but the man in the kitchen had."

"It's probably an old Irish remedy," I said.

"Are you Irish?"

"Yes. With the name Malloy I couldn't be anything else."

"Howdia do. My name is Hackley. Thanks very much. I wonder what it does, butter?"

"It does something for the skin. I guess it's the same principle as any of the greasy things."

"Of course. And it's cooling. It's such a stupid accident. I thought I closed the cover, but I guess I didn't." He hesitated. "Are you stopping here?"

"No, staying at the Ritz, but I have a guest card from Mr. Ellis in New York."

"Oh, of course. Where did you know *him?*"

"His son is a friend of mine."

"You're a friend of Charley's? I see. He's had another child, I believe. A daughter, this time."

"Yes. They wanted a daughter. I'm one of the godfathers of the boy."

"Oh, then you know him very well."

"Very," I said.

"I see. At Harvard?"

"No, after college. Around New York."

"Oh, yes. Yes," he said. Then: "Oh, *I* know who you are. You're the playwright. Why, I saw your play night before last."

"That wasn't a very good night to see it," I said.

"Oh, I didn't think it was so bad. Was I right in thinking that one fellow had trouble remembering his lines? The bartender?"

"Indeed you were."

"But aside from that, I enjoyed the play. Had a few good chuckles. That what-was-she, a chorus girl? They do talk that way, don't they? It's just that, uh, when you hear them saying those things in front of an audience. Especially a Boston audience. You know how we are. Or do you? We look about to see how the others are taking it. Tell me, Mr. Malloy, which do you prefer? Writing books, or writing for the stage?"

"At the moment, books."

"Well, of course with an actor who doesn't remember lines. A friend of mine in New York knows you. She sent me two of your books. I think one was your first and the other was your second."

"Oh? Who was that?"

"Polly Williamson is her name."

So here he was, the serious-minded widower who had been Polly Williamson's only lover. "That was damn nice of Polly. She's a swell girl."

"You *like* Polly. So do I. Never see her, but she's a darn nice girl and I hear from her now and again. Very musical, and I like music. Occasionally she'll send me a book she thinks I ought to read. I don't always like what she likes, and she knows I won't, but she does it to stimulate me, you know."

I had an almost ungovernable temptation to say something coarse. Worse than coarse. Intimate and anatomical and in the realm of stimulation, about Polly in bed. Naturally he misread my hesitation. "However," he said. "I enjoyed your first book very much. The second, not quite as much. So you're James J. Malloy?"

"No, I'm not James J. Malloy. I'm James Malloy, but my middle initial isn't J."

"I beg your pardon. I've always thought it was James J."

"People do. Every Irishman has to be James J. or John J."

"No. There was John L. Sullivan," said Hackley.

"Oh, but he came from Boston."

"Indeed he did. But then there was James J. Wadsworth. I know he wasn't Irish."

"No, but he was sort of a friend of Al Smith's."

"*Was he really?* I didn't know that. Was—he—really? Could you by any chance be thinking of his father, James *W.* Wadsworth?"

"I am. Of course I am. The senator, James *W.* Wadsworth."

"Perfectly natural mistake," said Hackley. "Well, I have to be on my way, but it's been nice to've had this chat with you. And thank you for the first-aid. I'll remember butter next time I set myself on fire."

On the evening of the next day I was standing in the lobby of the theatre, chatting with the press agent of the show and vainly hoping to overhear some comment that would tell me in ten magic words how to make the play a success. It was the second intermission. A hand lightly touched my elbow and I turned and saw Polly Williamson. "Do you remember me?" she said.

"Of course I remember you. I told you once I'd never forget you." Then I saw, standing with but behind her, Mr. Hackley, and I was sorry I was quite so demonstrative. "Hello, Mr. Hackley. How's the hand?"

He held it up. "Still have it, thanks to you."

"Just so you can applaud long and loud."

"The bartender fellow is better tonight, don't you think?"

"Much better," I said. "I'm glad you can sit through it a second time."

"He has no choice," said Polly Williamson.

"I hadn't, either," said Hackley. "I'll have you know this lady came all the way from New York just to see your play."

"You did, Polly?"

"Well, yes. But I don't know that I ought to tell you why."

"Why did you?" I said.

"Well, I read excerpts from some of the reviews, and I was afraid it wouldn't reach New York."

"We've tightened it up a little since opening night. I think the plan is now to take it to Philadelphia. But it was awfully nice of you to come."

"I wouldn't have missed it. I'm one of your greatest fans, and I like to tell people I knew you when."

"Well, I like to tell people I know you."

"I suppose you're terribly busy after the show," said Hackley.

"Not so busy that I couldn't have a drink with Polly and you, if that's what you had in mind."

They waited for me in the Ritz Bar. Two tweedy women were sitting with them, but they got up and left before I reached the table. "I didn't mean to drive your friends away," I said.

"They're afraid of you. Frightened to death," said Hackley.

"They're pretty frightening themselves," I said, angrily.

"They are, but before you say any more I must warn you, one of them is *my* cousin *and* Charley Ellis's cousin," said Polly Williamson.

"They thought your play was frightful," said Hackley.

"Which should assure its successes," said Polly. "Maisie, my cousin, goes to every play that comes to Boston and she hasn't liked anything since I don't know when."

"*The Jest,* with Lionel and Jack Barrymore, I think was the last thing she really liked. And not so much the play as Jack Barrymore."

"I don't think she'd *really* like John Barrymore," I said.

"Oh, but you're wrong. She met him, and she does," said Hackley. It seemed to me during the hour or more that we sat there that he exerted a power over Polly that was effortless on his part and unresisted by her. He never allowed himself to stay out of the conversation, and Polly never finished a conversational paragraph that he chose to interrupt. I was now sure that their affair was still active, in Boston. She had occasion to remark that he never went to New York, which led me to believe that the affair was conducted entirely on his home ground, on his terms, and at as well as for his pleasure. I learned that he lived somewhere in the neighborhood—two or three minutes' walk from the hotel; and that she always stayed with an aunt who lived on the other side of the Public Garden. Since they had not the slightest reason to suspect that I knew any more about them than they had told me, they unconsciously showed the whole pattern of their affair. It was a complete reversal of the usual procedure, in which the Boston man goes to New York to be naughty. Polly went to Boston under the most respectable auspices and with the most innocent excuses—and as though she were returning home to sin. (I did not pass that judgment on her.) Williamson was an ebullient, arrogant boor; Hackley was a Bostonian, who shared her love of music, painting, and flowers; and whatever they did in bed, it was almost certainly totally different from whatever she did with Williamson, which was not hard to guess at. I do know that in the

dimly lighted bar of the hotel she seemed more genuinely at home
and at ease than in her own house or at the New York parties where
I would see her, with the odd difference that in Boston she was willingly under the domination of a somewhat epicene aesthete, while in
New York she quietly but, over the years, noticeably resisted Williamson's habit of taking control of people's lives. After fifteen years
of marriage to Williamson she was regarded in New York as a separate and individual woman, who owed less and less to her position
as the wife of a spectacular millionaire. But none of that was discernible to me in her relations with Hackley. She did what he wanted
to do, and in so doing she completed the picture of her that Charley
Ellis had given me. In that picture, her man was missing. But now I
saw that Hackley, not the absent Williamson, was her man.

It was hardly a new idea, that the lover was more husband than
the husband; but I had never seen a case in which geography, or a
city's way of life, had been so influential. Polly not only returned
to Hackley; she returned to Boston and the way of life that suited
her best and that Hackley represented. There was even something
appropriately austere about her going back to New York and Williamson. Since divorce was undesirable, with Williamson, the
multi-millionaire, she was making-do. The whole thing delighted
me. It is always a pleasure to discover that someone you like and
have underestimated on the side of simplicity turns out to be intri-
cate and therefore worthy of your original interest. (Intricacy in
someone you never liked is, of course, just another reason for dis-
liking him.)

"I have to go upstairs now and start working on the third act," I
said.

"Oh, I hope we didn't keep you," said Hackley.

"You did, and I'm very glad you did. The director and the manager have had an hour to disagree with each other. Now I'll go in
and no matter what I say, one of them will be on my side and the
other will be left out in the cold. That's why I prefer writing books,
Mr. Hackley . . . Polly, it's been very nice to've seen you again.

Spread the good word when you go back. Tell everybody it's a great play."

"Not great, but it's good," said Polly. "When will you be back in New York?"

"Leaving tomorrow afternoon."

"So am I. Maybe I'll see you on the train."

There was a situation in my play that plainly needed something to justify a long continuing affair, something other than an arbitrary statement of love. In the elevator it came to me: it was Polly's compromise. In continuing her affair with Hackley, Polly—and the woman in my play—would be able to make a bad marriage appear to be a good one. The character in the play was a movie actress, and if Polly saw the play again she never would recognize herself. The director, the manager, and I agreed that we would leave the play as-is in Boston, and open with the new material in Philadelphia. Only three members of the cast were affected by the new material, and they were quick studies. One of them was Julianna Moore.

I had said to my wife: "Would you object if I had Julie read for the part?"

"No. You know what I'd object to," she said.

"Well, it won't happen. There won't be any flare-up. Kenworthy is doing the sets, and they seem to be making a go of it."

There was no flare-up. Julie worked hard and well and got good notices in Boston, and I got used to having her around. I suppose that if she had come to my room in the middle of the night, my good intentions would have vanished. But we had discussed that. "If people that have slept together can never again work together," she said, "then the theatre might as well fold up. They'd never be able to cast a play on Broadway. And as to Hollywood . . ."

"Well, if you get too attractive, I'll send for my wife," I said.

"You won't have to. Ken will be there most of the time," she said. "Anyway, Jim, give me credit for some intelligence. I know you thought this all out and talked it over with your wife. Well, *I* talked it over with Ken, too. He hates you, but he respects you."

"Then we're in business," I said, and that was really all there was to it. I made most of my comments to the actors through the director, and Julie was not the kind of woman or actress who would use acquaintance with the author to gain that little edge.

Polly Williamson was at the Back Bay station and we got a table for two in the diner. "Do you think Mr. Willkie has a chance?" she said.

"I think he did have, but not now. Roosevelt was so sure he was a shoo-in that he wasn't going to campaign, and that was when Willkie had his chance. But luckily I was able to persuade the President to make some speeches."

"You did?"

"Not really," I said. "But I did have a talk with Tim Cochran in August, and I told him that Roosevelt was losing the election. I was very emphatic. And then one of the polls came out and showed I was right."

"Are you a New Dealer? I suppose you are."

"All the way."

"Did you ever know Jack Preswell? I know you know Nancy, Nancy Ellis, but did you know her first husband?"

"I once went to a baseball game with him, that's all."

"That's a tragic story. You know how he was killed and all that, I'm sure, but the real tragedy happened several years before. Jack was a brilliant student in Law School and something of an idealist. He had a job with Carson, Cass & Devereux, but he quit it to get into the New Deal. I probably shouldn't be saying this . . ."

"You can say anything to me."

"Well, I *want* to. Nancy is married to my cousin and I know you and he are very good friends, but all is far from well there, you know."

"No, I didn't know. I haven't seen them lately."

"Nancy and her father hounded Jack Preswell. They were very contemptuous of his ideals, and when he went to Washington Nancy wouldn't go with him. She said it would be a repudiation of everything she believed in and her father believed in and everything

Jack's *family* believed in. As a woman I think Nancy was just looking for an excuse. Nancy is *so* beautiful and has been told so *so* many times that she'd much rather be admired for her brains. Consequently she can be very intolerant of other people's ideas, and she made Jack's life a hell. Not that Jack was any rose. I didn't agree with him, but he had a perfect right to count on Nancy's support, and he never got it. Not even when he got out of the New Deal. She should have stuck by him, at least publicly."

"Yes, as it turned out, Preswell became as anti-New Deal as she was, or Old Man McMinnies. I knew a little about this, Polly."

"Well, did I tell it fairly? I don't think you could have known much of it, because she was at her worst in front of his friends. She's a very destructive girl, and now she's up to the same old tricks with Charley. You don't know *that,* do you?"

"No."

"She's gotten Charley into America First. You knew that?"

"No, I didn't."

"Yes. And even my husband, as conservative as he is, and his father, they've stayed out of it. What's the use of isolationism now, when we're practically in it already? I agree with you, I think Roosevelt's going to win, although I just can't vote for him. But he'll get in and then it's only a question of another *Lusitania,* and we'll be in it too. So I don't see the practical value of America First. We ought to be getting stronger and stronger and the main reason I won't vote for Mr. Roosevelt is that he's such a hypocrite. He won't come out and honestly say that we're headed toward war."

"A little thing about neutrality and the head of the United States government."

"Oh, come. Do you think Hitler and Mussolini are hoping for a last-minute change of heart? Roosevelt should be uniting the country instead of playing politics. This nonsense about helping the democracies is sheer hypocrisy. There is no France, there's only England."

"You're very fiery, Polly."

"Yes. We have two English children staying with us. Their father was drowned coming back from Dunkerque. Nancy has Charley convinced that their presence in our house is a violation of neutrality. She said it wouldn't be fashionable to have two German children. When have I ever given a darn about fashion? That really burned me up."

I became crafty. "How do they feel about this in Boston? What does Mr. Hackley think?"

"Ham? The disappointment of his life was being turned down by the American Field Service. He'd have been wonderful, too. Speaks French, German, and Italian, and has motored through all of Europe. He'd make a wonderful spy."

"They'd soon catch on to him."

"Why?"

"If he burnt his hand, he'd say 'Son of a bitch,' and they'd know right away he was an American."

"Oh, yes." She smiled. "He told me about that. He's nice, don't you think?"

She was so nearly convincingly matter-of-fact. "Yes. He and I'd never be friends, but of his type I like him. Solid Boston."

"I don't know," she said. "Charley's almost that, and you and he have been friends quite a long time. Poor Charley. I don't know what I hope. Oh, I do. I want him to be happy with Nancy. I just hate to see what I used to like in him being poisoned and ruined by that girl."

"And you think it is?"

"The Charley Ellis I used to know would have two English children staying with him, and he'd probably be in the Field Service, if not actually in the British army."

"Well, my wife and I haven't taken any English children, and I'm not in the Field Service, so I can't speak. However, I'm in agreement with you in theory about the war. And in sentiment."

"Look up Charley after your play opens. Talk to him."

"Do you think I'd get anywhere in opposition to Nancy?"

"Well, you can have a try at it," she said.

I did have a try at it, after my play opened to restrained enthusiasm and several severe critical notices. Charley and I had lunch one Saturday and very nearly his opening remark was: "I hear you caught up with Polly and her bosom companion?"

I was shocked by the unmistakable intent of the phrase. "Yes, in Boston," I said.

"Where else? He never leaves there. She nips up there every few weeks and comes home full of sweetness and light, fooling absolutely no one. Except herself. Thank God I didn't go to Oxford."

"Why?"

"Well, you saw Hackley. He went to Oxford—after Harvard, of course."

"You sound as if you had a beef against Harvard, too."

"There are plenty of things I don't like about it, beginning with der Fuehrer, the one in the White House," he said. "Polly fill you up with sweetness and light, and tell you how distressed she was over Nancy and me?"

"No, we had my play to talk about," I said.

"Well, she's been sounding off. She's imported a couple of English kids and gives money to all the British causes. She'd have done better to have a kid by Hackley, but maybe they don't *do* that."

"What the hell's the matter with you, Charley? If I or anyone else had said these things about Polly a few years ago, you'd have been at their throat."

"That was before she began saying things about Nancy, things that were absolutely untrue, and for no reason except that Nancy has never gone in for all that phony Thoreau stuff. Nature-lover stuff. You know, I think Polly has had us all fooled from 'way back. You fell for it, and so did I, but I wouldn't be surprised if she'd been screwing Hackley all her life. One of those children that Junior thinks is his, *could* very well be Hackley's. The boy."

"Well, I wouldn't know anything about that. I've never seen their children. But what turned you against Polly? Not the possibility of her having had a child by Hackley."

"I've already told you. She's one of those outdoor-girl types that simply can't tolerate a pretty woman. And she's subtle, I'll give her that. She puts on this act of long-suffering faithful wife, while Junior goes on the make, and of course meanwhile Polly is getting hers in Boston."

"But you say not getting away with it."

"She got away with it for a long time, but people aren't that stupid. Even Junior Williamson isn't that stupid. He told Nancy that he's known about it for years, but as long as she didn't interfere with his life, he might as well stay married to her. Considering the nice stories Polly spread about Preswell and Nancy, I think Nancy showed considerable restraint in not making any cracks about Hackley and Polly's son. Nancy has her faults, but she wouldn't hurt an innocent kid."

The revised portraits of Junior Williamson, tolerating his wife's infidelity for years, and of Nancy Ellis, withholding gossip to protect a blameless child, were hard to get accustomed to. I did not try very hard. I was so astonished to see what a chump Nancy had made of my old friend, and so aggrieved by its effect on him, that I cut short our meeting and went home. Three or four months later the war news was briefly interrupted to make room for the announcement that Mrs. Ethridge Williamson, Jr., had established residence in Reno, Nevada. "A good day's work, Nancy," I said aloud. Much less surprising, a few months later, was the news item that Mrs. Smithfield Williamson, former wife of Ethridge Williamson, Jr., millionaire sportsman and financier, had married Hamilton Hackley, prominent Boston art and music patron, in Beverly, Massachusetts. The inevitable third marriage did not take place until the summer of 1942, when Lieutenant Commander Williamson, USNR, married Ensign Cecilia G. Reifsnyder, of the Women Accepted for Volunteer Emergency Service, in Washington, D. C. It seemed appropriate that the best man was Lieutenant Charles Ellis, USNR. The bride's only attendant was her sister, Miss Belinda Reifsnyder, of Catasauqua, Pennsylvania. I gave that six months, and it lasted twice that long.

* * *

My war record adds up to a big, fat nothing, but for a time I was a member of an Inverness-and-poniard organization, our elaborate nickname for cloak-and-dagger. In Washington I moved about from "Q" Building to the Brewery to South Agriculture and houses that were only street addresses. One day in 1943 I was on my way out of "Q" after an infuriatingly frustrating meeting with an advertising-man-turned-spy, a name-dropper who often got his names a little bit wrong. In the corridor a man fell in step with me and addressed me by my code nickname, which was Doc. "Do I know you?" I said.

"The name is Ham," said Hackley.

"We can't be too careful," I said.

"Well, we can't, as a matter of fact, but you can relax. I called you Doc, didn't I?" He smiled and I noticed that he needed dental work on the lower incisors. He had grown a rather thick moustache, and he had let his hair go untrimmed. "Come have dinner with Polly and me."

"I can think of nothing I'd rather do," I said.

"Irritating bastard, isn't he?" he said, tossing his head backward to indicate the office I had just left.

"The worst. The cheap, pompous worst," I said.

"One wonders, one wonders," said Hackley.

We got a taxi and went to a house in Georgetown. "Not ours," said Hackley. "A short-term loan from some friends."

Polly was a trifle thick through the middle and she had the beginnings of a double chin, but her eyes were clear and smiling and she was fitting into the description of happy matron.

"You're not at all surprised to see me," I said.

"No. I knew you were in the organization. Charley told me you'd turn up one of these days."

"Charley Who?"

"Heavens, have you forgotten all your old friends? Charley Ellis. Your friend and my cousin."

"I thought he was at CINCPAC."

"He's back and forth," she said. She put her hand on her husband's arm. "I wish this man got back as often. Would you like to see Charley? He's not far from here."

"Yes, but not just now. Later. I gather you're living in Boston?"

"Yes. My son is at Noble's and my daughter is still home with me. How is your lovely wife? I hear nothing but the most wonderful things about her. Aren't we lucky? Really, aren't we?"

"We are that," I said. Hackley had not said a word. He smoked incessantly, his hand was continually raising or lowering his cigarette in a slow movement that reminded me of the royal wave. I remembered the first time I had seen him and Polly together, when he would tack on his own thought to everything she said. "Are you still with us?" I said.

"Oh, very much so," he said.

"Can you tell Jim what you've been doing?"

"Well, now that's very indiscreet, Polly. Naturally he infers that I've told you, and he could report me for that. And should," said Hackley. "However, I think he can be trusted. He and I dislike the same man, and that's a great bond."

"And we like the same woman," I said.

"Thank you," said Polly.

"I've been in occupied territory," said Hackley. "Hence the hirsute adornment, the neglected teeth. I can't get my teeth fixed because I'm going back, and the Gestapo would take one look at the inside of my mouth and ask me where I'd happened to run across an American dentist. Hard question to answer. So I've been sitting here literally sucking on a hollow tooth. Yes, I'm still with you."

"I wish I were with *you*—not very much, but a little."

"You almost were, but you failed the first requirement. I had to have someone that speaks nearly perfect French, and you took Spanish."

"I'm highly complimented that you thought of me at all. I wish I did speak French."

"Yes, the other stuff you could have learned, as I had to. But without the French it was no go. French French. Not New Orleans or New Hampshire."

"Do you go in by parachute—excuse me, I shouldn't ask that."

"You wouldn't have got an answer," said Hackley. He rose. "I wonder if you two would excuse me for about an hour? I'd like to have a bath and five minutes' shut-eye."

As soon as he left us Polly ceased to be the happy matron. "He's exhausted. I wish they wouldn't send him back. He's over fifty, you know. I wish they'd take me, but do you know why they won't? The most complicated reasoning. The French would think I was a German agent, planted in France to spy on the Resistance. And the Germans would know I was English or American, because I don't speak German. But imagine the French thinking I was a German. My coloring, of course, and I *am* getting a bit dumpy."

"Where are your English children?"

"One died of leukemia, and their mother asked to have the other sent back, which was done. John Winant helped there. The child *is* better off with her mother, and the mother is too, I'm sure."

"Ham wants to go back, of course," I said.

"I wonder if he really does. Every time he goes back, his chances—and the Germans are desperate since we invaded Italy. It's young men's work, but a man of Ham's age attracts less attention. Young men are getting scarcer in France. Oh, I'm worried and I can't pretend I'm not. I can to Ham, but that's because I have to. But you saw how exhausted he is, and he's had—"

"Don't tell me. You were going to tell me how long he's been home. Don't. I don't want to have that kind of information."

"Oh, I understand. There's so little I want to talk about that I'm permitted to. Well, Charley Ellis is a safe subject. Shall I ask him to come over after dinner?"

"First, brief me on Charley and Nancy. I haven't seen him for at least a year."

"Nancy is living in New York, or you could be very sure I'd never see Charley. I didn't want to ever again. It was Nancy that stirred up the trouble between Junior and me, and I'm very grateful to her now but I wasn't then. Junior'd had lady friends, one after another, for years and years, and if he'd been a different sort of man it would have been humiliating. But as Charley pointed out to me, oh, twenty years ago, there are only about half a dozen Junior Williamsons in this country, and they make their own rules. So, in order to survive, I made mine, too. I really led a double life, the one as Mrs. Ethridge Williamson, Junior, and the other, obviously, as Ham's mistress. You knew that, didn't you?"

"Well, yes."

"I didn't take anything away from Junior that he wanted. Or withhold anything. And several times over the years I did stop seeing Ham, when Junior would be going through one of his periods of domesticity. I was always taken in by that, and Junior can be an attractive man. To women. He has no men friends, do you realize that? He always has some toady, or somebody that he has to see a lot of because of business or one of his pet projects. But he has no real men friends. Women of all ages, shapes, and sizes and, I wouldn't be surprised, colors. He married that Wave, and the next thing I heard was she caught him in bed with her sister. Why not? One meant as much to him as the other, and I'm told they were both pretty. That would be enough for Junior. A stroke of luck, actually. He's paying off the one he married. A million, I hear. And she's not going to say anything about her sister. What will those girls do with a million dollars? And think how much more they would have asked for if they'd ever been to the house on Long Island. But I understand he never took her there. That's what he considers home, you know. Christmas trees, and all the servants' children singing carols, and the parents lining up for their Christmas cheques. But the Wave was never invited. Oh, well, he's now an aide to an admiral, which should make life interesting."

"Having your commanding officer toady to you?"

"That, yes. But being able to pretend that you're just an ordinary commander, or maybe he's a captain now, but taking orders and so on. An admiral that would have him for an aide is the kind that's feathering his nest for the future, so I don't imagine Junior has any really unpleasant chores."

"Neither has the admiral. He's chair-borne at Pearl."

"Yes, Charley implied as much. I've talked too much about Junior, and you want to know about Charley and Nancy. Well, Nancy stirred up the trouble. I never would have denied that I was seeing Ham, if Junior'd asked me, but that isn't what he asked me. He asked me if Ham were the father of our son, and I felt so sick at my stomach that I went right upstairs and packed a bag and took the next train to Boston, not saying a single word. When I got to my aunt's house, Junior was already there. He'd flown in his own plane. He said, 'I asked you a question, and I want an answer. *Entitled* to an answer.' So I said, 'The answer to the question is no, and I never want to say another word to you.' Nor have I. If he was entitled to ask the question, which I don't concede, he was entitled to my answer. He got it, and all communication between us since then has been through the lawyers."

"What about Nancy, though?"

"Oh, bold as brass, she told people that she thought my son's father was Ham. Which shows how well she doesn't know old Mr. Williamson. The boy looks exactly like his grandfather, even walks like him. But she also didn't know that Mr. Williamson is devoted to the boy, wouldn't speak to Junior for over a year, and worst of all, from Mr. Williamson's point of view, I have my son twelve months of the year and at school in Boston, so his grandfather has to come to Boston to see him. I refuse to take him to Long Island. And Mr. Williamson says I'm perfectly right, after Junior's nasty doubts. Doubts? Accusations."

"But you and Charley made it up," I said.

"Yes and no. Oh, we're friends again, but it'll never be what it used to be. Shall I tell you about it? You may be able to write it in a story sometime."

"Tell me about it."

"Charley was getting ready to ship out, his first trip to the Pacific, and he wrote me a letter. I won't show it to you. It's too long and too—private. But the gist of it was that if anything happened to him, he didn't want me to remember him unkindly. Then he proceeded to tell me some things that he'd said about me, that I hadn't heard, and believe me, Jim, if I'd ever heard them I'd have remembered him *very* unkindly. He put it all down, though, and then said, 'I do not believe there is a word of truth in any of these things.' Then he went on to say that our friendship had meant so much to him and so forth."

"It does, too, Polly," I said.

"Oh, James Malloy, you're dissembling. You know what he really said, don't you?"

"You're dissembling, too. I know what he used to feel."

"*I* never did. I always thought he was being extra kind to an awkward younger cousin," she said. "And he never liked Junior. Well, since you've guessed, or always knew, you strange Irishman, I'll tell you the rest. I wrote to him and told him our friendship was just where it had always been, and that I admired him for being so candid. That I was hurt by the things he had said, but that his first loyalty was to Nancy. That I never wanted to see Nancy again, and that therefore I probably would never see him. But since we lived such different lives, in different cities, I probably wouldn't see him anyway, in war or peace."

"But you did see him."

"Yes. We're friends again. I've seen him here in Washington. We have tea together now and then. To some extent it's a repetition of my trips to Boston to see Ham. Needless to say, with one great difference. I never have been attracted to Charley that way. But I'm his double life, and the piquancy, such as it is, comes from the fact that Nancy doesn't know we see each other. Two middle-aged cousins, more and more like the people that come to my aunt's house in Louisburg Square."

"Do you remember the time we came down from Boston?"

"Had dinner on the train. Of course."

"You said then, and I quote, that all was far from well between Nancy and Charley."

She nodded. "It straightened itself out. It wasn't any third party or anything of that kind. It was Nancy reshaping Charley to her own ways, and Charley putting up a fight. But she has succeeded. She won. Except for one thing that she could never understand."

"Which is?"

"That Charley and I like to have tea together. If she found out, and tried to stop it, that's the one way she'd lose Charley. So she mustn't find out. You see, Jim, I don't want Charley, as a lover or as a husband. I have my husband and he was my lover, too. As far as I'm concerned, Charley is first, last and always a cousin. A dear one, that I hope to be having tea with when we're in our seventies. But that's all. And that's really what Charley wants, too, but God pity Nancy if she tries to deprive him of that."

For a little while neither of us spoke, and then she said something that showed her astuteness. "I'll give you his number, but let's not see him tonight. He doesn't like to be discussed, and if he came over tonight he'd know he had been."

"You're right," I said. "Polly, why did you divorce Williamson?"

"You're not satisfied with the reason I gave you?"

"It would be a good enough reason for some women, but not for you."

She looked at me and said nothing, but she was disturbed. She fingered her circle of pearls, picked up her drink and put it down without taking a sip.

"Never mind," I said. "I withdraw the question."

"No. No, don't. You gave me confidence one day when I needed it. The second time I ever saw you. I'll tell you."

"Not if it's an ordeal," I said.

"It's finding the words," she said. "The day Junior asked me point-blank if he was the father of my son, I had just learned that I was pregnant again. By him, of course. One of his periods of domesticity. So I had an abortion, something I'd sworn I'd never do, and I've never been pregnant since. I had to have a hysterectomy, and Ham and I did want a child. You see, I couldn't answer your question without telling you the rest of it."

* * *

After the war my wife and I saw the Ellises punctiliously twice every winter; they would take us to dinner and the theatre, we would take them. Dinner was always in a restaurant, where conversation makes itself, and in the theatre it was not necessary. Charley and I, on our own, lunched together every Saturday at his club or mine, with intervals of four months during the warm weather and time out for vacations in Florida or the Caribbean. Every five years on Charley's birthday they had a dance in the ballroom of one of the hotels, and I usually had a party to mark the occasion of a new book or play. We had other friends, and so had the Ellises, and the two couples had these semi-annual evenings together only because not to do so would have been to call pointed attention to the fact that the only friendship was that of Charley and me. Our wives, for example, after an early exchange of lunches never had lunch together again; and if circumstances put me alone with Nancy, I had nothing to say. In the years of our acquaintance she had swung from America First to Adlai Stevenson, while I was swinging the other way. She used the word valid to describe everything but an Easter bonnet, another favorite word of hers was denigrate, and still another was challenge. When my wife died Nancy wrote me a note in which she "questioned the validity of it all" and told me to "face the challenge." When I married again she said I had made the only valid decision by "facing up to the challenge of a new life." I had ceased to be one of the authors she admired, and in my old place she had put Kafka, Kierkegaard, Rilke, and Camus. I sent her a copy of Kilmer to make her velar collection complete, but she did not think it was comical or cute.

Charley and I had arrived at a political rapprochement: he conceded that some of the New Deal had turned out well, I admitted that Roosevelt had been something less than a god. Consequently our conversations at lunch were literally what the doctor ordered for men of our age. To match my Pennsylvania reminiscences he provided anecdotes about the rich, but to him they were not the rich.

They were his friends and enemies, neighbors and relatives, and it was a good thing to hear about them as such. Charley Ellis had observed well and he remembered, and partly because he was polite, partly because he had abandoned the thought of writing as a career, he gave me the kind of information I liked to hear.

We seldom mentioned Nancy and even less frequently, Polly. If he continued to have tea with her, he did not say so. But one day in the late Forties we were having lunch at his club and he bowed to a carefully dressed man who limped on a cane and wore a patch over his left eye. He was about sixty years old. "One of your boys," said Charley.

"You mean Irish?"

"Oh, no. I meant O.S.S."

"He must have been good. The Médaille Militaire. That's one they don't hand out for traveling on the French Line."

"A friend of Ham Hackley's. He told me how Hackley died."

All I knew was that Hackley had never come back from France after my evening with him in Washington. "How did he?" I said.

"The Germans caught him with a wad of plastic and a fuse wire in his pocket. He knew what he was in for, so he took one of those pills."

"An 'L' pill," I said.

"Whatever it is that takes about a half a minute. You didn't know that about Ham?"

"I honestly didn't."

"That guy, the one I just spoke to, was in the same operation. He blew up whatever they were supposed to blow up, but he stayed too close and lost his eye and smashed up his leg. You wouldn't think there was that much guts there, would you? He knew he couldn't get very far, but he set off the damn plastic and hit the dirt." Charley laughed. "Do you know what he told us? He said, 'I huddled up and put my hands over my crotch, so I lost an eye. But I saved everything else.' We got him talking at a club dinner this winter."

"I wish I'd been here."

"Not this club. This was at the annual dinner of my club at Harvard. He was a classmate of Ham's. I don't usually go back, but I did this year."

"Did you see Polly?"

"Yes, I went and had tea with her. Very pleasant. Her boy gets out of Harvard this year. Daughter's married."

"We got an announcement. What does Polly do with her time?"

"Oh, why, I don't know. She always has plenty of things to do in Boston. A girl like Polly, with all her interests, she'd keep herself very busy. I must say she's putting on a little weight."

"What would she be now?"

"How old? Polly is forty-one, I think."

"Still young. Young enough to marry again."

"I doubt if she will," said Charley. "I doubt it very much. Boston isn't like New York, you know. In New York a woman hates to go to a party without a man, but in Boston a woman like Polly goes to a party by herself and goes home by herself and thinks nothing of it."

"Nevertheless she ought to have a husband. She's got a good thirty years ahead of her. She ought to marry if only for companionship."

"Companionship? Companionship is as hard to find as love. More so. Love can sneak up on you, but when you're looking for companionship you shop around."

"Maybe that's what Polly's doing, having a look at the field."

"Maybe. There's one hell of a lot of money that goes with her, and she's not going to marry a fortune-hunter. Oh, I guess Polly can take care of herself."

"Just out of curiosity, how *much* money is there?"

"How much money? Well, when Polly's father died, old Mr. Smithfield, he left five million to Harvard, and another million to a couple of New York hospitals, and a hundred thousand here and a hundred thousand there. I happen to know that he believed in tithes. All his life he gave a tenth of his income to charity. So if he followed that principle in his will, he was worth around seventy million gross.

I don't know the taxes on that much money, but after taxes it all went to Polly. In addition, Ham Hackley left her all his money, which was nothing like Cousin Simon Smithfield's, but a tidy sum nonetheless. I also know that when Polly divorced Junior Williamson, old Mr. Williamson changed his will to make sure that the grandchildren would each get one-third, the same as Junior. That was quite a blow to Junior. So all in all, Polly's in a very enviable position, financially."

"Good God," I said. "It embarrasses me."

"Why you?"

"Don't you remember that day I told her I loved her?"

"Oh, yes. Well, she took that as a compliment, not as a business proposition. She's never forgotten it, either."

"Well, I hope Polly holds on to her good sense. When I was a movie press agent I made a great discovery that would have been very valuable to a fortune-hunter. And in fact a few of them had discovered it for themselves. Big stars, beautiful and rich, would come to New York and half the time they had no one to take them out. They depended on guys in the publicity department. I never would have had to work for a living."

"How long could you have stood that?"

"Oh, a year, probably. Long enough to get tired of a Rolls and charge accounts at the bespoke tailors. Then I suppose I'd have read a book and wished I'd written it. I knew a fellow that married a movie star and did all that, and he wasn't just a gigolo. He'd taught English at Yale. He took this doll for God knows how much, then she gave him the bounce and now he's living in Mexico. He's had a succession of fifteen-year-old wives. Once every two or three years he comes to New York for a week. He subsists entirely on steak and whiskey. One meal a day, a steak, and all the whiskey he can drink. He's had a stroke and he knows he's going to die. I could have been that. In fact, I don't like to think how close I came."

"I don't see you as Gauguin."

"Listen, Gauguin wasn't unhappy. He was doing what he wanted to do. I don't see myself as Gauguin either. What I don't like to think of is how close I came to being my friend that married the movie actress. That I could have been."

"No, you were never really close. You were no closer than I was to marrying Polly. You thought about it, just as I did about marrying Polly. But I wasn't meant to marry Polly, and you weren't meant to steal money from a movie actress and go on the beach in Mexico."

"Go on the beach? Why did you say that?"

"It slipped. I knew the fellow you're talking about. Henry Root?"

"Yes."

"Before he taught at Yale he had the great distinction of teaching me at Groton. You know why he *stopped* teaching at Yale? Bad cheques. Not just bouncing cheques. Forgeries. There was one for a thousand dollars signed Ethridge B. Williamson, Junior. That did it. He had Junior's signature to copy from, but that wasn't the way Junior signed his cheques. He always signed E. B. Williamson J R, so his cheques wouldn't be confused with his father's, which had Ethridge written out. Henry was a charming, facile bum, and a crook. You may have been a bum, but you were never a crook. Were you?"

"No, I guess I wasn't. I never cheated in an exam, and the only money I ever stole was from my mother's pocketbook. And got caught, every time. My mother always knew how much was in her purse."

"Now let me ask you something else. Do you think Henry Root would ever have been a friend of Polly's? As good a friend, say, as you are?"

"Well—I'd say no."

"And you'd be right. When she was Polly Smithfield he'd always give her a rush at the dances, and it was an understood thing that Junior and I would always cut in. I don't think we have to worry about Polly and fortune-hunters, or you about how close you came to being Henry Root. I don't even worry about how close that damn story of yours came to keeping Nancy from marrying me."

"Oh, that story. 'Christiana.' No. 'Telemark.' That was it, 'Telemark.' "

"You don't even remember your own titles, but that was the one."

"I may not remember the title, but the point of the story was that two people could take a chance on marriage without love."

"Yes, and Nancy was so convinced that you were wrong that she had it on her mind. You damn near ruined my life, Malloy."

"No I didn't."

"No, you didn't. My life was decided for me by Preswell, when he walked in front of that taxi."

I knew this man so well, and with his permission, but I had never heard him make such an outright declaration of love for his wife, and on my way home I realized that until then I had not known him at all. It was not a discovery to cause me dismay. What did he know about me? What, really, can any of us know about any of us, and why must we make such a thing of loneliness when it is the final condition of us all? And where would love be without it?

From

THE CAPE COD LIGHTER

♦

PAT COLLINS

♦

N ow they are both getting close to seventy, and when they see
each other on the street Whit Hofman and Pat Collins bid each
other the time of day and pass on without stopping for conversation. It may be that in Whit Hofman's greeting there is a little
more hearty cordiality than in Pat Collins's greeting to him; it may
be that in Pat Collins's words and smile there is a wistfulness that is
all he has left of thirty years of a dwindling hope.

The town is full of young people who never knew that for about
three years—1925, 1926, 1927—Whit Hofman's favorite companion was none other than Pat Collins. Not only do they not know of
the once close relationship; today they would not believe it. But then
it is hard to believe, with only the present evidence to go on. Today
Pat Collins still has his own garage, but it is hardly more than a filling station and tire repair business on the edge of town, patronized
by the people of the neighborhood and not situated on a traffic ar-
tery of any importance. He always has some young man helping out,
but he does most of the work himself. Hard work it is, too. He hires
young men out of high school—out of prison, sometimes—but the
young men don't stay. They never stay. They like Pat Collins, and
they say so, but they don't want to work at night, and Pat Collins's
twenty-four-hour service is what keeps him going. Twenty-four
hours, seven days a week, the only garage in town that says it and
means it. A man stuck for gas, a man with a flat and no spare, a man
skidded into a ditch—they all know that if they phone Pat Collins he

will get there in his truck and if necessary tow them away. Some of the motorists are embarrassed: people who never patronize Pat Collins except in emergencies; people who knew him back in the days when he was Whit Hofman's favorite companion. They embarrass themselves; he does not say or do anything to embarrass them except one thing: he charges them fair prices when he could hold them up, and to some of those people who knew him long ago that is the most embarrassing thing he could do. "Twelve dollars, Pat? You could have charged me more than that."

"Twelve dollars," he says. And there were plenty of times when he could have asked fifty dollars for twelve dollars' worth of service—when the woman in the stalled car was not the wife of the driver.

Now, to the younger ones, he has become a local symbol of misfortune ("All I could do was call Pat Collins") and at the same time a symbol of dependability ("Luckily I thought of Pat Collins"). It is mean work; the interrupted sleep, the frequently bad weather, the drunks and the shocked and the guilty-minded. But it is the one service he offers that makes the difference between a profit and breaking even.

"Hello, Pat," Whit Hofman will say, when they meet on Main Street.

"Hyuh, Whit," Pat Collins will say.

Never more than that, but never less . . .

Aloysius Aquinas Collins came to town in 1923 because he had heard it was a good place to be, a rich town for its size. Big coal interests to start with, but good diversification as well: a steel mill, a couple of iron foundries, the railway car shops, shoe factories, silk mills, half a dozen breweries, four meat packing plants and, to the south, prosperous farmers. Among the rich there were two Rolls-Royces, a dozen or more Pierce-Arrows, a couple of dozen Cadillacs, and maybe a dozen each of Lincolns, Marmons, Packards. It was a spending town; the Pierce-Arrow families bought small roadsters for their children and the women were beginning to drive their own cars. The Rolls-Royces and Pierce-Arrows were in Philadelphia territory, and the franchises for the other big cars were already spoken for, but Pat Collins was willing to start as a dealer for one of the many makes in the large field between Ford-Dodge and Cadillac-Packard, one of the newer, lesser known makes. It was easy to get a franchise for one of those makes, and he decided to take his time.

Of professional experience in the automobile game he had none. He was not yet thirty, and he had behind him two years at Villanova, fifteen months as a shore duty ensign, four years as a salesman of men's hats at which he made pretty good money but from which he got nothing else but stretches of boredom between days of remorse following salesmen's parties in hotels. His wife Madge had lost her early illusions, but she loved him and partly blamed life on the road for what was happening to him. "Get into something else," she would say, "or honest to God, Pat, I'm going to take the children and pull out."

"It's easy enough to talk about getting another job," he would say.

"I don't care what it is, just as long as you're not away five days a week. Drive a taxi, if you have to."

When she happened to mention driving a taxi she touched upon the only major interest he had outside the routine of his life: from the early days of Dario Resta and the brothers Chevrolet he had been crazy about automobiles, all automobiles and everything about them. He would walk or take the "L" from home in West Philadelphia to the area near City Hall, and wander about, stopping in front of the hotels and clubs and private residences and theaters and the Academy of Music, staring at the limousines and town cars, engaging in conversation with the chauffeurs; and then he would walk up North Broad Street, Automobile Row, and because he was a nice-looking kid, the floor salesmen would sometimes let him sit in the cars on display. He collected all the manufacturers' brochures and read all the advertisements in the newspapers. Closer to home he would stand for hours, studying the sporty roadsters and phaetons outside the Penn fraternity houses; big Simplexes with searchlights on the running-boards, Fiats and Renaults and Hispanos and Blitzen-Benzes. He was nice-looking and he had nice manners, and when he would hold the door open for one of the fraternity men they would sometimes give him a nickel and say, "Will you keep your eye on my car, sonny?"

"Can I sit in it, please?"

"Well, if you promise not to blow the horn."

He passed the horn-blowing stage quickly. Sometimes the fraternity men would come out to put up the top when there was a sudden shower, and find that Aloysius Aquinas Collins had somehow done it alone. For this service he wanted no reward but a ride home, on the front seat. On his side of the room he shared with his older brother he had magazine and rotogravure pictures of fine cars pinned to the walls. The nuns at school complained that instead of paying attention, he was continually drawing pictures of automobiles, automobiles. The nuns did not know how good the drawings were; they only cared that one so bright could waste so much time, and their complaints to his parents made it impossible for Aloysius to convince Mr. and Mrs. Collins that after he got his high school diploma, he wanted to get a job on Automobile Row. The parents sent him to Villanova, and after sophomore year took him out because the priests told them they were wasting their money, but out of spite his father refused to let him take a job in the auto business. Collins got him a job in the shipyards, and when the country entered the war, Aloysius joined the Navy and eventually was commissioned. He married Madge Ruddy, became a hat salesman, and rented half of a two-family house in Upper Darby.

Gibbsville was on his sales route, and it first came to his special notice because his Gibbsville customer bought more hats in his high-priced line than any other store of comparable size. He thus discovered that it was a spending town, and that the actual population figures were deceptive; it was surrounded by a lot of much smaller towns whose citizens shopped in Gibbsville. He began to add a day to his normal visits to Gibbsville, to make a study of the automobile business there, and when he came into a small legacy from his aunt, he easily persuaded Madge to put in her own five thousand dollars, and he bought Cunningham's Garage, on Railroad Avenue, Gibbsville.

Cunningham's was badly run down and had lost money for its previous two owners, but it was the oldest garage in town. The established automobile men were not afraid of competition from the newcomer, Collins, who knew nobody to speak of and did not even have a dealer's franchise. They thought he was out of his mind when he began spending money in sprucing up the place. They also thought, and said, that he was getting pretty big for his britches in choosing to rent a house on Lantenengo Street. The proprietor of Cunningham's old garage then proceeded to outrage the established dealers by stealing Walt Michaels' best mechanic, Joe Ricci. Regardless of what the dealers might do to each other in the competition to clinch a sale, one thing you did not do was entice away a man's best mechanic. Walt Michaels, who had the Oldsmobile franchise, paid a call on the new fellow.

A. A. Collins, owner and proprietor, as his sign said, of Collins Motor Company, was in his office when he saw Michaels get out of his car. He went out to greet Michaels, his hand outstretched. "Hello, Mr. Michaels, I'm Pat Collins," he said.

"I know who you are. I just came down to tell you what I think of you."

"Not much, I guess, judging by—"

"Not much is right."

"Smoke a cigar?" said Pat Collins.

Michaels slapped at the cigar and knocked it to the ground. Pat Collins picked it up and looked at it. "I guess that's why they wrap them in tinfoil." He rubbed the dirt off the cigar and put it back in his pocket.

"Don't you want to fight?" said Michaels.

"What for? You have a right to be sore at me, in a way. But when you have a good mechanic like Joe, you ought to be willing to pay him what he's worth."

"Well, I never thought I'd see an Irishman back out of a fight. But with you I guess that's typical. A sneaky Irish son of a bitch."

"Now just a minute, Michaels. Go easy."

"I said it. A sneaky Irish son of a bitch."

"Yeah, I was right the first time," said Collins. He hit Michaels in the stomach with his left hand, and as Michaels crumpled, Collins hit him on the chin with his right hand. Michaels went down, and Collins stood over him, waiting for him to get up. Michaels started to raise himself with both hands on the ground, calling obscene names, but while his hands were still on the ground Collins stuck the foil-wrapped cigar deep in his mouth. Three or four men who stopped to look at the fight burst into laughter, and Michaels, his breath shut off, fell back on the ground.

"Change your mind about the cigar, Michaels?" said Collins.

"I'll send my son down to see you," said Michaels, getting to his feet.

"All right. What does *he* smoke?"

"He's as big as you are."

"Then I'll use a tire iron on him. Now get out of here, and quick."

Michaels, dusting himself off, saw Joe Ricci among the spectators. He pointed at him with his hat. "You, you ginny bastard, you stole tools off of me."

Ricci, who had a screwdriver in his hand, rushed at Michaels and might have stabbed him, but Collins swung him away.

"Calling me a thief, the son of a bitch, I'll kill him," said Ricci. "I'll *kill* him."

"Go on, Michaels. Beat it," said Collins.

Michaels got in his car and put it in gear, and as he was about to drive away Collins called to him: "Hey, Michaels, shall I fill her up?"

The episode, the kind that men liked to embellish in the retelling, made Pat Collins universally unpopular among the dealers, but it made him known to a wider public. It brought him an important visitor.

The Mercer phaeton pulled up at Pat Collins's gas pump and

Collins, in his office, jumped up from his desk, and without putting on his coat, went out to the curb. "Can I help you?" he said.

"Fill her up, will you, please?" said the driver. He was a handsome man, about Collins's age, wearing a brown Homburg and a coonskin coat. Pat Collins knew who he was—Whit Hofman, probably the richest young man in the town—because he knew the car. He was conscious of Hofman's curiosity, but he went on pumping the gasoline. He hung up the hose and said, "You didn't need much. That'll cost you thirty-six cents, Mr. Hofman. Wouldn't you rather I sent you a bill?"

"Well, all right. But don't I get a cigar, a new customer? At least that's what I hear."

The two men laughed. "Sure, have a cigar," said Collins, handing him one. Hofman looked at it.

"Tinfoil, all right. You sure this isn't the same one you gave Walt Michaels?"

"It might be. See if it has any teeth marks on it," said Collins.

"Well, I guess Walt had it coming to him. He's a kind of a sorehead."

"You know him?"

"Of course. Known him all my life, he's always lived here. He's not a bad fellow, Mr. Collins, but you took Joe away from him, and Joe's a hell of a good mechanic. I'd be sore, too, I guess."

"Well, when you come looking for a fight, you ought to be more sure of what you're up against. Either that, or be ready to take a beating. I only hit him twice."

"When I was a boy you wouldn't have knocked him down that easily. When I was a kid, Walt Michaels was a good athlete, but he's put away a lot of beer since then." Hofman looked at Collins. "Do you like beer?"

"I like the beer you get around here. It's better than we get in Philly."

"Put on your coat and let's drink some beer," said Hofman. "Or are you busy?"

"Not that busy," said Collins.

They drove to a saloon in one of the neighboring towns, and Collins was surprised to see that no one was surprised to see the young millionaire, with his Mercer and his coonskin coat. The men drinking at the bar—working-men taking a day off, they appeared to be—were neither cordial nor hostile to Hofman. "Hello, Paul," said Hofman. "Brought you a new customer."

"I need all I can get," said the proprietor. "Where will you want to sit? In the back room?"

"I guess so. This is Mr. Collins, just opened a new garage. Mr. Collins, Mr. Paul Unitas, sometimes called Unitas States of America."

"Pleased to meet you," said Paul, shaking hands.

"Same here," said Collins.

"How's the beer?" said Hofman.

Paul shook his head. "They're around. They stopped two truckloads this morning."

"Who stopped them? The state police?" said Hofman.

"No, this time it was enforcement agents. New ones."

Hofman laughed. "You don't have to worry about Mr. Collins. I'll vouch for him."

"Well, if you say so, Whit. What'll you have?"

"The beer's no good?"

"Slop. Have rye. It's pretty good. I cut it myself."

"Well, if you say rye, that's what we'll have. Okay, Collins?"

"Sure."

Hofman was an affable man, an interested listener and a hearty laughter. It was dark when they left the saloon; Collins had told Hofman a great deal about himself, and Hofman drove Collins home in the Mercer. "I can offer you some Canadian Club," said Collins.

"Thanks just the same, but we're going out to dinner and I have to change. Ask me again sometime. Nice to've seen you, Pat."

"Same to you, Whit. Enjoyable afternoon," said Collins.

In the house Collins kissed Madge's cheek. "Whew! Out drinking with college boys?" she said.

"I'll drink with that college boy any time. That's Whit Hofman."

"How on earth—"

She listened with increasing eagerness while he told her the events of the afternoon. "Maybe you could sell him a car, if you had a good franchise," she said.

"I'm not going to try to sell him anything but Aloysius Aquinas Collins, Esquire. And anyway, I like him."

"You can like people and still sell them a car."

"Well, I'm never going to try to make a sale there. He came to see me out of curiosity, but we hit it off right away. He's a swell fellow."

"Pat?"

"What?"

"Remember why we moved here."

"Listen, it's only ha' past six and I'm home. This guy came to see me, Madge."

"A rich fellow with nothing better to do," she said.

"Oh, for God's sake. You say remember why we moved here. To have a home. But *you* remember why I wanted to live on this street. To meet people like Whit Hofman."

"But not to spend the whole afternoon in some hunky saloon. Were there any women there?"

"A dozen of them, all walking around naked. What have you got for supper?"

"For *dinner,* we have veal cutlets. But Pat, remember what we are. We're not society people. What's she like, his wife?"

"How would I know? I wouldn't know her if I saw her. Unless she was driving that car."

They had a two weeks' wait before Whit Hofman again had the urge for Pat Collins's company. This time Hofman took him to the country club, and they sat in the smoking-room with a bottle of Scotch on the table. "Do you play squash?" said Hofman.

"Play it? I thought you ate it. No, I used to play handball."

"Well, it's kind of handball with a racquet. It's damn near the only exercise I get in the winter, at least until we go South. If you were a good handball player, you'd learn squash in no time."

"Where? At the Y.M.?"

"Here. We have a court here," said Hofman. He got up and pointed through the French window. "See that little house down there, to the right of the first fairway? That's the squash court."

"I was a caddy one summer."

"Oh, you play golf?"

"I've never had a club in my hand since then."

"How would you like to join here? I'll be glad to put you up and we'll find somebody to second you. Does your wife play tennis or golf?"

"No, she's not an athlete. How much would it cost to join?"

"Uh, family membership, you and your wife and children under twenty-one. They just raised it. Initiation, seventy-five dollars. Annual dues, thirty-five for a family membership."

"Do you think I could get in? We don't know many people that belong."

"Well, Walt Michaels doesn't belong. Can you think of anyone else that might blackball you? Because if you can't, I think I could probably get you in at the next meeting. Technically, I'm not supposed to put you up, because I'm on the admissions committee, but that's no problem."

Any hesitancy Pat Collins might have had immediately vanished at mention of the name Walt Michaels. "Well, I'd sure like to belong."

"I'll take care of it. Let's have a drink on it," said Whit Hofman.

"We're Catholics, you know."

"That's all right. We take Catholics. Not all, but some. And those we don't take wouldn't get in if they were Presbyterian or anything else."

"Jews?"

"We have two. One is a doctor, married to a Gentile. He claims he isn't a Jew, but he is. The other is the wife of a Gentile. Otherwise, no. I understand they're starting their own club, I'm not sure where it'll be."

"Well, as long as you know we're Catholics."

"I knew that, Pat," said Hofman. "But I respect you for bringing it up."

Madge Collins was upset about the country club. "It isn't only what you have to pay to get in. It's meals, and spending money on clothes. I haven't bought anything new since we moved here."

"As the Dodge people say, 'It isn't the initial cost, it's the up-keep.' But Madge, I told you before, those are the kind of people that're gonna be worth our while. I'll make a lot of connections at the country club, and in the meantime, I'll get a franchise. So far I didn't spend a nickel on advertising. Well, this is gonna be the best kind of advertising. The Cadillac dealer is the only other dealer in the country club, and I won't compete with him."

"Everything going out, very little coming in," she said.

"Stop worrying, everything's gonna be hunky-dory."

On the morning after the next meeting of the club admissions committee Whit Hofman telephoned Pat Collins. "Congratulations to the newest member of the Lantenengo Country Club. It was a cinch. You'll get a notice and a bill, and as soon as you send your cheque you and Mrs. Collins can start using the club, although there's no golf or tennis now. However, there's a dance next Friday, and we'd like you and your wife to have dinner with us. Wear your Tuck. My wife is going to phone Mrs. Collins some time today."

In her two years as stock girl and saleslady at Oppenheim, Collins—"my cousins," Pat called them—Madge had learned a thing or two about values, and she had style sense. The evening dress she bought for the Hofman dinner and club dance was severely simple, black, and Pat thought it looked too old for her. "Wait till you see it on," she said. She changed the shoulder straps and substituted thin black cord, making her shoulders, chest, and back completely bare and giving an illusion of a deeper décolletage than was actually the case. She had a good figure and a lovely complexion, and when he saw her ready to leave for the party, he was startled. "It's not too old for you any more. Maybe it's too young."

"I wish I had some jewelry," she said.

"You have. I can see them."

"Oh—oh, stop. It's not immodest. You can't see anything unless you stoop over and look down."

"Unless you happen to be over five foot five, and most men are."

"Do you want me to wear a shawl? I have a nice old shawl of Grandma's. As soon as we start making money the one thing I want is a good fur coat. That's all I want, and I can get one wholesale."

"Get one for me, while you're at it. But for now, let's get a move on. Dinner is eight-thirty and we're the guests of honor."

"Guests of honor! Just think of it, Pat. I haven't been so excited since our wedding. I hope I don't do anything wrong."

"Just watch Mrs. Hofman. I don't even know who else'll be there, but it's time we were finding out."

"Per-*fume!* I didn't put on any per*fume.* I'll be right down."

She was excited and she had youth and health, but she also had a squarish face with a strong jawline that gave her a look of maturity and dignity. Her hair was reddish brown, her eyes grey-green. It was a face full of contrasts, especially from repose to animation, and with the men—beginning with Whit Hofman—she was an instant success.

The Hofmans had invited three other couples besides the Collinses. Custom forbade having liquor bottles or cocktail shakers on the table at club dances, and Whit Hofman kept a shaker and a bottle on the floor beside him. The men were drinking straight whiskey, the women drank orange blossoms. There was no bar, and the Hofman party sat at the table and had their drinks until nine o'clock, when Hofman's wife signalled the steward to start serving. Chincoteagues were served first, and before the soup, Whit Hofman asked Madge Collins to dance. He was feeling good, and here he was king. His fortune was respected by men twice his age, and among the men and women who were more nearly his contemporaries he was genuinely well liked for a number of reasons: his unfailingly good manners, no matter how far in drink he might get; his affability, which drew upon his good manners when bores and toadies and the envious and the weak made their assaults; his emanations of strength, which were physically and tangibly demonstrated in his expertness at games as well as in the slightly more subtle self-reminders of his friends that he *was* Whit Hofman and *did have* all that money. He had a good war record, beginning with enlistment as a private in the National Guard for Mexican Border service, and including a field commission, a wound chevron, and a Croix de Guerre with palm during his A.E.F. service. He was overweight, but he could afford bespoke tailors and he cared about clothes; tonight he was wearing a dinner jacket with a white waistcoat and a satin butterfly tie. Madge Ruddy Collins had never known anyone quite like him, and her first mistake was to believe that his high spirits had something special to do with her. At this stage she had no way of knowing that later on, when he danced with his fat old second cousin, he would be just as much fun.

"Well, how do you like your club?" he said.

"My club? Oh—*this* club. Oh, it's beautiful. Pat and I certainly do thank you."

"Very glad to do it. I hope you're going to take up golf. More and more women are. Girl I just spoke to, Mrs. Dick Richards, she won the second flight this year, and she only started playing last spring."

"Does your wife play?"

"She plays pretty well, and could be a lot better. She's going to have a lot of lessons when we go South. That's the thing to do. As soon as you develop a fault, have a lesson right away, before it becomes a habit. I'm going to have Pat playing squash before we leave."

"Oh."

"He said he was a handball player, so squash ought to come easy to him. Of course it's a much more strenuous game than golf."

"It is?"

He said something in reply to a question from a man dancing by. The man laughed, and Whit Hofman laughed. "That's Johnny King," said Hofman. "You haven't met the Kings, have you?"

"No," said Madge. "She's pretty. Beautifully gowned."

"Oh, that's not his wife. She isn't here tonight. That's Mary-Louise Johnson, from Scranton. There's a whole delegation from

Scranton here tonight. They all came down for Buz McKee's birth-day party. That's the big table over in the corner. Well, I'm getting the high sign, I guess we'd better go back to our table. Thank you, Madge. A pleasure."

"Oh, to me, too," she said.

In due course every man in the Hofman party danced with every woman, the duty rounds. Pat Collins was the last to dance with Madge on the duty rounds. "You having a good time?" he said.

"Oh, *am* I?" she said.

"How do you like Whit?"

"He's a real gentleman, I'm crazy about him. I like him the best. Do you like her, his wife?"

"I guess so. In a way yes, and in a way no."

"Me too. She'd rather be with those people from Scranton."

"What people from Scranton?"

"At the big table. They're here to attend a birthday party for Buz-zie McKee."

"Jesus, you're learning fast."

"I found that out from Whit. The blonde in the beaded white, that's Mary-Louise Johnson, dancing with Johnny King. They're dancing every dance together."

"Together is right. Take a can-opener to pry them apart."

"His wife is away," said Madge. "Where did Whit go?"

Pat turned to look at their table. "I don't know. Oh, there he is, dancing with some fat lady."

"I don't admire his taste."

"Say, you took a real shine to Whit," said Pat Collins.

"Well, he's a real gentleman, but he isn't a bit forward. Now where's he going? . . . Oh, I guess he wanted to wish Buzzie McKee a happy birthday. Well, let's sit down."

The chair at her left remained vacant while Hofman continued his visit to the McKee table. On Madge's right was a lawyer named Joe Chapin, who had something to do with the admissions commit-tee; polite enough, but for Madge very hard to talk to. At the moment he was in conversation with the woman on his right, and Madge Collins felt completely alone. A minute passed, two minutes, and her solitude passed to uneasiness to anger. Whit Hofman made his way back to the table, and when he sat down she said, trying to keep the irritation out of her tone, "That wasn't very polite."

"I'm terribly sorry. I thought you and Joe—"

"Oh, *him*. Well, I'll forgive you if you dance this dance with me."

"Why of course," said Hofman.

They got up again, and as they danced she closed her eyes, pretending to an ecstasy she did not altogether feel. They got through eighteen bars of "Bambalina," and the music stopped. "Oh, hell," she said. "I'll let you have the next."

"Fine," he said. She took his arm, holding it so that her hand clenched his right biceps, and giving it a final squeeze as they sat down.

"Would you like some more coffee?" he said. "If not, I'm afraid we're going to have to let them take the table away."

"Why?"

"That's what they do. Ten o'clock, tables have to be cleared out, to make room for the dancing. You know, quite a few people have dinner at home, then come to the dance."

"What are they? Cheap skates?"

"Oh, I don't know about that. No, hardly that."

"But if *you* wanted to keep the table, they'd let you."

"Oh, I wouldn't do that, Madge. They really need the room."

"Then where do we go?"

"Wherever we like. Probably the smoking-room. But from now on we just sort of—circulate."

"You mean your dinner is over?"

"Yes, that's about it. We're on our own."

"I don't want to go home. I want to dance with you some more."

"Who said anything about going home? The fun is just about to begin."

"I had fun before. I'm not very good with strangers."

"You're not a stranger. You're a member of the club, duly launched. Let's go out to the smoking-room and I'll get you a drink. How would you like a Stinger?"

"What is it? Never mind telling me. I'll have one."

"If you've never had one, be careful. It could be your downfall. Very cool to the taste, but packs a wallop. Sneaks up on you."

"Good. Let's have one." She rose and quickly took his unoffered arm, and they went to the smoking-room, which was already more than half filled.

At eleven o'clock she was drunk. She would dance with no one but Whit Hofman, and when she danced with him she tried to excite him, and succeeded. "You're hot stuff, Madge," he said.

"Why what do you *mean?*"

"The question is, what do *you* mean?"

"I don't know what you're *talking* about," she said, sing-song.

"The hell you don't," he said. "Shall we go for a stroll?"

"Where to?"

"My car's around back of the caddyhouse."

"Do you think we ought to?"

"No, but either that or let's sit down."

"All right, let's sit down. I'm getting kind of woozy, anyhow."

"Don't drink any more Stingers. I told you they were dangerous. Maybe you ought to have some coffee. Maybe I ought to, too. Come on, we'll get some coffee." He led her to a corner of the smoking-room, where she could prop herself against the wall. He left her, and in the hallway to the kitchen he encountered Pat Collins on his way from the locker-room.

"Say, Pat, if I were you—well, Madge had a couple of Stingers and I don't think they agree with her."

"Is she sick?"

"No, but I'm afraid she's quite tight."

"I better take her home?"

"*You* know. Your first night here. There'll be others much worse off, but she's the one they'll talk about. The maid'll get her wrap, and you can ease her out so nobody'll notice. I'll say your good-nights for you."

"Well, gee, Whit—I'm sorry. I certainly apologize."

"Perfectly all right, Pat. No harm done, but she's ready for beddy-bye. I'll call you in a day or two."

There was no confusing suggestion with command, and Pat obeyed Hofman. He got his own coat and Madge's, and when Madge saw her coat she likewise recognized authority.

They were less than a mile from the club when she said, "I'm gonna be sick."

He stopped the car. "All right, *be* sick."

When she got back in the car she said, "Leave the windows down, I need the fresh air."

He got her to bed. His anger was so great that he did not trust himself to speak to her, and she mistook his silence for pity. She kept muttering that she was sorry, sorry, and went to sleep. Much later he fell asleep, awoke before six, dressed and left the house before he had to speak to her. He had his breakfast in an all-night restaurant, bought the morning newspapers, and opened the garage. He needed to think, and not so much about punishing Madge as about restoring himself to good standing in the eyes of the Hofmans. He had caught Kitty Hofman's cold appraisal of Madge on the dance floor; he had known, too, that he had failed to make a good impression on Kitty, who was in a sour mood for having to give up the Buz McKee dinner. He rejected his first plan to send Kitty flowers and a humorous note. Tomorrow or the next day Madge could send the flowers and a thank-you note, which he would make sure contained no reference to her getting tight or any other apologetic implication. The important thing was to repair any damage to his relationship with Whit Hofman, and after a while he concluded that aside from Madge's thank-you note to both Hofmans, the wiser course was to wait for Whit to call him.

He had a long wait.

Immediately after Christmas the Hofmans went to Florida. They returned for two weeks in late March, closed their house, and took off on a trip around the world. Consequently the Collinses did not see the Hofmans for nearly a year. It was a year that was bad for the Collins marriage, but good for the Collins Motor Company. Pat Collins got the Chrysler franchise, and the car practically sold itself. Women and the young took to it from the start, and the Collins Motor Company had trouble keeping up with the orders. The bright new car and the bright new Irishman were interchangeably associated in the minds of the citizens, and Pat and Madge Collins were getting somewhere on their own, without the suspended sponsorship of Whit Hofman. But at home Pat and Madge had never quite got back to what they had been before she jeopardized his relationship with Whit Hofman. He had counted so much on Hofman's approval that the threat of losing it had given him a big scare, and it would not be far-fetched to say that the designers of the Chrysler "70" saved the Collins marriage.

Now they were busy, Pat with his golf when he could take the time off from his work—which he did frequently; and Madge with the game of bridge, which she learned adequately well. In the absence of the Whit Hofmans the social life of the country club was left without an outstanding couple to be the leaders, although several couples tried to fill the gap. In the locker-room one afternoon, drinking gin and ginger ale with the members of his foursome, Pat Collins heard one of the men say, "You know who we all miss? Whit. The club isn't the same without him." Pat looked up as at a newly discovered truth, and for the first time he realized that he liked Whit Hofman better than any man he had ever known. It had remained for someone else to put the thought into words, and casual enough words they were to express what Pat Collins had felt from the first day in Paul Unitas's saloon. Like nearly everyone else in the club the Collinses had had a postcard or two from the Hofmans; Honolulu, Shanghai, Bangkok, St. Andrew's, St. Cloud. The Hofmans' closer friends had had letters, but the Collinses were pleased to have had a postcard, signed "Kitty and Whit"—in Whit's handwriting.

"When does he get back, does anyone know?" said Pat.

"Middle of October," said the original speaker. "You know Whit. He wouldn't miss the football season, not the meat of it anyway."

"About a month away," said Pat Collins. "Well, I can thank him for the most enjoyable summer I ever had. He got me in here, you know. I was practically a stranger."

" 'A stranger in a strange land,' but not any more, Pat."

"Thank you. You fellows have been damn nice to me." He meant the sentiment, but the depth of it belonged to his affection for Whit Hofman. He had his shower and dressed, and joined Madge on the terrace. "Do you want to stay here for dinner?"

"We have nothing at home," she said.

"Then we'll eat here," he said. "Did you know the Hofmans are getting back about four weeks from now?"

"I knew it."

"Why didn't you tell me?"

"I didn't know you wanted to know, or I would have. Why, are you thinking of hiring a brass band? One postcard."

"What did you expect? As I remember, you didn't keep it any secret when we got it."

"You were the one that was more pleased than I was."

"Oh, all right. Let's go eat."

They failed to be invited to the smaller parties in honor of the returning voyagers, but they went to a Dutch Treat dinner for the Hofmans before the club dance. Two changes in the Hofmans were instantly noticeable: Whit was as brown as a Hawaiian, and Kitty was pregnant. She received the members of the dinner party sitting down. She had lost one child through miscarriage. Whit stood beside her, and when it came the Collinses' turn he greeted Pat and Madge by nickname and first name. Not so Kitty. "Oh, hel*lo*. Mrs. *Col*lins. *Nice* of you to come. Hello, Mr. Collins." Then, seeing the man next in line she called out: "Bob-bee! Bobby, where were you Tuesday? You were supposed to be at the Ogdens', you false friend. I thought you'd be at the boat."

The Collinses moved on, and Madge said, "We shouldn't have come."

"Why not? She doesn't have to like us."

"She didn't have to be so snooty, either."

"Bobby Hermann is one of their best friends."

"I'm damn sure we're not."

"Oh, for God's sake."

"Oh, for God's sake yourself," she said.

The year had done a lot for Madge in such matters as her poise and the widening of her acquaintance among club members. But it was not until eleven or so that Whit Hofman cut in on her. "How've you been?" he said.

"Lonely without you," she said.

"That's nice to hear. I wish you meant it."

"You're pretending to think I don't," she said. "But I thought of you every day. And every night. Especially every night."

"How many Stingers have you had?"

"That's a nasty thing to say. I haven't had any. I've never had one since that night. So we'll change the subject. Are you going to stay home a while?"

"Looks that way. Kitty's having the baby in January."

"Sooner than that, I thought."

"No, the doctor says January."

"Which do you want? A boy, or a girl?"

"Both, but not at the same time."

"Well, you always get what you want, so I'm told."

"That's a new one on me."

"Well, you can *have* anything you want, put it that way."

"No, not even that."

"What do you want that you haven't got?"

"A son, or a daughter."

"Well, you're getting that, one or the other. What else?"

"Right now, nothing else."

"I don't believe anybody's ever that contented."

"Well, what do *you* want, for instance?"

"You," she said.

"Why? You have a nice guy. Kids. And I hear Pat's the busiest car dealer in town."

"Those are things I have. You asked me what I wanted."

"You don't beat about the bush, do you, Madge? You get right to the point."

"I've been in love with you for almost a year."

"Madge, you haven't been in love with me at all. Maybe you're not in love with Pat, but you're certainly not in love with me. You couldn't be."

"About a month ago I heard you were coming home, and I had it all planned out how I was going to be when I saw you. But I was wrong. I couldn't feel this way for a whole year and then start pretending I didn't. You asked me how I was, and I came right out with it, the truth."

"Well, Madge, I'm not in love with you. You're damn attractive and all that, but I'm not in *love* with you."

"I know that. But answer me one question, as truthful as I am with you. Are you in love with your wife?"

"Of course I am."

"I'll tell you something, Whit. You're not. With her. With me. Or maybe with anybody."

"Now really, that *is* a nasty thing to say."

"People love you, Whit, but you don't love them back."

"I'm afraid I don't like this conversation. Shall we go back and have a drink?"

"Yes."

They moved toward the smoking-room. "Why did you say that, Madge? What makes you think it?"

"You really want me to tell you? Remember, the truth hurts, and I had a whole year to think about this."

"What the hell, tell me."

"It's not you, it's the town. There's nobody here bigger than you. They all love you, but you don't love them."

"I love this town and the people in it and everything about it.

Don't you think I could live anywhere I wanted to? Why do you think I came back here? I can live anywhere in the God damn world. Jesus, you certainly have that one figured wrong. For a minute you almost had me worried."

He danced with her no more that night, and if he could avoid speaking to her or getting close to her, he did so. When she got home, past three o'clock, she gave Pat Collins a very good time; loveless but exceedingly pleasurable. Then she lay in her bed until morning, unable to understand herself, puzzled by forces that had never been mysterious to her.

The Hofman baby was born on schedule, a six-pound boy, but the reports from the mother's bedside were not especially happy. Kitty had had a long and difficult time, and one report, corroborated only by constant repetition, was that she had thrown a clock, or a flower vase, or a water tumbler, or all of them, at Whit at the start of her labor. It was said, and perfunctorily denied, that a group of nurses and orderlies stood outside her hospital room, listening fascinatedly to the obscene names she called him, names that the gossips would not utter but knew how to spell. Whatever the basis in fact, the rumors of hurled bric-a-brac and invective seemed to be partially confirmed when Kitty Hofman came home from the hospital. The infant was left in the care of a nurse, and Kitty went to every party, drinking steadily and chain-smoking, saying little and watching everything. She had a look of determination, as though she had just made up her mind about something, but the look and decision were not followed up by action. She would stay at the parties until she had had enough, then she would get her wrap and say goodnight to her hostess, without any word or sign to Whit, and it would be up to him to discover she was leaving and follow her out.

Their friends wondered how long Whit Hofman would take that kind of behavior, but no one—least of all Pat Collins—was so tactless, or bold, as to suggest to Whit that there *was* any behavior. It was Whit, finally, who talked.

He was now seeing Pat Collins nearly every day, and on some days more than once. He knew as much about automobiles as Pat

Collins, and he was comfortable in Pat's office. He had made the garage one of his ports of call in his daytime rounds—his office every morning at ten, the barber's, the bank, the broker's, his lawyer, lunch at the Gibbsville Club, a game of pool after lunch, a visit with Pat Collins that sometimes continued with a couple of games of squash at the country club. On a day some six weeks after the birth of his son Whit dropped in on Pat, hung up his coat and hat, and took a chair.

"Don't let me interrupt you," he said.

"Just signing some time-sheets," said Pat Collins.

Whit lit a cigarette and put his feet up on the windowsill. "It's about time you had those windows washed," he said.

"I know. Miss Muldowney says if I'm trying to save money, that's the wrong way. Burns up more electricity. Well, there we are. Another day, another dollar. How's the stock market?"

"Stay out of it. Everything's too high."

"I'm not ready to go in it yet. Later. Little by little I'm paying back Madge, the money she put in the business."

"You ought to incorporate and give her stock."

"First I want to give her back her money, with interest."

"Speaking of Madge, Pat. Do you remember when your children were born?"

"Sure. That wasn't so long ago."

"What is Dennis, about six?"

"Dennis is six, and Peggy's four. I guess Dennis is the same in years that your boy is in weeks. How is he, Pop?"

"He's fine. At least I guess he's fine. I wouldn't know how to tell, this is all new to me."

"But you're not worried about him? You sound dubious."

"Not about him. The doctor says he's beginning to gain weight and so forth. Kitty is something else again, and that's what I want to ask you about. You knew she didn't have a very easy time of it."

"Yes, you told me that."

"How was Madge, with her children?"

"I'll have to think back," said Pat. "Let me see. With Dennis, the first, we had a couple false alarms and had the doctor come to the house one time at four o'clock in the morning. He was sore as hell. It was only gas pains, and as soon as she got rid of the gas, okay. The real time, she was in labor about three hours, I guess. About three. Dennis weighed seven and a quarter. With Peggy, she took longer. Started having pains around eight o'clock in the morning, but the baby wasn't all the way out till three-four in the afternoon. She had a much harder time with the second, although it was a smaller baby. Six and a half, I think."

"What about her, uh, mental state? Was she depressed or anything like that?"

"No, not a bit. Anything but."

"But you haven't had any more children, and I thought Catholics didn't believe in birth control."

"Well, I'll tell you, Whit, although I wouldn't tell most Protestants. I don't agree with the Church on that, and neither does Madge. If that's the criterion, we're not very good Catholics, but I can't help that. We had two children when we could only afford one, and now I don't think we'll ever have any more. Two's enough."

"But for financial reasons, not because of the effect on Madge."

"Mainly financial reasons. Even if we could afford it, though, Madge doesn't want any more. She wants to enjoy life while she's young."

"I see," said Whit Madge. The conversation had reached a point where utter frankness or a change of the subject was inevitable, and Whit Hofman retreated from candor. It then was up to Pat Collins to break the silence.

"It's none of my business, Whit," he began. "But—"

"No, it isn't, Pat. I don't mean to be rude, but if I said any more about Kitty, I'd sound like a crybaby. Not to mention the fact that it goes against the grain. I've said too much already."

"I know how you feel. But nothing you say gets out of this office, so don't let that worry you. I don't tell Madge everything I know. Or do. She made some pretty good guesses, and we came close to busting up. When I was on the road, peddling hats and caps, I knew a sure lay in damn near every town between Philly and Binghamton, New York. Not that I got laid every night—but I didn't miss many Thursdays. Thursday nights we knew we were going home Friday, salesmen. You don't make any calls on Friday, the clients are all busy. So, somebody'd bring out a quart."

"Did you know a sure lay in this town?"

"Did I! Did you ever know a broad named Helene Holman?"

"I should say I did."

"Well, her," said Pat Collins.

"You don't see her now, though, do you?"

"Is that any of your business, Whit?"

"Touché. I wasn't really asking out of curiosity. More, uh, in-credibility. *Incredulity.* In other words, I've always thought you behaved yourself here, since you've been living here."

"I have. And anyway, I understand the Holman dame is private property. At least I always see her riding around with the big boot-legger, Charney."

"Ed Charney. Yes, she's out of circulation for the present, so my friends tell me."

"Yes, and you couldn't get away with a God damn thing. You're too well known."

"So far I haven't tried to get away with anything," said Whit Hofman. "How would you feel about a little strenuous exercise?"

Pat Collins looked up at the clock. "I don't think any ripe pros-pect is coming in in the next twenty minutes. Two games?"

"Enough to get up a sweat."

They drove to the country club in two cars, obviating the contin-uance of conversation and giving each man the opportunity to think his own thoughts. They played squash for an hour or so, took long hot showers, and cooled out at the locker-room table with gin and ginger ale. "I could lie right down on that floor and go to sleep," said Whit. "You're getting better, or maybe I'm getting worse. Next year I'm not going to give you a handicap."

"I may get good enough to take you at golf, but not this game. You always know where the ball's going to be, and I have to lose time guessing." They were the only members in the locker-room. They could hear occasional sounds from the kitchen of the steward and his staff having supper, a few dozen feet and a whole generation of prosperity away. The walls of the room were lined with steel lockers, with two islands of lockers back-to-back in the center of the room, hempen matting in the passageways, a rather feeble ceiling lamp above the table where their drinks rested. It was an arcane atmosphere, like some goat-room in an odd lodge, with a lingering dankness traceable to their recent hot showers and to the dozens of golf shoes and plus-fours and last summer's shirts stored and forgotten in the lockers. Whit, in his shorts and shirt, and Pat, in his B.V.D.'s, pleasantly tired from their exercise and additionally numbed by the gin and ginger ales, were in that state of euphorious relaxation that a million men ten million times have called the best part of the game, any game. They were by no means drunk, nor were they exhausted, but once again they were back at the point of utter frankness or retreat from it that they had reached in Pat's office, only now the surrounding circumstances were different.

"Why don't you get it off your chest, Whit?"

Whit Hofman, without looking up, blew the ash off his cigarette. "Funny, I was just thinking the same thing," he said. He reached for the gin bottle and spiked Pat's and his own drinks. "I have too damn many cousins in this town. If I confided in any of them they'd call a family conference, which is the last thing I want." He scraped his cigarette against the ash tray, and with his eyes on the operation said, "Kitty hates me. She hates me, and I'm not sure why."

"Have you got a clear conscience?"

"No," said Whit. "That is, *I* haven't. When we were in Siam, on our trip, Kitty got an attack of dysentery and stayed in the hotel for a couple of days. I, uh, took advantage of that to slip off with an American newspaper fellow for some of the local nookie. So I haven't got a clear conscience, but Kitty doesn't know that. Positively. I don't think it's that. I *know* it isn't that. It's something—I don't know where it began, or when. We didn't have any fights or anything like that. Just one day it was there, and I hadn't noticed it before."

"Pregnant."

"Oh, yes. But past the stage where she was throwing up. Taking it very easy, because she didn't want to lose this baby. But a wall between us. No, not a wall. Just a way of looking at me, as if I'd changed appearance and she was fascinated, but not fascinated because she *liked* my new appearance. 'What's this strange animal?' That kind of look. No fights, though. Not even any serious arguments. Oh, I got sore at her for trying to smuggle in a ring I bought her in Cairo. I was filling out the customs declaration and I had the damn thing all filled out and signed, then I remembered the ring. I asked her what about it, and she said she wasn't going to declare it. She was going to wear it in with the stone turned around so that it'd look like a guard for her engagement ring. So pointless. The ring wasn't *that* valuable. The duty was about a hundred and fifty dollars. An amethyst, with a kind of a scarab design. Do you know that an amethyst is supposed to sober you up?"

"I never heard that."

"Yeah. The magical power, but it doesn't work, I can tell you. Anyway, I gave her hell because if you try to pull a fast one on the customs inspectors and they catch you, they make you wait, they confiscate your luggage, and I'm told that for the rest of your life, whenever you re-enter the country, they go through everything with a fine tooth comb. And incidentally, an uncle of Jimmy Malloy's was expediting our landing, and he would have got into trouble, no doubt. Dr. Malloy's brother-in-law, has something to do with the immigration people. So I had to get new forms and fill out the whole God damn thing all over again. But that was our only quarrel of any consequence. It did make me wonder a little, why she wanted to save a hundred and fifty when it wasn't even her money."

They sipped their drinks.

"The day she went to the hospital," Whit Hofman continued, "it was very cold, and I bundled her up warm. She laughed at me and said we weren't going to the North Pole. Not a nice laugh. Then when we got to the hospital the nurse helped her change into a hospital gown, but didn't put her to bed. She sat up in a chair, and I put a blanket over her feet, asked her if she wanted anything to read. She said she did. Could I get her a history of the Hofman family? Well, there *is* one, but I knew damn well she didn't want it. She was just being disagreeable, but that was understandable under the circumstances. Then I sat down, and she told me I didn't have to wait around. I said I knew I didn't have to, but was doing it because I wanted to. Then she said, 'God damn it, don't you know when I'm trying to get rid of you?' and threw her cigarette lighter at me. Unfortunately the nurse picked that exact moment to come in the room, and the lighter hit her in the teat. I don't know what came over Kitty. 'Get that son of a bitch out of here,' and a lot more on the same order. So the nurse told me I'd better go, and I did." He paused. "Kitty had an awful time, no doubt about it. I was there when they brought the baby in to show her. She looked at it, didn't register any feeling whatsoever, and then turned her face away and shut her eyes. I have never seen her look at the baby the way you'd expect a mother to. I've never seen her pick him up out of his crib just to hold him. Naturally she's never nursed him. She probably hasn't enough milk, so I have no objection to that, but along with hating me she seems to hate the baby. Dr. English says that will pass, but I know better. She has no damn use for me *or* the child." He paused again. "The Christ-awful thing is, I don't know what the hell I *did.*"

"I agree with Dr. English. It'll pass," said Pat Collins. "Women today, they aren't as simple as they used to be, fifty or a hundred years ago. They drive cars and play golf. Smoke and drink, do a lot of the same things men do."

"My mother rode horseback and played tennis. She didn't smoke that I know of, but she drank. Not to excess, but wine with dinner. She died when I was eight, so I don't really know an awful lot about her. My father died while I was still in prep school. From then on I guess you'd say I was brought up by my uncle and the housekeeper and my uncle's butler. I have an older brother in the foreign service, but he's too close to me in age to have had much to do with bringing me up. He was a freshman when our father died."

"I didn't know you had a brother."

"I saw him in Rome. He's in the embassy there. Both glad to see each other, but he thinks I'm a country bumpkin, which I am. And since I don't speak French or Italian, and he has a little bit of an English accent, you might say we don't even speak the same language. He married a Boston girl and you should have seen her with Kitty. Every time the Italian men flocked around Kitty, Howard's wife would act as an interpreter, although the Italians all spoke English. But I don't think that has anything to do with why Kitty developed this hatred for me. Howard's wife disapproved of me just as heartily as she did Kitty. We were all pretty glad to see the last of each other. Howard's wife has twice as much money as he has, so he doesn't exactly rule the roost, but in every marriage one of the two has more money than the other. That's not what's eating Kitty." He sipped his drink. "I've been thinking if we moved away from here. Someone told me that this town is wrong for me."

"They're crazy."

"Well, it's bothered me ever since. This, uh, person said that my friends liked me but I didn't like them back."

"That *is* crap."

"As a matter of fact, the person didn't say like. She said love. Meaning that as long as I lived here, I wouldn't be able to love anybody. But I've always loved Kitty, and I certainly love this town. I don't know what more I can do to prove it."

"As far as Kitty's concerned, you're going to have to wait a while. Some women take longer than others getting their machinery back in place after a baby."

Whit Hofman shook his head. "Dr. English tells me Kitty's machinery is okay. And whatever it is, it started before the machinery got out of place. It's me, but what in the name of Christ is it? It's getting late, Pat. Would you have dinner with me here?"

"If you'll square me with Madge. It *is* late. I'm due home now."

234 ♦ JOHN O'HARA

"You want me to speak to her, now?"

"We both can."

There was a telephone in the hall off the locker-room and Pat put in the call.

"I knew that's where you'd be," said Madge. "You could just as easily called two hours ago."

"I'm going to put Whit on," said Pat, and did so.

"Madge, I take all the blame, but it'll be at least an hour before Pat could be home. We're still in our underwear. So could you spare him for dinner?"

"Your wish is our command," said Madge.

Whit turned to Pat. "She hung up. What do you do now?"

"We call Heinie and order up a couple of steaks," said Pat.

It was not only that the two men saw each other so frequently; it was Pat's availability, to share meals, to take little trips, that annoyed Madge. "You don't have to suck up to Whit Hofman," she would say. "Not any more."

"I'm glad I don't."

This colloquy in the Collins household resembled one in the Hofmans'. "Not that it matters to me, but how can you spend so much time with that Pat Collins person?" said Kitty.

"What's wrong with Pat? He's good company."

"Because your other friends refuse to yes you."

"That shows how little you know about Pat Collins," he said. "You don't seem to realize that he had hard going for a while, but he never asked me for any help of any kind."

"Saving you for something big, probably."

"No. I doubt if he'll ever ask me for anything. When he needed money to expand, he didn't even go to our bank, let alone ask me for help. And I would have been glad to put money in his business. Would have been a good investment."

"Oh, I don't care. Do as you please. I'm just amused to watch this beautiful friendship between you two. And by the way, maybe he never asked you for anything, but did he ever refuse anything you offered him? For instance, the club."

"He would have made it."

"Has he made the Gibbsville Club?"

"As far as I know, he's not interested."

"Try him."

"Hell, if I ask him, he'll say yes."

"Exactly my point. His way is so much cagier. He's always there when you want him, and naturally you're going to feel obligated to him. You'll want to pay him back for always being there, so he gets more out of you that way than if he'd asked for favors. He knows that."

"It's funny how *you* know things like that, Kitty."

She fell angrily silent. He had met her at a party just after the war, when he was still in uniform and with two or three other officers was having a lengthy celebration in New York. Whit, a first lieutenant in the 103d Engineers, 28th Division, met a first lieutenant in the 102d Engineers, 27th Division, who had with him a girl from New Rochelle. She was not a beauty, but Whit was immediately attracted to her, and she to him. "This man is only the 102d and I'm the 103d. He's only the 27th and I'm the 28th," said Whit. "Why don't you move up a grade?"

She laughed. "Why not? I *want* to get up in the world."

He made frequent trips to New York to see her. She was going to a commercial art school, living at home with her family but able to spend many nights in New York. Her father was a perfectly respectable layout man in an advertising agency, who commuted from New Rochelle and escaped from his wife by spending all the time he could in sailing small boats. His wife was a fat and disagreeable woman who had tried but failed to dominate her husband and her daughter, and regarded her husband as a nincompoop and her daughter as a wild and wilful girl who was headed for no good. One spring day Kitty and Whit drove to Greenwich, Connecticut, and were married. They then drove to New Rochelle, the first and only time Whit Hofman ever saw his wife's parents. Two days later the newly married couple sailed for Europe, and they did not put in an appearance in Gibbsville, Pennsylvania, until the autumn. It was all very unconventional and it led to considerable speculation as to the kind of person Whit Hofman had married, especially among the mothers of nubile girls. But a *fait accompli* was a *fait accompli,* and Whit Hofman was Whit Hofman, and the girls and their mothers had to make the best of it, whatever that turned out to be.

In certain respects it turned out quite well. The town, and indeed the entire nation, was ready to have some fun. There was a considerable amount of second-generation money around, and manners and customs would never revert to those of 1914. Kitty Hofman and the Lantenengo Country Club appeared almost simultaneously in Gibbsville; both were new and novel and had the backing of the Hofman family. Kitty made herself agreeable to Whit's men friends and made no effort in the direction of the young women. They had to make themselves agreeable to her, and since their alternative was self-inflicted ostracism, Kitty was established without getting entangled in social debts to any of the young women. A less determined, less independent young woman could not have achieved it, but Gibbsville was full of less determined, less independent young women whom Whit Hofman had not married. And at least Whit had not singled out one of their number to the exclusion of all the others, a mildly comforting and unifying thought. He had to marry somebody, so better this nobody with her invisible family in a New York suburb than a Gibbsville girl who would have to suffer as the object of harmonious envy.

Kitty did nothing deliberately to antagonize the young women—unless to outdress them could be so considered, and her taste in clothes was far too individualistic for her new acquaintances. She attended their ladies' luncheons, always leaving before the bridge game began. She played in the Tuesday golf tournaments. She precisely returned all invitations. And she made no close friendships. But she actively disliked Madge Collins.

From the beginning she knew, as women know better than men know, that she was not going to like that woman. Even before Madge got up to dance with Whit and made her extraordinary, possessive, off-in-dreamland impression with her closed eyes, Kitty

Hofman abandoned herself to the luxury of loathing another woman. Madge's black dress was sound, so much so that Kitty accurately guessed that Madge had had some experience in women's wear. But from there on every judgment Kitty made was unfavorable. Madge's prettiness was literally natural: her good figure was natural, her amazing skin was natural, her reddish brown hair, her teeth, her bright eyes, her inviting mouth, were gifts of Nature. (Kitty used a great deal of makeup and dyed her blond hair a lighter shade of blond.) Kitty, in the first minutes of her first meeting with Madge, ticketed her as a pretty parlor-maid; when she got up to dance with Whit she ticketed her as a whore, and with no evidence to the contrary, Madge so remained. Kitty's judgments were not based on facts or influenced by considerations of fairness, then or ever, although she could be extremely realistic in her observations. (Her father, she early knew, was an ineffectual man, a coward who worked hard to protect his job and fled to the waters of Long Island Sound to avoid the occasions of quarrels with her mother.) Kitty, with her firmly middle-class background, had no trouble in imagining the background of Madge and Pat Collins, and the Collinses provided her with her first opportunity to assert herself as a Hofman. (She had not been wasting her first years in Gibbsville; her indifferent manner masked a shrewd study of individuals and their standing in the community.) Kitty, who had not been able comfortably to integrate herself into the established order, now rapidly assumed her position as Whit's wife because as Mrs. Whit Hofman she could look down on and crack down on Madge Collins. (By a closely related coincidence she also became a harsher judge of her husband at the very moment that she began to exercise the privileges of her marital status.) Kitty's obsessive hatred of the hick from West Philadelphia, as she called Madge Collins, was quick in its onset and showed every sign of being chronic. The other young women of the country club set did not fail to notice, and it amused them to get a rise out of Kitty Hofman merely by mentioning Madge Collins's name.

But the former Madge Ruddy was at least as intuitive as Kitty

Hofman. Parlor-maid, whore, saleslady at Oppenheim, Collins—
the real and imagined things she was or that Kitty Hofman chose to
think she was—Madge was only a trifle slower in placing Kitty.
Madge knew a lady when she saw one, and Kitty Hofman was not
it. In the first days of her acquaintance with Kitty she would willingly enough have suspended her judgments if Kitty had been moderately friendly, but since that was not to be the case, Madge
cheerfully collected her private store of evidence that Kitty Hofman
was a phony. She was a phony aristocrat, a synthetic woman, from
her dyed hair to her boyish hips to her no doubt tinted toenails.
Madge, accustomed all her life to the West Philadelphia twang, had
never waited on a lady who pronounced third *thade* and idea *ideer*.
"Get a look at her little titties," Madge would say, when Kitty appeared in an evening dress that had two unjoined panels down the
front. "She looks like she forgot to take her hair out of the curlers,"
said Madge of one of Kitty's coiffures. And, of Kitty's slow gait,
"She walks like she was constipated." The animosity left Madge free
to love Kitty's husband without the restraint that loyalty to a friend
might have invoked. As for disloyalty to Pat Collins, he was aware
of none, and did he not all but love Whit too?

Thus it was that behind the friendly relationship of Pat Collins
and Whit Hofman a more intense, unfriendly relationship flourished between Madge Collins and Kitty Hofman. The extremes of
feeling were not unlike an individual's range of capacity for love and
hate, or, as Madge put it, "I hate her as much as you like him, and
that's going some." Madge Collins, of course, with equal accuracy
could have said: "I hate her as much as I love him, and *that's* going
some." The two men arrived at a pact of silence where their wives
were concerned, a working protocol that was slightly more to Whit's
advantage, since in avoiding mention of Madge he was guarding
against a slip that would incriminate Madge. He wanted no such slip
to occur; he needed Pat's friendship, and he neither needed nor
wanted Madge's love. Indeed, as time passed and the pact of silence
grew stronger, Whit Hofman's feeling for Madge was sterilized. By

the end of 1925 he would not have offered to take her out to his parked car, and when circumstances had them briefly alone together they either did not speak at all or their conversation was so commonplace that a suspicious eavesdropper would have convicted them of adultery on the theory that two such vital persons could not be so indifferent to each other's physical presence. One evening at a picnic-swimming party at someone's farm—this, in the summer of '26—Madge had had enough of the cold water in the dam and was on her way to the tent that was being used as the ladies' dressing-room. In the darkness she collided with a man on his way from the men's tent. "Who is it? I'm sorry," she said.

"Whit Hofman. Who is this?"

"Madge."

"Hello. You giving up?"

"That water's too cold for me."

"Did Pat get back?"

"From Philly? No. He's spending the night. It's funny talking and I can't really see you. Where are you?"

"I'm right here."

She reached out a hand and touched him. "I'm not going to throw myself at you, but here we are."

"Don't start anything, Madge."

"I said I wasn't going to throw myself at you. You have to make the next move. But you're human."

"I'm human, but you picked a lousy place, and time."

"Is that all that's stopping you? I'll go home now and wait for you, if you say the word. Why don't you like me?"

"I do like you."

"Prove it. I'm all alone, the children are with Pat's mother. I have my car, and I'll leave now if you say."

"No. You know all the reasons."

"Sure I do. Sure I do."

"Can you get back to the tent all right? You can see where it is, can't you? Where the kerosene lamp is, on the pole."

"I can see it all right."

"Then you'd better go, Madge, because my good resolutions are weakening."

"Are they? Let me feel. Why, you are human!"

"Cut it out," he said, and walked away from her toward the lights and people at the dam.

She changed into her dress and rejoined the throng at the dam. It was a good-sized party, somewhat disorganized among smaller groups of swimmers, drinkers, eaters of corn on the cob, and a mixed quartet accompanied by a young man on banjo-uke. Heavy clouds hid the moon, and the only light came from a couple of small bonfires. When Madge returned to the party she moved from one group to another, eventually staying longest with the singers and the banjo-uke player. "Larry, do you know 'Ukulele Lady'?"

"Sure," he said. He began playing it, and Madge sang a solo of two choruses. Her thin true voice was just right for the sad, inconclusive little song, and when she finished singing she stood shyly smiling in the momentary total silence. But then there was a spontaneous, delayed burst of applause, and she sat down. The darkness, the fires, the previously disorganized character of the party, and Madge's voice and the words—"maybe she'll find somebody else/ bye and bye"—all contributed to a minor triumph and, quite accidentally, brought the party together in a sentimental climax. "More! More! . . . I didn't know you were a singer . . . Encore! Encore!" But Madge's instinct made her refuse to sing again.

For a minute or two the party was rather quiet, and Kitty had a whispered conversation with the ukulele player. He strummed a few introductory chords until the members of the party gave him their attention, whereupon he began to play "Yaaka hula hickey dula," and Kitty Hofman, in her bare feet and a Paisley print dress, went into the dance. It was a slow hula, done without words and with only the movements of her hips and the ritualistic language of her fingers and arms—only vaguely understood in this group—in synchronous motion with the music. The spectators put on the knowing smiles of the semi-sophisticated as Kitty moved her hips, but before the dance and the tune were halfway finished they stopped their nervous laughter and were caught by the performance. It hardly mattered that they could not understand the language of the physical gestures or that the women as much as the men were being seduced by the dance. The women could understand the movements because the movements were formal and native to themselves, but the element of seductiveness was as real for them as for the men because the men's responsiveness—taking the form of absolute quiet—was like a held breath, and throughout the group men and women felt the need to touch each other by the hand, hands reaching for the nearest hand. And apart from the physical spell produced by the circumstances and the dance, there was the comprehension by the women and by some of the men that the dance was a direct reply to Madge's small bid for popularity. As such the dance was an obliterating victory for Kitty. Madge's plaintive solo was completely forgotten. As the dance ended Kitty put her hands to her lips, kissed them and extended them to the audience as in a benediction, bowed low, and returned to the picnic bench that now became a throne. The applause was a mixture of hand clapping, of women's voices calling out "Lovely! Adorable!" and men shouting "Yowie! Some more, some more!" But Kitty, equally as well as Madge, knew when to quit. "I learned it when Whit and I were in Hawaii. Where else?" she said.

Madge Collins went to Kitty to congratulate her. "That was swell, Kitty."

"Oh, thanks. Did you think so? Of course *I* can't *sing,*" said Kitty.

"You—don't—have—to—when—you—can—shake—that—thing," said Bobby Hermann, whose hesitant enunciation became slower when he drank. "You—got—any—more—hidden—talents—like—that—one—up—your—sleeve?"

"Not up her sleeve," said Madge, and walked away.

"Hey—that's—a—good—one. Not—up—her—sleeve. Not—up—your—sleeve—eh—Kitty?"

In the continuing murmur of admiration for the dance no one—

no one but Madge Collins—noticed that Whit Hofman had not added his compliments to those of the multitude. In that respect Kitty's victory was doubled, for Madge now knew that Kitty had intended the exhibition as a private gesture of contempt for Whit as well as a less subtle chastening of Madge herself. Madge sat on a circular grass-mat cushion beside Whit.

"She's a real expert," said Madge. "I didn't know she could do the hula."

"Uh-huh. Learned it in Honolulu."

"On the beach at Waikiki."

"On the beach at Waikiki," said Whit.

"Well, she didn't forget it," said Madge. "Is it hard to learn?"

"Pretty hard, I guess. It's something like the deaf-and-dumb language. One thing means the moon, another thing means home, another means lonesome, and so forth and so on."

"Maybe I could get her to teach me how to say what *I* want to say."

"What's that?" said Whit.

"Madge is going home, lonesome, and wishes Whit would be there."

"When are you leaving?"

"Just about now."

"Say in an hour or so? You're all alone?"

"Yes. What will you tell *her?*"

"Whatever I tell her, she'll guess where I am. She's a bitch, but she's not a fool."

"She's a bitch, all right. But maybe you're a fool," said Madge. "No, Whit. Not tonight. Any other time, but not tonight."

"Whatever you say, but you have nothing to fear from her. You or Pat. Take my word for it, you haven't. She's watching us now, and she knows we're talking about her. All right, I'll tell you what's behind this exhibition tonight."

"You don't have to."

"Well I hope you don't think I'd let you risk it if I weren't positive about her."

"I did wonder, but I'm so crazy about you."

"When we were in Honolulu that time, I caught her with another guy. I'd been out playing golf, and I came back to the hotel in time to see this guy leaving our room. She didn't deny it, and I guessed right away who it was. A naval officer. I hadn't got a good look at him, but I let her think I had and she admitted it. The question was, what was I going to do about it? Did I want to divorce her, and ruin the naval officer's career? Did I want to come back here without her? That was where she knew she had me. I *didn't* want to come back here without her. This is my town, you know. We've been here ever since there was a town, and it's the only place I ever want to live. I've told you that." He paused. "Well, you don't know her, the hold she had on me, and I don't fully understand it myself. There are a lot of damn nice girls in town I might have married, and you'd think that feeling that way about the town, I'd marry a Gibbsville girl. But how was I ever to know that I was marrying the girl and not her mother, and in some cases her father? And that the girl wasn't marrying me but my father's money and my uncle's money? Kitty didn't know any of that when I asked her to marry me. She'd never heard of Gibbsville. In fact she wasn't very sure where Pennsylvania was. And I was a guy just out of the army, liked a good time, and presumably enjoying myself before I seriously began looking for a job. The first time Kitty really knew I didn't have to work for a living was when I gave her her engagement ring. I remember what she said. She looked at it and then looked at me and said, 'Is there more where this came from?' So give her her due. She didn't marry me for my money, and that was somewhat of a novelty. Are you listening?"

"Sure," said Madge.

"That afternoon in the hotel she said, 'Look, you can kick me out and pay me off, but I tried to have a child for you, which I didn't want, and this is the first time I've gone to bed with another man, since we've been married.' It was a good argument, but of course the real point was that I didn't want to go home without a wife, and have everybody guessing why. I allowed myself the great pleasure of giving her a slap in the face, and she said she guessed she had it coming to her, and then I was so God damned ashamed of myself—I'd never hit a woman before—that *I* ended up apologizing to *her*. Oh, I told her we were taking the next boat out of Honolulu, and if she was ever unfaithful to me again I'd make it very tough for her. But the fact of the matter is, her only punishment was a slap in the face, and that was with my open hand. We went to various places—Australia, Japan, the Philippines, China—and I got her pregnant."

"Yes. But what was behind this hula tonight?"

"I'd forgotten she knew how to do it. The whole subject of Honolulu, and ukuleles, hulas—we've never mentioned any of it, neither of us. But when she stood up there tonight, partly it was to do something better than you—"

"And she did."

"Well, she tried. And partly it was to insult me in a way that only I would understand. Things have been going very badly between us, we hardly ever speak a civil word when we're alone. She's convinced herself that you and I are having an affair—"

"Well, let's."

"Yes, let's. But I wish we could do it without—well, what the hell? Pat's supposed to be able to take care of himself."

"I have a few scores to settle there, too."

"Not since I've known him."

"Maybe not, but there were enough before you knew him. I used to be sick with jealousy, Monday to Friday, Monday to Friday, knowing he was probably screwing some chippy in Allentown or Wilkes-Barre. I was still jealous, even after we moved here. But not after I met you. From then on I didn't care what he did, who he screwed. Whenever I thought of him with another woman I'd think of me with you. But why isn't Kitty going to make any trouble? What have you got on her, besides the navy officer?"

"This is going to sound very cold-blooded."

"All right."

"And it's possible I could be wrong."

"Yes, but go on."

"Well—Kitty's gotten used to being Mrs. W. S. Hofman. She

likes everything about it but me—and the baby. It's got her, Madge, and she can never have it anywhere else, or with anybody else."

"I could have told you that the first time I ever laid eyes on her."

"I had to find it out for myself."

There is one law for the rich, and another law for the richer. The frequent appearances of Whit Hofman with Madge Collins were treated not so much as a scandal as the exercise of a privilege of a man who was uniquely entitled to such privileges. To mollify their sense of good order the country club set could tell themselves that Whit was with Pat as often as he was with Madge, and that the three were often together as a congenial trio. The more kindly disposed made the excuse that Whit was putting up with a great deal from Kitty, and since Pat Collins obviously did not object to Whit's hours alone with Madge, what right had anyone else to complain? The excuse made by the less kindly was that if there was anything *wrong* in the Whit-Madge friendship, Kitty Hofman would be the first to kick up a fuss; therefore there was nothing scandalous in the relationship.

The thing most wrong in the relationship was the destructive effect on Madge Collins, who had been brought up in a strict Catholic atmosphere, who in nearly thirty years had had sexual intercourse with one man, and who now was having intercourse with two, often with both in the same day. The early excitement of a sexual feast continued through three or four months and a couple of narrow escapes; but the necessary lies to Pat and the secondary status of the man she preferred became inconvenient, then annoying, then irritating. She withheld nothing from Whit, she gave only what was necessary to Pat, but when she was in the company of both men—playing golf, at a movie, at a football game—she indulged in a nervous masquerade as the contented wife and the sympathetic friend, experiencing relief only when she could be alone with one of the men. Or with neither. The shame she suffered with her Catholic conscience was no greater than the shame of another sort: to be with both men and sit in self-enforced silence while the man she loved was so easily, coolly making a fool of the man to whom she was married. The amiable, totally unsuspecting fool would have had her sympathy in different circumstances, and she would have hated the character of the lover; but Pat's complacency was more hateful to her than Whit's arrogance. The complacency, she knew, was real; and Whit's arrogance vanished in the humility of his passion as soon as she would let him make love to her. There was proficiency of a selfish kind in Pat's lovemaking; he had never been so gentle or grateful as Whit. From what she could learn of Kitty Hofman it would have been neatly suitable if Pat had become Kitty's lover, but two such similar persons were never attracted to each other. They had, emotionally, everything in common; none of the essential friction of personality. Neither was equipped with the fear of losing the other.

It was this fear that helped produce the circumstances leading to the end of Madge's affair with Whit Hofman. "Every time I see you I love you again, even though I've been loving you all along," she told Whit. Only when she was alone with him—riding in his car, playing golf, sitting with him while waiting for Pat to join them, sitting with him after Pat had left them—could she forget the increasingly insistent irritations of her position. Publicly she was, as Whit told her, "carrying it off very well," but the nagging of her Catholic conscience and the rigidity of her middle-class training were with her more than she was with Whit, and when the stimulation of the early excitement had passed, she was left with that conscience, that training, and this new fear.

The affair, in terms of hours in a bed together, was a haphazard one, too dependent on Pat's unpredictable and impulsive absences. Sometimes he would telephone her from the garage late in the afternoon, and tell her he was driving to Philadelphia and would not be home until past midnight. On such occasions, if she could not get word to Whit at his office or at one of the two clubs, the free evening would be wasted. Other times they would make love on country roads, and three times they had gone to hotels in Philadelphia. It seldom happened that Whit, in a moment of urgently wanting to be with her, could be with her within the hour, and it was on just such occasions, when she was taking a foolish chance, that they had their two narrow escapes in her own house. "You can never get away when I want you to," said Whit—which was a truth and a lie.

"Be reasonable," she said, and knew that the first excitement had progressed to complaint. Any time, anywhere, anything had been exciting in the beginning; now it was a bed in a hotel and a whole night together, with a good leisurely breakfast, that he wanted. They were in a second phase, or he was; and for her, fear had begun. It told on her disposition, so that she was sometimes snappish when alone with Whit. Now it was her turn to say they could not be together when she wanted him, and again it was a truth and a lie of exaggeration. They began to have quarrels, and to Whit this was not only an annoyance but a sign that they were getting in much deeper than he intended. For he had not deceived her as to the depth or permanence of their relationship. It was true that he had permitted her to deceive herself, but she was no child. She had had to supply her own declarations of the love she wanted him to feel; they had not been forthcoming from him, and when there were opportunities that almost demanded a declaration of his love, he was silent or noncommittal. The nature of their affair—intimacy accompanied by intrigue—was such as to require extra opportunities for candor. They were closer than if they had been free and innocent, but Whit would not use their intimacy even to make casual pretense of love. "I can't even wring it out of you," she said.

"What?"

"That you love me. You never say it."

"You can't expect to *wring* it out of anyone."

"A woman wants to hear it, once in a while."

"Well, don't try to wring it out of me."

He knew—and she knew almost as soon as he—that his refusal to put their affair on a higher, romantic love plane was quite likely to force her to put an end to the affair. And now that she was becoming demanding and disagreeable, he could deliberately provoke her into final action or let his stubbornness get the same result. It could not be said that she bored him; she was too exciting for that. But the very fact that she could be exciting added to his annoyance and irritation. He began to dislike that hold she had on him, and the day arrived when he recognized in himself the same basic weakness for Madge that he had had for Kitty. And to a lesser degree the same thing had been true of all the women he had ever known. But pursuing that thought, he recalled that Madge was the only one who had ever charged him with the inability to love. Now he had the provocation that would end the affair, and he had it more or less in the words of her accusation.

"You still won't say it," she said to him one night.

"That I love you?"

"That you love me."

"No, I won't say it, and you ought to know why."

"That's plain as day. You won't say it because you don't."

"Not *don't. Can't,*" he said. "You told me yourself, a long time ago. That people love me and I can't love them. I'm beginning to think that's true."

"It's true all right. I was hoping I could get you to change, but you didn't."

"I used to know a guy that could take a car apart and put it together again, but he couldn't drive. He never could learn to drive."

"What's that got to do with us?"

"Don't you see? Think a minute."

"I get it."

"So when you ask me to love you, you're asking the impossible. I'm just made that way, that's all."

"This sounds like a farewell speech. You got me to go to a hotel with you, have one last thing together, and then announce that we're through. Is that it?"

"No, not as long as you don't expect something you never expected in the first place."

"That's good, that is. You'll let me go on taking all the risks, but don't ask anything in return. I guess I don't love you *that* much, Mr. Hofman." She got out of bed.

"What are you going to do?"

"I'm getting out of this dump, I promise you that. I'm going home."

"I'm sorry, Madge."

"Whit, you're not even sorry for yourself. But I can make up for it. I'm sorry for you. Do you know what I'm going to do?"

"What?"

"I'm going home and tell Pat the whole story. If he wants to kick me out, all he has to do is say so."

"Why the hell do you want to do that?"

"You wouldn't understand it."

"Is it some Catholic thing?"

"Yes! I'm surprised you guessed it. I don't have to tell him. That's not it. But I'll confess it to him instead of a priest, and whatever he wants me to do, I'll do it. Penance."

"No, I don't understand it."

"No, I guess you don't."

"You're going to take a chance of wrecking your home, your marriage?"

"I'm not very brave. I don't think it is much of a chance, but if he kicks me out, I can go back to Oppenheim, Collins. I have a charge account there now." She laughed.

"Don't do it, Madge. Don't go."

"Whit, I've been watching you and waiting for something like this to happen. I didn't know what I was going to do, but when the time came I knew right away."

"Then you really loved Pat all along, not me."

"Nope. God help me, I love you and that's the one thing I won't tell Pat. There I'll have to lie."

It was assumed, when Pat Collins began neglecting his business and spending so much time in Dick Boylan's speakeasy, that Whit Hofman would come to his rescue. But whether or not Whit had offered to help Pat Collins, nobody could long go on helping a man who refused to help himself. He lost his two salesmen and his book-keeper, and his Chrysler franchise was taken over by Walt Michaels, who rehired Joe Ricci at decent wages. For a while Pat Collins had a fifty-dollar-a-week drawing account as a salesman at the Cadillac dealer's, but that stopped when people stopped buying Cadillacs, and Pat's next job, in charge of the hat department in a haberdashery, lasted only as long as the haberdashery. As a Cadillac salesman and head of the hat department Pat Collins paid less attention to business than to pill pool, playing a game called Harrigan from one o'clock in the afternoon till suppertime, but during those hours he was at least staying out of the speakeasy. At suppertime he would have a Western sandwich at the Greek's, then go to Dick Boylan's, a quiet back room on the second story of a business building, patronized by doctors and lawyers and merchants in the neighborhood and by recent Yale and Princeton graduates and near-graduates. It was all he saw, in those days, of his friends from the country club crowd.

Dick Boylan's speakeasy was unique in that it was the only place of its kind that sold nothing but hard liquor. When a man wanted a sandwich and beer, he had to send out for it; if he wanted beer without a sandwich, Boylan told him to go some place else for it; but such requests were made only by strangers and by them not more than once. Dick Boylan was the proprietor, and in no sense the bartender; there were tables and chairs, but no bar in his place, and Boylan wore a suit of clothes and a fedora hat at all times, and always seemed to be on the go. He would put a bottle on the table, and when the drinkers had taken what they wanted he would hold up the bottle and estimate the number of drinks that had been poured from it and announce how much was owed him. "This here table owes me eight and a half," he would say, leaving the bookkeeping to the customers. "Or I'll have one with you and make it an even nine." Sometimes he would not be around to open up for the morning customers, and they would get the key from under the stairway linoleum, unlock the door, help themselves, and leave the money where Dick would find it. They could also leave chits when they were short of cash. If a man cheated on his chits, or owed too much money, or drank badly, he was not told so in so many words; he would knock on the door, the peephole was opened, and Boylan would say,

"We're closed," and the statement was intended and taken to mean that the man was forever barred, with no further discussion of the matter.

Pat Collins was at Dick Boylan's every night after Madge made her true confession. Until then he had visited the place infrequently, and then, as a rule, in the company of Whit Hofman. The shabby austerity of Dick Boylan's and Boylan's high-handed crudities did not detract from the stern respectability of the place. No woman was allowed to set foot in Boylan's, and among the brotherhood of hard drinkers it was believed—erroneously—that all conversations at Boylan's were privileged, not to be repeated outside. "What's said in here is Masonic," Boylan claimed. "I find a man blabbing what he hears—he's out." Boylan had been known to bar a customer for merely mentioning the names of fellow drinkers. "I run a san'tuary for men that need their booze," said Boylan. "If they was in that Gibbsville Club every time they needed a steam, the whole town'd know it." It was a profitable sanctuary, with almost no overhead and, because of the influence of the clientele, a minimum of police graft. Pat Collins's visits with Whit Hofman had occurred on occasions when one or the other had a hangover, and Boylan's was a quick walk from Pat's garage. At night Whit Hofman preferred to do his drinking in more elegant surroundings, and Pat Collins told himself that he was sure he would not run into Whit at Boylan's. But he lied to himself; he *wanted* to run into Whit.

At first he wanted a fight, even though he knew he would be the loser. He would be giving twenty pounds to a man who appeared soft but was in deceptively good shape, who managed to get in some physical exercise nearly every day of his life and whose eight years of prep school and college football, three years of army service, and a lifetime of good food and medical care had given him resources that would be valuable in a real fight. Pat Collins knew he did not have a quick punch that would keep Whit down; Whit Hofman was not Walt Michaels. Whit Hofman, in fact, was Whit Hofman, with more on his side than his physical strength. Although he had never seen Whit in a fight, Pat had gone with him to many football games and observed Whit's keen and knowing interest in the niceties of line play. ("Watch that son of a bitch, the right guard for Lehigh. He's spilling two men on every play.") And Whit Hofman's way of telling about a battle during one of his rare reminiscences of the War ("They were awful damn close, but I didn't lob the God damn pineapple. I *threw* it. The hell with what they taught us back in Hancock.") was evidence that he would play for keeps, and enjoy the playing. Pat admitted that if he had really wanted a fight with Whit Hofman, he could have it for the asking. Then what *did* he want? The question had a ready answer: he wanted the impossible, to confide his perplexed anger in the one man on earth who would least like to hear it. He refused to solidify his wish into words, but he tormented himself with the hope that he could be back on the same old terms of companionship with the man who was responsible for his misery. Every night he went to Dick Boylan's, and waited with a bottle on the table.

Dick Boylan was accustomed to the company of hard drinkers, and when a man suddenly became a nightly, hours-long customer, Boylan was not surprised. He had seen the same thing happen too often for his curiosity to be aroused, and sooner or later he would be given a hint of the reason for the customer's problem. At first he dismissed the notion that in Pat Collins's case the problem was money; Collins was selling cars as fast as he could get delivery. The problem, therefore, was probably a woman, and since Collins was a nightly visitor, the woman was at home—his wife. It all came down to one of two things: money, or a woman. It never occurred to Dick Boylan—or, for that matter, to Pat Collins—that Pat's problem was the loss of a friend. Consequently Dick Boylan looked for, and found, all the evidence he needed to support his theory that Collins was having wife troubles. For example, men who were having money troubles would get phone calls from their wives, telling them to get home for supper. But the men who were having wife trouble, although they sometimes got calls from women, seldom got calls from their wives. Pat Collins's wife never called him. Never. And he never called her.

It was confusing to Dick Boylan to hear that Pat Collins's business was on the rocks. Whit Hofman did not let his friends' businesses go on the rocks. And then Boylan understood it all. A long forgotten, overheard remark about Whit Hofman and Madge Collins came back to him, and it was all as plain as day. Thereafter he watched Pat Collins more carefully; the amount he drank, the cordiality of his relations with the country clubbers, the neatness of his appearance, and the state of his mind and legs when at last he would say goodnight. He had nothing against Pat Collins, but he did not like him. Dick Boylan was more comfortable with non-Irishmen; they were neither Irish-to-Irish over-friendly, nor Irish-to-Irish condescending, and when Pat Collins turned out to be so preoccupied with his problems that he failed to be over-friendly or condescending, Dick Boylan put him down for an unsociable fellow, hardly an Irishman at all, but certainly not one of the others. Pat Collins did not fit in anywhere, although he got on well enough with the rest of the customers. Indeed, the brotherhood of hard drinkers were more inclined to welcome his company than Collins was to seek theirs. Two or three men coming in together would go to Pat's table instead of starting a table of their own and inviting him to join them. It was a distinction that Dick Boylan noticed without comprehending it, possibly because as an Irishman he was immune to what the non-Irish called Irish charm.

But it was not Irish charm that made Pat Collins welcome in the brotherhood; it was their sense of kinship with a man who was slipping faster than they were slipping, and who in a manner of speaking was taking someone else's turn in the downward line, thus postponing by months or years the next man's ultimate, inevitable arrival at the bottom. They welcomed this volunteer, and they hoped he would be with them a long while. They were an odd lot, with little in common except an inability to stand success or the lack of it. There were the medical men, Brady and Williams; Brady, who one day in his early forties stopped in the middle of an operation and had to let his assistant take over, and never performed surgery again; Williams, who at thirty-two was already a better doctor than

his father, but who was oppressed by his father's reputation. Lawyer
Parsons, whose wife had made him run for Congress because her
father had been a congressman, and who had then fallen hopelessly
in love with the wife of a congressman from Montana. Lawyer
Strickland, much in demand as a high school commencement
speaker, but somewhat shaky on the Rules of Evidence. Jeweler
Linklighter, chess player without a worthy opponent since the death
of the local rabbi. Hardware Merchant Stump, Eastern Pennsylvania trapshooting champion until an overload exploded and
blinded one eye. Teddy Stokes, Princeton '25, gymnast, Triangle
Club heroine and solo dancer, whose father was paying blackmail to
the father of an altar boy. Sterling Agnew, Yale ex-'22, Sheff, a re-
mittance man from New York whose father owned coal lands, and
who was a part-time lover of Kitty Hofman's. George W. Shuttleworth, Yale '91, well-to-do widower and gentleman author, currently at work on a biography of Nathaniel Hawthorne which was
begun in 1892. Percy Keene, music teacher specializing in band in-
struments, and husband of a Christian Science practitioner. Lewis
M. Rutledge, former captain of the Amherst golf team and assistant
manager of the local branch of a New York brokerage house, who
had passed on to Agnew the information that Kitty Hofman was
accommodating if you caught her at the right moment. Miles Lassiter, ex-cavalry officer, ex-lieutenant of the State Constabulary,
partner in the Schneider & Lassiter Detective & Protective Company, industrial patrolmen, payroll guards, private investigators,
who was on his word of honor never again to bring a loaded revolver into Boylan's. Any and at some times all these gentlemen
were to be found at Boylan's on any given night, and they constituted a clientele that Dick Boylan regarded as his regulars, quite
apart from the daytime regulars who came in for a quick steam,
drank it, paid, and quickly departed. Half a dozen of the real regulars were also daytime regulars, but Boylan said—over and over
again—that in the daytime he ran a first-aid station; the sanctuary
did not open till suppertime. (The sanctuary designation originated
with George Shuttleworth; the first-aid station, with Dr. Calvin K.

Brady, a Presbyterian and therefore excluded from Boylan's generalities regarding the Irish.)

For nearly three years these men sustained Pat Collins in his need for companionship, increasingly so as he came to know their problems. And know them he did, for in the stunned silence that followed Madge's true confession he took on the manner of the reliable listener, and little by little, bottle by bottle, the members of the brotherhood imparted their stories even as Whit Hofman had done on the afternoon of the first meeting of Whit and Pat. In exchange the members of the brotherhood helped Pat Collins with their tacit sympathy, that avoided mention of the latest indication of cumulative disaster. With a hesitant delicacy they would wait until he chose, if he chose, to speak of the loss of his business, the loss of his jobs, the changes of home address away from the western part of town to the northeastern, where the air was always a bit polluted from the steel mill, the gas house, the abattoir, and where there was always some noise, of which the worst was the squealing of hogs in the slaughterhouse.

"I hope you won't mind if I say this, Pat," said George Shuttleworth one night. "But it seems to me you take adversity very calmly, considering the first thing I ever heard about you."

"What was that, George?"

"I believe you administered a sound thrashing to Mr. Herb Michaels, shortly after you moved to town."

"Oh, that. Yes. Well, I'm laughing on the other side of my face now. I shouldn't have done that."

"But you're glad you did. I hope. Think of how you'd feel now if you hadn't. True, he owns the business you built up, but at least you have the memory of seeing him on the ground. And a cigar in his mouth, wasn't it? I always enjoyed that touch. I believe Nathaniel would have enjoyed it."

"Who?"

"Nathaniel Hawthorne. Most generally regarded as a gloomy writer, but where you find irony you'll find a sense of humor. I couldn't interest you in reading Hawthorne, could I?"

"Didn't he write *The Scarlet Letter?*"

"Indeed he did, indeed so."

"I think I read that in college."

"Oh, I hadn't realized you were a college man. Where?"

"Villanova."

"Oh, yes."

"It's a Catholic college near Philly."

"Yes, it must be on the Main Line."

"It is."

"Did you study for the priesthood?"

"No, just the regular college course. I flunked out sophomore year."

"How interesting that a Catholic college should include *The Scarlet Letter.* Did you have a good teacher? I wonder what his name was."

"Brother Callistus, I think. Maybe it was Brother Adrian."

"I must look them up. I thought I knew all the Hawthorne authorities. Callistus, and Adrian. No other names?"

"That's what they went by."

"I'm always on the lookout for new material on Nathaniel. One of these days I've just got to stop revising and pack my book off to a publisher, that's all there is to it. Stand or fall on what I've done—and then I suppose a week after I publish, along will come someone with conclusions that make me seem fearfully out of date. It's a terrifying decision for me to make after nearly thirty years. I don't see how I can face it."

"Why don't you call this Volume One?"

"Extraordinary. I thought of that very thing. In fact, in 1912 I made a new start with just that in mind, but after three years I went back to my earlier plan, a single volume. But perhaps I could publish in the next year or two, and later on bring out new editions, say every five years. Possibly ten. I'd hoped to be ready for the Hawthorne Centenary in 1904, but I got hopelessly bogged down in the allegories and I didn't dare rush into print with what I had then. It wouldn't have been fair to me or to Nathaniel, although I suppose it'd make precious little difference to him."

"You never know."

"That's just it, Pat. He's very real to me, you know, although he passed away on May eighteenth or nineteenth in 'sixty-four. There's some question as to whether it was the eighteenth or the nineteenth. But he's very real to me. Very."

This gentle fanatic, quietly drinking himself into a stupor three nights a week, driven home in a taxi with a standing order, and reappearing punctually at eight-thirty after a night's absence, became Pat Collins's favorite companion among the brotherhood. George was in his early fifties, childless, with a full head of snowy white hair brushed down tight on one side. As he spoke he moved his hand slowly across his thatch, as though still training it. Whatever he said seemed to be in answer to a question, a studied reply on which he would be marked as in an examination, and he consequently presented the manner, looking straight ahead and far away, of a conscientious student who was sure of his facts but anxious to present them with care. To Pat Collins the mystery was how had George Shuttleworth come to discover whiskey, until well along in their friendship he learned that George had begun drinking at Yale and had never stopped. Alcohol had killed his wife in her middle forties—she was the same age as George—and Boylan's brotherhood had taken the place of the drinking bouts George had previously indulged in with her. "The Gibbsville Club is no place for me in the evening," said George. "Games, games, games. If it isn't bridge in the card room, it's pool in the billiard room. Why do men feel they have to be so strenuous—and I include bridge. The veins stand out in their foreheads, and when they finish a hand there's always one of them to heave a great sigh of relief. That's what I mean by strenuous. And the worst of it is that with two or possibly three exceptions, I used to beat them all consistently, and I never had any veins stand out in *my* forehead."

As the unlikely friendship flourished, the older man, by the strength of his passivity, subtly influenced and then dominated Pat Collins's own behavior. George Shuttleworth never tried to advise or instruct his younger friend or anyone else; but he had made a life for himself that seemed attractive to the confused, disillusioned younger man. Ambition, aggressiveness seemed worthless to Pat Collins. They had got him nowhere; they had in fact tricked him as his wife and his most admired friend had tricked him, as though Madge and Whit had given him a garage to get him out of the way. He was in no condition for violent action, and George Shuttleworth, the least violent of men, became his guide in this latter-day acceptance of defeat. In spite of the friendship, George Shuttleworth remained on an impersonal basis with Pat Collins; they never discussed Madge at all, never mentioned her name, and as a consequence Pat's meetings with his friend did not become an opportunity for self-pity.

The time then came—no day, no night, no month, no dramatic moment but only a time—when George Shuttleworth had taken Whit's place in Pat Collins's need of a man to admire. And soon thereafter another time came when Pat Collins was healed, no longer harassed by the wish or the fear that he would encounter Whit. It was a small town, but the routines of lives in small towns can be restrictive. A woman can say, "I haven't been downtown since last month," although downtown may be no more than four or five blocks away. And there were dozens of men and women who had been born in the town, Pat's early acquaintances in the town, who never in their lives had seen the street in the northeastern section where Pat and Madge now lived. ("Broad Street? I never knew we had a Broad Street in Gibbsville.") There were men and women from Broad Street liberated by the cheap automobile, who would take a ride out Lantenengo Street on a Sunday afternoon, stare at the houses of the rich, but who could not say with certainty that one house belonged to a brewer and another to a coal operator. Who has to know the town as a whole? A physician. The driver of a meat-market delivery truck. A police officer. The fire chief. A newspaper reporter. A taxi driver. A town large enough to be called a town is a complex of neighborhoods, invariably within well-defined limits of economic character; and the men of the neighborhoods, freer to move outside, create or follow the boundaries of their working activities—and return to their neighborhoods for the nights of delight and anguish with their own. Nothing strange, then, but only abrupt, when Pat Collins ceased to see Whit Hofman; and nothing remarkable, either, that three years could be added to the life of Pat Collins, hiding all afternoon in a poolroom, clinging night after night to a glass.

"What did you want to tell me this for?" he had said.
"Because I thought it was right," she had said.
"Right, you say?"
"To tell you, yes," she said.
He stood up and pulled off his belt and folded it double.
"Is that what you're gonna do, Pat?"
"Something to show him the next time," he said.
"There'll be no next time. You're the only one'll see what you did to me."
"That's not what I'm doing it for."
"What for, then?"
"It's what you deserve. They used to stone women like you, stone them to death."
"Do that, then. Kill me, but not the strap. Really kill me, but don't do that, Pat. That's ugly. Have the courage to kill me, and I'll die. But don't do that with the strap, please."
"What a faker, what a bluffer you are."
"No," she said. She went to the bureau drawer and took out his revolver and handed it to him. "I made an act of contrition."
"An act of contrition."
"Yes, and there was enough talk, enough gossip. You'll get off," she said.
"Put the gun away," he said.

She dropped the revolver on a chair cushion. "You put it away. Put it in your pocket, Pat. I'll use it on you if you start beating me with the strap."

"Keep your voice down, the children'll hear," he said.

"They'll hear if you beat me."

"You and your act of contrition. Take off your clothes."

"You hit me with that strap and I'll scream."

"Take your clothes off, I said."

She removed her dress and slip, and stood in brassiere and girdle.

"Everything," he said.

She watched his eyes, took off the remaining garments, and folded her arms against her breasts.

He went to her, bent down, and spat on her belly.

"You're dirty," he said. "You're a dirty woman. Somebody spit on you, you dirty woman. The spit's rolling down your belly. No, I won't hit you."

She slowly reached down, picked up the slip and covered herself with it. "Are you through with me?"

He laughed. "Am I through with you? Am *I* through with you."

He left the house and was gone a week before she again heard from him. He stayed in town, but he ate only breakfast at home. "Is this the way it's going to be?" she said. "I have to make up a story for the children."

"You ought to be good at that."

"Just so I know," she said. "Do you want to see their report cards?"

"No."

"It's no use taking it out on them. What you do to me, I don't care, but they're not in this. They think you're cross with them."

"Don't tell me what to do. The children. You down here, with them sleeping upstairs. Don't you tell me what to do."

"All right, I won't," she said. "I'll tell them you're working nights, you can't come home for dinner. They'll see through it, but I have to give them some story."

"You'll make it a good one, of that I'm sure."

In calmer days he had maintained a balance between strict parenthood and good humor toward the children, but now he could not overcome the guilt of loathing their mother that plagued him whenever he saw the question behind their eyes. They were waiting to be told something, and all he could tell them was that it was time for them to be off to school, to be off to Mass, always time for them to go away and take their unanswerable, unphrased questions with them. Their mother told them that he was very busy at the garage, that he had things on his mind, but in a year he had lost them. There was more finality to the loss than would have been so if he had always treated them with indifference, and he hated Madge the more because she could not and he could not absolve him of his guilt.

One night in Boylan's speakeasy George Shuttleworth, out of a momentary silence, said: "What are you going to do now, Pat?"

"Nothing. I have no place to go."

"Oh, you misunderstood me. I'm sorry. I meant now that Overton's has closed."

"That was over a month ago. I don't know, George. I haven't found anything, but I guess something will turn up. I was thinking of going on the road again. I used to be a pretty good hat salesman, wholesale, and when I was with Overton I told the traveling men to let me know if they heard of anything."

"But you don't care anything about hats."

"Well, I don't, but I can't pick and choose. I can't support a family shooting pool."

"Isn't there something in the automobile line? A man ought to work at the job he likes best. We have only the one life, Pat. The one time in this vale of tears."

"Right now the automobile business is a vale of tears. I hear Herb Michaels isn't having it any too easy, and I could only move four new Cadillacs in fourteen months."

"Suppose you had your own garage today. Could you make money, knowing as much as you do?"

"Well, they say prosperity is just around the corner."

"I don't believe it for a minute."

"I don't either, not in the coal regions. A man to make a living in the automobile business today, in this part of the country, he'd be better off without a dealer's franchise. Second-hand cars, and service and repairs. New rubber. Accessories. Batteries. All that. The people that own cars have to get them serviced, but the people that need cars in their jobs, they're not buying new cars. Who is?"

"I don't know. I've never owned a car. Never learned to drive one."

"You ought to. Then when you go looking for material for your book, you'd save a lot of steps."

"Heavens no," said George Shuttleworth. "You're referring to trips to Salem? New England? Why it takes me two or three days of walking before I achieve the proper Nineteenth Century mood. My late lamented owned a car and employed a chauffeur. A huge, lumbering Pierce-Arrow she kept for twelve years. I got rid of it after she died. It had twelve thousand miles on the speedometer, a thousand miles for each year."

"Oh, they were lovely cars. Was it a limousine?"

"Yes, a limousine, although I believe they called it a Berliner. The driver was well protected. Windows on the front doors. I got rid of him, too. I got rid of him *first*. Good pay. Apartment over the garage. Free meals. New livery every second year. And a hundred dollars at Christmas. But my wife's gasoline bills, I happened to compare them with bills for the hospital ambulance when I was on the board. Just curiosity. Well, sir, if those bills were any indication, my wife's car used up more gasoline than the ambulance, although I don't suppose it all found its way into our tank. But she defended him. Said he always kept the car looking so nice. He did, at that. He had precious little else to occupy his time. I believe he's gone back to Belguim. He was the only Belgian in town, and my wife was very sympathetic toward the Belgians."

"Took his savings and—"

"His plunder," said George Shuttleworth. "Let's not waste any more time talking about him, Pat. You know, of course, that I'm quite rich."

"Yes, that wouldn't be hard to guess. That house and all."

"The house, yes, the house. Spotless, not a speck of dust anywhere. It's like a museum. I have a housekeeper, Mrs. Frazier. Scotch. Conscientious to a degree, but she's made a whole career of keeping my house antiseptically clean, like an operating surgery. So much so, that she makes me feel that I'm in the way. So I'm getting out of the way for a while. I'm going away."

"Going down South?"

"No, I'm not going South. I'm going abroad, Pat. I haven't been since before the War, and I'm not really running away from Mrs. Frazier and her feather dusters. I have a serious purpose in taking this trip. It has to do with my book. You knew that Nathaniel spent seven years abroad. Perhaps you didn't. Seven years, from 1853 to 1860."

"You want to see what inspired him," said Pat.

"No, no! Quite the contrary. He'd done all his best work by then. I want to see how it spoiled him, living abroad. There were other distractions. The Civil War. His daughter's illness. But I must find out for myself whether European life spoiled Nathaniel *or* did he flee to Europe when he'd exhausted his talent. That may turn out to be my greatest contribution to the study of Hawthorne. I can see quite clearly how my discoveries might cause me to scrap everything I've done so far and have to start all over again. I've already written to a great many scholars, and they've expressed keen interest."

"Well, I'll be sorry to see you go, George. I'll miss our evenings. When do you leave?"

"In the *Mauretania,* the seventh of next month. Oh, when I decide to act, nothing stops me," said George Shuttleworth. "I want to give you a going-away present, Pat."

"It should be the other way around. You're the one that's leaving."

"If you wish to give me some memento, that's very kind of you.

But what I have in mind, I've been thinking about it for some time. Not an impulse of the moment. How much would it cost to set you up in a business such as you describe?"

"Are you serious, George?"

"Dead serious."

"A small garage, repairing all makes. No dealership. Gas, oil, tires, accessories. There's an old stable near where I live. A neighbor of mine uses it to garage his car in. You want to go on my note, is that it?"

"No, I don't want to go on your note. I'll lend you the money myself, without interest."

"Using mostly second-hand equipment, which I know where to buy here and there, that kind of a setup would run anywhere from five to ten thousand dollars. Atlantic, Gulf, one of those companies put in the pump and help with the tank. Oil. Tools I'd have to buy myself. Air pump. Plumbing would be a big item, and I'd need a pit to work in. Anywhere between five and ten thousand. You can always pick up a light truck cheap and turn it into a tow-car."

George Shuttleworth was smiling. "That's the way I like to hear you talk, Pat. Show some enthusiasm for something. What's your bank?"

"The Citizens, it was. I don't have any at the moment."

"Tomorrow, sometime before three o'clock, I'll deposit ten thousand dollars in your name, and you can begin to draw on it immediately."

"There ought to be some papers drawn up."

"My cheque is all the papers we'll need."

"George?"

"Now, now! No speech, none of that. I spend that much every year, just to have a house with sparkling chandeliers."

"Well then, two words. Thank you."

"You're very welcome."

"George?"

"Yes, Pat."

"I'm sorry, but you'll have to excuse me. I—I can't sit here, George. You see why? Please excuse me."

"You go take a good long walk, Pat. That's what you do."

He walked through the two crowds of men and women leaving the movie houses at the end of the first show. He spoke to no one.

"You're home early," said Madge. "Are you all right?"

"I'm all right."

"You look sort of peak-ed."

"Where are the children?"

"They're out Halloweening. They finished their home work."

"I'm starting a new business."

"You are? What?"

"I'm opening a new garage."

"Where?"

"In the neighborhood."

"Well—that's good, I guess. Takes money, but it'd be a waste of time to ask you where you got it."

"It'd be a waste of time."

"Did you have your supper?"

"I ate something. I'm going to bed. I have to get up early. I have to go around and look for a lot of stuff."

"Can I do anything?"

"No. Just wake me up when the children get up."

"All right. Goodnight."

"Goodnight."

"And good luck, Pat."

"No. No, Madge. Don't, don't—"

"All right. I'm sorry," she said quietly. Then, uncontrolled, "Pat, for God's sake! Please?"

"No, Madge. I ask you."

She covered her face with her hands. "Please, please, please, please, please."

But he went upstairs without her. He could not let her spoil this,

he could not let her spoil George Shuttleworth even by knowing
about him.

"Hello, Pat."
"Hyuh, Whit."
Never more than that, but never less.

From

THE HAT ON THE BED

◆

NINETY MINUTES AWAY

♦

I t was a very cold night in February. More snow was expected, but apparently it was waiting for the temperature to go up a little. In the streets the going was rough; snow piled high in the gutters, ruts in the roadway frozen solid, and the sidewalks were hazardous with patches of ice. Not many people were to be seen on the streets of South Taqua, although it was the night before Washington's Birthday and the mines would be idle the next day. The people who had gone in to Taqua to see a movie were already home. The store window lights were out. The only illumination was from overhead arc-lights at three intersections, and from the Athens, the all-night restaurant. A few cars were parked near the Athens, as near as they could get.

Harvey Hunt paid his check at the Athens, folded his muffler over his chest, turned up his overcoat collar, put on his hat and went out. He took a few steps on the sidewalk, and someone called to him from the doorway of the Athens. "Hey, Harve, you forgot your arctics."

"I'll be back for them later," said Harvey Hunt. "But thanks."

He resumed his walk to the borough hall, a block away, sliding where there was enough ice, walking flatfooted where the ice was patchy. Halfway to borough hall he covered his nose with the muffler; the wind was strong and cold and made breathing difficult.

He entered the borough hall though the side door marked Police. The room he entered was warm, small, and crowded with desks,

269

chairs, filing-cases, fire extinguishers, assorted traffic signs and stanchions, a gun closet, a small telephone switchboard, a couple of rubber tires, an oxygen tank, new and old first-aid kits, clothestrees, several pairs of hip boots. There was only one human being in the room, sitting at the desk near the switchboard. He was a rather handsome man who was getting thick through the middle. He wore a dark blue woollen shirt with sergeant's chevrons and a silver-plated shield. In one hip pocket was a .38 revolver, encased in a pocket holster. In his shirt pockets were three or four fountain pens and pencils. "Shut the door, shut the door," he said.

"Let me get inside first," said Harvey Hunt. "What's doing, Ken?"

"You'll find out soon enough," said the sergeant.

Harvey Hunt took off his overcoat and hat and hung them on a clothestree. "All right, what's doing?"

"Nothing, yet, but there will be," said Ken. "Just keep your shirt on. I wouldn't get you here on a false alarm."

"What kind of a story is it?"

The policeman looked up at the wall clock. "It's a raid."

"A Prohibition raid?"

"I wouldn't get you down here on a Prohibition raid," said Ken.

"I noticed you looking at the clock. Is the raid going on now?"

"Yes. I wouldn't of told you that much if it wasn't."

"Are you afraid I'd have tipped off somebody?"

"Not intentionally. But by accident you could have."

"The raid was supposed to start at eleven o'clock?"

"Five after eleven. Eleven-five," said Ken. "They'll be coming in pretty soon."

"Then tell me what it's all about."

"All right, I guess it's all right now," said Ken. "You know Buddy Spangler's place, out there by the freight yards."

"Sure. I know every saloon in the county. I haven't been to Spangler's much, but I know the place. It's back off the main road."

The cop nodded. "That's where the raid is."

"Who's raiding it? Not just your fellows."

"All our fellows are in it, but the raid was partly our fellows, partly the state cops. The orders came from the county attorney's office. They didn't tell us anything about it till around nine o'clock. They didn't want any leak. There isn't any of our fellows would spill the beans, but the county attorney wanted to make sure."

"Now maybe you're ready to tell me what *kind* of a raid it is."

"It's a dirty show. Spangler imported in some women from Allentown and Bethlehem, and they're putting on a dirty show. Spangler didn't invite any of the local men, or anyway only two or three. He's charging five dollars a head admission. Men from Gibbsville and Reading, Hazleton. Business men. Sports. Somebody tipped off the county attorney, and he notified the state cops. They got here around nine o'clock and told us about it so we wouldn't look bad. McCumber, Jefferson, O'Dwyer, and Snyder. Those are our men. The state cops are some in uniform and some in plain clothes."

"Who will they arrest? Spangler and the women. But those business men, they won't arrest them."

"No, they won't arrest them. But the county attorney, Millner, he's there and he'll recognize them, most of them, anyway."

"How nice for Millner. He's going to run for judge this year."

"You don't have to look at it that way. Millner's doing his job. And he could of left us out in the cold. We get just as much credit as anybody else. Millner's all right."

"Well, this won't do him any harm. Raiding a dirty show, and getting something on all those business men. They'll shell out when he starts running for judge."

"Why shouldn't they? You always take the opposite side. You don't believe any cop is honest. Or politician."

"As far as I know, *you're* honest, Ken."

"I'm pretty honest. And I don't like dirty shows in this town. McCumber don't either. This is a pretty clean town, considering. We got a lot of church people here."

"You don't have to tell me," said Harvey Hunt. "Are they bringing them in here, the prisoners?"

"Bringing them here, then we gotta wake up Squire Palsgrove if he's home asleep. They'll get a hearing, and I guess most likely keep them here overnight. Take them to the county jail tomorrow. It depends on if they get somebody to go their bail tonight."

"Depends on how high the bail is."

"It'll be as high as Squire Palsgrove can make it. That you can be sure of."

"You say the women came from Allentown?"

"Allentown and Bethlehem, according to what I heard. Three of them and their pimp. They're supposed to come from Allentown, but who knows where they come from originally? Allentown is what they say, Allentown and Bethlehem. But they might as well come from New York City."

"Or South Taqua," said Harvey.

"There you go again, always taking the opposite side."

"I was just kidding you, Ken."

"I don't say we don't have some immoral women in South Taqua. That wouldn't be true. You'll come across immoral women everywhere you go, I guess. That's been my experience. But we never had a whorehouse in South Taqua since McCumber was chief of police. McCumber won't tolerate it, and I won't either. The people don't want a whorehouse in this town."

"It would save some of the men a trip to Taqua."

"Taqua and South Taqua are a very different thing. They got three times our population in Taqua. Maybe we get a black eye for having this raid in South Taqua, but it'll be worth it to get rid of Buddy Spangler. He don't care anything about the reputation of this town, or else he wouldn't let them put on a dirty show in his place."

"What kind of a dirty show is it?"

"How should I know what kind? They're all the same, aren't they?"

"Did you ever see one?" said Harvey.

Ken paused. "Yes, I saw one."

"Not here in town, though."

"No, not here in town. Wilkes-Barre, when I was a young fellow.

Before I was a police officer. Some little town outside of Wilkes-Barre. There was things went on you wouldn't believe if you didn't see them with your own eyes. You'd wonder how a woman could stoop so low. I was around nineteen or twenty at the time, and I never forgot it."

"What were *you* doing there?"

"What was I doing? You mean why did I go? Well, in those days I wasn't married, and just like all the young fellows my age I was after all I could get. We all went after as much as we could get. I had a friend of mine had an auto. It was a big old second-hand Chandler. We used to drive around every Sunday afternoon, him and I. Half of those girls never had a ride in an automobile, and all we had to do was open the door and they'd get in. I used to raise a lot of hell in those days."

"And you were a good-looking fellow before you began to put on that weight."

"I sowed my wild oats. But as soon as I got married I settled down. With some fellows it's just the opposite. They get married, and they're no sooner married than they start chasing after other women. I don't believe in that. You marry a woman, you ought to settle down. Unless *she* won't settle down. But that don't often happen . . . Car outside. I guess that's them."

The office door opened and the newcomers streamed in. There were three women, each carrying a small overnight bag and keeping close to each other; there were five men. It was easy to tell which man was Spangler, and which was Millner, the county attorney. Spangler was wearing a suede windbreaker and a hunting cap. He was dissolute-looking and harassed, and except for Millner the other men pushed him around. Millner was very much in charge, better dressed than the others, who were police officers in plain clothes.

"Here they are, Sergeant," said Millner. "Will you call up Squire Palsgrove? I'd like to get them committed as soon as possible."

"Snyder, you call the squire. I want to book these people. Your name?" said Ken.

"You know my name."

"Come on, Spangler. Answer my questions. I don't know your first name."

"Marvin J. Spangler."

"Age?"

"Thirty-seven."

"Occupation?"

"Hotelkeeper."

"You don't have a license to run a hotel."

"Then put down—restaurant proprietor."

"Rest. Prop.," Ken wrote in the book. "Address?"

"You know that. Washington Street."

"You ever been arrested before?"

"Plenty."

"What's the charge, Mr. Millner?" said Ken.

"Chief, do you want to make the charges?" said Millner.

"Conspiring to give an indecent performance," said McCumber. "Disorderly conduct. Resisting arrest. Illegal possession of firearms. Selling intoxicating liquor without a license. Lewd and immoral conduct. Running a bawdyhouse. We got him on about ten counts. Lock him up, Snyder."

Snyder, one of the plainclothes policemen, took Spangler's arm and led him out of the office to a cell.

"All right, young woman," said Ken. "Your name."

"Gloria Swanson."

"Don't get fresh here. I said your name."

"Mary Smith."

"Mary Smith, huh," said Ken. "Age?"

"Twenty," said Mary Smith. The others laughed.

"You must of had a hard life," said Ken. "Occupation?"

"Manicurist," said Mary Smith.

"She really is, too," said one of the other women.

"I didn't ask you," said Ken. "Address?"

"Bellyvue Stratford Hotel, Philadelphia. Bellyvue. Get it?" The men and women laughed.

"Ever been arrested before?" said Ken.

"Never," said Mary Smith, and the women laughed.

"How many times you been arrested before, Mary Smith?" said Ken.

"I don't know. I didn't keep a diary."

"What's the charge, Chief?" said Ken.

"Against all three of these women, indecent performance, indecent exposure, soliciting, illegal possession of narcotics. No, strike that out. We only found narcotics on this one. Jefferson, take her back and put her in Cell Two."

"You're not gonna put me in a cell with that Spangler gorilla," said Mary Smith.

"You'll be with the other women," said McCumber. He nodded to Jefferson, who led her out.

A second woman now stood before Ken. "My name is Jane Doe, age twenty, address Seventh and Hamilton, Allentown, PA. Occupation, artist's model. No previous arrests. And did anybody ever tell you you look like Bryant Washburn, because you do?"

"Seventh and Hamilton?" said Ken. "That's where the monument is."

"I know. I live up there on top of the monument."

"Cut the comedy," said Ken. "Snyder, put her in with the other one, Cell Two."

"Do I get anything to eat here? I'm hungry. If I pay for it myself can I send out for something to eat?" said Jane Doe.

"What do you want?" said Ken.

"Steak tartare with a raw egg on top. Here's a buck, that oughta take care of it. And tea with lemon and sugar."

"We'll see. Go on, beat it," said Ken. "Chief, I understood they had a pimp with them."

"He got away," said McCumber. "We don't know how he got away, but he got away all right. He won't get far, the state police'll pick him up."

"All right, you, young woman," said Ken. "Your name."

"Jean Latour."

"How do you spell that?" said Ken.

"J, e a, n, capital L, a t, o, u, r."

"Age what?"

"Seventeen."

Ken looked at her. "I almost believe you. How old *are* you?"

"I'll be eighteen on my next birthday."

"You're starting early," said Ken.

"Huh. I started before this."

"How many arrests?"

"None. I was never arrested before."

"Where do you live? On top of the monument with that Smith woman?"

"That was Jane, that lived on top of the monument. Mary lives at the Bellyvue. Bellyvue. Funny." She giggled.

"We book this one on the same charges, Chief?" said Ken.

"This one was the worst," said McCumber.

"The best, you mean. I get the most pay," said Jean.

"You'll need it," said Ken. "What occupation?"

"Dancer and actress. And *singer,*" said Jean.

"Put down prostitute for this one," said McCumber.

"All right, put down prostitute. I don't give a damn. Put down whore if you want to."

"The youngest, and the worst," said McCumber.

"Give me a cigarette, somebody," said Jean.

Harvey offered her his pack, as the others remained still. "You don't look like a cop. What are you, a lawyer?"

"I'm a reporter."

"Oh, are you gonna take my picture?"

"No."

"Then give me a good writeup, if you're not gonna take my picture. What paper is it gonna be in?"

"The Taqua *Chronicle.*"

"The what?"

"The Taqua *Chronicle.*"

"I never heard of it," she said. "Is that just local?"

"That's all," said Harvey.

"Oh, *well.* The hell with *that.* I thought maybe you were on some big paper, from Philly. But you're just a hick reporter, like these hick cops." She spat the smoke out of her lungs. "I have a proposition. You're the chief, huh?"

"I'm the chief," said McCumber.

"But he's higher than you," said Jean, pointing the cigarette at Millner. "Who do I have to talk to to get out of this?"

"Save your breath," said Millner.

"I don't want to spend the night with those other girls. I never saw them before tonight. How about if you get me a room in the hotel? I don't care which one of you. I'll give you a good time."

McCumber and Millner were silent, but she did not give up.

"All right. I tell you what I'll do. Get me a room in the hotel, and whatever I make I'll split with you, fifty-fifty."

Millner and McCumber were still silent.

"Then how about this? You can have all I make over ten dollars." The silence continued.

"What's the *matter* with you? Don't you have any manhood? You? Reporter? Will you help me out?"

"I don't have the say," said Harvey.

"Take her back and put her in a cell," said Ken.

The telephone rang, and Ken answered it. "Police headquarters, Sergeant Dunlop. Yeah. Yeah. Oh. All right, Mrs. Palsgrove." He hung up. "That was Mrs. Palsgrove. Squire couldn't get his car started, and she don't want him out in this cold. He won't be here tonight. Now what do we do, Chief?"

"Up to Mr. Millner," said McCumber.

"Nothing we can do. Leave these people here tonight and give them a preliminary hearing in the morning. We can hold the women for a medical examination anyway, that's the law. We'll take all four of them to Gibbsville tomorrow and put them in the county jail."

"You're not gonna put me in any jail," said Jean. "I want a lawyer."

"You can get one tomorrow, but you're still going to jail. You admit you're a prostitute," said Millner.

"You can't prove it. I was never arrested before in my whole life, you dirty son of a bitch," said Jean. "You. Reporter. You put it in the paper that I asked for a lawyer, and they wouldn't let me have one. You didn't arrest any of those johns. Who was that hot-pants funnyman that got up on the stage, that respectable business man? He was as much in the act as anybody. But I don't see *him* here. You let him put his clothes on and get away, but he was as much in it as we were."

"Who was it, Millner?" said Harvey, grinning.

"Never you mind, Hunt," said Millner. "Don't you start poking your nose in where it doesn't belong."

"That's what I do for a living, Millner," said Hunt. "If this broad finds out who the business man was, she could subpoena him when she goes to trial."

"Who's going to help her find out? You?" said Millner.

"Well, I could," said Harvey.

"Yes, I suppose you could," said Millner.

"And you don't want that, do you?" said Harvey. "If this kid gets herself a smart lawyer, somebody like Bob Dockstader, Dockstader could subpoena your business man and maybe he could even subpoena some of the other sports, the ones you didn't arrest."

"Say, Hunt, are you a reporter or what are you?" said Millner. He turned to McCumber. "What about this fellow, Chief? Is he in some kind of a racket?"

"Not that I know of, but he's very contrary," said McCumber.

"He's against everything," said Ken. "If you're *for* something, he'll be against it. He's an againster."

"Oh, one of those," said Millner. "Well, Hunt, what is it you want? Not that I couldn't get you fired in one phone call. Your boss is a man I know better than you do."

"You could get me fired, all right. But if you did, then believe me I'd go right to Bob Dockstader, and the two of us would have a lot of fun with you when you get into court. You just threatened me, Millner, so now I'm not on your side at all. Maybe I was before, but I'm not now."

"I didn't threaten you. I said I *could* get you fired, but I never said I was going to," said Millner.

"Nuts. I know what you're thinking, Millner. You're thinking this kid and Spangler and the others will plead guilty and there won't be any trial. That's the way it always works in these cases. But you respectable lawyers don't think much of Dockstader, and he doesn't like you either. Dockstader would plead them all not guilty just for the fun of it."

"Everybody knows what Dockstader is," said Millner. "These are the kind of people he has for clients. What I want to know is, what do you want? Speak up. You want something."

"Let this kid off," said Hunt.

"Let her off? You're crazy. She was the worst of all four of them," said Millner.

"That's right, there were four. The pimp you let get away. All these South Taqua cops and the state police, but the pimp eluded your grasp. The pimp and your business man were the only ones that got away. Can you imagine Dockstader when he gets you all in court. I can just see it. The courtroom'll be crowded. Probably Number Three Courtroom. And Dockstader starts asking a lot of embarrassing questions. The whole thing will be embarrassing anyway. Millner, you taking charge of the raid personally, and Dockstader will want to know why. Chief, you letting the pimp get away. And all these prominent guys under subpoena."

"What are you trying to do, Hunt?" said Millner.

"I don't know. But I never like it when some politician says he'll get me fired. Oh, I know I'll be out of a job tomorrow, but I've been out of work before."

"Just out of curiosity, why do you want me to go easy on this Latour woman?" said Millner.

"I didn't say I wanted you to go easy on her. I said let her go."

"Why? What's she to you?" said Millner.

"Yeah, I don't understand it myself," said Jean Latour. "I never saw him before I came in here."

"Because she's pretty, and I like pretty dames," said Harvey.

"That's not your reason," said Millner.

"Then you tell me what my reason is. I don't know. She said she was never arrested before, and I believe her. Maybe that's the reason."

"Maybe she was never arrested before, although I doubt that. But if you could have seen her an hour ago you wouldn't worry so much about whether she was arrested or not. Ask any of these police officers. This young woman has absolutely no morals. In all my—"

"That's a speech you can save till you take her to court," said Harvey.

"You didn't even pay your way in, did you, Mister?" said Jean. "What are you squawking about? The johns that were there all paid to get in. And it was private."

"Hunt, even you can see that this young woman has no morals. The only thing that counts with her is money. No guilty feelings, no regrets. Only money."

"You know, Millner, you put your finger on it. I've been trying to dope out why I'm on her side, and you found the reason for me. She has no morals."

"Then what are you defending her for?" said Millner.

"Because I never saw anybody like her before. She isn't like those other dames. She doesn't even look like them. She's a very unusual dame. But if you throw her in the clink, she'll be just like all the others."

"I told you," said Ken to Millner. "He likes to be different. Always different. He comes in here every day and there's hardly a day he don't come out with some new idea. Wants to be different. I think he's a Socialist, into the bargain."

"The hell I am," said Harvey. "But different, yes. Come to think of it, I voted for you, Millner. Because it didn't look like you had a chance."

"Appreciate that, I'm sure," said Millner.

"That's all right. I won't vote for you for judge."

"Hunt, we've had enough talk from you. You're only a reporter, and you wouldn't be here if you didn't work for the *Chronicle.* So shut up. You have your story, so shut up and get out." The speaker was McCumber, the police chief.

"Okay," said Harvey. "But Millner knows where I'm going tomorrow morning, first thing. I know I won't have a job tomorrow, but I'm sure as hell going to call on the Honorable Mr. Dockstader. Then we'll watch the fur fly."

Millner was frowning, deep in thought and trying to make a decision. "Chief," he said to McCumber. "We have Spangler and those two women in there. I'll let them plead guilty and go to prison. But if this fellow and Dockstader get together, there'll be a court trial and a lot of pretty well-known men will have to appear. You know what Dockstader is like when he gets somebody on the stand, and a lot of reputations will be ruined. If this goes to trial there'll be no stopping Dockstader, you know that."

"That shyster lawyer," said McCumber. "He ought to be disbarred."

"And some day maybe he will be. I'd like to help bring that about," said Millner.

"And I'll tell him you said that in front of five police officers, Millner," said Harvey. "I just want to remind you, Millner. Dockstader has never been up on charges before the Bar Association, but you and the chief have been making statements about him, *in front of witnesses,* that he could sue you for. These cops are officers of the law, and they won't all perjure themselves to protect you and McCumber."

Millner realized he had made a mistake. "I'd be glad to take my chances if Dockstader wanted to sue."

"You're bluffing. These are good cops, and they won't lie on the stand to save your neck. Also, Millner, you're from Gibbsville, not South Taqua. Here they don't like Gibbsville people very much. But you were saying something to the chief, and I don't want to interrupt that."

"I'd like to give you a punch in the nose, but I'll deny myself that luxury," said Millner. "Chief, if you have no serious objection, I'm willing to let this Latour woman go. Provided that she leaves here tonight, right away, and this fellow Hunt goes with her."

"Hey, Reporter! You got me off," said Jean Latour. "Do you have a car?"

"Not so fast," said Harvey.

"Now what do you want?" said Millner.

"Two weeks' pay, at thirty-five dollars a week. That's what the paper would give me if they fired me. I've been with them three years."

Millner took a roll of bills from his pants pocket. "Here's your seventy dollars. On your way."

"And don't come back," said McCumber. "You or the woman. Snyder, you go with them and see that they leave town."

"I want to go to the boarding-house and get my other suit."

"See that he packs his suitcase and is out of town in a half an hour," said McCumber. "Go on, get them all out of here." McCumber was displeased with Millner's deal. He hardly looked at Millner.

"You gotta give me more than a half an hour, McCumber," said Hunt. "I have to stop and get my arctics at the Athens, and I don't know how long it'll take me to get my car started."

"Go on, get out. Just get out," said McCumber.

"Well, Miss Latour," said Harvey. "Fate has thrown us together."

"Yeah," she said. "Well, goodbye, boys, no hard feelings."

"Goodbye, you guys," said Harvey.

The cops did not respond, vocally or otherwise.

"Come on, little one," said Harvey.

"One thing," said Jean to the men. "I still never been in jail."

Snyder gave Jean and Harvey a couple of hard nudges, and all three left the room. "Wow, is it always as cold as this?" said Jean.

"I have to stop and get my arctics," said Harvey.

"I oughta brought along a pair of arctics," said Jean. "What kind of a car do you have? I hope it's a closed car."

"It's a Ford coop."

"Does it have a heater in it? Where we going?"

"Where do you want to go?"

"I got a friend of mine I can stay with her, in Allentown."

"Where do *you* live? Where is home base for you?" said Harvey.

"You mean where do I keep my wardrobe?" she said. "I got most of it in my room, in Philly. I got a room in a hotel there. I didn't bring much tonight. You don't need much on this kind of a job."

"No, I guess not." They were outside the Athens. "Here's where I left my arctics. Do you want a cup of coffee? Snyder, how about you? You want a cup of coffee?"

"My orders are to—"

"Aw, come off it, Snyder. Have a cup of coffee with us," said Harvey.

"Listen, you," said Snyder. "Quit stalling around. Get your arctics and then we go to your boarding-house, and you get the hell out of town."

"What are *you* so sore about all of a sudden?" said Harvey.

"This here little tramp ought to be run out of town on a rail, and you're no better. I should of known all along what you were. A lousy pimp."

"I'll be right out," said Harvey. He entered the Athens, put on his arctics, and returned to the sidewalk, where the girl and the policeman were staring at each other.

The cold wind discouraged conversation during the three-block walk to Harvey's boarding-house. "If you're in such a hurry, Snyder, you can see if you can get my car started. The key's in it. Kid, you can sit in the car with him while he warms up the engine."

"She don't sit in any car with me," said Snyder. "She can wait inside with you. And you be out in ten minutes or I'll come and get you."

In about fifteen minutes Jean and Harvey were ready to drive away. "Well, Snyder, South Taqua is safe once more. No more sin in South Taqua."

"Birds of a feather flock together," said Snyder.

"Goodbye, copper. Keep your knees together," said Jean.

"Get outa here, you little bum."

"We're off!" said Harvey. "Off in a cloud of dust."

"Where to?" said the girl.

"Well, we'll try Allentown first. Maybe if the roads aren't too bad we can make Philly tonight."

"Let's try to get to Philly," she said.

It was about thirty-five miles to Allentown and the road was sometimes blown clean by the valley winds, sometimes they had to proceed in low gear through snow and ice. The girl fell asleep ten minutes out of South Taqua and stayed asleep until Harvey found a garage in Allentown that was still open. Drowsy, the girl said she wanted to continue to Philadelphia, and almost immediately fell asleep again.

On North Broad Street, when they were getting closer to City Hall, Harvey shook her knee until she came awake. This time she was fully awake. "Why look where we are. Old Willie Penn. Boy, I'm glad I'm not sitting up there with him, like Jane. What's on top of the monument in Allentown?"

"Do you want to go back and look?" said Harvey. "Where is this hotel you stay at?"

"You go around City Hall and then on Market Street I'll show you," said Jean Latour. "They'll be surprised to see *me*."

"They may be surprised to see me, too," said Harvey.

"Not as much," she said.

It was not a hotel of faded elegance; it was an establishment that had never had any grandeur, built and furnished for the brief accommodation of transients. The atmosphere, and the night clerk, proclaimed the motto: No questions asked.

"Hello, Jean," said the night clerk. "Back already?"

"I couldn't stay away from you," she said. "You know that, Albert. Any messages for me?"

"Not since I came on. I'll look in your box. No. Nothing there. Do you have your key?"

"I got my key."

"The elevator's out of order again. You'll have to walk up," said Albert. "Your friend gonna register?"

"No, he's with me," said Jean.

"That'll be one dollar," said Albert.

"If you don't register you have to give Albert a dollar," said Jean.

"Either that or I have to charge her the double rate," said Albert.

"But this goes into your pocket," said Harvey.

"Yeah, I get a dollar. The other way, she has to pay the double rate, or else I have to register you and charge you for a single."

"Oh, I don't mind paying the buck. I just didn't understand the racket, but now I do," said Harvey.

"Where's Henry?" said Jean. "He ought to be here to carry our baggage upstairs. I give him enough tips."

"I sent him home early. He was coughing, coughing, coughing, and I didn't want to catch his God damn cold."

"All right, we'll carry our own."

Her room was three flights up but they were not long flights. Above the main floor the rooms were low-ceilinged. In Jean's room there was a double brass bed. Harvey looked at the bed and said, "What's this going to cost me?"

"Well, I know you only have around seventy dollars on you," she said.

"Not only *on* me, but that's my entire bankroll. I have to get a job quick, and probably sell my car."

"What would you say to five dollars? I usually get more. Twenty-five I been getting. I only take a few regulars."

"Five is all right," he said. "Maybe if I get a job in Philly I'll get to be one of your regulars."

"Maybe, who knows?" she said.

"At least it's warm here," he said. "This is where you make your headquarters?"

"It's one of the places. Why, because you don't see my wardrobe?"

"Not only that. It doesn't look as if you spent much time here."

"You're very observing," she said. "All right, I'll tell you. I got a keeper, an old guy around fifty years of age. He has an apartment. That is, I have, and he pays for it. That's where I live, mostly."

"Where is he now?"

"In Florida. Palm Beach, Florida. But I couldn't bring you to the apartment. I don't trust the elevator man. He spies on me."

"How can you take a chance on lousing up that arrangement?"

"You mean like working for Spengler, or Spangler, or whatever his name is? How much do you think I got tonight? Well, I'll tell you. I got a hundred dollars from Spengler-Spangler, and if it wasn't for those cops I would have picked up easily another hundred. Easily. There was one guy there tonight, I think he was a bootlegger. I could of got a hundred from just him. He was flashing money around there like it was going out of style. He gave Mary ten dollars just to sit on one guy's lap. He wanted to see what the guy would do if he got a naked girl on his lap."

"What did he do?"

"Oh—started to wrestle around with her. This bootlegger wanted me to go back to Griggsville with him."

"Gibbsville."

"Yeah. He had some scheme. I don't know what."

"But you were taking a big chance, going up to South Taqua. As it was, you got pinched."

"I know. But *you* sit around doing nothing, going to the movies, and the elevator man spying on you. See how long before *you* went crazy. I heard about this chance to make a few dollars and have a little fun, and Spangler guaranteed me there wouldn't be any trouble. That Spangler, I shoulda known he was a small-time smallie. I hope they give him ten years. Do you know what he got those other girls for? Twenty-five apiece. And what will they get out of it? What kind of a rap will they get, do you know?"

"Oh—six months, maybe. They'll plead guilty and get off pretty light."

"Six months! You call that light?"

"They could get more, if Millner wanted to get tough with them. But he's only after two things. He wants to put Spangler away, and he wants to have this hanging over some of those men that were there. He's going to run for county judge, and that costs money in Lantenengo County. Every little bit helps."

"I didn't trust him either. All that time he was calling me names, if there was nobody else there I could tell by the way he was looking at me."

"I'm not so sure. Millner's supposed to be a family man. In politics he's a double-crosser and everything else. But I never heard about him and the women."

"You make me laugh," she said. "You stood up for me, but I know why and so do you. There's only the two kinds of men. The real queers, that get sick if a woman touches them. They can't help it, they were born that way, and I'm afraid of some of *them*. But the others, I don't care if they're a family man or a priest or what, if they can like one woman they can like them all. And if they don't like me, believe me, I know what they are. All those cops tonight, I could of got a week's pay out of all of them. Even the old chief, he was afraid to look at me."

"What about the fellow behind the desk? The sergeant?"

"Him? Oh, boy. He was kind of handsome-looking, too. I bet I could have got him to let me go before the night was over."

"Where did you get all this information? When did you start finding out so much about men?"

She laughed. "They always want to know that. Simple. When I was a kid, one of the towns where I lived there was a man there that if I put my hand in his pocket he let me keep what I found. The son of a bitch, he used to put five or ten pennies there ahead of time, never anything big like a quarter. Cheap thrill for him, but I didn't care. I used to pester him to let me put my hand in his pocket. It's a wonder I have any teeth left, I used to eat so much candy."

"Did you know what he was doing?"

"What he was doing, or what I was doing? Sure. How could I help it? The penny game. I knew what was there besides those pennies. It wasn't his *coat* pocket, for God's sake. I probably would have got him up to a dollar bill, most likely, but we had to move to another town. Otherwise I probably wouldn't have a tooth left in my head. I used to eat those penny creams, and do you remember those peanut-butter bolsters, all covered with chocolate? Every day after school. One day I ate ten of those penny creams and I got sick, and that took away my taste for creams. But carmels I liked. I guess they were good for my teeth, you had to chew carmels. Look. See my teeth? I have these two fillings and that's all."

"And what did you do in the next town?"

"The next town? You mean when we moved from Pittsburgh?"

"Wherever the guy was that you played the penny game with."

"That was Pittsburgh. Then we moved to Buffalo, New York, but we didn't stay there very long. My old man worked on the railroad and he got his leg cut off."

"Did he lose his job?"

"His job? He got killed."

"How old were you?"

"When my old man got killed? Search me. Ten? Eleven? I don't remember."

"Who took the place of the guy that gave you the candy money?"

"Where did I get money from? Why do you want to know that for?"

"Don't tell me if you don't feel like it," said Harvey.

"Oh, well, I might as well tell you. You couldn't report me to the police for that. I used to steal. Some boy I knew, the two of us used to go around and steal stuff. We used to steal things out of cars, and off of clotheslines. The five-and-dime. The most we ever got was five dollars, a fur neckpiece we swiped off a clothesline. The other kid used to take the stuff to some hockshop near where the boats came in. We never got what the stuff was worth. I'll bet you that fur neck-piece was worth a hundred dollars. Maybe more. But we only got five for it. Or that was what he said, the other kid. Maybe he was holding out on me. But we didn't stay there very long. My mother divided us up. I and my two older sisters went to live with my aunt and uncle. Paterson, New Jersey. And the three youngest to another aunt and uncle in Cleveland, Ohio."

"Where did your mother go?"

"Oh, she got sick. Consumption. She died, too. That was after I ran away. They wouldn't give us any money, and my two older sisters went to work in the mills. But I knew where he hid his money, my uncle, and I took a hundred and fifteen dollars and went to New York. He kept his money in a cigar box under the bathtub. I had a hard time finding it, but I knew it was somewhere in that house, so I used to search every room when they were out. They used to go to the eight o'clock Mass every Sunday, and I went to the nine. The children's Mass. So while they were out I gave that house a good going-over till I found out where he kept the money. There was over three hundred dollars in the box, but I only took a hundred and fif-teen."

"Why a hundred and fifteen?"

"It was five twenties and three fives. Eight bills. In case he got back early from Mass I didn't want him to notice that some of it was gone. You know, if he took a quick look, he wouldn't notice only eight bills were gone. Unless he counted. If he counted, I was licked. But he came home from Mass, and I started out for the nine, only I never went to the church. I rode on a couple of trolleys and got to Newark and took the Tube to New York and went to the movies. The Rivoli. I sat in the back till my eyes got used to the dark and I could see better. Then I waited a while till I picked out some john that was there alone, and I got up and sat next to him."

"And then you were on your way," said Harvey.

"Not with the first one. He got up and changed his seat. But the next one I didn't have to do anything. He started on me, the second one. He sure did. He was a john, all right." She laughed. "He took me to some hotel, a dump like this, and around ten o'clock that night I cried and said I was afraid to go home. My father would kill me. Kill him, too. I said I was gonna give myself up to the police. Well, we argued back and forth till finally he gave me all he had on him, sixty or seventy dollars, and said I was to stay there till Tuesday and he'd come and take me away. To Florida. I knew he was never coming back, the son of a bitch, and I didn't care. I had about a hundred and eighty dollars, and I wasn't worried."

"Then what happened?"

"Well, the fellow that ran the hotel came to the room the next day. He said I had to get out, and I said the john was coming to get me the next day. The manager knew damn well he wasn't, but he said he'd give me till the next day. Well, about a half an hour later this woman came in my room. She pretended to feel sorry for me and all, but she was just sizing me up. Finally she said to me, she said she knew I was a little hooker and if I wanted to do business I had to do business with her. I swore up and down I didn't know what she was talking about, and I didn't know very much, to tell the truth. I could tell she wasn't sure whether I was telling the truth or not. She just couldn't figure me out. Then I said to her, I wasn't what she thought I was, but I ran away from home and the police would be looking for me. I said I had to stay there for a while and I had thirty dollars that the john gave me. I said I was a virgin, but if there was no other way to make money, I'd work for her. She fell for it. She said I didn't exactly have to work for her, but some johns liked it if a young girl was there to watch. And that was how I really got started."

"How long did you work there?"

"A week. She paid me fifty dollars for the week and my room rent, and at the end of the week I went down to Florida with her boy friend. He and I got married down there. He ran a clip-joint in Miami, and that was where I started singing."

"Oh, you sing?"

"You heard me tell those cops I was a singer. I sing as good as anybody around. I ought to be getting a thousand dollars a week. I can sing rings around Ruth Etting, *or* Helen Morgan. I traveled all over the country with a couple bands. Teddy Bryer. You ever hear of Teddy Bryer?"

"Yes, I heard of him."

"He came in the joint one night and heard me sing. Came back every night for a week, and when the band was going north I went with them."

"What about your husband?"

"Him. I walked out on him. He wanted Teddy to buy up my contract, a thousand dollars. Teddy hit him so hard I thought he killed him. Teddy knew I didn't have any contract. You don't know Teddy, I can see that. He punches first and argues after. He gets in trouble with everybody. The union. The dance-hall managers. He'll go right down in the crowd, come down off the bandstand, and punch some stranger and you won't ever know what Teddy had against him. That's what finally broke up the band, his bad temper. He beat up the piano player for making a play for me, and they took it up with the union. Teddy was fined and he refused to pay the fine."

"So that's what happened to Teddy Bryer. He used to play at the parks, near the place where you were tonight."

"Then I went with Bobby Beach and the Beach Boys. I made two records with them. I did the vocal on one and the other was a duet with Bobby. I did the vocal on 'Sunny Side of the Street.' The trouble with that was we made it for one of the small companies, and it was a lousy arrangement. Bobby wouldn't spend money for an arranger. He'd take the stock arrangements and fool around with them himself, to save a dollar. If I could have stayed with Teddy six more months he was just beginning to get in good with Victor again. He had some fight with them, too. He fought with everybody."

"Well, you're a girl of many talents," said Harvey.

"You think you're sarcastic, but I do have one talent, and that's singing. I know what you had reference to, but some day you can forget all about that. You and everybody else. Because I'll tell you something, boy. The way those cops looked at me tonight, and you saw them. That's the way the people look at me when I sing, even with a lousy band like Bobby Beach behind me. You ask the musicians. What girl singer is the best? They'll name off Ruth Etting, Helen Morgan, Lee Wiley, half a dozen others. But the musicians that heard me, they'll tell you. And they know."

"Well, you're still young."

"You bet I am. Some day you'll be bragging that you laid Jean Latour. And people won't believe you."

"Well, so far I don't believe it myself. And you know what, kid? I'm dead tired."

"You mean you just want to sleep?"

"You had a nap in the car."

"Yes, I'm ready to go. I can stay up the rest of the night."

"How about if I grab about an hour? What will you do?"

"I'll take a bath," she said.

"Just give me about an hour," he said. The long day, the cold drive, the warmth of the room made sleep, just a little sleep, more desirable than the girl. There was, in fact, and considering the girl's build, a strange absence of urgency in his desire for her. He had not yet touched her body, although he had every intention of doing so. He was not going to leave this room unsatisfied, and his willingness to postpone his pleasure with her now, in favor of sleep, was so that when he awoke he would be strong and virile.

"I'm gonna turn on the water in the bathtub," she said. "Will it keep you awake?"

"Nothing'll keep me awake, now," he said. He got out of his suit and shirt and lay on the bed in his B.V.D.'s. He heard the water plunging into the tub, and in two minutes he was dead asleep.

When his sleep was over, that first heavy sleep, the room was dark, but he was a man who had slept in many places and at odd times of day and night, and he awoke knowing exactly where he was. He looked at his wristwatch, glowing in the dark, and guessed that he had been unconscious about two hours. His next conscious thought was the irritating observation that he was alone in the bed.

He would have liked to wake up with her beside him and to give her a good lay, perhaps even before she was fully awake. He fumbled around for a match or a light switch. He could find neither, and he got out of bed and by following the length of the bed went straight to the hall door, and now he found the light switch in the wall. He went to the window and pulled the shade aside. First light had come. Now he had a look in the bathroom and saw that there were still a couple of inches of water in the tub and it did not appear to be water that anyone had used for a bath. No human body had been in that water, and the soap in the dish was dry and hard, the rubber sponge was brittle.

Little by little he began to realize that when she left the room she had taken away everything that belonged to her. There were some cigarette butts in the ash trays, and in the bathroom a small bottle containing a couple of powdery aspirins. But everything else was gone, and he remembered now that there never had been much of hers in the room. Immediately he made a couple of quick steps to his suit, which lay on an easy chair. As he knew it would be, his wallet was empty of money; in his pants pockets she had left a five-dollar bill and eighty-four cents in coins.

"Not even rolled," he said aloud. He laughed angrily at himself. "Not even rolled, not even laid, not even got a hangover." He took the receiver off the hook and waited for the switchboard to respond. He waited and waited before he got a response.

"Hello?"

"Hello, Albert. Did I interrupt your sleep?"

"No, I had the buzzer off. I didn't take notice to the light flashing," said Albert.

"Did our young lady leave any message for me?"

"No, she didn't say anything. I got her a taxi and she left here about an hour ago, I guess it was."

"Do you know where she went? Not that you'd tell me."

"Well, I don't know for sure *where* she went."

"But you have a pretty good idea," said Harvey.

"I guess that's right."

"But you wouldn't tell *me*," said Harvey.

"No."

"Why did she take all her stuff with her? I understood she had this room on a permanent basis."

"All her stuff? She didn't have much stuff. She paid up for the last couple days and checked out. You can stay there till tonight if you want to. The room's paid for till six o'clock tonight."

"She walked off with my bankroll, but you don't know anything about that, do you?"

"No, but what the hell? You weren't born yesterday. You didn't look to me like some college kid. You been around, I could see that."

"I'd like to get that money back, or some of it. I'll give you ten bucks for her address and phone number."

"You don't *have* ten bucks, you just said. No, I don't know her phone number, so I couldn't give you that if I wanted. And I wouldn't give you her address. Not for ten bucks, anyway."

"Did you ever lay her, Albert?"

"Why?"

"I just wondered whether it was because you liked her personally, or the little tips you get."

"Oh, well I guess it's both. I laid her one time."

"Only once? Wouldn't you like to again?"

"Well, she's pretty. She sure is built. But I could get fired if I let her stay here free."

"She's too expensive for you," said Harvey. "When do you guess she'll be back here again?"

"I wouldn't want to make a guess on that. She comes and goes. Like maybe I won't see her for weeks at a time, then she'll have the room for a whole week. She had some piano player here for over a week one time. He was a piano player in some orchestra down on South Broad Street. A baldheaded fellow. He'd roll in here drunk every night, and she'd be here all day, till it was time for him to go to work. I'd come on about my usual time, eight o'clock, and they'd just be leaving."

"I understand she's a pretty good singer," said Harvey.

"That's the first I ever heard of it, but that wouldn't prove anything. I only know her from coming in here. She has some rich guy, but she sure is the little two-timer."

"And yet I like her, don't you?"

"Well, yes, I guess so, and she's only a kid. But when it comes to money—oh, boy. They ought to have her over at the Bourse."

"Well, I guess you're not going to help me out with her address," said Harvey.

"No. You gotta find that out for yourself, but this is a big city. If I was you, buddy, the best thing is to forget about it. You got taken. Too bad. But look at me. I got asthma. I think I get it from the soap they use here, scrubbing the floors."

"If I get my money back I'll buy you a bottle of cologne," said Harvey. "It's all right for me to leave my suitcase here?"

"Till six o'clock tonight. If you want a cheaper room, I got one for a dollar and a half a night. It's an inside room, quiet. And the weekly rate is nine dollars, the same as if you were getting one night free. You share a toilet and a shower with another guy, but he's away a good deal of the time. He's a salesman, an elderly bachelor or maybe a widower, I don't know which. That's as good as you'll find anywhere in town."

"And I may run into Jean if she comes back here. I'll let you know tonight," said Harvey.

As a reporter he was pleased with the information he had extracted from Albert, and reasonably confident that in one or two further conversations he would be successful in his attempt to learn Jean Latour's address. He went back to bed and slept until ten o'clock. He shaved and dressed and went out and had a good breakfast; fried eggs, French fries, toast and coffee. He was going to need all his strength.

He first went to the garage where he had left his car, and asked for the boss. "How much will you give me for the Ford coop?" said Harvey.

"I wouldn't give you five dollars for it," said the manager. "I can't use it."

"I paid six hundred for it a year ago, and it's in pretty good condition. Give me four hundred for it."

"No sale."

"Look at the rubber. Those are all new, all four."

"I can see that, but I'm not buying."

"Give me two hundred for it," said Harvey. "You can make yourself a quick hundred and a half on that. You know you can. I think you could probably get five hundred dollars for this car."

"Then you get it."

"Make me an offer. I need money quick. Or how much would you *lend* me on it?"

"I wouldn't lend you a nickel on a Lincoln phaeton," said the manager. "I'll give you seventy-five dollars for the car."

"Make it an even hundred."

"You got the papers on it?"

"I have the bill of sale, the registration, and my driver's license. I'm a newspaper reporter, and I just lost my job. Will you give me a hundred?"

"All right, I'll give you a hundred dollars," said the manager. The papers were signed, the money handed over.

"I'll be interested to see what price you put on it," said Harvey.

"I'll show you," said the manager. He took a piece of soap and wrote on the windshield: "For Quick Sale—$495."

"Nice going," said Harvey.

"What the hell, you would of taken seventy-five," said the manager. "You got no kick coming."

"Only one thing more. Will you kiss me? I like to be kissed when I'm getting screwed," said Harvey.

"So long, buddy, I'm a busy man," said the manager.

Harvey returned to the hotel and paid a week's rent on the $1.50 room, commencing that night after six. He then went to Jean's room and made half a dozen telephone calls to newspaper offices. He had some luck. A day rewrite man on the *Public Ledger* agreed to meet him for a drink late in the afternoon; a copyreader on the *Inquirer* said he would nose around and see if there might be a job for him; a sportswriter on the *Evening Ledger* invited him to go to the fights that night and have drinks later with a fight promoter who was a soft touch for newspaper men. All at once Philadelphia was a warm and friendly town. At least it was a town of *brotherly* love, he told himself.

In a few days he had a job as a rewrite man on the morning *Ledger*. It paid forty dollars a week. It was not exactly what he wanted; he preferred to be a leg man, but he did not know Philadelphia too well; his personal acquaintance with the geography of the city was only less limited than his contacts with the police and other such news sources. But rewrite was a job he could hold down, and live on, while he was getting better acquainted in the city. Accidentally Jean Latour had done him a couple of favors by getting him out of South Taqua and by stealing his money, but they were not favors he would have to return.

In the succeeding weeks he could find no one among his newspaper acquaintances who had ever heard of the girl, and he guessed that Albert had tipped her off that he was living at the Royal, which was the uninspired name of the hotel. Another guess that concerned Albert was a wrong one; Albert kept the secret of Jean's address, and with the occupational suspiciousness of a night clerk he refused to be drawn into conversation about the girl. Often at night Harvey would stop for a chat with Albert before going upstairs to bed. The Royal had no kitchen, and Albert brought his own lunch, to be eaten at midnight. Henry was always sent out to get hot coffee, and Harvey would sometimes order a container for himself. He had begun to like the Royal; it was certainly a more inviting place than the rooming-house in South Taqua, a cheerless room in a cheerless house, that he had gone to only for sleep. The Royal had the smell that went with the unending war against vermin, but it had the fascinatingly unwholesome human traffic of its lobby and elevator and halls. The majority of the male guests were horse-players, including two men who worked in bookmaking establishments. The women were anybody's women, trying not to think of the day when nobody would want them. It was an orderly place; the police had their instructions from the ward leaders, who got their own instructions from the landowners' representatives at district headquarters. Out in Chestnut Hill the real owners of the Royal were pleased with any property that paid its own way and showed a little profit; over on the Main Line it might not have pleased Mr. Gaston Pennington to learn that indirectly he was a minor contributor to the income of his cousins who owned the Royal. Gaston Pennington was the gentleman who supported Jean Latour.

For Harvey Hunt this was a period of contentment. The three years in South Taqua had been easy and not unpleasant, and should have provided contentment but had actually been a period of unrest. In South Taqua he did his work, the pay was not bad; he was given passes to the movie theater in Taqua and small discounts at the store where he bought his clothes. The business department helped him to buy a car. He was rewarded for small favors with the small graft that was a perquisite of small-town newspaper reporting. He gave the name and address of Levy's store when writing that Levy's daughter had won a mathematics prize at State, and Levy would pay for the puff with a free pair of shoes, Bostonians worth ten dollars a pair, retail. Harvey got a complimentary weekly five-dollar meal ticket at the Exchange Hotel for remembering to mention the hotel in his accounts of Rotary luncheons. He was not much of a drinker, but he would run up a bill for pints of whiskey at Mac McDonald's Pharmacy, and McDonald would forgive the debt in appreciation of an occasional news item that tied in with a paid advertisement of a shipment of exotic French perfumes and Eastman Kodaks.

Literary brilliance would have been wasted in the columns of the *Chronicle,* and Harvey Hunt was not the man who could supply it. He had not gone into the game as a trainee in belles-lettres. Until senior year in high school he had more or less wanted to try for an appointment to West Point or Annapolis, but his Congressman lived in the next county, and neither Harvey nor his father or mother knew exactly how to go about getting the appointment. It had not been a burning desire in any case. Harvey's father was station agent for the New York Central at Elk City in one of the sparsely populated northern counties of Pennsylvania, and he had wanted Harvey to learn a trade, but Harvey's mother had insisted on the boy's finishing high school.

The Hunts lived in an apartment on the second story of the Elk City railway station, and Mrs. Hunt earned three dollars a week on the local paper by reporting the comings and goings of her fellow citizens. It had not occurred to her that there might be a future in journalism for her son, but when Harvey wrote an account of an accident to a circus train a couple of miles down the track, she brought the article with her to the newspaper office. It was printed in its entirety, and the publisher of the paper said that Harvey had a real knack. Harvey received no payment for the article, but he was given his first byline, and his fate was sealed. At the end of high school he became a reporter at double his mother's salary.

The paper died three years later. It was not a paper that was much better or much worse than many others. It had been publishing for forty years, into the second generation of the family that founded it. It had never known any extensive prosperity. It had served the community reasonably well, but only as a convenience. There had rarely been any reason for a citizen to read the paper unless he were personally involved in the content, and between such personal involvements the citizen would lose interest in the paper. It made no difference to him whether the paper came out or not, and when finally publication was suspended no one asked, "What will we ever do without the *Constitution?*" The *Constitution* would be missed, they said, but there was no sense of emergency, no dramatic effort to revive the paper while there was still a chance. The publisher wept privately, settled with his creditors for fifteen cents on the dollar, and took a job in the county office of the Sealer of Weights and Measures. Only then did he realize that for fifteen years he had neglected to send away copies of his paper to be bound.

Paper by paper Harvey Hunt made his way southward through

the Commonwealth, making friends with other newspaper men, but acquiring no other assets. On one paper he received pay for one week out of five; on another he was fired for using the publisher's office for a rendezvous with a young woman; on another paper he quit because he was not given a single day off during a twenty-one-day stretch. In Reading he was fired for lying about his salary on his previous job; in Allentown he was offered a five-dollar raise by the publisher of the Taqua *Chronicle,* who liked a story he wrote about a South Taqua mining disaster. There had never been any complaints about his work as such, and during his time in South Taqua he was given good reason to believe that he could stay there forever, eventually to take over as the publisher retired.

The publisher was a man who had other and more profitable interests than the *Chronicle:* a stone quarry, the gas company, half a block of business properties, and, through his wife's inheritance, a nice income from electric power and light. John Barringer was the *owner* of the *Chronicle,* and he made it pay. His interest in the paper was in making it pay, just as he made his stone quarry and his real estate pay, and if he was only vaguely aware of the existence of Munsey and Ochs, Pulitzer and Northcliffe, he was even less aware of the Kents and Chapins and Wattersons and Whites. He was an owner-publisher and not an editor-publisher. Nevertheless he ran a successful paper, because he published the kind of paper he liked to read and his preferences reflected the tastes of most of the solvent readers of his paper. To that extent he was a good editor by accident. When by accident something got into the *Chronicle* that he did not like, he nearly always learned next day that his readers had not liked it either. The *Chronicle* seldom carried a story longer than one column, and almost never was there a story that was given a two-column headline.

For Harvey Hunt that meant a lot of work; many news stories rather than one or two big ones. It was the best sort of training. Because he was under restrictions of space, he was prevented from acquiring bad stylistic habits. Because he was expected to bring in quantities of items, he learned not to waste time in useless questions.

John Barringer, who literally could not have named the capital of Maryland and had never heard of Bonar Law, described Harvey Hunt as the best reporter he had ever known, and from time to time he would drop a clumsy hint that Harvey ought to settle down with a nice local girl and get ready to take over the managing of the *Chronicle.* Barringer was a man of his word, and Harvey Hunt knew that if he stayed on in South Taqua, Barringer would make it easy for him to buy the *Chronicle.* But Harvey grew restive under the gentle pressure from John Barringer. Without knowing what it was, without trying very hard to understand it, there was something about the life he led in South Taqua that was worse than being broke and jobless, and he never experienced the slightest regret either for leaving South Taqua or for the manner of his leaving. John Barringer would not have fired him for quarreling with Millner, but John Barringer would not have been able to help him understand why he wanted to come to the defense of a girl like Jean Latour. An older man ought to be able to understand such things, but John Barringer only understood that it was time to settle down with a nice local girl as a step toward taking over the *Chronicle.*

In Philadelphia, sitting behind the switchboard with Albert and listening to the horse-players' lies, Harvey Hunt was more truly at home than he had ever been. The Market Street trolleys did not have to make so much of a clangor, but at least they made it all the time, all through the night, so that you needed nothing else to tell you that South Taqua was past and gone. You could wake up in the dark of four A.M. and some angry motorman would stomp his bell for you, and you would go back to sleep. In a big city like Philadelphia there was always enough news to fill the paper. You did not have to worry about the news supply, as you did on a small-town paper. Harvey Hunt was appalled at the waste of news by the big city papers. In Philadelphia they had a Chinatown that should have provided hundreds of fascinating news items but was practically ignored; the city was a seaport, with ships arriving and sailing for places all over the world, but nobody ever did a story on the seaport. There was surely one good news story a day in each of the big department stores; stories in the theaters, among the highbrow musicians, in the fancy hotels. You simply could not have two million persons living together without creating the frictions that result in news items. To a man who had worked in the small towns of eastern Pennsylvania the city was inexhaustibly rich with unwritten columns of wonderful, exciting stuff. To Harvey Hunt, blasé was a word that went with long cigarette holders and the magazine *Vanity Fair,* and in the excitement of his first year in a big city he felt the need to live forever.

He saw a tall man in a brown broadcloth greatcoat with a fur collar, brown spats, brown Homburg, waxed moustache, and monocle. He saw the man again, and noticed that in the band of the Homburg, the man wore a tiny feather. He had never seen any such man in Allentown, but he saw him half a dozen times, and as the weather improved the man was in different costume but always had the glass in his eye or dangling from a thin cord. There was an elderly lady who rode around in a baby Renault towncar, which had a chauffeur and footman. There was no such turnout in Reading or Bethlehem. In the dead of winter he saw young men carrying oddly shaped tennis racquets, escorting young women carrying similar racquets. He had never seen any such racquets in Scranton or Wilkes-Barre. He had never seen a Negro policeman, or a Boy Scout wearing bare-kneed shorts, a subway or an "L" train, a fire-fighting water tower, an eight-oar shell or a single sculler, four Japanese couples in evening dress at a theater together, a department store with its own bugle corps, a house of prostitution where men went to meet other men, a butler in knee breeches (perhaps the father of one of those Boy Scouts?). He had never seen so many rich people, so many poor people, so many people, and he wanted to know all about all of them.

He began with the obvious ones, the men and women who worked on the paper with him. He had heard of them because of their bylines—the general news reporters, the political reporters, and the sports writers. They never looked the way he expected them to. Walter J. Bright, who covered major crimes of violence, should not have looked like a policeman but he might at least have looked like a private detective. Instead he was a short stout man who wore a slouch hat in and out of the office and believed that every man and woman was guilty as charged, should be sent to the electric chair, and would be so if it were not for the bungling and venality of the prosecutors. He was married and had a homely daughter who worked in the classified-ad department.

Theodore N. Kruger, the top political writer, was thin to the point of emaciation, and owed at least part of his success to his ability to sit up all night, drinking whiskey with the politicians and remembering what they told him when they, but not he, got drunk. He had a modest fortune, acquired by being let in on state and municipal real-estate deals. He would buy a piece of property, sell it to the city, and divide his profits with the proper officials, whose names were kept out of the original transactions. He was a Swarthmore graduate and eventually the one to enlighten Harvey Hunt on the oddly shaped tennis racquets.

Martha Swanson came as a surprise to Harvey Hunt. The stories he read under her byline were so completely unadorned with feminine touches—they were, in fact, stories that would not ordinarily have been assigned to a woman—that during his first weeks in the office he had her confused with Miss Pitney, a secretary in the financial department who affected Eton collars and Windsor ties, and wore rimless pince-nezs. Martha Swanson, although she usually wore tailored suits, was abundantly feminine. She wore single-pearl earrings and a seed-pearl necklace, and whether she had on one of her cashmere pullovers or a shirtwaist, her bosom was distracting. Between assignments she would sit at her desk, bent over a Modern Library volume, chain-smoking, not taking off her hat, always at the ready, so to speak. She was a trifle overweight, completely at home in her surroundings, and Harvey Hunt guessed that all romantic notions between her and the men on the staff were a thing of the past. They referred to her as Swanson behind her back, and she was always good for a five- or ten-dollar touch. She appeared to be lazy, but when she went out on a story she worked hard and efficiently. In time Harvey Hunt learned that she was the daughter and only child of O. C. Swanson, a San Francisco newspaper man and magazine writer who was a friend of Herbert Hoover's *and* Woodrow Wilson's. She was divorced from Don Bushmiller, the one-time Stanford football and track star, and when Harvey Hunt asked her to have dinner with him she smiled and said, "I don't see why not."

They went to a more or less open speakeasy in an alley, where the steaks and chops were reasonably priced and the liquor was safe. She knew the waiters by name, and they knew her tastes in food and drink. "You come here often?" he said.

"Force of habit," she said. "It was the first place I went to when I started working in Philly."

They had visitors from other tables, and the bill came to fourteen dollars. "Have you got enough?" she said. "I have some money, and there's no reason why you should buy drinks for my friends."

"I can swing it," he said.

"Well, if you're sure. The next time we'll go Dutch. I make more money than you do, and it isn't fair to have you pay for those extra drinks. I mean it. Here, why don't we start now? I'll pay half."

"All right, if you insist."

"You have to watch out for that Morton fellow. He'll sit all night and never pay for a drink. He's that kind."

They walked to her flat—in another alley—and he was overwhelmed by the presence of her books. From floor to ceiling three walls were covered with filled shelves. "They're not all mine," she said. "Some of them were my father's. I got rid of a lot when I left San Francisco, but they're beginning to pile up again. I hate to part with a single one of them, but I have no room for my pictures." In her bedroom the wall space was taken by a profusion of Japanese prints and American moderns. "All from San Francisco. The prints are good. They were my father's and he knew what he was doing. The others are mine, and it's too soon to say whether they'll stand the test of time. I'm beginning to get tired of some of them. The ones I liked the most when I bought them, I bought them for their colors, but they're going to be the first to go the next time I move. Do you care anything about pictures?"

"Not very much," he said.

"If you want to use the bathroom, there it is. Would you like a drink? I have some gin and some rye. I'm going to have a rye and ginger ale. You?"

"Okay," he said.

While he was in the bathroom she stood behind a screen and changed into a pajama suit. "Your drink is on the brass tray. I'll be with you in a minute."

She rejoined him presently and sat with her legs folded under her on a studio couch.

"Do you mind if I ask, is that a picture of you in the bathroom?"

"The nude, you mean? Yes, that's me. As I was six years ago. Seven."

"Who painted it?"

"People always ask that. It was painted by a man that didn't like women, obviously, but I think it's pretty good."

"Why would you pose for a man that didn't like women?"

"Oh, he wasn't the only one I posed for. Wouldn't you pose if someone asked you to?"

"I'd never pose for a woman that didn't like men," he said.

"Very few women artists that don't like men. That is, women artists that would ask a man to pose in the nude."

"I never thought of that," he said.

"There's always sex in it when a woman asks a man to pose, at least I think there is. No matter what they say. But men *and* women can have a woman pose without sex entering into it."

"Do you think so?" he said.

"I know so. I used to pose for just about anybody and everybody that asked me to."

"I'll never be an artist," he said. "I couldn't keep my hand steady if I had a naked girl in the same room with me."

"Well, then, don't be an artist."

"I couldn't be anyway," he said. "I have no talent for it."

"Are you writing a novel?"

"Hell, no. I have no talent for that either. I'd never have the patience to write fiction. Are you writing one?"

"Oh, I've written two. Neither one published. One I wouldn't even show to anyone. Some day, when I have enough money, I'm going to take a year off and write one good novel. Just one. I'll publish it under an assumed name and then go back to the newspaper business. I couldn't publish it under my own name because I'd never have any peace. I could never cover another story without having all the other reporters saying I was the one that wrote that novel. But I know I can write one good novel. Just one."

"About your own life?"

"Well, mostly."

"Then wouldn't people recognize it anyway, even if you used a phony byline?"

"Some people would recognize themselves, but they'd keep quiet about it. They wouldn't brag about being in it. What I wouldn't like would be every reporter and rewrite man trying to go on the make for me because I wrote the book. That would get to be a bore, and I like this business. I expect to stay in it all my life."

"You don't intend to get married again?"

"Later on, maybe. When I'm thirty-five or forty I might marry a newspaper man and the two of us can settle down with a small paper somewhere."

"Where have I heard *that* before?" he said.

"You probably heard yourself say it."

"Not me. No more small-town papers for me," he said. "From here I go to New York, get a job on the *News*. The big money."

"And then what?"

"Oh, I don't know. By the time I'm forty I'll be ready to take over as managing editor. I'll either stay with Patterson, or Hearst will make me an offer."

"How can you be so sure of yourself?"

"I never was till I came to Philly, but I'm a city man. I wasn't here two days before I knew that. I was a different person. It was as different as day and night, working upstate and working in the city. You wouldn't understand that, coming from San Francisco, and your father a big shot."

"Oh, it isn't hard to understand," she said. "I'm not overawed by Philly, but it's the East, and I guess I was a little nervous about that. In San Francisco everybody knew who my father was, even people he'd never met. But here the only people that knew of him were a few newspaper men and some of the big politicians. So his reputation didn't help me much here. San Francisco is a real newspaper town. Philly isn't."

"Why?"

"Well just tell me one newspaper man in Philly that has the same standing my father had. Don't waste your time. There isn't any. What have they got here that corresponds to the Bohemian Club? Certainly not the Union League, and certainly not The Rabbit or the Fish House. Or the Philadelphia Club. My father belonged to the Pacific Union, which corresponds to the Philadelphia Club, but what newspaper man could ever get in the Philadelphia Club?"

"I'm not much for clubs. I've never belonged to one and never wanted to."

"You'll change your mind about that when you start making big money."

"I doubt it."

"What's the most you ever earned?"

"What I'm getting now. Fifty."

"Then you haven't started making real money. And incidentally, you're getting forty, not fifty. They don't pay fifty for your job, and you won't get fifty till you've been on the paper five years. If then. You're wise to think ahead. New York. You could probably start at seventy-five on the *News,* but wait a while and start at a hundred. I could get a hundred on the *News,* but I'd hate the kind of assignments they'd give me. I don't want to cover those love-nest stories, but that's what I'd get on the *News.* One of the reasons why I stay here is because they let me do general assignments."

"You're trying to be your father all over again."

"Not a chance. But at least I'm covering stories they don't usually give to women. I showed them I could in San Francisco, and when they took me on here they knew I could."

"Yes, you're good," said Harvey Hunt. "You're as good as any of the men."

"I'm better than most of them. I'd had several offers from magazines. *Collier's. Cosmo.* But they offer me two or three hundred for pieces they'd pay a man five hundred or a thousand. And I told them so. When they pay me men's prices, I'll write for them, but not before."

"It's nice to be able to afford your independence."

"Yes, my father took care of that. Insurance, and some stocks and bonds. I could have got alimony, too. Don's family have money. But I'm against alimony for women that have no children."

"Why did you break up?"

"None of your business."

"The only way to find out is to ask questions."

"You're not on a story now," she said.

"Not for the *Ledger,* but for my own curiosity. I never knew anybody like you before."

"What's so different about me?"

"Damn near everything. The way you think. Your independence."

"I think it's time for you to go home now, Hunt."

"I was thinking just the opposite."

"I know you were. That's why I'm sending you home."

He got up and sat beside her, but she would not put down her highball. "You're going to spill my drink," she said.

"Then let me put it somewhere out of the way."

"Why? I'm not going to go to bed with you."

"Why not? Because you make sixty-five a week and I make forty?"

"Partly that, I guess."

"Put the God damn drink away and give it a chance," he said.

She smiled, then placed the drink on the floor. "All right," she said. "Now show me how irresistible you can be."

"No I won't," he said. "If you don't want it, I don't want it either. You're so God damn independent, you ought to know that much."

"Well, you're not as sure of yourself as I thought you were."

"I'm sure of myself, but now I'm not so damn sure of you. You like wearing pants because it comes natural to you. Goodnight, Swanson old boy."

"Goodnight," she said. She was angry. She remained immobile until he had closed the door behind him.

He did not see her during the next three days. She was in Atlantic City on a bankers' convention, a "must" story that even she could not make readable. On the third day she returned to Philadelphia on an early afternoon train. He saw her come in the office, have a few minutes' chat with the city desk, collect her mail, go to her desk, toss her hat on the desk and run her fingers through her hair to fluff it up. She lit a cigarette and examined her mail, half of which she dropped into the wastebasket unopened. So far she had not looked in his direction. She read her letters, and apparently answered one immediately, or so he judged by the fact that she put some notepaper in her typewriter, tapped out a few lines, and copied the address before signing and sealing the letter. Now she looked around the room, and he averted his gaze just a fraction of a second before her eyes fixed on him. He could see her slowly get up and slowly make her way to his desk.

"Hello," she said.

"Oh, hello. When did you get back from the shore?"

"Just now. I'm going to cash an expense-account cheque. Do you want to have dinner?"

"I can't leave here before nine, nine-thirty."

"That's all right. I have a lot of little things to do. Will you stop for me when you can get away, or would you rather meet me at Kessler's."

"Kessler's, a little after half-past nine."

"I brought you some salt-water taffy."

"You did?"

"Of course not. I've had the most boring three days—but I won't inflict that on you. Nine-thirty, then?"

She was at the restaurant when he arrived. She was wearing a light blue bouclé dress, as simple in design as all her clothes, but made more feminine by the color and the material. "Well, sorehead, what have you been doing for excitement?" she said.

"Reading those stories of yours from the convention."

"Never mind," she said. "It's a front-office must, and the first time they ever let a woman cover it."

"How did the bankers feel about *that?*"

"One or two of them thought it was a great idea."

"Those were the ones that didn't bring their wives."

"None of them brought their wives, not while the convention was on. Some of the wives began showing up this morning."

"A good time for you to get out of town," he said.

"Aren't you going to say you missed me? Try to say something nice, can't you? After all, I invited you to dinner. I have my expense-account cheque—and this."

"What's that?"

"A twenty-five-dollar bonus, from upstairs."

"You don't deserve it."

"You don't think so, but the convention chairman did. He called the paper to say so, hence the bonus."

"Then you'll be getting a lot of bankers' conventions from now on."

"Not if I can help it," she said. "Let's order. Anything but seafood in any form. Let's have something like Wiener schnitzel. Or spaghetti. Just so it doesn't come out of the ocean."

They arrived at steaks and beer, and when she finished her tenderloin she said, "As a matter of fact I had a steak yesterday, but no matter what I ate in Atlantic City it all seemed like lobster Newburg."

"I went there for a week when I was a kid. My old man was a

station agent and we used to get passes. We went to quite a few places that way, but we never had enough dough to stay very long. We stayed at a hotel on South Carolina Avenue, all three of us in the same room. We didn't have as much privacy as we did at home, and I always liked my privacy, even when I was little."

"So did I," she said. "I still do. Don never understood that. My husband. He wanted to do everything together, and I *mean* everything. He wanted our house to be like a locker-room, and it was."

"Is that why you broke up?"

"No. Although that may have been at the base of it. We had a good-sized house down on the Peninsula, and it wasn't a question of being in cramped quarters."

"I spent eleven years in a sort of an apartment on the second story of a railroad station, but I always had my own room."

"How could you sleep, with those trains going by at all hours?"

"I never heard them. That is—I knew when they were late, so I heard them that much. But the noise didn't bother me. It's a funny thing. I like my privacy, but I don't mind noises. Where I live now is about as noisy as any place in the city—except maybe the Baldwin Locomotive Works. But noises mean people, and I like to be near people. With my privacy, but knowing that people are somewhere around. I'd go crazy on a farm. I never wanted to be a cowboy, not after I found out how much time they spend miles away from anybody."

"I'm the same way, I guess. I don't mix much with people, but I like being in the midst of them, where things are going on. Then I like to go home to my flat and be alone. But not really alone. I just want to be able to shut people out when I feel like it. I suppose everybody is more or less the same way, really. Although I'm not so sure about that. My father wasn't. He was really gregarious, always on the go, loved his clubs. He would even have had a good time at that convention. And they would have loved him. He would have come away from there with a hundred new friends."

"Did you?"

"Me? I have no friends."

"I don't have so many myself."

"Everybody has a best friend, some people have two or three best friends, but not me. I was a terrible pain to the girls in my sorority. They were to me, too. But they used to give me lectures on the subject of cooperation, and friendship and loyalty. I had nothing against loyalty, but cooperation meant practically nothing to me. And as for friendship—I was bid to four sororities, and I know exactly why. They were the best. The richest and the most social. But I was bid because everybody knew who my father was. Friend of Mr. Hoover's and Woodrow Wilson's. Pictures in the paper with Lloyd George and Clemenceau. I didn't have to be rich. The rich people cultivated my father. It was a mark of being somebody to say you were a friend of O. C. Swanson. Not only on the Coast, either. He went to New York and Washington two or three times a year, and to Europe on assignments, and when he came home he'd have all sorts of offers to move back East. But he had California all to himself, and if he'd gone back East he would have lost some of his individuality. So when O. C. Swanson's daughter went to Stanford the parents and the alumni saw to it that I was rushed."

"Did you know that was why it was?"

"Of course. I'd known it all my life, practically. It wasn't only because my father was a famous reporter. Even before he won the Pulitzer prize or was given the Legion of Honor, my father attracted people by sheer force of personality. When we were still living at a small hotel we always had famous visitors, every Sunday night. Opera singers. Politicians. Writers. Stage people. When I was about eight years old I played a duet with Paderewski. He was there on a concert tour, and I had no idea who he was. Madame Schumann-Heink always had supper at our apartment, whenever she was in San Francisco. They all could have gone anywhere they liked, but they came to our apartment in the Belvedere."

"Was your mother artistic or anything like that?"

"My mother? No, not a bit. She was educated, the University of Minnesota. Her father was a dairy farmer, Swedish. But she stayed in the background. Nothing to contribute. Well—*contribute?* They used to quarrel about money, how much those parties used to cost, and all he had was his reporter's pay till the paper began to realize that Mr. Hearst had his eye on him. That was when Daddy's boss, Mr. Stewart, invited Margaret Anglin to his house for supper and Anglin said she was having supper with us. Made it a rule whenever she came to San Francisco. A *rule*. They gave my father a raise and something extra for the parties. But I'll say this for my father. He never invited Mr. and Mrs. Stewart to our parties, and he never went to the Stewarts'. When Daddy was put up for the Bohemian Club he never even asked Mr. Stewart for a letter. Got in without him. If you want to know where I got my so-called independence, it was from him. Then that wonderful day when Daddy went to see Mr. Stewart about a raise, and Mr. Stewart said he thought Daddy was entitled to more money and offered him two hundred a week. 'I thought that was about as high as you'd go,' Daddy said, and walked out without another word. That same day he signed his first big contract with *Collier's*. When Mr. Stewart heard about it he was wild. Came to see my father and accused him of all sorts of ingratitude and so forth. 'You'll see how far you get without the paper,' said Mr. Stewart. And Daddy said, 'So will you, Charlie, you tight-fisted bastard.' Mr. Stewart tried to keep Daddy out of the Pacific Union, but he didn't get very far with that. The men that put my father up were much more important than Mr. Stewart ever was and he just didn't have the nerve to go against them. And Daddy *looked* more like a Pacific Union member than Mr. Stewart. He was six-foot-one and never an ounce of fat. Spent a lot of money on clothes. You should have seen him all dressed up for some big banquet. Full dress, of course, and he had a medal that hung around his neck and the Legion of Honor badge. It was no wonder the women fell for him."

"I was going to ask you about that."

"Well, he couldn't help it. My mother should have made more of an effort, but she was really a farm girl. If she'd had her way—I can remember her trying to persuade him. 'Olaf, let's go back to Min-ney-*saw*-ta!' Minney-*saw*-ta. My grandfather wanted Daddy to take

over the farms. My mother's father, that is. My paternal grandfather was a carpenter, nicely fixed but nowhere near as much money
as my mother's family. When they had those spats over how much
the Sunday night suppers were costing, my mother would threaten
to leave him. She complained that she was paying for the parties,
which I guess was true, but all she ever did was threaten him. And
she didn't really like it when he began making more money. She
didn't have that hold over him any more."

"He liked the ladies," said Harvey.

"The *ladies* liked *him*. Even when I was a little girl I could see
that, and that was behind my mother's bickering about money. He'd
go on those long trips, especially when *Collier's* used to send him
abroad, and when he got home you'd think she'd be glad to see him
but instead of that they hardly spoke for several days. I know why,
now. She was accusing him of having other women, and I suppose
he didn't deny it. But she didn't make any effort to live up to what *he*
was. She was pretty, and she spoke three languages. English,
French, and Swedish. She played the piano and the organ. She could
have been more of a help to him, and I'm sure *Collier's* would have
been glad if they'd moved to New York and did a lot of entertaining.
But Daddy didn't really want to live in New York, and Mama didn't
even want to live in San Francisco."

"Well, if your old man was running around with other women, he
was smart to keep your mother in San Francisco."

"That isn't why he wanted to stay there. I told you before, he had
California all to himself."

"Sure. But he was away on trips a good deal of the time."

"You've got it all wrong. If she'd made the effort to keep up with
him—but she wouldn't."

"Didn't she ever try to get a divorce?" said Harvey.

"What?"

"Why didn't she divorce him? All those women, she could have
taken him for plenty, and she certainly would have got custody of
you."

"Don't you know? I thought you knew."

"Knew what? She *did* divorce him?"

"She committed suicide," said Martha Swanson.

The casualness of her statement made it no less abrupt. "No, I didn't know that. How would I have known it?"

"I guess I thought everybody knew it. I've always thought everybody knew everything about my father."

"He was a big name to me, but I never knew much about his personal life," he said. "O. C. Swanson, on the cover of *Collier's,* and you always see his name with Richard Harding Davis, Frank Ward O'Malley, Irvin S. Cobb. And I've seen pictures of him. But I never knew anything about his family life. Now I think of it, I sort of had the idea he was a bachelor."

"He was no bachelor. He was a wonderful father," she said. "He came home that day, late in the afternoon, and the maid said my mother left word she didn't want to be disturbed, not even for lunch. She was going to stay in bed all day. She did that sometimes, and the maid knew why. So did my father. So did I."

"Hitting the booze?"

"Yes," said Martha Swanson. "She'd do it for two or three days at a time, pretending to have a sick headache but actually just locking herself up with a bottle. She'd been doing that for a couple of years, every few weeks. Their friends didn't know it, but Daddy did, and I did, and the maid was a Swedish woman that they got from one of my grandfather's farms. Practically a member of the family. So my father went to their room and he found her there, hanging from the big four-poster. She'd been dead six or seven hours, maybe a little longer."

"Any letters or anything like that?"

"No," said Martha Swanson. "So my father cut her down and phoned the police, and said he wouldn't be there when they got there. They ordered him to stay, but he said he'd be back around eight o'clock. They asked him where he was going but he wouldn't tell them, and hung up on them. He went out and got in his car and drove as fast as he could to Stanford. I was a junior. He wanted to get there and tell me before anyone else did."

"How far was it?"

"Oh, under thirty miles. I'd just finished supper and was listening to some records. He came in and beckoned to me. The other girls started making a fuss over him, the way they always did, but he told them they'd have to excuse him. I don't know *what* he told them, but they knew something was up and they behaved I will say very sensibly. He took me to the car and we drove away, and then he stopped the car and told me what'd happened. He said there were only the two of us now, and that whenever I got over the shock he'd let me do whatever I liked. Stay in school, or quit, or go abroad. But I wasn't shocked. My first reaction, to tell you the truth, was anger."

"Angry with him, or with your mother?" he said.

"With her. It was like publicly blaming him for all her own deficiencies. That's really what it was, too. Have you covered many suicides?"

"A few," he said.

"Isn't that what most of them are? Blaming the world, or some individual? Getting even with somebody?"

"I guess some of them are," he said.

"Most of them," she said. "And the way she did it. Taking all her clothes off and hanging herself to the bed. She knew that's how he'd find her, and she made sure Minnie wouldn't be the one to find her."

"Strange she didn't leave a note," he said.

"That was part of it. People could make up their own stories, and you can be damn sure they did. Horrible stories. And you can imagine Stewart had a field day. Don't think he'd miss a chance like that. 'The nude body of Mrs. O. C. Swanson,' up in the lead. The other papers were bad enough, but Stewart was awful. You know how they can tell you to play up a story, play down certain angles and so forth. Stewart must have stood over the rewrite man and made sure my father got all the worst of it. A lot of people stopped speaking to Stewart, but of course there were some jealous ones that relished every minute of it."

"What happened to you? Did you stay in school?"

"I never went back. I didn't even go back to get my clothes. I had another girl bring them to my house. If my mother'd lived I'd have stayed to graduate, but only because I didn't want to be at home with her. I'd had a few dates with Don before my mother committed suicide, and he came to see me during the notoriety. He graduated that year, and he was so nice and easygoing that I married him. Worse luck for both of us."

"Why?"

"He was a wild bull. Do you remember the Wild Bull of the Pampas?"

"Luis Angel Firpo," said Harvey Hunt. "The Argentine boxer."

"Yes," she said. "Don was known as the Wild Bull of the Campus, but he'd never been that way when I went out with him. Quite the opposite, in fact. Maybe because I wouldn't neck with him, not at all. Other girls would come back from dates with him and tell these awful stories, but I'd go out with him and there'd be nothing like that. It wasn't only that I wasn't a necker. It was Don himself, and he worshiped my father. He was always disappointed if my father wasn't home when he came to our house. Don was a famous athlete, but he wanted people to think he had brains, and most of all he wanted Daddy to think he wasn't just a big football hero. 'What did your father say about me?' he used to ask. He'd read Daddy's pieces in *Collier's* and bore the hell out of Daddy, trying to discuss inflation in Germany and things like the trouble between Peru and Chile. Way over his head. But Daddy treated him as though he were the Secretary of State. Nobody ever knew it when they bored Daddy. He used to say to me, 'You'll never know when some dull bastard's going to turn out to be very useful.' "

"And so you married the dull bastard."

"Well, he was better than that. For one thing, he was a beautiful specimen of manhood, whether he was in a track suit or a Tux. He was almost as striking-looking as Daddy, although in a different way, and girls made fools of themselves over him. And he knew it. He knew he had that power over women. Animal magnetism."

"But not over you."

"Yes he had. But I'd met a lot of famous people for a girl of my

age, and a Stanford athlete didn't turn my head the way it did some
girls. I never have been one to show what's going on inside of me.
Also, I knew my father expected a great deal of me. When I asked
him for permission to marry Don he said he considered Don a fine
boy, good family, well off financially, popular. The only thing he
wanted to be sure of was that I'd seen enough of the world to be sure
I was ready to settle down to being Don's wife. What a wonderful
man! He was trying to tell me that he understood me better than I
understood myself, but at the same time he didn't want to frighten
me off marriage. So we were married, quietly, because of my
mother. And on my wedding night I wanted to run away."

"You were a virgin?"

"Of course. Not a dumb virgin. I knew what it was all about. But
I'd married a man that had had dozens of affairs, if not hundreds,
and he expected me to be as sophisticated as he was. Well, I just
wasn't. In the first place, his uncle had lent us his yacht for our wedding trip. Well, even if it was a big yacht, I was the only female
aboard and there was a crew of four or maybe five. It was like being
in a hospital for an operation, with all those men knowing we were
just married and staring at me. The yacht would slow down for
meals, so's not to spill things, I guess, but I wanted to stop completely so I could go for a swim. I just felt that if I could put on a
bathing suit and dive into the ocean I'd feel better. But Don said
we'd have plenty of time for swimming when we got to Honolulu.
That was one small thing, and I couldn't explain it to him without
sounding ridiculous, so I went without my swim. And felt dirty all
the way to the Islands. In Honolulu I insisted on staying at a hotel.
Anything to get away from that boat. If there had only been one
other woman aboard, a maid, they'd have had someone else to stare
at. I tried to persuade Don to come back on a steamship, and he
thought I was crazy. I should have pretended I got seasick, but I
couldn't have got away with it. If anything I was a better sailor than
Don, having sailed small boats most of my life. So we didn't exactly
get off to a good start. And then before we had our first wedding
anniversary I had a stupid affair with an artist and Don found out

about it. That gave him all the excuse he needed, and that was the story of our marriage. *Well!* Did you ask me the story of my marriage? You got it anyway."

"And what ever happened to Don?"

"Why, he's happy as a clam. He has two five-handicaps, one at golf and one at polo. Trying to raise the one and lower the other, and he will, make sure of that. And he has a five-year-old son."

"Five seems to be his lucky number."

"Exactly. No doubt he has five girl friends, too. He married a dumb little girl from Santa Barbara, with all the money in the world, and he doesn't have to pretend any more that his brains are going to waste. I hear from him now and then."

"Do you ever see him?"

"What you really want to know—yes. After we were divorced, and I'd had one or two affairs of my own. That was what finally made me quit my job in San Francisco. I wasn't very proud of myself, listening to him tell me how much he loved me when I knew his dumb little wife was having a baby. He was telling the same thing to other women, and really believing it."

"But *you* didn't love *him.*"

"Of course not. But I never refused to see him, and as long as I stayed in San Francisco that's the way it was going to be. When my father died the only person I could bear to talk to was Don. The only living human being I wanted to be with. The night of the funeral I went away with Don. We drove to Elko, Nevada, and stayed two days. If we could have stayed in Elko, who knows? I might have been there yet. No, that's silly. But I was happier those two days with Don than I've ever been with anyone. I'm a Swede. We like a little misery with our pleasure."

"I guess I do too, and I'm Scotch-Irish," he said.

"There was a fascinating little tramp in Atlantic City. I couldn't figure out who she was with, because I never saw her with any of the bankers. They all wore badges with their names on them. She was there with one of them, I'm sure of that, but she never appeared in public with him. Whenever I saw her she was alone, riding on the

Boardwalk in a wheel chair, and I saw her several times in the elevator. She must have been staying at the Marlborough, where I was."

"Why was she so fascinating?"

"Because I think she just this minute came in with that big fellow.
Do you know Gaspar Pennington? Does that name mean anything
to you? It isn't Gaspar, it's Gaston. Gaston Pennington."

"Yes, I've seen the name and I've written it in some connection or
other," said Harvey Hunt.

"Old Philadelphia, Main Line."

"Oh—the fellow with the monocle? Standing at the bar between
us and the girl?"

"Yes, you can't see her till he gets out of the way."

"I've seen him around, and wondered who he was," said Harvey.

"Gaston Pennington. One of the few loafers in Philadelphia.
Most of them have jobs, but Pennington keeps busy doing nothing.
He knew my father *and* my ex-husband."

"Have you ever been out with him?"

"No, he steers clear of the press. You can be sure he didn't come
here because he wanted to. The girl must have brought him."

"How did you meet him?"

"I never have met him, actually. He called me up one day at the
office, four or five years ago. Said he'd been to San Francisco and
someone had told him to look me up. He'd been there a lot, to play
polo at Burlingame, and had met my father and Don. He was leaving for Florida the next day, but he'd like to take me to lunch when
he got back. That was the last I ever heard from him. That's a great
custom in Philadelphia, in case you haven't run into it yourself.
They invite you, but they don't say when, and they feel they've done
their duty. So Pennington hasn't the least idea what I look like."

"You're right about the dame. She's a tramp," said Harvey
Hunt. "Her name is Jean Latour."

"She could have been more imaginative than that. You know
her?"

"Yes."

"You've had business dealings with her?"

He laughed. "Wasn't for her I wouldn't be sitting here tonight."

The room was dark enough for anyone who wanted to pretend not to see anyone else to pretend to blame it on the dim lighting. Jean Latour now did just that. She recognized Harvey Hunt, but gave no sign.

"Did you see that?" said Martha Swanson. "Either she's very near-sighted or she doesn't want to have any more dealings with you. Tell me about her. I gave you *my* life history."

"Let's watch and see what she does," he said.

Pennington, standing behind Jean Latour, leaned down to hear what she was saying. Obviously he was protesting, then he shrugged his shoulders in controlled exasperation, dropped some money on the bar, and followed the girl to the door. Kessler, the proprietor, hurried to them, concerned by their sudden decision to leave.

"Kessler doesn't often get a Gaston Pennington in his place," said Martha Swanson.

Kessler, giving up, went back to the bar and questioned the bartender, who was very busy and impatient with Kessler's agitated interrogation.

"Kessler doesn't know who to blame," said Martha Swanson. "If he knew it was you, you'd most likely get a Mickey Finn. *After* he found out what you had to do with it. On second thought, maybe he *wouldn't* give you a Mickey. He'd wonder what you knew that could upset Pennington, or the girl, and no matter what you told him, he wouldn't believe you. He'd always think you were holding out on him. *I'm* pretty curious *myself.*"

"You sure have made a study of Kessler," said Harvey Hunt.

"He's one of the biggest phonies I've ever known. He doesn't give a damn about us. It's the people we bring in that count with him. The sports writers bring the prizefighters and baseball players, the rest of us bring the politicians. It was the same in San Francisco. The newspaper people find a place they like and can afford, and pretty soon the place is popular and the prices go up, and the newspaper crowd can't go there any more."

"We're here now."

"We're not here every night, not any more," she said. "Get back to your friend with the phony French name. She looks to me like a Polish girl from the coal regions. Is that where you knew her? She's awfully young, but then most of them are, and anyway you wouldn't mind that, would you?"

"She claims to be seventeen."

"I don't think she *is* much more," said Martha Swanson. "But why are you stalling me off? Where do you fit in?"

"I never did fit in, if you know what I mean," he said.

"I'd have to be stupid *not* to know what you mean," said Martha Swanson. "*At all?* Why did she look at you that way?"

"It's a long story," said Harvey Hunt.

"Well tell it, for heaven's sake. Kessler stays open till four."

He told his story of Jean Latour as fully as it came to him, and Martha Swanson was so quiet that he needed her interruptions—to reorder a drink, to light a cigarette—to reassure him of her attention. Her interruptions were never in the form of questions, and when he finished the story she remained silent. Her silence made him uneasy.

"Are you still awake?" he said.

"Yes, I'm awake," she said.

"I thought maybe you'd fallen asleep."

"No, I didn't fall asleep," she said.

"You sure seemed it," he said.

"Well, that was because right at the beginning I wanted to ask you a question, but I didn't like to interrupt."

"What was the question?" he said.

"The question was, why did you want to play a sort of Sir Galahad for this girl? Why did you want to go to bat for her?"

"I honestly don't know. I've had almost a year to figure that out, and I still don't know."

"Just obeyed an impulse," she said.

"She wasn't an ordinary, banged-up whore," he said. "And she wasn't the usual run of sixteen-seventeen-year-old tarts. I've seen plenty of them, plenty. You do, in the places where I've worked. The coal towns, where the girls quit school at thirteen or fourteen and get work in the stocking factories. And places like Reading and Allentown, they get jobs in the silk mills and so forth, and they have to bring home all their pay. If they hold out a buck or two they get hell beaten out of them, and they soon find out that there're other ways of making a little money on the side. Some of them run away, some of them are sent to the Catholic Protectory. This kid didn't happen to come from the anthracite region, but the background was the same. But *she* wasn't the same. She was worse—but she was better."

"You didn't know all that when the police brought her in."

"No. But if she wanted to stay out of jail, I wanted to help *keep* her out. I don't *know* why. Maybe just because it was what she wanted."

"In other words, you fell for her," said Martha Swanson.

"That's just it. I don't think I did. But maybe I did."

"Well, you did a nice thing—"

"And I got what I deserved," said Harvey Hunt.

"She's sorry, though. She has it on her conscience. I saw her look at you."

"I'd hate to bet on that."

"But you wish it were so," said Martha Swanson. "Let's ask Kessler what he knows about her."

Kessler, when questioned, became suspicious. "Why do you want to know about *her?*"

"Now, Kessler, you know better than that," said Martha. "If you have nothing to say, all right."

"Oh, I got no objections," said Kessler. He plainly could not bear to be left out of things, even to be left out by his own doing. "Martha, you can always wheedle me around your little finger. Lemme sit down a minute here. Now, you want to know who she is and all? Too much I can't tell you because there's a lot I don't know. She showed up around town a couple years ago, not in my place so much but I seen her around. First with guys from dance orchesters. Then lo and behold she stard once in a while I seen her with Gaston Pennington. Pretty big stuff for her. Then the next I heard he was paying the rent. A lotta little girls would give their eyeteeth to have Gaston Pennington pay the rent, but there's one thing with Gat. That's what they call him. Gat. A girl that he pays the rent, she gotta be there, at his beck and call. He's not an every-night guy, but they gotta be there. He don't come in here much because he don't like the newspaper reporters, so she come in here with other guys, and I said to myself I bet her days are numbered because she's two-timing Gat, and one of these nights she won't be there when he wants her. But I guess she was lucky so far. He's always going away some place, but she don't know when he'll be back. Gat's a very close-lipped guy. What I call very close-lipped."

"Why did they suddenly leave here tonight?" said Martha.

"Oh, you know. Gat's the kind of a guy, he's changeable. Very changeable. I seen him order a whole meal and send it all back because he decide he wanted something else. He'll pay for it. No trouble about paying. But very, very changeable. Very changeable. You take now tonight, maybe he decide he didn't want to eat with her. And I gotta yumor him or he could raise my rent. He owns all the way to Spruce Street."

"Does he own the building where she lives?" said Harvey Hunt.

"That I'd have to guess, because I don't know where she lives. I asked her, but she clammed up on me."

"You could follow her home," said Harvey.

"Yes, I could. And I could not only get my rent raised, but he could refuse to renew my lease. And it ain't like I could move next door or across the street. She's a nice little dish, but first I gotta think of my business. No broad is worth that much to me, not with what I got coming in here from all the shows. Not to mention I'm a married man and Miss Latour looks at all the angles. All the angles, that kid." He looked to the right, to the left, and behind him, leaned forward and lowered his voice. "I could ask where was she yesterday and the day before and I *know* where she was and who with. But I don't want her sore at me. Not her. You know, some day she's liable to turn up with somebody I don't want to tangle with. I don't mean like Gat Pennington. I mean—well, shall be nameless."

"You mean one of the big boys in the racket?" said Martha Swanson.

"Draw your own conclusions," said Kessler.

"Oh, don't be so mysterious," said Martha Swanson. "If you mean Choo-Choo Klein why don't you say so? Is that who she was with in Atlantic City?"

"Wuddia wanta know all this for, Martha? You starting a big exposé?"

"You hit it," she said. "We just discovered that the Wanamaker Bugle Corps are taking over South Philly. It's going to mean a new gang war."

Kessler looked at her without changing his frozen half smile. He tapped the table with his fingertips. "Martha, where you from originally?"

"San Francisco," she said. "Why?"

"Oh, yeah. They got a big Chinese population out there. Bigger than here."

"Yes, why?"

"Did you ever cover a story where a man got his head cut off? Did you ever *see* a man with his head cut off?"

"No."

"Well, I did. Don't kid around about gang wars, Martha. Just don't kid around."

"Or I'm liable to get hurt?" she said.

"If it was you I wouldn't give a damn," said Kessler. "I don't care what happens to you. But I care what happens to me. Just don't kid around about gang wars, and keep your nose out of where it don't belong. You're liable to say the wrong thing and it wouldn't be *you* that got hurt."

"I'm sorry, Kessler," she said. "But you're not going to get hurt over anything I say."

"As usual, you don't know a God damn thing. Even the cops know more than you newspaper reporters. I had one of the owners of a paper in here one night and he stard shooting off his mouth about Choo-Choo Klein. And all the time you know who was sitting at the next table? Choo-Choo Klein. Choo-Choo knew who *he* was, but the newspaper fellow didn't know Klein when he saw him. Would you know Choo-Choo?"

"Of course."

"How about you, Hunt? Would you reccanize him?"

"I met him the second night I was in Philly. Sure I'd know him. That's not saying he'd know me."

"Would you know his brother? Either one of you?" said Kessler.

"I didn't know he had a brother," said Martha Swanson.

"Well, he has a brother. He has a brother is a respectable business man. But the brother that's a respectable business man, *he* has Choo-Choo Klein for his brother, if you follow me." Kessler was in a conflict between the urge to shut up and the compulsion to talk. "Martha, you was down't the shore? Then did you happen to see a fellow there looked like Choo-Choo only heavier set and darker complected?"

"I didn't happen to notice. But that was Choo-Choo's brother?"

"Draw your own conclusions. I din tell you nothing. Have a drink on the house." He stood up and left them.

"I've found him very unreliable. He never knows as much as he likes you to think he knows, but in this case he produced a few facts. Very interesting, your little tramp two-timing Gaston Pennington with the gangster's brother. When I go home tonight I'm going to go through the handouts from the convention, see if I can find Choo-Choo Klein's respectable brother."

"It must be pretty well known that he has a brother."

"Yes, but I didn't know it, and neither did you. Shall we wait for the free drink or would you like to go home and listen to some records?"

They went to her apartment. "I have all of Art Hickman and the early Whiteman records. Whenever I get homesick for San Francisco I play them. Well, not all of them, that'd take all night. But they were both friends of Daddy's. I'll see if I can find the dope on Klein. Meanwhile, help yourself to a drink, and fix me a rye and soda, please?"

He prepared the drinks, and she found a publicity sheet from the convention. "Uh-huh," she said. "M. A. Klein, president, Barnegat Bank and Trust Company, Hamilton Bays, New Jersey. That must be near Atlantic City, Barnegat."

"Say any more about him?"

"No, this is just a list of the men attending the convention, and where they were staying. But M. A. Klein doesn't give a hotel address."

"Why are we so interested in M. A. Klein?"

"I thought you'd be," said Martha Swanson.

"Do you know what I think? I think you're interested in Gaston Pennington."

"And why do you say that?" she said.

"A hunch."

She took a long, deep breath. "That's twice tonight you surprised me. First when you told me about your reaction on seeing that girl in the police station. And now, Gaston Pennington. If you surprise me one more time I'm going to have to change my impression of you."

"What's your impression of me?"

"That you were just another newspaper man on the make."

"Maybe that's all I am, but what's wrong with that? I don't pretend to be an O. C. Swanson. I'm a fast, accurate rewrite man, without any flowers, or I'm a damn good reporter. If I can get off rewrite I'll show this town what a good reporter I am. In fact, I'd like to go out on a story against you, Martha. I'd come back with stuff you never thought of."

"Maybe you would. I don't feel like arguing. Play 'Rose Room,' and imagine yourself in San Francisco."

"It makes me think of Joe Nesbitt at Harveys Lake."

"All right. I'll think of San Francisco, you think of Harveys Lake, whatever that is. But don't let's argue."

When the record was finished she asked him to play it over again, and the second time it was finished he looked at her, implying the question, did she want it again? She shook her head. He sat beside her and took her in his arms and kissed her, and she was acquiescent. With their faces close together she looked at him. "I don't know," she said.

"What don't you know?" he said.

"Why I like you. But I do. Will it be all over the city room tomorrow?"

"No."

"I'd hate that. They've all tried, and got nowhere. A year from now you can talk, but don't for a while, will you please?"

"I won't."

"You've been pretty lonely, too. God knows *I* have. God *knows* I have."

There were three weeks, nearly four, of their well-kept secret, achieved by their meeting only in her apartment and staying apart when they were in the office. When they made love they spoke of love, but they avoided the committal declarations and plans. There was a continuing passion that carried them from day to day and that enabled them to postpone the calmer declarations and long-range plans. His hours were later than hers, and he would go to the flat and eat her dinner and stay until she had left in the morning. At the Royal the change in his routine had been noticed by a vaguely resentful Albert. "Don't see as much of you these last couple nights," said Albert.

"Well, as long as I pay my rent," said Harvey Hunt.

"Oh, I wasn't thinking about the rent," said Albert. "Y'aren't the only one keeps their room and don't sleep in it, much."

"I know. I remember. She been in lately?"

"Yesterday. And asked about you," said Albert.

"Asked about me? She didn't leave an envelope with seventy bucks in it, did she?"

"Not with me. And there's nothing in your box that I can see, so I guess she didn't. I thought maybe you run across her somewhere."

"No."

"That's what I thought, though. Something she said made me al-

329 MINUTES AWAY ♦ 329

most positive, like as if she was expecting to see you. Maybe she was just looking for you."

"She wouldn't be looking for me, Albert. And I'm not looking for her. Only the seventy bucks she swiped, that's all I ever want from Miss Latour."

"Yesterday was the first time she was here since you checked in. Well, maybe not the first. But not more than twice or three times since you checked in. Other times she didn't want to run into you, but yesterday she particularly asked for you. Maybe she had the seventy on her and wanted to pay you back, I don't know."

"As much chance of that as a celluloid cat in hell," said Harvey. "Just tell her to leave the money in an envelope, and I'll give you ten of it."

"Ten dollars, or ten percent?"

"Dollars, Albert."

"Didn't run across her anywhere, hey?"

"And don't want to," said Harvey. "I'll have some laundry I want done."

"You can leave it here on your way out and it'll be taken care of."

"Thanks, Albert," said Harvey Hunt.

He did not always see Albert when he went to the Royal to change his linen. On some mornings he slept past Albert's time to leave. On one such morning it was close to ten o'clock before he got to the room at the Royal, and when he let himself in, she was there.

"Kind of late," she said.

"Well, so are you. Damn near a year. Have you got seventy dollars that belongs to me?"

"Right there it is, on the dresser. Seven tens. Count them to make sure."

"Thank you. Anything else you want?"

"You don't have a cigarette on you? I smoked all mine, waiting for you to show up."

"If you want a Fatima."

"Yeah, for a change. Beggars can't be choosers. And a light, please?"

"Take the pack and the matches."

"Trying to get rid of me?"

"I want to change my clothes and go to work."

"You don't have to be bashful with me. I've seen everything you have."

"So you have. All the same, I'd just as soon you let me have some privacy."

"Don't be such an old maid," she said. "I'll go as soon as I finish my cigarette. For seventy bucks I'm entitled to that."

"All right, if you put it that way."

"Why didn't you give me a tumble at Kessler's that night?"

"It seemed to me, you got the hell out of there fast when you saw me."

"I tried to say hello to you."

"No you didn't."

"I did so, but you were sneaking a feel with that dame, I guess. Is that who you're getting it from that you're so bashful? I didn't think much of her. Big tits, that's all. Probably hangers, too. Takes off her brazeer and *blump,* down they go. Is that what you like?"

"Smoke your cigarette."

"Don't hurry me. I don't like to be hurried. I like to take it slow— and easy. Slow—and easy."

He laughed. "I was just thinking of you and your dude with the monocle. That must be a funny sight."

"That dude could buy and sell you *and* your paper. You know Kessler's? He owns all that land. He happens to be one of the richest men in Philly."

"I know all about him. And M. A. Klein, too, for that matter."

She was startled. "Who did you say?"

"You heard me, you're not handcuffed. I said M. A. Klein, the president of the Barnegat Trust Company. Whose brother—"

"Where did you get all that? From Kessler? That son of a bitch Kessler. He talks too much." She was confused by fear. "You got it from Kessler, didn't you? Listen, please tell me. I gotta know, for certain reasons I gotta know. I'll do anything you want, but only tell me, was it Kessler?"

"I won't tell you anything. You're a two-timing, triple-timing little bitch, and—"

"I know, but this is different. Harvey, I'll get in that bed and give you the biggest thrill you ever got from any woman. You want a thrill, and you like me. I know you do, the minute you saw me. You gave up your job for me. And I like you, too, even if I did steal a few dollars from you. Honey, let me show you how I can give you a thrill. Will you let me show you?"

"No."

"You're sore at me, that's it." She looked about her from place to place, then rushed to him and pulled his belt out of the loops and handed it to him. "Beat me. You want to beat me. Look, I'll take everything off and you can hit me with your belt. I'll like it if you do, Harvey."

"Stop! Cut it out!"

She sat wearily on the edge of the bed. "A fellow wanted to give me a thousand dollars if I let him, and I wouldn't. A thousand dollars. I don't know what else I can offer you, Harvey. If I give you this ring will you tell me?"

"Why do you want to know that so much? What difference does it make who told me?"

"Oh, if you only knew," she said. "Please tell me if it was Kessler."

"First you tell me why it's so important to know where I found out."

"I can't, I can't, I can't. I can't tell you anything. Don't you see I'm scared?"

"Look, you're not going to get anything out of me. And I have to go to work, so beat it. What the hell did you come here for?"

"I don't even remember that," she said. "Oh, I remember all right. I came here to pay you back the money, and then we could be friends again."

"We never were friends," he said.

"Yes, you liked me. There was something going, don't deny that."

"Well, it didn't last very long."

"No. I always louse things up. But that's all I came here for, I swear to God."

"You're a natural-born liar."

"I know," she said. Behind the conversation it was apparent that she was thinking of something else. "But this is one time I'm going to tell you the truth. This part will be the truth. Will you believe me?"

"I doubt it, but go ahead and try."

She waited, and in her manner and appearance there was so much defeat, so complete a lack of her young arrogance—the kind that had made her so defiant in the South Taqua police station—that she was half convincing even before she began to speak. "You know how I got started and all that, way back. You know all about me, or a hell of a lot. And I never claimed to be a Sodality girl. And you know I got this Pennington fellow keeping me, and I cheat on him. I admit all that, and why shouldn't I? Who do I have anything to hide from? Even Pennington isn't that much of a chump that he thinks I sit home all the time, waiting for him to get horny. We have a kind of an understanding, where he don't ask me questions because he knows I'll just fill him full of lies. Oh, he's all right, Pennington."

"Gat," said Harvey Hunt.

"That's what they call him," she said. "Then I don't know, several months ago I met a fellow and I didn't know very much about him except he had money and he lived out of town. How I happened to meet him was Pennington took me to New York and then he went to Boston and I was on the train back to Philly and I saw this fellow. He rode with me as far as Broad Street Station and I gave him my phone number. He said his name was Mr. Little. The *L* didn't go with the initials on his suitcase, but I didn't think I was ever gunna see him again, but I did. A week or so and he called me up and I went out with him in his car. We had dinner out near Paoli, out in that direction, and I liked him and we went to some apartment of a friend of his. That's the way it was for a couple months. Then one day I was home and the doorbell rang and this stranger came in and asked me if I knew him. I said I didn't. I didn't know him, and why should I? He said he was Max Klein's brother and I said I didn't know any Max Klein and to get the hell out or I'd call the cops. He laughed at that. Well, he called me a lot of names till I finally convinced him I didn't know any Max Klein, but from the description I figured out he was talking about my friend Little. This took about an hour, I guess, and it finally dawned on me who this fellow was. 'Are you *Choo-Choo* Klein?' And he said he was. Well, *then* I knew who he was all right. I said I was pleased to meet him and he got friendlier. No pass, but flattered me a little. He said he could easily understand how his brother could go for me and all that. Then came the payoff, why he was there. The brother was legitimate, ran a bank down at the shore, and had a wife and kids and all. I was to give him up. Give him up? Outside of a few meals and maybe two or three hundred dollars for presents I didn't have anything to give up. Little was nothing in my young life. Two or three hundred bucks and a couple bottles of per-*fume.* Choo-Choo peeled off four hundred-dollar bills. 'For your trouble,' he said. The next time the brother called I was to brush him off and make it stick. Then Choo-Choo got a little nasty again, just a little but enough so I remembered who I was talking to. He said if I did see his brother again a lot of things could go wrong for me. Like I could get in a taxi some night and it'd be a long time before I got home again. He wanted that brother respectable, he wanted that bank respectable. He didn't want his brother playing around and getting talked about. On the other hand, if I was a nice kid and did what he said, I'd get a little bonus at Christmas when he handed around his other bonuses. I said I didn't want a bonus, but maybe he could fix it so I could sing in a club. I was fed up with hanging around with nothing to occupy my time. He said that could be arranged."

"You always land on both feet, don't you?" said Harvey Hunt.

"The next time Little phoned I said I was all sewed up. I couldn't give him any more time. He knew about Pennington and he said he'd top what Pennington was giving me, but I said it wasn't only the money. I made up a story that Pennington wanted to marry me, and Little said he'd match that offer too. He'd marry me. I said Pennington's both offers were better than his, and all bets were off. I hung up, but a couple days later he was on the phone again and I almost told him to go talk to his brother, but I didn't. I hung up on him that time and the next, but then I realized he was hanging around Philly getting drunk, and what good was that doing me? So I said I'd see him once more, and I did. That was when I told him about Choo-Choo coming to see me, and believe me, that scared him. He told me Choo-Choo didn't give a damn about him, but wanted him respectable to please their mother. Choo-Choo worshiped the old lady, even if she treated him like dirt. She called Choo-Choo a gunsel and some other Jewish name, but Max was a good boy. So I said I didn't want to get my little ass in a sling because of some old lady I never even heard of. Well, he didn't want any trouble with Choo-Choo either. He went home the next day and I thought that would be the last of him, but no.

"I had guys stuck on me before, carrying the torch. But Max Klein was different. Why different? Well in some ways they're all different and in some ways they're all the same, only Max was more different than anybody. He'd sit and look at me and say did I realize what we were? According to him we were a tragedy. A tragedy? I didn't want to be any tragedy. He said we were doomed, and I didn't want to be doomed. This guy ran a little bank down at the shore and he had a brother the top guy in the mob. I didn't get it, this tragedy, this doomed. I was just a girl trying to get along, and I didn't want any of this Shakespeare. He said we were invented by Shakespeare, and I'm lucky I even heard of Shakespeare. But he must of appealed to me, because otherwise why would I take all those chances? I always said I wouldn't see him again, but he could always talk me into it. And God knows there was nothing in it for me. A fifty-dollar bill once in a while. And as far as being the great lover, this guy was on a par with—well—"

"Albert, at the Royal?"

"All right, Albert. To tell you the truth, Albert was better. At least with Albert he didn't kid around. I wouldn't have him again, but he can satisfy a woman, and that's more than you can say for most of them. Albert told you, hey?"

"Sure."

"Well, all right, if he wants to brag about it. If I said he was a liar nobody'd believe him, so I don't worry about Albert ruining my reputation."

"Go on about Klein," said Harvey Hunt.

"Nobody caught on, because I made him go on the wagon and pay attention to his bank. He had to do that or I'd get in trouble with Choo-Choo, and so would he, and if he didn't I wouldn't meet him. We never went to the same place twice, in case Choo-Choo was suspicious. We went to Trenton, Baltimore, Wilmington, Reading. A different hotel every time, and only for the one night. It was costing him money, but it was costing me almost as much. Why did I want to take all these chances with a guy that was a lousy lay. He was, he was a lousy lay. And all he could talk about was the sword of democracy hanging over us. Jesus! I don't know. Did I get a kick out of taking the chances? I must of. I don't know what else. What the hell was in it for me, I'll never know. Oh, maybe I got a kick out of outsmarting Choo-Choo. I guess there was that. I guess so. I don't like to take orders from anybody, whether he's a big-shot racket guy or a wealthy millionaire, I don't like to take orders. And Choo-Choo never got wise. Every so often I'd be out with Pennington and I'd see Choo-Choo and he'd just give me a little tumble, just enough to get it across to me that I was doing great. Then like a stupid dumbbell I said I'd meet Max at that convention down at the shore. There was three or four hundred guys there and I could of been with any one of them, the way Max figured it, and that made it safe, according to him. But safe? You know about it, that broad knows about it, and who else? If Choo-Choo Klein finds out, me there with his brother and all those bankers, in one of the big Boardwalk hotels—I'm finished. I'd be afraid to take a taxi, I'd be afraid to walk on Walnut Street in broad daylight. And if you found out from Kessler, that's as good as Choo-Choo finding out, because Kessler made a play for me and I said I'd rather get in bed with his busboy." She had come to the end of her speech, and she was now in an attitude of waiting.

"It was Kessler," said Harvey Hunt.

"Yes, I guess I knew it all along," she said. "If it was anything else I could go to Pennington. He very seldom turns me down when I ask him something. But I can't ask him to get me out of this."

"Probably not," said Harvey Hunt.

"Ten o'clock in the morning and I'm afraid to go out on the street," she said. "All of a sudden I don't have any place to go."

"Do you think it's as bad as all that?"

"Yes. The minute Kessler opens his mouth, and maybe he opened it last night."

"How do you think Kessler found out?"

"What's the difference, how? Maybe it was something that broad said that was with you. Maybe he saw us in Baltimore a month ago and we didn't see him. Kessler's like an old-maid gossip. He hears plenty, and he has to be in on everything. What he don't know he makes guesses at."

"Well, what do you do next? I mean today."

She opened her purse, turned it upside down to dump the contents in her lap. "A hundred and forty-two dollars, and some cents," she said.

"Plus seventy."

"No, you keep that. It won't do me much good. This ring. My pin. The earrings. I got about six hundred dollars in the bank. Will you do me a favor?"

"If I can," he said.

"Will you put me on the train? Go all the way with me to the seat in the coach, and stay with me till the train leaves?"

"I never went all the way with you, and I never stayed with you," he said. "All right."

"I owe you that, don't I? Well, I made you a good offer and you turned me down."

"What happens when you get to New York?"

"New York? Don't you remember me telling how I started out in New York? New York's easy, and don't forget I learned a few things since the first time I went there."

"Well, be sure and let me know how you make out."

"Let you know? Read the papers. Or *I* know. I got a better idea. You come with me."

"Sure. Great," he said.

"Listen, I'm gonna need a press agent. Don't get stuck here all your life. You're still young."

"A minute ago you were shaking."

"I know I was, but all of a sudden I can hardly wait to hit the big town again. Harvey, this is a chance for you, too. We just pull out of here and get a whole new start. Will you do it? Harvey, I know I'm right. I go by feelings, and I got a feeling. This is the exact minute for both of us."

"For you, not for me. Or maybe for me, too, but I don't have the same feeling."

"Oh, I see. You know what's gonna happen to you, don't you? You'll end up marrying that dame and living out in West Philly, and five years from now I'll come here with some big show and you'll wish you went with me today."

"It's a possibility," he said.

From

WAITING FOR WINTER

♦

ANDREA

♦

Nearly everything she said was truthful, but because she laughed
so much her friends often believed she was joking and remained her friends. She had beautiful teeth, even and strong all
the way back, and some of her friends had been known to remark
that it was such a pleasure to look at her teeth that it actually did not
matter much what she said. There were, of course, a few people who
were not deceived by her laughter or diverted by the display of her
teeth, and those people hated her. "How can you hate someone like
Andrea Cooper?" her more constant friends would say. "There's no
one around that brightens up a room the way she does." But Andrea
had left many wounded souls along her merry way, and there were
men among them as well as women.

Throughout her lifetime Andrea's popularity had always been
more immediate and durable with boys and with men. It was said of
her that her frankness, her honesty, appealed to the males. It was
certainly true that if she had ever been ill at ease with the opposite
sex, it did not show. One of the first things I noticed about her when
I began to notice her at all was her quick decision, at a party or on
the club verandah, to join the young men in preference to the girls. If
there were two or three young men standing together she would go
up to one of them and tug his sleeve. "Andrea's here," she would
say, and she would be sure of her welcome. In those days a lot of
girls were borrowing a line from a movie called *Young Man of Manhattan,* in which Ginger Rogers (or maybe it was Toby Wing) said,

"Cigarette me, big boy." I never heard Andrea say just those words, but then I did not often hear Andrea use a line that was not her own.

She was then about sixteen years old, maybe fifteen but not seventeen. Her mother and father had come to town the year before, leaving Andrea and her brother in school in California while Mr. and Mrs. Cooper found a suitable place to live. Mrs. Cooper had inherited the second largest department store from her grandmother, and Mr. Cooper, who had been working in a bank in Santa Barbara, was going to try his hand at managing the store. Everyone agreed that King's needed new blood and that Mr. Cooper could not do any worse than the previous managers. With his banking experience he might even put King's back on its feet again. Much to everyone's surprise he did just that, although the results were slow in coming. Mr. and Mrs. Cooper were young, still in their thirties, and young for their age. He possessed a California affability that could have affected people either way, but in his case it worked favorably on the other business men. Mrs. Cooper, a native Pennsylvanian who had grown up on the West Coast, was a rather diffident woman who let her husband do most of the talking. She was obviously devoted to him, had no designs on other women's husbands, and the Coopers fitted in much more quickly than most newcomers to the town. In their first year in town they won the mixed doubles in the club tennis tournament, knocking off a much younger couple who had two legs on the cup and were believed to be invincible.

They had Andrea finish out the year in a Santa Barbara school before transferring her to one in New England, and what with one thing and another, I did not get a good look at Andrea until after her mother and father had been living in town for the better part of two years. *"Who is that?"* I said, when I first saw her. She was obviously too young for me; I was already halfway through law school and had been having an affair with a married woman in West Philadelphia. Nevertheless my first reaction on seeing Andrea, with a golden band in her pale blond hair, those teeth, her breasts as firm as fists under her sequined white dress, was of civic pride. This radiant creature had come to live in my home town, and I had seen nothing like her at the Philadelphia parties. It may have been that she was overdressed for her age, but as someone said, she would have looked good in a sweatshirt.

I cut in on her at that first dance, and she flattered me by knowing who I was. "Hello, Judge," she said. "Thanks for rescuing me."

"What do you mean, *judge*?" I said.

"Isn't that what you're going to be?"

"It's a long way off if I am," I said. "But how did you know?"

"I made a point of knowing," she said.

"You mean it was love at first sight?"

"No, I didn't say that. I just said I make a point of knowing *if* they're at all attractive," she said.

"Score one for the common people," I said. "You build me up and then knock me down."

"Didn't knock you down," she said. "How could I? You saved my life. That horny man you cut in on, he's older than my father."

"Peter Hofman," I said.

"He didn't want to dance, he wanted to wrestle."

"That's the price you pay," I said. "You're the belle of the ball. Peter Hofman is always out to show us young fellows that he's the best dancer, the greatest lover."

"I've seen his wife, *and* his children. He ought to keep them in hiding. They're not much of an ad for him."

The music stopped. "Are you thirsty?" I said.

"No, but if you are, go ahead. You want to go out to the smoking-room."

"Not necessarily."

"I'm not supposed to go there," she said. "My parents issued strict orders."

"Do you always obey your parents?"

"Of course, especially when they're in the same room and keeping an eye on me."

"Oh, I haven't seen them," I said. "They're here?"

"They're probably in the smoking-room. Daddy probably having a ginger ale and Mother the same. But I'm sure that's where they are. You go on, I won't mind."

"No, I can get a drink any time."

"Then how would you like to take me out on the porch and give me a cigarette? I've also been told not to smoke, although they know I do smoke. But it's unbecoming, very unbecoming for a young girl to smoke."

"They're pretty strict with you," I said, as we moved toward the verandah.

"They have to be," she said. "Otherwise there's no telling what I'd do. I might be out in the car, wrestling with Mr. Hofman."

"Would you wrestle very hard?"

"If it was Mr. Hofman I'd kick him, you know where," she said.

"Where it would do the most good, but not for old Peter," I said. "I have a car out there."

"Then we won't have to freeze on the porch," she said.

"I've even got a pint of prescription liquor."

"You think of everything, don't you? Unfortunately, they'll smell it on my breath when I kiss them goodnight. Then they won't let me go to the other dances. I'm not supposed to drink till I'm eighteen."

We got in my car, an Essex speedster in which you practically sat on the floor, and I lit her cigarette. "I'll never get used to the weather in the East," she said. "Maybe I'll never get used to the East, period."

"Did you have a heavy beau in California?"

"About your weight, I guess," she said.

"A hundred and seventy-four," I said.

"No, it isn't just him. There's something different about Easterners. Even Mother, brought up in California, she's different than Daddy, the way they look at things. She was born here, but she left when she was a little girl. Do you know who's like us? The Swedes. So it isn't just the climate."

"How are you like the Swedes?" I said. "Have you known many Swedes?"

"My heavy beau was from a Swedish family. They all moved to Southern California from Minnesota. His father and his uncles and aunts, and cousins. I must know a hundred or more. And they're always picked out as typical Southern Californians. People used to think I was one of them, when I went to their parties. But my mother's family were from the North of Ireland, and Daddy's people came from Iowa."

"Aren't there a lot of Swedes in Iowa? They spilled over from Minnesota."

"I didn't know that. Then I may *be* part Swedish. I've never been to Iowa."

"You do look rather Swedish," I said. "I've been there, on the North Cape cruise. You could be taken for a Swede."

"They like to have a good time, and so do I," she said. "I'd give anything for a drink."

"No, you don't want to miss the other parties."

She looked at me, frowning and studying me as though I were some strange specimen that she was having trouble identifying.

"What?" I said.

"I'm not sure," she said, still studying me.

"About what?"

"You. Do you care whether I miss the other parties?"

"I don't, but you do," I said. "I won't even *be* here, but two of the parties are bound to be good, and there's the Assembly."

"I can't go to the Assembly. I'm too young."

"Well, there are the other two. You wouldn't want to miss them. Markel's for one, and Sherbo for the other."

"I suppose they're orchestras," she said.

"You'll soon find out," I said.

"We have Arnheim's. I don't know the Eastern orchestras unless they're on records. It's nice of you to care whether I miss the parties, it really is. Is it because you like me, or what? I mean—me especially?"

"Yes. And I think you'd be a great addition to the parties. You're what we call new talent."

"Thank you," she said. She was thinking. "You're not at all what I expected."

"No?"

"Maybe because you're older. Maybe because you're so Eastern-ish. Both, I guess. Why do you wear those pumps? I thought you only wore them with tails."

"I always wear them. I always have."

"And that kind of a collar. Daddy always wears those collars that open at the neck. Wings?"

"I'll wear a wing collar with tails, but not with a Tuck."

"Daddy says Tux. You say Tuck. I'll have to tell my brother these things. He's not here for Christmas, but next year he's entered in Andover. What do you think of Andover?"

"Good."

"Where did you go?"

"I went to a small church school called St. Bartholomew's."

"Oh, come on. A small church school. I've heard about St. Bartholomew's. Then where did you go? Yale?"

"Williams," I said.

"And now you're at the U. of Penn," she said.

"Jesus, don't call it the U. of Penn. Penn, or the U. of P., but not the U. of Penn. Ugh."

"So sorry. When my brother comes here next summer, will you help him out? Show him things?"

"I'm afraid I won't be here next summer," I said. "I have a job in Philadelphia. Anyway, the kind of things you're thinking of, he'll learn them at Andover."

"I'd like him to know them before he goes to Andover."

"How old is this boy?"

"Fourteen."

"Hell, he has plenty of time," I said. "And he might resent my telling him things."

"No he wouldn't. I'd see to that. He listens to me. He adores me, he really does."

"Well, you are rather adorable."

"If you think I am now, wait'll you see me in a bathing suit."

"I can hardly wait," I said.

"You *should* be making passes at me," she said.

"Oh, I don't know."

"Mr. Hofman would be making passes at me," she said.

"Not after you kicked him."

"But you're not afraid I'd kick you."

"No. But you couldn't kick anybody in this car."

"Then why haven't you made a pass at me?"

"Do you really want to know?"

"Yes," she said.

"Because you're a virgin."

"That's never stopped anyone else from making passes at me."

"It stops me."

"Oh, you have to go all the way?" she said. "How do you know I wouldn't go all the way?"

"It would be almost physically impossible in this car."

"You don't approve of necking? Heavy necking?"

"Do you?"

"Morally, I don't. But I've done it."

"But you've managed to stay a virgin. You must have given that Swedish boy a bad time."

"He didn't think so," she said. "He didn't expect me to go all the way. The night before I came East I would have, but he didn't know that."

"Then you were lucky," I said.

"Yes, but I didn't think so at the time. Now I do, but then. I was sure he didn't love me."

"And now you're sure he did?"

"No, and I don't love him any more. We don't even write to each other. I was really glad to get out of California. Not so much glad to get out of California as to be moving back East. Everything is new and different here."

"Maybe not as different as you think," I said.

"Have you ever been there?"

"No," I said.

"Then how can you tell?"

"There are differences, but I don't think they matter so much when you come right down to it," I said.

"Oh, are *you* ever wrong!" she said. "If you went to California you'd find out. I wish I could fall in love here, but I feel like such a stranger."

"That's not why you haven't fallen in love. Use your head. When you're ready to fall in love, the geography isn't going to make any difference. It's the person, not the location."

"It must be the location. I've been ready to fall in love ever since I got here, but the people are so different."

"Don't rush things."

"Why not? I want to rush things."

"Then you probably will, and you won't be a virgin much longer."

"That would suit me," she said.

"Even if you weren't in love?"

"I've thought about that. And I've come to the conclusion that I am not going to wait till I'm in love."

"You're just going to give the fair white body to some guy with a dimple in his chin?"

"Oh, no. I hate dimples in chins."

"Well, then one of us lucky guys without a dimple in our chins."

"You're razzing me, but I'm serious."

"You'd better be, about this. You might have a little accident."

"Not me. I'm not that naïve," she said. "You know, I haven't even called you by your first name. I know it's Philip. But do you know why I'm so relaxed with you? Telling you so much?"

"No, why?"

"Because when you said I oughtn't to take a drink and miss those parties, that was the first time since I came East that anyone was really human. And the funny thing is, you didn't seem very human. You and that collar and those pumps. Studying to be a lawyer. Cold as an icicle. And you're not really."

"No, I'm not."

"Where do you live in Philadelphia? At a fraternity house?"

"No, I share an apartment with two friends of mine. Why, were you thinking of paying me a visit?"

"Naturally. Why else would I ask?"

"We have a thing in the Commonwealth of Pennsylvania called statutory rape."

"It wouldn't be rape if I went there of my own accord," she said.

"Yes, I'm afraid it would. Your father and mother aren't the kind of people that would have me arrested, but frankly you're a bit young for me."

"Look, is this young?" She pulled down the straps of her evening dress and bared her breasts.

"Cut that out," I said.

"Kiss them," she said.

"God damn it, I said cut that out."

"You're a son of a *bitch,*" she said. She replaced the straps, and began to weep. I said nothing for a while, then passed her my handkerchief. She took a deep breath and said, "I guess we ought to be going back."

"All right with me," I said.

"You have every right to be cross with me," she said.

"Well, God damn it."

"I *want* somebody."

"*I* want *you,*" I said. "But for God's sake."

"I know, I know."

"No, you don't know, Andrea. You really don't."

"Yes I do. I honestly do, Philip. Honestly and truly, I know everything you could say to me."

"I doubt that but let's forget about it."

She shook her head. "I won't and you won't. Is your number in the telephone book, in Philadelphia?"

"Yes. I could say no, but if you looked you'd find it."

"Right," she said. "What's a good time to call you?"

"After four o'clock, and any evening."

"Next week?"

"Yes," I said.

"You'd be better for me than some guy with a dimple in his chin," she said. She was smiling now, and I put my arms around her and kissed her.

"That's better," she said. "You could love me, you know. I know it, if you don't."

"Oh, I know it now," I said.

We went back to the clubhouse, and several of my friends looked at me in mock disapproval and said things about robbing the cradle. But I told them to grow up, and I think I deceived them by not dancing again with Andrea. I had never been much of a parked-car Romeo, and my reputation for good conduct was paying off. The next week, on a Tuesday afternoon, Andrea came to our apartment on Walnut Street, and I committed statutory rape. Six years later, the week before she was to be married, she came to another apartment I had on Spring Garden Street; and ten years after that, when she had been divorced a second time, she was still the only woman I could not do without.

She had a way of turning up just as I was beginning to convince myself that I ought to put an end to my bachelorhood. Two or three times as much as a year would pass without my hearing from her except for a message scribbled on a Christmas card. In Philadelphia, and I suppose in any other city, a busy man who likes his work is not uncomfortably conscious of the passage of time. I had all the legal practice I could handle, and I was making a good deal of money. From my office on South Broad Street I would alternate between clubs for lunch on working days, and on Sundays I would join a group of men who foregathered to eat and drink and play shuffle-board. My evenings were as socially active or filled with work as I wished to make them, and it did not matter to me that I was sometimes called a selfish pig and a stuffed shirt. Some of the wives who called me a selfish pig for not marrying a suitable divorcée or widow were also pleased to have me as an extra man. And as for my being a stuffed shirt, the epithet was most often conferred upon me by other lawyers who had not done their homework as thoroughly as I. I was an upstate carpetbagger as well, but some of the men who called me that were also known to have remarked that it was too bad I was single and could not run for high public office. There were moments when bachelorhood seemed less desirable than matrimony, but I found that such spells of weakening usually coincided with the end of a long period of silence on the part of Andrea. Days would come when I became so obsessed with the need of her presence that only habit and routine kept me from chucking my practice and seeking her out. But then I would hear from her, remarkably soon and even on the very same day, and we would be together for a while. Only once did we discuss marriage. I proposed to her, and she said, "No, never to you, Phil. It would be pure hell for both of us. I'd rather keep coming back to you than keep running away from you every few months. That's the difference. I actually consider myself faithful to you all these years. And as far as that goes, I consider you faithful to me." There was no more to be said, unless I cared to admit that my fine legal mind had not summarized our situation as precisely as hers.

We had good times together. Between us there were no sexual inhibitions, and almost no twinge of jealousy. She would tell me about the problems she was having in breaking in a new man and she would talk freely and coolly about her husbands and lovers, one after another doomed to failure. "It makes me so cross when you say they call you a selfish pig," she once said. "You were never that with me, never for an instant. But they weren't with us back in that little car of yours. Oh, I love you, Phil. Andrea Cooper Et Cetera loves you."

"And I love Andrea Cooper—without the et cetera," I said.

"Yes," she said. "We have a love. Love, love, love, love, love. Now tell me something about your latest. How is she peculiar?"

"Not very peculiar," I said.

"You're holding out on me," she said.

"Well, one peculiarity," I said. "She likes to drive around with nothing on under her fur coat."

"Oh, yes, I've heard of that. That's fairly common. What does she do in the summertime? A raincoat?"

"I should imagine so," I said.

"My theory is that they want to be raped, but don't want to be, if you know what I mean. They're teasers, I think."

"Yes, that fits in. She's a teaser."

"Is she good at it?"

"Yes, I must say she is. She can be very aggravating."

"But satisfactory?"

"Eventually," I said.

"Is she living with her husband? I assume she's married."

"Oh, yes."

"Does he know about the fur coat business?" she said.

"He doesn't know anything about anything, from what I gather."

"You know what we are, you and I?"

"Among other things, what?" I said.

"What do they call those things? Safety valves. I wonder how many people there are that owe their sanity to us."

"Well, yes, but I owe my sanity to you."

"Oh, that goes without saying, you and I. But I was thinking of the other people."

"But what happens to them when you ditch them? In my case I don't think it matters too much. The women's peculiarities are rather minor things. Some like the phonograph playing, some don't. Some like to be hurt, others don't. But with men, there's the danger of violence."

"Yes," she said. "There is with women, too, but not as much as with men." She was silent.

"What?" I said.

"I was thinking of Stanley Broman. He's a man I had an affair with two years ago, until I broke it off. He's been calling me up late at night. If the Gibbsville operators ever listen in on those calls they must have a lovely opinion of me."

"Get an unlisted number, or turn off your phone," I said.

"I've done both. But what happens next? I'm afraid he may turn up some night."

"Tell him you're getting married again."

"I did, and that was a mistake. He said he was going to do everything to stop it."

"But you're not getting married again, are you?" I said.

"No. At least I have no plans to," she said.

"Then how can he stop what you have no intention of doing?" I said.

"I'm not worried about that. I just don't want to have him come near me again."

"What do you want me to do?" I said.

"I don't know. I was hoping you'd think of something," she said.

"Well, give me all the details and I'll bring in a private detective."

"I don't want to get you mixed up in anything," she said.

"I won't have to be," I said. "My man isn't a movie private eye. He's a member of the bar, a full-fledged attorney-at-law. Name is John MacIlreddy. Actually he was once a cop and studied law at night school. We use him for all sorts of things. Tell me about Mr. Broman."

"Well, he's a promoter. He has an office on Fifth Avenue and a house in Great Neck, Long Island. In his late forties. Married. Two or three children."

"What does he promote?"

"Various things. Sporting events, like prizefighting. Automobile races. I met him one night in the Stork Club, when he came to the table where I was having supper with some characters. You wouldn't know them, but Stanley did. 'The hell with the rest of you,' he said. 'I'm smitten by this lady,' meaning me. 'Well, I'm not smitten by you,' I said, 'so why don't you go back to your table.' But the others were amused, or impressed, or as I later found out, somewhat terrified by Stanley, and he stayed."

"Why were they terrified?" I said.

"Not really terrified, but afraid of him. Apparently he got into fights, and made scenes, and he certainly was mixed up with some very shady characters. In any event, he believed in the direct approach. He pulled a chair up beside me and began talking very dirty and invited me to go to his hotel with him. I stood as much of it as I could, then I excused myself to go to the ladies' room and never went back to the table. When I got outside on Fifty-whatever-it-is Street, he was waiting for me. Sitting in the first taxi. I was actually halfway in the taxi before I realized he was there. He grabbed my hand and pulled me in the rest of the way. Obviously the taxi driver knew him. In fact, he was part owner of a fleet of taxicabs. He's in all sorts of things. Loads of money. Spends a lot on clothes, and was probably a very handsome Jew when he was younger. Oh, let's face it, he had sex appeal. 'I'm gonna take you to your hotel and I'm gonna leave you there,' he said. 'But I just didn't want you to think you were outsmarting me.' And that's exactly what he did. He dropped me at the Barclay, where I was staying, and went on his way.

"The next morning, when they brought my breakfast, there were two dozen yellow roses. How he found that out, I don't know. But they're my favorites, as you know. I opened the envelope to look at the card, and there was this thin little diamond bracelet. No big diamonds, but it was narrow and beautiful. On the card was written, 'Think it over,' and it was signed with his initials. I looked him up in the phone book to know where to return the bracelet, but no Stanley Broman. Then I called up one of the people I'd been to the Stork Club with and found out that he was at the Waldorf. So I sent the bracelet back by messenger. Within half an hour he was on the phone. 'All I wanted you to do was think it over,' he said. 'That didn't take long,' I said. Oh, what's the use of telling you inch by inch? He was waiting for me in the Barclay lobby when I came down to go out for lunch. 'Lady, I told you I was smitten and I am,' he said. 'If necessary I'll move to Gibbsville P A.' I couldn't have dinner with him that night, but I did the next. He took me to the Colony and the theater and El Morocco, behaved like his idea of the perfect gentleman, and left me at the Barclay."

"And then you had an affair with him," I said. "How long did that last?"

"Oh, maybe six months. He never came to Gibbsville. I was firm about that. But he used to send a private plane to take me to New York, and sometimes I'd stay a week at a time. His friends were unbelievable. The women were almost worse than the men. They all looked like whores that had struck it rich, and did they ever hate me! Where did I get this, where did I get that? If it wasn't a personal question, but how much did this cost? What infuriated them most was knowing that Stanley wasn't keeping me. He paid for the plane and I stayed in his suite at the Waldorf, but my clothes were my own and I refused his expensive presents. After all, I have some very nice things I got from you and other people."

"The affair lasted six months, then what? Why did you give him the air?" I said.

"Because my bloomers got warm for someone else, to put it delicately," she said.

"But you don't get rid of people like him that easily," I said.

"I found that out. 'Who is this guy? I'll kill him,' he said. And I said I'd like to see him try. The new man was half a head taller and—and Stanley isn't small—and does boxing every day to keep in shape. Doesn't drink, doesn't smoke. He played football at Holy Cross University, and he could probably go out and play now. He's a lawyer, too, although actually he's a politician."

"Where?"

"In Brooklyn. Not really Brooklyn. Queens, sort of a part of Brooklyn, but closer to Great Neck, where Stanley lives when he goes home. Stanley knew right away who he was, and stopped making threats or trying to see me."

"You told him about Stanley?" I said.

"No. I didn't have to, and the affair with Jack Spellacy didn't last long enough to get to the exchange-of-confidences stage. However, it did last long enough to get rid of Stanley. Till about two months ago, when the phone calls began. He called up one night and said he was sending the plane next day. They called me from the airport, and I sent the plane back to New York."

"And the calls have persisted. It's odd that a man like that hasn't showed up in Gibbsville. I'll have to look into that," I said. "In fact, I'll do it right now."

"At this hour? All the offices are closed," she said.

"Watch me spring into action," I said. I telephoned the office of the Philadelphia *Bulletin* and was put through to George Taylor, the financial vice-president, with whom I occasionally had lunch. "George, I'd like to know what you have on a man named Stanley Broman. He's a New Yorker. A promoter. Will you see if you have any clippings on him?" George Taylor promised to call me back or to have someone in the *Bulletin* "morgue" give me the information. I hung up and waited.

"You're marvelous," said Andrea.

"I impress you, do I?" I said.

"This is the first time I've ever seen you in action. That kind of action."

"I know a lot of people," I said. "You never know when they'll come in handy. I have no friends, but I never have had."

"That's your fault. You could have. Or maybe you couldn't. No, I think you've learned to get along without them. I have no *women* friends. That's why you and I have love, love, love."

The telephone rang. It was a man in the *Bulletin* office. He said he had quite a batch of clippings on Stanley Broman. Did I want him to read them all? It was against the rules to take them out of the building, although in my case they might make an exception. "Just read the headlines and I'll tell you which ones interest me," I said.

He read a dozen or so before he came to one in particular. "Hold it," I said. "Read the whole article, please." He did so, and I asked him to read several others pertaining to the same topic. I thanked him and we hung up. "As I suspected," I said.

"I have never in my life seen you look so smug," she said. "What is it?"

"Good news for you," I said. "Your Mr. Broman will never

bother you in Gibbsville. At least that's a reasonable assumption. He faces a lawsuit if he sets foot in our glorious Commonwealth. Under the statute of limitations, as it applies to this case, you're safe for four more years. Apparently he owes a lot of people a lot of money. I know the lawyer who represented him here, and I could find out all there is to know, but that won't be necessary, or desirable, from your point of view."

"You're absolutely clever," she said. "You spotted that right away."

"There had to be some very good reason why a man like that stayed away from Gibbsville. I suggest you say nothing to him about this. What he doesn't know won't hurt us. You'll have to put up with the telephone calls, but at least you can rest easy about his appearing in person. He'll get over you in four years. His kind of ego can't endure defeat, and pretty soon he'll be able to convince himself that you're not worth bothering about. However, I'm glad we found out about the lawsuit. If it weren't for that I might have recommended your taking out a pistol license."

"How can I thank you?" she said.

"In various ways. And you do."

"We just won't say that we love each other."

"We say it all the time," I said. "But we have sense enough to know that our way is the best way for us. When I'm eighty and you're seventy I'll propose to you again."

"And I'll accept your proposal. I would now, but you don't want that hanging over you."

"It would be interesting to announce our engagement now, and say that the wedding will take place in the spring of 1986. I can just see it in the Evening Chat column in the *Bulletin*. Actually, you know, in my business I project myself into the future every day. Bond issues maturing at such and such a date. Wills. Trust funds. Ninety-nine-year leases. Then on the other hand, we're always having title searches that go back to 1681. In case you've forgotten, that was the year William Penn was granted his charter."

"Oh, I knew that all along," she said.

358 ♦ JOHN O'HARA

"In a pig's ass you did," I said.

"You can be so *vulgar,*" she said. "Thank God."

That was shortly after the end of World War II. She vanished again and I did not see or hear from her until about a year later. My secretary said that Mrs. Andrea Cooper—she had adopted her maiden name—wished to speak to me. Ruth, of course, knew that any call from Andrea had top priority.

"Have you been listening to the radio?" said Andrea.

"Naturally," I said. "I come to the office every day to listen to the radio. We get such good reception here. Why are you so breathless?"

"I just heard over the radio that Stanley Broman's been murdered. Is there anything I ought to do?"

"Well, obviously you didn't do it, so if I were you I'd open a small bottle of champagne. Who gets the medal for this public-spirited act?"

"They don't know. They found him in his car, in the meadows near Newark, New Jersey. The car was on fire, and he was shot and stabbed. Shot *and* stabbed."

"They really wanted to get rid of him, didn't they?"

"Is there anything I ought to do? Am I liable to get mixed up in it? I don't *want* to get mixed up in it, especially now."

"Romance in the air?"

"Very much so. I'm on the verge of marrying my doctor."

"With what *he* must know about you, it must be true love," I said. "No, you have nothing to worry about. You didn't write the late Mr. Broman any letters, did you? You've never been much for letters."

"No, he never put anything in writing if he could help it, either."

"Then I would say that the New Jersey gangsters have given you a very nice wedding present. I'll admit now that I was always a trifle apprehensive about Broman. Just a trifle."

"Don't think *I* wasn't."

"Are you coming to see me before you go to the altar with your doctor?"

"I will if you want me to," she said.

"I always want you to," I said.

"Then I'll come down this afternoon. He's dead, but he frightens me, that man. I have to be back here tomorrow. Is that all right?"

"Of course it's all right," I said.

She was remarkable. She was thirty-three years old, give or take a few months, yet when she arrived at my apartment she was fresh and unstained and—radiant. I always went back to that word to describe her to myself. She almost never wore a hat and she was not wearing one now. Her hair was cut in a longish page-boy style, and I said to her, "Tell me something. Do you dye your hair?"

"I have it touched," she said. "But I'm a light blonde and you damn well know it. What kind of a greeting is that? *Do I dye my hair?*"

"We're very hostile today. I was only curious," I said.

"I drove a hundred miles to see you. I expect a nicer welcome than that. Would it be too much to offer me a drink?"

"You can have anything but a Martini. I won't give you a Martini when you're in this mood."

"I don't want a Martini. Give me a bourbon with ice, no water. Please."

"My question about your hair was in the nature of a compliment. I have a favorite word for you. Radiant. In addition, I was thinking that you had driven ninety-four miles—not a hundred, by the way—and not a hair was out of place."

"I ran a comb through it in the elevator."

I handed her the drink. "Which doctor is it you're going to marry? One of the newer ones?"

"Not so new," she said. "He came there after you left, but he's been there about ten years. Sam Young."

"I know the name, but I've never met him. You know how often I get back there. Maybe once in five years, since Mother died."

"Yes, people have been known to say that the old town isn't good enough for you," she said.

"They're right. It isn't," I said. "The last time anything interesting happened there was when you arrived."

"Are you trying to get me back in a good mood?"

"Trying as hard as I can," I said. "We only have tonight, and then it may be years before we see each other again."

"Oh, I want to sleep with you. You needn't worry about that," she said.

"Well, I was worrying about it," I said.

"I'll always sleep with you," she said. "You were my first, and maybe you'll be my last. Who knows?"

"Why are you marrying Dr. Young?"

"First of all, because he's nice, and if you're going to live in Gibbsville it's better to be married."

"But why go on living in Gibbsville?"

She stretched out on the sofa. "Yes, why? It's home, with Mother and Daddy there, and my kid brother married and raising a family. I've lost all contact with my friends in California. I've been married and divorced twice, and I don't think those marriages did me any great harm, but I can't go on getting married and divorced. Stability. I need some stability, and I'd never get it if I moved away from Gibbsville. Look at what happened to me in New York. I fell in love with a gangster."

"You're dramatizing that," I said. "You didn't fall in love with him, and he wasn't a real gangster."

"Yes he was. I saw enough of him to find that out. He was a gangster. Maybe he didn't go around with a machine-gun in his hand, but they don't do that any more."

"Someone did, or he wouldn't be lying in the Jersey meadows," I said.

"He was a modern gangster. He made his money in the black market during the war. Not nylons and things like that. He used to call himself a steel executive. Rubber. Steel. Building materials."

"You knew a lot more than I thought you did."

"He thought I was a dizzy blonde that didn't know what was

going on. And maybe I was. But I couldn't help but overhear some of his conversations."

"Now I see why you were so worried. You're afraid you might be called on to testify. That's doubtful. If he lived, and there was some kind of Congressional investigation, they'd have the F.B.I. visit you. It's still a possibility, but very remote."

"That's what I want to know," she said. "What do I do if they come and start asking me a lot of questions?"

"The first thing you do is ask for their credentials. I mean that. The F.B.I. men have a kind of wallet, with their picture in it. Take your time about examining it. If you have any reason to be doubtful, tell the man that you're going to call their office to check. If he's a phony, he'll give you an argument. If not, and if you're satisfied that he's the real thing, give him all the information he asks for. Sometimes there are two of them. Make them both identify themselves. One man can put on a convincing act, but when there are two of them it's not so easy. Your instinct will warn you. But once you're satisfied, tell them everything. You can trust them. Above all, don't lie to them. You may just happen to lie about something they know all about, in which case you make everything you say suspect."

"Can't I simply say I don't want to talk to them?" she said.

"Yes. But if you do, be sure and call me right away," I said. "By the way, does Dr. Young know about me, you and me?"

"Nobody knows about you and me," she said.

"Still?" I said.

"I've never told anyone. Maybe you have, but I haven't. They all want to know who my first was, and I tell them it was a boy in California. For some reason they don't seem to mind that. California is so far away. So is my virginity."

"You're feeling a little better now," I said.

"Well, for Christ's sake, starting out with 'Do you dye your hair?' What did you expect? By the way, *you're* getting a bit grey."

"I'm getting grey in your service," I said.

"Yes, I guess that's true," she said. "What I said about Gibbsville and stability—as long as I have you, I have *some* stability. I wouldn't want to live any place that was too far from you."

"I'll never be farther away than the telephone and the airplane. You're announcing your impending nuptials. Well, I have an announcement of my own, just for you. I am never going to get married."

"When you're eighty and I'm seventy?"

"Then, yes, but not before. When I was still in my thirties, I could have adjusted to marriage. But now I'm only seven years from fifty, and my habits are frozen. The first time I ever danced with you, you called me Judge. I was in law school."

"The night I did my strip tease," she said.

I nodded. "And they're even better now than they were then."

"By an inch and a half," she said.

"I wish I could say the same for my own measurements," I said. "Anyway, I remember telling you that a judgeship was a long way off for me. Now it isn't, and that's my ambition, my goal. It always has been. By the time I'm fifty I'll have enough money for one man."

"Don't forget us when we're married," she said.

"I won't. There'll be enough for the two of us," I said. "Do you want to hear about my ambition, or don't you?"

"Yes, dear. I promise not to interrupt any more."

"There are two things I can't discuss with anyone but you. My sex life and my ambition. Naturally I'd like to be an associate justice of the U. S. Supreme Court, but that's out of the question. They don't appoint my kind of lawyer to the Supreme Court any more. I've handled too many cases for large corporations. But I've been sounded out on running for a state job, which I won't do. Before they sound you out they study your qualifications, so mine must be all right. I'm being over-modest. They're damn good. Too good for the job they want me for. However, they did come to me, spontaneously, and they'll come again. And again. Then I'll tell them that I'll run if unopposed."

"You mean if nobody runs against you?"

"Yes. You can't be permanently appointed, you have to be

elected. But you can be unopposed. I'm a hell of a good lawyer, you know, with a hell of a good record. The public doesn't know much about me, but the other lawyers do. I've never lost a case in the U. S. Supreme Court, and only two in the state court. And I'm not getting any dumber."

"Just think of you sitting up there in those black robes. I'll go and make faces at you."

"I'll have you held in contempt," I said.

"You do, and I'll tell your guilty secret. What kind of rape was that?"

"Statutory," I said.

"I knew it wasn't statuary. I was anything but statuary. Well, I'll be proud of you. I really will. I am anyway. I can't tell people I've been your girl all these years, but I'm secretly proud. And you're getting grey hairs. And I also notice you're wearing your Phi Beta Kappa key. I never knew you were one."

"I was wearing the key the first night I danced with you," I said.

"Maybe you were, but I didn't know what it was. I never knew what it was till my brother made it. But you must have stopped wearing it."

"Vests are coming back," I said.

"That's not why you're wearing it. You're running for judge. Don't try to fool me, Phil."

"That would be a great mistake, I guess. Besides, I never wanted to fool you."

"We must never try to fool each other," she said. "Let there be two people in the world that don't."

"How about your mother and father?" I said. "You've always had great admiration for them."

"Have I? Not in recent years. Not since I've been able to think for myself, instead of being a yes-man to them. He's cruel, my father. He dominates her in every little thing. For instance, she never wanted to leave California, but he did. He didn't want to be stuck in the bank in Santa Barbara. He wanted to be the manager of King's department store."

"He's done very well, though," I said.

"The store has, I have to admit that. But Mother has aged terribly. She hates the climate, she doesn't like the people. Consequently, she comes to see me every day, not because she wants to see me but because she knows where I keep the vodka. 'Oh, I think I'll have a little cocktail,' she says. Then you ought to see what she pours herself. Right up to the top. One cube of ice, the rest straight vodka. Her little cocktail. Then she has another little cocktail. I tried watering the vodka, but she noticed it right away. Insisted that I get a different brand and offered to pay for it. My mother has become a quiet lush. My brother's no help. He says he's very sorry, but he doesn't want Mother coming to his house and criticizing the way his wife is bringing up their kids. Mother knows she's not welcome there, so I get her every afternoon."

"What if you and the doctor have children?"

"We won't. He's sterile. I didn't say impotent. He can get it up all right, but he's sterile. And I doubt if I could have children now. Three abortions since I was nineteen."

"Beginning with mine," I said.

"Yes, and each of my husbands. The last one the doctor didn't want to do it, but I told him if he didn't do it I'd have to go to some butcher. That was Sam Young. So you see he knew me pretty well before he knew me at all, so to speak."

"A moment ago you spoke of stability," I said. "You said you stayed in Gibbsville because it offered stability, and you mentioned your parents. Then a bit later you gave me a quite unhappy picture of them. He's cruel, she's an alcoholic. What kind of stability do you call that?"

"It's stability. It isn't happiness, but it's stability. What kind of a lawyer's trick is this, going back to things I said before?"

"It's a lawyer's trick, all right," I said. "I'm doing it for a reason. I want to find out why you're marrying your doctor. Does he represent stability?"

"Yes," she said.

"You don't love him."

"No."

"What do you like about him, besides the dream of stability?"

"Are you going to try to argue me out of marrying him?" she said.

"I know better than that," I said.

"Then what are you trying to do?" she said. "You can't make me a better offer."

"No, I can't. But I've always seemed to take the role of uncle, or big brother, with you. You don't remember this, but that first night we sat in my car together—"

"You told me not to take a drink or my parents wouldn't let me go to the other dances."

"You do remember," I said.

"I ought to. That's what got us in the hay together. But I don't see what you're trying to do now."

"It would help if you answered my question, what do you like about the doctor?"

"Well, he's a man. All man. He was married before and his wife died of leukemia, the year he went into private practice. Then he went into the Navy for three years, and after that he came back to Gibbsville, reopened his practice. When I got the flu I sent for him, having already been his patient once before. The abortion. He annoyed me by throwing in a piece of advice that I hadn't asked for. It was part medical and part moral. He said that a woman with my record of abortions ought to have periodic checkups for T.B., and I told him to mind his own business. We became friends, and lovers. He had other women, but I was it, he said."

"What makes either of you think you'll make a good doctor's wife?"

"You *are* trying to talk me out of it," she said.

"All right, maybe I am. Three abortions aren't good for you, but neither are four marriages."

"This will be my third marriage!"

"Which will last two years, then there'll be a fourth. And quite possibly a fifth."

"You're jealous! You pretend you're not, but you are. You don't show it because I go away. You want me to go away so I won't see how jealous you are!"

I waited, and went on. "And there might even be a sixth."

She threw her glass at me, a heavy piece of Steuben. It missed me and broke against the paneling of the wall behind me. The dent in the woodwork was half an inch deep. I got up and stood over the largest piece of glass, which lay on the carpet. I was being dramatic while trying to think of the right thing to say. I was also frightened. Retroactively I could hear the thud of the glass on the woodwork, and imagine what it would have done to my skull. Looking down at the broken glass I was avoiding looking at her, and I did not see her coming toward me. When she touched me I reacted out of fear; I sprang away from her.

"Phil! Phil! I could have killed you!" She put her arms around my waist and held on to me, and then for only the second time in our life together she began to cry. I put my arms around her and held on to her, and she kissed me time after time, on the lips, on my neck, my hands, passionately but without passion. Now, having retroactively heard the glass smashing against the wall, I could retroactively see it passing over my shoulder, and though I was safe I was impotent with the effects of fear. I could feel impotence in my genitals and age in my soul. She stopped kissing me and looked at me. The tears streaked down her cheeks but she had stopped crying. "Are you all right?" she said.

"I want to sit down," I said.

"You're pale," she said.

"Odd," I said.

She held my hand on her bosom and drew me to the sofa, and I sat down. She sat on the edge of the sofa, waiting for whatever was next, act or words. "Think I'll have a cigarette," I said. I was recovering rapidly, but I had to know what to do. It had to be right, or I had lost her forever; that much I knew. It was like that moment in a jury trial when you are addressing the twelve good men and true, and something tells you to stop, or to go on, you're not sure which but you are sure that in two seconds you will have them or have lost them, regardless of whatever else you do or have done, say or have said.

I hesitated, and I guess she read into my hesitation some other emotion than the vestige of fear. Deep disappointment, disillusionment perhaps. She got the cigarette for me and put it in my mouth and lit it. "I would rather die than hurt you," she said. "Than hurt you in any way. If that glass had hit you I'd have jumped out your window. See my hand?" Her hands were shaking. She got up and used the letter-opener and pencil tray from my desk to sweep up the broken glass fragments. She took them and the larger pieces of glass to the kitchen. "I put them in the garbage pail," she said. She was standing in the middle of the room. "Do you want me to go?"

"No," I said.

"What do you want me to do? Shall I fix you a drink?"

"No thanks," I said.

"Please tell me what to do. I can't think," she said.

"Why don't you just come here and sit down?" I said.

She sat beside me and gently put her head on my shoulder and I put my arm around her. We stayed that way for a full two minutes, which can be a long time of silence for two such people as she and I; I suddenly older, she as suddenly younger. "I feel as though I'd thrown something at God," she said.

"I'm not God. I'm not even a very minor god," I said. "I'm not even a good first baseman or I'd have caught the damn thing. Would you mind if we just stayed here and didn't go out for dinner?"

"Oh, I don't *want* to go out for dinner. I'd be almost sure to burst into tears, and embarrass you. Would you like me to show you what a good cook I am?"

"I know what a good cook you are. Let's sit here a while and later on you can make one of your omelettes. Do you want to listen to some records?"

"No thanks," she said. "When you're ready, we'll talk. You have something you want to say, and so have I."

"I haven't much to say, but what there is is fairly important," I said. "I'm all right now but I have to tell you, I'm a different man from five or ten minutes ago. I never thought so before, but I'm a middle-aged man. I don't want to exaggerate anything, but there it is. And you know it. That's why you somehow got me confused with God, because I happen to know you don't believe in God."

"No, I don't. I stopped believing in God when I changed my mind about my father."

"And I suppose I took their place. Father. God. And perennial lover."

"I guess that's right," she said.

"An all-purpose man in your life," I said.

"And what have I been to you? Perennial mistress and what else? Not your mother, or the Virgin Mary."

"Well, there've been hundreds of times when I was a child at your breast."

"You're feeling better now, aren't you?"

"I told you, I'm all right," I said. "But you have to know that when that glass went whizzing by me, my reflexes were slow and one of the slow reflexes was fear. I wasn't afraid till after it was over. A young man's reflexes protect him. I didn't move. I played first base when I was in school but tonight I was rigid. With a kind of anticipatory fear, I guess."

"I threw the glass without any warning," she said.

"A prep school pitcher does the same thing, trying to pick a runner off first base. No signal. No warning. Or a first baseman misses the signal that the pitcher's going to throw to him."

"What has all this stuff about baseball got to do with us?"

"I'm trying to explain what's happened to me. I'll be brief, if you like. In a word, I got old."

"All right, if you insist. You're forty-three years old. I never have any trouble remembering your age."

"But let me go on, Andrea. This is important. I'm forty-three, but *you* suddenly *lost* a batch of years. Your reaction was very young, and you practically said so when you said it was like throwing something at God."

"I'll agree with that, too. It was childish."

"Young-girlish, not childish," I said.

"I've decided not to marry Sam Young," she said.

Her statement was so out of order that in a courtroom I would have requested a recess. For the truth was I had been leading up to a repudiation of my earlier opposition to her marriage. It was frustrating and confusing to have her brush aside my speech before it was made.

"You've decided *not* to marry him?" I said.

"It wouldn't work out. Not even for two years," she said. "It would be very bad for both of us. For him and me, that is."

"What convinced you of that?" I said.

"Something you said, of course," she said. "You asked me why either of us, Sam or I, thought I'd make a good doctor's wife. Actually, we never talked about that. I mean about the doctor's-wife part of it. We've always talked about ourselves and each other, but being a doctor's wife is something special. He must have thought about it, but he avoided bringing it up. I'd make a terrible doctor's wife. He'd lose every patient he has."

"Would he? Why?"

"Because he would, that's why. I'm not cut out for that kind of a life. My mother could have done it, but not me."

"What about all that business of living in Gibbsville and stability and so on?"

"I can always find good reasons for doing something I want to do," she said. "Even now I can think of a good reason for throwing a glass at you. You taunted me, you went too far. You should know better than to make me angry. I'm a very impulsive girl. If I'd hit you, I *would* have jumped out the window. That would have been great, you with your head bashed in, and me lying on the sidewalk in Rittenhouse Square. And all because you needled me when I was tired from a long drive."

"Yes, of course, of course," I said. "Is this final, your decision not to marry Young?"

"Absolutely," she said. "Just as final as my decision not to marry you."

"I was coming to that," I said. "Just thinking out loud, as the advertising people say. Just as a trial balloon, how would it be if you and I got married and kept it secret—don't interrupt me, please—and thereby prevented you from a hasty marriage to someone else?"

"We're not married now, and I prevented myself from a hasty marriage, as you call it."

"So you did. But you're quite liable to find yourself in the same situation again, and marry the man."

"You're quite liable to get another glass thrown at you," she said.

"Not so soon," I said. "Let's speculate as to the advantages for you. I don't know how close you ever came to marrying that gangster. Not very close, I guess. He had that wife in Great Neck or wherever it was, and Jews generally, even gangster Jews, don't go rushing to the divorce courts. But you're impulsive, by your own admission, and the record speaks for itself. Two marriages, two divorces. Both of your ex-husbands married again and I believe they've stayed married?"

"Yes," she said.

"And you were about to marry a widower until you suddenly, impulsively changed your mind. Doesn't all this seem to indicate that it'd be to your advantage to have a legal husband to protect you from your own impulses? Don't start throwing things. I'm asking you to consider the matter."

"I'm considering it. What's the advantage for you?"

"For me? Well, I could say that I was looking ahead to the time when I become a judge. Stability and all that. I'll never marry anyone but you, that's a certainty. But I'd like to be sure of having you, when that time comes."

"You're just so God damn jealous."

"You've probably put your finger on it. Our hidden motives we won't admit to, even to ourselves sometimes."

"The answer is no," she said. "I'm not giving up Sam Young to marry you."

"There would be financial advantages, too," I said. "What do you live on now? It's mostly your stock in King's store, isn't it?"

"Mostly," she said. "I had alimony from my first husband, but that stopped when I married again. I got no alimony from my second husband. I was the guilty party there. Yes, my income is from the store."

"I happen to know something about economic conditions in the coal region. They're not getting any better. I don't know much about King's, but how long do you think they can compete against Stewart's, which is bigger and older, and the new Sears? King's is in the middle there. And no matter how efficient your father may be, the economic facts of life are running against him. Sears has the big buying power and lower prices. Stewart's has four other stores besides Gibbsville, and third-generation charge accounts. They make money with their charge accounts, because they're not the old-time charge accounts. Stewart's is really in the same business as a loan company. Selling on the installment plan, and collecting their pound of flesh by financing the retail purchases."

"I've heard Daddy talk about that, but it's too deep for me," she said.

"You ought to try to understand it, because it's going to affect you. I don't want to frighten you, but if King's had two or three bad years they'd have to go out of business. I assume that Dr. Young makes pretty good money."

"About twenty thousand a year. He told me."

"And you?"

"Last year, around ten."

"Is that all?" I said.

She nodded. "Daddy told me to expect less this year."

"You spend it all, of course," I said.

"Oh, do I! I'm continually overdrawn. But I work, you know."

"I didn't know," I said.

"Before Easter I help out in ladies' ready-to-wear. Four weeks. And before Christmas in the toy department or wherever they send me. I get a hundred dollars a week, which just about covers what I owe Daddy."

"I'll *bet* it does," I said.

"Not entirely. He gives me the rest as a Christmas present."

"Encouraging bad habits," I said.

"That's exactly what he says."

"Does he worry about you?"

"Not about me. He'd wet his drawers if he knew his little daughter's ex-boy friend was killed by gangsters, but he wouldn't be worrying for me. For himself and Bud, my brother, Bud. I love Bud, but I hate what my father's doing to him. When Bud graduated from Colgate my father gave him a present of a trip abroad, and Bud came back thinking he'd get a job on a newspaper, in hopes of becoming a foreign correspondent. My father talked him into taking a quote temporary unquote job in the store. It was a job anyone could have done, not a Phi Beta Kappa with a knack for languages. What Daddy really wanted was a doubles partner, and Bud had been captain of the Colgate tennis team. So Bud gave in, and got himself married, and then the war came and he quit his job to go to O.C.S. and they sent him to England with the O.S.S. because he knew German. After the war he wanted to live over there, but he already had one child and his wife was producing another. Well, Daddy began working on him again, a year at a time. You can imagine what happened. Bud could have lived abroad with a wife and one child, on his income. But with a wife and three he had to have more than that. Kids are expensive, so are young American wives. The sad thing, but funny, ironical, is that now Daddy plays golf, and Bud doesn't even get to the semi-finals in the singles any more."

"Let's hope your father doesn't turn the store over to him just before it folds up," I said.

"He would if he thought of it."

"You don't want to marry me for my money?" I said.

"No."

"Or to keep yourself out of trouble?" I said.

"No."

"Or to possibly be of some help to your brother if the store goes out of business?" I said.

"No."

"Or because you know that eventually you will marry me," I said.

"You're more sure of that than I am," she said.

"Only if we both live long enough. I'm not talking about when I'm eighty. I honestly believe we'll be married before that, and unless I'm very wrong, you believe it too."

"You don't know what it's like to be married, Phil. I do. It takes a long time to get used to living with someone, and we both like our privacy. We both like to come and go as we please. You can't do that, and you can't have your privacy, when you're someone's wife. Maybe I was cut out to be an old maid. Not the usual kind of old maid that looks under beds. But an old maid with plenty of memories. I'm not going to marry you just so you'll have a wife in reserve for when you're a judge."

"All right," I said.

"I'm going to get you some supper. Do you mind if I unpack first?"

"Did you bring a bag?"

She laughed. "No, I'm kidding. I didn't even bring a toothbrush. I know you always have extras, and I count on wearing your pajamas. You have your bath and I'll have your supper ready by the time you're out of the shower. Then we can have a quiet evening at home. The kind that makes you think you'd like to be married to me."

I took a shower and put on pajamas and dressing-gown. She had set the table and lighted the candles in my small diningroom. We had the omelette and toast and a bottle of Rhine wine that she found in the refrigerator. "Do you still get your own breakfast every morning?" she said.

"Coffee," I said. "I usually stop at the drug store at Broad and Locust and have bacon and eggs."

"And lunch at your club. When you're having dinner alone what do you do?"

"One of the other clubs, or I can have it sent in from the hotel across the way. But usually at the Racquet Club. Why?"

"That's the life you like, you see? You could afford a much larger apartment and a full-time servant, but you prefer this. I do too, really. The difference being that I do my own cooking, make my own bed and so on. Once a week I have a woman come in to give the place a good cleaning. Are you simply dying to give me a present?"

"Yes."

"They're going to raise my rent from seventy-five to a hundred dollars a month. I could get a cheaper apartment but I don't want to, and so I've been wondering where I could economize, to make up the difference. I figured out that I could save ten dollars a month by going to the hairdresser twice a month instead of once a week. But then what? I went over all my bills and I was amazed to discover that I spend about fifty cents a day on perfume. It comes to that, about fifty cents a day. Fifteen dollars a month. Now if you would like to leave a standing order with your drug store to send me a bottle of perfume once a month, I could go on staying in my apartment and smelling nice, too."

"Write down the name of the perfume, or I'll forget it," I said.

"It's a hundred and eighty dollars a year," she said.

"I'll be able to swing it," I said.

"In case I should happen to impulsively marry someone else, I'll tell the drug store to stop sending it to me."

"It would be a waste of time to offer you money, wouldn't it?" I said.

"Don't try *too* hard," she said. "Actually, the way I feel about it is, if I really need more money, I can get a job. Me, that never wears a hat, I have a standing offer to work in a millinery shop. There's a new little fairy on Market Street near the Y.M.C.A. who thinks I'm just *per*fectly *ador*able, and he'll pay me two hundred dollars a month, five days from ten to four. He calls me Butch, or did till I told him I knew what it meant in fairy talk."

"What does it mean?"

"It means a bull-dike."

"Well, you're certainly not that," I said.

"No, that's the least of my problems. I've had my palm scratched by several women, but that's as far as they ever got. Actually, you know, I think I'm under-sexed. I can go awfully long without it, and the man always has to be somewhat unusual. I know a girl at home that gets tight and she frankly admitted to me that it might just as well be a broom-handle, for all the difference it makes. She doesn't give a damn about the preliminaries, or giving the man any pleasure."

"Do you call me somewhat unusual?"

"I should say I do. Anybody that's put up with me all these years. I'm sure I know you better than anyone else does, but how well is that? Sometimes when I leave you after spending the night with you, I say to myself, 'What does he really think of me? Or does he think of me at all?' I know that we have love, love, love, but sometimes I think I'm just a lay, lay, lay, although I know better. I don't think I could live without knowing that you were somewhere on the same earth."

"How are you going to break it to the doctor?" I said.

"I don't know," she said. "We hadn't set an actual date. Vaguely sometime in the next few months. What I'll probably do is wait till he says something about a definite date, and then I'll put him off. Then the next time he brings it up again, I'll put him off again. On the other hand, I might just tell him tomorrow. I don't know."

"The fair thing to do would be to tell him tomorrow," I said.

"Yes, that would be the fair thing. So I may. On the other hand, what has fairness got to do with it?"

"That's entirely up to you and how you feel about him."

"If I went out with someone else a few times, he might get the message."

"I should think so," I said. "As a doctor's wife in Gibbsville you'd be expected to give up dates with other men."

"If I were going to marry him, I wouldn't have dates with other men, but since I'm not going to marry him, I think I'll have a few dates and let him tell me that that has to stop. Then I'll say I'm sorry, but it isn't going to stop, and that will give him a good out. Result—no wedding bells, but no hard feelings. I like him, and I don't want to lose him as a friend. Also, I want him to go on being my doctor."

"It sounds to me as though Dr. Young might turn into a Gibbsville version of me," I said.

"No, but he might turn into a Gibbsville version of Dr. Young. You see, I can tell you about him but I could never tell him about you. It always comes down to that. I never tell them about you. You're private and personal to me. There's probably some very good psychological reason for that, but offhand I wouldn't know what it is."

"If I were just a little older I might say that you were ashamed of me," I said.

"I see what you mean, yes, but not a woman that's had two husbands and liable to have six," she said. "I wonder, Phil, if we saw each other oftener, would we always spend so much time talking about what's kept us together?"

"No, not if we saw each other oftener."

"We meet, and we're like a child studying its own belly-button," she said. "I was twelve years old before I understood that, either. I still don't understand why men have nipples, but they *would* look very strange without them, now that I've got used to them. Have you got a lot of work to do?"

"It doesn't have to be done tonight," I said.

"If I weren't here, it would be, though."

"Yes," I said.

"Well, let me do the dishes and put things away, and I'll have a bath and get into a pair of your pajamas. Then we can go to bed early and get a good night's sleep and I'll get your breakfast in the morning. You won't have to go to the drug store."

"That seems like a very sensible program," I said. We even made sensible love that night, and at seven-thirty in the morning she brought me a cup of coffee. She was already dressed in a sweater and the skirt of her Glen plaid suit. "Couldn't you sleep?" I said.

"As if I'd been pole-axed, till about six o'clock," she said.

I put my hand under her skirt and felt her leg. She stood still. "Do you think that's wise?" she said.

"What do you think?" I said.

"Whatever you want. All this can come off in no time," she said.

"Are you trying to spare me because I suddenly got old?"

"Well, something like that," she said. "But if you keep doing that, I'm not going to give a damn how old you are."

"Let's see how quickly you can take that stuff off," I said.

"Before you can change your mind, that's how quickly," she said.

"Remember a tune by Vincent Youmans? 'Day will break and you'll awake'?"

"No singing before breakfast," she said. "Supposed to be very bad luck."

"If you don't believe in God you can't believe in foolish superstitions," I said.

She lay on top of me. "Stop being so bossy so early in the morning. If there's anything I hate it's a bossy old man."

"If there's anything I love it's you," I said.

"I know," she said. "That—I know."

I remembered to place the order for her perfume, and for seven or eight months the only communication I had with her—if it could be called that—was the monthly bill from the drug store. Then my firm took a case involving some mineral rights near Gibbsville and I volunteered to confer with one of the principals, a boyhood chum of mine. We were not at all sure that we wanted to go into court with the case, and someone had to explain the delay. Accordingly, I drove up to Gibbsville and spent the day with my friend. "It was damn nice of you to come," he said. "But I wish they'd told me it was going to be you. Mary and I could have had some of the old crowd in for dinner."

"That's just what I didn't want," I said. "I'll have a little look around, and I may even drive back tonight."

My look around consisted of finding Andrea's telephone number and a visit, on foot, to her apartment. She was pleased but not overjoyed to see me. "Am I wrong, or am I getting a cool reception?" I said.

"No, you're right," she said.

"Did I louse up other plans?"

"I had to get out of something else," she said.

"Dr. Young?"

"Oh, no. Not that kind of thing. It's my brother. If it isn't my brother it's my mother, and in between it's my father. The store is in trouble, and my mother is hitting the bottle and Bud's had a fight with Daddy. The last time I saw you you told me some things about the store. I wish you'd told me more."

"I didn't know more. I was only conjecturing," I said.

"My father is turning out to be a crook. At least that's what Bud thinks."

"Whose money is he stealing?" I said.

"Ours. Mother's and Bud's and mine, among others. I don't want to talk about it," she said.

"I do. It's obviously what's uppermost in your mind, and as long as it is, there's no use talking about anything else."

"All right," she said. "It's complicated, and it's nothing he can be arrested for. But it's crooked. As I understand it, from Bud, Daddy is deliberately letting the store go to hell. They've had an offer to sell it to a chain of stores, with Daddy to be manager if they sold. But Daddy hasn't got any stock in the company. It's all Mother's and Bud's and mine and some cousins'. Bud is our advisor. Before that we always did exactly what Daddy said, but Bud found out that the chain store people had offered some ridiculously low price for King's, and Daddy was trying to persuade us to accept it. He had Mother all but talked into it."

"I begin to get the picture," I said.

"Oh, there's a lot more, but that's the gist of it. Bud wants us to fire Daddy, but Daddy has a contract with the company that we all voted for without reading it. Twenty-five thousand dollars a year for life, a share in the profits, et cetera. Can you imagine anybody being such a son of a bitch? According to Bud, Daddy gets some kind of a bonus if the chain stores buy King's. That's why he's so eager to have us sell. That, and an agreement that he'll be the new manager. Daddy has cut down the inventory so that the chain stores won't have to pay for goods on the shelves, and there *are* no goods on the shelves. Customers ask for things, and we're out of them. The chain store of course can buy everything cheaper than we can."

"You're learning something about business," I said.

"I wish I had earlier. I'm working. I have a job in a hat store on Market Street."

"The new little fairy?" I said.

"Oh, did I tell you about that? I guess I did."

"You probably have a case against your father if you wanted to sue him."

"Bud would, but Mother won't, and she can outvote everybody else. Such a hypocrite, my father. He'd never allow us to take a discount at the store unless we were actually on the payroll. Things like that. But he has a Cadillac that the company paid for and his expense account is something you wouldn't believe, according to Bud. He never spends a cent of his own money if he can help it. Mother paid all of Bud's expenses through college, and their house is in his name, although she paid for it. That's enough. Who are you suing? Anybody I know?"

"This isn't that kind of case. It has to do with mineral rights. Mighty dull stuff at this stage of the game," I said.

"How long are you going to be in town?" she said.

"That depends on you. I may go back tonight," I said.

"You can stay, but you have to be out of here before daylight. You can't be seen leaving at eight or nine o'clock in the morning. And you'd be recognized. This building is full of people you used to know. In fact, you may have made a mistake coming here in the first place, but I wasn't thinking very clearly when you phoned."

"I take it you've had your dinner," I said.

"Yes, I was just putting the dishes away when you arrived," she said.

She took a cigarette out of a box and tapped it, a gesture which was not habitual with her. "Listen, are you sore at me?" I said. "And if so, what for?"

"No, I'm not sore at you, but if you stay here tonight I'm going to be more careful. The last time, you knocked me up. That morning when I was all dressed and ready to give you your breakfast. I was unprepared, but I took a chance. Bingo! That's twice you've got me pregnant."

"Why didn't you let me know?" I said.

"What for? You couldn't come and hold my hand."

"Don't tell me Dr. Young performed the abortion," I said.

"Well, he did, and that solved the problem of whether to tell him I wasn't going to marry him. Neatly. 'By the way, Doctor, I'm not going to marry you, and while I'm here will you take care of this little problem?' "

"You didn't say that," I said.

"No, it wasn't as easy as that. He took it rather big. It wasn't any fun at all for either of us. And right about then Bud began telling me what was going on at the store. So you see I'm not sore at just you. I'm sour on the world, and have been for months. The only person I can let down my hair with is my boss. The little fairy. He's the most sympathetic man, woman, or child I've ever known."

"You told him about your abortion?"

"After it was all over and I went to work for him, he asked me one day if I was having love-trouble, and he was so kind that I burst into tears and told him everything but names. He's like a mother hen. Makes me sit down and rest between customers. Takes me to the movies, and dinner at the hotel. Next month we're going to New York together on a buying trip. He's the only bright spot in these last few months, I must say."

"What's his name?"

"His real name is John W. Metz, from Swedish Haven. But he calls himself Jacques. The name of the shop is Jacques, no last name. He studied to be a schoolteacher, but they expelled him in his second year in spite of having good marks and everything. He had a very hard time getting a job. In fact, at one time he worked as a stock-boy at King's, and that was how he got interested in millinery. His father wouldn't have anything to do with him, but he had a sister that helped him get started in business. He's a very good businessman, too. That's the Pennsylvania Dutch, I guess. He reads everything. Books. *The New Yorker. Time. The Wall Street Journal!* You should see his apartment. There's nothing else like it in Gibbsville. It's on the third floor of the building the shop's in, and when you get inside you can't believe you're not in New York or Paris. Très moderne, ness pa? I *love* him."

"Why, I think you do," I said.

She shook her head. "He has boy friends. One's a politician, a really quite horrible man, looks as if he ought to be a priest. He's not, though. He even has the nerve to bring his wife to the shop and sit there while she tries on hats. The only good thing is he can keep Jack out of the clutches of the law. Once in a while they have parties on Saturday night that get a bit raucous. Not that it's a residential neighborhood any more, but they do get noisy."

"I'm very sorry about the pregnancy," I said.

"It was worse on Sam than on anyone else. The blow to his pride, to start with. As I said, he took it big. But just as bad was the fact that he didn't want to do the abortion. He'd warned me once before, and this time he asked me please to go to someone else. He recommended two other doctors. But I said I was frightened. He even tried to get me to have the baby. Even if the father was a married man, I ought to have the baby. And he said frankly he was just as frightened as I was. I said that if anything happened to me, they'd never be able to trace it to him. *I'd* never tell on him. So, there in his office, without a nurse or anyone to assist him, he did it. Nothing went wrong then, but he'd warned me about these fits of depression, and he was certainly right. On top of which, came all this business about the store."

"I feel left out," I said.

"My troubles aren't your troubles," she said.

"I have no troubles to compare with yours," I said. "And besides, you're wrong. Your troubles are my troubles, as far as my wanting to share them is concerned. Apart from the fact that I was the one that got you pregnant. Apart from the fact that I'm not married and would gladly have married you. Dr. Young was right, there."

"Don't *you* start telling me I should have had the baby. It's a little late for that," she said. "It's easy to say now."

"There's never been a moment in the last fifteen years when I wouldn't have married you if you'd said the word."

"Oh, that's a lie, Phil. That's such a lie that it should have stuck in your throat."

"There were times when I was more ready than others, but I *don't* lie to you. What it comes down to is that you preferred dying to marrying me."

"That's something you just thought up to put me in the wrong. You love to argue, and twist what I say," she said.

"Half true. I love to argue with you, and I suppose I enjoy the give-and-take. But I play fair, and I don't reinforce my arguments with untruths. From force of habit a lawyer is probably more aware of truth and untruth than anyone else."

"Oh, lawyers are no more honest than other people," she said.

"I didn't say anything about honesty. I only said we were more aware, from force of habit, of the truth. We can distort it, in various ways, but we're accustomed to speaking for the record and extremely conscious of such things as perjured testimony, and disbarment proceedings, and so on. Honesty, ethics—that's another matter."

"Oh, shut up," she said.

"Very well," I said. "We're also pretty good at controlling our tempers."

"I said, shut up."

"If we're not going to talk, there's no point in my staying here."

"There's no point anyway," she said. "What you really came here for you're not going to get."

"You haven't even got a very high opinion of yourself, have you? I came here to see you. Sex isn't the only thing that's kept us together all these years." I stood up. "I'll leave you with this thought, my girl. What if I'd come to Gibbsville and not telephoned you? Sex or no sex. Goodnight, and I'm very sorry."

Never in a million years would she have called me back after I closed the door, and knowing that, I took my time in making my departure. But she let me go, and the walk back to the hotel was a dreary one. There were not many people on the street; it was just after the dinner hour for most of them. But at one time I had known the ownership of every house in the ten blocks to the hotel, and I had been inside a good many of them, played in their back yards. In a couple of days all my old friends would know that I had been in town on business, and some of them would be hurt or annoyed because I had not looked them up. But I had reconciled myself to that before leaving Philadelphia; what I did not like was this furtive walk from Andrea's apartment to the hotel. I wanted to drive back to the city, but I was too tired physically and my visit to Andrea had not revived me. At the hotel I asked to have dinner in my room and was told that room service was not available after eight o'clock, and so I had to throw my weight around with the manager, whom I did not know but who knew who I was. He assured me that *of course* in my case I could have dinner in my room. When it arrived the soup was tepid and the chicken and vegetables were not even as warm as that. "Be sure and put the tray out in the hall, will you?" said the waiter. No "please" and no "thank-you" for the tip. And no "goodnight." I got out some transcripts of testimony in old mineral rights cases, and wished I was back in Rittenhouse Square. At six o'clock in the morning—I must say I slept well—I asked the telephone operator if I could have a cup of coffee in my room. He, probably a bellboy, said the kitchen wasn't open yet but if a cup of coffee was all I wanted, he himself would bring me that and a cinnamon bun. In five minutes he was at my door, with a thermos of hot coffee and a bun. I gave him five dollars, but I almost kissed him too. "You know this is a five?" he said.

"I know it's a five," I said.

He laughed. "This don't even go on your bill," he said. "They got no way to charge you till the checker comes on in the kitchen. But thanks."

"Not at all. Virtue must not go unrewarded," I said.

"Didn't you used to be here in town?" he said.

"I was born here," I said.

"You's smart to get out. There's nothin' here no more. Nothin'. You used to have the house out Lantenengo, between Fifteenth and Sixteenth?"

"That's right," I said.

"Delivered groceries there, many a time," he said. "I remember that kitchen. A big coal stove, you could of put a thirty-pound turkey in that oven. You had a colored woman for a cook. I used to sit there and get warm."

"You must have worked for Frank Snodgrass."

"For Frank Snodgrass is right. Christ, all them old stores went out of business. The out-of-town chains. I tell you, there's nothin' here. Nothin'."

"I'm afraid you're right," I said.

"Well, I gotta start wakin' them up. Thanks for the fin."

I had no idea who he was, I don't think I had ever seen him before. He probably had been the Snodgrass delivery man during my years at prep school and college. But he remembered Rhoda Hume, our cook, and our Buckeye range, and as far as I was concerned he was right about Gibbsville. For him and for me there was nothin' there, nothin'.

I wrote a note to Andrea. "It is now 7:30 A.M. and I am about to leave. Too early to telephone you. I have finished my business here and will not be coming back. If you need me, or if I can do anything for you, you know where to reach me. I am going abroad next month for about seven weeks, but will leave word with my secretary to forward any messages from you. Love, Phil." I posted the note on my way out of the hotel.

For almost twenty years, now, our love affair had consisted of brief meetings and absences that varied in length. On my part, and I

am sure on hers, there had been no deceitfulness; no broken promises of fidelity since there had been no promises. A certain amount,
probably a great deal, of honesty ensued as an accompaniment of
the freedom we granted ourselves. I was able, for instance, to admit
to myself without shame that it was very pleasant to have a love affair with a stunning young woman who came and went and did
nothing to disarrange my comfortable bachelorhood. If I occasionally accused myself of selfishness, I defended myself on the ground
that she had more than once refused to marry me. Equally true, I
could defensively argue, was the fact that I was a convenience for
her. In her somewhat raffish life I was the one consistently dependable man to give her the emotional security that she seemed to reject
by her conduct with the others. So much so that morally I was probably bad for her. She could always turn to steadfast me, and she
always did.

But it was her nature to pass herself around among men, and she
would have done so whether I was in her background or not. It was
therefore a spurious twinge of conscience that I sometimes allowed
myself. Long ago she had told me the complete details of her love
affair with the boy in California, and though I was the first male
with whom she experienced true copulation, she and the boy had
gone from fellatio to coitus interruptus, which she was pleased to
call heavy necking. It also pleased her (and my masculinity) to re-
gard me as the taker of her virginity, but the distinction was to at
least some extent honorary. We had something besides the sexual
relationship, and had had it from the start. But, circumstances per-
mitting, we had always had intercourse at some point during our
sporadic reunions. It was customary, and we had always taken it for
granted. As usual, I had taken it for granted when I visited her in her
apartment, and my dissatisfaction with our meeting was two-fold: I
had not gone to bed with her, as I had been looking forward to
doing, and our conversation had not brought out a physical reason,
meaning the after-effects of her latest abortion, for her coolness. I
was inclined to believe that she had not been to bed with anyone
since the abortion, and I tended to substantiate my belief with her

account of her fondness for her pansy employer. I had known a Philadelphia girl who, after a bad abortion, took up with a band of homosexuals and became one herself, never to return to heterosexuality. At the moment I had no such fears for Andrea, but I did not give the matter much thought. I was more deeply concerned with my overall relationship with her, and disturbed by the appearance of a coolness that was without precedent. We had had quarrels aplenty, but coolness never. As I drove back to Philadelphia I tried to correlate the new coolness with the angry outburst in which she had thrown the glass at me. It was possible that a deep-seated resentment of me had existed that far back, despite the fact that we went on that night to make love with tenderness and consideration. Although I cared for no one else in the world, I realized that I did not know her, and in self-preservation I began to make preparations for the contingency of life without her.

That, however, was not easy. I said I began to make preparations, but no specific preparations occurred to me. How do you go about making plans to live without something you never really had? If she had been really my mistress, I most likely would have had some possessions of hers in my apartment, to put in a box and send back to her. But I did not have so much as a douche bag, a toothbrush, to get rid of. The only thing of that sort that I could do would be to tell the drug store to stop sending her that monthly bottle of perfume, and I briefly considered that move to remind her that she had banished me. But in addition to its being ridiculously petty, such a move would have been effective as a reminder just once. Oddly enough, though, I had hit upon a most significant detail. A couple of days after I got back from the Gibbsville fiasco, the drug store, one of the last of the old-time ethical pharmacies, sent me a letter to notify me that at the request of Mrs. Cooper, they were discontinuing monthly delivery of the perfume. So she had put me out of her life.

Fortunately for my state of mind, I had made my plans for the trip abroad, which was to combine pleasure and business. My passage had been booked in both directions, my hotel reservations made, and the exact time of my business appointments in London,

Paris, Brussels, and Berlin was set. On the social side, I had accepted
invitations for the two weekends I would be in England, as well as
for the weekend that I would be in France, and it was a safe guess
that my overseas acquaintances would wish to entertain for me as
the representative of clients. My schedule was tight, but for once I
welcomed the restrictions on my free time. I would not have to
brood about that little bitch.

I began brooding about her the moment the *Queen Mary*
sounded its horn and backed into the channel in the North River.
The sound of the horn went right to my guts and standing alone
on the boat deck I ignored the Manhattan skyline and stared out
toward the Jersey meadows, where her lover had been done in, and I
tried to guess the precise direction of a straight line to Gibbsville,
Pennsylvania, where at this moment she would be in all likelihood
having lunch at the Y.M.C.A. cafeteria. People like her, in jobs like
hers, all had lunch at the "Y" cafeteria. I would be having mine
shortly in the Verandah Grill of the *Queen Mary,* with a Boston lawyer and his wife who were on their way to a world convention of
breeders of Dandie Dinmonts at Edinburgh. I had a feeling that I
was going to see a lot of Mr. and Mrs. Wallen, and I was right. She
introduced me to her sister, another Dandie Dinmont fancier, and
the four of us played bridge all the way to Southampton. By skill,
luck, and intense concentration on the cards, I won sixty-five dollars.

The whole trip was like that, more or less. In Brussels, where my
business acquaintance was a fat bachelor, I was provided with a tall
young blonde who could have worn any item of Andrea's clothes.
She was very pleasing to the eye and to the senses, and was under
strict orders to accept no money from me. But I gave her fifty dollars
anyhow so that she would not think the less kindly of gentlemen
from Philadelphia. She knew of Philadelphia as the home town of
Grace Kelly, of the cinema, and of Eddie Fisher, a singer. No, I had
never met Miss Kelly or Fisher, and I had to assure the young
woman that it was not so much because I was a *snopp* as that Philadelphia was a large city, about twice as many people as Brussels,

which she manifestly did not believe. She was a very competent professional, kept busy by the delegates to the Benelux Customs Union, and was moderately pleased when I told her that she reminded me very much of a young woman I knew in the United States. "Your mistress?" she said, and I said yes, and let it go at that. She had guessed immediately that I was not married, and could not explain her guess other than to say that she had never yet been wrong. Intuition. I could not reasonably argue with that; intuitively I had guessed that she was a high-class whore.

She was my only physical contact with her sex throughout my trip, and just what I wanted. I wanted no involvement with a nonprofessional, no polite wooing for the privilege of the bed. Twice I had conversations with my secretary on the overseas telephone, and she would not have failed to report a message from Andrea. The distance and the time that had intervened since my Gibbsville fiasco now seemed very great indeed. I attributed that notion to my realizing, retroactively, that Andrea intended the rupture to be permanent. If that were the case, three weeks and three thousand miles were only the beginning, and if so, I would do well to make a more serious effort to dismiss her from my thoughts. That I had never done, neither on this trip nor in the past, when she had stayed away from me for a year at a time.

Going home, in the *Queen Elizabeth,* I played bridge with other men for higher stakes than I had played for with the Wallens. I hate to lose at anything, particularly at bridge, and I suggested the ten-cents-a-point game because it was the only way I knew to divert me from the excitement I had begun to feel as soon as I boarded the ship. I drank a little more than I usually do; not enough to have a noticeable effect on my bridge game, but enough to make me ready for sleep when our nightly game was over. There was nothing— meaning no one, meaning Andrea—waiting for me at home, and yet the excitement demanded some attention. Several nights I went to bed quite sozzled, the result of nightcaps following the bridge games. On totting up the score on the night before we were to land, I was delighted to find that I had won more than a thousand tax-free dollars, and I was gratified to discover that the bridge and the whis-key had had the desired palliative effect. One disturbing note: as he paid up, one of my bridge-game companions said, "For a man that put away as much Scotch as you did, you played awfully good bridge." He was a New Yorker, a member of my New York club, and I was glad he was not Philadelphian. At home no one had ever had occasion to comment on my intake of whiskey. I had actually never been a heavy drinker by the standards of the men whom I saw every day. Yet the bridge companion had seen fit to comment on the quantity of my drinking and not on the effect on me.

The next day one of our clients sent a company limousine to meet me at the pier and transport me to Philadelphia, and I was home in time for lunch at the club. Lunch at a club was the antithesis of the kind of excitement that I had been subduing on the ship. I took my seat at the large, common table, and the man next to me said, "I missed you the last couple days," and the man on the other side of me asked me if I had had a good trip. That was par for the course, and I was home again, back in the old routine. From the club I walked to my office, spent an hour with my secretary and another hour with my partners. By quitting time it was hard to believe that I had been in New York that morning, and the most surprising thing of all was that as I slipped back into my routine, I almost believed that Andrea was where she had always been as a sort of offstage character in the comedy-drama of my life. Everything else was the same; why not she? But she refused to stay put in the customary role.

The next few weeks were busy ones for me. After all, I had spent about $7,000 of other people's money, and they were entitled to their conferences and my reports and opinions. I found that it was taking as long to report on the trip as the trip itself had taken, and one day I happened to notice on my calendar that four months had passed since my visit to Gibbsville. It did not seem possible. Meanwhile the mineral rights case had been turned over to Whitman, one of our junior partners, and it was trudging along as such cases tend to do. It could and might go on for years. Two teams of accountants were working on the basically same set of figures and coming out with wildly disparate results, a normal condition when the accountants are on opposite sides of the fence. At a senior partners' weekly meeting, during which we regularly go through the list of our cases, I said, "What about Southern Anthracite? Any progress there?"

Joe Sloan, one of the senior partners, said, "Slow as molasses, Phil. You wouldn't like to have another go at it?"

"Isn't Whitman doing all he can?" I said.

"No criticism of Whitman, but he's young. If we want to goose them, one of us will have to go. It must be six months since you went up to Gibbsville—"

"It's four," I said.

"Well, do you want to wait another two months and then go up? This thing may drag along and drag along till nobody gets any money out of it but the accountants. I was thinking that we could have our accountants do a pressure job, work overtime if necessary, and finish up well ahead of their accountants. Then if you went up to Gibbsville with the final figures you could get both litigants together and say, 'Here it is, let's sit down and work this out.' They won't take our figures as gospel, but they'll have a basis to work on. And I'm afraid you're elected, Phil. You're the only one they'll all listen to. I'd like to get this case finalized. I hate to see all that money going to the accountants, and not to us."

"Joe, you're just greedy," I said.

"I know I am. My one besetting sin," he said.

"I'll think it over and let you know tomorrow," I said.

If Joe Sloan's one besetting sin was greed—which it was not— mine was curiosity. I agreed to go to Gibbsville, and arranged to have a little article printed in the Gibbsville papers to the effect that the Southern Anthracite mineral rights dispute might be reaching its final stages ("Settlement Looms," the paper said) with the arrival of the noted Philadelphia attorney, meaning me, for several days of conferences. The dispute was of sufficient local interest to warrant its being printed on the front page, where Andrea would not miss it. This time everybody in town would know I was coming.

Before departing I received hasty invitations from the Lantenengo Bar Association, the Gibbsville Chamber of Commerce, and the Gibbsville Rotary Club to say a few words. With my judicial ambition in mind, I accepted the Bar Association invitation. They promised that their meeting would be informal, one of their regular monthly dinners, and that they were not asking me to prepare a speech. Anything I cared to say. Off the record. Intra-professional. No questions relating to the Southern Anthracite case or the subject of mineral rights. Just a hastily planned get-together in tribute to one of the county's most distinguished sons.

In theory, I was only the attorney for one party to the mineral rights dispute, but obviously during the first all-day conference I was in command. Whenever anyone was speaking, he would address me, and I slowly assumed the position of arbiter. I had Whitman with me to dig the appropriate papers out of his attaché case, and until late afternoon I did not say a word. Then, shortly after five o'clock, I said, "Gentlemen, this thing has gone on long enough. Here we are, eight men who are reasonable men, men of good will and personal integrity, here to serve the best interests of the people we represent. If that were not the case, I would not do what I am about to do." I paused and looked at each man, excluding Whitman. Across the table was a shyster who should have been disbarred years ago; a johnny-come-lately to the coal industry who had once been a bootlegger; a weak sister of a fellow whose family name was as old as the mining of hard coal; a man from Wilkes-Barre who had been in a lot of trouble for violations of the safety regulations. On our side of the table, besides Whitman and me, were our clients. I reached in my inside coat pocket and drew out a sheet of paper. "This is a memorandum that we prepared in my office. It is confidential, but I am going to read it to you." I then recited, or intoned, an almost day-to-day list of the expenses of the dispute between the two parties: accountants' fees, accountants' expenses, our disbursements, and so on and so on. I gave them five minutes of $125 for this, $54 for that, and finished up by saying, "That comes to sixty-two thousand, nine hundred and twelve dollars and twenty-seven cents. Sixty-two thousand, nine hundred and twelve dollars and twenty-seven cents. That's a lot of coal, gentlemen. A lot of coal. But you haven't even heard the half of it. You may have noticed that I did not mention legal fees. I don't know what our fee will be, but I doubt if it will be less than the accountants' fees. Let's say it will be the same. Sixty-three thousand dollars. That comes to, in round numbers, one hundred and twenty-six thousand dollars. That's *our* side of it. Let's say that your side of it matches that figure. That means that two hundred and fifty-two thousand dollars has been spent by both sides so far. *So far!* At the rate we're going, we could go well over the half-a-million-dollar mark. A half a million dollars is a lot of coal, a lot of coal. You could build a breaker for that kind of money. You could buy fifty trucks. But that's not all. If we go into court, the legal expenses on both sides will be staggering. Staggering. And even *that* isn't all, because I assure you gentlemen, if our side loses, we are going to appeal, and if our side wins, your side will probably appeal." I paused, to let the financial points sink in, and then I continued: "We have all had a tough day. I suggest we adjourn until ten o'clock tomorrow morning." I then, in my capacity as unofficial arbiter, stood up to give the signal for the others to stand up. They did so. If they had not done so, my argument would have been futile, but I had been silent all day and studying the opposition's shyster. They all got up automatically, and the meeting broke up then and there.

"That was masterful," Whitman whispered to me as he was putting his papers back in the attaché case.

"Maybe it was, but I hope you don't think it was the argument that did it. It was the timing and the psychology. Let's get out of here quick," I said.

I had won the case and I knew it. The details would be worked out later. I felt like one of those football players who, having scored a touchdown, leave the ball on the ground for the umpire to pick up. "Tomorrow you take over," I said to Whitman.

"You're not going to be there?" said Whitman.

"That's part of the psychology," I said. "I'll be at the hotel if you need me, but I have no intention of facing that shyster Spockman.

He'll spend the night thinking up arguments against me, but they're not going to be any good if I'm not there. You go to the meeting as though we'd all agreed to behave sensibly, and I think you'll find that Spockman will be the only hold-out. Care to join me for a drink?"

"No sir, I have to call Mr. Sloan, but thanks."

"I'll be at the Gibbsville Club, then there's a Bar Association dinner that I'm going to. Look in if you feel like it," I said. "It's at the hotel."

I saw some old friends at the Gibbsville Club, where I had retained my non-resident membership. I stayed there until it was time to go to the Bar Association dinner, at which I arrived in a very very cheerful mood. Somehow the rumor had spread that I had conducted a highly successful meeting in the mineral rights case, and I was compelled several times to say that congratulations were premature; but I was a lawyer among lawyers, and they were aware, and pleased, that I had outsmarted Mr. Spockman. He, of course, stayed away from the dinner.

When it came my turn to speak, I played it safe. I was not drunk, but I had had a lot to drink, and this seemed to be a good opportunity to dispel the notion that I was a stuffed shirt. I therefore confined my remarks to professional jokes and anecdotes about old-time members of the county bench and bar. I turned the meeting into a social evening, and when it was over I was told repeatedly that it was the liveliest session they had had in years. About a dozen of us repaired to the taproom to reminisce. At midnight I grew weary of their adulation and obsequiousness, and said goodnight.

There were two identical telephone messages under my door. I checked the number in the telephone book, and it was Andrea, who had not left her name. "Please call 625-1181," and the calls had been received during the time I was at the Gibbsville Club. I called her, and I woke her up. Her speech was slow, heavy with sleep, and I had trouble making her understand that it was I who was calling. "I took a sleeping pill," she said, obviously with an effort.

"Go back to sleep," I said.

394 · JOHN O'HARA

"All right," she said, and hung up. She was no good to me that night, and I took a bottle of Scotch out of my bag and poured a nightcap. She was no damn good to me, full of sleeping pills and dead to the world.

In a way, to be perfectly truthful, I was relieved. I had come to Gibbsville on the early morning train, had gone almost immediately to the morning meeting, lunched with Whitman and our clients, returned to the afternoon meeting, and built up to the climax of the meeting which was my speech to Spockman and the others. Then instead of slowing down, I had kept going at the Gibbsville Club and the Bar Association dinner. More than eighteen hours of more or less intense effort. I was annoyed but at the same time grateful that for that night there would be no more demands on my physical and mental resources. I got into bed without finishing my nightcap, and fell asleep with the light on.

From another world came the ringing of my telephone. It rang several times, stopped, and then was rung again with renewed vigor. "For Christ's sake," I said, and answered it. It was my old friend the night man who had delivered groceries for Snodgrass. "There's a lady to see you, sir."

"To *see* me? You mean downstairs?"

"Yes sir, she says you sent for her and she won't go away," he said. In a lower tone, barely audible, he added: "It's somebody you know."

"All right, send her up," I said.

I had time to splash some cold water on my face and run a comb through my hair, but I was unsteady and drowsy when the rap came on the fireproof door. Behind her stood the night man, waiting to see if I was going to let her in. "Hello, come in," I said, and the door closed behind her.

"You did send for me, didn't you?" she said.

"No, I didn't, but you're here," I said.

"Did I imagine it? You did call me, didn't you?"

"Yes, but you were full of sleeping pills, you said."

"One. Not pills, just one."

"I might as well be," I said. "My sleeping pill was Scotch."

"So I see," she said, looking at the unfinished nightcap.

"Do you want some?" I said. "Did I hear three o'clock strike?"

"You could have. It's after four, now."

"Then I didn't hear three o'clock strike. I was really pounding away. Do you want a drink of Scotch? And tap water? It's all I can offer you at this hour."

"And you're not offering that very graciously. No thanks," she said. "Go on back to bed," she said. "I woke up thinking you'd sent for me, but if you didn't—the hell with it."

"How'd you get here?"

"On my Flexible-Flyer," she said. "What do you mean, how did I get here? I have a car. It sits out in front of my apartment all night, case some traveling salesman gets horny. *How* did I *get* here!"

I was coming to, and I knew it by the fact that desire for her was growing in me. I closed the windows, and put on my dressing-gown. "I'm not going to pull a knife on you," I said. "There's no use watching me that way."

"I'm not going to pull a knife on *you,* either."

"Well, why don't you take off your coat?"

"Because it's still cold in here," she said.

I turned up the thermostat. "Take off your coat," I said.

"Are we going to go to bed?" she said.

"That's always up to you," I said.

"No, it isn't," she said. "That's what I came here for, but that was when I thought you'd sent for me. However, you deny that. You *didn't* send for me, and I was laboring under a misapprehension."

"If I ask you now, politely and unequivocally, will you go to bed with me?"

"Are either one of us going to get any pleasure out of it?" she said. "I don't think I'll be any good."

"Well, then let's talk," I said. "Frankly, I thought I was never going to see you again."

"I thought I was going to have to struggle along without you, too," she said.

"And you seem to have," I said. "Are you still working at the hat store?"

"Thank *God* I am. Otherwise I would be waiting for horny salesmen to call me at night," she said. "You heard about King's?"

"No."

"Bankruptcy, or receivership. Anyway, it's going out of business. Daddy flew the coop, taking all the cash with him. Mother is living with Bud, my brother. She rented her house, furnished, and that's all she has to live on. Fortunately, she doesn't have to spend much money on food. Just give her a bottle of vodka every day and she's happy and contented."

"That must be pretty tough on your brother. What is he living on?"

"He's a substitute teacher in the high school, and his wife's family are giving them something. There are so many people around here having financial difficulties, it's becoming quite the thing. I hate this hotel. It's always filled up with people from out-of-town, squeezing the last dollar out of Gibbsville."

"What about the hat store?"

"It's amazing. Women can always scrape up twelve-ninety-five for a hat."

"And your fairy friend, your boss?"

"One of the few prosperous men in town," she said.

"And you still love him dearly?" I said.

"Of course I do," she said. "If he was a man, I'd marry him. And he says the same thing about me."

"What about the doctor?"

"He comes to see me once in a while. We go out to dinner together."

"And?"

"Oh, sure," she said.

"Then you might marry him after all," I said.

"No. We don't even discuss marriage any more. We have dinner together. Sex. And he goes home. He's seriously considering going back in the Navy again. If they'll take him back as a lieutenant commander, and let him take a two-year course in urology, he'll go. He's in the reserve, and apparently they need doctors."

"He's willing to give up twenty thousand a year?"

"It's less than that now, and he wouldn't have to pay rent and a secretary and all that. It makes a lot of sense."

She stood up and took off her coat and folded it on the back of a chair. Then she kicked off her shoes and lay beside me on the bed. "Rather crowded in here," she said. She put her arms around me and kissed me on the mouth. "We're getting there," she said.

"I missed you," I said.

She nodded. "Yes," she said. She got up and took off her clothes and got back into bed with me. "Don't you think it'd be polite if you took yours off too?"

"It wouldn't be polite, exactly. I'm getting a paunch. But it'd be more comfortable."

"Well, then be comfortable," she said. She watched me. "You're not *getting* a paunch, you have one. What is it? The booze?"

"It's the booze," I said.

"Is that my fault?"

"If I want to put the blame on someone else, yes," I said.

"Don't become a drunkard on account of me," she said.

"I don't intend to become a drunkard," I said.

"You'd better be careful, then," she said.

"I'm careful," I said.

"No," she said. "You got drunk tonight, didn't you?"

"How did you know?"

"You didn't even finish your last drink," she said. She began to make love to me, startlingly like the Belgian girl, the girl in Brussels who had made me think of her. "Maybe if we went to sleep for a little while," she said.

"No," I said. "Unless you want to."

"Suddenly you lost interest," she said.

"It'll come back," I said.

"Oh, I know that," she said. She sat up. "There's something on your mind. Either that, or you're too tired. Which is it?"

I could not lie to her, so I told her about the Belgian girl.

"Well, it almost had to be something like that," she said. "Now we can forget about her—or, if you want to think about her, turn out the light."

"I don't want to think about her," I said.

"That's good. Don't think about me, either. The hell with thinking. It's me, Phil. Your girl." She nestled down, and slowly we returned to our old selves and now everything was all right.

"That was good," she said. "It's still good. With you it's never over so soon. There's always something left. Something nice. I don't know. Something nice. You have it for me, and I guess I have it for you."

"It'd be too obvious to call it love," I said.

"It obviously isn't love, either," she said. "Love quits on you. At least it always has on me. I guess you're my steady. How many years is it?"

"Oh—twenty."

"Then it certainly isn't love," she said. "Although it certainly is."

"We don't have to have a name for it," I said.

"Phil and Andrea, Incorporated," she said.

"Or as the French say, Société Anonyme," I said.

"I don't quite get it," she said.

"Americans say incorporated, the British say limited. The French say société anonyme, using the initials s.a. You probably thought they stood for sex appeal."

"You've lost me," she said.

"Well, the next time you look at a bottle of perfume—speaking of which, you sorehead."

She smiled. "Yes, that was sorehead. Now you can tell them to start sending it again. What was that horrid noise?"

"It sounded like a bus."

"That's exactly what it was. It's getting daylight," she said. "You have time for a few hours' sleep. And I have time to get out of here before everybody in Gibbsville sees me. Will you take me to dinner tonight, or come to my apartment?"

ANDREA ♦ 399

"Whatever you like."

"Come to my apartment. Société anonyme."

"All right, fine," I said.

I lay in bed and watched her get dressed, an operation that was almost as fascinating as watching her undress. "Shall I open the windows?" she said.

"If you don't mind," I said.

"Of course I don't mind. We have to have a clear head," she said. She kissed me on the forehead and went to the window and opened it. Then she went to the other window and opened it, and I don't know what happened because I was not watching. But when I did look she was not there, and I did not believe that until I heard a most awful scream. Then I believed it, and it is all I have left to believe.

James Francis and the Star

♦

J ames Francis Hatter, the writer, having eaten his usual large breakfast and finished with the Los Angeles newspapers, took a second cup of coffee and the Hollywood trade papers out on the terrace, and inside of two minutes the day that had started so well—well, it was utterly ruined for him. All because of one little item in one of the chatter columns. "Town buzzing over chic dinner party tossed by Rod Fulton to celebrate his return to local scene. Rod just back from three years abroad and three pix in Italy and London. His new Holmby Hills manse a real smasher," said the item, and followed with a dozen names of Fulton's guests. The names were old and new, but all big.

James Francis Hatter knew, of course, that Rod was back. That news, accompanied by photographs taken at the airport, had been in all the papers. Not too long ago James Francis Hatter would have been at the airport to greet him. A very long time ago James Francis would have been at the Pasadena station when Rod came in on the Super-Chief. And still longer ago Rod Fulton would have been at the station to meet James Francis, helping James Francis with his luggage and leading the way to James Francis's car. Rod would have got the girls and reserved the table at the Troc for James Francis's first night home. He would have washed James Francis's Packard convertible, and on the ride down from Pasadena to Beverly Hills, Rod would have read off a complete and accurate list of the important telephone calls that had come in during James Francis's absence.

Things had changed, as they were bound to change, as James Francis had often said they would change. "Don't *worry* about it, fella," he would say to Rod. "You need two good pictures, one right after the other, and you're in, I tell you. Then the dough you're in me for can come out of your first week's salary."

"I wish *I* thought so," Rod had said. "I'm about ready to go back and start hitting the managers' offices in New York."

"Not till you click here," said James Francis. "I won't let you. These muzzlers out here gave Gable the same kind of a run-around. Tracy. Astaire. I could name you a dozen. With a dame it's different. A dame can make it on her back, whereas there aren't many producers that are fairies. So be patient a little while longer."

"I owe you eighteen hundred dollars, not to mention what I'd owe you if you charged me for board and room."

"The money you will pay me back, I know that. The rest, I lived off friends of mine before I began hitting the *Post*. Twenty-two stories I sent them before they finally accepted one. Then things began to happen fast, and they will for you, too. I know when people have something and when they haven't, and you have, Rod. I'll try to get you the gangster's brother in this one I'm working on now. Then you'll need something else good, not necessarily big, right after that. Meanwhile, keep yourself in good condition. The people in makeup can always make you look dissipated if the part calls for it, but if you *are* dissipated they can't make you look healthy. So watch the booze, and the rich food. Not only for now but for later. You don't want to have to take character parts when you're forty, just because you made a pig of yourself when you were thirty."

"Well, fortunately I like to take exercise, and if I never had another drink I wouldn't miss it."

"Fortunately for me, my living doesn't depend on how I look."

"You do all right with the dames."

"*Some* dames," said James Francis. "If you can't make a score in

402 ♦ JOHN O'HARA

this town, the next stop is Tahiti. Or Port Said. Or maybe a lamasery in Thibet."

"What do they have there?" said Rod.

"What they don't have is dames."

"Oh," said Rod. "What did you say that was?"

"A lamasery. The same as a monastery."

"Do you think I ought to read more, Jimmy?"

"Well, it wouldn't hurt you to try. But you don't have to. Some directors would rather you didn't. But some of *them* don't read any more than they have to."

"I wish I could have been a writer."

"I wish I could have been a good one," said James Francis. "But failing that, I can be a fat one."

"Well, you're getting there, slowly by degrees. You're the one ought to start taking the exercise, Jimmy. I mean it."

"Oh, one of these days I'm going to buy a fly swatter."

"A fly swatter? You mean a tennis racket?"

"No, I mean a fly swatter."

"You bastard, I never know when you're ribbing me," said Rod Fulton.

The cash debt had mounted to three thousand before Rod was able to start repaying it, and it took three pictures rather than two for his career to get in high gear. But thereafter there never was any doubt about it. He was a star, a big, dumb, youthful man whom women wanted to go to bed with and men wanted to go fishing with or to give him a good punch in the mouth. He bought a house of his own on North Roxbury, quite a distance from James Francis Hatter's house high above the Sunset Strip, but he did not cease to be grateful to James Francis. "This is the guy, this is the *one* guy that had confidence in me when I didn't have it in myself," he would say. And he would express it in other ways than words.

If James Francis happened to be working on the same lot, he and Rod would have lunch together every day. When James Francis was working somewhere else Rod would call him on the telephone just to chin, or to talk about getting a couple of broads. James Francis went along for the ride when Rod took a trip to Oregon to fish for steelheads, and at Rod's request, his studio paid all of James Francis's expenses on Rod's first visit to Europe. It was only James Francis's second, but Rod had the studio believing that James Francis had traveled as much as Lowell Thomas. Actually the studio was relieved that Rod had not insisted on taking some broad. He was at the moment having a secret romance with a waitress at the Beverly Derby as well as a widely publicized affair with Doris Arlington, and the studio wanted the European public to think of him as unattached.

The only unpleasantness of the trip occurred when an Englishwoman of title invited Rod to her house for the weekend, and Rod said he would have to ask Jimmy. "Jimmy? Is that Hatter?" she asked. "But surely you don't take your orders from your secretary?"

"He's not my secretary."

"Oh, I *see.*"

"He's my friend."

"Yes, exactly. Well, in that case that does change things, doesn't it?"

"He happens to be one of the highest-paid writers in Hollywood. He got me started in pictures."

"Oh, yes. Well, you see I hadn't really counted on having an extra man. I thought it would be just you and I and another couple, friends of mine. Mr. Hatter being there would complicate things, wouldn't it?"

"I don't know. Would it?"

"Yes, rather. My friends aren't married, to each other, that is. *She* has to be awfully careful, and I'm afraid she'd back out if a total stranger—"

"*I'm* a total stranger," said Rod.

"Not to me."

"Well, no," said Rod. "Get another girl for Jimmy."

"A *girl?*"

"Well of course a girl. He may be getting fat, but he's one of the greatest swordsmen in Hollywood."

"He *is*? You couldn't be mistaken about that, of course."

"What the hell are you hinting at? You don't think Jimmy is a fag, do you?"

"As a mattrafact I did."

"Then what does that make me?"

"Oh, now, Rodney, don't put me in the spot."

"*On* the spot. In the spot is lighting. On the spot is what you're trying to say."

"I don't know *what* I'm trying to say," she said. "Yes I do! I'm just afraid that as we can't possibly have Mr. Hatter, and I've promised Sybil—she has to be *so* careful now—I'm going to have to disinvite you, dear boy."

"Six, two, and even Sybil would end up in the kip with Jimmy, whoever Sybil is."

"If only you knew, you'd be bloody well impressed, Mr. Fulton."

"Not me. I don't know these English broads. Jimmy does, but I don't."

"Then all the more reason for not having your Jimmy person. No, you and I must make other plans."

"We don't *have* to. Anyway, I don't like you inferring about Jimmy and I."

"My fault, really. I should have known. He doesn't *look* like a secretary." She was talking to herself. "Darling, you will have lunch with me Tuesday. At my flat? One-ish?"

"No can do. All day Tuesday I'll be at Elstree."

"You and Jimmy?"

"That's right, me and Jimmy," he said.

The countess's suspicions of James Francis were as natural to her, as automatic and unthinking as Rod's defense of him. Nevertheless now that someone had come right out and said it, thus showing that someone else had thought it, Rod admitted to himself that he had wondered a little about James Francis. Various kinds of homo were nothing new to Rod, particularly after he had got his first job as a chorus boy in the road company of a Broadway musical. On several occasions, when the money was low, he had allowed them to seduce him, and at the beginning of his friendship with James Francis he had half expected more of the same. But when weeks passed and James Francis had continued to treat him as half-brother, half-servant, and unemployed friend, Rod stopped waiting for that other shoe to drop. The actor who had told Rod to look up James Francis was an older, fortyish, hard-drinking, saloon-brawling man, who had a speaking part in the road show. His tastes, like James Francis's, were for women and booze. He completely ignored the queens among the chorus boys. If Rod had had no show business experience he might never have had the slightest suspicion of James Francis, and such as he had soon vanished. James Francis had never married and he was often content to sit alone and listen to highbrow music on the phonograph. He read a lot. But he was a writer, the first successful writer Rod had ever become acquainted with, and writers were *supposed* to be intellectual. One of the best things about James Francis was that regardless of how successful a writer he was, he did not look down on people who couldn't even write a good letter. He wore expensive cashmere jackets and doeskin slacks, and horn-rim glasses, and looked more like a writer than a bank clerk; but directors and cameramen and high-priced film cutters dressed the same way. For a man making the kind of money he made, James Francis Hatter was God damn democratic. And a great sense of humor. He kept the whores laughing for hours at a time, just by the things he said. He was a great guy.

And the countess was a bitch, twenty-four karat, to revive those forgotten suspicions. She was something new for Rod. In her taking for granted that he and James Francis were sweethearts she had shown not the slightest bit of surprise or censure. Her only concern was for the Sybil broad, who did not want to get caught with her boy friend. (They had some divorce law in England which they nicknamed the Decree Nazi.) She trusted Rod, because he was a prominent film star, but she did not have sense enough to trust James Francis. She was a bitch, and he kept thinking about her long after he returned to Hollywood. He was determined that nothing she had said would affect his gratitude and friendship for James Francis; he saw Jimmy as much as ever. As Rod's fame expanded and his pictures made more money, there were inevitable changes in their relationship. Publicly, Jimmy became the uncaptioned companion of the big movie star; in the industry, he was the man you had to talk to if you wanted to get to Rod Fulton; privately, he was the only person whom Rod could rely on to tell him the truth. Hollywood, after John Barrymore's memorable performance as Svengali, applied the nickname Trilby to Rod Fulton, but not within his hearing. He had got too big for that; the only person who could talk that way to Rod Fulton was Svengali Hatter. Moreover, even Hollywood, which enjoyed its moments of sentimentality, was aware that this was a remarkable friendship. It gave the lie to the charge that movie stars are ungrateful.

Then in 1942 the alert Public Relations men of the Air Force beat the Marine Corps to it with a firm offer of a captaincy to Rod Fulton. The Navy ran a poor third. There was a certain amount of apprehensive discussion among the Air Force brass. Jimmy Stewart was a fully qualified peacetime pilot and properly belonged in the Air Force. Clark Gable was not a pilot and had no better education than Rod Fulton, but was given a commission. What then if all three big movie stars got killed? What would be the effect on military and civilian morale? It was decided that the chance was worth taking on the theory that as far as service personnel were concerned, movie stars were expendable, and that if all three men got killed, the civilian population would know that we were in a war. Public Relations hoped that if anyone got killed it would not be Stewart or Gable.

They sent Rod on enough missions to qualify him for his Air Medal, and then kept him on the ground. Having visited London before the war, he was not a stranger to the West End, and he found his way back to the countess. Angela was fatigued by the war, the hazards and the austerity program, and one night Rod Fulton found that he had asked her to marry him and had been accepted. He was never quite sure how it happened; he had no James Francis in London whom he could turn to for advice, and who could think up a way to get him off the hook. So the marriage took place, with Sybil as matron of honor and Angela's brother as best man. The union was generally regarded as propitious, a sweeping away of class distinctions and a more than symbolic alliance of two typical representatives of Britain and America. Public Relations could not complain about that, and did not. At the earliest opportunity Angela was given a fairly high priority to fly to Los Angeles, there to do splendid work for the Red Cross and the U.S.O. while, in the words of her fellow-Briton Ivor Novello, keeping the home fires burning.

An early visitor was James Francis Hatter, who welcomed her with black market steaks, cigarettes, and nylons. "I don't know *when* I've had steak," she said. "You *are* a dear, Hatter."

"Yes, ma'am," he said. "Will there be anything else, ma'am?"

"Why are you imitating a film butler? That *is* what you're doing, isn't it?"

"Very good, ma'am. Yes, it is, you got it," he said. "Why I guess because I'm not used to having a woman call me by my last name."

"What shall I call you?"

"Jimmy. Or Mr. Hatter. Or Svengali. Baby, I don't care what you call me. If you want anything, I'll try to get it for you. Rod asked me to. But let's not you and me kid ourselves or each other."

"All right," said Angela. "In other words, if I need anything, you'll get it as a favor to Rod, not to me. I'm for that. Have you any influence with the airline people?"

"Some. Not as much as the studio transportation department. Why?"

"I know about the studio transportation people. Rod told me. But if I could go to New York next week without having to ask the studio's help, I'd be ever so."

"I might be able to fix it," said James Francis.

"And no questions asked?"

"Would I get a truthful answer?"

"This time you might, but I shouldn't count on it every time," she said. "It's rather relaxing not to have to pretend, don't you find it so?"

"Very. It was my idea. I couldn't see putting on an act with you. Life's too short for that, old girl."

"If I promise not to call you Hatter, will you agree not to call me old girl?"

"It's a deal."

"I'm two years older than Rod, if you must know. But I'm not twenty years older, or ten or even five. On the other hand, I'm not so young as to not mind being called old girl. I didn't object when you called me baby, although that's slightly disrespectful as you say it."

"Slightly," said James Francis.

"By the way, I know there's never been anything naughty between you and Rod. You hate me because I thought there had been. But I promise you, it wouldn't have made the slightest difference to me."

"Well, why should it? You've had girl friends, and it won't be long before you have some here, judging by the group you latched onto."

"I much prefer boy friends, but Rod wouldn't take kindly to that. How do you know so much about me, Jimmy? Rod doesn't know that."

"Rod doesn't know anything."

"He doesn't, does he?" said Angela.

"Maybe he will by the time you get through with him, but I doubt it."

"That may be a long ways off. I adore this climate."

"It can get monotonous."

"Oh, but I hope not," she said. "I love my England, but there's not much to be said for our weather. I could soak in this sunshine forever. This is only my third week here, but there's only a tiny bit of me that's my original color. Imagine. In February. You're quite brown, too. You must come and have a swim with me. I won't try to seduce you."

"Why not?"

"Well, if you put it that way, I will. Rod told me you were quite a swordsman, and we don't have to like each other, you know. I don't suppose you and I ever will like each other, but you brought me those nylons, and the cigarettes, and the steak, without liking me. I think I'll sit on your lap. May I?"

"Sure."

"Shall I just close this door so that we won't have any untimely interruptions?"

"I was going to suggest that," said James Francis.

"You see, we think alike in some respects." She got up and turned the latch in the door. On the way back she shed her pajamas. "I know I'm going to like this, and you are too," she said. "How much do you think I weigh?"

"Eight stone," he said.

"Extraordinary! One pound off. And you must be sixteen stone."

"Just about," he said.

"How too perfectly matched we are. You're *very* obliging, Jimmy. I was rather hoping this would happen, but you were awfully forbidding at first, with that chip on your shoulder. And now you've got a chippie on your lap. I'd never call myself a chippie to Rod." The frivolity disappeared. "He *doesn't* know anything, *does* he? He's a crashingly dull man."

"The hell with him, baby."

"I say so too, the hell with him," she said, and stopped talking.

Later she said, "Wouldn't it be better if I went to your house? Hereafter? You could never possibly spend the night here. I adored having a quickie with you, but that's not the real fun, is it?"

"No, and if you lock the sitting-room door you might just as well hang a sign out and tell the servants what you're doing. My house is much better. A taxi is better than your own car, too. You don't leave a taxi standing out all night, where everybody can see it. Not to mention gas rationing."

"Do you like me any better? A smidgeon better?"

"Well, I feel more kindly toward you."

"Me too. I can hardly wait to get into an enormous bed with you. You have one, I'm sure."

"Yes."

"There's so much of you—and there really is, you know. More than sixteen stone."

"Closer to seventeen. I don't watch my weight. It always goes up, never goes down."

"Oh, what an opening for a funny. Two funnies. I'm full of funnies today. Most likely because Rod told me years ago that you kept the whores laughing with your jokes. 'It always goes up, never goes down.' Unlimited possibilities there. Do you adore puns? My father adored puns, and I was the only other member of the family that did. Adore them. And of course the filthier they are, the more I treasure them. After I was married Daddy felt free to tell me some of the *mildly* filthy ones. In limericks, mostly. I've always adored talking dirty, and obscene picture postcards. I was sent down from my school, not for having them but for drawing them. I've never really had any inhibitions, you know."

"Who were you married to?"

"Oh, a chap. A stinker. Died ten years ago, but he was a stinker."

"How would a guy qualify as a stinker in your book?"

"He ruined my father, or very nearly. Money. He was a stockbroker. The title wasn't very old, but old enough to get him his job in the City. He persuaded Daddy to buy shares in a mining something or other in Rhodesia. Actually not to buy them but to give him the money to buy them. Never did buy them. Then when he got found out he shot himself, and a fat lot of good that did anyone. Only added to the mess he'd already created. Oh, he *was* a stinker."

"Were you in love with him?"

"Was I in love with him? Yes, I suppose I was, in the beginning. He was much older, and I was much younger. All the naughty things I was curious about were right in his line. He had me get girls for him. That sort of thing. I complied willingly enough. But he sent me to bed with a friend of his and then blackmailed him. Threatened to divorce me and name his friend, which would have been fatal to his friend's career. Then for the first time I realized that it wasn't all fun and games. If you ever want to write a scenario about a real stinker,

I can supply you with quantities of material. Quantities of it. Piled high and very malodorous."

"They might have trouble with the casting."

"I quite see what you mean."

"And the last picture I worked on was for Nelson Eddy. Nelson Eddy and Jeannette MacDonald."

"I rather think she'd balk at playing me. Have you ever spoken to her? Had conversation with her?"

"Sure, why?"

"Does she speak, or does she sing? Lalalala lala. How do you do do do?"

"Not a bad dame," said James Francis. "Not the worst in this town."

"Who *is* the worst?"

"You've met her. She's in that group you've latched onto."

"Oh, tell me. Don't be a stick," said Angela.

"No, you find out for yourself. And you will," he said.

"Indeed I shall. Does everyone know she's the worst?" said Angela. "I mean to say, is she someone notorious?"

"No, you wouldn't call her notorious. As a matter of fact, she has quite a good reputation."

"Quite a good reputation? Then she's in the films? Not one of the wives? You can tell me that much."

"She's in the films."

"Ah, then I think I know which one you have in mind. Dining at her house Friday week. Will you be there, by any chance?"

"Hell, no. I'm not a member of that set," said James Francis. "You'll find out all about the Hollywood caste system as you go along."

"But you make pots of money."

"For a writer, I do all right. But it isn't all money, in that set. Gene Autry makes more than most of them, but he's not a member."

"Is that the cowboy that sings?"

"Yes. He sings all the way to the bank, as they say out here. There are a couple of actors in your set that don't make as much money as I do, and one producer that's in hock for the rest of his life. No, money's important, but it isn't the whole story. You'll find out."

"Would you *like* to be in that set?"

"Well, truthfully, nobody likes to be kept out of anything. I've never turned down one of their invitations. They used to invite me, at the last minute, out of desperation. You know, they'd go through their lists and see my name. Jimmy Hatter. Fat writer. Single. Salary, twenty-five hundred. Has Tux, will travel."

"Oh, now really!"

"Just about," he said. "I'd always go, and we'd all pretend I went there all the time. But gradually even the last-minute invitations got scarcer and scarcer."

"Do you know why?"

"Yes, I think I do. The women. They want *chic,* and I was never *chic.* It's the only word I can think of to explain it, and who can explain *chic*? You knew I didn't have it the first time you met me, that time Rod and I were in London. Rod didn't have it then, either, but he's acquired it since then. And as a dame you had a hunch that potentially he had it."

"Yes, he had it. The potential. He was so gauche, and he's frightfully dull, you know. I'm not sure that it's *chic* that he has, and yet I know exactly what you mean. It's true in London, too. That stinker I was married to had it, loads of it, although he had practically no chin and a figger like a scarecrow's. In spite of which, girls were mad for him. Just as they're mad for Rod, who *does* have a chin and a wedge-shaped figger. I have another explanation that isn't *chic.* It's the thing that goes on in a woman's mind, or elsewhere, her response when she sees a man, or a woman, or a thing. Does she want to possess it, to have it around, so to speak? No, I don't suppose that is a very good explanation. *Chic* is better. Not quite it, but better. Whatever name you give it, I know I have it, while much prettier women haven't. That ladies' luncheon I went to the other day, that got into the papers and supplied you with your information about my set—Louise Parsons's column, isn't it?"

"Louella. Yes, that's where I read it."

"There were four or at most five women that had it, this thing you're trying to define. And it's a dead cert that they'll be my pals. Birds of a feather, you know. Not because we're all naughty. After all, everyone's naughty when the door is closed, don't you agree?"

"Probably."

"Definitely. At all events, I have found my pals and they have found me, and so I propose to stop in this lovely California sunshine. When this ugly war is over, and Rod comes back and takes up his wonderfully lucrative career again, I shall be the one who says what's *chic* and what isn't. And I'll see to it that you're *chic,* Jimmy."

"Baby, it isn't going to be that easy."

"Easy? I didn't say it was going to be easy. But you didn't come here with any intention of committing adultery with your best friend's wife. And I certainly had no intention of seducing you. But these things happen."

"Hollywood isn't going to be a pushover."

"No, but when I go after something, I get it. Rod, for instance. Wasn't a woman in London that would have said no to him. But I got him. Two years older, no money to speak of, no steaks or whiskey to lure him with, and he's never yet told me that he loves me. Nor I him. But here I am. And here we are. Shall I come see you tonight?"

"Sure."

"After the eleven o'clock news. I'll just pop in, and if you're asleep I won't disturb you. Ha ha. The hell I won't. Isn't it nice, though, how things have turned out?"

"Damn nice," said James Francis.

"And you mustn't have a guilty conscience, Jimmy. I seduced, you, you didn't seduce me. Rod wouldn't like it either way, but I'm not going to tell him, and you're not, certainly."

"It's an interesting stalemate."

"Now don't imply that I planned it that way. I didn't. When Rod comes home and starts asking those dreary questions, I'm not going to mention you at all. If there's anyone else, I'll tell him, because I can hardly expect those London bitches to stay away from him, and he'll have to answer my dreary questions, too. But I'll keep you out. Of course it occurs to me that he won't believe me if I say there wasn't anyone. I'm afraid he knows me too well for that. Whom would he mind the least?"

"He knows you go for girls."

"Oh, brilliant, Jimmy! Of course. Think of a girl that he had an affair with and still rather likes. Are there any in my set?"

"Oh, yes."

"Be rather fun, you know. Writing and telling him that I'm seeing a lot of Susie Ramsbottom, his old girl friend, and then having him *force* the admission out of me that, yes, Susie and I did have a *little, tiny* whatchamacallit. He won't believe it was a little-tiny, but he'd rather believe that than have me tell him about some man."

"You know, Angela, I think you must be the worst woman I ever knew."

She paused in the midst of lighting a cigarette. "That would be more of a distinction if I knew more about your women. I only know about your whores, and they were *paid* for being naughty."

"I wasn't thinking of the whores."

She shook the matchstick long after the flame had gone out. "I'd also have to know who you considered the *best* woman you've ever known. Your mother, no doubt."

"My mother was somewhere in between the worst and the best. She had the morals of a reformed hooker. A whore that got religion late in life, but went right on stealing junk off the counters in the five-and-dime."

"Your mother was actually a whore?"

"No, I didn't say that. My father was a linotyper, a printer in a newspaper plant in Chicago and elsewhere. My mother was a book-keeper. She was married once before she married my father, and her first husband died. My old man was a periodic drunk, but he made pretty good money when he was working. Men used to come to the house when my old gent was on a toot, and I've always assumed that she was putting out. Laying them. For money or not, I don't know. Maybe the old boy got drunk because she was putting out. That I don't know either. But they sent me to college for two years, and during my second year she went back to the Catholic Church. My old man wasn't a Catholic and I never was, but she was brought up one. The old man died, and she went back to work, and I quit college and got a job as a reporter. She earned her own living and I earned mine. She used to try to get me to turn Catholic, but I didn't want any of that. She was at me all the time, trying to convert me, until finally I had to move out."

Her interest was diminishing. "Then she wasn't the best woman you've ever known nor yet among the worst, down here with me. Is it sex things that make a woman naughty?"

"Not always, but often."

"But it's what you had in mind when you decided I must be the worst. Weren't you thinking that I have no morals?"

"Well, have you?"

"Yes, oddly enough I have. But not where sex is concerned. We have this business between our legs—you have yours, and I have mine—and obviously they were intended to fit together. Animals and Eskimos are born knowing that. But I've never considered myself an animal, or an Eskimo. I've always enjoyed tinkering with other people and letting them tinker with me, for pleasure. What does it matter if you get the pleasure from a man or a woman? Who *said* it has to be one way and not the other? A woman tinkering with another woman is not going to produce a child, nor a man tinkering with another man. But you see I believe that this thing is so strong within us that procreation is only a small part of the story. I produced one child. I never knew for certain whether it came from my husband or someone else. More than likely, my husband. I haven't seen it since it was two years old. It wasn't something you'd proudly display to the uncles and aunts. It died in a nursing home when it was eleven. I of course had jolly well seen to it that I'd never have another. But I'm not any worse off than a great many of my friends who've produced healthy, so-called normal offspring. Some of them turned out to be little stinkers. Some were killed in the war. And *all* of them were demanding, selfish, and rather ungrateful, even those with the good manners to pretend otherwise. I suppose all this adds fuel to your fire, your belief that I'm the worst woman you've ever known. If it does, I assure you I couldn't care less."

"That I'm sure of," said James Francis.

"What shocked you was my flight of fancy concerning Susie Ramsbottom. That I could be so—calculating. No more calculating than I was in marrying Rod Fulton. I wasn't calculating when I took off my pajamas and sat on your lap, though you may find that hard to believe. That was impulse, and being hard up. However, you could be forgiven for suspecting me of something else. Whatever I may have had in mind, you and I have cuckolded Mr. Fulton, and you're far more likely to feel guilty about it than I. My only suggestion is that as you're going to feel guilty anyhow, you might as well hang yourself for a sheep as a goat. You and I may as well keep the home fires burning till our boy comes home. Agreed?"

"I've already agreed. You're coming to my house at eleven."

"After the news broadcast," she said. "Don't try to lock me out. I'll climb in through a window."

Major Rod Fulton's predicted inquisition did no harm to his pride. "You probably knew this," he said to James Francis. "But you know who she cheated on me with? Melina Waltham. The two of them got talking about me one time, and before they knew it they were in the hay together. All the time I was banging Mellie I never knew there was any dike there. Did you?"

"How would I know?" said James Francis. "I don't move in that set."

"It's a funny thing now, to go to dinner at Mellie's and look at her and Angela, putting on this act as if they were like two Pasadena housewives."

"I don't even move in that set—the Pasadena housewives. Or the

Santa Ana housewives. Don't complain. You're lucky she didn't fall
for some filling-station attendant."

"Complain? Who's complaining? I just think it's funny. I
couldn't complain. There was plenty of gash in London, and I admitted that I got some of it, but I didn't tell her how much. Do you
remember me telling you about one named Sybil, that time you and
I were there?"

"Yes."

"She was my Number 1 Priority. I went up in the world, from a
countess to a duchess."

"Well, you went in as a captain and came out a major. You were
entitled to a promotion."

"Yeah, son of a bitch I got browned off on that. I thought I
should have got bird-colonel. I think of some of these bastards that
rank me. Not even lieutenant-colonel. Major. Wait till they want
something from me."

"Did you get into any trouble? Is that why?"

"Well—there was a buck general after Sybil. He didn't help me
any, I guess," said Rod. "He as much as told me that the R.A.F.
boys were taking a *deem veeiew* of the duchess and I. And I said to
him, 'General, is it the R.A.F. or something closer to home?' Meaning him, of course. He got it. And I got my travel orders to a dump
in Northern Ireland. The same as Siberia. So I came out a major. I
must owe you a pisspotful of dough."

"Not a nickel."

"I mean for all that black-market stuff. Angela says you really
took care of her—in a nice way, of course. Steaks, nylons, and butter and all."

"It came to exactly seventy-five thousand eight hundred and
twenty-four dollars and fifteen cents."

"No, seriously, Jimmy."

"Oh, for Christ's sake," said James Francis.

"It'd be funny if Mellie Waltham got some of those nylons."

"I hope not," said James Francis.

"She has a nice pair of gams," said Rod. "Well, now it's back to the old grind. And you know who's going to be in my first picture? If you don't know, you can guess."

"Miss Melina Waltham."

"You knew?"

"No, I guessed."

"I wonder how that's gonna be? The real acting won't get on film. It'll be Mellie and I between takes."

"Why kid around? It'll come out the first time you give her a jump."

"I wasn't sure I *would* give her a jump."

"Now you're kidding yourself."

"Maybe you're right. You usually are."

"It doesn't take much to be right about you and Mellie."

"Jimmy, I think you knew she was a dike and you knew it all along."

"As far as I'm concerned, personally, she's a virgin. If she ever wants to prove otherwise, you can give her my number. Whatever she is, it's nice pussy, and you're not going to pass that up."

"When you think of it, why should I? We're gonna be three weeks in the High Sierras, and Angela wants to go to Palm Springs. She's nuts about that sunshine. She says she's never going back to England. I'm not either, if I don't have to. Korda wants me for a picture there, but the studio wants me to do at least three for them before they loan me out. Did you know I was big in England?"

"Sure, didn't you?"

"Oh, not like when we were there. I mean really big."

"How are you in Northern Ireland?"

"You son of a bitch, the same old Jimmy. I tell you, guy, it's good to be back," said Rod. "Wuddia say you come up to the High Sierras with me? You can just fart around, do some writing. Maybe make a score with Mellie."

"No, I was thinking of going to the desert."

"The Springs?"

"Or Indio. Twenty-nine Palms. It'll probably be The Springs. The Racquet Club and the Chee-Chee Bar. I'm a creature of habit."

"Why don't you plan your trip the same time as Angela's going to be there?"

"Oh, she's probably seen enough of me to last her for a while."

"Nuts. She's thinking of taking Ed and Mary Veloz's house. There'd be plenty of room for you, and you'd save a few bob on the rent."

"A few what?"

"A few bob. All right, that's limey talk. Anyway, that'd be a good chance for me to pay you back for some of those steaks and stuff."

"You'd better talk to Angela first."

"All right, I will," said Rod.

In due course Rod departed for the High Sierras, and Angela and James Francis settled down in the Veloz house in Palm Springs. "I'm beginning to think you're married to the All-American chump," said James Francis.

"I never thought otherwise," said Angela. "And this is the end, the living end. Very uncomplimentary to you and to me. Especially as Mellie promised to let me know the moment he comes creeping into her tent."

"You should see that tent. It's what you English call a caravan. Electric lights. Shower. Flush can. All the comforts of home. Rod gets one, too. They'll use his, because her maid sleeps in hers."

"There's nothing her maid doesn't know about her," said Angela. "I sometimes wonder about all this. Do you?"

"Yes, I do. We're all outsmarting each other, and the pay-off has to come sooner or later," said James Francis. "In some form or another. Is that what you meant?"

"Yes. I adore this life—the sunshine, and never having to worry about money and so on. But lately I've begun to realize how difficult life was before I married the film star. There was always something, you know. Money. My father growing feeble-minded. My mother giving me dark looks. My stinker of a husband. My child. The bloody war. But here I have nothing to worry about."

"Then don't worry."

"It isn't as easy as all that. The English weather makes us appreciate a few sunny days. By the same token, my troubles made me enjoy my fun. You see what I mean, of course?"

"I see that you're a restless dame that always will be restless," he said.

"I adore having you as my lover. But if I should bring home one of those tennis players, you wouldn't mind a bit."

"Are you thinking of bringing home one of the tennis players?"

"I did, yesterday. I wasn't going to tell you, but it belongs in this conversation."

"While I was playing dominoes at the club," said James Francis.

"I'll never have him here again. I'll never *have* him again. He was crude. And to top it all, he walked off with two hundred and thirty-four dollars out of my purse."

"I'm not sure which made you sore. The crudeness or the theft."

"Both. I've never had to actually pay money, you know. If anything, it's been the other way round. I've been given some awfully nice presents in my time. But this creature *expected* me to reward him. He put on his flannels and his blazer. I was still lying in bed. He picked up my purse and reached inside it and said, 'I'll just take this, lady. I'll be back next weekend, if you care to look me up.' Then it began to dawn on me that he'd always expected to be paid, and that at last I was one of those women. That if I'd been ugly and fat and unattractive, he'd still have come home with me. A gigolo in a Wimbledon blazer is a gigolo nonetheless. And a woman that he *expects* payment from is—one of those women. Am I one of those women, Jimmy? Have I reached that stage?"

"He's about twenty-two or -three, and you obviously picked him up."

"We'd been introduced, quite properly introduced. He should have known that I wasn't one of those women. I was much the most attractive *lady* at the club. You always tell Rod the truth—"

"Not always."

"You know what I mean. You're candid with him. Be candid with me. We're friends."

"What is there to be candid about, Angela? You know how old

you are. You got hot pants for a tall young kid that you'd been watching playing tennis, where he's at his best. You invited him here, and both of you knew what you wanted him for. He must be used to that by this time, and if you're over twenty-five, he expects to get paid in some way or another. At least you got off without promising him a Lincoln Continental."

"I had a lovely affair with an Italian tennis player. Davis Cup. *Years* ago. This creature yesterday had never heard of him."

"There you are," said James Francis.

"But you? You're not cross with me?"

"If you mean, am I jealous? No. Would you be jealous if I brought someone home with me?"

"No. *Yes!* If you brought her here, yes. Unless you were bringing her here for both of us."

"That's different," said James Francis. "I am a little cross with you, though. This quick lay with your tennis player may get back to Rod, and if it does he's going to be sore at me *and* you."

"Why?"

"Because he's gotten really big, especially in the head, and out here he's royalty. He's not going to like having his princess get in the sack with a lowly tennis player. They're a dime a dozen in California."

"And why will he be cross with you?"

"Because I'm here to keep an eye on you. I am your duenna, while he's up there screwing Mellie Waltham, getting even with you and her for cheating on him during the war."

"He didn't mind that a bit. It rather amused him."

"That's what *you* think. That head has gotten so big that he wants to run all our lives."

"We could shrink that head, you and I. Shall we?"

"I don't want to. He'd be so bewildered if we told him about us, when he finally got around to believing it he'd be left with nothing. Nothing."

"You really love him, don't you?"

"Yes, I do."

"Why? Is it something in him, or something in you?"

"In me, I guess. When I first knew him he was pathetic, but at the same time I was sure he was going to get there. Whatever he has, I saw it in him, and I was the first to see it. I've never been an envious man, not even of other writers. I know my limitations there. I'm not as good a writer as Hemingway, but I doubt if year in and year out he makes as much money as I do, and your own Dr. Johnson said that a writer who didn't write for money was a damn fool, or words to that effect. I'm doing all right. Whenever I'm tempted to worry about the future, I tell myself that this is the future. I make so much money writing for pictures that I actually can't afford to write any more *Saturday Evening Post* stories."

"But your future that isn't writing—what about that?"

"I have none. One of these days the ticker will give out. Rich food, and booze, and mattress calisthenics—"

"Mattress caliswhat? Oh, mattress calisthenics. I see. I get it."

"When that happens, I'll give up writing and devote my remaining energy to loose living. At present, half of my energy goes into my work. But once I've had a stroke or something like that, I'll just keep sticking my finger down my throat, and some morning I won't wake up."

"I've never really, *really* thought of doing away with myself."

"Well, you have something to live for," said James Francis.

"Oh? What?"

"Pleasure. All-out, selfish pleasure," he said.

"Yes. I never thought of it that way, but it's quite true."

"Don't weaken, just because some jerk tennis player wounded your pride. You've been honest with yourself so far. You've never given much of a thought to anyone else. I'd hate to think you were going to spoil that record just because you're afraid of getting old. Some people do, you know. They reform, out of fear. But don't you."

"Are you being sardonic?"

"Not a bit," said James Francis.

"What you say about me is perfectly true, but it sounds so awful when put into words."

"I've known some women in their sixties that still get a great kick out of being wicked."

"I'm not wicked. I'm naughty, but not wicked."

"You can graduate to wicked."

"A wicked old woman. I'm not so sure I'd care to be that. What do they *do?*"

"Nothing very different from what they've always done, but the fact that they're doing it at sixty-five makes it wicked and therefore exciting. All their contemporaries are behaving like professional grandmothers, but they still get a bang out of seducing a willing bell-boy."

"Or a tennis player."

"Or a tennis player. Or a young doctor. Or a clergyman. If they can't do it on the grand scale, with Lincoln Continentals, they do it with candy for the neighbors' children."

"Were you ever given candy by a wicked old woman?"

"I wasn't, but one of my chums was. He not only got the candy, but he used to tell me how the old lady made him *feel* good."

"Oh, yes," said Angela. "We had some of that at home, come to think of it."

"I'm sure it wasn't confined to my neighborhood in Chicago."

"And so you suggest that I save the little boys for my old age?"

"If that happens to please you. Mind you, it doesn't have to be sex. Some of them abandon sex for other pastimes. As in the case of my mother trying to convert me to her religion. Or those old women who louse up their children's marriages. Or go around bullying people by threatening to leave them out of their wills."

"But in my case it's more apt to be sex?"

"That's where you've operated mostly," said James Francis.

"It has been my speciality."

"Why do you say speciality? The word is specialty."

"No, the word is speciality. *Specialité.* I refer you to the French."

"You know, you're kind of wonderful. You're practically illiterate, but you'll argue with a writer over the pronunciation of a word. The arrogance. I'm not going to worry much about you."

"It just happens that I was right and you were wrong."

"There's something else about you. A couple of times in my life I've lived with various dames. Shacked up with them for fairly long periods of time. But those ersatz marriages—to put it another way, I've come closer to the real thing with you than with anyone else in my whole life."

"That's rather nice. I like you, too. You're not like anyone I've ever known before. I've come to completely trust you, and that's a new experience for me. Even my father, sweet as he was, was rather ineffectual and not the tower of strength one hopes a father will be. He never cared much what I did, and you do. You tell me to go on being naughty, and give little boys candy to let me tinker with them. But that's you showing off, to prove to me how frightfully sophisticated you are. Actually, you're as sound as the Bank of England, and what *I* like is that you make *me* feel warm. Comfy. Protected. Are you by nature protective, Jimmy? You were with Rod, and now you are with me. I like it, and I've never known it before. Some night you may roll over on me and squash me to death, but with my dying breath I'll forgive you because I'll know you could never be cruel. It's the blind cruelty of men that I like the least about them. The tennis player. Rod. My other stinker of a husband. But never you. I really love you, and I almost wish I could say it without saying *really.*"

"I know that," said James Francis. "I'd do anything for you, baby."

They were impulsively silent, the busyness of their thoughts for once dominated by the nearness of an emotion.

"Odd that we haven't heard anything from the High High Sierras," she said. "The High C's in the High Sierras. What made me think of that was Miss Waltham. At certain moments of ecstasy she hits high-C. She's a noisy piece. Rather common."

"Common to you and your husband, at least."

"Oh, shut up," she said.

"Mind your manners," he said. "What do you want to do to-night? Do you want some Chinese food? And then the Chee-Chee Bar?"

"Yes, let's be out when they telephone. They'll be so disappointed, whichever one it is. She'll be dying to break the news to me, and I think I'd like to take some of the fun out of it for her."

"He's getting under your skin, baby."

"Yes, as dear Cole Porter says, 'Don't you know, you fool, you never can win.' "

"I will take you out and get you slightly intoxicated."

"And when we come home I'll turn off the telephone, and sleep, sleep, sleep. Don't let me take any cognac. My heart thumps and keeps me awake. I've never really cared for spirits. My saving grace, that I never became a dipso. I may get tight as a nun's cunt on wine, but don't make me have those liqueurs with you."

"All right," he said. "Anything you say."

"Dear man," she said. "Dear friend Jimmy."

"Whom you really love."

"Whom I really love. It isn't quite the same, is it? If I say, 'I really love you,' it means not quite. But if I say, 'Whom I really love,' it means very nearly."

"And the French say *specialité*. Go take your bath, baby. Let's be ready in an hour," he said. "I have to eat an awful lot of Chinese food before the temple bells start ringing."

"The temple—"

"Before my stomach gets the message," said James Francis.

They returned from their night out shortly after one o'clock in the morning. "What time is it in the High-C Sierras?" said Angela.

"The same as here. Same time zone. But they'll have gone to bed hours ago, separately or together. They have to get up at half past four or five. We won't be hearing from them tonight, but I advise you to turn your phone off anyhow. They might decide to call you at nine o'clock in the morning. How do you feel?"

"Terribly sleepy. Not a bit tight, but terribly sleepy."

"Well, then I'll not foist my attentions on you," he said.

"I don't think I'd be much good," she said.

"I could use the sleep, too," said James Francis.

She was taking off her rings and bracelets as she spoke, and she opened the dressing-table drawer. "Someone's been here!" she said. "My jewel box is empty!"

"Uh-oh. What did they take?"

"I know exactly. The best things are at home, thank heaven. But my star sapphire's gone. My star sapphire. Gold wristwatch. A little pearl necklace. Five or six gold pins, costume jewelry. My small gold cigarette case that holds six. That sunburst I wear with a beret."

"Not exactly junk. What was the star sapphire worth?"

"For insurance purposes, a thousand pounds."

"Well, let's say six thousand dollars. Wristwatch?"

"Oh—probably a thousand dollars. The pins were worth at least a hundred apiece, dollars. The cigarette case can't be replaced. It once belonged to a grand duke and had his crest on it. I adored it. I bought it from a man in the Ritz Bar, in Paris. At least it was bought for me. Actually it was bought for Sybil, and she gave it to me for my birthday. How infuriating! Weren't we told that we didn't have to lock up?"

"Yes, but you don't leave ten thousand dollars' worth of jewelry lying around," said James Francis. "You make a list, and I'll call the cops."

"Do we want to do that? Call the police?"

"If you ever want to get any of it back."

"You know, of course, who I suspect," she said.

"Sure. The tennis player. He probably dropped in for a retake with you, and when you weren't here, he helped himself."

"At least he didn't find me *too* repulsive, did he?"

"Always look on the bright side, Angela. That's my girl. I suggest that we call the cops right now and lay it on the line with them."

"Tell them who we suspect?"

"Yes. This town doesn't like bad publicity, and if you play ball with them, they'll play ball with you."

"It's on your head," said Angela. "I wash my hands of it. Frankly, I think you'll be making a most awful mistake, but I'm a foreigner here."

The police car arrived in ten minutes. James Francis greeted the two patrolmen, identified himself and Angela, and gave an account of the burglary as he knew it. The sergeant, a man named Wittenberg, had dealt with Hollywood people before, but James Francis, a former newspaper man, had likewise dealt with police. "Here's the situation, Sergeant," he said. "Mrs. Fulton rented the house from Mr. and Mrs. Edmund Veloz—"

"We know that, all right," said Wittenberg.

"They're great friends of Mr. and Mrs. Fulton."

"We know that, too. Mr. Veloz told us all that," said Wittenberg. "And we know who you are, too, Mr. Hatter."

"Good. Now I'm going to level with you, because Mrs. Fulton is a foreigner. English. The wife of my best friend. She hasn't been over here very long, and her husband would want me to go to bat for her, so to speak. Yesterday she was followed home from the tennis club by a young fellow named Glenn Slaymaker—"

"The tennis player," said Wittenberg.

"Right," said James Francis. "Apparently Mrs. Fulton had said to him something about coming to see her sometime, in a polite English way. And he took her literally. In any case, she came home and five minutes later, Mr. Glenn Slaymaker appeared, and made some advances to Mrs. Fulton. She repulsed him and sent him on his way, but before he left he helped himself to all her cash, amounting to over two hundred dollars. He made no bones about it. He opened her purse and took out the money. She of course was only too glad to get rid of him. As you can see, Mrs. Fulton would be no match for Slaymaker in a real struggle, and two hundred dollars was a small price to pay, possibly for her life. She was still nervous and overwrought when I came home, and I had a hard time getting the whole story out of her. Naturally, I wanted to notify the police immediately, but Mrs. Fulton didn't want any publicity that might adversely affect her husband. She hadn't been harmed physically, and it was only a couple of hundred dollars."

"Sure," said Wittenberg.

"However, there's one thing that might interest you gentlemen. It seems that Slaymaker told Mrs. Fulton that he was going away, but that he'd be back next week, and told her or *threatened* her with another visit. That's interesting to me, because he wanted her to think he wouldn't be here last night. In other words, my theory is—for what it's worth—Slaymaker was preparing a sort of alibi."

"Yeah, that could be," said Wittenberg.

"At the *same* time, warning her that he was coming back."

"Uh-huh."

"Now of course all this is pure speculation on my part. It may be absolutely worthless if it turns out that Slaymaker did go away, and didn't steal this jewelry. But he's my prime suspect."

"Use your phone?" said Wittenberg.

"Go right ahead," said James Francis. "This one, or there are others if you'd rather."

"This'll be all right," said Wittenberg. He dialed a number and spoke. "Norm? It's Frank Wittenberg, out at the Veloz house on that burglary. Find out if Glenn Slaymaker, the tennis player, is anywhere around. I just want to make sure if he's in town. No, don't pick him up just yet. I'll be back to you in ten minutes. Okay, Norm. Over."

"Could we offer you gentlemen a cup of coffee?" said James Francis.

"No thanks," said Wittenberg. "Itta been better if you notified us when he took that money yesterday. Guys like that, you know, they count on people being afraid of publicity. If we picked him up yesterday, he probably would of told an altogether different story. Like inferring that Mrs. Fulton gave him the money, and didn't force his attentions on her. We'd like to put this fellow away for a while, but if we don't get the right cooperation there isn't much we can do."

"You have a sheet on him?" said James Francis.

"No, we don't have a sheet on him. Well, we have a sheet on him, but it's unofficial. Not even an arrest. Were you ever a cop?"

"No, but I was a police reporter, back East."

"Oh. Well, if we could hit him with a grand-theft rap, we could put him away for a while. His kind of a guy will go right on as long as you people let him get away with it."

"Only too true," said James Francis. "But you know what the press would make of this. And there's that other angle. The Palm Springs angle."

"What angle is that, Mr. Hatter?" said Wittenberg.

"Oh—I've been coming here a long time, so I know a little bit about The Springs. How they don't like to have any bad publicity any more than a big star like Rod Fulton. The motion picture industry has always been sort of the mainstay of Palm Springs, from the very beginning. Looking at it realistically, it's always been a case of you scratch my back and I'll scratch yours. You know what I mean, Sergeant."

"Yeah, but I'd still like to put that fellow away for a while. We won't have any trouble getting him to leave town. But I'd like to see him in Q."

"The sergeant is referring to San Quentin. That's one of our prisons," said James Francis. "Well, I'll tell you, Sergeant. Both Mr. and Mrs. Rod Fulton usually listen to my advice. If you hang it on this guy Slaymaker, so that you have a real open-and-shut case against him, I'll advise Mrs. Fulton to cooperate completely. All you care about is sending him away. You don't care whether he cops a plea or not, do you?"

"He'll get a shorter sentence that way."

"What do you care, and what does Palm Springs care? As long as you hang it on him, it's not going to make any difference to you or to Palm Springs if he goes away for a year or five years. He'll be marked as a jailbird, and he won't be coming around here again."

"Well, we may be jumping pretty far ahead. We're not sure he did it."

"No, you couldn't go into court with what you know now. But as man to man, as an experienced police officer to an old-time reporter, I'll bet that's the way it turns out. Slaymaker's your man."

"I'm inclined to think so, but I'm a cop, not a lawyer."

"Bring him in for questioning. You'll know inside of ten minutes whether he did it or not. Just forget about the legal technicalities. Go by your experience with criminals. I think this guy'll scare pretty easily, too. He's used to frightening women, but he hasn't had to face experienced police officers."

"Uh-huh," said Wittenberg. "Mrs. Fulton, we'll want a detailed description of the stolen articles. The more detailed the better, like if you can give us little sketches of the design. Where the stuff came from. Any initials or other engraving."

"I should be delighted," said Angela. She was back at being a countess, on the side of law and order and gentility. She gave a performance that could not have been imitated by a mere actress. The cops, James Francis could see, were impressed. "There we are, Sergeant," said Angela when she had completed her list. "The money value may be high on some and low on others. The sapphire ring is the most valuable single piece, and the cigarette case has the greatest sentimental value. It once belonged to a grand duke, who was assassinated in the Revolution. It was given me by a friend of his. Actually she was a cousin, not a friend. I never knew the grand duke, but my late husband knew him. They were in the war together."

"Yes, ma'am," said Wittenberg. "Well, I hope we get it back for you, and the other articles. The drawings will be a lot of help."

"Thank you. You sound as if you went in for sketching. Do you?"

"Well, not any more, but I used to," said Wittenberg. "You folks won't be hearing any more from us tonight, but I'll call you first thing in the morning if we have anything."

The cops departed. "Another five minutes and you'd have had his fly open," said James Francis.

"Less than that, if you hadn't been here. You and the other

policeman. Actually, I didn't flirt with him. I was being my most garden-party-and-parasol, slightly unbending."

"You gave a performance worthy of Norma Shearer, with a touch of Dame May Whitty. Knowing something about police procedure, I imagine this place will be under surveillance for a while. So for the next few days don't walk around without any clothes on."

"Thank you for taking charge, Jimmy. You were marvelous, really you were."

"We were both pretty good. That crap about the grand duke's cigarette case, that convinced the sergeant that he wasn't dealing with some Hollywood broad."

"I *had* to convince him that anything Slaymaker told him was a lie. About me, that is."

"He was partly convinced by the fact that I phoned him right away. If you'd have been afraid of what Slaymaker'd say, you wouldn't have let me phone. And that's why I phoned. It's Slaymaker's word against yours, and they won't want to believe Slaymaker. If he had any sense he'd be in Tia Juana by now, but I'll bet you he's still in Palm Springs. He's greedy."

"Do you think he might come back here?"

"Yes, and if he does he's on his way to San Quentin."

"Why would he come back here? He's taken all the jewelry I have with me."

"He didn't take what you wore tonight. That ring is worth more than all the rest of the stuff put together."

"Rod's wedding present," she said. "Yes, that's much the most valuable thing I own. I know he paid ten thousand guineas for it. I'm never without it."

"And charm-boy saw it yesterday," said James Francis. He got up and wandered about, opening and closing drawers. He left the room and came back with a snub-nosed revolver in his hand. "This is what I was looking for. I was sure Ed Veloz would have one somewhere."

"Please put it away. I hate them."

"Listen, I don't want to tangle with a trained athlete. Slaymaker would knock me out cold with one punch."

"But you said the police would be nearby."

"And they probably will be, but just in case," said James Francis. "Do you know how to shoot it?"

"Christ, yes. I'm not Dead-Eye Dick, but I've fired plenty of them."

"Then please put it away, Jimmy. I'm really most awfully frightened of them."

"Just forget about it. I'll keep it in my room. Now you go to bed. Take a sleeping pill, and I'll see you in the morning."

"I haven't got any. Have you?"

"No, I don't use them," said James Francis. "Take a hot bath and I'll heat you some milk."

"Do you really think he might be back tonight?"

"I'm not ruling out the possibility," said James Francis. "If he does come, he won't stay when he sees this. As I told the sergeant, Slaymaker is used to threatening women, not a man with a .38 in his hand."

"I hope they catch him before he gets here."

"Devoutly, so do I," said James Francis.

She took her warm bath and he brought her a glass of warm milk. "I put a little nutmeg on top, and a teaspoon of sugar. It'll go down more easily."

"I really love you, Jimmy," she said.

"I know. Really. How many men have put you to bed with a glass of warm milk?"

"Not one. That's why I really love you," she said.

"Goodnight, baby."

"Are you staying up?"

"For a while. I have all the magazines to catch up on," he said.

He left her as she was slowly sipping the milk, her bedside lamp still burning. He got some magazines from the sitting-room and took them to his bedroom, undressed, propped up some pillows and sat in bed, reading. It was not long before drowsiness set in, and from force of habit he turned off his light. In two minutes he was asleep.

It was not a sound that made him come awake. He was awake, his eyes open in the dark, and *then* listening for a sound. But his instinct cautioned him to be as quiet as the quiet house. He reached under his pillow for the .38, and even the barely audible rustling of his hand on the bedlinen was still the loudest noise in the house. Angela's room was on the other side of the sitting-room, and he tuned his hearing for sounds from there. He got out of bed in the dark and in his bare feet. His vision was adjusting to the light in the sky and he began to discern the outlines of furniture. In the sitting-room he paused, and he saw that the light from Angela's room spilled out onto the turf beside the house.

He went out through the sitting-room door and walked on the turf until he was standing just outside the door of Angela's room. She was sitting upright in bed, and fear had made her modest; she was holding the bedclothes neck-high and watching Slaymaker go through a drawerful of lingerie, throwing it piece by piece to the floor. "You've got everything, I tell you," she said. "Take the ring and please go."

"I want to know where the other stuff is," said Slaymaker.

"I tell you it's in Beverly Hills, I swear it."

"Don't talk so loud, you'll wake that fag creep," said Slaymaker.

James Francis pushed the door open. "All right, I'm a fag creep," he said. "Back up against the wall. Angela, phone the cops."

Slaymaker rushed toward him, and James Francis fired the .38. Slaymaker was momentarily stopped, but momentum carried him forward and James Francis fired again. This time the impact of the bullet on his chest—higher than the first shot—knocked Slaymaker back and he fell over. "Jesus, I am Dead-Eye," said James Francis. Slaymaker looked up at him from the floor, and then the life went out of his eyes. "Never mind, I'll call the cops," said James Francis. Angela was weeping and muttering to herself, unintelligibly and childishly, like a little girl who has just been snatched out of the path of a nasty boy on a bike.

Sergeant Wittenberg found a .25 automatic in a side pocket of Slaymaker's blazer, and Angela's wedding-present ring in the breast pocket. "We were here till about an hour ago," said Wittenberg. "Then we got a call to the other end of town. Is that your revolver?"

"No, it belongs to Ed Veloz," said James Francis.

"I'll take it, please," said Wittenberg. He looked down at Slaymaker's body. "He sure takes up a lot of room here, doesn't he?"

"He was a big one, all right," said James Francis.

"He had enough stuff stashed away in his room to start a small jewelry store. All of your stuff, Mrs. Fulton, plus a lot of things were reported stolen. His wife came in while our men were having a look. One more day and she'd have had it over the border. Acapulco."

"He had a wife, eh?" said James Francis.

"And a kid on the way, judging by her appearance. A nice little doll, aged about eighteen maybe. Now the kid gets born in Tehachapi, most likely. 'I was born in Tehachapi, and my father was a famous tennis player.' That's what the kid'll be saying all its life. Well, we got things to do here."

"Let me brew some coffee," said Angela.

"Yeah, there'll be no more sleep here the rest of the night," said Wittenberg. "You know, the worst of it is, he had every opportunity. My kid idolized this bum. Idolized him."

"Can we go back to Los Angeles today?" said James Francis.

"Today? I don't know why not, as soon as you get the word from the Riverside County authorities. There won't be any charge against you, but they'll want to know where they can get in touch with you."

"Till the coroner's jury returns a verdict, as I recall it," said James Francis.

"That's about it. A couple weeks, then you're free to go anywhere in the world."

"In line of duty, did you ever have to kill a man?"

"Yes, I did."

"I was just wondering when it would begin to hit me, and how long it stays with you."

"Well, with me it's different, Mr. Hatter. I have a gun on my hip most of the *time*. I was a cop six years before I ever fired it at anybody. I winged him. I guess I felt worse about that than the one that died. Ask Merle. Merle had to kill a guy the second week he was a cop."

"Part of the job," said the other cop. "It was him or me. Crazy drunken wet-back come at me with a machete. There was his wife lying on the floor with her head half cut off. I gave him five slugs and he still nicked me just below the elbow. Twenty-four stitches. They were afraid I was gonna lose the arm through infection. You know they don't exactly sterilize those machetes. The arm was out like this."

"The second week he was a cop," said Wittenberg.

"It's part of the job," said Merle. "With this bum, it was him or you, Mr. Hatter. He had that jealous wife in his pocket."

"Our name for the .25 automatic," said Wittenberg. "They never seem to miss, either. A little old woman that never had a gun in her hand before, she'll point it at a guy and get him right through the heart. One slug."

"I'd like to get out of here, if you don't mind," said James Francis. "Let's go in the other room."

"You stay here, will you, Merle?" said Wittenberg. He lowered his voice. "You want to be sick, Mr. Hatter?"

"No, I just want to get out of this room. I have a feeling he's listening to us. Slaymaker."

"Right," said Wittenberg. "The fellow'll be here to take the necessary photographs, and then the body can be removed."

"The sooner the better," said James Francis.

"Right," said Wittenberg. They sat in the sitting-room, and Wittenberg lit a cigarette, first offering his pack to James Francis. "You didn't know Slaymaker, did you?"

"Only to see. I watched him play tennis a few times. He was good. Jesus! Now it's beginning to get me. I just thought of the thousands of people that paid to see him play, and now he never will again. Thanks to me."

"Wait a minute. Thanks to himself. Think of how many women he was blackmailing. You don't know it, but there's going to be plenty of them will heave a sigh of relief when they read the papers today. All over the country. Over in Europe, too. Mexico. This bum started a long time ago. First with a prominent business man in L.A., till the older guy had a stroke. Slaymaker was around seventeen then. Then there was a movie actress that I won't mention her name. You'd probably know her. But you see none of these people would ever sign a complaint. That's the kind of people he always picked on. He had a regular gift for—oh, thanks very much, Mrs. Fulton. Just sugar, no cream, thanks. Hard to get used to having sugar whenever you want it."

"Did you have *any* sleep, Jimmy?" said Angela.

"I had some."

"It couldn't have been much. Sergeant, don't you think Mr. Hatter ought to get some more sleep before—can't you *order* him to rest before they all descend upon us? The press, and the authorities and so on?"

"Well, he *looks* pretty peak-ed, but I can't order him to do anything. Our people will be here any minute, and then maybe you could go to some friend's house. Those reporters'll track you down, that's for sure, but if you had some friend's house you could go to, that'd be all right with us."

"I say let's get it over with and then I'll call the studio and they'll do what they can for you, Angela. The old Hollywood slogan. The studio can do anything. I'm free-lancing at the moment, but I have my car and I know my way around."

Thus, eventually, it was arranged. A chartered airplane took Angela to Santa Barbara, where she obtained a hotel room under an alias. James Francis left his own car at the Veloz house and rented a Chevrolet. He eluded the reporters and established his temporary headquarters in the bordello on Crescent Heights Boulevard. The madam was out shopping when he got there, but the colored maid let him in. "Early in the day for you, Mr. Hatter," said the maid.

"Miss Bonnie is over to the Farmers Market, and all the girls is either asleep or out."

"That's all right, Lily. All I want now is a room with a telephone."

"With a telephone? Let me think. Yes sir, I guess Room 9 there's a phone in there."

"Didn't you hear about me, Lily? I'm hot."

"There's something I should hear about you, Mr. Hatter? I don't only seldom read the newspapers, and my little radio is on the blink. Wud you do now, Mr. Hatter?"

"I killed a man," said James Francis.

"That's serious—if you're serious. You done killed one, for sure? You always kidding around."

"Don't worry, Lily. I'm not really hot, but I don't want to be bothered with newspaper reporters."

"Then you come to the right place, that's for sure. I take you up to Room 9. You care for liquid refreshment? A sandwich?"

"If you have any cold beer, and a ham sandwich, maybe. Anything you can rustle up. I'll leave it to you."

Now began a couple of hours of revelation and frustration, unlike any he had ever known. He telephoned eight men—other writers, a producer friend, a saloonkeeper, his agent. The agent was playing golf. All the others wanted to talk about the shooting in Palm Springs. But not one of them would offer or even agree to put him up for a few days. Each of them had a sound excuse, some of which may have been true, but no one would stretch a point for him. "Every son of a bitch I called owes me a favor," he said to the madam on her return. "I'm just as hot as if I were guilty of a crime."

"I don't know, Jimmy," said Bonnie. "I just don't know."

"What don't you know?"

"Well, anybody gets in a jam—"

"But who's in a jam? Didn't you see the papers? I'm not a lammister. I wasn't even put under technical arrest. The cops actually helped me dodge the newspaper guys."

"I read all the papers and I been listening to the radio. The guy you shot was a bum, that's for sure. He never come in here, but you hear talk. All the same, though, Jimmy, I kind of understand what they're all thinking."

"Do you want me to get out of here?"

"No, no, no. You can stay. You *can* do *me* a favor. Tonight, when the customers start dropping in, I just as soon you didn't sit around the bar. You can stay a week if you feel like it, but they come here for a good time, you know. You ought to know."

"Oh, big deal. Big deal. How much do I owe you for the use of the room and the phone calls?"

"I wouldn't charge you if you stayed a week. I'd let you stay if you *were* hot. All I'm asking is if you keep out of the bar, that's all."

"My home away from home," said James Francis. "They were all local calls, so maybe I owe you a buck for the telephone. Two bottles of beer, that's two bucks. The sandwich, another two bucks. The use of the room, I don't know how to figure that when you didn't supply any entertainment. What do you figure it, Bonnie? I never came out of here for under fifty bucks, but this time you and Lily were the only females I talked to. Here's twenty bucks."

"I won't take your money. I only asked you one small favor and right away you get a fig up your rear end."

"Yes, I have a fig up my rear end. I shouldn't have come here in the first place. But I promise you this, Bonnie. I'll never set foot in your palace of joy again. The years I've *been* coming here I probably blew around fifty gees, but that, as they say, is water under the bridge."

He dropped a twenty-dollar bill on the table and left the house. He drove out to the Strip, up the hill to the vicinity of his house. But from a block away he saw a small group of bored men and women, some of them with camera kits slung over their shoulders, clustered across the street from his driveway entrance. He continued on his way, without being sure what that was. He was a marked man, and the mark was Cain's.

* * *

It was often said in later years that Rod Fulton, whether you liked him or not, had stood by James Francis Hatter when Jimmy got in that jam in Palm Springs. That was the jam where Jimmy Hatter shot and killed a guy. There were a lot of stories at the time about how Jimmy happened to shoot him. The official version, of course, was that the guy was a thief, who had come to steal some jewelry from Rod Fulton's wife, the former English countess that Rod was then married to. Angela Somebody. Rod divorced her a couple of years later, and there were a lot of stories about that, too. She went completely Lesbo, according to one story, and Rod gave her a bundle and sent her back to England. There was another version that she had been banging the guy that stole the jewelry, and that he and Jimmy had a fight in the course of which Jimmy shot him. There were all sorts of rumors and the story never did get straightened out. One of the cops on the case ended up as the head of the security department at Rod's studio. Fellow named Wittenberg. Well liked. The other cop on the case, Merle Billings, was murdered in cold blood by his own wife, who shot him with a .25 automatic. The only reason people remembered that was because the wife's defense was said to have been based on her insane jealousy of Angela Fulton, but there was no testimony to that effect in court. If anybody should have been jealous of Angela Fulton, according to the Palm Springs gossip, it was Mrs. Wittenberg.

After Rod Fulton married Melina Waltham, and they became the first husband-and-wife team to win the Academy Award as co-stars in the same picture, Rod really settled down to serious acting. There was that one bomb, in which he played Plato, but he and Melina appeared in a string of successes. They had a tiny theater on their ranch in The Valley, where they gave Sunday night readings of Shakespeare and Molière and Sheridan, and what-not, for a few invited friends who shared their intense interest in the drama. They were coached by Olga Chapman-Lang, formerly of the Royal Academy, who was a close friend of Melina Waltham's. Their ultimate aim was a New York production of *Macbeth,* which was announced prematurely and, of course, canceled forever by the tragic death of

Melina by lung cancer. Rod was inconsolable. He asked for, and obtained, the postponement of the film he had hoped to do with Melina and which, they both knew, was to be their last co-starring vehicle.

He had seen very little of James Francis Hatter during his marriage to Melina. Olga Chapman-Lang had been frank to say that she considered Hatter a gross voluptuary, whose influence on Rod was disruptive and destructive to his serious preparations for the next phase of his career. "We cannot work, we cannot think, when that man is near," said Olga Chapman-Lang. "He must be kept away or I cannot go on working with you. He has no respect for anything he does not understand." As she had a strong ally in Melina Waltham, her wish prevailed; James Francis was not invited to the Rod Fulton house until after Melina's death. But he came as soon as he was asked, and Olga Chapman-Lang was seen no more at the Fulton ranch.

"How about going away with me for a while?" said Rod.

"Where to?" said James Francis.

"Up to Oregon, for the steelheads. I'll have to buy all new tackle. I gave mine all away."

"I can't do it, Rod," said James Francis. "No more roughing it for me. The old bones won't take it."

"Then let's go someplace else, just so we get out of here."

"Well, we could take an apartment in New York, and you could let the word get out that you're looking for a play."

"That'd be no more different than staying here," said Rod.

"Have you given up the idea of conquering the legitimate?"

"You know something? I wouldn't walk out in front of a Broadway audience for a million dollars cash. Those critics would tear me to pieces."

"Yes, in Shakespeare they would. You *and* Mellie. But you were safe. That Chapman-Lang dike knew better than to let you play *Macbeth.* She had a good thing going for her as long as you did your acting in the back yard."

"I used to wonder about that, but Mellie had her heart set on it. Olga had us both hypnotized. Mesmerized. Something."

"She sure did," said James Francis. "To convince Mellie Waltham that she could play Lady Macbeth. One of the greatest con acts I ever saw. Mellie, with her cute little nose and those gams, believing she could be Judith Anderson. And you. You went for it too."

"Well, we used to enjoy those Sunday evenings. Those readings."

"I heard about those readings, Rod," said James Francis. "Nobody got in that Chapman-Lang didn't approve of. Her own hand-picked stooges. They'd come out here and stuff themselves with your food and your booze, and then go to your little jewel-box of a theater and applaud on cue."

"It wasn't always as bad as that."

"Yes it was. Sometimes it was worse than other times, that's all. I used to hear about it from some of the stooges. They delighted in telling me, because they figured you and I were on the outs. Just out of curiosity, what did you pay Olga?"

"Oh—maybe a couple of hundred dollars a week."

"Like five hundred a week?"

"I guess it was about five. She charges ten dollars an hour, you know."

"Well, that's less than a Powers model, which she certainly ain't. And much less than a head-shrinker. Which in a way she was. But five hundred a week isn't bad at all, considering that you supplied her with a car and most of her meals. Did she have totin' privileges?"

"What's that?"

"You never heard of totin'? That's a time-honored custom, by which the servants are allowed to take home as much as they can carry. Sugar. Butter. Meat."

"You don't have to put the blast on Olga," said Rod.

"I think I do," said James Francis.

"All right, but lay off Mellie."

"No, I won't lay off of Mellie, either."

"She had a very hard time there towards the end."

"She gave a lot of other people a hard time all her life."

"But not me, Jimmy. That you'll never understand. You didn't see us together, so you don't know how it was with she and I. We were right for each other."

"Well, maybe you were," said James Francis.

"It took a while, but after we were married about a year or so we began to level with each other. Angela was the big aristocrat, and she never let me forget that I wasn't. But Mellie was from the same kind of people I came from. Mildred Walsh, from Valley Stream, Long Island. Her old man a car inspector on the Long Island Rail Road, and she was knocked up by a booking agent when she was seventeen years old. She was a straight woman for a magician and God knows what else before she got in pictures. But once she was in pictures, boy, she was in her element. She played it their way, as tough as they come, and fighting all the way."

"Oh, so you fell in love with her? That must have been a surprise."

"Yes, I fell in love with her, and she fell in love with me. Not right away, mind you. But gradually it was there, and I didn't care if I never saw anybody else. I *did*. Once in a while I'd give a little screw to somebody or other. I laid Angela the night before she went back to England, and I told Mellie I did. But Mellie was so much smarter than I was, she would have guessed it. And she didn't give a damn. Mellie was a pro, a real pro. More than I ever was or ever will be. Angela was a bum. She had nothing going for her but being a bum. Well, Mellie was no angel. But she had something else going for her. Acting. Being a movie star. That's not supposed to be much, is it? Making faces in front of a camera. But for over twenty years people all over the world paid to see her make faces, and she was bigger at the end than she ever was. What the hell difference did it make if she didn't have any morals? She was Mellie, Melina Waltham. Over in Japan—*Japan,* mind you—three fans of hers committed suicide when she died. You ought to see some of the letters I got. Over eigh-

teen thousand letters. I don't know how it is with a writer. But with
Mellie, and to a certain extent with me, you get a feeling that you're
with those people every minute of the time. They know who you are,
you're in their thoughts, and you multiply that by two hundred million people—two—hundred—million—people—and there gets to
be some kind of a thing in the air. We never knew about radio till a
few years ago. Well, it's that kind of a thing. It goes back and forth
between you and those people. Only it doesn't exactly go back and
forth. It stays there. It's there. Yes, and Mellie had it, whatever it is.
I had it, too, without knowing I had it till I married Mellie. The two
of us had it together, and with all those people. Back and forth, but
at the same time just staying there. It would take a writer to explain
it, but I don't know if writers ever feel it, and if you don't feel it you
can't explain it. I feel it, and I can't explain it. I had a letter from a
young girl fan of mine, which she was embarrassed to sign only her
initials. She asked me if I went to the toilet. Well, I used to wonder
the same thing about George Washington, and here was a kid asking me. So I wrote on the bottom of her letter and said, 'Just like
everyone else, signed, Rod Fulton,' I don't answer much mail, but I
answered that one. With Mellie this thing was as close as she came
to a religion. She was a Catholic when she was little, but she lost it
on the road, when she was getting kicked around in vawdaville. For
a while she tried Science. Christian Science. They had those booklets
backstage. I remember them, in a tin box nailed to the wall. Help
yourself. She tried that for a while. No go. Then she came out here
and got to be a star, and instead of a regular religion she got this
feeling towards the public. Towards picture business and the public,
the two of them combined. They kid around about 'I belong to my
public,' but by Christ there's something to it. There's positively
something to it, and radio is the closest I can come to describing it.
But explain radio! The ether. The airwaves. The oscillation. I got
some of that in the service, but it was too deep for me. The Norden I
could understand. The bomb-sight. They wanted you to understand
that in case the bombardier and the navigator got hit, and there
wasn't much to it. But the whole air full of guys talking from one

airplane to another, and once in a while you'd get one kraut talking to another. That's too much for me. I can put out my hand here, now, and make a fist. You know what I'm doing when I make a fist? I'm squeezing the hell out of a lot of human voices and music, all in the air. This I never would have thought of but for the fact that I married Mellie and we used to exchange ideas. She was way ahead of me. I guess nobody else ever knew that side of her." He had come to the end of his soliloquy, and the subsequent silence was a part of it that James Francis respected by his own silence.

"Well, what are you thinking, Jimmy?"

"I'm thinking that you've begun to grow up," said James Francis.

"Well, wasn't it about time?" said Rod. "How would you like to come and live here. You could have the guest cottage all to yourself."

"Nope. This place belongs to Mellie."

"You're right," said Rod. "I think I'll put it up for sale. You and I go abroad, and when I come back I'll live in a hotel. You're absolutely right, it belongs to Mellie, and if I stayed here I'd start talking to myself."

"That can get to be very dull conversation, I can assure you from experience. I've often tried to explain to a tennis player that I didn't mean to kill him. They don't listen. They're not tuned in."

"You know, I never even think about that, the Palm Springs thing. But I guess you do. Does it bother you?"

"No worse than if I'd killed somebody," said James Francis.

"But you did—oh, I get it. Well, we both need a trip. You be my guest."

"No."

"Then how about if I get the studio to buy some story of yours? Some old story you never could sell any place else?"

"That would be different. That I'll go for," said James Francis. "The old saying is that the studio can do anything. My version of it is, the studio can do anything—and damn well should."

They were companionable again, each knowing that the conditions of the relationship had been changed, had been compelled to change during their separation. The circumstances of Rod's coming under the influence of Melina Waltham, and of James Francis's guilt neurosis, affected each man individually; as a pair of individuals they could function as friends if there were a tacit understanding that the once dominant James Francis was now the dominated. Perhaps the subtle difference was most evident in the fact that where James Francis had once made all the arrangements to suit his own convenience and pleasure, he now continued making the arrangements but to gratify the wishes of his friend. Rod frankly used him, almost to the point of abuse.

Rod was taken up by Society, the Society of the post-war gyrations in Florida, Long Island, and the ski runs. He got into some famous houses and some well-known beds, and James Francis became accustomed to being left behind. On only one occasion did he protest—when Rod went to Sun Valley. Sun Valley implied skiing, and Rod simply announced to James Francis that he was off to Sun Valley for a week. Before the week was up there were pictures in the newspapers of Rod Fulton and Ernest Hemingway in shooting clothes. "Why didn't you tell me you were going shooting with Hemingway—the one guy I wanted to meet?" said James Francis.

"I didn't think of it. You don't like to shoot," said Rod. Then realizing the tactlessness of the remark, he made it worse. "I mean, I thought you wouldn't want to be around guns."

"One way or the other, you're a liar," said James Francis.

"Well, the next time I'm going to see him I'll take you along. But don't call me a liar."

"You are a liar, and now I don't want to meet him. If he can stand your gibberish for a week, he's fallen pretty low in my estimation." James Francis stormed out of Rod's apartment in the Beverly-Wilshire. It was five or six days before Rod—as though nothing had happened—invited him to accompany him to the races at Santa Anita. James Francis, as though nothing had happened, accepted.

But something had happened, and things like it were happening rather frequently. "One of the papers called me," said James Francis one day. "They wanted to know if it was true you were going back to work."

"What did you tell them?"

"I said there was nothing to it," said James Francis.

"Good. They're going to make the announcement Friday, for release in the Monday papers."

"You *are* going back to work?" said James Francis.

"Yes. It was all very hush-hush. We didn't want to make any announcement till it was all set."

"You have a story?"

"A great story! An original written by some refugee. He used to be a playwright in Vienna. Or maybe it was Budapest. I can never remember his name. Vlas-loss or something like that. Nagly Vlas-loss. You probably know who I mean."

"Not from your description. What about my story?"

"Oh, don't worry. They're going to pay you for it. But they don't want it for me."

"You mean you don't want it for you."

"Hell, what do you care? You're getting your money. A hundred and twenty-five gees, I understand."

"I wanted the credit on your first picture back at work."

"Well, they might be able to work you in somehow. Split the credit on the screenplay."

"I don't split credits. My name goes up there by itself."

"Not always."

"Damn near always. What did he write it in? Hungarian?"

"I guess originally. I read it in English."

"That's for sure," said James Francis.

"No use getting a fig up your ass about this, Jimmy. This is a story you couldn't have written anyway. It's about a guy in the Resistance Movement."

"Where was your Hungarian resisting? In Malibu?" said James Francis.

But The Star, as James Francis sometimes called him, was as unpredictably considerate as he was carelessly tactless. On James

Francis's fiftieth birthday Rod said, "I have a present for you, if you'll have dinner with me tonight."

"Sure. We were going to have dinner anyway," said James Francis.

"Well, I wanted to make sure. What size Cadillac do you wear?"

"You're kidding," said James Francis.

"I'm just throwing you off. Now you won't expect a Cadillac."

They met at Romanoff's, their usual table. The proprietor came and sat with them for a moment. "Old boy, Rod tells me it's your birthday," said Romanoff.

"Yes, Mike. Don't tell me you're going to break down and buy a drink?"

"I have no such intention. However, I may take it under advisement. See you later, old boy."

Rod and James Francis had a couple of drinks. "Well, God damn it, where's my present?" said James Francis.

"It'll be along," said Rod.

"Then let's order."

"No hurry," said Rod.

They had another drink, and then Romanoff came back to the table. "I believe all is in readiness," he said to Rod.

"Come on, fat writer," said Rod. "Upstairs."

They went to the large room on the second floor, and as they made their entrance an orchestra played the birthday ditty. The words were sung by the highest-priced chorus in the land—every major star from every studio in Hollywood, producers and their wives, writers, some directors, starlets, cameramen, old-timers from all occupations, faces, and faces. James Francis lost his breath. He turned to Rod. "You son of a bitch. *You* did this?"

"Mike helped," said Rod.

It was one of the great parties. Everyone there had known James Francis at some time or other, in varying degrees of past intimacy and contemporary indifference, but they had known him. He was the common denominator, no cause of envy, and a recognized—just now recognized—veteran of picture business. They all wanted to speak to him. "Rosemary Theby, for God's sake. How's Harry? . . .

Regis Toomey. Read this to me, Regis Toomey. I always have to say that . . . Vilma. How's your golf, Vilma? . . . C. Aubrey, bless my soul . . ." He had special whispered thanks for those who had written to him during the Palm Springs mess, and he refrained from embarrassing those who should not have been invited and those who should not have come. The party began to thin out at ten o'clock— early calls—and again at midnight, and at three o'clock they called it quits.

James Francis and Rod walked the few steps to Rod's hotel apartment. "You going to be able to make it home all right?" said Rod.

"What do you mean? I never made the load. Not many did, come to think of it."

"I was ribbing you. I meant, now that you're fifty going on fifty-one," said Rod.

"Oh, that's another story. By the way, I never got my present."

"Your present? I'll send you the receipted bill for the party," said Rod. "It's not deductible, either."

"You know, I wondered about that."

"My tax man said I'd have a hell of a hard time explaining a deduction for a birthday party for a fat writer. If you were Sidney Skolsky, I might be able to get away with it. But you're not, not by a half a ton."

"I'd still like a birthday present."

"All right, you son of a bitch, if it'll make you sleep better, you're getting one."

"What?"

"It's a book. A kind of guest-book. It was signed by everybody that was there tonight."

"Where is it now?"

"It's locked up in Mike's safe, overnight. I didn't want anything to happen to it."

They were in Rod's apartment. "You know that guest-book is going to be like my Oscar, only more so. I got my Oscar for a picture I didn't think much of. The studio spent a lot of money getting Oscars for the stars and the director, and I got a free ride on their publicity."

"Where was I when you got an Oscar? I never knew you had one."

"You were in England, in the service. I was kind of pissed off that I never heard from you, but then I remembered they weren't accepting congratulatory telegrams. You never knew I got an Oscar?"

"Never till this minute. It must have been for that Pearl Harbor picture, that I never saw."

"It was."

"Where do you keep it?"

"In my study, over the fireplace."

"Jesus, is it that long since I've been in your house?" said Rod. "I used to empty the ash trays in that house. I even washed your car."

"You remember that?"

"Well, why the hell do you think I threw this party tonight? I been working on this party for over a month. You should have seen the time we had tracking down some of those people. Some of those old-timers, not even Casting knew where to reach them. And swearing them all to secrecy, in *this* town."

"How did you do that?"

Rod considered. "That part you won't like."

"Go ahead, tell me."

"We told them that ever since the Palm Springs thing you were adverse to publicity."

"Yes, I'll bet that's exactly what you told them. Adverse. The word is averse."

"Well, that's what we told them. That if any word of it leaked out, you wouldn't show. You'd leave town."

"I probably would have, too," said James Francis. "When I killed Slaymaker I developed a passion for anonymity. You do."

"Well, after tonight you don't have anything to worry about. You have more friends in this town than you think you have."

"Yes, as a matter of fact it's going to be hard to adjust myself to it. All these years thinking I was a friendless soul."

"Except for me, I hope."

"Except for you."

"I don't have many friends. I never did have. The people that pay to see my pictures, that has nothing to do with friendship. Dwight D. Eisenhower."

"Is he a friend of yours?"

"Hell, no. I never got higher than major. I met him, in London, and he used to look at me and I knew he was thinking, 'Where do I know this guy from?' No, what I mentioned his name for, there was another guy that everybody in the world knew him, but how many friends can you have in that spot? When they were planning the invasion, he couldn't even be friends with Churchill. Friendly, but not friends. I'm no Eisenhower. But take for instance, Churchill had *his* ideas about the invasion, and Eisenhower had his. If they got to be too good friends, Eisenhower would start giving in to Churchill. The thing is, they all want something from you."

"Well, I never want anything else from you. After tonight, we're all square. I never did want anything from you, but it always bugged you that I helped you get started. Now you're in the clear."

"That's not why I did it, but if you want to think so, all right," said Rod Fulton. He stood up. "You want to shack up here instead of going home?"

"Thanks, but I think I'll go home and cry a little. All by myself. Do you realize that we ended up this evening without a couple of broads? And the worst of it is, I didn't even think about it till now. That's really being fifty."

"I don't know," said Rod. "It's kind of nice to just be able to hit the sack when you want to. I can get laid any time. And any*where*. That's the worst of it."

"Boy! We're getting there."

"Well, once in a while I get tired of women looking at me and saying—not in words but by the way they look at you—they say, '*I* will, honey, *I* will.' As if I couldn't get it any time and any place, whenever I felt like it."

"You need a month in Death Valley, without any women. As

soon as your guide, or the burros, begin to look good—come home."

"I need more than that, but what it is I don't know," said Rod. "In the service I used to think all I wanted was to get the damn war over with and come back here. Life would be simple. It *was* kind of simple, with Mellie. But I'm not looking for another Mellie. I don't know what the hell I *am* looking for, and that's just the trouble. I just for Christ's sake don't know."

"Well, at four o'clock in the morning, after a great party, I'm not going to try to tell you. If you find out, maybe *you'll* tell *me,*" said James Francis.

Now that Rod was, as James Francis said, in the clear, he made rather a point of limiting their times together. Frequently a week would go by with no communication between them. Rod had achieved that degree of importance at which the studio no longer dared urge him to romance a co-star for the publicity; James Francis therefore assumed that the gossip items which coupled Rod's name with that of his current leading woman were accurate. She was, in the classic Hollywood phrase, a "New York actress," meaning a stage actress who had not acquired a motion picture reputation. Her name was Gwen Hickman, and the studio was unable to persuade her to change it, or her nose, or her indifference toward the Hollywood press. Her posture in relation to Hollywood was only her variant of the attitude of Garbo, Hepburn, and Margaret Sullavan, but she was affecting it twenty years later than they. She was rather dirty-looking, and the money she might have spent on clothes found its way into funds for liberal causes and through them into activities more sinister. But she had a keen sense of publicity values, particularly of the value of the Rod Fulton association. When he refused to take her to a movie premiere unless she changed into an evening dress, she put on an evening dress; when he refused to give any money to one of her causes, she did not press the point. When she asked him to marry her, he told her he was too old to get married to a woman not yet thirty. When she heard that he had a very large piece of the picture in which they were appearing, she accused him of romancing her for the exploitation. "Well, it hasn't done you any harm, has it?" he said. It was her first experience of the Hollywood *droit de seigneur,* and when the picture was completed she went back to New York and in a series of articles for an afternoon paper she allowed herself to be described as an escapee from the Rod Fulton harem. "Never again!" she said. And she was correct.

"What about that cunt?" said James Francis.

Rod Fulton snorted. "I read one of the articles," he said. "So I sent her a present. A dozen bars of soap, with my card. Just my card. Nothing written on it. But I'll say this for her, she helps the picture. She's supposed to have been gang-raped by a bunch of Nazis, and you don't have a hard time believing it. *On* the screen, that is. Off-screen, she was never raped by anybody."

"You gave her a lot of your time," said James Francis.

"I guess I did," said Rod. "But I got a guarantee of six hundred thousand dollars and a percentage of the producer's gross. If I went broke today, I'd still have a nice start for the future. This picture's gonna be big everywhere, and I wouldn't be surprised if she got an Oscar. If you don't vote for *her,* it'd be the same as voting *for* the Nazis. I'm thinking of becoming a star-maker. Get these unknowns for my leading lady, and meanwhile I get the cash."

"It worked with Barthelmess," said James Francis.

"It'll work with me. What have you been up to lately?"

"History is repeating itself," said James Francis. "A young actor came to me with a letter from Joe Shapiro, a guy I used to know in New York. Joe's retired now, but this young guy is a nephew of Joe's sister."

"This is where I came in," said Rod.

"Well, not quite. The kid came to see me, with the letter. I gave him a meal. Studied him. He had all the mannerisms of Julie Garfield, but none of the charm. The laugh. The toughtalk. It was like watching Julie with the Lane Sisters, before he made *The Postman.*"

"In other words, he had nothing," said Rod Fulton.

"Maybe it's me," said James Francis. "But when you showed up, I was sure you had it. This guy—no."

"What *did* I have, Jimmy?"

"I've often wondered," said James Francis. "I've come up with seventy-five different answers. The obvious answer is that I was queer for you. I don't rule that out entirely, but that only explains me. It doesn't explain what you had."

"You were never a queer, were you?"

"Very queer. And afraid of it, hence the broads."

"I had my hat blown a few times, when I was a chorus boy. But they were swish fags. I was never sure about you, but do you know who was? I mean sure that you weren't?"

"Angela."

"Who?"

"Oh, Angela," said James Francis.

"She told me you killed that guy because you were jealous of him."

"Is that what she told you? Well, maybe she was right."

"You were banging Angela, and I never knew it. But she told me before she went away."

"That was nice of her," said James Francis.

"She laid it all on the line because I was generous to her. You were in love with her, for God's sake."

"Well, not for God's sake. We can leave God out of it. But she's the only woman that—if I wasn't in love with her, she obsessed me. And she still does."

"I know that, and she knew it. That was her argument. That you were a one-woman man, and she was the woman."

"That's true. I don't care if I never see her again, but that's probably because I killed a guy on account of her. If I think of her, immediately I start thinking of him. Him, and his pregnant wife, and their kids. So I only think of her every day of my life. Every God damn day of my miserable fucking life."

"Oh?"

"Sometimes I'll be somewhere and somebody will be staring at me. 'What the hell are *you* staring at?' Only a couple of weeks ago, in the studio commissary. I called a guy that I thought was staring at

me. A dress extra, he was. All through lunch I thought he was staring at me, and finally I went over and called him on it. What was he
staring at? The woman with him burst out laughing. Staring? He
couldn't see that far without his contact lenses. He wasn't staring at
anybody, just giving his eyes a rest, she said. So then I had to apologize, and I never apologize, and I'm not very good at it. You'd know
the guy. I think he's been a dress extra since Griffith made *Hearts of
the World.* He has pure white hair."

"Oh, sure. I think I know which one it is. He gets work in every
picture that Harry Hawthorne directs."

"That's the guy, all right. Well, if you want to know how he rests
his eyes, he rests them by staring at me. Do you know anybody that
rests their eyes by staring at you?"

"Plenty," said Rod.

"Yeah, but they're car-hops that say, '*I* will, *I* will.' "

"Christ, you never forget anything, do you?"

"Nothing worth forgetting," said James Francis.

"Well, I guess I won't be seeing you for a while," said Rod.
"Starting the first of February I'm doing a picture in Italy. Venice."

"I saw you were," said James Francis.

"Then when we wind that up, I get a vacation in Norway, for
some fishing. Then starting around the first of October I'll be in Ireland on an independent production of my own."

"You going in for the three-year tax dodge?"

"I'm going to try to," said Rod. "It's a long time to be out of the
country, but I have nothing to keep me here. So why not make four
or five or six million dollars that I can hold onto? I've been talking
to an architect about building a new house."

"Where?"

"Here, somewhere. First we have to find out where they're going
to build new super-highways. No use buying the land and getting a
house halfway up and they come along and condemn it. So we'll
have to wait and see. But we're going ahead with the plans for the
house. Something to look forward to when I get back."

"You figure it'll be three years from now?"

"Three years from February, if I work the tax dodge."

"When you get back, I'll give a party for you. If I'm still around."

"All right, it's a deal. By that time you'll know all the new people and I won't know any."

"Will I see you before you go?" said James Francis.

"Oh, hell yes. I won't be leaving till the middle of January."

"That's not so far off," said James Francis.

"No, but we'll keep in touch," said Rod Fulton.

The day before he took off for Venice, Italy, he telephoned James Francis. "Well, guy, I'm off tomorrow," he said.

"Yes, I saw that," said James Francis.

"I'm sorry everything got so jammed up at the last minute," said Rod. "Is there any chance of your coming abroad?"

"So little you could stick it under your eyelid," said James Francis.

"Well, you know where I'll be."

"I'll just ask any gondolier," said James Francis.

"Right. Just ask any gondolier. Well, keep punching, and let me know what gives."

"Right," said James Francis. "Oh, say, Rod. Before you go?"

"What?"

"You wouldn't have time to wash my car?"

"Oh, very funny! *Verr*-ry *fah*-nee!" said The Star.

Natica Jackson

♦

One afternoon on her way home from the studio in her cream-yellow Packard 120 convertible coupe Natica Jackson took a wrong turn, deliberately. Every working day for the three years that she had been under contract at Metro she had followed the same route between Culver City and her house in Bel-Air: Motor Avenue, Pico Boulevard, Beverly Glen, Sunset Boulevard, Bel-Air. In the morning it was Bel-Air, Sunset Boulevard, Beverly Glen, Pico Boulevard, Motor Avenue, Culver City, the studio. She was fond of saying that she knew the way in her sleep, because many mornings she might as well have been asleep as the way she was. In the afternoons and early evenings, tired though she was, it was not quite the same. The reason it was not the same was that when she got through working it was like being let out of school. In those days she was still close enough to high school to have that feeling. It had not been so long since a Warner talent scout saw her in a school play in Santa Ana and wafted her the fifty thousand miles from Santa Ana to Hollywood. They gave her a seven-year contract beginning at $75 a week, and in six months she was released, just before they would have had to pay her $125 a week. Then she got an agent who helped someone at Metro discover that she could sing and dance; and pretty soon the public discovered that there was something in the spacing between her eyes and the width of her upper lip that made her stand out, made them want to know who she was. Among beautiful women and cute girls she was the one that the public liked. She

456

became everybody's favorite niece, and she also looked extremely well in black opera-lengths. The studio teamed her up with Eddie Driscoll in two dreadful musicals, the second so dreadful that it was scrapped halfway through, but Jerry B. Lockman saw enough of it to want her for a straight, non-musical comedy he was doing, and she walked away with the picture. Walked away with it. In the executives' diningroom they could not agree that Natica Jackson had star quality, but no one could deny that she was ready for stardom. Not Garbo stardom, not Myrna Loy stardom, but sure as hell Joan Blondell stardom, and maybe, in the right pictures she would develop into another Jean Arthur. The God damn public liked her. She couldn't carry a picture by herself, but whenever she was in a picture the people would come out of the theater saying how wonderful she was.

She bought the house in Bel-Air with money she had not yet earned, but her agent knew what he was doing when he helped her finance it. "I don't want you rattling around some apartment on Franklin," he said. "I'm thinking of ten years from now, when you ought to be making easily a couple hundred thousand dollars a year. Move your mother in with you and stay out of the night spots."

"And have no fun," said Natica.

"Depends on what you mean by fun. You have Jerry Lockman."

"He can't take me out anywhere," she said.

"I'll take you anywhere you ought to go. Anywhere I can't take you, you shouldn't be there."

"Don't try to make me into something I'm not," said Natica.

"How do you know what you're not? You know Marie Dressler?"

"Tugboat Annie, you mean?"

"You know who she pals around with? Vanderbilts and Morgans, those kind of people. And you should make a year what she makes."

"Well, I hope she has more fun than I do."

"I hope you have as much fun when you're her age. Over sixty and making what she makes. Well loved throughout the entire civilized world. If all is not well with you and Jerry, get yourself a younger fellow. Only don't go for some trap drummer in a cheap night club. I'll look around and see if I find the right kind of a fellow for you. I coulda told you a few things about Jerry, but you didn't take me into your confidence till it was too late. But we can get rid of Jerry. You *graduated* from his type pictures. I got great confidence in your future, Natica. Not just next week or the week after. I'm talking about 1940, 1950, 1960!"

Natica had already been around Hollywood long enough to have respect for her agent, and she obeyed him in all things. Morris King was a rich man, an agent by choice, and not one of the artists' representatives who waited hopefully for a permanent connection with one of the studios. Morris had turned down offers of producer jobs. "I'll take L. B. Mayer's job, should they offer it to me, but not Eddie Mannix's or Benny Thau's," he would say. He had a big house in Beverly Hills, a 16-cylinder Cadillac limousine with a Negro chauffeur who wore breeches and puttees, and he had Ernestine, his wife, who according to other agents was the real brains of the Morris King Office. Ernestine would sit with Morris at the Beverly Derby, the Vine Street Derby, Al Levey's Tavern, the Vendome, Lyman's downtown, with her fat forearms resting flat on the table and her hands clasped, her eyes sparkling as she followed the men's conversation. She would wait, she would always wait, until Morris or one of the other men asked her what *she* thought, and her opinions were always so clever or so completely destructive that the men would nod silently even when they did not agree. She had opinions on everything; who was going to be the boss at Universal, who was going to win the main event at the Legion Stadium, why was Natica Jackson worth Morris King's personal attention. "Ernestine thinks like a man," said one rival agent. "I was having a discussion with her and Morris the other night. We happen to be talking about something, and in the mist of it I pulled a couple cigars outa my pocket and accidentally I offered one to Ernestine. I didn't mean anything by it. It was just like I said, she thinks like a man, and I done it like you offer a coupla men a cigar. Did she get sore? No, she didn't get sore. You know what she said? She said, 'The supreme compliment.' I don't say she's *all* the brains, but when it comes to thinking I give her credit for fifty-one percent. I give her the edge. Incidentally, she *took* the cigar. She don't smoke, but she wanted the cigar for a souvenir, a memento."

The Kings had no children, and at forty-four Ernestine was as reconciled to childlessness as at twenty-two she had been fearful of pregnancy. They loved Morris's business, going out every night, and each other. But Morris thought he saw through Ernestine's interest in Natica Jackson. "She's a little like you, Teeny," he said. "If you had a daughter that's what she'd be like. She even resembles you facially."

"You think you're smart, don't you?" said Ernestine.

"Maybe not smart, but not dumb either," said Morris. "It's all right if you don't want to tell me. I got my own two eyes."

"I know you have, honey," she said. "But I was never as pretty as Natica Jackson. That I can't claim."

"I only said she resembles you facially. I didn't say she was the exact duplicate."

"What if she was the exact duplicate? Would you go for her?"

He rubbed his chin as though he were stroking a Vandyke. "You know what I think? I think you're trying to find out if I *do* go for her. Like I saw the facial resemblance back there two-three years ago, and said to myself here was a modern-day version of Ernestine Schluter. Well, if that's what you're thinking, you're all wrong. The first time I saw her I took notice she had a pair of legs like Ruby Keeler and a kind of a face on the order of Claudette Colbert, only not as pretty."

"Claudette has a pair of legs on her."

"I'm telling you what *I* thought, not what you're thinking now, if you'll let me continue," said Morris. "So I did a little selling job at Metro. Then *you* liked her and the public liked her, and you more or less took her under your wing. As to me going for her like Jerry Lockman went for her, you got no cause to be suspicious."

"I know, Morris, I know. I was just kind of putting you on the pan," said Ernestine.

"Sure. But you got something on your mind, whatever it is," he said.

"It isn't much. The way some of you men buy a prizefighter and have him for a hobby, that's my interest in Natica."

"You wanta buy her from me? I'll sell you her contract and let you service her?"

"Not me. If there's anything I don't want to be it's a woman agent. But I'd like to have the say in her career, just for a hobby."

"All right."

"Starting with getting rid of Jerry Lockman."

"That's easy. She's fed up to here with Jerry."

"So am I, and she's been with him long enough. Everybody in town knows about Jerry and how he's peculiar, but if Natica keeps on being his girl they'll think the same of her. Get her a new fellow. An Englishman, or a writer, or I don't care if you get her an out-and-out pansy. But somebody that can be her escort."

"You want me to find a new girl for Jerry?"

"That shouldn't be hard. They're a dime a dozen in this town. The next new girl comes into your office, send her out to Jerry."

"Well, I guess I can do that," said Morris. "But you find a guy for Natica."

"All right," said Ernestine.

She found an Englishman who was also a writer and an out-and-out bisexual, who was more than willing to act as Natica's escort and lover. It was not the ideal arrangement for Natica, but they kept her busy at the studio, gave her bonuses for waiving vacations, and sent her home at night too tired to think. Alan Hildred, her English beau, sold the studio two original stories for Natica Jackson pictures, and one of them, *Uncles Are People,* was actually produced and did well. Twenty-five thousand dollars, less Morris King's ten percent, more than made up for the times when Natica did not wish to see him—or for the times when she did wish to see him. It became an understood thing that Alan Hildred was to make *some* money, as author of the original or collaborator on the screenplay, on every Natica Jackson picture. Natica's mother, who would have liked being a dress extra, was persuaded to take a job as saleslady in a florist's shop owned by Ernestine King. Natica's father, a brakeman on the Southern Pacific, went right on being a brakeman, but he had been separated from his wife for a good ten years. No one knew where Natica's brother was. Last heard from as a deckhand on one of the Dollar Line ships. But he was bound to turn up sometime and when he did he would have to be taken care of. Natica's maternal uncle, who had moved into the Jackson household when Natica's father left, was employed as a gardener at Warner Brothers. He had expected to move into the Bel-Air house, but there Natica put her foot down. "That dirty old son of a bitch can stay away from here," said Natica.

"That's no way to talk about your own flesh and blood," said her mother.

"Listen, Mom, there's no law says *you* have to live here either," said Natica. "You're making seventy-five a week."

"Yes, but for how long? My arthritis."

"Don't kid me, with your arthritis. If you have the arthritis I'll send you to the desert. Go see the doctor, and if he says you have the arthritis I'll get you a place to stay. But if Uncle Will thinks he's moving in here, you just tell Uncle Will it was Mr. King got him the job at Warners', and the same Mr. King can get him kicked out on his big fat can."

"I don't see why Mr. King can't get me a job as a dress extra. Then I wouldn't have to be in and out of that refrigerator all day."

"Well, I'll tell you why," said Natica. "They don't want you on the lot is why. And another reason is because they give those jobs to people that can act. Professionals. The only acting you ever do is putting on this act with the arthritis. Don't you exhaust my patience, Mom. Just don't you exhaust my patience."

"Sometimes I wish we never left Santa Ana."

"Here's fifty bucks," said Natica. "Go on back."

"Yes, you'd like to get rid of me, wouldn't you?"

462 ♦ JOHN O'HARA

"Oh, cut it out. I'm tired," said Natica. "I get up at five o'clock in the morning and get pushed around all day, and when I get home evenings I have to listen to your bellyaching."

It was a day or two later that Natica Jackson, on her way home from the studio in her little Packard, deviated from her customary route. There was a point on Motor Avenue where the road bore to the right. At the left there was a street—she didn't know its name— that formed the other arm of a Y. She had wondered sometimes what would happen if she turned in at that street. Not that anything would happen except that she would be a little later getting home and she would have seen a Southern California real estate development that she had never seen before. But at least she would have gone home by a different way. And so she turned left into a street called Marshall Place.

She had to slow down. Marshall Place was a winding road, S-shaped and only three-car width and a tight squeeze at that. The houses were quite close together and English-looking, and Natica wondered if the street had been named after Herbert Marshall, the English actor. The cars that were parked in Marshall Place were cars that were suitable to the neighborhood: Buicks, Oldsmobiles, a Packard 120 like Natica's, a LaSalle coupe, an oldish foreign car with a name something like Delancey. It was a far superior neighborhood to the section of Santa Ana where Natica had lived, but she had so quickly become accustomed to Bel-Air that Marshall Place seemed almost dingy. She came to another turn in the road and now she could see Motor Avenue again, and she was not sorry to see it. Marshall Place was certainly nothing much, and whatever curiosity she had had about it was completely satisfied. Just another street where people who worked in offices lived. Fifty yards from Motor Avenue and farewell to Marshall Place—and then her car banged into a Pontiac.

The Pontiac was pulling out from the curb and she hit it almost broadside. It was a noisy collision in the quiet street. The driver of the Pontiac shouted, "What the hell?" and other things that she did not hear. She backed her car away and he reversed to the curbstone and got out. "What do you think you were doing?" he said. "Didn't you see my hand? I had my hand out, you know."

"I'm sorry," she said. "I didn't see your hand. It's kind of dark. I'm covered with every kind of insurance." She was wearing a silk scarf over her head and tied under her chin.

"Aren't you Natica Jackson, the actress?" he said.

"Yes," she said.

"I thought so," he said. "Well, my name is H. T. Graham, and I live in there, Number 8 Marshall Place. I suppose you have your driver's license and so forth? You'd better pull up to the curb or you'll be in the way of any cars that want to get through."

"Listen, Mr. Graham, don't start bossing me around like you were taking charge here. You say you had your hand out, but I don't have to take your word for it. The insurance company will pay for your damages, only don't start bossing me around. Here. Here's my driver's license and you can look on the steering if you want to copy down the registration."

"Don't pull any movie actress stuff on me," he said. "You were completely in the wrong and the condition of the two cars proves it. I didn't smack into you. You smacked into me." He took out a fountain pen and wrote down her name and address and various numbers in an appointment book. "Have you got a pencil?"

"No," she said.

"All right. Then I'll copy it all down for you." He did so, and tore a sheet out of his appointment book and handed it to her. "Some people would get a whole new car out of this, a crackup with a movie actress," he said. "But all I want is what I'm entitled to."

"Big-hearted Otis," she said.

"You movie people, you wonder why you're so unpopular with real people, but I'll tell you why. It's the way you're behaving now. Like a spoiled brat. You think a cheque from the insurance company is all that's necessary. This time you can drive your car home and tomorrow you can buy a new one. But the next time you may kill somebody. This is a narrow street, residential, small children. Luckily they're all home having their supper now, but a half hour

earlier this street would have been full of children. I read all about
that drunken director that killed three people down in Santa
Monica. He should have been put in the gas chamber."

"Listen, Mr. Graham, all I did was wrinkle your fender and put a
few dents in your door."

"But if the window'd been up you could have blinded me with
flying glass. Stop trying to make this seem like nothing."

"You stop trying to make it seem like a train wreck."

"Oh, go on home," he said. "And try and get home without killing anybody. Go on, beat it."

"I can't," she said.

"Naturally, your motor isn't running. Step on the starter."

"It isn't that," she said.

"Are you hurt?"

"No, not that either. I just don't want to drive. Would you mind
going in your house and calling a taxi? Suddenly I lost my nerve or
something. I don't know what it is."

"Are you sure you didn't bang your head on the windshield?" He
looked at her closely.

"I'm not hurt. Please, will you just call me a taxi and I'll send
somebody to pick up my car."

"No, no, I'll drive you home. You feeling faint or anything?
Come on in and I'll get you a glass of water. Or maybe a brandy is
what you need."

"Honestly, all I want is if you'll get me a taxi and I'll be all right.
I'm doing a delayed take, I guess, but I positively couldn't drive
home if you paid me."

He got in her car and drove it to Bel-Air. She spoke only to give
him directions in the final stage of the ride. "Now I'll get *you* a taxi,"
she said, when they reached her house. "Can I offer you a drink?"

"No thanks," he said.

"I guess you expectèd me to have a big car with a chauffeur."

"It'd go with this house, all right," he said.

"It's too big for just my mother and I."

"Aren't you married?"

"No." She telephoned the taxi company. "There'll be a cab in five minutes," she said. "I'm sorry I was such a jerk back there."

"I was pretty rough on you."

"Oughtn't you to tell your wife where you are?"

"She's away. She and the kids are down at Newport."

"Oh, then I guess you were on your way out to dinner when I bumped into you."

"I was going over to Ralphs in Westwood. I usually go there when I'm batching it."

"How about a steak here? I have dinner by myself and go to bed around nine. My mother doesn't wait for me. She eats early and then goes to the show."

"So I'm all alone with a movie star. This is the first time that ever happened to me. I have a confession to make, though. I've never seen you on the screen. I recognized you from the ads, I guess. I don't go to the movies very much."

"Well, what do *you* do for a living? Maybe I don't buy what you sell, either."

"No, I don't guess you do. I'm a chemist with the Signal Oil Company."

"I buy oil," she said.

"Well, my job isn't the kind of oil you use. I'm supposed to be developing certain by-products."

"Whatever that means. Wouldn't you like to make a pass at me?"

"You mean it?" he said.

"Yes. If you don't, I'm liable to make a pass at you," she said. "Come on over and sit next to me."

"I don't get it," he said.

"Neither do I, but I don't care. I don't even care what you think of me. I'll never see you again, so it won't matter. But when the taxi comes, here, you give him this five-dollar bill and tell him you won't need him. That's him now. They're very prompt."

"You sure you want to go through with this?"

"Well, not if we start talking about it. Will you send the cab away?"

"Sure," he said. He went to the door and dismissed the taxi. "What about your mother?"

"My room's in a different part of the house. We can go back there now." She stood up and he embraced her, and they knew quite simply that they wanted each other. "See? You did want to make a pass at me."

"Sure I did, but I wouldn't have," he said.

"Well, I would have," she said. "Come on."

They went to her room and he stayed until eleven o'clock. "I wish you didn't have to go, but I have to be up at five o'clock. And I guess you'll probably want to phone your wife. Do you phone her every night?"

"Just about."

"Well, tell her you didn't phone her earlier because you were in bed with a movie star."

"Shall I say who?"

"No, maybe you better not. You're going to have to tell her about the accident, and that's the first thing she'll think of, is what happened after the accident. Do you realize something?"

"What?"

"You're never going to be able to mention my name again without her thinking you did go to bed with me. That's always going to be in the back of her mind."

"No."

"Yes. Believe me. That's what I'd think, and that's what she's going to think. That maybe, *maybe* that night you had the accident and didn't phone her, *maybe* you spent the night with that Natica Jackson."

"I don't know but that you could be right," he said. "You have her figured out pretty well, for somebody that never saw her."

"That's because I think I know the kind of a girl you'd be married to. Did she ever know you were untrue to her?"

"Well, there was only one other time and that was in Houston, Texas."

"But I'll bet she watches you like a hawk."

"Yes, she's inclined to be jealous."

"And so are you."

"Yes, I guess I am," he said.

"Well, Hal Graham, I guess it's time you went home," she said. "I'll call you another cab." She did so.

"Where is your mother now?" he said.

"My mother? I guess she's in her room. Why?"

"I just wondered," he said. "You know, she'd think it was strange if she was sitting out there in the livingroom and I walked by."

"Well, she might," said Natica. "It doesn't happen all the time."

"That's what I meant."

"Don't get me wrong. It does happen. But not all the time," said Natica. "That is, I don't have a strange man here every night."

"I could tell that," he said.

"How?"

"Oh—it's hard to say. But you know these things. This house is so quiet, I got the impression that it's always quiet, and you're lonesome. Lonely, I guess is the better word. I get an altogether different impression than I had before."

"Of how a movie star lives?"

"Yes."

"Yes. Well, of course some of them are married. Most of them are," she said. "But I never got that lonely, that I wanted to marry the kind of a guy that wanted to marry me. I wouldn't marry an actor, even if I was in love with him. But if I didn't marry an actor, who else would I marry? Regular people don't understand the way we have to live. The only person for me to marry is a director. Then I wouldn't be always wondering whether he married me because I was a movie star, because I made a lot of money. I'd be willing to marry a big director, but they all have somebody. A wife or a girl friend. Or both. Or they're queer."

"You wouldn't marry a queer," he said.

"No, I guess not. Of course some of them are double-gaited, and some of the double-gaited ones are just as masculine as anybody."

"Do you speak from experience? You sound it," he said.

"Don't start asking me about my experiences. By tomorrow morning you'll be one of my experiences. And I'll be one of yours."

"The big one. Practically the only one. I don't know whether I'll be able to take it so casually."

"Yes you will. You will because you have to. Maybe not casually, offhand. But don't look at the dark side. Look on the bright side. From now on you'll be able to say to yourself, these movie stars are just like anyone else."

"The only trouble with that argument is I didn't think of you as a movie star. I never would have made a play for a movie star."

"You didn't have to. The movie star made a play for you."

"I had other girls make a play for me."

"But you didn't go to bed with them."

"Before I was married I did, but not after I was married. Except for the girl in Houston, Texas."

"And she was a whore," said Natica.

"No. She was the wife of a friend of mine."

"Oh, I thought she was some girl you met at one of those conventions."

"It was a convention, but I knew her before. She and her husband live there in Houston. He's another chemist. I went to Cal with him, and she was there at the same time, a couple classes behind us."

"Was she your girl at Cal?"

"No. I didn't have a girl at Cal, till senior year. The girl I married."

"Oh, so the one in Houston—"

"Was never my girl. But when I showed up at the convention and we all had a lot of drinks, that's all it was. Her husband passed out completely, and she said we ought to make up for lost time."

"Was he your best friend?" said Natica.

"No, just a friend. A fraternity brother. He was never my best friend. I don't have a *best* friend. I have guys I like to go fishing with, and others I work with at the lab, and there's two or three of us that play tennis together. But for instance I don't have anybody that I could tell what happened tonight, even if I thought they'd believe me. You're the first person I ever told about the girl in Houston."

"Then maybe I'm your best friend," she said.

He smiled. "Well, at least temporarily," he said.

"Did you ever stop to think that maybe we're both kidding ourselves?"

"How so?"

"About never seeing each other again," she said.

"Well, we oughtn't to," he said.

"You're weakening," she said.

He stared at the empty fireplace. "Possibly," he said.

"I've weakened already," she said. "I go by your house every day, twice a day, only a half a block away. Today I just happened to feel like turning off Motor Avenue into Marshall Road."

"Place. Marshall Place. Yes, you told me," he said.

"Why?" she said.

"Because you were tired of taking the same route every day. You told me."

"But I didn't say why, because I don't *know* why," she said. "Why did I turn off today instead of last week, when your wife was home? Why did you happen to be starting your car just at the same exact moment that I came along? Why did you feel like going to Ralphs at just that exact moment? If you stopped to tie your shoe or change your necktie, you wouldn't have been in your car when I hit it. It would have been sitting there at the curbstone, and I would have driven right by your house."

"The laws of probability."

"I don't know what that means," she said.

"Oh, I was just thinking of probability and chance, in mathematics. There wouldn't be any way to work it out mathematically, that I know of. So it comes down to luck, which is beyond our comprehension. Good luck or bad luck, or a little of both."

"Mathe-*matics?*"

"I use mathematics in my work, quite a lot."

"I thought you were a chemist, with test tubes full of oil."

"Actually I'm a chemical engineer, in research. It saves time to say I'm a chemist, since nobody knows or cares what kind of work I'm doing. Not even my wife. She was an English major, and if I told her what I did at the lab on any given day, she wouldn't understand it any more than you would. Plus the fact that it's a team operation, with five other men working on it."

"You have five men working under you?"

"As a matter of fact, I have," he said. "But how did you know I was in charge?"

"Just guessed," she said. "Then you must be pretty important."

"I'll be pretty important if I get the right results."

"And rich?"

"Rich? Well, no, not rich, but I'll be set for life. I probably am anyway. That is, I'll always make a pretty good living."

"What do they pay you now?"

He laughed. "Well, if you must know, eighteen thousand a year."

"I guess that's a lot in your business," she said.

"It's a lot in any business except yours, and I don't consider movies a business."

"Money is money," she said. "They don't look at a ten-dollar bill and say, 'Oh, this is Signal Oil Company money. That's worth twice as much as Metro money.'"

"No, they don't. But what will you be earning twenty years from now?"

"Two hundred thousand dollars a year," she said.

"What?"

"That's what Morris King says."

"Who the hell is Morris King?"

"My agent, and a multye-millionaire."

"Well, I hope he's right, for your sake," he said.

"He usually is. He advanced my career from seventy-five a week to seventy-five thousand a year, and next year I get more, and the year after that and the year after that."

"A young girl like you making that much money."

"Shirley Temple makes more, and she's a lot younger," said Natica. "But I'm getting started, according to Morris."

"Is that what you want most? Money?"

"I know God damn well I never want to be without it," she said.

"What about love? A home? Children?"

"Yeah, what *about* love? And a home and children. You picked a fine time to ask."

"Yes, I did, didn't I?"

"You have a home and children, and I suppose you love your wife, but you're still not satisfied."

"No, I guess I'm not," he said.

"Well? What do *you* want most?" she said. "Not money."

"No, not money for its own sake. I want to do certain things in my work, and I guess that's uppermost. And have a nice home and educate my children."

"And every once in a while somebody like me," said Natica.

"Yes."

"But not too often," she said. "You'd like to have your home and children and someone like me, off to one side, and your work uppermost. That's funny, me in the same category with your wife and kids. That would get a laugh in Culver City. But I guess that's the way most men would like to have it, and that's why I don't get married. I'm too independent, I guess."

"Maybe," he said.

"But I'm not independent," she said. "I have to get up at five o'clock in the morning and drive to Culver City. I'll toot my horn when I'm passing your house."

"You'd better have them check your alignment. You hit my car just hard enough to knock yours out of line."

"No, I think I'll just trade mine in on a new LaSalle. So the next time I run into you I'll have a new car. How early do you have to get up?"

"Oh, generally around seven," he said.

"You'll sleep soundly tonight," she said.

"I'll say I will."

"So will I," she said. "Be funny if all we got out of this experience was a good night's sleep for both of us. But don't count on it."

"I won't. What you started to say about if I stopped to tie my shoe, or put on a different necktie. We got sidetracked, but there's something in it."

She scribbled on a piece of paper. "Here. This is the number of my dressing-room. It's private, doesn't go through the Metro switchboard. If I don't answer it'll be my maid, but don't tell her anything. She gossips plenty about other girls she worked for, so she's sure to gossip about me. Tell her Mr. Marshall called, and I'll know who it was."

"I'll give you my number at the office," he said.

"No, I don't want to know it. You think it over, and if you want to see me again, call me up. But think it over first. You have the most to lose. Besides, *I* may not want to see *you*. But don't count on that, either."

"What's a good time to phone you?" he said.

"You have to keep trying. I never know when I'll be in my dressing-room or on the set." She looked at him, standing with his hand on the doorknob.

"What are you thinking?" he said.

"Wondering," she said. "But not really wondering. I know."

"So do I," he said.

"Left, and then straight down the hall," she said.

She heard the taxi pulling away. She reached out her hand to the table beside her bed and picked up a typescript, opened it to the next day's scene. "No," she said aloud and replaced the script and turned out the light.

At half past five the next morning she left her house, went down Sunset Boulevard, turned in at Beverly Glen and across to Pico and from Pico to Motor Avenue. She slowed down when she came to Marshall Place. She turned right and moved along in second gear. His car was at the curb. The left door and the running board had been given quite a banging. She looked up at the second-story windows. Two of them were wide open. His bedroom, without a doubt. He was sleeping there, and without a doubt he was sleeping heavily. If she tooted her horn she would wake up the whole neighborhood. She did not mind waking up the whole neighborhood, but it would be cruel mean to wake him. And so she kept going, through Marshall Place to the other end where it led into Motor Avenue, and ten minutes later she was on the Metro lot.

The early workers were already at their tasks and Natica Jackson was soon at hers, which began with the arrival of the young man from Makeup. "Somebody didn't get enough sleep last night," he said.

"You're so clever," said Natica.

"Oh, it's not bad," he said. "Not hopelessly bad. You're young. Not like some of these hags I have to bring to life again. Actually I love to work on you, Miss Jackson, especially around your eyes. But get your eight hours, always try to get your eight hours. And here's some of those drops for when you start shooting. Remember now, don't put them in your eyes till you're ready to shoot, and use them sparingly. They're very strong, and I don't want you to get used to them." He prattled on, and his prattling and professional ministrations returned her to her movie-actress world, and she stayed there all day. Lunch was brought to her in her dressing-room. She read the gossip columns in the newspapers and the trade papers. She was visited by a man who owned a chain of theaters in New England, who was being given a tour of the studio. He wanted her *personal* autograph and not just one of those printed things that meant nothing. She asked him if he would care for a sandwich or something, but he thanked her and said he was having lunch with William Powell and Myrna Loy. She resumed eating her lunch and was interrupted by a girl from Publicity who wanted her to give an interview to the Hollywood correspondent of some paper in Madrid. "Don't do it if you don't feel like it," said the publicity girl. "But if you do, make sure you don't get alone with him. He's a knee-grabber." A stout man with a cigar tapped twice on her screendoor and pushed it open. "May I come in? Jason Margold, from New York City. I see you're eating your lunch," he said. "Would you rather I came back in ten-fifteen minutes?"

"Who did you say you were?"

"Jason Margold, from New York City. But I don' wanna disturb you while you're— I see you got a preference for cottage cheese. You know what's good with cottage cheese? Try a little Major Grey's chutney."

"What's this all about? Who are you?"

"My card," he said. "My business card."

She read it aloud. "Jason Margold, vice-president, Novelty Creations, New York, London, Paris. So what?"

He removed the day's newspapers from a folding chair, placed them on the floor, and seated himself. "You mind the cigah?"

"Quit stalling around, will you?" she said.

"I won't take but a minute of your time, Miss Jackson," he said. "It jus' happened I said to Jerry Lockman, I said who in his opinion was the real coming star on the Metro-Goldwyn lot."

"Oh, you know Jerry Lockman?"

"Jerry jus' happens to be my brother-in-law, once-removed. His sister, the former Sylvia Lockman, is married to George Stern. George used to be married to my sister Evie till she passed away of heart trouble several years ago."

"And?"

"So I asked Jerry, who was the young star that they were banking on the most here at Metro-Goldwyn. And without a moment's hesitation he named you. Miss Natica Jackson. So I said right away I wanted to have this talk with you for the purpose of sounding you out on this excellent proposition whereby, whereby we could work this out to our mutual advantage and profit."

"Is this a tie-in?"

"Well, you might call it a tie-in, but tie-in usually means a product gets tied in to a certain motion picture and like they run your picture in the ads and the actress never gets a nickel out of it, only the publicity for the motion picture. We'd be willing to pay you a royalty on every item we sold bearing your name."

"What is the item? A pessary?"

"Huh?"

"You're so God damn mysterious, I thought you didn't want to come out and say what it was."

"Well, it isn't anything like what you mentioned, Miss Jackson. It's an item of hand luggage that we expect to sell up in the millions."

"If I got five cents on every pessary I'd make a lot of money, too. The Natica Jackson pessary."

"You got a sense of humor, I'll give you that," he said.

"I need it, in this business," said Natica. "Just a sec'." She dialed a number on the intra-studio telephone. "Me speak to Mr. Lockman. It's Natica Jackson."

"You checking on me?" said Margold.

"Hello, Jerry? This is my lunch-hour and I'm supposed to get some rest. What the hell do you mean sending some jerk relation of yours to my dressing-room? Come and get him out of here before I call the studio cops. That's *all.*" She hung up daintily.

"Now*way*da minute. Why did you have to go and do that?" said Margold.

"Miss Garbo's dressing-room is down the way. Try *her,*" said Natica Jackson.

"You din even listen to my proposition," said Margold.

"Screw, bum," she said. "Take a powder."

Margold left. It was fun to have Jerry Lockman in such an embarrassed position. She could imagine how he was stewing now, for fear that she would tell other executives about his brother-in-law once-removed. Let him stew. Let him roast in hell.

"The car's downstairs," said her maid.

It was an elderly Cadillac limousine, to take her to the back lot. "You ready to go? You got everything?" said Natica.

"I think I got everything," said the maid. "Two packs of Philip Morris, makeup box, your mules, two packs of Beech-Nut gum."

"Do you have the eye drops?"

"In the makeup box."

"We're off," said Natica. She was in a bathing suit and a bathrobe, ready for the scene on the back lot, in which she was to drive a motorboat a distance of forty feet. The scene had originally been written to take place in a diner, but it had been changed to give her an opportunity to wear the bathing suit. They had shot the scene five times that morning and it had never been right. They were afraid to expose her to the sun for more than a few minutes at a time. The last thing they wanted was for her to acquire a natural sunburn that would not match her body makeup. The shooting schedule called for a ballroom scene the next day, and two hundred extras had been hired for it, but if the fair skin of Natica Jackson was reddened by the sun in the motorboat scene, they would have to shoot around her. Moreover, the natural light changed at three o'clock in the afternoon, and if they didn't get the motorboat scene right before three they would have to come back and shoot it again sometime. The complications had nothing to do with acting, but Natica was used to that. Acting was the last thing you did after everything else was ready, and you did that for two minutes at a time. Then they glued those two minutes together until they had eighty minutes that made sense—and then they put you in another picture. She could not understand how people got an impression of you from this collection of two-minute, one-minute, thirty-second snatches, but they did, and if they liked you that was all that mattered. Of all the girls she had known in Santa Ana she was the only one who could say, "I'm going to get a new LaSalle," at eleven o'clock at night and be sure that it would be delivered to her the next afternoon. She was certainly the only Santa Ana girl who had been kissed by Robert Taylor, and Garbo had smiled at her. Life was funny.

They did the motorboat scene three times while the light was still right. The director rode back to Natica's dressing-room with her. "I think the second take'll be the one, but I won't know till I see the dailies," said the director. "Let me have a look at your nose."

"It feels all right," said Natica.

"Yeah, it looks all right," said the director. His name was Reggie Broderick and he had grown up in the business. He spoke the jargons of the camera and lighting crews, he knew or could improvise sight gags that were not in the script, and he loved to direct motion pictures. He was not quite an artist, but his pictures always displayed ironic touches that other directors admired. "You got a new fellow, Natica?" he said.

"Maybe," she said. "Why?"

"Maybe, meaning you're not sure he's going to be your fellow?" said Reggie Broderick.

"Something like that," she said.

"Well, that's all right," said Reggie. "But send him home early, in time to get your eight hours. It's a good thing we didn't have any close-ups today, or you'd have been a total loss."

"I'm sorry," she said.

"No harm done, but tonight go to bed early."

"Was it my eyes?" she said.

"It wasn't only your eyes. You went around all day with your buttons showing."

"My buttons? In a bathing suit?"

"Your nipples, dear," he said. "You were a woman fulfilled, today. You can hardly wait to get back to this guy, whoever he is. Which is all right, as long as you get your sleep."

"I never even thought about him, all day," she said.

"Subconsciously you never thought of anything else," he said.

"Well, maybe you have something there," she said.

"We only have twelve more days on this picture, kid. As a favor to me will you postpone any emotional crisis? Only twelve more days."

"You know what I said to him last night?" she said.

"No, I can't even *guess* what you said to him last night."

"We were talking about marriage—he's married. And I said the only kind of a guy that I ought to marry is a director. I wouldn't think of marrying an actor, and the only person I could think of marrying was a director."

"Well, I tell you what you do. You finish this picture for me and I'll marry you. Unless you had some other director in mind."

"I didn't even have *you* in mind," she said.

"I must be losing my grip," he said.

"You never showed any interest, that way," she said.

"That's because this is our first picture together," he said. "The next time we do one, I'll see to it that we have a couple weeks on location. Where would you like to go? Don't say Catalina. That's too near. How about the High Sierras?"

"Why does it have to be on location?"

"Because I have to go home at night otherwise," he said.

"Oh, this wasn't going to be marriage," she said.

"I thought we got away from marriage," he said.

"I'm back to it," she said. "I think you ought to marry me and see that I get to bed early."

"Or vice versa. But meanwhile what about this guy that kept you up last night? What do we do about him?"

"That's going to be a problem," she said.

"Who is he? Can you tell me? I'm not butting in, but you went serious on me all of a sudden. How is he going to be a problem?"

"I guess I *was* thinking about him all day, subconsciously. I expected him to phone me, and he didn't," she said.

"He might have phoned while there was nobody here," he said.

She shook her head. "I expected him to keep trying. I was here all during the lunch break, and my phone never rang. And we've been sitting here over half an hour."

"And there's some reason why you can't phone him," he said.

"I told him I wouldn't. That he had to phone me. I don't even know his number. I know where to reach him, but I told him I wasn't going to try, that it was up to him."

"Are you going to sit here all evening in case he does phone? I don't think that's such a good idea."

"No, if he hasn't phoned me by this time, he isn't going to," she said.

"How would you like to come home and take pot-luck with the Brodericks? Mona's a great fan of yours. If you don't mind eating dinner with two small boys, aged seven and ten."

"I can't figure you, Reggie," she said. "Are you a family man, or aren't you?"

"I'm a family man," he said.

"And a Catholic, I guess, with that name."

"A family man and a Catholic," he said. "But I've had some things to tell in confession. And not just eating meat on Friday."

"Then why didn't you go for me?"

"I don't always go for the girls in my pictures. Not even most of the time. Very seldom, in fact. It interferes with the work, and this is my job."

"But you like me. I can tell that. You've been nicer to me than any director I ever worked with," she said.

"Yes, I like you. I asked to do this picture, you know. They had me down for something else, but I wanted to work with you."

"Who was in the other picture?" she said.

"A prima donna. Somebody I never worked with, but I heard all about her from another director. And *she* wanted *me*. The studio got a little tough when I said I wanted to do this picture and not hers. They would have put me on suspension if they hadn't been afraid of the bad publicity. Not the bad publicity for me. They didn't give a damn about that. But it would have got out that I preferred working with you, and that would have given her a black eye. So they told her I was off on one of my benders and wouldn't be in shape by the starting date of her picture."

"Were you off on a bender?"

"No, but I'd have gone on one," he said.

"Why did you want to work with me?"

"Because so far all they've done is photograph you. I looked at every picture you ever made, including one dog you made at Warner's."

"And was that ever a dog!" she said.

"Then I saw you in a dumb musical they made here, and a comedy Jerry Lockman produced. You used to be his girl."

"Yes."

"I can well understand why you gave him the air. They've never known what to do with you around here. This picture we're doing now. It isn't the greatest thing in the world for you, but I've made a good try with it. It's a common-ordinary program picture that'll make some money, but the pleasure I get out of it is what it'll do for you, and therefore for me. You're going to be surprised when you see this picture. How much have you seen?"

"Most of the footage that I'm in, but that's all," she said.

"Well, there's a lot more to the picture than that. By this time I can pretty well visualize the whole thing, the final cut. From now on you can figure to be in pictures the rest of your life. You have a career."

"I thought I *had* a career," she said.

"Two years? Three years? You'd be surprised how many women had two or three years at a big studio, and then disappeared. I don't mean disappeared to Republic. I mean disappeared entirely. And you never quite know why. They brought a girl out from New York. She was beautiful, she could act. She'd been a hit in two big plays on Broadway, and they signed her to a contract that was something fantastic. Five thousand a week. They gave her a deal that was absolutely unheard of for somebody that'd never been before a camera, but they wanted her. Do you know where she is now? She's back in New York, living in a hotel and waiting for Hollywood to come to their senses. She was in exactly two pictures. The first one was one of the most expensive pictures they ever made here. The story costs alone amounted to over two hundred thousand dollars. A top director. An expensive cast. The works. And it wasn't bad. It really wasn't a bad picture. But nobody went to see it. The people didn't care whether this girl had a Broadway reputation, or how many writers worked on the picture. They couldn't knock her looks. She photographed beautifully, and she had a good voice. *I* couldn't figure out why the picture laid such an egg. Then I happened to be in New York about a year ago and I was having lunch at the Algonquin and this girl came in. I never knew her when she was in pictures, and I asked the guy I was having lunch with what she was doing. The guy was a playwright, knew all the Broadway crowd, and when I asked him about this dame he said—as if I was supposed to know—he said she had a new girl friend. She was a Lez. I'd never known that, and I don't think most people in Hollywood knew it. But do you know who did know it? Those people that pay to go to see movies. Most of them have never heard of the word Lesbian. Wouldn't know what I was talking about if I said some actress was a Lez. But they knew something was wrong, something was missing. Some warmth that wasn't there. As soon as I got back to the Coast I ran that picture, and there it was. But only after I'd been told. I called up the director, a friend of mine, and asked him about this dame. I put it to him straight. Did he know she was a Lez when he was working with her? He said no, never suspected it for one minute. He knew there was something lacking, but he blamed himself. He never knew about her till after she washed up in pictures, and then some New York actress told him."

"You should have asked me," said Natica.

"You know who I'm talking about?"

"Sure. Elysia Tisbury."

"Now how did you know? A high school kid from Santa Ana?"

"My feminine instinct," said Natica.

"No, I won't buy that. No."

"Well, I was given a hint," said Natica. "She used to go out with Alan Hildred."

"Oh, your English boy friend. So she did. So she did."

"But that doesn't mean I'm that way," said Natica.

"You know, if I ever found out that you were, I think I'd start wondering about myself," he said. "You're about the last person in the world I'd ever think that about."

"Ooh, but when I get to be a big star," she said.

"You're planning to turn Lez?"

"I'm thinking of it," she said. "Alan says I'm terribly unsophisticated."

"Well, he's not."

"I know. He tries to sophisticate me."

"A guy like that could sophisticate you right out of pictures. Or would, if you didn't have so much common sense."

"Well, I'll say this for Alan. He's fun to *be* with. Not all the time. But I never knew anybody like him in Santa Ana. There *isn't* anybody like him in Santa Ana."

"There aren't very many like him in Hollywood," he said.

"You don't like him, but you're not a woman. If I was just one of those girls I went to high school with, I never would have understood a person like Alan. All they ever wanted was to marry a boy that had a father that owned a bank or something. That wasn't what I wanted. I wasn't even sure what I did want till I got this offer from Hollywood. Then I knew what I wanted, all right."

"What?"

"To have every big star know who I was," she said. "Not for me to know every big star. But every big star to know me."

"Well, they just about do," he said.

"G.G. spoke to me one day. Not exactly spoke to me, but nodded her head and smiled. I think she knows me now."

"All right. What's next?"

"To have my name in lights on the Statue of Liberty."

"That seems reasonable enough," he said. "Then what?"

"After that? Well, maybe a statue of me there."

"That'll probably happen. The Goddess of Liberty doesn't look very American, and you do. After that, what?"

"You know Joan of Arc?"

"Not personally."

"I'd like to be something like her," she said.

"You don't want to be barbecued."

"No, I guess I wouldn't go for that part. Who were some of the other famous women?"

"Cleopatra, but she got a snake to bite her right on the teat."

"No. Who else? Queen Elizabeth."

"Too late. She was known as the virgin queen."

"Do you think she really was? How old was she?"

"You can forget her. She wasn't very pretty. Mata Hari, but she got shot."

"It'd be fun to be a spy, but if I was famous I couldn't be a very good spy. They all seem to get in some jam. Martha Washington, but they only know about her through George."

"And Lincoln's wife went off her rocker," he said.

"My big trouble is, I'm not very glamorous. You can be famous without being glamorous. I'm pretty famous now, I guess, but people think they know all about me. America's niece, is what Alan calls me."

"You'll be more than that when we finish this picture."

"But not glamorous."

"No, but not all sweetness and light, for a change. The sexiest shot of you, you're wearing that housedress. I hope it gets by."

"I know which one that is. That was what you had the wind-machine for. Where I'm standing on the roof."

"That's the one. Better than a skin-tight bathing suit. You should have heard them in the projection room when they saw that shot."

"What did they say?"

"They said, 'Wow!' And they meant every word of it," he said. "Tomorrow they'll see you in a bathing suit and it won't mean a thing. But in that housedress, with the wind against you, you might as well have been soaking wet. But at the Hays Office they watch out for dames in soaking-wet dresses. This way I may sneak it by them."

"Was Jerry Lockman at the rushes?"

"Jerry Lockman? Jerry Lockman, the way he stands now, couldn't get in a projection room if he paid admission. You don't keep up with your old boy friends. I hear they offered him the job of producing travelogs, and if he's smart he'll take it. They've gone sour on him."

"Oh, dear. Why?"

"You never know the real reason."

"Maybe the public found out that he's a Lez," she said.

"You may be kidding, but the things that turn the big shots against a man make just about as much sense. You and I, what they call the talent people, we tend to overlook the fact that our jealousies are nothing compared to what goes on among the big shots. Now Jerry Lockman, for instance. He more or less discovered you, with a little help from Morris King. So Jerry was instrumental in helping your career. Fine. But there are fifteen other supervisors on the lot that *didn't* discover you. Every single one of them thinks that's a black mark against *him.* So there are fifteen supervisors, or associate producers, or whatever they want to call themselves, that automatically hate Jerry. One of them happens to be Joe Gelber, the man that's producing our picture. He particularly hates Jerry because you were Jerry's discovery, so Joe has to go after Jerry hammer and tongs. Joe absolutely has to see to it that Jerry gets none of the credit if our picture turns out well. Which it will, don't worry about that. It'll make nice money. But Jerry Lockman mustn't be able to claim that he had even a tiny pinch of the credit for you. For the last six months, ever since Joe Gelber was assigned to this picture, he's had to put the knock on Jerry Lockman. Not only where you're concerned, but in every direction you can think of. I've heard him. He'll make fun of his clothes. Drops little jokes about his sex life. I heard him say it was very odd, very strange that Jerry went abroad on the *Europa* a couple years ago."

"What's wrong with that? I remember that," said Natica.

"The *Europa*? That's one of Hitler's boats. In case you're thinking of taking a trip abroad, young lady, don't book passage on the *Europa* or the *Bremen.* Not while you're under contract here. Hitler isn't very popular in Hollywood."

"Oh, *Hitler.* He's against the Jews," said Natica.

"Hitler's against the Jews, that's right."

"But Jerry's a Jew," she said.

"Sure he is. But what kind of a Jew will travel in a boat owned by Hitler? Every opportunity Joe gets, he puts the rap on Jerry. And when a guy like Joe Gelber goes to work on somebody, he never loses his temper or says things that aren't true. He'll point out a hundred little faults that nobody ever noticed before, or that never bothered anybody. Jerry Lockman's neckties are no worse than L. B.

Mayer's. But if you keep hammering away, calling attention to any man's shortcomings, you can finally get somewhere. And Joe Gelber has finally done a job on Jerry Lockman."

"Isn't it childish?"

"Yes. Childish and vicious. And it's exactly what Jerry would have done to Joe Gelber if he'd had the chance."

"You bet he would," said Natica. "A phony intellectual is what Jerry used to call him."

"If there's anything intellectual about Joe Gelber, it sure is phony."

"I wouldn't know," she said. "He has all those books in his office. I wondered when he got time to read them, but I didn't say anything."

"Well, he's on my side now. And yours. By the way, why did you ask me if Jerry was at the rushes?"

"I was wondering what he'd say when they all said 'Wow.' He would have been the only one that knew what was underneath that dress."

"Would you care what he said?"

She hesitated. "I guess I wouldn't," she said. "Not any more. A few years ago I would have. But you know I discovered something. When a man and a woman have something peculiar about their sex life, people always laugh at the man. They make fun of the man, but not of the woman. Have you ever noticed that?"

"I never thought of it before, but you may be right."

"Do you know why that is?" she said.

"No. I'd have to think about it."

"It's because men aren't supposed to be that much interested in sex. They should be more busy with their work and stuff. Sex is all right for women, but men ought to have it and forget about it."

"To rise supremely above it?" he said.

"I'm serious! A man that thinks about sex all the time, like Jerry, or Alan Hildred, I think he ought to have something else to think about."

"You're just restating an old poetic theory. 'Man's love is of his life a thing apart, 'tis woman's whole existence.' "

"Yes, we had that in high school," she said. "But look at the way a woman is constructed. She's built for sex. And a man—well, a man only partly. You never saw anybody put a brazeer on a man. Except at a drag. And even a drag! What do they do at a drag? They dress up like women."

"Do you really like sex, Natica?"

"I love it, but I'm a woman. I don't think men ought to like it so much. And yet every man I ever slept with does. Except that son of a bitch that didn't call me all day. Never gave me a jingle. And I know why. I was the one that made the first pass."

"Make a pass at *me,* dear heart, and *I'll* phone you tomorrow," he said.

"You know, I almost would. If we were at my house I would, but not here. Even in Jerry's office, when he'd lock the door and shut off the phone, I never felt right about it." She looked around her dressing-room, and shook her head. "Just a lousy chaise-lounge."

"For purity," he said. "Well, how about coming home and having dinner with us?"

"I just remembered. I'm supposed to have a brand-new LaSalle waiting for me." She dialed a studio number. "This is Miss Jackson. Natica Jackson. Do you have a car there for me? You have? How does it look? Does it have white-walls? Fine. Thank you. Okey-doke." She hung up.

"It's there?" he said.

"It's been there since early this afternoon. I'm glad. I loved my Packard, but I'm glad I don't have to see it again. Once I make up my mind to get rid of a thing, I don't care to see it any more. I wish I could be the same way about people."

"Who says you're not?" he said.

"It's not as easy with people," she said. "I'll give you the first ride in my new car."

"And have dinner with us?"

"I'd love to," she said.

"Let me call Transportation and I'll have somebody drive my car home, and maybe I ought to tell Mona you're coming. She won't want to have her hair up in curlers when you arrive."

"I won't mind."

"A figure of speech. I've never seen her hair up in curlers."

On the walk to the parking lot she was always half a step ahead of him. They admired the new car from all sides, and the parking attendant showed her the starting and lighting controls.

"Well, off we go," she said. Darkness had come.

She was a good driver and was taking pleasure in her new car. "Your new pony cart," he said.

"I never had one," she said.

"Hey! Straight ahead," he said. "Pico is straight ahead."

"This is Marshall Place, where I had my accident yesterday," she said. She had slowed down.

"Oh."

"He lives at Number 88. There, on the right. And there's his car. See the door, where I hit him? House all lit up. Maybe his wife came home unexpectedly. And maybe I'm just making excuses for him." She blew her horn, held her hand on the button, and drove away. "Well, so long to you, Mr. Hal Graham."

"He isn't one of our people," said Reggie Broderick. "Don't lose any sleep over him."

"Oh, you just don't want me to lose any sleep," she said.

They went to Broderick's house in Beverly Hills, and she was affable. The Broderick sons were delighted with her, the Broderick wife—after one hard look—was friendly. Natica gave the boys a ride in her new car (they chose to sit in the rumble seat), and when she brought them home again she did not get out of the car. She said goodnight to all the Brodericks and went home to Bel-Air. She lay in her warm, perfumed bath and wondered what the hell.

They finished the picture a day ahead of schedule, and Natica went away with Alan Hildred, to a borrowed cottage at a place called San Juan Capistrano. The water was too cold for her to swim in but Alan went in three or four times a day. They observed silences. He would take a pipe and a book and be self-sufficient until mealtime, sitting in the sand close enough to hear her if she called him. She slept late every morning, had breakfast of orange juice, toast and coffee; read the newspapers until lunchtime. After lunch she would read magazines and detective stories until sleep overtook her. She would nap for an hour, have coffee, and do some telephoning and letter-writing, and then it would be time for cocktails. He would have five, she would have two Martinis, and then dinner. The owners of the house, California friends of Alan's, had left behind an assortment of phonograph records as heterogeneous as the books on the shelves. Some good, some bad, and some cracked. At eleven o'clock, never later, she would go to bed and Alan would come in and make love to her, and for her it was a combination of sensation and detached remote observation. So it went for four days, as pleasant a stretch of time as she had ever known. On the fifth afternoon she went out and lay, belly-down, on the sand beside him. "Do you want to go home?" she said.

He took the pipe out of his mouth. "I suppose it's time we were thinking about it. Are you getting restless?"

"I could stay here forever, just like this," she said.

"Oh, really? I know *I* couldn't. I've got to think about making some money. So have you, for that matter. Don't they expect you for fittings next week?"

"Tuesday," she said. "Oh, I'm not kidding myself. I'm not rich enough to stop working, and wouldn't want to anyhow. But I've been so relaxed, Alan. That was you. I never knew anybody that was so relaxing. You can just sit and read, and smoke your pipe, off by yourself, and be perfectly content."

"You didn't know that side of me," he said.

"How would I? I guess I never knew you till now," she said. "Were you ever married, Alan?"

"Oh, yes."

"You never mentioned your wife. I just took for granted you were always a bachelor."

"Oh, no, I had a wife. Would you like to hear about it?"

"I'm dying to," she said.

"Well, it isn't much of a story, actually," he said. He sat cross-legged, tailor-fashion, and ran sand through his hands. "I'm older than you think."

"I was sure you were older than you look."

"Mm, thanks. I'm thirty-seven."

"You had to be, to've been to all the places you've been to," she said.

"Well, in some of them I didn't stop very long." He laughed. "In one place they wouldn't even let me land. Apparently my reputation had preceded me."

"What were you then? Were you a writer then, too?"

"Not, uh, recognized as such. I'd written a very bad novel, but I believe it stopped selling at two hundred copies. It was reviewed in a Yorkshire paper, and a pal of mine mentioned it in *Sketch*. No, I wasn't a writer. Various other things, but not a writer. Odd jobs, some of them very odd indeed."

"How did you meet your wife?"

"That was just after the war. I'd been in it, and I was still wearing His Majesty's uniform. I had a week or two to go before I was required to get back into cits, and I took every advantage of that situation. There were a great many parties in London, and crashing them wasn't at all difficult. I was, let me see, twenty-two. Been to a *fairly* good public school. Had two pips on my shoulder straps, and I'd acquired the M.C., the Military Cross. By purchase. It made all the difference, you know. No one asked how I got it, but they'd look at the ribbon and nod approvingly and *compel* me to drink some more champagne. It was too good to last, and I was only too well aware of that fact. Consequently, when I was introduced to Miss Nellie Ridgeway, the soubrette, who'd just been divorced from one of our more solvent bookmakers, I confessed to an undying devotion to her. There was some truth to that. I'd seen her in one or two shows, and I remembered one of her best songs. 'You and I in Love,' it was called. She was forty. Or she may have been forty-two. Perhaps a trifle thick through the middle, and not too firm up above, but the legs were good. Well, she consented to be my bride. Her money was unfortunately tied up in real estate holdings, not easily converted to cash, and I had one hell of a time getting my hands on any of it. She gave me ten quid a week, pocket money, but out of that I had to pay her cab fares and odds and ends, and she was extremely disagreeable because she didn't have a show that season and was having to spend her non-theatrical income. Actually, she was quite a chiseler, as so many actresses are apt to be. Always economizing on food and drink unless it was for show. A great one for professional discounts, too, and my tailor didn't give professional discounts."

"Was she good in the hay?"

"In a word, no. But insatiable. Stingy women are apt to be, I've found."

"So you divorced her."

"I left her. I took a few things. Her best gewgaws were locked up in a safe to which I didn't have the combination, but I realized about a thousand pounds on cigarette cases and vanities and that sort of thing, and off I went. I left a note, saying I was going to Scotland to try to think things out and do some writing, and she'd hear from me soon. That gave me time to board a rusty old tub that was bound for South Africa. Very astute of me. Naturally she didn't quite believe the Scotland story, but expected me to head straight for the French Riviera. I wasn't the tramp steamer type, and certainly not the South Africa type. I was one of the Mayfair boys, or so she thought. I'd never given her any reason to think otherwise."

"How long were you married?"

"How long did we live together? Less than a year. We were never divorced. She died while I was on tour with the Miller Brothers-101 Ranch Circus. I read about it in the newspapers."

"What were you doing with the circus?"

"I was a Cossack."

"Could you ride?"

"Of course I could ride. I could do all those things. My father was a very keen sportsman, and as I was the only son amongst five daughters, I had a vigorous boyhood. Riding. Boxing. Shooting.

Fishing. Not to mention the defense of my chastity against the on-slaughts of the elder sisters. A nasty pair, they were. The English public school has a lot to answer for, but the upper middle-class English home such as mine, with five daughters and one rather pretty son—between the two I'll take the public school. It's possible to buy off an older boy with money or sweets, but two predatory older sisters are unbribable."

"Oh, well that's not just England. There was a girl on our street that had her little brother a nervous wreck, and her parents never caught on. Did you ever get married again?"

"No. The other side of me, that you've seen these past few days, has kept me from marriage or any similar involvement. I must have my privacy."

"Is that the way you pronounce it? You make it sound like an outdoor toilet. A Chic Sales. I say pry-vacy."

"Very well."

"What would you think of marrying me?" she said.

"Is that a proposal of marriage? I'd like you to state it more un-equivocally."

"You mean lay it on the line? All right. Would you marry me?"

"Thank you very much, but no," he said. "I only wanted you to say it so it could go in my memoirs. October the somethingth, 1934. Received proposal of marriage from lovely young movie star. Why would you want to marry me, Natica? You know I've pimped and buggered my way around the world all these years. I know you're a lonesome kid, dissatisfied. But don't for heaven's sake get yourself into anything like that."

"If I didn't like it, I could get out of it," she said.

He lit a cigarette. "May I offer two bits' worth of advice?"

"Sure," she said.

"Don't marry before you're fifty," he said.

"*Fifty?*"

"Take lovers, and make a lot of money, but don't marry. It'll only complicate your life, and it isn't as if you had to prove some-thing by getting a husband. That presents no problem."

"You're wrong. No one ever asked me to marry him."

"Well, that's a quibble, isn't it? You could have a husband if you liked. These few days down here have been very pleasant for both of us. But they're only a holiday, and you can take a holiday when you feel like. Not always in such charming company, it's true, but the charming company can also be very difficult." He looked away. "I might bring a friend home with me. And he might be hard to get rid of. That *has* happened, you know."

"Oh."

"I can't help it, Natica," he said. "I seem to have a limited capacity for feminine companionship, and then I turn to someone of my own sex. Isn't that putting it delicately?"

"You get tired of girls, and then you go for the boys," she said.

"I was afraid you might have put it more crudely, but I should have known better," he said. "You don't seem to mind."

"I never said I didn't mind, but it was sort of none of my business."

"Well, of course it wasn't, was it?" he said. "The Kings, or at least Ernestine King, made it worth my while to officiate as your gentleman-in-waiting. Unhappily, as I made more money, I spent more. Old friends turned up that I hadn't seen in years. One of them came to stay, or so he thought."

"How did you get rid of him? How do you get rid of people like that?"

"In this case, I took him for a ride. A modification of the Chicago gangster method. We drove up beyond Oxnard and I stopped the car on the roadside. It was late evening, and I daresay I'd given him the impression that I had romantic notions. But I got out of the car and pulled him out, and my old boxing lessons stood me in good stead."

"You beat him?"

"Unmercifully," he said. "A boy for whom I'd once had a feeling of real tenderness. I couldn't stop punishing him. When he could no longer stand up, I gave him my boot. I left him there. What ugliness."

"Well, I guess he asked for it," she said.

"Oh, yes," he said. "He was no rose."

"That's another side of you I never saw," she said.

"And I hope you never do." He got to his feet and peeled off his sweatshirt. He was a slender man, with overdeveloped biceps and forearms that seemed to have been attached to the wrong torso. He walked slowly to the water and stood at knee depth, and when he was good and ready he dived in and swam out a long distance. She had seen him do that before, and the first time she was frightened, but when he returned, and she told him he had scared her, he had only smiled and said, "That's one thing I *can* do, my dear." Now she could see him, doing the dead man's float, and she was not worried about his ability to get back. But she knew with sudden clarity that one day—and it could be soon—he would not want to come back. He was—what was he? Thirty-seven—and ageless. He got older, because we all get older by the day, but he already spoke of his life, the events of his life, as though they had no relation to the present. An end had been put to his life, and the thing that had put an end to it was not an occurrence, a nasty event or a tragic occurrence, but simply the exhaustion of his will to live. She had never known anyone who caused her to think such thoughts. Everyone else spoke of things to come, for them, for her. But for Alan Hildred she had always been dimly aware that it was all over, and that she had forced or demanded the continuation of his existence. She had often put him aside, but she had always picked up with him again, and during this stretch of peace she had reached a state that she wanted to prolong by a marriage that could only be prolonged under precisely the conditions of these five days. If, this minute, he came out of the water and said he would marry her, she would go through with it. But the man floating in the troughs of the waves was going to stay there. He had tried to tell her that he was empty of desire for her, and it did not really matter now where he went next. She would let him go, and she would not ask him to come back.

She rose from the sand and returned to the house and took a bath. She put on a suit of lounging pajamas and went to the sitting-room, and presently he appeared, dressed in his blue blazer and slacks and rope-soled espadrilles. He had a scarf at his neck.

"Martini time?" he said.

"Sure," she said.

"It's a bit early, but the gin may warm me up," he said. "Besides, I have a rather important announcement to make."

"What's that?" she said.

"I'm leaving Hollywood," he said. He stirred the drinks and poured them.

"For good?"

"If you mean permanently, yes." He sipped his drink and obviously he was in a good mood. "I arrived here, in Hollywood, with something under two hundred dollars. I'm leaving with just under twenty thousand. I call that a successful sojourn, especially as the money was paid me for services rendered. Nothing illegal about it. They gave me twenty-five thousand apiece for the stories they bought for you, and they paid me to work on the scenarios. But it isn't going to last forever, is it? I imagine I could find someone a great deal less attractive than you to squire about, but you've spoiled me for the Nellie Ridgeway types. And I'm afraid the time has come when you're ready to give me my walking papers."

"What made you think that?"

"Your proposal of marriage, oddly enough. As I was lying out there in the deep blue sea, I asked myself what was behind your proposal. The good time we've had this week, obviously. But you've got to be back in town Tuesday next, and this relationship will never again seem as pleasant to you as it's been here. You had a premonition of that, too. I'm very happy to've made you at all happy, Natica, and in these four or five days I have given you some happiness, if that's not too big a word."

"Yes, you have," she said.

"Then forgive me if I desert you before you give me the air," he said.

"All right," she said. "You're under no obligations to me."

"Sensible girl," he said. "Extraordinarily sensible girl."

"Where will you go?"

"Sensible girl, asks the sensible question, too. I'm going home to England. I've been naughty, but my peccadillos have been committed in far-off lands. There's no one back home who's apt to turn me in for stealing Miss Ridgeway's gold lighters and ivory cigarette holders."

"And what will you do there?"

"Oh, we have a film industry in England, too, you know. And I have several imposing screen credits on Natica Jackson pictures. I shouldn't have too much trouble finding gainful, legitimate employment. And it's fifteen years since I've been home."

"Have you missed it?"

"Not in the beginning. But I don't want to die out here."

"Are you planning to die in England?" she said.

"Yes," he said. "And planning to is the word. My father cut me off when I married Miss Ridgeway, and all I'll have is the money I take back with me. I can live on that reasonably comfortably for four years without working in the films, without doing a tap. But I'm not going home to scrounge around or work as a dustman. I shall live at a certain scale, and when my money runs out, I'll shoot myself. Nothing terribly dramatic about that. Life isn't very dear to me anyhow. Look at mine. Look at me. Look what it's always been, and now I'm thirty-seven. Life has had its chance to be attractive to me, and I say it's failed dismally."

"I don't know whether you're joking or not," she said.

"I believe you know I'm *not* joking," he said. "I wish I could make love to you now, Natica, and have it mean much more than it ever has. But unfortunately all passion's spent. Will you accept that rather tired bouquet?"

"I accept it," she said.

"Will you also forgive me if I nip off first thing in the morning?"

"In whose car? You can't have mine."

"I'll hire one."

"I guess I might as well go too," she said. "I wouldn't want to stay here by myself."

"Splendid. Then let's get an early start, shall we?"

"Okay by me," she said.

They had dinner, and he drank more than usual. He finished the batch of Martinis, had sherry with his soup, and a Mexican red wine with his steak. He put a bottle of cognac at his side while he had coffee, and she saw that he was determined to get drunk. "I'm going to bed if we're getting up early," she said. "Did you tell Manuel we were leaving in the morning?"

"He's heartbroken," said Alan. "Rita's heartbroken, too, but not as much so as Manuel. He hopes we will come back many times and stay longer."

"Will you tip them in the morning?"

"Whatever you wish, my dear. I suggest twenty dollars, ten apiece."

"I'll give it to you in the morning," she said. "Goodnight."

In the morning her car was gone. Alan was gone, but his clothes had not been packed. She telephoned Morris King and had him send a Tanner Cadillac for her. When she arrived at Bel-Air her brand-new LaSalle was parked in her driveway, without a scratch on it. But she never knew what Alan did with her car in the meanwhile. She never heard another word from him, ever, and neither did anyone else in picture business.

"I could fix it so he'd never get work at Gaumont-British," said Morris King.

"Why would you want to do that?" said Natica.

"I thought maybe you'd want me to," said Morris.

"What did he do to me? I wouldn't want to keep anyone out of a job."

"Well, he sort of humiliated you," said Morris.

"I think you got that idea from Ernestine," said Natica. "He sort of humiliated her, because he didn't turn out right. But I have nothing against him."

"Then okay, we'll forget about him," said Morris. "You go in Tuesday for fittings, right?"

"Right," she said.

"I worked them for a $5,000 bonus," said Morris.

"You did? Good for you, Morris."

"And it's all yours. No commission. That make you feel better?"

"Five hundred dollars better," she said.

"Buy yourself something nice with it, with my compliments. You can consider it my bonus for being a good girl. However, Natica, you gotta be ready to go on suspension after the next picture."

"I do? Why?"

"Because when this one's in the can, then I'm going after a new ticket. Tear up the present contract and write a new one for you. This they will not do without some cries of anguish, including they'll put you on suspension. They gotta do that, Natica. The suspension gimmick is something a studio gotta do to keep people in line. Not you, so much as other people. They'll make it look like it's costing you a lot of money to turn down your next picture, but you'll get the money back in the long grun. That'll be taken care of. But I'm just forewarning gyou now, that this picture you work as hard as you ever worked in your whole life. Give them no cause for complaint, you see what I mean. Then they come around with a picture to follow this one and down we turn it. Flat. They turn around and say you don't work anywheres else, and so forth. Well, *we* know that. You're under contract to Metro, and you'll still owe them a couple more pictures under that contract. You can't work anywheres else. We know that. But in this business you strike while the iron is hot. I'm not waiting till they offer you a new contract, two pictures from now. I'm hitting them as soon as you finish this next one. They moan and wail, and they hit you with a suspension. But when they get done crying and threatening, I go in and talk to them and say who's the loser? And they know who's the loser. They are. You lose a few thousand dollars' salary on suspension, but it's big money if your suspension holds up a picture, and that's when New York starts calling gup. Straighten out that Jackson contract and quit futzing around, New York says."

"Well, I hope you're right," she said.

"Natalie, you're on the verge of—"

"Natica."

"Yeah, Natica. A slip of the tongue, when I get all enthused. Anyway, dear, we're gonna get you a contract that frankly you're not entitled to yet. Frankly, you're not. But we're only getting you what you'll be entitled to two or three years from now. I'm gonna fight to get you the kind of money they pay bigger stars than you are, but I'm doing git for a reason. You want to know what that reason is?"

"Sure."

"That reason is because your whole life is gonna be in pictures. Don't ever come to me and say get you out of a contract so you can do a Broadway play. If you do, you're gonna have to look for representation elsewhere. To me you are motion pictures and no place else. I don't want you to as much as walk on a Broadway stage. I don't want you monking around with Broadway."

"I'm not a stage actress. I know that," she said.

"You know it now, but these Broadway managers come out here and put the con on picture people. Art. The Theater. And all they do is stir up trouble. I got clients I *want* to go back and do a Broadway play every once in a while. *Let* them go back and take fifteen hundred a week or less. But that's for the actors and actresses that started on Broadway. I got all the confidence in the world in you, Natica, but I never want to see some Broadway critic take a crack at you because you're a movie star. You know why? Because I'll tell you why. Because I been going through the reviews of all your pictures since you were at Metro, and I never came across one single review that was a rap. Here and there they rap the picture, but never you. Everybody likes you. You. But some hundred-a-week guy on a New York paper is just liable to rap you because he don't like picture people."

"Well, that wouldn't kill me."

"Kill you, no. But out here they never saw a bad notice for you. They never *saw* one. And I don't want them to ever see one. But if some hundred-and-a-quarter critic on a New York paper raps you, the spell is broken, Natica. And we got a fortune at stake. Human nature is human nature, and once somebody takes a rap at you, others will follow suit. It's human nature, and I won't allow it. I got actors on my list that they go back to Broadway, and if they get one good notice in some New York paper, it keeps them alive for a year. They come back here and work in pictures, make some money, and they start itching for Broadway again. So all right. They're not picture stars. They're Broadway people. You are a film star, and you stay that way."

"Morris?"

"What?"

"Is somebody trying to get me for Broadway?"

"Huh? What makes you ask that question at this particular time?"

"Are they?"

"Hell, there's always some manager wishing to capitalize on a picture reputation."

"What is it? A musical comedy, or a play without music?"

"You know, for a young girl that was never outside of the State of California, I have to hand it to you," he said. "Ernestine often said to me, she said one of these days you'd surprise me with how sharp you were."

"I learned it all from you, and Ernestine. You still haven't said what the offer was."

"A musical comedy," he said. "I told them to get lost. They wanted to pay you a thousand a week and no guarantee of any kind whatsoever. They wouldn't even guarantee me they'd open in New York. You could spend all that time in rehearsal, anywheres from three weeks to a couple months out of town, and they could close the show in Baltimore. I told them to get lost. Imagine you coming back here after closing a show on the road, and I go into L. B. Mayer's office and start telling him why you ought to have a new contract. It makes me positively sick to think of it."

"What did Ernestine say?"

"She was positively nauseous, the gall they have coming out here and making an offer like that. The guy said it was a chance to prove what you could really do. And Ernestine said to him right to his face, 'Fifty million people go to the movies every week, and they're all that much farther ahead of you, Mister.' "

"Mr. What?" said Natica.

"You want to know his name? It's a fellow named Jay Chase. If that name don't appeal to you he used to have another one when I knew him in the old days. But what the hell, I had a different name then myself, and Natica Jackson used to be Anna Jacobs if I'm not mistaken."

"Getting me off the subject of Jay Chase, Morris," she said.

"Yeah, I was. But I'll get you back on the subject I wanted to talk about. You and pictures. Natica, I see you—do you know what I see you as? I see you as like Garbo. Gable. Lionel Barrymore. Crawford. I see you as much a part of the Metro organization as Mr. Schenck. L. B. Mayer. The lion. Wally Beery. Them. Some of my clients I can never hope for such an arrangement, whereby they got a home lot and it's a regular second home to them. You think of Metro and automatically you think of Natica Jackson. You think of Natica Jackson and automatically you think of Metro. That's the way I want it to be, because that way you're set for life. I want that for you before you start getting married and maybe you marry a fellow that gets you all discontented. But if you got a permanent home lot, that much of your life is all taken care of."

"You want me to marry Metro."

"Exactly. Or Metro to marry you. I don't care how you put it."

"Some people say a star is better off independent," she said.

"Yeah, that's what they say. You hear that all the time, from actors that it don't look so good for their next option. You hear it from actors that the studio only wants them for one picture. You hear it from agents that can't land a contract for more than one picture. Yeah, a star is better off independent, once he got about two million stashed away and don't care if he never works. But that won't be you for another ten years or so. You're a working girl, Natica."

"That's the only thing you said so far that makes any sense to me.

I'm a working girl," she said. "Morris, you and Ernestine stop filling me up with big talk. All of a sudden I'm not a kid any more. I was eighteen and got into pictures, and almost got out. Then you and Jerry Lockman and Joe Gelber and a half a dozen pictures, and this guy and that guy. And my folks sponging off of me, and I get overcharged in the stores. And nearly all the girls I went to high school with are married and started a family. And I'm nearly twenty-four years old. A woman. Not a girl any more. Sixty million girls would like to trade places with me, and I'd be one of them if I wasn't Natica Jackson. I'm lucky, and I know it. But one of these days don't be surprised if I blow my lid."

"You're entitled," he said.

"Just don't be surprised, that's all," she said.

"What are you thinking of doing?"

"I've been thinking of going after something *I* wanted, for a change."

"A fellow?"

"What else? I can buy nearly anything else," she said. "This one I couldn't buy."

"Oh, you got him picked out. Well, you talk to Ernestine and next week we'll take him to the fights. Is he—"

"Oh, no, Morris. You and Ernestine have to stay out of this."

"Who is the fellow? How did you conceal him from us?"

"You put your finger right on it," she said. "You and Ernestine and the studio have to know everything I do. But this was one time I got away with something. Imagine. I slept with a fellow, and you and Ernestine didn't know about it."

"When did you have time to?" he said.

"I get a kick out of this," she said. "I got you puzzled."

"Just don't get yourself into any trouble."

"I know. A fortune's at stake."

"And you want to be sure he's worth it. Don't do nothing you'll be sorry for."

"I sure will," she said. "I am already, but I didn't know how good that can feel. The only thing I *have* felt, these last couple of years."

"Married, this fellow?"

"The works. Married. A good job. Respectable."

"What does he get out of it? What good's it gonna do him?"

"Him? It may not do him any good at all," she said.

The new picture went into production and Natica Jackson was a dream to work with. Everybody said she was a dream to work with: the director, the other actors and actresses, the producer, the unit man from the publicity department, the script girl, the assistant director, the little people from Wardrobe and Makeup, the little people from Central Casting, the little people from Transportation. She had always been easy to work with, but now she was a dream. She was cooperative, tractable, patient, and cheerful; and she was punctual and always knew her lines. She was also good. There is in Hollywood a legendary tribute to a scene well played. It is that moment when a performer finishes a scene and the grips and the juicers burst out in spontaneous applause. It is a phony. It does not happen. But there is the real thing, which happens no more than once or twice in a dozen pictures. It is that moment when a performer has finished playing a scene, and for perhaps a count of three seconds no one on the set speaks. There is complete silence on the part of everyone who has been watching the scene. The silence is usually broken by the director, who says—and does not need to say—"We'll print that." Then all the people on the set go about their business once again, the better for having witnessed a minute-and-a-half of unrecapturable artistry. Natica had two such moments in the new picture. One was during the scene in which she hears shots that she knows will kill her brother. The other was in a church pew, kneeling beside the gangster who she knows has killed him. In the one she blinks her eyes as though she were receiving the shots in her own body. In the other she is full of fear and loathing of her brother's murderer. Both were routine bits of screen writing, but they were redeemed by her potentially explosive underplaying. "This girl can go," said the director. "She can really go."

"Oh, she can go, all right," said Joe Gelber.

"Reggie Broderick told me she could go," said the director. "But you know how it is, Joe. One director can get it out of an actor, and the next director can't."

"You're getting it out of her, Andy," said Gelber.

"I know I am, but it had to be there in the first place," said Andrew Shipman. "What was she doing with that English fag?"

Gelber shrugged his shoulders. "What was she doing with Jerry Lockman?"

"That's true," said Shipman. "And who else did she have?"

"I don't know. Reggie Broderick, maybe."

"No, he said no," said Shipman. "He said she'll talk about it, but that's about as far as it gets."

"Well, you have over a month to find out."

"She may be what I call a cucumber," said Shipman. "Show business is full of cucumbers, but particularly in our business. They look good as hell, the answer to all your wildest dreams. But you get in bed with them and that's when you discover the cucumber. No steam. No blood. It's all an accident of how they photograph. Either that, or they save it for their acting. This girl may be a cucumber, but I hate to think so."

"She may be. Jerry Lockman, and the English fag. That's all we got to go on."

"Pending further investigation," said Shipman. "You're sure you never looked into the matter, Joe?"

"Listen, I'd tell you in a minute," said Gelber.

"Yes, I guess you would," said Shipman.

"I'd tell you quicker than you'd tell me. You held out on me before this."

"Only temporarily," said Shipman.

"Well, you want to know the truth, Andy," said Gelber. "I like them prettier than her. Either they gotta be prettier or so God damn perverted I don't want to be seen in public with them."

"You're as bad as Jerry Lockman," said Shipman.

"Maybe worse, but everybody found out about Jerry. I operate different. One big-mouthed dame spread it around about Jerry, because she was a star. Who would of listened to her if she wasn't a star? My motto is—well, I don't know. I guess I don't have any motto."

"I have. My motto is, if at first you don't succeed, you're wasting your time. I'll give you a report on Miss Jackson later on. But meanwhile, the kind of report the studio's interested in is all good. She can really go."

Every shooting day the girl who could really go drove her LaSalle past the Marshall Place intersections of Motor Avenue and was pleased with herself. Now the temptation to reenter Marshall Place and Hal Graham's life was completely controlled. Her mind was made up, she would call the shots. Early in the morning, on her way to the studio, as she came to the Marshall Place entrance she would call out, "Sleep well, get your beauty sleep, Mr. Graham. I'll be with you in a little while." First she must finish this picture, working hard and well and cheerfully. Then Morris King would make his demands, suspension would follow, and her time would be free. Homeward bound in the evenings, she would call out, as she came to Marshall Place, "Another day, another dollar, Mr. Graham. See you soon, Mr. Graham." She was happy. They were wonderful to her at the studio, they let her know they were pleased with her, and Morris King confided to her that he was planning to adjust his demands upward, so that her suspension might be longer than his original guesses of four to six weeks.

"The things I been hearing about your performance," said Morris. "If they were just a little smarter, the studio, they'd come to me and they'd offer to voluntarily tear up your contract. Imagine how good that would make them look? But the studio mind ain't constituted that way, so what'll happen is naturally I'll go in some day and they'll be able to tell by the look on my face that I didn't come in for any social call. But wouldn't they be so much smarter if they anticipated me?"

"And you say to them, you have all your other clients that will never work for Metro unless they give me a new contract," said Natica.

"You *think* it, and you get the thought across so *they* think it. But with Metro you don't threaten. RKO you can threaten. Universal you can threaten. Republic you don't even answer your phone. But Metro, the lion is the king of beasts, you know. You threaten without saying ganything. Jack Warner you can threaten, Harry Warner you don't. Harry Cohn threatens you first, and bars you from the lot. Sam Goldwyn don't use enough people, so when he wants somebody you let him come to you. He'll scream at your price, irregardless of what it is, but when he wants somebody he wants them, so you wait till he calms down and you knock off a few dollars and you got a deal. Agenting is a great business as long as they can't bully you. Nobody can bully me any more, and even Metro knows it, but all the same I'm careful who I threaten. None of these guys are using their own money, and I am."

"You're using my money if I get put on suspension," she said. "I'm the one that's not getting paid."

"You'll get it all back in the long grun. Just don't lose your confidence in yourself. And don't lose your confidence in me."

"I'm kidding," she said. "I've never been so confident in my whole life."

"Yeah, and it makes me wonder," said Morris. "Also it worries Ernestine. If you got one real friend in this business, it's Ernestine. So don't go antagonizing her too far. Everybody has to have one real friend in this business."

"Morris, you handle the studio, and let me ruin my own life," she said.

"I'll let you run your own life, but it sounded as if you said *ruin* your own life, by accident."

"Ruin is what I said," she said.

"All right, have it your own way," he said.

She invented, and rejected, a dozen ruses which would bring about her next encounter with Hal Graham. Some of them were neat and logical, and some relied on sloppy coincidence. They were all pleasant time-killers, anticipating the actual event, which she was willing to postpone because the postponement was in her hands. She was on the final week of the picture and beginning seriously to consider her plans for Graham and herself, and one afternoon Andrew Shipman told her she might as well go home early, that there was nothing more for her to do that day. "I'll need you in the morning," said the director. "Made up and on the set at eight-thirty."

"Eight-thirty? That's practically the afternoon," she said.

"Well, this won't take long. It's a retake of the long shots in front of the church. You might as well get used to loafing again."

"Thanks," she said. She did not point out to him that it would be close to five-thirty by the time she left the studio. Five-thirty was still better than seven-thirty.

She took off her makeup and changed into her slack suit and left the studio. It was still daylight as she drove up Motor Avenue, and as she proceeded she noticed that a pest was following her in a black Buick convertible. She was familiar with the type. They hung around the studio parking lots until they saw an actress leaving by herself. Sometimes they were impossible to shake until she got to the gate at Bel-Air, but once there she could stop and ask the watchman to intervene.

This one was the playful type. He began blowing his horn, and made no pretense whatever of not following her. She stepped on the gas, hoping to lose him, but he kept the same distance, and at Pico he even drove through the stop signal to keep up with her. Instead of turning in at Beverly Glen she kept on to Westwood Boulevard, hoping that the added distance would enable her to lose him in the Pico traffic. The strategy did not work. She was driving through the university campus, with Sunset Boulevard in sight, when he drew up beside her and maintained her speed.

"Do you want me to call a cop?" she shouted at him.

"No," he said.

Then she recognized him. He was grinning. "How do you like my new car?" he called to her.

She pulled over and stopped her car, and he did likewise. He got out and came to her car. "So it was you," she said. "I thought it was some high school goon."

He put one foot on her running board and his elbows on the right-hand door. "How've you been?" he said.

"Oh, eating my heart out because you never called," she said. "You know, I've forgotten your name."

"Hal Graham," he said. "I've been reading a lot of compliments about you."

"You have? I thought you didn't like picture people."

"I don't, but you're the one I knew," he said. "This is *your* new car, eh?"

"Not so new. I got it the day after you ran into me."

"I ran into you," he said. "Well, we'll skip that. How do you like my chariot? I just took delivery on it last week. I almost got a LaSalle, but the resale value is better on a Buick. Of course you don't have to worry about that angle."

"Do you want to get in and sit down, or would you rather follow me home?"

"Whatever you want me to do."

"If we stay here the autograph hounds will start collecting," she said.

"Yeah, these kids are UCLA. Up at Cal we have more sense."

"If you're going to be unpleasant—"

"No, just joking." He went back to his car, and when she pulled away his followed her to her house.

"Is your mother home?" he said.

"Why?"

"I don't know. I just asked," he said.

"No. She's down at Santa Ana at some funeral. Would you like a drink?"

"Are you having one?"

"No."

"Then I won't."

"The last time you were here, your wife was down in Balboa or some place. Did she ever get back?"

"The next day. One of the kids took sick and she came home."

"And that's why you decided not to call me?" she said.

"Partly. Not entirely," he said.

"You were ashamed of yourself."

"Yes, I guess so. There was no percentage for you or me."

"Then why did you follow me today, blowing your horn like a God damn idiot kid? Going through that light at Pico. All those people from the Fox lot. You could have killed a dozen."

"I just wanted to see you, that's all. To talk to you," he said.

"What about, for God's sake?"

"Listen, don't be so stupid. In the first place, you're not that stupid. As soon as I saw you I would have followed you to Santa Barbara."

"Why not make it San Francisco? Santa Barbara isn't very far. Well, what shall we talk about, Mr. Graham?"

"Nothing, if you're not more friendly."

"Don't expect me to be as friendly as the last time. I learned *my* lesson. You should have learned yours, too."

"Well, I didn't. I thought I did, but I didn't," he said.

"I guess not. Not if you were willing to follow me all the way to Santa Barbara. That must be a hundred miles. You *are* romantic."

"No, it isn't a hundred miles," he said. "It's closer to sixty."

"I have no sense of distance," she said.

"You're sore at me because I didn't phone you that time. I'll make it worse. The kid didn't get sick. I made that up. The fact of the matter is, if I would have seen you the next day I never would have stopped seeing you."

"Is that so?"

"Well, as far as I was concerned."

"So you went back and worked on your invention," she said. "You had some kind of an invention you were working on. How did it come out?"

"It's coming along. It isn't an invention. It's a process."

"Tell me all about it, but some other time. So you went back to your process, and the wife and kiddies. Have you had any more kiddies?"

He hesitated.

"Don't *tell* me," she said.

"There's one on the way," he said. "I got a raise, and my wife decided we could afford another child."

"Oh, it wasn't that you were so ashamed of yourself that you had a guilty conscience, and became attentive to her?" she said.

"I wonder."

"You're stupid, aren't you?" she said.

"In some things, I guess I am," he said. "I don't pretend to be very good about people. I remember telling you I didn't have any close friends. My wife says I'm too wrapped up in my work, but why shouldn't I be? I know I'm good and I'm headed for somewhere. They gave me a raise, and next year the company's doubled my appropriation. My work is showing results two years ahead of time."

"Why, it's just like bringing a picture in ahead of schedule," she said. "You're stupid enough to be an actor, and you're almost good-looking enough to rate a screen test. You know you're good-looking, don't you?"

"So I've been told."

"Well, you are."

"Looks don't mean anything in my job. I never think about my looks, one way or the other. And it sure as hell wasn't my looks that you went for. You're with those movie actors all day."

"I want to ask you something. Is your wife pretty?"

"Oh, yes."

"Has she got a good shape?"

"Terrific. Beginning to get big now, with the kid on the way, but she has a great figure."

"Then why don't you get in your new Buick and dash home and jump right in the hay with her?"

"Because I don't feel like it."

"And why don't you feel like it?"

"Because I never got over you," he said.

"Oh, nuts," she said.

"That's true. And you never got over me. I told you, maybe you forgot, but I remember telling you I had plenty of girls before I was married."

"And then you quit, except for one girl in Dallas."

"Well, it was Houston, but I see you remember," he said. "I remember everything, too. I can tell you every word you said to me. I could draw you a sketch of the headboard on your bed. I am stupid about some things, because I don't care. But I remember everything about you."

"Well, do you want to refresh your memory?"

"If I do, Natica, this time we're starting something that may be hard to finish. I'm not going to just think about you all the time. So send me home now if you don't believe me."

"I believe you," she said.

"My wife's going to catch on, and she's going to make trouble."

"I know that. She would."

"Bad trouble, for you *and* me."

"Oh, stop talking about it. *Bad* trouble. What other kind is there?"

"Well, if I didn't love you it wouldn't be so bad. But I do."

"Do you? I never even thought about that," she said. "Well, maybe I did. Maybe I never thought about anything else."

"Why are you smiling?"

"Something a director said. It was about my buttons," she said. "I'll tell you later."

"Order me the hamburger and baked potato," said Morris King. "I want to go over and talk to Leo McCarey a minute."

"It'll get cold," said Ernestine.

"Well, order me one anyway and tell the girl to save it for me," he said.

"All right," said Ernestine. She turned to Natica. "What do you feel like having, Natica?"

"I think I'll have the avocado with the Russian dressing, to start with. Then I'll have the hamburger too."

Ernestine shook her head. "Where does it all go to? If I had the avocado—well, I'll have it anyhow." She waved the menu to summon the waitress.

"Good evening, Mrs. King. You decided?"

"Hello, Maxine. Yes, there'll be two avocados with the Russian dressing, and two hamburgers with the baked potato. Then also I want you to hold a hamburger and baked potato for my husband. He's over with Mr. McCarey."

"And coffee with?" said Maxine.

"Yes, I'll have coffee," said Natica. "How are you, Maxine?"

"I'm fine, thanks. I was home last Tuesday. They were all asking me did I ever see you. I said you come in once in a while."

"I didn't know you two knew one another," said Ernestine.

"We went to high school together," said Natica.

"Yeah, but what a difference," said Maxine. "I end up in a balloon skirt and look where she is today. Well, we're all proud of her. Nobody begrudges her success."

"Thank you," said Natica.

Maxine left. "She's cute," said Ernestine.

"Yes. She took a fellow away from me or maybe I would have married him."

"How could she take a fellow away from *you*?"

"By being cute. She married him, too, but I guess it only lasted a little while. Joe Boalsby. As dumb as they come, but awful pretty. Blond curly hair and built like a Greek god."

Ernestine put her elbows on the table, and looked at Natica. "I had a visit from your mother, Natica. She's fit to be tied."

"Well, get a rope and tie her."

"Is it true what she said? She said you put her out of the house."

"It's true," said Natica. "I got her an apartment on Spaulding. Eighty-five a month, furnished, and a colored woman to come in five days a week."

"Yes, well, Morris and I are kind of worried about that. You remember when we helped you with the house in Bel-Air, it was the understanding that your mother was to live there."

"I know," said Natica. "And I owe money on the house. But if my mother stays, I go. I'll take the apartment on Spaulding."

"She's in the way. Is that it?"

"That's part of it. I don't care where I live, but it's got to be alone. No member of my family is going to live with me. I can be out of the Bel-Air house tomorrow. Morris can sell it, and give me what I put into it."

"You're too big a star now to have a dingy little apartment on Spaulding."

"It isn't a dingy little apartment. It's a duplex with plenty of room, and the furniture is better than what my mother bought for the Bel-Air house. Listen, Ernestine. Let's quit beating about the bush. I have a new fellow. He's married, and has a job and all like that. He has no intention of marrying me, and I have no intention of marrying him. So far his wife hasn't gotten wise to it, but she will sooner or later, and then I don't know what'll happen. But the way I feel now, I'll trade places with Maxine if necessary. You can take Metro-Goldwyn-Mayer and stick it. I'm crazy mad for this fellow, and I never was that way for anybody. You have Morris, that you were married to for twenty years, but all I ever had was Joe Boalsby, that ditched me for Maxine, and Jerry Lockman, and Alan Hildred, and this one and that one in between. Do you want me to shock you? Or maybe it won't. Maybe it won't shock you at all. But to show you how hard up you can get, I asked Alan Hildred to marry me. I think that's what frightened him off, the poor bastard."

"Yes, it would," said Ernestine. "Not because he's a fag. But because he's a snob. You knew he married that English actress, older than he was."

"He finally told me, but I had to ask him," said Natica.

"He was ashamed of it. He's ashamed of his whole life, because he's a snob. Everything about his life he's ashamed of. You know who seduced him, don't you? His older sisters. And he turned fairy when he went away to prep school."

"You had the same conversation with him I had."

"Uh-huh."

"You're not trying to tell me he was *your* boy friend," said Natica.

"The only one," said Ernestine.

"Why? Did Morris cheat on you?"

"Not that I know of. Maybe he did. But that wasn't my excuse. I didn't have any excuse, except that I wanted to have a lover, and Alan showed up at the right time. Maybe I would have gone for him no matter when he showed up. I know for a while there I had Alan Hildred on the brain. Brain, nothing. I was like any silly middle-aged dame that gets stuck on a younger man."

"How did you get to know him?" said Natica.

"Oh, he came in the office one day, trying to get Morris to handle him. About four years ago, this was. He had a copy of some book he wrote, and he gave it to Morris and said he didn't think there was a picture sale in it, but he understood the movies were looking for new writers. Morris never reads anything, so he took the book and said he'd have someone in the office look at it. Meaning me, of course, only he didn't say so. Well, you know how Alan could be, when he wasn't having one of his homo spells. Charming. And I was having a hard time keeping from making passes at elevator boys. So we walked out of the office together and we went to a speakeasy, and he began sizing me up, and the first thing I knew I was lending him a hundred dollars. Me! I never lend anybody a nickel, without a promissory note, but here I was giving this total stranger a hundred dollars that I knew I'd never get back. But it wasn't only the hundred dollars. Morris and I were worth well over a million and I could afford it. But that Alan, he knew my psychology. 'Wouldn't you like to see where I live? It's only a few steps from here,' he said. And I went. One room in a little bungalow just off Vine. So I had my lover. He never asked for too much. I told Morris to get him a job polishing English dialog. They were doing a lot of English plays that they got American writers to adapt, but the dialog was too American. So that's how Alan got in pictures. Two hundred a week. Three hundred. Never any screen credit, but a living, and learning a little about writing for pictures."

"And then you palmed him off on me," said Natica.

"Well, later. I got a little afraid that he'd tell one of his boy friends about Mrs. Morris King. I wasn't afraid of Alan. I always trusted him. He was a gentleman. But some of his boy friends were real scum. Male whores. And I was afraid I might get a disease, and give it to Morris. That frightened me as much as blackmail, so I gave him up."

"I could have got a disease," said Natica.

"You were old enough to look out for yourself," said Ernestine.

"Then *let* me look out for myself," said Natica. "If I was old enough then, I'm that much older now."

"You're right, you are," said Ernestine. "Well, I had to talk to you, though. Morris wanted me to, and I'll always do what he says. Tomorrow's the day he goes to Metro and hits them for a new contract, and he wanted me to talk to you."

"And you did," said Natica.

"And I didn't get you to change your mind."

"You didn't want me to, did you?"

"I'd like to been able to tell Morris I got you to change your mind. But in a thing like this, one woman trying to change another woman's mind is only wasting her breath. I just hope you come out of this no worse off than I did with Alan Hildred. I could of got myself into a lot of bad trouble, but instead of that I only made a fool of myself in my own eyes."

"Bad trouble. That's what he says we have to be ready for," said Natica.

"Well, if he knows that maybe he'll have some sense, or at least be a little more careful," said Ernestine. She patted the back of Natica's hand. "I'm with you, if you need anybody."

"Thanks, Ernestine. I guess all you can do is pacify my mother. Keep her out of my way."

"If it was all as easy as that," said Ernestine. "Three days' work as a dress extra and she'll be glad to go back to the flower shop. Your mother is one of the dumbest dumbbells I ever knew."

"And one of the meanest."

"Yes, I'll bet she is," said Ernestine. "There's Bing Crosby sitting down at McCarey's table. I better get Morris away from there or he won't have sense enough to leave them alone. *Maxine, will you tell my husband we want him back?*"

They sneak-previewed the new picture in Long Beach and Van Nuys and the comments were so good that the studio was in an awkward position, torn between the urgency to spread the word in the industry and the wisdom of postponing the happy news until Natica's contract was renegotiated. "They're playing it very smart," said Morris. "They can't suspend you till you turn down the next picture, so they don't seem like they're gonna show you a script. So you're still on salary. They may keep you on salary a long time without sending you a script. They can afford that. But on the other hand they want to be able to announce you in a new picture for next season. Sometimes they're smarter than I give them credit for."

"Well, what do you want me to do?"

"Keep out of trouble," he said. He was firmer, closer to anger, than she had ever seen him. "Get yourself in a scandal and all my work goes for nought. This fellow you're sleeping with, he's just about the perfect example of what a movie actress should lay off of. A young professional man, with a wife and kids and an excellent reputation. The All-American ideal husband, with the All-American ideal home. Broken up by a movie actress."

"Oh, you found out who he is," she said.

"You wouldn't tell me yourself, so I got someone else to find out for me. Yeah, a detective. The license number of his car, parked in your driveway. I got his credit rating, how much he earns, what he's working on. I guess you knew his father-in-law is a Presbyterian minister in Oakland."

"No, I didn't know that," she said.

"His uncle that he's named after, the same identical name, is the superintendent of schools in Whittier. Oh, I got it all, believe me.

Your boy friend Graham, as far as I've been able to find out, there isn't a member of his family on either side that got so much as a parking ticket."

"Well, you don't want me getting mixed up with some saxophone player."

"You can lay off the sarcasm, too," said Morris. "You ever meet his wife?"

"No."

"Well, I got pictures of her when they were married and a trip they took the year before last. You know what type woman she is? The Irene Dunne type. In other words, he don't have the excuse of being married to some homely broad. This is a good-looking woman, and to cap the climax, she's having another kid. Oh, you picked good this time. What ever made you give up that English fag?"

"Graham."

"Well, what'll make you give up Graham?"

"Nothing. Nothing except Graham," she said.

"I wonder what'd make him give you up?"

"Right now, nothing. I don't say it's going to last, but we want it to."

"You just won't listen to anybody, will you?"

"I'll listen. I'm listening now," she said.

"This guy has a clean record, Natica. I spent over two thousand dollars checking, and outside of some college-boy dates, the only woman he ever got mixed up with was his wife."

"That may be," she said.

"You can count on it. Also, her record is even cleaner. She was a studious type and didn't have dates till she started going out with him. She wrote poems. She got some prize for writing a poem. People like that, you know, they're not like people in our business. They take things big. I'm trying to warn you."

"I've been warned. By Graham. I'll take the consequences."

"Big talk. What consequences? How much sleep are you gonna lose if you break up a home with three children?"

"Don't try that argument, Morris. I had to grow up without both my parents. I'm in love with this guy, and I don't want to think about anything else."

"All right. I give up."

"That's good. Don't try any fast ones," she said.

"When the roof falls in, I'll get you a good lawyer. That's all I can do now."

Beryl Graham's poetry prize was a certificate, eight inches by ten, made of a simulated parchment stock, and matted and framed. It rested, rather out of sight, on top of the built-in bookshelves of the den at 88 Marshall Place. The text of the document stated that the eighth annual first prize for poetry of the San Luis Obispo County Poetry Society was awarded to Miss Beryl Judson Yawkey for her sonnet, "If I at Dawning." The certificate shared space atop the bookshelves with Beryl's Bachelor of Arts degree, Hal Graham's Bachelor of Science degree, his commission as second lieutenant in the Army Reserve, and the Grahams' high school diplomas.

It should have been a comfortable room. The chairs were chosen for comfort; well cushioned and with pillows. An effort had been made, too, to create a comfortable relaxed atmosphere, with a sampler that said "God Bless Our Home," and the coats of arms of the Sigma Nu fraternity and the Pi Beta Phi sorority on the walls; a portable phonograph, a small radio, a portable typewriter, a magazine rack filled with recent copies of *Time* and *The Saturday Evening Post,* three silver-plated tennis trophies, half a dozen framed photographs of the Graham family. But everything in the room had been given its carefully selected place, and once given its place had never been put anywhere else. The room had acquired a stiffness that was the opposite of the intended effect. It was just like all the other rooms in the house, from kitchen to bedroom. The nubbly counterpanes had to be where they belonged at ten o'clock every morning, and at one P.M. the Venetian blinds on the west windows were closed against the strong afternoon sun.

Beryl Graham could not have lived any other way, no more than she could have permitted herself the fifteenth line of a sonnet. Sometime in the first year of her marriage she had arrived at a personal ritual of lovemaking, with limits beyond which she would not go, and the ritual remained constant throughout the succeeding years. She did not wish to hear of other women's and other men's variations. She accepted Hal's admiration of her body as a proper compliment not only to herself but to all womankind, and she would speak generously of another woman's "lovely" figure without going into detail that might cause her husband to dwell upon the individual woman as an individual. Beryl made herself the guardian of all women's mysteries. Being a woman was something that no man could ever understand, and he must be prevented from violating women's secrets. It was quite enough for him to be a partner to her climax. He must be satisfied with that intimacy, and he must then go to sleep, gratefully.

She was happiest in the company of other women. It was always a clouding conclusion to a pleasant afternoon when a husband would appear to call for his wife after a bridge game. It was a male intrusion into a feminine world, an end for that day to the pleasing gentleness of women's voices and the pretty sight of feminine things. Beryl loved her kitchen and her bathroom, the tapestries in her hall, the chinaware in her diningroom, and the husband and children that so admirably completed her establishment, *her* establishment among the establishments of other women. She had a son as well as a daughter, but a son was a boy and a boy was a child that was not a girl and children belonged to the mother, a woman. A boy was not a man, and even when he became a man he would become the husband of a woman. It would be nice if her boy went into the ministry. There was still time to direct his steps. He worshiped her, even if he did understand the terms of his father's profession. Howard in a pulpit was an inspiring dream. The Reverend Howard Yawkey Graham. She could see his name in white letters under glass on the sign on a church lawn up North. Sacramento. Fresno. Oakland. San Francisco. The Reverend Howard Yawkey Graham will preach on "Woman's Role Today."

Jean, of course, was already so much like her mother that Hal sometimes would jokingly refer to her as little Beryl. He could just as well have referred to Beryl as big Jean, for with the exception of the overt sexual relationship there was little difference in his treatment of the one and the other. Correspondingly, their treatment of him was tolerantly maternal. The daughter had learned fast.

Howard was nine years old, Jean was seven, and they had been told to expect a new little brother or sister. The age gap between Jean and the unborn child worried Beryl not at all. She fully expected the older children to assume a proper responsibility toward the child that she had tentatively named Emily, after Emily Dickinson. The difference in ages between Emily and the older children was perfectly calculated, she felt. One of the women in her group (whom she did not like very much) had introduced her to the term, sibling jealousy, which turned out to be a name for the hitherto nameless concern that Beryl had disposed of before undertaking her third pregnancy. She disposed of it by deciding firmly that Howard and Jean must learn to love "Emily" before she was born. In this she was succeeding nicely, and for a little while she had no unnecessary worries. In spite of the obstetrician's reassurances Beryl discontinued conventional lovemaking with Hal and they went back to the "heavy necking" that was as much as she would allow in the weeks before the formal announcement of their engagement and the wedding ceremony. Hal's protests were mild, and then he told her that he had decided to stay away from her until after the baby was born. He would sleep in the guest room.

It was such a sensible idea that she playfully accused Hal of suddenly acquiring the ability to read her mind. No man on earth could read her mind, she was certain, but she had so strongly wished that Hal would come to just that decision that she wondered if she did not possess some extra-sensory powers that could be as effective as the spoken word. In many marriages the husband and wife often found themselves thinking the same thought simultaneously, and Hal's decision might only be an extension of this common coincidence. The power of her wish had been undeniable, and if it had not been such an intimate matter, she would have mentioned it to her father as bearing a close relation to the power of prayer. It was too bad, in a way, that she had never discussed those things with her father. But then she had never discussed them with her mother either. She had never really discussed them with anyone, not excepting Hal. She was much too proud of being a woman to relax her own reserve. The same pride had often served her well when Hal made love to her; it was unthinkable that she would ever let him know that *he* could leave *her* unsatisfied. No woman should be that dependent on a man.

But nearly seven years had intervened since Hal had slept in the guest room, and in all those years not a single week had gone by without his getting in bed with her. It was healthy for him. Five years ago, when she had her appendix out, he had slept alone for five or six weeks, but that did not count. She remembered it, though, because he had been so nervous and irritable in spite of himself and his good intentions; and there had been a remarkable demonstration of men's dependence on sex when the doctor said it was completely safe for her to allow Hal to make love to her again. Overnight he became cheerful and relaxed and his old sweet self. Now that he had once again betaken himself to the guest room she began to look for indications of a return of his nervous irritability. At the end of the second week of his celibacy—a fair test—she could see no bad effects, physically or spiritually. He was neither constipated nor petulant. She kept track of his bowel movements and she watched his manner with herself and the children. He was normal. And then she knew, for a fact beyond the suspicion stage, that Hal Graham was having sexual relations with another woman.

She did not need proof. She did not want proof, in the usual sense of the word. Hal Graham was all the proof she needed. She knew him like a book, a man who did complicated equations in a laboratory and could speak for an hour on problems so abstruse that not a hundred men in the entire State of California could follow him for five minutes. That was all there was to him, really, all that set him apart from the race of men. Otherwise he was a vapid, uninspiring person who drove a certain kind of car, played certain games, wore certain clothes, said certain things, and was now indulging certain animal instincts with a certain inferior type of female. Beryl Graham's contempt for her husband had never had occasion to be expressed. The feminine woman, to avoid being a freak, required a husband, a male to fertilize her and to signify his responsibility to her by giving her his name. The inconveniences attendant upon this convention were bearable so long as the relationship was not cheapened by disrespect. But sexual infidelity was disrespect of the most grievous kind. It placed the wife on equal terms of messy intimacy with the husband's mistress. The unfaithful husband sought in his mistress the thrilling shudder that was the proud woman's weakest moment. The cheap and traitorous woman gave him what he sought, and while she was a pitiable and contemptible person, she must be punished for her disloyalty to her sex.

The punishment, however, must be carefully thought out. It need not be visited directly upon the traitorous woman. It should unquestionably be administered indirectly through the offending, disrespectful man. And under no circumstances should it be of a character that would further lower the dignity of the offended wife. Beryl Graham almost automatically discarded the notion of divorce. There was no dignity in becoming the self-proclaimed victim of Hal Graham's disrespect. She next ruled out financial punishment. She could impose upon him a financial burden that he would carry all his life, but two factors decided her against that: fundamentally he cared very little about money, and, secondly, he was so indispensable to his company that they would make some arrangement to help him. It was quite possible, too, that the woman, whoever she was, had money of her own. She was certainly not costing Hal any money now. Beryl knew where every penny went.

No, the usual forms of punishment and revenge were not acceptable to Beryl Graham. They were insufficient, inadequate to the offense, and they were *unsubtle, unfeminine.* They were the thinking of men, the thinking of lawyers, and most lawyers were men.

In her present condition Beryl had plenty of opportunity for calm reflection. Her pregnancy gave her an excuse to give up tennis with the women of Marshall Place, and now that she was convinced of Hal's disrespect to her she used her pregnancy as an excuse to give up the enjoyment of her afternoon bridge games. After she sent the children off to school in the mornings she did her housework and was left with the entire day in which to be alone with her thoughts. When Marshall Place neighbors dropped in she would let them stay only a little while, and she soon discouraged their casual visits. It was not long before she had almost the whole day to herself, and she went through her household duties mechanically while occupying her mind with the problem of dealing with Hal and his unknown woman. It was not a problem that could be solved as he would solve one of his chemical formulae, if he solved chemical formulae. It was not a mathematical thing or a test tube thing; it was not a materialistic matter. It was a problem for a poet.

"How are you getting along?" he said to her one night, when the dishes were put away and the children had been put to bed.

"Me? Fine, thanks. Why?" said Beryl.

"I just wondered," he said. "You have any trouble with little Emily?"

"Not a bit," said Beryl.

"Do you feel life?"

"Of course I feel life," she said. "Men don't understand those things."

"I guess not," he said. "Well, I guess I'll say goodnight."

"Goodnight," she said. She gave him her cheek to kiss.

"Are you sure everything's all right?" he said.

"Why shouldn't it be?"

"I don't know," he said.

"If there's something bothering you, for heaven's sake tell me."

"Well, something is," he said.

"Oh? What?"

"The children. Well, not both children. But Howard said he hoped you'd have the baby soon."

"Why?" said Beryl.

"Because you're acting strangely. He didn't say that, but he thinks it."

"What *did* he say?"

"He said you talk to the baby as if it was alive."

"Well, it is alive."

"I know, but he doesn't understand that."

"And what did you tell him?"

"Well, I tried to explain that the baby's alive, and that it had to grow a little more before it was ready to be born."

"He knows that. I've told them that."

"But he doesn't understand why you'd talk to it now."

"Well, do *you*?"

"I do, because you used to talk to *him* before he was born, and Jean, too."

"I suppose I did," said Beryl. "I believe mothers *should* talk to their babies."

"They don't usually, before they're born," he said.

"Don't they? How would you know? There we are again, you see. A man is so different from a woman that it's just hopeless for him to try to understand us."

"All the same, Beryl, you have to admit it's kind of confusing to a young boy Howard's age, to overhear his mother talking to someone and you can't even see who she's talking to."

"I don't admit anything of the kind. It may be confusing to Howard, because he's a boy. But I'm sure it isn't confusing to Jean."

"I don't know," he said. "She hasn't mentioned it, but she wouldn't anyway. She doesn't confide in me, and never has."

"Naturally. If she had anything to say, she'd say it to me."

"I guess so," he said.

"Oh, I know so," said Beryl. "And there's nothing else on your mind?"

"No."

"Nothing out of the ordinary at the lab?"

"Not a thing," he said. "The usual slow progress. We try one thing, and if it doesn't work, we start all over again and try something else. But we know we're in the right direction."

"That must be such a great satisfaction, knowing you're at least in the right direction," she said. "But what if you found out some day that you were going in the wrong direction?"

"What do you mean by that?"

"Just what I say. Suppose you discovered that these last five years' work was all wasted? That you were completely wrong?"

He smiled. "That would be impossible, now. This is scientific work, you know. Every step is experimental, yes, but when we've proved something by one experiment, that's scientific fact. Then we take up the next experiment. Step by step, experiment by experiment, we accumulate our scientific facts. Those are things you can't deny. Certain elements behave certain ways under certain conditions. Those aren't laws that man made. Man only discovers them."

"But what if something new comes along and proves you were wrong?" she said.

"Nothing new comes along. It was always there, but we hadn't discovered it. Where we can go wrong is through ignorance. But the things we've proved, scientifically, are never wrong."

"You're all so conceited. So sure you're right."

"Not for one minute," he said. "We're sure that the laws are right. The laws of physics, I mean. But the man that's sure *he's* right, disregarding those laws, doesn't belong in the lab. He *is* conceited, and we don't want him around."

"How interesting," she said.

"You're getting bored. I'll let you go to bed," he said. "Goodnight."

"Goodnight," she said.

He closed the door of her bedroom and she sat with the pillows propped up behind her and a limp-leather volume of Wordsworth's poems lying open at her side. She had a feeling that she was getting closer to the solution of her problem. Whatever it was, it would certainly involve his destruction. This blindly conceited man, with his prattle about laws, must be rendered harmless. There must be a castration of his egotism, so that he could never again take that superior tone. How he had gloated over her and her unconscious, innocent habit of talking to the child in her womb! Did *he—he—* presume to judge her strange?

On the morning of the second Friday after the preceding conversation Beryl waited until Hal had left the house and then announced to the children that she had a surprise for them. They were not to go to school that day, but instead she was taking them to Newport a day early. Daddy, she said, would join them the next day.

She drove them to their cottage, had them get into their bathing suits, and informed them that as a special treat she was taking them for a ride in a motorboat. They went to Red Barry's pier, where the Grahams customarily hired boats, and Red gave them a new Chris-Craft because he trusted Beryl's ability to handle it.

They took off into the San Pedro Channel, which was calm, and when they were about five miles from shore, Beryl stopped the boat and told Howard he could go for a swim. The boy dived in, and Beryl then told Jean that she could go in too. The girl was somewhat reluctant, but she lowered herself into the water. Beryl then started the motor and pulled away. She made a wide circle until she saw first the boy and then the girl disappear beneath the surface. She circled again several times before turning back to shore.

In the words of Red Barry: "She brought the boat in all right, and tied it up herself. And then I thought to myself, 'Hey, wait a minute,'" and I asked her. I said where were the two kids? And she looked at me like I was asking some kind of a dumb question, and said, 'They're out there somewhere.' And I said to her what did she mean by out there somewhere, and did she mean she had some kind of an accident? You know, I thought she was out of her mind from shock. But she was just as calm as if nothing happened, and I took notice her dress wasn't wet. Her hair was dry. In other words, she hadn't been in the water. And I thought, Jesus Christ, what *is* this? So I right away went to my shack and phoned the police. I didn't know what the hell else to do. Now there's a woman I been dealing with, her and Graham, five or six years at least. I would of trusted her with my own kids. And it isn't as if she wasn't a great swimmer. Pregnant, yes, but maybe that's the cause of it. You know, when a woman's expecting, and it's six or seven years since she had a child, it's hard to say. In fact, if you ask me, it's hard to tell about them anyway. Like I thought, well the first thing I better do is repaint that boat a different color, but I'm a son of a bitch if there wasn't a party of four wanted to take it out the following Sunday. They asked specially for it. I couldn't let them have it, though. The police impounded it. And how would you like to be Graham the rest of your life? He wasn't even here, but how do you live that down? Because right away people began saying he must of had something to do with it. A guy is married to a crazy woman, a real monster, but they try to shift the blame on him. Well, I guess if I didn't know him I'd probably think the same thing."

Morris and Ernestine King came out of the Beverly Derby, the one-legged newsboy handed Morris the folded morning papers and was handed a fifty-cent piece. "You want to go to the Troc for a little while?" said Morris.

"I don't know. For a little while," said Ernestine.

"Yeah, we might as well go for a little while. It's early."

Their car was crossing from the parking lot.

"What's the headline? There's a big headline," said Ernestine.

"There's always a big headline," said Morris. " 'Mother Held in Tots' Drowning.' Now that's nice. To practically accuse a mother of drowning her kids."

"Let me see it," said Ernestine.

He handed her the *Examiner,* and she read the big story. "If I live to be a hundred, I'll never get used to Newport being in California. To me, Newport—wait a minute. Oh, *wait* a *minute.* Morris. What's the name of Natica's boy friend?"

"The name of Natica Jackson's boy friend? Some name like Hamilton. One of those names. Why?"

"Hamilton," said Ernestine. "You're sure it isn't Graham?"

"Graham is what it is," said Morris King.

"Harold T. Graham?"

"Yeah, why?" said Morris.

"Get in the car," said Ernestine. She spoke to the chauffeur. "Eddie, take us out to Miss Jackson's house."

"Natica Jackson, in Bel-Air?" said the chauffeur.

"Yes, and I'm sorry, Eddie, but don't figure on getting home at a decent hour tonight," she said.

"That's all right, ma'am, as long as I can have tomorrow off," said Eddie.

"Don't even count on that," she said.

Morris was reading the newspaper under the dome light of the town car as they proceeded out Wilshire Boulevard. He finished the *Examiner* and read the *Times.* Before they had got as far as Beverly Glen he refolded both papers and put out the light. "You got any ideas?" he said.

"First we have to find Natica," said Ernestine.

"Yeah, first we find her, then what?"

"What's the use of ideas till we had a chance to talk to her?"

"I guess so," said Morris. "I was thinking we ought to secrete her someplace. I hope we can secrete her before she finds out about this."

"We don't know anything, where she is or what she knows. Have a cigar to steady your nerves."

"A good stiff hooker of brandy is what my soul cries out for at this particular moment," said Morris.

"You're behaving admirably, Morris," said Ernestine. "Considering what's going on inside. When the chips are down, I have to hand it to you."

"And a hell of a lot of chips are down right now. A matter of two hundred thousand dollars, our end. A million-eight for Miss Natica Jackson. And from the studio's point of view, *you* guess. Now when we get there, I'm gonna let you handle the situation. One woman to another, till we find out where we are. But I want to be in the room all the time."

"If she's there," said Ernestine.

"If she ain't there, I want to go somewhere and get pissy-assed drunk."

"No, you don't want to do that," said Ernestine.

"There you're wrong. I won't do it, but I'll want to. I want to now. If I wasn't afraid of you thinking I was a kyoodle, I'd quit the business tonight."

"Never would I think that, Morris," she said.

The car halted at Natica's door and they got out. Morris pushed the doorbell button, and after a pause the door was swung open by Natica, who closed it quickly behind them. "I had to be sure who it was," she said. "I apologize for making you wait."

"You got a peephole?" said Morris.

"Yes. It isn't in the door. It's off to one side so it won't show the light. It's in the lavatory."

"Oh, good idea," said Morris. "You had any other visitors?"

"No," said Natica. "I phoned you, but they said you were out for the evening."

"We came out of the Beverly Derby and Ernestine happen to take a glance at the morning papers."

"Oh, you found out that way," said Natica. "Can I get you both a drink?"

"You wouldn't have any celery tonic?" said Morris.

"What's that?" said Natica.

"If you have a Coke or some ginger ale," said Ernestine. "Morris'll get it. Dearie, bring me a ginger ale with maybe a little twist of lemon peel."

"What do you want, Natica?" said Morris.

"A big slug of brandy, but I guess I better stick to Coke," said Natica. "Thanks, both of you, for showing up like this."

"Yeah. Well, you two talk while I get the drinks," said Morris.

Natica sat down and lit a cigarette. They were in a small room which contained a portable bar, and ordinary conversational tones sufficed. "He was supposed to come here around five," she said.

"This is Graham, you're talking about?" said Morris.

"Uh-huh. I had a hair appointment for three o'clock, but I decided the hell with it and lucky I did or I wouldn't of been here when he phoned. He was phoning from some gas station on the way to Newport. The police down there notified him what happened and told him he better get there right away. That was after he got back from lunch. He usually has lunch with some fellows on LaCienega every Friday, and then he goes back to the lab. The laboratory. So the police finally got in touch with him around ha' past two. He told me what they told him. That the two children met with an accident and his wife was at the police station. He asked them to put her on, but they said she was in custody. The poor guy, he asked them what they meant by that and all they'd say was he better get down there as soon as he could. They wouldn't even tell him if the kids were alive or dead. They said they didn't know for sure. And he started to tell them he thought his wife and the kids were still home. They weren't supposed to leave till tomorrow. But the cop said he didn't want to talk any more on the phone, and for Hal to get there as soon as possible. The rest I got by listening to the radio."

"We have the morning papers," said Ernestine. Morris served the drinks and took a chair. "And naturally you haven't heard any more from Graham?" said Ernestine.

"No. And he said for me not to try and get in touch with him. He said it looked very bad, and he didn't want me to get mixed up in it. God, I don't want to get mixed up in it either, but I'd like to help him."

"And the way to help him is to stay the hell out of it," said Morris. "The only way."

"Oh, sure. I know that," said Natica. "There isn't any doubt about it, is there? I mean, she did drown the two kids?"

"Wait till you read the papers and you'll be convinced of that," said Morris. "They're holding her on an open charge, but the whole thing is there for anybody to read. They got him quoted saying he didn't know why she'd do it. The grief-stricken husband and father, it says. The pregnant mother showed no signs of remorse or even awareness of the tragedy. The father went out on a Coast Guard boat to join in the search, which already attracted more than fifty small craft containing volunteers and curiosity-seekers. The *Times* has an aerial photograph of the boats, and there's a statement here from a veteran fishing captain who says it may be days before the children's bodies are found. A man named Barry rented her the boat and he's the one that reported it to the police. He refused to talk to reporters, but it was learned that he observed her return to his pier and questioned her as to the whereabouts of the children, and she is alleged to have told Barry that he would find the children 'out there.' He then telephoned the police. Mrs. Graham was taken into custody while returning on foot to the attractive cottage which the family had rented annually for the past five years. And so forth. I'd say the woman was what they call criminally insane."

"She talked to herself," said Natica.

"She did?" said Ernestine.

"And not to herself, really. She talked to the baby in her womb. She worried the poor kids, according to Hal. But he wasn't as worried as they were, because he remembered she did the same thing when she was carrying the boy *and* the girl."

"She'll get off," said Morris.

"They'll put her away somewhere," said Ernestine. "It's too bad they didn't a long time ago."

"Yes, you're right," said Morris. "But now let's talk about you, Natica. First, who knows you were sleeping with Graham?"

"Well, you two do. She didn't. That I know for a fact. She never accused Hal of sleeping with anybody. Not once, and she wasn't the kind that would let him get away with it."

"She wasn't the kind that would murder her two children, either. That's how well Graham knew her," said Morris. "So we don't know what she knew. Who else?"

"Nobody, unless Hal told some friend of his, and he said he didn't."

"It'd be pretty hard for a guy like that to not brag about getting in the hay with Natica Jackson," said Morris.

"He wasn't the bragging kind," said Natica.

"And he had something to lose," said Ernestine. "How about you? Who did *you* tell?"

"A long time ago, Reggie Broderick, but I never told him who the guy was," said Natica.

"What about your servants? Your mother?" said Ernestine.

"My mother doesn't know a damn thing about him. The cook and the maid, if he gets his picture in the paper—"

"Which you can be damn sure he will, tomorrow," said Morris.

"Let me finish. The cook never saw him. The maid could have, if she hid somewhere and watched him leave, a long time ago. Lately he never came in the front door, or left by it. I have a door in my bedroom that opens out into the garden and then through the back gate. I'm not worried about the maid. And if he had to phone me he used the name of Mr. Marshall. There's one person that does know, Morris."

"Who's that?"

"Your detective," said Natica.

"God damn it, that's the thing that's been plaguing me. I knew there was somebody. I knew it, God damn it."

"He has his name. License number. Address. Every damn thing about him and his wife," said Natica. "So, it's up to you, I guess."

"It's absolutely up to me," said Morris.

"Who was it? Rosoff?" said Ernestine.

"Yeah."

"Well, how much can you trust him? He never popped off before."

"No, but he never had anything as big as this," said Morris.

"How much do you think he'd settle for?" said Ernestine.

Morris shook his head. "Who knows? A pension, the rest of his life."

"Well, he wouldn't be the first in this town to get that kind of a pension," said Ernestine. "Do you have his number?"

"Yes, I guess so. You mean with me? Yes. Why?"

"I have an idea," said Ernestine. "Get him on the phone, tonight. Right away. Tell him you have a big job for him, but don't say right away what it is. Find out if he connects up this Graham with the one he investigated."

"He will."

"All right, suppose he does. I have to think a minute," said Ernestine. They were all three silent, until Ernestine tapped her kneecap. "This is what you do. The minute he thinks you're buying him off, you're in for it. He'll bleed you, he'll bleed Natica. I wouldn't even be surprised if he tried to take the studio."

"That he better not try, if he wants to walk around on two legs," said Morris. "Me and Natica he can take, but the studio won't fool around with a small-time operator like Rosoff."

"So you don't want him thinking you're buying him off. Instead of that, you want him thinking you want him to do a little dirty work. You're in it together. You pretend you're taking him into your confidence. 'Rosie,' you say—now let me think." She paused. "I got it. You tell him you're worried about Natica getting mixed up in this thing. Be frank, like. And you say you got a tip that Mrs. Graham, Beryl, went to Europe several years ago and had a child by somebody that wasn't her husband. You aren't sure whether it was Paris, London, or Monte Carlo. But you want him to go abroad right away, as quick as he can, and check the hospital records of all the private hospitals in Paris and London. You'll pay all expenses and fifty dollars a day, or whatever he charges. But he has to do it right away or you'll have to get someone else."

"It won't work," said Morris.

"I guarantee you it will, Morris. Fifty dollars a day and all expenses? I know Rosie well enough to know he won't pass up a chance like that. That's uh, for two months that's three thousand dollars plus his living, plus a little larceny on the expense account. And a nice de luxe trip to Europe."

"You're spending my money, Teeny, but what for? What do I get out of it?"

"Jesus Christ! The one thing you want right now. Time. *Time.* You get this goniff out of the way for the next five, six, seven weeks. He won't find anything, but he won't be around here making trouble. By the time he gets back to L.A., Mrs. Graham will be put away somewhere. And by that time there'll be five other scandals for the newspapers to occupy their attention. If Rosie wants to blackmail us then, we laugh in his face. But I wouldn't laugh in his face tonight, or next week. Tonight I'm afraid of him. Tomorrow I'm afraid of him. I'm afraid of him till he gets on board The Chief and I'm still afraid of him till he gets on board the *Ile de France.* Then I begin to rest easy."

"It'll work," said Morris. "It'll positively work. Natica, where's your phone?"

"Right there where you're sitting," said Natica.

Within an hour Morris had tracked down Rosoff at a gambling house on the Sunset Strip. "Rosie? You winning, gor losing? Well, can you meet me at the Vine Street Derby in three-quarters of an hour? I need your very urgent help in a matter, and it won't keep till tomorrow. Right, Rosie. If you get there first you tell Chilios I'm on my way, and if I'm there first I'll wait there. But be a good boy now, Rosie, and don't you keep me waiting." Morris hung up. "He says he's winning. I say he's losing or he wouldn't answer the phone. You couldn't get him away from that blackjack game if he was winning. I seen him on two or three occasions blow a couple months' pay inside of an hour. So did you, Teeny."

"Yes, I did," said Ernestine. "He's a chump from the word go. You want me to come with you?"

"This time, no. If you were there, he'd smell a rat. No offense, sweetheart. But you know. He'd be looking for an angle. With just me there, he don't get suspicious. You ladies wish to sit and talk, keep one another company till I phone you?"

"If Natica wants my company," said Ernestine.

"Of course I do, you silly," said Natica.

"All right. Then get going, Morris. And good luck," said Ernestine.

"Too bad Natica's not a hunchback. I could rub it for luck. Why wouldn't it be just as lucky to give you a little rub in front?" said Morris. "Wuddia say, Natica?"

"Get out of here," said Ernestine.

"Ah, she knows I'm only kidding."

"Yeah, but do *you* know it?" said Ernestine.

He left.

"There goes a nice little fellow," said Ernestine. "Tough. Shrewd. He'll murder you in a business deal. He'll have the gold out of your teeth before you open your mouth. But if he likes you, once he gets to liking you, you never saw such real, genuine loyalty. And he likes you, Natica."

"I'm positive of that," said Natica.

"How do you feel?" said Ernestine.

"I feel all right. I felt panicky till you and Morris got here. I couldn't think who to turn to. The only person I could think of was Reggie Broderick. All the people I know in Hollywood, and the only ones I had to turn to were you and Morris and Reggie. I would of phoned Alan Hildred if I knew where he was."

"Yes, in a spot like this you could count on Alan. A no-good English fag, but you could count on him in this kind of a situation. Well, that's four people. That's not so bad."

"I ought to feel worse about those two little children, but I don't. He was crazy about them, Hal. But the mother never let him get very close to them."

"What do you know about her?" said Ernestine.

"Hardly anything, it turns out. I thought I knew a lot, mostly from knowing him. But he didn't know much about her either. Married all that time and that's as well as they ever got to know each other. You'd think a married couple would know each other better, but they didn't. I know one thing about her he told me."

"What?"

"She never wanted to look at his private parts. He could look at her, but she wouldn't look at him. She wasn't modest about herself, but he always had to keep covered up till they turned out the lights. She wasn't a Lez, but she hated men."

"She was a Lez," said Ernestine.

"That's what I said, but he said no. She liked to be laid, but she didn't care what happened to him. It was all for her. I don't know, Ernestine. I often felt the same way with Alan. Maybe I'm like her."

"I doubt that," said Ernestine.

"I was with Alan."

"But not with Graham," said Ernestine.

"No, not with Graham."

"Well, you see I was just the opposite with Alan," said Ernestine. "If he told me to—one time he did tell me to do something terrible in front of one of his boy friends, and I did. That was the last time I had anything to do with him, but he had that power over me. That was why I had to stop seeing him. But he had no power over you, and Graham did."

"I would have done anything Graham wanted me to, anywhere, any time. And I would now."

"Well, with me it was Alan. Starting with the first time I ever met him, when I lent him a hundred dollars."

"How did you have the strength to break it off?" said Natica.

"I don't know. Fear, I guess. Not strength. If he could make me do that in front of his boy friend, what next? Those kind of people, people like Alan, that have that much power over a person, maybe the good Lord only gives them so much power. If they had a little more power—but they don't. And that's how the good Lord protects us. You see what I mean?"

"Yes, but how do we protect ourselves from ourselves?"

"Search me. I guess we don't till we get frightened."

"You think I'm gonna get frightened?"

"Yes, I do," said Ernestine.

"You're right. I am frightened. I'm frightened of that crazy woman with the child in her womb."

"Of what she'll do, or what she'll say?"

"Neither one. I don't think she can do anything, locked up in an institution. And nobody'll pay much attention to what she says."

"Then what are you frightened of?" said Ernestine.

"Her. I never even saw her, and I probably never will. But I'll be afraid of her for the rest of my life, like she was some kind of a ghost. Her and those two children, but mostly her. I want to talk to Reggie Broderick."

"What the hell for, Natica?"

"He's a Catholic."

"I'm Jewish. You can talk to me."

"No, I remember those Catholic girls I grew up with. They'd get into trouble—not just knocked up, but other kinds of trouble—and they weren't as afraid as the rest of us."

"It only seemed that way. They were just as afraid, if not more so. And anyway, is Reggie Broderick going to get rid of your ghost? I doubt that, Natica. Him *or* his religion. Think it over before you start spilling everything to Reggie."

"Well, maybe you're right," said Natica. "Right now I don't know my ass from first base. I wish to hell I could get drunk. I wish Hal Graham would walk in this room. Only I don't. A terrible thing is I don't want to see him and maybe I never will want to again, with that damn crazy murderess looking over his shoulder at me. That's my ghost, Ernestine."

"Yes, I see what you mean," said Ernestine.

"What happens to her baby when it's born?"

"I don't know what the law says about that."

"I wasn't thinking about the law. I was wondering about the child's future."

"I imagine the father will be given custody, and I suppose he'll move away. Maybe change his name. Get a new job and so forth."

"Do you know something, Ernestine? As sure as we're sitting here, he's never going to see me again. He'll want to, maybe, but the kind of man he is, he'll have a ghost, too. Not only his wife locked up in an institution, but a child to raise. And he'll never try to see me. And all of a sudden I'm beginning to realize that that crazy woman knew what she was doing."

"What?"

"Just as if she called me on the phone and told me. Maybe she doesn't know my name, even, but I get it inside me, Ernestine. She's telling me."

"Telling you what, dear?" said Ernestine.

"She's saying, 'This is what you have to live with. Ann Jacobs or Natica Jackson, or whatever you call yourself, this is what you have to look forward to.' "

"I wish I didn't believe that," said Ernestine.

"But you do," said Natica.

"I won't lie to you. It's the only thing to believe that makes any sense," said Ernestine.

They were silent for a moment, then Natica spoke. "I told him once, if he hadn't stopped to put on a necktie I never would have smacked into his car."

"I don't get it," said Ernestine.

"Oh, I'll tell you sometime, but not now," said Natica.

"We ought to be hearing from Morris," said Ernestine.

"No hurry. I can wait," said Natica. "I have complete confidence in Morris."

THE SKELETONS

♦

George Roach went to the club every day, had his lunch, played his bridge, and returned home late in the afternoon. That was all right. He kept out of sight most of the day, and that, among other things, is what clubs are for. But his brother Norman, who was only two years younger than George, was not a member of the club, and the people of the town could see Norman going from place to place, doing nothing but go from one place to another, idling, trying to make conversation with busy people. "Uh-oh, here comes Norman Roach," they would say, and take action to avoid being buttonholed by him.

There was no sad reason why Norman Roach was not a member of the club. He had resigned from it in 1931, when many men were making such economies all over the country. "A hundred dollars a year isn't going to break you," said his brother George. "Two dollars a week."

"Will you give me two dollars a week for the pleasure of my company?" said Norman.

"I will not," said George.

"Then mind your own business," said Norman.

"All right, but I just want to remind you, if you stay out two years you won't be able to get back in without paying the initiation. That's two hundred and fifty."

"I may not want to get back in, and if I do, let me worry about how much it'll cost me," said Norman. "There's also the possibility

THE SKELETONS ♦ 539

that two years from now there won't be any club. And the further possibility that you won't be able to afford it either."

George laughed. "I'll always be able to afford it as long as my pigeons bid no-trump."

"You don't win that much playing bridge," said Norman.

"That's where you're wrong. I do win that much. As long as I've been in the club I'd never had a losing year, and one year I came out six hundred dollars ahead."

"I'd be ashamed to admit it if I were you," said Norman.

"Well, you're such a lousy bridge-player," said George.

"I have better things to do with my time," said Norman.

"Such as what? Such—as—what?"

"Well, for one thing, we have a very sick mother. If you'd pay a little more attention to her instead of every afternoon stopping at the club and playing cards with a bunch of nitwits. You don't show her the slightest consideration, and she'll be lucky to last out the year. If you want to know what I think, you're an ungrateful bastard."

"And you're a sanctimonious son of a bitch. You go see Mother every day because you think it's your duty—"

"It *is* my duty, and yours too."

"I haven't finished. You go there, and sit with her, and you never let her forget that you're being a dutiful son. But I'll tell you something, Norman. You bore the Christ out of her. You're going to bore her to death, and in less than a year at that."

"If you want to make excuses for yourself," said Norman.

"No. I got it straight from Mother."

"You're a liar, too. Mother would never make such a statement."

"As good as. And to me. 'Norman shouldn't feel that he *has* to come every day,' she said. So don't be so God damn high and mighty. Give the old girl a break, and stop boring her every afternoon. You're not exactly jolly company at best."

"She knows I care for her. That's more than she ever gets from you. And I'm not going to forget this conversation, George. You've said some things to me that aren't going to be easy to take back."

They were in their middle thirties. The Roach brothers. People who had not known them all their lives sometimes mistook the younger for the older. The looks, people said, had all gone to George, and it was not only the better nose and set of the eyes and chin. The older brother had more pep, as people said in those days, and Norman seemed to be continually watching him in mystification, baffled by his exuberance and his ease with the human race. It came so easy to George; to Norman it came not at all. Their mother dressed them alike throughout boyhood, in matching clothes that came from a rather special shop in Philadelphia; but the uniform attire was nearly the only thing they had in common. The boys were different from each other in so many respects that their clothes produced no fraternal effect. When they were old enough to select their own suits and haberdashery the brothers made their personal declarations of independence, and they extended their individuality in 1917 when George joined the navy and Norman the army. George was assigned to a gun tub in an army transport and never saw a submarine; Norman returned from France with two battle stars. But once again George in his officer's cape was a more dashing figure than Norman with his Croix de Guerre (avec paume).

In such cases the stodgy one is expected to be the more reliable, more substantial citizen, but Norman was neither a more nor a less successful man of business. They both had the same amount of money from the equal division of their parents' estates, and neither George nor Norman was conspicuously enterprising as a member of the business community. Their father, Patrick Roach, had made his fortune as a capitalist, by being there with the cash at the right time. He diversified. He went to work as office boy in a law firm at fifteen, with a parochial school education that had included bookkeeping and shorthand. He was accomplished in penmanship and made a few pennies by writing calling cards. He read law and in time was admitted to the bar, but he saw that the making of money in a law firm was a slow process for a young man who was not related to the partners. Through his experience as rent-collector for the firm's clients he became interested in real estate; as the firm's office boy he had paid almost daily visits to the local banks, where he had made a favorable impression for his neatness and politeness. He was, of course, scrupulously honest. Thus when he decided to open his own office as a lawyer specializing in real estate, he commenced with the blessing of some of the bankers. There were a few murmurs by his former employers as certain clients transferred their real estate affairs to the ambitious young Patrick Roach, but he had been careful not to influence the officials of the corporation clients, the coal company and the iron foundry, and publicly the old firm wished him well. Now, for the first time in his life, he was on his own.

By the time he was thirty he owned at least one building in each of the eight blocks of the principal business section, and he had married Sophie Richardson, daughter of one of the old families of the county. They were married in the First Presbyterian Church, and Patrick's mother, a County Limerick girl, refused to attend the nuptials. The Roaches, however, were represented by Patrick's brother and two sisters, who had been told that Sophie was taking instructions in Catholicism. She was doing no such thing, but she had told Patrick that some day she might, and Patrick was more in a hurry to get married than to make a convert of his bride. Thereafter Patrick Roach became by degrees a man without a church, and when he died room was found for him in the Richardson plot in the Presbyterian cemetery. His mother stayed away from that ceremony too, but her absence was not noticed by many of the leading citizens and their wives, come to pay their last respects.

The Roach brothers grew up without knowing their Roach cousins. It might even be said that they grew up without knowing their father, who went to his office every day of the week including Sunday. The citizens on their way home from church would see his Winton 6 standing at the curb and say, "Pat Roach—upstairs counting his money." It was a fair comment. He took no one into his confidence, and when it was said that Pat Roach was all business, there was very little left to say. His wife and his sons belonged in the large stone house on Lantenengo Street (that had once been owned by a corrupted judge), and he went home to see them. But he had no interest in Sophie's friends or in the details of his sons' upbringing. His games were played with other men, in offices. He joined the club because he was Sophie's husband and he remained a member because there were certain gatherings of certain men that more desirably were held at the club than in the good hotel. After such meetings Patrick Roach would return to his office or to the stone house out the street, without socializing, without the need to socialize.

Sophie chose the boys' schools. Lawrenceville because the Presbyterian minister thought well of it; Lehigh for George because her father had gone there, and Cornell for Norman because her brother had gone there. George joined Chi Phi because his grandfather had been a Chi Phi; at Cornell, where it was almost impossible to be overlooked by a fraternity, Norman joined Delta Upsilon in his junior year. None of this mattered to their father. "You could just as well send them to Harvard," he told Sophie. "I have the money."

"They have no roots in Harvard," said Sophie. "My mother's uncle went there, but he died a bachelor. We have nobody to write letters for them."

"All right, I leave that entirely up to you," said Patrick Roach. He had said the same thing so many times that she knew it was what he was going to say in this instance. Indeed, he would not have known how to oppose her; he was not sure of the dates of their birth, of their age at any given moment. It was the kind of thing he left entirely up to her. When she finally discovered that his bookkeeper had been his mistress, her only real curiosity was about where they had *gone,* where was the *bed*? And he refused to tell her. "I've admitted it," he said. "You don't have to know any more." He died without telling her that for fifteen years he had kept a room in the Roach Building to which only he and the bookkeeper had a key.

"Did you ever know that the old man had an apartment at 214?" said George to his brother.

"An apartment? What kind of an apartment?" said Norman.

"An apartment, to live in."

"Well, I guess if he wanted to have an apartment—although I

don't know what he'd want it for. He had that big sofa in his office if he wanted to take a nap."

"I'll tell you what *I* think," said George. "It wasn't for taking a nap."

"*Him?* You mean there was a woman involved?"

"I'll take you down and show it to you. A bed. Chairs. A toilet."

"I don't wish to see it."

"Sheets all folded up in the closet. I'll bet it was he and Irma Michaelson."

"The bookkeeper? Quit your kidding."

"I'll bet anything."

"Well, you can't prove it by her. She croaked before he did. It doesn't surprise me, though."

"You acted surprised," said George.

"I am surprised in a way, but anything he did wouldn't surprise me. I just hope Mother never found out, that's all I care about. And don't you ever let on."

"I'll bet she did know," said George.

"You're crazy. She wouldn't have tolerated it for a minute."

"No? Who had the money?" said George.

"She has her own," said Norman.

"Nowhere near what he had. Nowhere near. I don't know what she has, but he had over six hundred thousand dollars. It may turn out to be a lot more. He owned stocks in companies I never heard of."

"I'll never touch a cent of it," said Norman.

"Oh, horsefeathers. You'll take all that's coming to you," said George.

George's prediction was accurate. Norman believed such things as he was saying them, but having said them, having registered his protest, he never again wished to be reminded of them. Not to accept his share of his father's estate would have made life uncomfortable for him, as it would have for his brother to have renounced his share. The Roach brothers, notwithstanding their differences in character, had a similar attitude toward work. They never quite got started in real jobs. Each of them had been left $100,000 by their father, and the income was just enough to keep them from having to earn a living. They had, moreover, expectations; half a million would be divided between them when their mother died. George improved his financial situation by marrying Elsie Stokes, who was really rich and had never considered marrying anyone else. Norman married Bertie Smith, whose family were not rich, but as a substitute for money she brought with her the habit of frugality and a lack of style that made for compatibility with Norman's. Of the brothers it was said that George was a gentleman of leisure and that Norman didn't do anything.

George and Elsie never invited Norman and Bertie to their parties, and Norman and Bertie never gave parties. Consequently the brothers might as well have been living in different towns. That was literally true for half the year, when George and Elsie were in Florida or Maine or traveling abroad. After two miscarriages Elsie had a hysterectomy and devoted herself to golf and the maintenance of her position as one of the town's outstanding hostesses. Having done no one any harm, having given people a few laughs, she suddenly died of cancer at the age of forty-two, and the gloom that afflicted the town was the greater because even George had not known the true nature of the operation on her gall bladder. Without being told to do so, the steward at the country club lowered the flag to half-staff, and George Roach was so benumbed that for months thereafter he failed to comprehend the universality of the sadness over Elsie's death. Now he was a rich man with nothing to do and no one to do it with.

He had been everywhere that he wanted to be, and in any case travel without Elsie was unthinkable. The war came, and he tried to get back in the navy, but they would not take him. The army took Norman, who had not had as many cocktails or eaten so much good food between wars, and Norman was shipped to North Africa as a staff officer in the belief that a man who had been decorated by the

French in 1918 might be useful in liaison work. He came home in 1945 a lieutenant-colonel and wearing three ribbons that had not existed during the earlier war. "What are they?" said George.

"This is the Legion of Merit, this is the American theater, and this is the African campaign," said Norman.

"The Legion of Merit? Is that ours?"

"Certainly. Haven't you ever heard of it?" said Norman.

"I guess I've heard of it. Very impressive. Congratulations. I got one, for serving on the draft board."

"They gave medals for that?" said Norman.

"I was surprised, too. One day it came in the mail. However, I don't think I'll ever wear it. At least not when you're around."

"If they gave it to you you must have earned it," said Norman.

"Norman, why is it that you can be such a patronizing bastard even when you're trying to be nice?"

"Well, I must say you haven't changed much yourself."

"Probably not," said George.

"I hear you have a new lady friend. I was glad to hear that. You brooded too much over Elsie."

"I'd rather you didn't talk about Elsie. As for my having a new lady friend, undoubtedly Bertie was referring to Mrs. Green. But as usual Bertie is a little late with her gossip. Mrs. Green is back with her husband, running a poultry farm down near Reading. It never was a great romance, you know. Just a couple of middle-aged crows trying to hold on. What did you do while you were overseas, Norman? About women, I mean."

"If you knew me better you wouldn't even ask that question."

"I guess I shouldn't have. But you were gone three years. Weren't there any WACS, or nurses? Never mind, never mind. As far as I know, the breath of scandal never touched Bertie, either."

"If I'm not permitted to speak about Elsie, I'd rather you didn't speak about Bertie."

"That's a very good thrust. A point well taken. And to change the subject, what do you contemplate doing between now and the next war? If it comes soon enough you'll undoubtedly end up a general."

"I thought of entering politics. I got so disgusted with what I saw that I'm seriously thinking of it. I may run for Congress."

"Well, that seems like a good idea. It'll cost you a lot of money, but I'll be glad to help some. Have you sounded out the right people?"

"I haven't said a word to anybody, and don't you. I'm going to wait and have a look first."

"Yes, but they're not going to come to you, you know. And you'll want to take advantage of your war record. You might even want to run as a Democrat. The old man was a Democrat."

"You're not serious. They're the ones I want to get rid of."

"Just a suggestion. If you decide to run, you'll want to win, and they're winning everything these days."

"I would like to reverse that trend," said Norman.

"Well, good luck to you," said George.

Thereafter Norman thought of himself as a man engaged in politics, but the politicians did not sense his availability and he did nothing to alert them. The years passed, two at a time, one Congressional election after another, and no one thought to ask Norman to run for office. In a state where politics was every man's second, if not his first, occupation, Norman's comments and opinions did not draw attention to himself. But then Norman had the great misfortune to make any conversational topic seem dull. He had inherited some of his father's secretiveness, and his mother had told him once or twice that it was not good manners to talk about oneself. The result was a habit of reticence that restrained him from full expression of the idea in his busy mind. Not even two World Wars had produced a single good story for him to tell; not even his own wife knew the circumstances that led to his getting the Croix de Guerre and consideration for the Distinguished Service Cross. He had no conversational assets and he had one incurable liability—head tones that made his simplest remarks sound like utterances from a Presbyterian pulpit.

Norman and Bertie had two daughters, Sophronia and Alberta,

who were never called anything else by their parents. They went from Gibbsville High to Wellesley and back to Gibbsville and jobs that did not take salaries away from young women who needed the money. Sophronia worked in the office at the Children's Home, and Alberta managed a gift shoppe that two friends of her Aunt Elsie's had opened as a hobby. It had never shown a profit, but it was a nice place to have a cup of tea, which Alberta served every afternoon, or to borrow an umbrella or go to the bathroom. Alberta loved the shoppe and its genteel clientele, who for the most part were women and girls with whom she rightly associated herself on quasi-social terms. With new customers who did not come from her acquaintanceship she was extremely polite. "Yes? Can I help you?" she would say. But even before the stranger had stated her needs Alberta would be smiling sadly, nodding pitiably, and she would interrupt. "I think I know what you have in mind, but we haven't carried it for ever so long," she would say. If the customer was persistent and asked if the item could not be ordered, Alberta would shake her head. "We're such a small shop," she would say. "You'd do much better to order it direct." The silent partners went on footing the bills, unaware that Alberta was maintaining the shoppe's prestige but fully aware that no one else would take the job for such small pay. And the toilet *was* spotless and the telephone was not a pay station.

Sophronia dropped in every afternoon on her way home from work, to hear about Alberta's interesting encounters with their mutual friends and strangers. Sophronia did not like her job at the Children's Home. The woman who superintended the Home was a former nurse, the only person the trustees could get at the salary, and Sophronia was frankly disgusted at the amount of food the woman put away. "She doesn't eat with the rest of the staff. Has hers cooked specially for her and served on a tray. But there's a darn good reason for that, let me tell you. We eat the same as the children, but Miss Mack has steak one day, roast chicken the next. But she pretends she's so busy she can't take time out for lunch. Busy, my foot. She has her nap after lunch till three o'clock every afternoon. Last month she had her sister staying with her for two weeks and this month it'll be her mother, fattening up at the Home's expense. She's trying to get the trustees to buy a station wagon, and here I am, a graduate of Wellesley, getting twenty dollars a week."

Alberta was sympathetic, but she did not respond to her sister's strong hints to be taken on as assistant in the shoppe. Sophronia, with her hair-sprouting moles on her chin and her not always clean fingernails, would not have added any daintiness to the shoppe, and might easily discourage the silent partners from dropping in. Alberta did not run the most successful shop in town, but it was the neatest. Also, in every respect but financial, the shop was her own. Notwithstanding a lifelong habit of obedience and respect to her parents' wishes, Alberta firmly resisted her mother's attempts to have Sophronia take part in the business. Fortunately Bertie understood Alberta's argument that the silent partners might be unwilling to support a losing proposition just to give employment to *two* Roach sisters. One, yes; two, no. "I wish we could go to your Uncle George," said Bertie. "He got all that money from your Aunt Elsie."

"No, Mother," said Alberta. "The only thing that keeps the shoppe in business at all is Aunt Elsie's friends. *Those* people. If they lost interest, we'd have to close."

"But you don't make a profit."

"No, but we don't show a very big loss either. The ladies come in and use the john, because they feel they have a right to. And they have. Then they buy something, and their friends do. But if they didn't own the business, they'd never come in. They'd wait till they got home to do wee-wee. The shoppe is just a comfort station, really."

"A strange way to put it," said Bertie. "Vulgar, to say the least."

"Not as vulgar as what I have to do there. But I'm perfectly willing to be a chambermaid, as long as they let me run the shoppe the way I like. It's a small luxury for them, the women that put up the money, and it's just wonderful for me. You have no idea how much I love it."

She did not often use the word love. It was not often used in the Norman Roach household. Such words as cabbage, and chair, and window, and rain, and dollars, and yesterday, and indigestion, and hairbrush, and rug got used, but not the word love. Soap was a word that they had used a thousand times more frequently. It was as far as they went in intimacy, and love as a word had taken on a bitter extra meaning as the girls grew into womanhood that promised nothing they had not already achieved.

"Then I'd go to Uncle George, if I were you. If it means that much to you. You want to be able to keep the shop when those ladies pass on."

"I want to do it *my* way, Mother, or not at all!"

"Oh, dear. You don't have to bite my head off."

"I'm sorry. I didn't mean to speak sharply. But—well, I'm sorry."

The conversation was too unusual not to be reported to Norman, and Bertie gave her account of it that evening. "Hmm. Last year I believe the loss was somewhere in the neighborhood of two thousand dollars," said Norman. "That's more than I'd care to underwrite."

"Of course it is," said Bertie. "And if you did, you'd have to give Sophronia the same amount. No, I wasn't suggesting that you put your money into the shop."

"Then what *did* you have in mind?"

"I don't exactly know. But if you spoke to George and got him to promise that he'd put up the money if the backers passed on, or decided to withdraw their support. In other words, just so we have some assurance that the shop isn't going to have to close."

"That seems like meddling, to me. Also, plus the fact that I'm not on very good terms with George."

"I didn't know you'd seen him lately."

"I haven't. About the only time I ever see him is if I happen to run into him on the street. I don't say we're on the outs or anything like that. But in a thing like this, going to him for a favor, I'd first want to be sure of where I stood with him."

"Oh, he's free with his money—and it's really Elsie's money, most of it."

"I know that, for heaven's sake. But what if he says it was Elsie and her friends that started the thing in the first place? Wasn't that enough for her to do? I don't know. If I happen to run into him, and he's in a good mood, maybe I'll mention it and maybe I won't."

"Not a word of this to Alberta, of course," said Bertie.

"Of course not. What do you think I am?" said Norman.

By a paradoxical misfortune George was in a jovial mood when Norman next encountered him; instead of a casual greeting and a quick leavetaking, with nothing much said in between, the brothers, at George's invitation, went to the hotel bar and had a beer together.

"What put you in such high spirits?" said Norman.

"If you thought a minute, you'd be able to figure it out for yourself. It's my birthday," said George. "Entering my sixtieth year."

"You're fifty-nine today? By gosh, that's right," said Norman. "Well, many happy returns and so forth. What are you doing to celebrate it? Anything special?"

"Well, tonight Dorothy Williams is having a few people in for dinner."

"Oh, is that on again? We heard something to the effect that you and Dorothy had broken off because you didn't want to get married."

"Always one little error in what you hear, Norman. *I* wanted to get married, and still do, but Dorothy doesn't."

"I should think you'd be quite a catch. Dorothy's no spring chicken. Let's see. She's about two years younger than I am, making her fifty-five."

"Yes. But she says we're both too set in our ways. We both like our independence, and she likes hers more than I like mine."

"I should think for companionship."

"My argument precisely. But she says what's the use of building up a companionship at this late date? One of us will outlive the other, and then be that much worse off later on. I see her point. It

took me a hell of a long while to get used to not having Elsie. There's
such a thing as getting too dependent on someone else. And at least
I can be sure that Dorothy won't marry someone else and take away
what we have. It would be nice to be living in the same house with
her, but it would probably have its drawbacks."

"You'd save money, having the one household."

"That was one consideration."

"A pretty big one, I should think. The size of your house, and the
size of Dorothy's. Cut down on servants. Taxes."

"Yes. Well, when Dorothy said no, she meant it. I'm going to get
rid of my house and probably buy a smaller one. I've had a very
good offer from Thomas Brothers."

"The undertakers?"

George nodded. "They like everything about it, particularly the
cellar. Did you ever know that undertakers are partial to houses
with a large cellar? And ours has a concrete floor and water fixtures
and so on. Ideal, they said. I won't get what Elsie paid for it, but
they named a good price and they'll go a little higher. I'm going to
give the money to the hospital or to cancer research. Not sure which.
I've wanted to do something like that for a long time."

"Leaving yourself enough to live on, I hope," said Norman.

"Oh, I'm not likely to become a public charge. Or to ask you for
assistance. I know approximately what you have, and you have to
think of your wife and daughters."

"I'm never sure when you're being sarcastic," said Norman.

"Most of the time," said George. "You bring out the sarcasm in
me, and always have."

"Oh, I don't mind it any more. It's just your way. The older
brother versus the younger brother."

"Very generous of you to take it that way. As we get older, and
this being my fifty-ninth birthday, I can look back and think of
times when I needn't have been quite so rough on you."

"It may have done me good," said Norman.

"Oh, now let's not get carried away, Norman."

"It's true, though. The three things that probably did the most for my character were *a,* being passed up by the fraternities my first two years in college. *b,* the army. And *c,* having you always take the wind out of my sails."

"I'd like you to elaborate. What did they do for your character?"

"Well, at Cornell I went there from a good prep school. Much better than most of the boys there. But Deke and Kappa Alpha and so on left me out in the cold, although they took in some fellows I'd gone to school with. Ithaca can be a pretty damn lonely place, I can tell you, and about the only friend I had there was a Chinaman. They had lots of Chinese there. They even had their own fraternity, and I'd have joined it if they'd given me a bid."

"Then came the army."

"That was altogether different. I wasn't a very popular officer. In fact, far from it. But I was a *good* officer. The same things that were against me at Cornell were in my favor during the first war. Namely, the fact that I had gotten used to being off by myself. If I had to send a couple of men out on patrol, I didn't have to think twice about whether a man was a particular favorite of mine. If it was his turn, and I could depend on him, I sent him. He would look at me and as much as say, 'You son of a bitch, you know I'm going to get killed.' But at least he couldn't accuse me of sending him and not somebody I liked better. I treated them all alike, and I ended up more respected than some officers that they liked better."

"This is the first time you ever talked to me about your army experience. How did you get your medal?"

"Oh, that's too long a story."

"I have all day," said George.

"No. It only makes me sore. I was up for the D. S. C., and all I got was the French medal. It was with palm instead of with star, but even so it griped me that the French would give me a medal and one of my own people—it must have been—fixed it so I didn't get the D. S. C. I think it was the major of my battalion. One of the popularity boys. A National Guard fellow from East Orange, New Jersey, and a graduate of Peddie. He always had it in for me after he found out I'd gone to Lawrenceville. But I'll tell you this much,

Brother George. I knew of cases where they gave the Medal of Honor for less than I did to get the Croix de Guerre. *I* know it, and a few of my men knew it, and I guess that ought to be enough satisfaction. Only it isn't."

"Then you wouldn't exactly call it helping to improve your character."

"That part didn't. But I look back on the army as a good thing for me, generally speaking. Altogether I spent nearly seven years of my life as an army officer. A lot of fellows, retreads like myself. You were a retread, but I guess the navy is different than the army."

"Very. And I wasn't a retread. I didn't get back in."

"That's right, you didn't. But anyway you tried."

"I'm an honorary retread," said George. "I wonder why you didn't stay in the army in 1919?"

"If I'd known better, maybe I would have. But I was just as anxious to get home as anybody. Bertie was waiting for me, and I wanted to settle down and raise a family."

"Well, you did that," said George.

"Yes. Yes, I did that," said Norman, and then he was overwhelmed by the impulse that he had been denying. "George, I—you're feeling pretty good and there's something I want to take up with you."

"Go ahead."

"Well, you know the little gift shop that Alberta runs. That Elsie and those others got started. It's not much of a money-maker, you know."

"I always understood it wasn't a money-maker at all."

"It isn't. It falls behind every year, and one of these days Norma Blair and Frances Cookson are going to stop supporting it."

"Yes. Frances Cookson especially. She's not going to be around much longer. Why?"

"That's just it. One or both of them won't last forever, and if you had any idea how much that shop means to Alberta. It's her *life*. She's there at half past eight every morning and never gets home before six. She only takes thirty-five a week salary out of the shop, and the amount of work she puts in. What I was wondering is, would you be willing to—in case anything happened to Frances or Norma, or both—would you be agreeable to becoming the backer?"

"Me? Why not you?" said George.

"Because you wouldn't miss the money, and I would. Two thousand dollars a year is nothing to you, but it is to me. But it isn't only the money. If people knew you were behind it they'd be more apt to patronize it than if they knew it was me. Those people are your friends, not mine."

"Somehow I don't see myself as a magnet drawing customers to a gift shop. It isn't the way I picture myself. On the question of money, I suppose I could buy out Frances and Norma and later on take some kind of a tax loss. I imagine Frances and Norma have some such arrangement. In my case, of course, the tax boys might complicate things because Alberta is my niece. Those are things I don't know too much about. On the other hand, Norman, is it such a good idea to have your daughter go on year after year, taking charity just to give her something to do? Wouldn't she be much better off if she got a real job?"

"Both girls are against taking jobs that other girls really need."

"That's going on the assumption that you're a lot richer than you are. Who gave them that idea? You did. Except for the army, you've never had a job. Neither have I, of course. But Elsie had more than enough for both of us. She backed the gift shop so that Alberta could be independent some day, but I know she never had any idea of making Alberta *dependent* for the rest of her life. Elsie helped a lot of people to help themselves, to get them started. But if she had known the shop was going to turn out this way, she wouldn't have put up a nickel. That being the case, I'm afraid my answer is no."

"By God, I never thought you'd be tight-fisted."

"Oh, very," said George.

"You think nothing of giving away large sums of money to the hospital, but when it comes to your own flesh and blood . . ."

"Alberta? That'll be news to Bertie. Or maybe I don't understand the term, flesh and blood. I'll tell you what I'll do. If Norma and

Frances have to stop supporting the shop, I'll *give* Alberta two thousand dollars if she'll promise to close the damn place, and go hunt for a job."

"Who are you going to leave your money to?" said Norman.

"A home for abandoned kittens."

"You're not serious," said Norman.

"No. There'll be small bequests to your daughters. But the major portions of it will be divided up among various institutions that Elsie was interested in. I'll enjoy the income while I'm alive, but when I depart it'll all be cut up."

"Some of that you inherited from Mother and the old man. It wasn't all Elsie's."

"You'd be surprised how little I had left when I married Elsie. I wasn't as careful as you, Norman. I almost had to go to work, and you know what a terrible thing that would be."

"You mean to say you squandered four hundred thousand dollars?"

"I took what you might call a post-graduate course in commerce and finance."

"Oh. The stock market."

"Foolish pride, it was," said George. "I thought I could run my little fortune up to somewhere near Elsie's. But when I was long, the market was short, and vice versa."

"You never told *me* you were losing in the stock market."

"It was hardly the kind of thing I wanted to brag about. I did everything wrong. Or everything right, except that I didn't do the right things at the right time. But I learned my lesson the hard way, and in all the time we were married I never gave a single word of advice to Elsie. Financial advice, that is. Well, one piece of advice. I told her never to pay attention to anything I told her about common stocks. And she didn't. In the long run that advice was worth over a million dollars to her. Not many husbands can make that claim. We knew any number of women who lost fortunes through taking their husbands' advice, but Elsie was always very proud of me as a non-advisor. Of course I helped her spend it. I was glad to cooperate there. We discovered a lot of places before the tourists spoiled them. Travel agent, that's what I should have been. A travel agent and a non-advisor to wealthy women. But I straightened out her slice."

"What was that?"

"Elsie. I was just trying to think of what I had done for her, and I remembered that when she took up golf I was the one that cured her slice."

"You had big things to worry you, you two," said Norman.

"*I* had, if I'd let them worry me. I'd taken a bad licking in the market. But I didn't let it worry me. With Elsie's money, the only thing to bother me was the fact that I was living off my wife. But she cured me of that, as effectively as I cured her slice. She pointed out to me a rather obvious fact, that the money I had had came from the old man and Mother. I didn't earn it. It was left to me, most of it by a man who happened to be my father but for whom I had no love."

"But he *was* your father," said Norman.

"Undoubtedly. But Elsie's point was that it was no worse to live off her, whom I loved and who loved me, than to live off my dear departed father, who had no love for me or you or Mother. Or even poor Irma Michaelson. It's no wonder you and I never developed the acquisitive instinct. He didn't make it seem very attractive, did he?"

"I'm still living off his money. I don't think I want to criticize him."

"Oh, God, you're pompous, Norman. Your whole life you've always talked as if you were afraid someone was taking down everything you say. Don't you know that no one cares?"

"I do. I have certain beliefs, certain standards. I don't consider that my life has been what I wanted it to be. But I can sleep nights—"

"I'll bet you do, too," said George.

"Well, I'm not sure how you mean that. Probably some reference to my home life, so I'll ignore it. I always remember the casual way you took it when we discovered about the old man and Irma Michaelson. Almost as if you were on his side."

"Not on his side. But I wonder how much Mother was to blame. She couldn't have been much fun."

"*Fun?* He didn't marry her for fun. He married her because she was Sophie Richardson and he was nobody."

"Yes, but why did *she* marry *him?* Sophie Richardson could have done a little better. Socially and financially, that is. Elsie used to say that Mother was itching to go out and have a good time, but didn't know how."

"That *sounds* like one of Elsie's ideas," said Norman.

"It was. I just told you. And like many of her ideas, or observations, very acute."

"I wouldn't have taken much stock in anything she had to say about Mother. I know she was very good at giving parties and that kind of life, but I wasn't aware that she had a serious side."

"Unfortunately, you didn't get to many of her parties, so you never really saw much of either side of her. But did you ever hear of Sven Svensen? The scientist? One of the men on the atom bomb project?"

"I may have read about him," said Norman. "Why?"

"We met him on the old *Kungsholm.* Saw quite a lot of him. He must have thought she had a serious side, because he turned up here one day for the sole purpose of getting Elsie to leave me and marry him."

"That was pretty fresh. What did you do?" said Norman.

"Well, first I had to make sure whether Elsie had given him any encouragement. And she conceded that a man like that might have got the impression that she was encouraging him. She had told him to come and see us when he came to America. And he took her literally, at her word."

"And you were satisfied with that explanation?"

"Not entirely. Not at all, really. But we'd been through something like it once before, only I was the one that had to make the explanations that time."

"So what did you do? With the Swede, I mean."

"Well, I took him to the club a few times. I showed him around the coal mines very politely. Then I insisted on having a dinner party for him. Elsie didn't want to, but I was adamant. I made up the list. The younger crowd. The prettiest girls in the county, and the big drinkers among the young men. It got a little out of control, I must say. But it gave Svensen a rather discouraging picture of the kind of life we led. You could almost see his mind working. If that was the way we lived, how long would it be before Elsie wanted to get back to that kind of carryings-on? There wasn't a soul there he could talk to. Elsie got a little tight, and tried to teach the guest of honor how to do the Lambeth Walk. Do you remember the Lambeth Walk? Nothing dirty about it, but nothing dignified, either. Like most Swedes, Svensen could put it away, but it only made him morose. As a matter of fact, he got rather disagreeable, and left the next day, with a terrible hangover and an extremely bad impression of Gibbsville society. It was the only time Elsie ever called me a son of a bitch. She knew what I was doing, all right. How could she not? But she forgave me. If I was willing to go to that much trouble to get rid of Svensen. She wasn't alive when they began writing about the men that built the atom bomb. I wonder if she would have been sorry she hadn't gone with Svensen. Her chance to go down in history."

"Yes, I remember the name now," said Norman. "He got the Nobel Prize."

"Oh, he'd already got it when we knew him. With someone else. But we didn't even know what he'd got it for, even after he told us. The Something Effect on Something of Heavy Water. Anyway, Elsie had her serious side. You've listened very patiently. Now would you care to tell me about Bertie's serious side?"

"That *is* sarcasm, and I think you're getting drunk. You'll be nice and drunk by dinnertime at the rate you're going."

"No, this is my usual time for my nap after lunch. What you think is intoxication is merely auto-intoxication. Fifteen minutes in a comfortable chair to let my food digest. Ten or eleven minutes of sound sleep, dead to the world, and I'm as good as new. You haven't got your car, have you?"

"No."

"It's only three blocks to the club, but I think I'll take a taxi."

"Why don't you go home?"

"In the middle of the afternoon? I'm never home in the afternoon."

"This would be a good day to go home. You're going to have to sooner or later, to change for dinner."

"Now that is a cogent argument. It makes so much sense that I wish I'd thought of it. But I'll give you the credit. Tonight at Dorothy's I'm going to make sure that you get proper credit for my well-rested appearance, my sparkle, my this, that, and the other. I'm sorry you won't be there to take a bow, but they aren't people you'd enjoy very much."

"No, they're all practically strangers to me, even though I don't know who's going to be there."

"As a matter of fact, Dorothy asked me if she should invite Bertie and you, but I said I couldn't imagine why. You've never had me to any birthday party of yours in the last fifty years."

"I haven't had one in that time, but if I had, I wouldn't have invited you. If I'd had any say in the matter you wouldn't have been invited to the ones when we were kids."

"Yes, we get along much better if we don't see each other. Every once in a while I think of asking you to have lunch with me, maybe even persuade you to come back to the club. But that would be a great mistake all around. A club is usually one of the places you try when you're looking for a man. 'Try him at the club,' they say. But in our case it works another way. You can be pretty sure that I'm at the club during certain hours of the day, therefore you don't have to worry about running into me someplace else."

"That's quite true. I *have* thought that."

"I'm not deliberately avoiding you. I have other reasons for going to the club. But if you were to rejoin, you'd feel that you had to go there to get your money's worth. And then we'd have to see each other. And then I *would* have to avoid you, deliberately. My friends, to be polite, and out of consideration for me, would feel they had to invite you to have a drink, or take a hand in a bridge game. Some of them might remember that you're a terrible bridge player, but they'd invite you anyway. And you might accept. Then you'd sit down and play a couple of rubbers, botching it. Leading from the wrong hand. Revoking. Misunderstanding the bidding. Arguing over the score. And before long you'd have a set of enemies that aren't your enemies now. Real enemies, too. In a club that's really a club a man likes to have everything just so. I'm sure you've heard about how a member can hate another member who sits in his favorite chair. That's been going on, I suppose, since the early days of White's Club."

"You mean Dick White?" said Norman.

"No, I don't mean Dick White. White's Club is a club in London, two hundred years old."

"Do you belong to it?"

"No, but I've been there."

"Does each member have his own special chair?" said Norman. "I wouldn't like to belong to a club where I couldn't sit where I pleased."

"If you're talking about White's, that's one thing you'll never have to worry about. You're as close now as you'll ever be to belonging to White's."

"I'm probably as close as I'll ever be to the Gibbsville Club. I never got anything out of it. I only joined the country club for my daughters, and they get very little use out of it. The swimming pool. That's about all. As far as I'm concerned, I go to the Y. M. C. A. three times a week, and that helps me keep in shape. That's why I was able to get back in the army without any trouble. I've always kept in shape. For someone my age, the doctors say I have the constitution of a man half my age. I walk at least a mile a day, rain or shine. Swim three times a week. I smoke, but I've never inhaled. Alcohol in moderation. Plain, wholesome food. Never any trouble with my bowels. First thing, right after breakfast, I'm on the can. That's the whole secret. Don't let yourself get constipated."

"What are you saving yourself for, Norman?"

"Saving myself? I don't know that I'm saving myself for any-thing."

"But you must be, to take such exceptionally good care of your-self."

"I wouldn't say that necessarily. I was given a good physique and I've always felt it was my duty to take care of it and not let it go to pot."

"That's not what you just said, but never mind."

"Whereas you should have taken warning when you couldn't pass the physical back in '42. Instead of which, you ought to con-sider yourself lucky to reach fifty-nine."

"I took warning when Elsie died. The warning was that a young person, comparatively young, who'd never had a serious illness, could get cancer and be dead in a few months. So what the hell was the use of going for walks in unpleasant weather, or playing vol-leyball at the Y. M. C. A., or giving up the good things to eat and drink? They told her she had cancer, and she kept it from me as long as she could. But *they* didn't. The doctors told me she had it, and so the two of us pretended she was going to have an operation and get well. Knowing better, both of us. It went to her brain, but at least she died thinking I'd been spared the truth. And at least I was able to be some comfort to her, up to the end. Now why should I change my ways? I couldn't possibly change my body. But what if I could? To restore my youthful vigor? And then what? Find myself at sixty, chasing after young women? Beating young men at tennis? What the hell for? Young women aren't very interesting in bed, and I'd done about as well at tennis as I ever cared to. I never had any trouble beating you, for instance. And I beat some fellows who were better than you. I didn't have to go out on the tennis court and show off my new vigor. Dorothy and I will go to bed tonight, if we haven't had too much to drink. If not tonight, maybe tomorrow night or the next. One of these days I won't have that any more, and when that time comes I hope I'll be ready for it. Although I suppose you never are."

"As a married man it's something I prefer not to talk about," said Norman.

"Why of course not, Norman. I wasn't hoping for an exchange of confidences on that subject. I've always thought of you and Bertie as fully clothed. In fact, with your hats on and maybe an umbrella."

"Don't go too far, George. Just don't go too far," said Norman. "I don't mind a little good-natured kidding, but leave my family out of it."

"But you can't object to what I just said. I always think of Bertie as fully clothed. If I'd said the opposite, then you would have every right to object. By the same token, I think of your daughters as virgins, which I'm sure they are. But if—"

Norman struck him. It was a clumsy and ineffectual blow of Norman's fist in the direction of George's face. But George was holding his drink halfway to his lips and Norman's fist struck his brother's arm. The glass was driven out of George's hand, the hand was driven against his chest, the contents of the glass spilled over his waistcoat.

"Now what did you do that for, you poor slob?" said George. The few other people in the tavern had not seen the actual punch, such as it was, but it was obvious that something unusual had occurred between the brothers. The onlookers waited in frozen attitudes for the next development. George addressed them: "It's perfectly all right, ladies and gentlemen," he said. "Slight altercation between brothers. This is my brother, Norman Roach, and I'm George Roach. It's my birthday. And we're half-Irish, you know. Now if you'll all just relax and mind your own God damn business, I'll be very much obliged." He had his handkerchief out and was sopping up the liquid on his waistcoat. The waitress handed him a napkin. "Thank you," he said.

"Would you care for a refill?" said the waitress.

"Ah, you understand about these things," said George. "But no thanks, Jennie. We know when we've had enough. You've had enough, haven't you, Norman?"

Norman had stood up during George's speech to the others. Now he reached in his pants pocket and took out some money. One by one he peeled off three dollar bills, then added a fourth, tossed the whole on the table and walked out.

"It came to a little more than that," George called to him, but Norman did not hear him. "Jennie, you take that."

"Jessie," said the waitress. "Thanks. Thanks very much. You want the check, Mr. Roach?"

"As soon as you call me a taxi," said George.

"You mind telling me what that was all about?" said Jessie. "You were sitting there peaceful and then all of a sudden."

"Just call me a taxi, Jessie," said George. "Chivalry, I am happy to say, is not dead."

"Who?"

"The taxi, Jessie, please. The taxi," said George.

The Roach brothers' quarrel over a woman who was supposed to have died but hadn't—a strangely unsatisfactory thing to quarrel about—did not long remain a topic of conversation in the town. The only accurate report of the altercation was given Dorothy Williams by George Roach, and her comment was, "You had it coming to you. You ought to know better than to tease a man like Norman. And especially over a thing like that. The virginity of two girls like Alberta and Sophronia is no joking matter. It's not a question of their morals, one way or the other. It's a reproach to their parents for not having produced someone more attractive. And it's a reminder to Norman that he's going to have to support them the rest of their lives. A man as stingy as Norman, not to mention a woman as stingy as Bertie—you should have known better. You must write him a letter of apology, this instant."

"You were going fine till you came to that," said George. "A letter of apology would be absolutely meaningless. And why wouldn't it be better all around if Norman and I disown each other? Now and forever. Thanks to Mother, I spent the first fourteen years of my life saying, 'I love my little brother.' When as a matter of fact I could hardly stand the son of a bitch. He had colds all the time. They took out his tonsils, but he still got colds. He always had something the matter with him, always suffering in silence, brave little man. But the brave little man always saw to it that everybody knew he was suffering. The only thing was, half the time there was nothing really the matter with him. The old man said to him one time, 'Norman, I believe you're a little faker,' and the little faker got sick to his stomach and threw up. He was of course a tattle-tale. We had a maid who used to let me watch her take a bath. Thanks to Norman, she got the sack, and eventually ended up in a house on Railroad Avenue. I've forgotten half the things he did that made me dislike him. 'I love my little brother,' I was forced to say. My father said one time, 'Sophie, maybe he doesn't love his little brother,' and my mother, in front of us, said, 'Kindly stop interfering.' Nothing ever convinced me that Mother was very fond of Norman, especially when we got older. But she had some notion that if I told that lie often enough, about loving my little brother, I'd begin to believe it was the truth. When he went to Cornell she made me write a letter to the Cornell chapter of my fraternity to try to get him a bid. She mailed the letter herself so that I wouldn't accidentally forget to. But I wrote a second letter, not exactly telling them to ignore the first letter, but quite frankly admitting that it had been written at the suggestion of a member of my family. They got the hint."

"I should think they would," said Dorothy.

"I've always been rather grateful to Bertie for marrying him. She didn't have much choice and it was a step upward for her in more ways than one. But they were so perfect for each other that they could have been living in another world. Think what it would have been like if she'd been some friend of Elsie's. Then we'd have had to see each other all the time and God knows what would have happened. I probably get along fairly well with most people because when I get through hating Norman, other people don't look so bad."

"Hate him? No, you don't hate him."

"Yes, I really do. I've come to that conclusion. And God knows, he hates me."

"I won't argue with you on that," said Dorothy. "But he hates everybody, without knowing it. Bores do. Bores are supposed to be pitiful, but I've never thought so. They can't help knowing that they're bores, but they go right on boring people because they hate them. It's their one weapon of revenge."

"Do people who hate people become bores? In other words, does it work both ways? I'd much rather do without the luxury of hating my brother than become a bore."

"Haters can be bores, but not because they're haters. On the other hand, people who don't hate anybody are the biggest bores. They're lacking in human emotion. Norman is more of a bore than a hater. He even bores me to talk about him," said Dorothy. Then, as an afterthought, she added, "But he doesn't hate you, George. Not you in particular. The one that would really hate you would be Bertie."

"Why do you say that?" said George.

"Speaking as a woman," said Dorothy. "If I were Bertie Roach, coming up from nowhere—"

"*To* nowhere," said George.

"Yes, to nowhere, but expecting more out of life than she ever got. Doing all the housework, raising those two hopeless specimens, and having to be Norman's wife. And all the time so near and yet so far from the fun you and Elsie had—I think Bertie must have had the dullest existence a woman ever had."

"It could have been worse," said George.

"Oh, it could have been. But she'd never think of that. She's had to spend her life thinking of how it could have been better. She's never really had anything. I almost feel sorry for her."

But now George began to tickle her in a way she liked to be tickled, and they quickly abandoned themselves to the special pleasures that the tickling usually produced. "You're *terrible*, George," she said.

"You think I'm terrible, Dorothy?" he said.

"Yes, I do. And I'm just as bad as you are, for liking it," said Dorothy. "Did you always know this was what I'd like?"

"Quiet," he said.

"Nobody else—"

"Quiet," he said.

The death of Frances Cookson was noted with suitable regret on the part of her limited circle of friends and acquaintances. It had been, as they said, a long time coming, which could have meant— but did not—that her friends were impatient to see her go. Her death put an end to her misery, but it was the beginning of active distress for Alberta Roach. Lawyers came to the shoppe and looked at her books; two sets of lawyers, one from the firm representing Frances Cookson's estate and the other representing Norma Blair. The settling of Frances Cookson's estate took more than a year, a year of harassment for Alberta, which told on her nerves, her appetite, her sleeping habits. The suspense was bad enough, but she got no relief when the problem was resolved by the agreement between Frances Cookson's and Norma Blair's lawyers. They decided that the shoppe must go out of business.

"It's cruel, it's cruel," said Alberta. "Mrs. Blair could have kept it going. I cut down the overhead to practically nothing. I was willing to have them reduce my salary. But Mrs. Blair said she didn't want to be bothered with it any more. Why did Father have to have that fight with Uncle George?"

"You must try to make the best of it," said Bertie. "It may turn out to be a blessing in disguise. With your experience, running your own shop, you shouldn't find it hard to get a job that will pay you much better, and you'll be able to do a lot of things you deprived yourself of."

The sisters were taking a more realistic view of jobs. Sophronia was no longer employed at the Children's Home, and the Roach girls no longer felt so strongly about competing with women who really needed money. Sophronia, with nothing else to do, had even offered her services as baby-sitter, with no takers. Alberta now discovered that her policy of running the shoppe for an exclusive clientele had made her an undesirable candidate for jobs in the larger stores. "Frankly, Miss Roach," said one manager, "you'd drive some customers away. You ran your own place for the country club crowd, and we don't get many of them in here." Alberta recalled now that the manager's own wife had been one of the women she had rebuffed.

"Something will come up," said Bertie Roach. "You have your degree from Wellesley."

"So has Sophronia," said Alberta.

"Well, you mustn't get discouraged."

"I *am* discouraged. What have I got to look forward to? Sitting home all day? Listening to Sophronia complain about her oily skin? And I wish you'd speak to her about rinsing out the tub. It doesn't do any good when I speak to her."

"Well, now you're not perfect either, you know. You could get into the habit of making your bed in the morning instead of leaving it till noon. It was different when you had to go to the shoppe every day. Your sister and I were more than glad to save you those few minutes. But each must do their share of the housework."

"Does that include Father? What does he ever do, I'd like to know. This house seems to be run for his convenience and comfort. Isn't he ever going to do anything?"

"What?" said Bertie.

"Yes, *what* is right. Lost his temper with Uncle George, and that ruined my chances of getting any help there."

Bertie Roach was not a subtle woman, but in matters that concerned her husband, her daughters, and her house she was perceptive. She liked watching pennies and bread crusts and fly specks and things that were in their proper place and things that were not in their proper place. She listened for the sounds that were the first signs of a cold in the head, for slightly prolonged gurgling in the water pipes that indicated trouble with the plumbing, for the variables in the pitch of greetings that revealed a mood or a change in mood. All her senses were continually at work, and little escaped her notice if it pertained to the objects and the beings in her house. She did not always or even often correct or improve what she observed; the effort would have been too great, and would have taken her away from her preoccupation with observation. Then too, her husband and her daughters treated her with a slight condescension that their formal respect for her did not altogether hide. But nothing got past her, and as the days and some months went by she had some new developments to watch.

These developments concerned Norman and Alberta, and affected Sophronia only indirectly. Norman, Bertie began to notice, would leave the house after breakfast, go for his walk in the shopping district, and return home before the morning was half gone. At first he would say he forgot something, and make a pretense of looking for a clean handkerchief or a pipe cleaner. But after a while he abandoned the making of excuses; he would turn up at home at ten o'clock, take his accustomed seat in the front parlor with his hat resting in his lap, and then abruptly announce that he was off again. He would be back in time for lunch, then leave once more. Bertie noticed that he seldom stayed away from the house for more than an hour. He offered no explanation for the changes in his former routine, and Bertie could not bring herself to the point where her curiosity would overcome her diffidence. If Norman wanted to be back and forth all through the day, there was no law against that. It was his house, and he was free to come and go as he pleased. In years past he had usually left the house after breakfast, come home for lunch, and then gone out for the afternoon. As men got older, they sometimes got bladder trouble, and Bertie made sure that that was not Norman's reason for the brevity of his absences from the house. She was not given much to finding the reasons for things, but Norman was her husband and whatever reason he had for a change in his habits was quite possibly important. She could not—though she tried—make herself believe there was no reason more important than caprice. Something was going on, something was happening.

When she learned the truth, she wished she had not. She wished she had remained ignorant and unashamed. The truth was, simply, that Norman had become a town character, an object of derision, a buffoon. In a most disrespectful way he had become known as *Norman,* with no need for further identification. One of the town drunks was known as Dory, one of the prostitutes was known as Mae. In like manner, Norman was Norman, a bore who had become an eccentric whom people laughed at behind his back and who would soon be laughed at to his face. It had taken time—a year or more—but she made the cruelly shameful discovery that her man, *her man*, was being called harmless! Not a harmless idiot, not a harmless nut, but "Norman, he's harmless." This strong man, well educated and brave, honest and decent, good husband and good father, with almost sixty years of blameless behavior to his credit, was being rewarded with the contempt of people who were not fit to lick his boots.

And he knew it.

He knew it before she did, and it was through his own small admissions that she pieced together the truth. First there were the occasional references to people who had got fresh; his being called Norman by people who had no right to call him Norman. Next came the incidents of impertinence in which he nearly lost his temper. Thinking back, Bertie realized that there must have been many such incidents and many times when he had come home to take temporary refuge from impertinent people. Her mind was unencumbered by the processes of psychoanalysis and her vocabulary was innocent of its jargon, but she recognized without being able to define his compulsion to return to the scenes of the abrasive attacks on his self-respect. He just couldn't keep away from those people.

Her method of dealing with Norman's problem was to observe silence, since she knew no other method. She could not tell him that he ought to stay away from people; to do so would have been the same as telling him that he was an outcast, and where was there to go that offered a race of people who were more understanding and tolerant? Here, at least, the enemies were not strangers. Here the bad people were not strangers who had never known that Norman was ever a brave and strong man. Another place would only be worse, cold and alien and seeing only the man he had become. There were just so many years a man could live (or a woman), and of the years that remained to Norman, some of them—the final ones—would be home years, when he would stay off the streets and away from the bad people. Some men got bladder trouble, some got the arthritis, and they sat in a chair and read books and took naps. Those were the home years, and as much as half the years remaining to Norman might turn out to be home years. Suddenly, and temporarily, Bertie had the material for a compromise that was not a solution, but was the next best thing to a solution of an unsolvable problem. When you know, and admit, that your husband bores people and inspires ridicule, you can plan for the day when you have him entirely to yourself. He did not, it must be remembered, bore Bertie. Long ago he had rescued her from a vegetable patch; for most of her life he had given her a house and the money to run it; and when she wanted him to, he made love to her. No one, it seemed, was going to do all these things for her daughters, and the bleakness of their future reminded her of what her life could have been.

For Sophronia there was no hope. She was a female, but men were repelled by her and thus had made her afraid of them. A certain few of the women of the town had friendships with other women that substituted for marriage. Bertie knew what they did; it had been described to her by Norman out of his limited supply of information. If Sophronia could have formed such an attachment, Bertie could have accepted the friendship part and deadened her imagination to ignore the secret kissings. In time Sophronia and her imaginary friend would be permanently designated as man-haters, and once so classified they would be forgotten. People were much more cruel to the fairies, as Norman called them—the men who corresponded to the women like Sophronia and her imaginary friend. It was sometimes argued that there was nothing but friendship between two such women, but the fairies were adjudged guilty, potentially if not actually. And, of course, they usually were. An odd sort of respectability attached to the female virgin perverts. In the history of the community none of them had ever been arrested, beaten up, or run out of town; whistled at, blackmailed, or driven to suicide by public scorn. Bertie did not know why this was so; she was not given much to finding the reasons for things. But she knew it was so, and if Sophronia could get someone, almost anyone, to be her companion and friend, Bertie would not stand in the way.

But women rejected Sophronia, and Sophronia was not constituted to make the effort of friendship. She was scornful of the people below her station in life, and jealous of those above it. The condescension she could not hide from her mother, a nobody, differed only in degree from her attitude toward her father, whose mother was a Richardson but whose father was undeniably Patrick Roach. And she had not tried to forgive Alberta for refusing to give her a job in the shoppe. Once, years ago, Sophronia had liked cats, but cat-hair made her father sneeze, and she was not allowed to keep one in the house. That had been years ago, a buried and forgotten oddment in the hideous history of Sophronia Roach, who had certain rights as a citizen of the United States of America that included her nullified right of the pursuit of happiness. God wasted no miracles on her.

Alberta at least had cried, and the shoppe was her hope. Had been her hope. A little store in an office building, full of trinkets and gadgets that were for sale more cheaply elsewhere; a place where nice women could borrow an umbrella and go to the bathroom and have a cup of tea. Almost a club for nice women, but nice women who had not appreciated it enough to support it. Bertie, thinking these things, progressed easily to intemperate thoughts of George Roach and his club and his failure to come through with the few dollars that would have kept the shoppe going, and his responsibility for what was happening to Alberta's hope and to Alberta. It was not hard to see what was happening to Alberta; before her time she was getting to be like her father. The details were not the same; Alberta had not yet become a laughingstock, a street bore. But when she telephoned the nice women they would not come to the phone or they would not return her call. Everybody—all the nice women— seemed to know that Alberta wanted to talk to them about starting a new shoppe. She had had to mention that project to only one or two of the nice women, and the others were told. The nice women were avoiding Alberta by telephone as the people on the street were looking the other way at the approach of her father. One day Bertie knew that that was so, no longer a truth to shrink from, but a hard, harsh fact to add to the other hard, harsh facts. As long as there was some hope for Alberta there could be some hope for Norman, for Sophronia, and for Bertie herself. It was a small family, and when there were only two children, if one of them turned out half well, the rest of the family could be sustained by that one's small hope. But Bertie had seen what those vigils beside the telephone had done to Alberta. ("Don't anybody use the phone this afternoon. I'm expecting a very important call.") The catalogs continued to come from the jobbers, and as though to add to the taunts the post office demanded its extra pennies for the insufficient postage on free samples of merchandise. ("I saw old Mrs. Reeves today. She told me how much she missed the shoppe—ha ha ha. I'll just bet she does. She used to bring things in to be rewrapped that she'd bought at the dime store.")

"What if we turned the front room into a shoppe?" said Bertie.

"It can't be done," said Alberta. "It's against the zoning laws, for one thing, and Father says it would put us in a different category with the insurance company."

"You spoke to your father? I didn't know that."

"Long ago. That was one of the first things I thought of, was having a shoppe here temporarily. Just to keep the business going."

"I wish you'd spoken to me first. I'd have known what to say to your father."

"It wouldn't have done any good. It would have cost around ten thousand dollars to get started again, and Father was against it. He won't touch his capital, because that's all we'll have to live on when he dies. He never took out life insurance, because he said you got better returns for your money in common stocks."

"Well, I never did know much about those things."

"After the holidays I'm going to start looking for a job. I was thinking of taking a course in shorthand and typing. Sophronia and I could take it together."

"Do you want to do that?"

"No, but for God's sake I have to do something or I'll go stark, staring mad!"

Her intensity frightened Bertie into silence.

"I mean it, Mother, and I'm not going to say I'm sorry, so don't expect me to. I'd rather wash dishes than sit around this house another year."

"You weren't given a college education to learn to wash dishes. But if that's what you want to do."

"It isn't what I want to do. But we'd have been better off if you hadn't given us a college education. It wasn't because we wanted it, but you and Father had a lot of ideas. That we were better than the girls in Gibbsville High and the rest of that baloney. Just because Father didn't have to work for a living. Well, if he hadn't deluded himself that he was a gentleman, he might have made enough money to do something for us. But he isn't a gentleman. He inherited money from his father, a cheap Irish skinflint who slept with his stenographer. Even so, if he'd been more like his father he could afford to live like a gentleman instead of what he is."

"What *is* he?"

"A tiresome old freak that people run away from. Oh, I know. I'm not blind."

"And what am I?"

"I wasn't talking about you," said Alberta.

"You were when you talk about your father that way, your own father. You might just as well call me a tiresome old freak too."

"Don't try my patience too much, Mother."

"Don't you try mine, either," said Bertie. But there was no force to her counter-threat. For thirty years she had ruled her children on the strength of her own belief in parental authority, with the result that in all that time they had not doubted or questioned her right to rule. But now neither she nor Norman could *do* anything for them; there was nothing now to take the place of feeding them, dressing them, binding their small wounds and performing all the other attentions that they needed as children. Bertie, when they were children, could find other children for them to play with, and did so by arrangement with other parents. No longer was that true. Bertie and Norman were of no use to their daughters. They were not even in the way.

Four lives were being lived in the Norman Roach house, four individual lives and not the collective family life that was Bertie's delusion. She did not wish to have any member separated from the family unit, and now that she was confronted with the accomplished fact of their individualities, the fact of her own individuality greatly disturbed her. She had not wanted to be alone, and through the years of her marriage to Norman she had not been alone. Now, however, the separate miseries of the others produced a separate misery for her, and she was unequal to the control of it. Upon discovering the collapse of her family as a unit, she rushed into the discovery that the collapse was also the destruction of the unit and of the individuals. *They* were deserting *her*. The spurious unity in which she had so long believed (and in which she had taken secret pride as the central factor) gave way to hysterical terror, in which every act of every individual was to be interpreted as protest, criticism of her, and, ultimately, persecution of her. The collapse of the unit was unreal because the unit as she understood it had never really existed; but there was nothing unreal about her belief in their persecution of her. It was real *because* she believed it, and could turn any word and any act into proof of it.

Soon—and very soon; it did not take long—the others noticed that Bertie was behaving strangely. She was snappish, she would argue over nothing, she would leave the table and lock herself in her room. Norman, with his massive ignorance of women, concluded that she was having a secondary menopause or had not graduated from an earlier one. As his knowledge of the climacteric consisted entirely of the information she had given him, and as she had refused to discuss it (reticence was her excuse, but her own ignorance was the reason), he had to be satisfied with his explanation of her conduct. One of the few things she had told him about the menopause was that it lasted an indefinite length of time and then it went away; she had not said anything about its coming back, but he convinced himself that she was having a recurrence. The *recurrence* would go away, and until it did he must be patient. The girls, too, must be patient, and he told them so. "Your mother is at a certain time of life," he told them. "I'm sure you know what I have reference to."

"I know what you have reference to," said Alberta. "But I thought that was over. And anyway—"

"I'd much rather we didn't discuss it," said Norman.

"I was going to say, whether it's change of life or not, it still doesn't give her the right to behave like this. She imagines things."

"Just you bear that in mind when you reach that age," said Norman. "Women, women."

"*Men! Men!*" said Sophronia.

"Now there, Sophronia, don't you be disrespectful," said her father. "*I'm* going for a *walk.*"

"Don't get lost, Father," said Sophronia. She grinned at him, half expecting to be slapped (as her mother would have slapped her), but unafraid.

Having more or less agreed that Bertie was a problem, the father and the daughters treated her as such, thereby confirming her suspicions of a union against her—the only unity in the household. She made up a bed in the attic and slept there. The protest she expected from Norman was not forthcoming, since he was doing everything to humor her. But the connotations of a bed in the attic did not escape the notice of Alberta and Sophronia; their mother had often sent them there to punish them when they were naughty, and only a woman who had something the matter with her would choose to sleep in a cold, dark room which had once been inhabited by bats. Every night at bedtime she would take her flashlight and retire, and Norman and the girls would exchange glances but say nothing. They would listen for the last sounds in the plumbing that indicated she was through in the bathroom and was on her way to the attic. The sounds had a relaxing effect on them. Norman could resume his reading of the *Congressional Record;* Alberta her study of the job-bers' catalogs, and Sophronia her endless knitting of scarves for the poor.

"Maybe you better go up and see how she is," said Norman one night at the beginning of Bertie's removal to the attic.

"And have her accuse me of spying on her? *You* go," said Alberta.

"Don't anybody go," said Sophronia. "That's what she wants—to get attention."

"I thought just the opposite, but maybe you're right," said Norman. "You may be right."

"Well, I'm glad I'm right for once, anyway," said Sophronia.

"Don't worry," said Alberta. "If there's anything wrong we'll hear from her."

"I suppose so," said Norman.

Interminable day followed interminable day for each and all of them, and yet they were sustained by a sense of waiting that was common to them all. At a quarter to seven one evening Bertie said, "I'm not going to wait dinner any longer. Sophronia's three quarters of an hour late as it is."

"Did she say anything to you about where she was going?" said Norman.

"She never tells me anything," said Alberta.

"It isn't like her," said Norman.

"It isn't like her to be late for a meal, if that's what you mean."

"And she was supposed to mash the potatoes," said Bertie.

"I'll mash them," said Alberta.

"No, I will. You stay where you are," said Bertie.

Sophronia did not appear all evening, and at eleven o'clock Norman announced that he was going to call the police station.

"I wouldn't if I were you," said Alberta.

"Why not? Is there something you're not telling us? You've been sitting pretty quiet all evening," said Bertie.

"Yes, out with it," said Norman.

"Out with nothing," said Alberta. "I just think it would be a mistake to call the police. She's not some sixteen-year-old juvenile delinquent. What would—"

At that moment Sophronia entered the house.

"Where on earth—" said Bertie.

"We were just about to call the police," said Norman.

"I was going to phone, but I didn't have any money," said Sophronia.

"I'm sure anybody in this town would lend you the price of a—" said Norman.

"Where *were* you?" said Bertie.

"Oh, leave me alone!" said Sophronia. "Can't a person go for a walk?"

"You could have walked to Reading by this time," said Norman. "You've been gone since two o'clock this afternoon."

"And what do you mean you didn't have any money? You had twenty dollars this morning," said Bertie.

"You're not going to get it out of her that way," said Alberta.

"Oh, you shut up, too," said Sophronia. "I'm going to bed."

"Have you had any dinner?" said Bertie.

"Are you still up? I thought you'd be in the attic," said Sophronia. She hurried upstairs and slammed the door of her room. Wherever she had been and whatever she had done, the only clue to her nine-hour absence was the delivery the next day of her purse. Mr. Grossman, the manager of the movie theater, delivered it in person. "It was turned in by the cleaning-woman," said Grossman. "There's seventeen dollars and forty-two cents in it. I guess she must of fell asleep."

"How did you know who it belonged to?" said Bertie.

"Oh, she always sits in the same place," said Grossman. "And I put two and two together. Miss Roach, I said, right away. We don't get that many customers for the matinee. Saturdays we do, but not on a weekday."

"Well, thank you very much. Here, give this to the cleaning-woman," said Bertie. She held out a dollar.

"Oh, that's all right," said Grossman. "Your daughter's a good customer."

"But the cleaning-woman ought to have something."

"Well—I'll make it a dollar if you make it a dollar."

"Isn't a dollar enough?"

"I guess a couple dollars is all right," said Grossman. "It comes to better than ten percent, if you want to look at it that way."

"Then let's give her five dollars."

"You mean you two and a half and me two and a half?" said Grossman.

"Yes," said Bertie. "Here's two-forty-two. I'll go get the other eight cents."

"Skip it, skip it."

"Or why don't we just give her two dollars apiece? Four dollars ought to be enough."

"Yes ma'am. Whatever you say," said Grossman. "Is she all right now, your daughter?"

"Yes. Why?"

"Well, you know she sat through four shows, pretty near."

"Oh, she did?"

"I guess she slept through part of them," said Grossman.

"Four shows. You didn't tell me that."

"Well, I seen her buy a ticket around ha' past two, and I noticed her going out when we broke about ten of eleven. Listen, she's no trouble, ma'am. That other time was water over the bridge, over and done with."

"What other time?"

"When her sister came and got her," said Grossman.

"Oh, *then,*" said Bertie. "Well, thanks, Mr. Gross. I'll see that she gets the purse and I'll explain that *I* took the two dollars."

"She's all right. She's *nothing* to some of the characters we get," said Grossman.

Alberta at first refused to enlighten her mother on the occasion of having had to go and get Sophronia.

"Is it that wicked?" said Bertie.

"I don't know whether it was wicked or not. The woman wanted to have her arrested."

"What woman?"

"The mother of the little girl. Don't you know any of this? Sophronia followed a little girl into the ladies' room and the child became frightened."

"At something Sophronia did?" said Bertie.

"I—don't—know. *I* wasn't there. Maybe it was something Sophronia did, and maybe it was just the child's imagination."

"Good heavens," said Bertie. "When was all this?"

"Oh, several years ago. After she lost her job at the Children's Home. She used to come in and hang around the shoppe and I finally told her I'd give her the money to go to the movies, and that's what she did. I couldn't have her annoying my customers. They used to come in and see her there and turn right around and walk out. You don't *know*."

"And she followed the child into the ladies' room and then what?"

"Oh, dear. Well, as near as I could make out, the child must have screamed and the mother ran in, passing Sophronia on the way out. The woman went to the manager, Grossman his name is, and said her child had been molested. For all I know, Sophronia may have been only trying to be nice to the kid, but her looks were against her. On the other hand, that dreadful woman at the Children's Home, Miss Mack, she spread some story around about Sophronia."

"I never heard it," said Bertie.

"How *would* you? You never see any of the trustees. Whether it was true or not, Miss Mack fired her and nobody, least of all Sophronia, made any fuss about it."

"Then what happened, at the picture theater?"

"The manager calmed her down, the mother, and sent for me. He knew me because we were both members of the Merchants Association. He was very nice. I think he was inclined to believe the woman's story, but the woman had nothing to go on but the word of a frightened child, and Grossman is only the manager of the theater.

580 • JOHN O'HARA

He wants to have a good record so he'll be promoted to someplace else. So he told me as much as he knew, and said he realized we were a prominent family and so forth and so on. In other words, he wanted us on his side. So I told him I'd see to that, all right. The Roaches would stand behind him in case there was any kind of trouble."

"Your father knew about this all along?"

"Father? Can you imagine me telling any of this to Father? It's hard enough to tell you, a woman."

"Sophronia is one of those degenerates," said Bertie.

"Probably."

"My daughter, one of those degenerates," said Bertie.

"Well, now maybe you'll understand why I didn't want her in the shoppe."

"I do," said Bertie. "You didn't have any pity for her."

"Pity! *Pity?* Where were you when I was covering up for her at Wellesley? You never knew till just now what she was like. Tagging along after me all her life. The only good times I was ever allowed to have were my two years at Wellesley before she arrived there. But she made up for those two years, don't think she didn't. My friends had to be her friends, she couldn't make any friends of her own. I couldn't go anywhere or do anything without her horning in. My senior year I didn't have a friend left, thanks to her. They couldn't *stand* her, and neither could I. Even the Lesbians didn't want her around."

"I don't like that word," said Bertie.

"You don't even know what it means," said Alberta.

"There you're wrong," said Bertie. "And if she's one, maybe you are too."

"I have been," said Alberta. "And I think you are. And God knows what Father is. You don't know. I wouldn't expect you to."

"If you say another word, I'll slap you."

"Do, and I'll leave this house," said Alberta. She put her head forward, held up her chin defiantly and irresistibly close to Bertie, and Bertie slapped her. Alberta laughed. "Now I can leave," she said.

She stood up, looked around at the articles of furniture, then left the room. An hour passed, long enough for Bertie to stop wondering what she was doing. At the foot of the stairs Bertie called out, "Alberta, I'm going next door to borrow their vacuum."

"Yes, Mother," she heard Alberta say.

"I have to borrow their vacuum. Ours is being fixed."

"Yes, Mother, I heard you," said Alberta.

When Bertie returned Alberta was gone. Bertie had heard and seen the taxi come and go, but the conversation attendant upon the borrowing of the vacuum cleaner involved the ritual of apology, of explaining the absence of the Roaches' vacuum, of a few words of conversation unrelated to the vacuum, of Bertie's promise to bring the vacuum back that very same day, and the consumption of a piece of home-made fudge that her neighbor pressed upon her. A good twenty minutes was spent in the ritual. Bertie went upstairs to Alberta's room to determine the extent of her packing. It was extensive. The dressing table had been stripped of silver-backed hairbrush and comb and manicure set; the bureau drawers were open and empty; the clothes closet contained only a few old dresses and shoes. Bertie looked everywhere for a note, but found none. There was nothing to do now but wait. She had neither bus nor train schedule, although she guessed that Alberta would be going southward toward Philadelphia. Northward were Scranton and Wilkes-Barre, of no interest to Alberta. Bertie wanted to be sick, but she did not want Norman to come home and find her being sick. Sophronia was probably at the movies.

Bertie plugged in the vacuum cleaner and started to do the front room. It was better than doing nothing while waiting for Norman to come home.

When he did come home she was doing the diningroom. "Don't stop, it's only me," he called to her. She switched off the vacuum and joined him in the front hall.

"Get ready for a shock," she said. "Alberta's run away."

"Run away? Where to? What do you mean *run* away?"

"Left. Packed her things and left. Where to, I don't know."

"You have some kind of a quarrel or something?"

"She was contemptible and I slapped her."

"Well, maybe she deserved it. She's been acting like an I-don't-know-what-lately. Where's Sophronia?"

"Dear knows."

"Didn't go with her, though. Well, we'll hear from Alberta when she runs out of money. Do you happen to know how much she had on her?"

"No."

"Her bank balance doesn't amount to much. I doubt if she has over a hundred dollars there, if that. You given her any lately?"

"No, did you?"

"Not since the first of the month. Her hundred dollars monthly allowance. That wouldn't leave her much. The bank's closed, so she couldn't cash a cheque, although I guess one of the stores would cash one for her."

"It wouldn't be for much, though," said Bertie.

"I'm going on the theory that she'd write a bad cheque," said Norman. "If she was going to run away from home, writing a bad cheque wouldn't faze her. At least I don't think it would. It wouldn't be the first time she was overdrawn, not by a long shot. Going back to her Wellesley days she formed bad habits. More careless than dishonest, but one's just as bad as the other at the bank. We'll hear from her."

"You don't seem very worried," said Bertie.

"What good does it do to worry now? She's not a young girl, she's a full-grown woman, and maybe it was a mistake to slap her for that reason. But I'm not holding that against you. Many's the time I felt like it myself, but I never spanked them when they were little and I couldn't begin now. The other one is just as bad. She never apologized or offered me any explanation for staying out that night. I'm frankly more worried about her than Alberta. God almighty! We've given them every advantage, decent home and a fine education, and the thanks we get. Compare that with the letter I got every year from the man I saved the life of in 1918. In 1918! An ignorant Italian fellow but they're famous for their politeness. Right up to the time he died. 'Dear Lieutenant.' Always lieutenant, never mister."

"Where are you going? Are you getting ready to go out again?"

"I thought I'd go and inquire if they saw her at the bus station. Ivor Jones there would recognize her. You'll be all right, won't you? Or would you rather I stayed?"

"Stay. There's no use letting outsiders know we're worried."

"I guess so. Where do you think she'd head for?"

"She probably didn't know herself."

"What did you quarrel about?"

"Oh, any number of things. We've been getting on each other's nerves."

"In other words you don't care to tell me."

"Not now," said Bertie.

"I could phone Ivor Jones and make up some story and maybe that way find out which bus she took."

"No, let's wait till we hear from her. If anybody asks, we can just say she went away for a few days."

"Yes, *if* anybody asks. That may be the root of the trouble. Nobody's liable to ask. I guess there are probably some poor people in town that envy us because we have a nice home and plenty to eat. But you can be as rich as Andrew Mellon and still have your troubles. You don't even have to go as far as Andrew Mellon. We have some in town with ten times our money and they're no better off. We all had it too easy, that was our trouble. Except you. In this whole family, you were the only one that really did anything. It isn't natural for a man to spend their lives like George and I. It wasn't natural, not in this country. Over on the other side, Europe, maybe they can get away with it, but not here. Here I am, getting to the age where most men think about getting ready to retire. But I've always lived retired. So has George. The two of us, as different as we can be, but neither of us ever did a tap of work and now there's George'll fall over dead some day in the midst of a game of bridge. Me, I'll fall over talking to somebody like Ivor Jones. That's the way it'll be for me, and that's the way it'll be for George."

"Why are you bringing his name into the conversation? It's the first time I heard you mention him in I don't know how long," said Bertie.

"Why do I mention him? Because I guess there's that connection between him and Alberta. He wouldn't offer to help her out, and now she's in some kind of trouble again."

"Do you know what she is? She's as good as having a nervous breakdown. I know of people that had nervous breakdowns, and they remind me of Alberta, or she reminds me of them."

"Who, for instance?" said Norman.

"Who?"

"Yes. There aren't so many people that have nervous breakdowns. I've seen men go suddenly haywire, but that was fear. Strain. Just before an attack. I saw a man climb up over the parapet and stand up full height. The machine guns practically cut him in half. That was a real nervous breakdown. I don't consider Alberta having a real nervous breakdown. You shouldn't use that expression for a female tantrum. You go move your things up to the attic, but I never considered that a nervous breakdown. That was a tantrum. That was like me going for a walk when I want to get out of the house. If you called it a nervous breakdown every time someone wanted to avoid some unpleasantness, everybody in the world is crazy."

"Maybe everybody is," said Bertie.

Norman smiled. "Well, sure they are, to a certain extent. I am. You are. Alberta. Sophronia. I see plenty of examples of it, of people acting a little crazy. But that wouldn't justify me calling them all crazy. The real nuts are the ones that think they're sane and everybody else is out of their minds. They're the real nuts. I have to admit I sometimes feel that way myself, when I look at the way things are going. They're spending all that money paving the North Side but in five more years there won't be anybody living there. A bond issue for that, mind you. Everybody I talk to agrees with me, but they're all going to vote for the bonds. They say it'll provide employment. Typical Gibbsville thinking, and it's just as bad or worse nationally. The trouble is we have no real leadership. Nobody wants to take any responsibility. They all agree with me, but they go right on electing the same people year after year. If the right people would only get together."

"Yes," said Bertie.

"Instead of spending that money paving the North Side, what they ought to do is cut down on the population. Australia is looking for people, paying people to go there. They have to be British subjects, but they'd take Americans I'm sure. I wrote to the State Department but I never got any answer. I had a scheme to send our unemployed to Australia. Operation Gibbsville, I called it. Give our people the fare to Australia without losing their American citizenship. It'd cost four or five hundred dollars apiece, but that's cheaper than paying them unemployment insurance. I never got any answer, although several people I talked to in town said they'd be willing to go. The people I'd send aren't paying taxes, they're on relief, not doing anyone any good. But if we sent them to Australia they'd be welcome there, and they'd be doing some good for themselves, for Australia, for the United States, and the world in general. I met quite a few Australians in Africa. They're a lot like Americans, once you get to know them."

"Maybe Alberta ought to go to Australia," said Bertie.

"I don't know whether they need women," said Norman. "As I understand it they're looking for married couples. Homesteaders. I wasn't thinking of Alberta when I concocted my scheme, but you remember Jamestown. And the Far West. Once they got started they sent for women. Not that Alberta fits into that category, but she might like Australia. You never know. I'll take it up with her when she calms down."

"Are you going to finance a trip to Australia for her?"

"Well, I don't want to commit myself that far. We don't even know where she is."

"Or if we're ever going to see her again," said Bertie.

"I'm not worried about that. As soon as she runs out of money, that's when we'll hear from her and not before."

"Why are you so sure? I'm not," said Bertie.

"Well, it's what I think," said Norman. "And more than half the time I'm right. I'm right a good deal more than half the time."

As is often the case with a man whose mind is always busy, Norman Roach was more frequently right than wrong. He was right now. The circumstances were not as he had envisioned them—a financially distraught Alberta telephoning from a distant city for the funds to pay her way home. But as he said, when she ran out of money, they heard from her.

Less than forty-eight hours after she left home, she returned, accompanied by Edgar Fleischer, a lawyer and former classmate of Alberta's at Gibbsville High. The doorbell rang at five minutes past six and Norman went to answer it. "Well, come in," he said. "You didn't have to ring. Hello, Edgar." Norman chuckled. "You didn't have to bring your lawyer," he said. "But come on in."

He held the door open for them, and when they were inside he called out to Bertie. "We have visitors."

Bertie came forward from the kitchen. "Alberta!" she exclaimed. "We were so worried."

"Mother, you know Edgar Fleischer," said Alberta.

"Is that who it is? I didn't recognize him in this light," said Bertie.

"She brought her lawyer," said Norman.

"Don't anybody say anything till I get back," said Bertie. "We're having calves' liver and it'll be burned to a crisp. Are you staying for dinner, or what?"

"No, we're not staying," said Alberta.

"I don't see why you had to bring a lawyer," said Norman. "I don't understand that at all."

"He's not my lawyer, he's my husband," said Alberta.

"Your husband? Since when?" said Norman.

"I won't say any more till Mother gets back from the kitchen."

"This once it doesn't matter," said Bertie.

"Calves' liver will smoke up the whole house," said Alberta. "Go on, take it off."

"I won't be but a minute," said Bertie. She hesitated and looked at Edgar Fleischer. "This isn't some kind of joke, is it?"

"No, she's serious," said Norman. "Go tend to the meat and come back. We won't say anything."

Bertie hurried away and was back so soon that Norman and Alberta and Edgar Fleischer were still standing in the front hall.

"All right, I guess we can go in and talk," said Norman. He led the way, pointed to chairs for each of the others, and sat down. "I understood you to say you were married to Edgar. When did this happen? You weren't secretly married to him all the time, were you?"

"No. We were married yesterday, in Shoemakersville," said Alberta. "Edgar has cousins there."

"I thought your mother came from Phoenixville," said Norman.

"No sir. Shoemakersville," said Edgar.

"Why did you have to go down there? You could just as easily got married here in town," said Norman.

"Alberta wanted it that way," said Edgar.

"Let me tell them," said Alberta. "When I left here the day before yesterday I realized I only had a little over thirty-five dollars. That wouldn't get me very far. So I tried to think of who I could borrow from and I remembered Edgar."

"Why Edgar? I don't understand that either," said Norman. "He was never our lawyer."

"No, but he was a friend," said Alberta.

"I didn't know that, either," said Bertie. "Of course we know Edgar, but when did you ever see him since high school?"

"I didn't, except to say hello to on the street. And he always used to wave to me when he passed the shoppe. But we were always friendly."

"Tell her what I said," said Edgar.

"You mean in high school?" said Alberta.

"Yes."

"In high school he said he wanted to marry me and didn't care how long he had to wait."

"Really?" said Bertie. "And he waited all this time? Didn't he ever propose again?"

"I never got much chance to," said Edgar. "We never went out together or anything."

"But you didn't go to his office and say you were ready to marry him, did you?" said Norman.

"No, no, no, no, no. I kept the taxi waiting while I went and asked him if I could have the loan of a hundred dollars."

"Oh, I see. Then before you knew it you were telling him what you wanted it for," said Norman.

"That's just about the way it was, Mr. Roach. That's just about the way," said Edgar Fleischer.

"But it doesn't tell how they got married," said Bertie.

"If you'd use your imagination," said Norman. "One word led to another, and Edgar said he'd always wanted to marry her. I can see how that would happen. Yes, I can understand that."

"But I want to know—" said Bertie.

"I'll tell you," said Alberta. "He suggested that we get married, and I couldn't think of any reason why not. If I knew him well enough to ask him for money, and he still wanted to marry me after all these years. So I said I would, and he went down and paid the taxi and I waited in his office till he got his car out of the garage."

"I phoned Shoemakersville," said Edgar.

"He phoned one of his cousins in Phoenixville. I didn't hear that conversation," said Alberta.

"I have this cousin by marriage, a judge in Common Pleas. He's married to my mother's first cousin, and a very likable man, although I don't see him very often. He said he'd take care of all the necessary preliminaries."

"That was while Alberta was waiting in your office," said Norman. "You'd paid the taxi and brought her luggage upstairs."

"Didn't anybody see you carry the luggage upstairs?" said Bertie.

"They could have without knowing it was Alberta's luggage,"

said Norman. "Mrs. Roach is wondering how many people know you eloped."

"Nobody in town knows it, so you don't have to worry about that," said Alberta.

"Where did you go from the office?" said Bertie.

Alberta looked at Edgar Fleischer and he looked at her. "We spent the night at a motel, near Reading," said Alberta.

"Oh, well, you were getting married the next day. I suppose you signed the register Mr. and Mrs. Edgar Fleischer."

"No. Mr. and Mrs. Edgar Fisher," said Edgar Fleischer.

"If you drove there in your car they could check your license," said Norman.

"What difference does that make?" said Alberta. "Good heavens, Father."

"Then the next day you went to Shoemakersville and your cousin married you?" said Bertie.

"The Methodist preacher," said Edgar Fleischer. "We were married in his house."

"Did you have any attendants?" said Bertie.

"Edgar's cousin, and the preacher's wife," said Alberta.

"What time of day was it?" said Bertie.

"What time was it, Edgar? I guess about quarter to twelve," said Alberta.

"Yes, we got there about eleven-thirty and we were out by twelve noon. It didn't take long."

"Then where'd you go?" said Bertie.

"To a motel. A different one. We were both exhausted. We stayed there till this afternoon. Then Edgar had to come back to see about things in his office."

"I'm supposed to be in court tomorrow morning," said Edgar Fleischer. "But I think I can easily get a postponement. It isn't anything big."

"Do you want Mrs. Roach and I to make the announcement tomorrow? Where were you thinking of living?"

"You could stay here," said Bertie.

"Edgar has a room at Mrs. Buckley's, but we're going to have to start looking for an apartment."

"You won't have any trouble finding one. Vacancies everywhere. Meanwhile why don't you make this your headquarters?" said Norman.

"No thanks," said Alberta.

"You'll stay for dinner, of course," said Bertie.

"No, we just wanted to tell you. And I wanted to see Father for a minute. Alone."

"All right," said Norman. "We can go back in the diningroom."

They did so, closing the sliding doors. "You want to talk about finances, no doubt," said Norman.

"Yes."

"Well, I guess if you'd had a regular wedding, with a reception, I don't know what that would amount to. But what would *you* say?"

"I don't know."

"Two thousand? Three thousand?"

"I guess so. It'd depend," said Alberta.

"Say three thousand. And I'll continue your allowance."

"That would be very satisfactory, if you did that."

"How much does Edgar make?"

"I didn't ask him. I know he supports his mother. She lives with his sister in Akron, Ohio, but he supports her."

"Maybe I ought to include Edgar in this conversation," said Norman.

"No, don't. Whatever you want to give me is all right. We know we're not going to have much to start with. But his mother is over seventy and probably isn't going to last much longer."

"You'll have some from me, later on. Not much, but some. Your mother will have a trust fund, then you and your sister will divide the principal. Of course no one knows when that will be, but maybe by that time Edgar will be better fixed. I never heard anybody say whether he was good or bad, as a lawyer, that is. I've never known much about him."

"Neither have I. But when I needed somebody I turned to him," said Alberta.

"Are you going to be—all right? I don't mean financially."

"I hope so. I'll try. I'll do my best."

"It isn't easy to talk about such things," said Norman.

"It probably doesn't do any good to talk about them. The two people have to work it out themselves."

"Yes, that's what I meant. They always have to work it out. If you have children, you think about them a lot. That saves you from thinking about yourself and the other person."

"Was Mother horrid to you, Father?"

"Oh, no. No no. Nothing like that. No, we seemed well suited to each other most of the time. They say that opposites attract, but similars attract too. My mother and father were opposites, and my brother and his wife were similars. And your mother and I were similars. Just as long as you don't expect too much, that's the thing to remember. Look at your Uncle George. He expected too much, and when Elsie died he didn't know what to do with himself. But you see I never expected too much. Well, I don't keep that much cash in my checking account, but I'll arrange tomorrow to have the three thousand put in your account. They'll accommodate me at the bank, and you can draw on it any time after tomorrow. I'll write you a cheque now for five hundred, and you can cash that tomorrow. That ought to tide you over. I'd like to give Edgar a wedding present, but I will later. I don't like to give him a post-dated cheque. Creates the wrong impression. You can tell him I'm going to give him a thousand dollars."

"Thank you. I will."

"You know, now that I think of it, Edgar was a D.U. We had a D.U. dinner at the hotel a few years back, and I remember seeing him there. Swarthmore. He was a member of the Swarthmore chapter."

"Yes, he went to Swarthmore."

"Not important. I just happened to think of it. Well, young lady.

Now you're a bride. A married woman. Customary to give the bride a kiss, I believe."

"All right," she said. She held up her cheek, and he brushed it with his thin, dry lips.

"Just don't expect too much, daughter. Nothing's the way we plan it," he said. "Where are you and Edgar staying, tonight?"

"We're taking a room at the hotel and then we're going to Atlantic City. Only for a week."

"A week. Well, I guess you'll be in and out of here. Or will you?"

"I'll be in and out to get my things, I guess."

"We ought to give some kind of a party for you," said Norman.

"I'd rather you didn't."

"I was thinking, that way Edgar could meet your friends, and that might be helpful to him professionally."

"They didn't help *me* much," said Alberta. "Edgar knows all those Roach cousins that we never had very much to do with. Those are the kind of people I'll be seeing more of."

"Well, they're good honest people, most of them. One or two bad eggs, but they average out pretty well. Are you going to wait for Sophronia?"

"Speaking of bad eggs?" said Alberta. "No. You can tell her all about it."

"Do you want me to do anything about your Uncle George? On the practical side, you know, he has a lot of money."

"He can read about it in the paper," said Alberta.

"That's what I was wondering. Will he like that?"

"If he wants to give us a wedding present, he will. But I'm not going to call him up and ask him for one. That's what it would amount to."

"I think he'll give you two thousand dollars. Why do I think that? Because that goes back to the time I had my quarrel with him. It would take too long to explain."

"Well, we've been in here long enough. I don't want to leave Edgar alone with Mother. There's no telling what she's liable to say. Or do. Anyway, thank you, Father."

"I wish there was more I could do, but it's too late for that. You're not even going to stay for dinner?"

"No."

"It isn't a bit the way I expected it to be," said Norman, shaking his head.

"Did you think you'd be wearing a cutaway? You said yourself, you're always saying, don't expect too much."

Bertie and Edgar were eagerly grateful for their return to the front room. "Everything all settled?" said Bertie.

"Everything," said Alberta.

"Well, anyway till after they get back from Atlantic," said Norman.

"Oh, you're going to Atlantic? Edgar wouldn't tell me," said Bertie.

"I didn't know whether Alberta wanted people to know," said Edgar.

"Ah, well that's nice," said Bertie. "It shows consideration."

The bride and groom soon departed. "How do you think they'll be?" said Bertie.

"I guess there's no telling this early in the game," said Norman.

"Did you notice he's a little cross-eyed?" said Bertie.

"I wasn't sure whether it was him or the lenses. He wears very thick glasses. They use their eyesight a lot in the legal profession. Fine print."

"No, he has a cast in one eye," said Bertie.

"I never knew what that meant, a cast in the eye," said Norman.

"I wasn't sure which eye to look at, and he gave me the impression of staring at me. What took you so long? Was she worried about money?"

"We took care of that," said Norman. "Did you ever have a long talk with Alberta about married life?"

"No, but girls nowadays get all the information from other sources."

"How did she seem to you?" said Norman.

"About that?"

"Yes," said Norman.

"Well, I guess he isn't very experienced, and they're new to each other. Why? Did she say anything about it to you?"

"Good Lord, no."

"Well, it's up to them," said Bertie.

"I couldn't tell anything. I guess they slept together both nights, but I'll just bet they didn't do anything."

"Well, we didn't either," said Bertie. "But at least you knew what we were supposed to do."

"So does Edgar, you can rely on that."

"But it isn't only knowing what you're supposed to do. Some women never get accustomed to it. He'll have to be very careful with Alberta."

"Good Lord, I thought we could stop worrying about her. You're holding something back from me. What is it?"

"It's only natural to worry about your own daughter. I won't be satisfied till she tells me she's having a child. She never took much interest in young men."

"I see. You're worried about her being frigid. But that's up to him now, and we have to stay out of it. If she has any trouble she can go see a doctor. So can he."

"If they tell him the truth. But there's no use in seeing a doctor if—"

"What the devil are you holding back from me? Out with it."

"Very well. If you insist. Alberta is a man-hater. She told me so herself."

"Rats! So were you till you found out you weren't."

"I thought I was a man-hater, but I was never a woman-lover. That's what Alberta is."

"You don't know what you're saying. She's too feminine to be that. Those kind of women wear a collar and tie, tailored suits. Over in France they even wear pants and men's hats. Why, they actually get all dressed up like men and pick up prostitutes."

"You told me all about that."

"It didn't sink in, or you'd know that Alberta isn't that kind."

"I'm going on what she told me herself."

"She said it to shock you, or else you misunderstood her."

"I misunderstood her, all right. I misunderstood both of them. I misunderstood everybody."

He paused. "I want to tell you about those women, something I didn't tell you before. Then maybe you'll realize what you're saying about Alberta. Those women, over in Paris and I guess other places too. They have a kind of a belt that they strap on, and it has a thing in front like a man's private parts, made of rubber. It's an exact fac-simile of a man's private parts, and they put it in a woman just as if they were a man and having intercourse."

"How do you know? Did you ever see them?"

"Of course I never saw them, but I heard it described to me more than once."

"Where would they buy a thing like that?"

"Listen, in Paris and when I was in Africa, they have things you could never imagine."

"What about the woman-lovers here in town? Do they have them? Not mentioning any names, but you know."

"How would I know that?"

"I don't think you know as much about such things as you let on you do."

"Well, maybe I don't want to know," said Norman. "There are plenty of other things to think about besides that. I want you to get such ideas out of your head about Alberta, and twisting things she said."

"She said she was a Lesbian."

"See? There you are. That's just what I mean. If she said she was an Amazon you wouldn't expect her to go around with a bow and arrow."

"She didn't *say* she was an Amazon. She said the other."

"Well, do you know what they were? They were a bunch of women in Greece that wouldn't have anything to do with men, and do you know why? Because they wanted to stop the men from going to war. So they told the men that if they didn't stop fighting, they wouldn't go to bed with them. That's *history*."

"It may be history, but that's not what Lesbians are."

"Are you going against history?"

"No, I'm not going against history. I'm not against it, and I'm not for it. But there are certain women in this town that like other women the same as there are certain men that like men."

"I could tell you what the men do, but I won't. We had them in the army. They had them in the navy, too. They say they were worse in the navy. In fact, they had them in prep school."

"Oh, I know what the men do. The women do the same thing."

"How could they? They're built differently."

"Oh, all right. Have it your way. Only you're wrong. I can see that I know some things that you don't know, especially where women are concerned."

"I should hope so. Not being a woman, I bow to your superior knowledge of the subject. Thank God I'm *not* a woman. Thank God for that."

"Thank God I'm not a man."

"I'll second the motion," said Norman.

"I'll third it," said Bertie.

"Now where is that Sophronia again? Don't tell me she's gone off and eloped too."

"If she only would," said Bertie.

"Not this year, I hope," said Norman. "I'll manage, all right, but Alberta is going to put a dent in my capital. Did you say we were having calves' liver?"

"I may have to throw it away and open a can of something," said Bertie.

"Anything at all. A quiet dinner. We've had enough excitement for one day. When Sophronia gets home, *you* tell her about her sister. I'll prepare the notice for the paper and take it there myself. Walk'll do me good. We don't happen to have a recent photograph of her, do we?"

"No, she never liked to have her picture taken," said Bertie.

"Call me when dinner's ready. I'll be at the desk."

The telephone rang. "That'll probably be Sophronia," said Bertie. "I'll answer it."

Norman stood beside her as she spoke into the telephone. "Yes. Where are you now? . . . You should have called sooner . . . All right." She hung up.

"Short and to the point," said Norman.

"Sophronia. She's having dinner with some friend of hers, she didn't say who or where, and I didn't bother to ask. She'll be home later."

"Then it's just you and me. We can eat in the kitchen. What does she *do* all day?"

"You're a fine one to ask," said Bertie.

From

AND OTHER STORIES

♦

A Few Trips and Some Poetry

♦

I t was a surprise to me to learn that there was a Turner living in
Turnersville. The village was so small—not on many maps—and
so out of the way—three or four miles from any road that we
used—that it had become a joke town, the next thing to a mythical
symbol of all country villages. Vaudeville actors who wanted to get
a local laugh would mention Turnersville in their monologues; year
after year the editors of the high school annual would have comical
references to Turnersville in the class prophecy ("And in our crystal
ball whom do we see but Ted Smith, our old classmate, still active in
politics as mayor of the metropolis of Turnersville?"). Once there
had been an industry in Turnersville, a powder mill owned by a family named Long; but in 1902 or '03 they had had an explosion in
which eight men were killed, among them Elias Long and his son
Ellis. The Widow Long moved away, and the mill went out of business.

I was one of the few boys in our crowd who had actually been in
Turnersville. My father had a farm, an expensive hobby, where we
spent the summers, and if you took the mountain road as a short
cut, you went through Turnersville at the foot of the mountain. It
was a narrow road; in places only wide enough for a single wagon;
and always in bad condition. Model T's would break their radius
rods and the leaves in their springs on that road, and the tires would
pick up horseshoe nails and pieces of glass from whiskey bottles that
farmers had tossed away. The farmers, who still had horses and

601

mules, would stop at the Mountain View Hotel on their way home from market or with a load of manure. They would have a few drinks at the Mountain View and buy a pint to drink on the road. It was all downhill from the Mountain View to Turnersville, and the farmers would set their brakes and the horses would head for home. If a farmer got so drunk that he fell off the wagon, that was his hard luck; the team would keep going without him. When the driverless wagon reached Turnersville, someone would stop the team and hold them until the owner got there on foot, *if* he got there. Not all of them did.

Turnersville had its own Farmers Hotel, a blacksmith shop, and a small country store that carried such things as stove polish and cough medicine and tobacco but was not in competition with the well-stocked general store in the nearby town of Fair Grounds. There was nothing else in Turnersville except the thirty or forty dwellings on the two sides of the road and one good-sized house of red brick, two and a half stories high, which I knew to be the Turner house. But as I had never seen anyone on the porch, and had never any reason to stop there, I did not know who lived in the Turner house and was not curious. Sometimes when I was on horseback I would stop at the trough in front of the Farmers Hotel and let my mare have a few sips of water, but I was too young to be a customer of the hotel saloon, and anyway I was Irish and in that Pennsylvania Dutch country they hated the Irish. The older men who sat on the porch of the hotel would say to me, "Hyuh, Irish," and snicker. They seldom said more than that, but when my mare finished her drink and I started off they would clap their hands to frighten her. But I was used to them, ready for them, and I had noticed that they never spoke disrespectfully to my father. They called him "Mister Doctor," and they were afraid of him because he was rich. I knew those things.

One day when I was about fifteen—so it must have been in 1920—I had stopped at the Farmers Hotel trough to water my mare. It was a day or two before the Fourth of July. Some men were on the porch, but this time they had not spoken to me at all. They were staring at me, but they were silent. A man with a bad limp, carrying a cane, was approaching the hotel. Suddenly he shouted, "Cut that out! You there, Faust, cut that out!" I looked about me and saw that one of the usual hangers-on was sneaking behind the mare with a giant firecracker in one hand and a match in the other. It was one of the six-inch "salutes," I think they called them, and if it had gone off under my mare's hind legs there is no telling what might have happened. The man Faust grumbled, but he did not light the firecracker. The man with the cane said, "You could have killed that horse—and where would you get five hundred dollars?" He then moved on toward the Turner house, and I followed him and thanked him. "Oh, that's all right," he said. "A horse can die of fright. Not a mule, but that's no mule you're riding." He did not stop walking as he spoke, and it was apparent to me that he did not wish to linger. I thanked him again, and he said, "That's all right. I know your father." I rode away at a trot, and when I looked back I saw him open the gate of the Turner property. I waved, but he was not looking in my direction.

That night I told my father what had happened. "Yes, I know that Faust fellow. I had him arrested for stealing a young bull. He's no good."

"Did they put him in jail?"

"No, they didn't put him in jail. But they made him work on the highway for sixty days. Pick and shovel. He'd rather have gone to jail, I imagine."

"Who was the nice man? Was that Mr. Turner?" I said.

"Samuel Turner. He thinks I made him a cripple. He hasn't spoken to me in twenty years."

"Then why did he come to my rescue?"

"Because, God damn it, a decent man is always decent," said my father. "That's something for you to remember."

"Why does he think you made him a cripple? Did you operate on him?" I said.

"Yes, and he wouldn't have that leg at all if I hadn't."

"Then why does he blame you?" I said.

"Oh, you ask too many questions," my father said. That was always the signal to shut up, and I said no more. Generally it meant that my father preferred not to continue a story that was very much in his favor or very much against him. In any event I got no more out of him, but there was always my mother, and I asked her to tell me about Samuel Turner.

"Samuel Turner, of Turnersville," she said. "Charles Carroll of Carrollton."

"You don't mean to say the Turners were signers of the Declaration."

"No, but they go back that far," she said. "There was a time when they owned all that land, where the powder mill used to be—"

"The landed gentry," I said.

"Well—they had the land. I don't know about the gentry part. We didn't have gentry this far north. It was just an old family that went back before the Revolution. Samuel Turner is a distant cousin of yours."

"On your side of the family," I said.

"His grandfather—now let me see—his grandfather and my grandfather were cousins."

"Oh, then you used to know Mr. Turner?"

"No, I never met him. But when he had his accident he told your father that I was a cousin. He had nothing to do but find out such things. When your father bought the farm, Samuel Turner took it upon himself to find out who we were. He knew your father was a doctor, but he wasn't a patient of ours. But when your father bought the farm we were the first Gibbsville people to buy land in the neighborhood. All the other people were Pennsylvania Dutch farmers."

"And Turner was an old busybody," I said.

"Well, he had nothing else to do. I don't think he was any more of a busybody than you are. You're asking all about him, and he asked all about us. And found out to his surprise that I was his cousin."

"How did he live? Where did the money come from?"

"There wasn't much. Enough for him to live on, but not on a very grand scale. He owned some farms, and the railroad bought some of his land."

"Did he ever get married?"

"No. He's always been a bachelor."

"And what about the accident, when Daddy made him a cripple?"

"Cripple! Your father saved his leg. I don't like that kind of talk."

"Go on, tell me about it," I said.

"To correct that impression, I'll tell you," she said. "Mr. Turner, Samuel, drank. And one day he'd been up to town, drinking, and on his way home he fell out of his buggy and got his leg all tangled up in the wheel. The horse came home, leaving Samuel lying on the road. Some people went looking for him and found him, and instead of taking him to the hospital they brought him home. Heaven knows what they must have done to his leg, carrying him from one place to another like that. Luckily for him your father was on the farm, and they came and got him. They made a sort of ambulance of a spring-wagon and your father rode with him to the hospital, and operated that night. Saved his leg."

"Why did he think Daddy crippled him?"

"Because they're all crazy, the Turners. Not really, but there's a streak of it in the family."

"You think Samuel Turner's not all there?" I said. "That's on your side of the family, Mother."

"He's not the only one. You have a closer cousin, Cousin George Gray."

"I always thought he was just a cheerful idiot," I said.

"Too cheerful."

"You always liked him," I said.

"Did I? Being polite to him didn't necessarily mean I liked him."

"What did he ever do that was crazy?"

"Things I'd rather not talk about," she said. When my mother used that expression it usually meant something to do with sex, and

606 ♦ JOHN O'HARA

this confirmation of my suspicions about Cousin George Gray disposed of him forever. George Gray was unattractive. Samuel Turner, on the other hand, had done me a favor and I looked forward to my next opportunity to talk with him. Now, whenever I rode through Turnersville, I would look more carefully to see if he was on the porch or somewhere in the yard. But the summers passed and I did not see Samuel Turner until I was eighteen years old. By that time I was no longer so young that I could not be a customer in the bar of the Turnersville Farmers Hotel.

Prohibition had not had much effect on such places. Some, but not much. You could still walk into the bar and be served beer and hard liquor. The beer was not good, the whiskey was raw, and applejack was said to give you the trots, but you could drink, and I was already a drinker. The Farmers Hotel in Turnersville was beginning to enjoy a certain limited popularity among our crowd. It was an out-of-the-way place and cheap, and the old jokes about Turnersville became passé; in a very few years the name of the village became synonymous with drinking. "Turnersville? Nine o'clock?" we would say, and it was all we needed to say. Almost any night you would see familiar cars parked outside: Joe Choate's Wills Ste. Claire, Charley Lloyd's Packard roadster, Mary Stauffer's Oakland coupe, Whit Hofman's Mercer phaeton, Stuffy Reifsnyder's Daniels, as well as the Dodges and Buicks of the boys using the family car. A dollar is a dollar, and the owner of the Farmers Hotel ignored the resentment of the villagers and farmers who had so recently been his only regular customers. One of the changes in the place was that my old enemy Faust was working as a help-out waiter, carrying trayfuls of drinks to the back room, and no more likable in his new obsequiousness than he had been as a tormenter of horses. With every trayful it was customary to give him a twenty-five-cent tip, and I so thoroughly despised him that I would sometimes drop the quarter on the floor and let him pick it up. "Be careful, Faustie, it might go off in your hand," I would say, and he would laugh, but he would stoop over for the money.

I suppose I was vaguely conscious of the presence in Turnersville of Samuel Turner, in the way that you are conscious of the President of the United States when you are in Washington, D.C. At least once a week I went to the Farmers Hotel with a girl or for stag drinking, but the Farmers Hotel at night was not Turnersville in the daylight, and I did not look in the direction of the Turner house. Then one night after we had been patronizing the hotel for about a year, I entered the bar and saw Samuel Turner sitting alone at a barroom table.

"Hello, Mr. Turner," I said. "Do you remember me?"

He nodded. "I do," he said. "I saw in the paper that your father died. Give my condolences to your mother, will you please?"

"Thank you," I said. "I will. She told me you're some kind of a cousin of hers."

"Therefore of yours," he said. "Would you care for a drink?"

"Come sit with us, in the back room," I said.

"Oh, you're with a party. I don't want to intrude," he said.

"Just a couple of fellows," I said.

"All right," he said. He used his cane to raise himself to his feet and accompanied me to the back room. He was much older than the rest of us, but soon after he sat at the table he was telling us stories about Turnersville, the old powder mill, the last panther shot in the neighborhood, the last Indian trapper, the Turner distillery that we had never heard of. I was proud of him. All the way home my friends kept saying he was quite a guy. The next time I went to the Farmers Hotel he was sitting at the barroom table and he joined us again, but he would never accept an invitation to sit with us when we had girls along. It was therefore a surprise when he said to me one night, "I would like to have some of your friends for dinner some evening, at my house."

"Great," I said. "How many?"

"Four or five couples."

"Oh, girls too?"

"Yes, let's do it up brown," he said. "Get out the good silverware and china. A lot of nice things in that old house that never see the light of day, and I don't think you boys would appreciate them but your girls would. *That* kind of girl."

"*That* kind of girl," I said. "Sure, that'd be great. When?"

"Well, it'd take a couple of weeks to get everything out and have it looking nice. Say two weeks from Sunday. I'll leave it up to you, who to invite."

I invited my girl and three other couples. Until we actually arrived at Samuel Turner's house the girls were not unconvinced that I was playing some kind of practical joke. They had never seen Samuel Turner, and none of us had ever been in his house. I was hardly less curious about the evening than the others, and they were looking forward to a dinner party that, no matter how it turned out, would not be a repetition of the parties we were accustomed to.

As it was a Sunday evening, we did not dress, but Samuel Turner greeted us in a black velvet smoking jacket, white silk shirt, and large, loosely knotted black bow tie. He had substituted an ebony stick with a fluted silver knob for the stout ash cane he usually carried. I wondered whether this elegance was customary. By prearrangement we arrived together, the eight of us, and as he was introduced to each of the girls he repeated her name and held on to her hand while he said something about her parents or made some little speech that kept the introductions from being perfunctory. He received us in the parlor, which was on the second story, and we were offered a choice of orange blossom cocktails and straight rye. He served the first drinks himself, moving about so carefully that his limp was not noticeable. Well, not very noticeable, and his bad leg gave him the excuse to carry the beautiful ebony stick, which became a subtle symbol, part scepter and part staff. In this house, on this occasion, Samuel Turner had me questioning my mother's accuracy as to her remark on the gentry. He was a confident and gracious host.

The parlor was full of objects for the girls to exclaim over. A spinet that had not been turned into a desk; miniature reproductions of mahogany rockers; a concert-size harp; a large German Bible in a thick leather binding, on a stand of its own; a Napoleon doll and a Marie Antoinette doll, under glass bells; a portrait of a beady-eyed bigot in clerical clothes. A story went with everything in the room, and Samuel Turner refilled our glasses as he talked. We did not have to force conversation. We had arrived at seven o'clock and it was close to eight when a stout, fiftyish woman came in and said, "Supper's ready."

Supper was chicken and waffles in abundance, washed down with a tame white wine that came out of a pair of Stieglitz bottles. The lighting was by candle. Dessert was mince pie with hard sauce. Nobody got tight, but there was constant chatter and laughter, no gaps of silence. It was a young group; in a few days all the other guests would be going back to school and college and it would be our last time together before the Christmas holidays. I was a working man, a reporter on a newspaper. After supper Turner told the girls that if they cared to powder their noses they could go upstairs; the young men would follow him to his room on the same floor as the parlor and diningroom, and that was how we discovered that Samuel Turner had his bedroom on that floor. Across the hall from the parlor was his study, and behind that his bedroom and bath. Obviously it was in this apartment that he spent most of his time. The study was lined with books from floor to ceiling—all kinds of books, from modern novels to the Eleventh Encyclopedia, the Memoirs of Ulysses S. Grant, and Diseases of the Horse; Carlyle, Thackeray, Longfellow, Wordsworth, Mark Twain, Harriet Beecher Stowe, and a poet named Walter Turner Herbein, whose volume was published by the Reading (Pa.) *Eagle.* Instead of a library ladder on a track, Samuel Turner had a long stick with a device that would grip a book on the topmost shelf. On the floor, in the kneehole of his desk, was a carpeted brick on which he could rest his right foot, that leg being shorter than the left. I began to realize how much his injury had handicapped him and why in all those years I had never seen him on the porch or in the yard: he spent most of his time in his house, and most of that in these few rooms of the house. I stopped to look at the guns in a glass-front closet in the bedroom: he had a double-barrel shotgun, a single-barrel shotgun, a 1906 Winchester .22 rifle, and a .30 caliber Savage rifle, as well as a .32 revolver and a Colt .45 revolver that hung on pegs in the closet. "I keep them under lock and key," he said. "I'll show them to you if you're interested."

"No thanks," I said. "I was just wondering what use you'd get out of the Savage. That's a lot of rifle for around here."

"I didn't do all my shooting around here," he said. "I killed a moose with that gun, up in Maine. Years ago."

I had, of course, said the wrong thing.

"If you'd ever like to borrow it," he said.

"I might take you up on that," I said. "I have four shotguns that belonged to my father, but the only rifle I have is a .22, like yours."

"You like guns?"

"I love guns," I said. "In fact, I love this house. If I ever have a house of my own, this is the way it'll be."

"No, your house'll be different," he said. "This house belongs to a hermit, and you'll never be that. Nobody's had a meal in the diningroom in almost twenty years."

"Really? It didn't seem that way."

"Yes, most of the things were put away. That's why we needed time to get everything out."

"Well, now that you got them out, you ought to keep them out."

"You mean stop being a hermit? I don't think so. Maybe. But I don't think so. A man gets used to certain ways," he said. "Well how about coffee? Does everyone want coffee?"

He was quite a different person from the man I had always seen before, who wore sternly conservative suits in the winter and fall and shiny black mohair in the summer, orthopedic shoes that had to be specially made, solid-color neckties, and carried canes that were strictly functional. In the course of the evening I ceased to wonder about the elegance of his smoking jacket and shirt and tie and the beautiful ebony stick. This, not the other man, was Samuel Turner. Probably every father I knew had been given a smoking jacket at some Christmas, put it on Christmas afternoon, and put it away forever on Christmas night. But Samuel Turner's velvet jacket showed signs of wear and it fell into the contours of his body. He was a trifle under medium height, thick through the middle, and, I guessed, had arrived at a certain weight and stayed there. He was bald except for some side hair that he let grow long and brushed across the top of his scalp. He shaved so close that there was no sign of his beard, but I had seen in the bathroom a shaving mug, two shaving brushes, and a leather case containing seven straight razors, the traditional set of one razor for each day of the week. Men who owned those sets took them to barber shops for honing. The backs of his hands were hairless; I found myself reminded of the hands of a fat nun who had taught me in sixth grade, whose fingers seemed to protrude from lumps of dough. It was not much of a jump from the recollection of the nun to a speculation as to the nature of his relationship with the woman who kept house for him. I guessed that there was nothing between them. We had not seen much of her, but in his manner toward her during the serving of the meal there was a pleasant, impersonal familiarity that defined the mutuality of their intimacy. Besides, she was not his type. We were beginning to use that phrase, and it still comes in handy. I would not have been able to say what his type was, but I would not have been surprised if he had produced an attractive mulatto or a Phi Beta Kappa from Wellesley or a dizzy blonde or a genteel lady down on her luck. I would not have said that *they* were not his type. On the other hand, I would readily have believed that a paid prostitute took care of his needs, or that he seduced the not unwilling farm girls in the neighborhood (who started early). Two things I would not believe: that he was sleeping with such an uninteresting woman as Gussie, or that he was celibate. The decency of which my father had spoken years before was of another kind than that which had to do with Samuel Turner's relations with women. His manner toward, his enjoyment of the presence of, the girls I had brought to his house convinced me that his bachelorhood meant only that he was not married. Besides, he had the hands of a sensualist, and the softness of his skin where he shaved his beard made me think of men I had seen in barber shops just before they went out on dates with women not their wives. They would rub their chins and cheeks as though already caressing the flesh of the woman they were to spend the evening with. No, Samuel Turner was not a celibate.

"Shall we have a fire?" he said, when we joined the girls in the parlor. "Let's have a fire." Going by the calendar, I would not have thought of having a fire with September only half gone, but the girls unanimously and enthusiastically approved. "There's quite a nip in the air," said Samuel Turner. "And I like my creature comforts, don't you, Isabel?"

"Yes I do," said Isabel Barley. "And we rode here with the top down."

"I should have had a fire for you early in the evening, but I was busy in the kitchen," said Turner.

"You *were*?" said Isabel.

"No, not really," said Turner. "I can cook, all right, but not when Gussie's here. She won't have anyone else in her kitchen." He was lighting the fire, already laid, with a long wax taper, and we all concentrated our attention on the logs until the fire caught. Turner, with no comment, went about the room and put out the lights until the sole illumination was from the fireplace. "I think I'll sit here with you, Isabel. May I?"

"But of course," said Isabel.

"Anybody know any ghost stories?" said Turner.

No, nobody could think of any just now.

"Neither can I," said Turner. "I could go into my library and find something by Edgar Allan Poe. But reading a story wouldn't be the same, would it? I've been trying to remember some of the things that have happened in this house that fall into that category. How would you like to live in a house like this, Isabel?"

"Well—since frankness is the fashion, I think I'd have to get used to it. I don't think I could live here by myself."

"Is frankness the fashion? I'm glad to hear it," said Turner.

"Oh, that's really just a saying we have. I don't suppose it's any more the fashion now than it ever was," said Isabel.

"It's usually the preface to saying something rude," said Edie

Watson. She made an exaggerated face at Isabel. "Not that Is needs any preface. She usually comes right out with it."

"Is that what you really think of me, Edie? Down deep?" said Isabel. "I always considered you one of my nearest and dearest. Mr. Turner is going to get an entirely erroneous impression of me."

"But I like frankness," said Turner. "I like good manners but I like frankness too."

"Can you have both?" said Isabel.

"Yes, I believe you can. In fact, I wonder if you can really have good manners without a certain amount of frankness."

"In limited quantities, the frankness," said Isabel. "As a matter of fact, this group, we all grew up together more or less, and we pass around the insults very freely. But that's because we know each other. We wouldn't dare say those things to people we didn't know."

"We're not really so darn frank with each other," said Mary Stauffer.

"You're not, because you have more to hide," said Isabel.

"That's a damn nasty thing to say, even in fooling," said Mary. "Talk about giving the wrong impression."

"Yes, Isabel. You ought to apologize," said Kitty Michaels.

"Another country heard from!" said Isabel.

"Well, while we're on the subject of frankness, we haven't heard a word from any of the gentlemen," said Turner.

"Frankly—notice I say frankly—we haven't had much chance to get a word in edgewise," said John Hall.

"Not while the women had the floor," said his brother Phil.

"No," I said.

"No," said Frank Day.

"They can all be frank enough when they want to be," said Isabel.

No one had any more to say about frankness, and the conversation encountered a lull, the first of the evening. Isabel, as she often did, took over. "You were going to say something about your house but we got sidetracked. In the category of ghosts."

"Oh, I never knew of any ghosts here, not in this house," said Samuel Turner.

"Would you believe in them anyway?" said Isabel.

"Not seriously," said Turner. "However, for those who do believe in them, there are some in the neighborhood. I don't suppose any of you are old enough to remember the powder mill. No, I don't think any of you were born then. There used to be a powder mill to the north of here, run by a family named Long. It was started back in the time of the Civil War, and for safety's sake it was in the deep woods, along the creek. They didn't want to have it too near the village, in case there was an explosion, but it was still close enough for the men in the village to walk to work, those who had jobs there. It was a very gloomy place. The woods so thick that the sun never got through. You'd never see a man walk through those woods without a stick or some kind of club in his hand, the snakes were so bad. That's still the case, by the way. Don't ever get the idea that the old powder mill site would be a nice spot for a picnic."

"Ugh-ugh," Isabel muttered. "I don't mind talking about ghosts, but not snakes, please."

"Some snakes are absolutely beautiful," said Mary Stauffer. "I've handled them."

"I don't doubt it for a minute," said Isabel.

"Some of them are beautiful," said Turner. "But they can't be counted on to share your friendliness, Mary."

"They're no different than some people I know," said Mary.

"Please get back to ghosts, Mr. Turner," said Isabel.

"Well, just after the turn of the century—October, 1902, as a matter of fact. October the fourth, to give you the exact date. Twenty minutes past three in the afternoon, to give you the exact time. The main building blew up and eight men were killed, including the owner and his son, Elias and Ellis Long. I happened to be in the woods at that moment, hunting deer on the side of the mountain."

"Then you saw the explosion?" said John Hall. "What caused it? Did they ever find out?"

"No, they never found out. There were various explanations. A workman smoking. The chemist doing something wrong. Spontaneous combustion. Even a barn full of hay will suddenly catch fire from spontaneous combustion, you know. That's why they sprinkle salt over it when they put it in the barn."

"Yes, I knew that," said one of the boys.

"What was it like, the explosion?" said Isabel.

"Just what you'd imagine it to be. A blast of flame and smoke, and brick and lumber flying through the air. And of course a noise like thunder, not as sharp as a clap of thunder but as loud, and you could hear it reverberating up and down the Valley."

"And then fire?" said John Hall.

"Not very much fire. It had been raining steadily all morning and the woods weren't a bit dry," said Turner.

"It must have been a horrible thing to see," said Isabel.

"Why, no, not really," said Samuel Turner. "Not from where I was."

"But all those people—" said Isabel.

"Ah, but I didn't see them. Actually there was very little left of them. There wasn't enough left in one piece to fill a single grave. That's where the ghost business originated. The people in the village began to believe that the woods were haunted, not by one ghost, but by the ghosts of all the dead men. Ellis Long, for instance. There was nothing left of him, nothing. His father, Elias, they *could* identify his head because he wore a beard. But they made no attempt to—to— uh—reconstruct a body. They had the same problem that they have to the north of here, when there's a mining disaster. Your family are in the coal-mining business, Isabel."

"Yes, and we had an accident at Number 8 this summer. I think there were two men killed, maybe three," said Isabel.

"I read about it," said Samuel Turner. "There were three. And the paper said they were mangled beyond reconstruction. It would have been even more confusing to try to reconstruct the bodies at the Long's Mill explosion. There were *eight* of *them.* They couldn't even find enough of Abe Lee, the one colored man. The deputy coroner, from over in Fair Grounds, wasn't a doctor, but he told the undertaker to go ahead and dispose of whatever they could find. Including Elias Long's head. Now they'll tell you that one of the ghosts has a beard, and one is colored, and so on. You couldn't pay a local man to spend the night in those woods. There's a man here in the village, his name is Faust."

"I know *him,* all right," I said.

"So do I. He's a waiter at the Farmers Hotel," said Mary Stauffer.

"Yes, he helps out there," said Samuel Turner.

"He's practically a moron," said Mary.

"Yes, but he wasn't always," said Turner. "Not that he was ever going to be a Rhodes scholar at Oxford or anything like that. He came from a poor family, inbred as a lot of these families are. His father never had a steady job, but managed to eke out a living as a day laborer. The son went to the township school till he was old enough to get working papers, and then he went to work for Schwab's store, over in Fair Grounds. Errand boy. Handyman. He kept that job till he was twenty-one, and I suppose he'd be there yet but he decided to join a lodge, one of the secret societies that everybody belongs to in this neck of the woods."

"The Ku Klux Klan," I said.

"Well, very much like it, without the white sheets. Exterminate the niggers and the Catholics and the Jews—and Wall Street. You can imagine how much they know about Wall Street, and there isn't a Jew this side of Gibbsville."

"We have plenty of them there," said Phil Hall.

"Only in the stores," said Kitty Michaels. "You never see them anyplace else."

"Be that as it may," said Samuel Turner. "Young Faust was accepted by the lodge and the night came for his initiation. There was always a good deal of cruelty and rough stuff in those initiations, but this time they outdid themselves. They blindfolded Faust and took him in a wagon out to the ruins of the old powder mill—and left him there. Goodness knows what he went through, but you can imagine waiting there in the dark, having no idea where he was. Taking off his blindfold, still not knowing where he was. And having to wait till daylight. Then beginning to recognize his surroundings, and making his way back to Turnersville. He was probably in those woods five or six hours, I don't know. I do know that when he got home he was hysterical, out of his head, trembling, weeping, making no sense whatsoever. His mother sent for the doctor, who put him to sleep. But when he came to he wasn't in much better shape, and the doctor had him taken to the insane asylum in Swedish Haven. He was there I guess about a month and then they let him go, but he's been in and out of trouble ever since."

"Didn't his lodge take care of him?" said John Hall.

"They did not," said Samuel Turner. "They even tried to deny that they'd had anything to do with it, but too many people knew they were lying. So they made up a story that he had jumped out of the wagon and got lost in the woods."

"Then I was right. He is a moron," said Mary Stauffer.

"Well, he isn't all there, there's no question about that," said Samuel Turner.

At that moment Gussie came in, wearing a shawl over her head. "You want anything else?" she said to Samuel Turner.

"Nothing more, thanks. Goodnight, Gussie."

"Goodnight," she said. "Goodnight, all." Some of us said goodnight, and we heard her close the front door and go down the outside steps.

"I hope you don't mind my saying so, but she fits into the spooky atmosphere," said Kitty Michaels.

"I don't mind a bit," said Samuel Turner. "She has every right to fit into the spooky atmosphere, or at least she fits into the story. She had a brother that was one of the men killed in the explosion. You see, in a place as small as Turnersville, the death of eight men all at once makes a considerable dent in the population. There wasn't anyone in the whole village that didn't lose somebody—a brother, a father, a son, a cousin. In proportion, it would be just as if the town of Gibbsville were to lose over five hundred men in one accident.

Will someone check me on that? Eight men is about one fortieth of three hundred, isn't it? Five hundred is a fortieth of twenty thousand?"

"Correct, sir," said John Hall.

"The explosion took away the lives of eight *men,* not just eight members of the population. Turnersville never recovered from that. We have only a little over a hundred population now, and the village has no real excuse for existing. The Turner family and the village named after us will go out of existence together. I'm the last of my line. The human race will survive, but that little tributary known as the Turner family ends with me."

"You don't seem to mind very much," I said.

"No. I used to, but not any more," said Samuel Turner. "When I was your age I had different plans, but I had to change them. I was going to fill this house with my heirs and heiresses, but I've had to content myself with ghosts."

He spoke without bitterness, or rather with no more bitterness than was habitual with him. He was having a good time, enjoying the evening and his role as host and especially the company of Isabel Barley. At this stage of her life—and of ours—she was at her most attractive. She had graduated from Wellesley that year and seemed to be in no hurry to get married. Her virginity was questioned by the boys in our crowd, but none of us was able to claim that he knew for sure, of his own knowledge and experience. There was a sort of intercollegiate information pool in those days; a boy at Yale, for instance, would learn that a certain girl at Smith was "putting out," and this information would sometimes come as a surprise to the Yale boy if he came from the same town as the Smith girl. Isabel Barley, according to the pool information, could be had, and had been had by two or three unidentified young men during her four years in New England. At home, however, she was classified as a heavy-necker-if-she-liked-you. She was pretty, very nearly a beauty; she wore her unbobbed flaxen hair brushed down tight, parted in the middle, and with a bun at the back and she had an absolutely flawless complexion. Her dress was modestly cut, but whenever she moved you could see the beginnings of her extraordinarily high, firm breasts. She had resisted the cutting of her hair and the fashion of the tight, flattening brassiere. Already you could guess how she would look when she reached forty. Notwithstanding the whispers about her and the fact that she had favored me with some long kisses and occasional exchanges of other intimacies, I was not in the least possessive toward her. She knew about boys, and she treated you fairly, but necking was as far as she would go—and not always that far. She was my girl only in the sense that she went out with me oftener than with anyone else, and we never spoke of love. She was about three years older than I; actually I was the youngest member of this group. It seemed to me that Isabel was not only remote from me but from our town and our time, that her life was being and always would be lived elsewhere. This theory could have originated in the knowledge that she was born in another town in another state; she had come to our town when she was about ten years old, from West Virginia, where her father had been a mining engineer. Duncan Barley quickly became one of the more successful independent coal operators, and the Barleys went right to the top, socially as well as financially. Sooner than most newcomers Mr. Barley was made a director of one of the better banks, a trustee of the larger hospital, a governor of the men's club and the tennis club (which grew into a country club). The Barleys had no roots in the community, but neither did they have to carry on family feuds from an earlier generation. Some of the girls in our crowd would occasionally remark that Isabel Barley had gone further in our town than she would have anywhere else, but it did not seem to me that it mattered as much to Isabel as to the girls who made the comment. Whatever the girls thought about Isabel, they would not have a party without inviting her. She was too much of a personage to be safely snubbed, and she had reached that status with no effort on her part.

It was no wonder then that Samuel Turner, the hermit, was attracted to her. As the evening wore on, however, I caught her several times looking at him, studying him as though he were at least a curiosity and a repellent one at that. At midnight the grandfather's

620 ♦ JOHN O'HARA

clock in the hall boomed out the hour, accompanied two thirds of the way by a ship's clock in Turner's study striking eight bells. "Good heavens," said Isabel to me. "You must take me home. I'm catching the early train to Philadelphia." I said nothing, because I knew that was not true. "I'm so sorry, Mr. Turner, but I'm getting the seven-five." She thereby broke up the party. We said our good-nights to Samuel Turner, who apologized for not accompanying us to our cars and thanked us for a truly delightful evening.

In the car I said to Isabel, "How are you going to be in Philadelphia and playing golf with my sister?"

"It's not going to be easy, is it?" she said. "I gave the first excuse that came into my mind."

"Why didn't you just tell him you had a golf date? Why tell him anything? It was twelve o'clock, and we'd been there since seven-thirty."

"He affected me that way," she said.

"What way?"

"I don't know. I preferred lying to him to telling him the truth," she said.

"I thought you were getting along fine, early in the evening. Then you seemed to change your mind about him. Did he make a pass at you?"

"Not exactly," she said. "He said something to me. Whispered it, twice. Once when we were leaving the diningroom, and once when we were sitting in front of the fire. Someone else had the floor for a change, and Mr. Turner put his hand to his mouth and whispered to me. No one else could possibly hear him. No one even noticed."

"Something dirty?" I said.

"I couldn't repeat it to you," she said. "It was something he wanted me to do."

"He wanted you to go to bed with him?" I said.

"Nothing quite as tame as that," she said. "Both times he said it to me in such a way that I thought I was imagining things, only I wasn't. It was something he wanted me to do, and let's not say any more about it. But let's never go there again."

"All right," I said.

About a week later I saw Isabel on the street. "Did you get a call from our friend Mr. Turner?" she said.

"No," I said.

"I did. He asked me to come to dinner and bring some of my young friends. I thought it was rather strange that he didn't mention you, and I inferred that he didn't want you. In fact, I inferred that he didn't want anybody that was there the other night."

"What did you tell him?"

"I told him that I was going to White Sulphur for a few weeks, and I'd let him know when I got back."

"But you're not going to White Sulphur," I said.

"No. But I'd rather lie to him than tell him the truth," she said. "I wonder what that is? What's your explanation for it?"

"Well, I have an explanation, a theory. I don't know how good it is. According to my theory, if you told him the truth, you'd be giving him a part of yourself. Does that make any sense?"

"It makes a lot of sense. You think, don't you? Most boys don't think."

"I think a lot about you," I said.

"Apple sauce, but all right," she said. "I'll treat you to a Coke."

"With pretzels?"

"With two cents' worth of Reading Butter pretzels," she said.

"Then I'll have a large Coke," I said. "You know, he reads the paper, Turner. He'll soon find out you didn't go to White Sulphur."

"Then maybe he'll get the hint," she said.

"He doesn't want to get the hint. You'll hear from him again."

"You don't like him either, do you?"

"The more I know about him, the less I like him," I said. "I told you I was related to him."

"Oh, when I was a girl they used to say all us white folks is related. That was West Virginia, but it's just as true here," she said.

"I hate to be so wrong about a guy," I said.

"Well, didn't you like him because he put out a firecracker or something? That was all you really knew about him. Now you're finding out a little more, getting a truer picture."

"Yes," I said. "When he phoned to invite you to dinner, did he say the same thing to you? The dirty thing?"

"Oh, no," she said.

"I think I can guess what it was he said."

"You probably can. It was supposed to shock me, and it did. But only the words, personally, to me. After all, we know everything, don't we? By the time we reach our age we've heard everything. Read about it. As a matter of fact, I didn't hear much in college that I hadn't already heard about in boarding-school. In college we had a more scientific vocabulary, that's all. Medical terminology instead of Mr. Turner's words."

"Do you happen to know whether he said anything like it to any of the other girls at the party?"

"I happen to know he didn't," she said. "Oh, I probed. But apparently he reserved that compliment for me. Should I feel flattered?"

"It was a tribute to your sex appeal, if you want to look at it that way."

"Just as soon he'd have flattered Mary Stauffer," she said. "She *would* have been flattered. But seriously, I've been thinking that—no."

"What?"

"Do you remember my saying something about 'frankness is the fashion'? But that was after dinner, sitting before the fire. And he'd already whispered his little nothing to me the first time. No, I won't blame myself."

"Listen, that's a very strange man. I think he's a bit wheely, living alone in that big house, semi-crippled, and God knows what all. If he calls you again, be sure and tell me, and I'll have a little talk with him."

"No, don't do that. I'm a big girl now, I can take care of myself."

"Well, he fascinates me, in a way. Some day I may write a novel about him. For instance, I think he had something to do with the explosion at the powder mill."

"You mean he set it off?"

"In my novel he will," I said.

"I'll bet I could get him to tell me if he did," she said.

"You could probably get him to do anything," I said.

"At this stage I probably could," she said.

I looked at her reflection in the soda fountain mirror, and she saw me looking. "Oh, I'm not going to," she said, and put her hand on mine.

Here, with an almost brutal lack of consideration for the line of my story, certain events of my life took place: I left town and got a job in New York. New interests, new friends, new loves separated me from the immediate past, and I was not making enough money to afford frequent homecomings. On my last evening with Isabel she was full of ambition for me. "I'm so proud of you, so pleased for you," she said. "At last you're getting out of here. I don't know why you stood it as long as you did." Actually I had been having a rather good time, all things considered, but there was no question that I was ready to move on. Her enthusiasm for my departure said a lot about her own state of mind. She gave me a silver cigarette lighter as a going-away present, noncommittally engraved with my initials and the date, and no more of herself than ever before. Six months later she invited me to her wedding, but I could not make it. She was marrying a young man from New Bedford or Fall River whom I had never seen but had heard her speak of. His name was Young and he had gone to Dartmouth, and that was all I knew about him. Her parents gave her a big wedding, suitably reported in the Sunday *Trib* and *Times,* and now she had made *her* move. I did not feel that it was quite what she wanted, or possibly what I wanted for her: marriage to a Dartmouth boy and domesticity in a New England mill town. But I reasoned that her husband had been one of the young men about whom there had been gossip, and that therefore she knew exactly what she was doing.

She had been married less than a year when her husband was fatally injured in an accident at his family's factory. They manufactured dyestuffs, and there was an explosion followed by a disastrous fire. I can remember reading about it without at first realizing that one of the fatalities was Isabel Barley's husband. By the time I connected her with the accident it was too late to send flowers, and I wrote her a long letter. One thing I kept out of the letter was the recurrent thought that she was not an ordinary girl to whom ordinary things happened: she had moved to a Massachusetts mill town and domesticity, but bizarre tragedy had assaulted her before she had been married a year. The reply to my letter was a black-bordered, formal card of acknowledgment. I heard through the grapevine that she was back with her parents, seeing no one, and going for horseback rides and drives in her car all by herself. It also transpired that none of us who had written letters had been sent replies other than the engraved acknowledgments—and that was not like Isabel.

My inclination was to respect her withdrawal, which was easy enough for me since I was working in New York. But about two years after her husband's death I went home for a brief visit and I telephoned her. Yes, she would see me. I had no car, so she came and called for me in her Ford coupe. She blew the horn outside our house, and when I went out she moved over and left the driver's seat to me. We shook hands. She was wearing a mink coat and a smart purple hat no bigger than a beret. "You've put on some weight," she said. "But it's becoming. You were always too thin. Where are you going to take me?"

"I thought I'd leave that up to you," I said. "I'm prepared to spend twenty dollars on you."

"Speaks well for your prosperity," she said.

"No. For my extravagance," I said. "And the fact that I'm glad to see you. I don't think I ever spent more than ten dollars on you in one evening."

"There's a new place on the other side of Reading. It was a private house, a farmhouse, and they've turned it into a restaurant.

Dinner is two dollars, but the food is good. Dancing on weekends. The most expensive drinks are a dollar, for planter's punches. Fifty cents for a martini, seventy-five for Scotch."

"Are you shilling for the joint?"

"Yes, if that means what I think it does," she said. "I discovered it quite by accident, on my way home from Philadelphia, and it's where I take my brother-in-law when he comes here. He has to come here on business. They still haven't settled my husband's estate. They began rebuilding right after the fire, but the insurance wasn't nearly enough to cover the loss. For the time being I'm living off Daddy again."

"No life insurance?"

"No. We'd only been married ten months, and it was one of the things Red hadn't gotten around to."

"Can you talk about it, or do you want to?" I said.

"Oh, I'll talk," she said. "What do you want to know? Was I happily married? Yes. Did I love my husband? I was getting to. Did he love me? He was getting to. I'll tell you anything you want to know."

"You will?"

"Yes, I think so," she said.

"Who are you sleeping with now?"

She smiled. "That's a logical question. I imagine a lot of people would ask it. I would, if the circumstances were reversed. Well, I had an affair with a man in New Bedford. Not my brother-in-law, but a business associate of theirs. I had slept with him once before Red was killed, and he was all for my getting a divorce. But Red and I were beginning to—I guess fall in love. The first few months were pretty stormy, but when I tried it with someone else I discovered that I wanted to be Red's wife. So that was the way it was when Red was killed. This friend of his came to see me, we both had a good cry together, because he was very fond of Red too. And then we sort of lapsed into an affair. He wanted to marry me, but I wanted to get away from New Bedford. I used to imagine I could smell that smoke every time I went out of the house, so I came back here. Also, my mother-in-law was quite upset that I wasn't carrying a wee one. There we'd been married ten months and nothing on the way. She and Red's father aren't too happy about my inheriting Red's stock in the company, considering that I'd only been in the family only such a short time—and never in the family way, if you'll forgive me."

"And who are you sleeping with now?" I said.

"Maybe you, before the night's over," she said.

"I don't believe that and neither do you," I said. "Whoever it is, you've decided you don't want to tell me. Okay, but don't play it that way, Isabel."

"Well, I don't know that I owe you any special consideration. Why should I tell you anything?"

"No reason, I guess."

"You didn't even come home for my wedding," she said.

"I would have if you'd sent me the fare," I said.

"You weren't as broke as all that," she said.

"Yes I was. But I knew you wouldn't miss me. In fact, I rather thought you didn't want me there, or you'd have written me."

"The big wedding wasn't my idea. It was my mother's, and Red was all for it, too. My mother wanted to show Gibbsville, and Red was a great one for parties. The first few months of our marriage we went out all the time. Didn't I give you that lighter?"

"That's the one," I said.

"I wonder how many girls that's lit cigarettes for," she said.

"Quite a few," I said. "Are you planning to live at home now?"

"I have to. I have no money of my own, only what Daddy gives me. He gives me an allowance. Not bad. And by living at home I can save up for trips."

"You don't see anybody, or so I'm told," I said. "And yet I find it hard to believe that you don't see *anybody.*"

"Who would be the most unlikely person for me to see, in your opinion?"

"The most unlikely? The most unlikely. Why, Mary Stauffer."

"Guess again. Not female."

"Not female," I said. "The most unlikely male? I give up. Samuel Turner."

"Was that a shot in the dark?" she said.

"Don't tell me you're seeing Samuel Turner?"

"I'll tell you. I wouldn't tell anyone else," she said.

"How did that come about?"

"He wrote me the nicest letter when Red was killed."

"I didn't think mine was so bad," I said.

"Yours was nice, but his was nicer. It was the only one I answered. He invited me to come and see him any time I felt like getting away from it all."

"And you went?"

"Obviously," she said.

"I thought he gave you the creeps," I said.

"He did. But at least he made me feel something. So I showed up unannounced one evening. He came to the door, with a book in his hand, and he made it very easy for me by pretending he was expecting me."

"He was alone in the house?"

"Yes. It was about nine o'clock at night. He gave me some coffee and we sat in that little room of his and I stayed about an hour. A little over an hour. At first I was very ill at ease—"

"Strange," I said.

"But he asked me questions and made me talk."

"All right, come to the point," I said.

"So far he hasn't made a pass or talked dirty. I see him about once a week."

"You get some kind of a kick out of seeing him, though," I said.

"Yes."

"What's going to happen when he asks you to take your clothes off?"

"I don't know," she said. "I've gone there thinking this will be the night, but it hasn't been so far. Actually I think he may be keeping me out of trouble. He's some sort of release for me."

"One of these nights the roof's going to fall in," I said.

"Well, I'm prepared for *something.* And after all, he's crippled. If
. anything does happen it'll be because I want it to."

"He's grotesque. But it wouldn't be the first time beauty and the
beast got together."

"You never met Red, my husband. He wasn't Apollo Belvedere,
either. Red hair, freckles, gap teeth, and talked through his nose.
And he wasn't particularly nice to me. You've always been much
nicer to me."

"And where's it got me?"

"Here, if you consider that getting you anywhere," she said.
"Maybe you don't. We could turn around and go home. But I hope
you say no to that."

"Oh, I say no to that. After all, I did bring you and Turner together, didn't I?"

"You're being sarcastic, but he's been very helpful to me," she
said. "He lets me talk, talk, talk as I haven't been able to talk to my
mother and father or anyone else."

"By the way, did you invite Turner to your wedding?"

"No," she said. She hesitated. "But he was there. Not at the reception, but at the church."

"You spotted him in all that crowd?"

"Yes. It wasn't hard. He was on the groom's side, in a back pew.
But I suppose I'd have seen him anyhow."

"Why?"

"Because he has a very strong personality," she said.

"Magnetic?" I said.

"You don't think so, but he has."

"What about your husband's friend that you had the affair with?
What was he like?"

"In looks, he was conventionally good-looking," she said.

"Therefore didn't appeal to your fondness for the grotesque," I
said.

"Probably," she said.

"If he came to town tomorrow, would you go to bed with him
again?"

"I might," she said. "I might not, but I might. If he wanted me to enough, I might. I was more or less planning to go to bed with you tonight, but you seem more interested in psychoanalyzing me. I haven't asked you—are you in love with somebody?"

"More or less," I said.

"That usually means less," she said. "You're not being faithful to this person?"

"Not really," I said.

"You're not engaged or anything?"

"God, no," I said.

"Then tonight's the night," she said. "After all those times I made you stop, this time I won't."

"Why did you always make me stop before?"

"Because I never went the limit with any Gibbsville boy. You all talked too much. Not only among yourselves, but you'd tell other girls. Some of you could hardly wait to tell me what a hot number Mary Stauffer was."

"Well, she is," I said.

"What if she is? I don't want to know about it. I could guess that. I was just as sure you told her all about me, but I wasn't going to let any Gibbsville boy be able to say I'd gone all the way with him."

"You sound just like your mother," I said.

"Anything wrong about that? I'm her daughter."

"You sound more southern than usual."

"Honey-lamb, Ah cain't he'p that. Ah'm a true doter of the old southland."

"West Virginia?"

"Mummy was born in Nashville, Tennessee. Daddy was born in West Virginia, but Mummy was born in Nashville."

I drove the car to the side of the road and stopped and kissed her. She was surprised but acquiescent. "Now why did you do that?" she said.

"I just wanted to," I said.

"The best reason in the world," she said. "But let's save it for later. This place where we're going, we can get a room all by our-selves."

I wanted to, but did not, ask her how she knew that. "They know me as Mrs. Young," she said. "They're not sure whether Sam is my husband or my father."

"Sam? Sam Turner?"

"Yes. Does that spoil it for you? I've taken him here for dinner a few times."

"Have you really?" I said.

"Now don't *you* spoil it for *me*," she said. "One thing I've never been able to put up with is jealousy."

"It's part of the scheme of things," I said.

"That may be, but as soon as I saw a boy or a man begin to show signs of jealousy, I had nothing more to do with him. Possessive-ness. The first sign of possessiveness. Red got possessive, and I went straight to bed with his best friend."

"Did Red know that?"

"No, but *I* did," she said.

"I don't know—it seems to me a bit of possessiveness on the part of a husband is a good thing."

"How would you like to be married to a possessive woman?" she said.

"I think I'd expect my wife to be possessive."

"You wouldn't like it. This girl that you say you're more or less in love with—you're not going to let her spoil our evening, are you? I've never known you to be faithful to any girl. Well, it works both ways."

"Isabel, how many men have you actually slept with?"

"You mean put their thing inside me?"

"Yes."

"Six," she said.

"That's about what I figured. Four before you were married, and two after."

"Three before Red, then Red, then two others. You'll make seven," she said. "Necking, of course, is another story."

"Did you ever lay two men in the same night?"

"How did you know that? Yes, Red and his best friend. Not in that order. His friend in the back of a car, and Red when I got home. It was quite a revelation to me. I'd necked two boys in one night. You *know* that. But I'd never thought I'd have two men all the way in one night."

"How was it a revelation?"

"If you want to know the truth, it was great. Not that I made a practice of it, but it happened more than once. In fact, almost every time I went all the way with Harry, I'd go home and go to bed with Red. I'd heard of a lot of girls doing it two or three times a night with the same man, but while I was having my affair with Harry I did it with two men."

"You'd warm up with Harry, and Red would get the full benefit."

"Just about," she said. "The last time I stayed with Harry, after Red was killed, I suddenly realized that I wouldn't be going home to Red, and I started to cry."

"In the middle of the proceedings?"

"Somewhere along the way."

"Did you stop?"

"Oh, no. No, I didn't stop. I couldn't have, and I wouldn't have anyway. Harry would have killed me—or maybe I'd have killed him!"

"You always knew when to stop with me," I said.

"But you and I'd never got that far. You're no virgin, you know the difference. And I always did *something* for you."

"Yes, I'll say that for you."

"I'm a terribly passionate girl," she said. "I don't think I'm immoral, but I know a lot more about myself than I used to. Do you feel—as I do—that nothing really happened to us before we went away from here? Even the sex I had before I left here didn't matter much. And even though I happen to be living here again, the place'll never be the same. My life'll never be the same. *I'll* never be the same. Those men that went away to the war in 1918, they had a hard time when they got back, trying to fit in again. It's only lately that they've been able to talk about it—how they didn't understand the people and the people didn't understand them. Well, it's much the same with me. I've been away, to a war of sorts, and I'll never be the same, no matter how long I live here."

"I don't expect you will live here very long," I said. "I know I couldn't."

It was about a fifty-mile drive to the Colonial Inn, Peter Stump, owner and proprietor, and the traffic in Reading slowed us down somewhat. During the latter part of the ride we talked less, and I began to believe that she had changed so much that I hardly knew her or that I had never known her at all. In spite of our friendship and our intimacies, the person she had presented to me had always been a girl who was governed by self-restraint and to her I was one of the Gibbsville crowd who talked too much. Now we were rather new to each other and had become so not through shared experience but through experiences shared with others. To say the least, the evening gave promise of continuing to be an interesting one.

The proprietor, Peter Stump, was a stout man in his forties, wearing trousers and vest without the jacket of his suit; with a second-generation heavy gold watch-chain strung across the upper part of his vest; his shirtsleeves were held in place by a frilly garter; an array of pencils, fountain pens, and haircomb protruded from the upper left pocket of his vest. On the third finger of his right hand he wore a gold ring which had a large script *S* applied to a dark stone. He wore a brown leather belt with a loop strap that held a detachable key ring so crowded with keys that it looked like a fan. "Mrs. Young," he said. "Such a pleasure. Such a real genuine pleasure." He carefully ignored me until we had been introduced. "Any friend of Mrs. Young I welcome. Your first visit, I set 'em up on the house." We stood at the bar; Isabel ordered a Manhattan; I ordered a Rob Roy, as much to test Stump's knowledge as to drink Scotch in a cocktail. He did not bat an eye, although in my whole life I had never heard anyone in Pennsylvania order a Rob Roy. Scotch in any form was not a popular drink. "Well, soon it'll be Holloween and before you know it, Thanksgiving already," said Stump. "Last week was a frost. I guess you had it up your way."

"Yes, we've had a frost," said Isabel.

"Such a beautiful time of the year, the different colors," said Stump. "I got my brother-in-law that supplies me with turkeys, a farm o'er in Lebanon County twenty *miles* away. Wednesday driving back from there I took notice all the different colors this time of the year. Such greens and browns and yellows." He was mixing the drinks as he spoke, addressing Isabel but including me. "The Manhattan cocktail for the lady, the Rob Roy for mister," he said. "The house takes a small beer." We all raised our glasses and drank. He finished his beer and sloshed his glass in the tank, and rested his forearms on the bar. He enjoyed having the right, as proprietor, to place himself on nearly equal terms with Isabel. As to me, he had not figured out where I stood, and out of a perverse impulse I decided to make him dislike me. I could have made him go the other way, but he irritated me. His looks, his get-up, his assumption of equality with Isabel, and his suspended judgment of me.

"I understand you have private diningrooms," I said. He had not yet been able to demonstrate his chumminess with Isabel, and my question at least established *my* relationship with him.

"Well, I ain't saying we do and I ain't saying we don't," he said.

"Oh, I thought you were the proprietor," I said. "Whom do I speak to about a private room?"

"Me," he said.

"I spoke to you, and I didn't get much of an answer," I said. "It doesn't matter."

"I only allow people to use the room if I know them," he said.

"It doesn't matter," I said. I raised my left wrist high in the air and looked at my watch. I turned to Isabel. "Shall we have another drink here and then move on?"

"I'd like another," she said.

"Another Manhattan and a Rob Roy," I said. "Not quite as

much vermouth in the Rob Roy, please." I turned again to Isabel. "Was yours all right?"

"Yes, mine was all right," she said.

There was a silence while Stump mixed the drinks, placed them on the bar, and watched as I tasted my cocktail. "Is better this one?" he said.

"Yes, this one is better," I said. I offered Isabel a cigarette, took one myself, lit Isabel's and mine. Stump reached in a lower vest pocket and took out a cigarette without taking out the pack. He lit his cigarette and inhaled such a long drag on it that he overestimated his lung capacity and had to cough. He moved away to the end of the small bar, but I had not yet finished with him.

"Why are you being so unpleasant?" said Isabel, just above a whisper.

"You'll see," I said.

"I don't know where else we can go," she said.

"We may not have to," I said. I knocked off the rest of my drink and snapped my finger at Stump, who was carefully not looking in our direction and carefully not listening to our words. "The bill, please," I said.

He went to the cash register and pressed the keys and pulled down a slip. I looked at the slip. The total was one-fifty. I gave him a five-dollar bill. Here was his last chance to sell two dinners and to make himself look good in the eyes of Isabel. He took his time making change. "One-fifty out of five," he said. "One-fifty, and fifty is two dollars, three dollars, four dollars, five dollars."

"Right," I said, pocketing the change. "Ready, Isabel?"

"Mm-hmm," she muttered.

"Let's go," I said. We turned and headed for the exit. "Now don't you say a word," I said to Isabel. We got outside, just outside, and Stump followed us.

"Mister, I don't want you going away mad. If I said anything, I apologize. Mrs. Young, you tell him. I was only making a little joke."

"Now wait a second," I said. "I asked you a perfectly reasonable question, and you gave me a snotty answer. Who the hell do you think you are?"

"I ain't nobody, and I apologize. I apologize to you, Mrs. Young. You brung him here and I don't want to make no trouble for you. Do me the favor and come back in."

"Well, what do *you* say, Isabel?"

"I'm sure he was only making a little joke," she said.

"Well—all right," I said. "We *have* come fifty miles."

"I guarantee you, if you ever ate a better dinner, I won't charge you a penny," said Stump.

He led us back through the diningroom to a small room upstairs. "Make yourselves comfortable and I bring you the menu card. The same drink as before?" he said.

"Well, it worked, whatever it was," she said, when Stump had gone.

"It was knowing the type," I said. "He couldn't see fifteen bucks fly out the window, and he wants to keep on your good side."

"But why did you do it? You were about as mean to him as you could possibly be," she said.

"He's the kind of kraut-head that wouldn't understand anything else. And when I want him to go away, he'll go away," I said. "This looks as if it used to be a bedroom. Do you suppose that's the door to a bathroom?"

"I know it is," she said.

"I thought you'd know," I said.

"Don't start using your psychology on me," she said.

"Start? I haven't stopped," I said.

"Balderdash!" she said. She disappeared into the bathroom, and by the time she came out Stump had brought the drinks and the menu. We ordered a plank steak for two, baked potatoes, and baby lima beans. No soup, no salad, no dessert. Of its kind it was as good a meal as ever I ate. We drank a bottle of Chianti, and with the coffee he brought a bottle of Scotch and a bowl of ice. "Ring when you want more ice," he said, and left us.

"Oh, Jesus, I feel good," I said. "Just enough of everything." I was sitting on the sofa and she came and lay down and rested her head in my lap and I put my hand down into her bosom. "I think the right one has gotten a little larger than the left."

"It's the way I'm lying. If I lie a little more to the left, the right one will seem larger."

"When did you stop wearing a bra?"

"Oh—about an hour ago. I got rid of excess baggage in the bathroom."

"You have nothing on under your dress?"

"Nothing. Wasn't that thoughtful of me?"

"You've always been very thoughtful," I said. "You have, you know."

"I try to be," she said. "For instance, this dress. The easiest thing in the world to get off. Much less trouble than all those things you have on."

"Yes, I'll need your help," I said.

We had never been naked together. To what we now became, we had never been anything together. In the midst of my excitement at seeing her stripped of everything but her rings, I almost failed to notice her smile, but it is what I remember best and will always remember. It began with her amusement at my being hypnotized by the beauty of her figure, and it continued when we both knew that I was inside her. It vanished then as she gave and demanded, gave and demanded, and then she smiled again as we collapsed into a breathless peace. I knew immediately that I would never love her and that she would never love me, but I am equally sure that she knew as I did that we would be loving each other for the rest of our lives. I kissed her on the lips.

"We've accomplished something," she said.

"Yes," I said.

"I'm not sure what it is, but we have accomplished something," she said.

"You don't have to know what it is, yet," I said.

"I guess it's just that we never accomplished anything before, and this time we did," she said. "When you get married you'll have to tell your wife about me, and the next time I get married I'll have to tell my husband about you. When I was married to Red I didn't have to tell him about you, because there was nothing to tell."

"Compared to this there was nothing," I said.

"But now there is something," she said. "When are you going back to New York?"

"Tomorrow," I said.

"Do you mind if I go with you, and spend tomorrow night with you? I don't want this to be just—this. I promise to leave in the morning, the day after tomorrow. But don't let's have only this room to remember. You can make up some story for your other girl. I'm sure you're good at making up stories."

"I'm very good at it," I said. "She's pretty good herself."

"Oh, it's that way?" she said.

"We pretend it isn't, but it is," I said. "She has a husband that she doesn't live with, but I know she sees him. She works in an advertising agency and he has a job in the advertising department at *Collier's*. They were separated once before and she went back with him. Maybe she plans to again."

"Would you mind?"

"When I'm with her, everything's fine. But if I don't see her for a couple of days—if she has to go to Detroit or someplace—I go on the make."

"Is she beautiful and attractive?"

"Yes. Both, actually. She also makes a hell of a lot more money than I do, and he makes more than she does. And they both have liberal expense accounts."

"I don't see much future in it for you," said Isabel.

"There is none. But when I'm with her I don't think of that angle," I said.

"Is she wonderful to sleep with?"

"That's what I've been trying not to say," I said. "I'll tell you all about her if you want me to, but you wouldn't like me any better if I did."

"Is she a Lesbian?"

"By God, you're pretty smart. She's not a flagrant Lez, but she has a very dear friend that wears a Tuxedo. They go to the Civic Repertory together and I imagine they hold hands."

"Is that all?"

"Of course it's not all, but she won't admit anything else. And God knows when she's with me, she's feminine enough."

"I had a girl that was crazy about me in college. Showered me with presents. Perfume. Theater tickets, things like that."

"And?" I said.

"Nothing, till senior year I spent a weekend with her at her family's house, a huge place overlooking the Hudson River. Nobody there but the servants. That was when she made her first pass at me."

"Did you go for it?"

"Yes," she said. "I never thought I would, but I rather liked it. At least with her. We were all alone in that great big house. The servants stayed out of sight most of the time, and Ginny—it was as if we were the only two people in the world. Have you ever been up there, on the Hudson, in those hills? You can look out for miles and not see another living soul. We had dinner and went to bed early the first night we arrived, she in her room and I in mine. She came in to say goodnight to me and open my windows. Ostensibly. She asked me if she could get in bed with me for a few minutes, and I said of course she could. We'd both had some champagne at dinner. Well, she got in bed and we lay there for a minute with our arms around each other, chatting, and then she kissed me goodnight. But before I knew it she was going down on me and I did nothing to stop her. I think I'd been wanting her to. There was something about the atmosphere of that big castle from the time we arrived. And maybe I'm just making excuses, because I didn't try to stop her. She left, and the next day not a word was said about it. But after dinner she put her arm around me and said, 'Shall we go upstairs?' and I agreed. This time there was no business about saying goodnight and opening my windows. And she stayed all night, till daylight."

"The inevitable question. What about you?"

"She didn't want me to. She had a nice little figure, and there we were, all alone in the world and she seemed to get so much pleasure out of it. But all she wanted was to make me come, and she could do that all right. Do you know, I've never told anyone about this chapter of my life. We were all suspicious of each other at college, especially of Ginny and me. But they never had anything to go on there. And after that one weekend she transferred her affections to a freshman, as blonde as I was and with almost as good a figure. I was a little miffed, frankly. But she took the freshman to her house for a weekend and then dropped her too, for another girl in our class. Ginny was a seducer, that's all. Well, she seduced me, and in New York, where there are thousands of pretty girls, she must be having a field day. She sent me a very expensive wedding present when I married Red. A silver tea service from Black, Starr. But she didn't come to the wedding, and I'm just as glad she didn't. I was disturbed enough seeing Sam Turner, whom I hadn't even invited, and my uncle from Tennessee, so drunk he was draped over the pew where everybody could see him. Passed out cold." On the word *cold* she got up and put on my shirt. "Not for the sake of modesty, but I don't want to catch cold."

"Can you imagine what your father and mother would think of this conversation?" I said.

"Easily. My mother would go into a tizzy. When I went away to boarding-school she warned me against girls that got too affectionate. Man-haters, she called them. She said there was a certain type of girl that tried to discourage other girls from getting married, especially pretty girls. My mother believed that anything that discouraged a girl from getting married should be declared against the law. The whole point of college wasn't to get an education but to meet eligible boys. But she wasn't so far wrong, you know. You could divide the girls at Wellesley into two classes—the ones who were waiting for a husband, and would-be schoolteachers."

"Where does that leave girls like your friend Ginny?"

"Well, she was pretty studious, so she belonged with the schoolteachers. Actually, Ginny was the most interesting girl I met the four years I was there. Her father was a very famous lawyer, but the money was on her mother's side. Her father was Roger Hillman."

"Oh, sure. Married one of the Berger clan. Edwin Berger, Percy Berger, Howard Berger, and there's a count in there somewhere."

"I don't know. I just know they're all enormously rich. Ginny's mother had a closet that was filled with nothing but fur coats. *Two* sable coats, two ermine. Unfortunately they didn't fit me, or I'd have been tempted to walk away with one—and I could have had it, that weekend. Ginny was rather undistinguished-looking except for her eyes and her hair. She had fierce black eyes and coal-black hair, and she wore eye-shadow, even at school. When she fixed those eyes on you you forgot that she wasn't very tall, or chic or anything."

"Would you spend another weekend with her?"

"I wonder. I really wonder. I've been staying with my family ever since Red was killed, on my very best behavior. But if Ginny had turned up instead of you, I'd probably be with her now. I've been accustomed to compliments and admiration since I was fifteen years old, and it isn't only men that appreciate feminine beauty. Women are more critical than men and therefore more appreciative. The three girls that Ginny seduced at college were the three prettiest blondes in the whole place. Me, and the other two. There may have been others that graduated in earlier classes, but I didn't know about Ginny till that weekend. There was one girl from Rochester, two classes ahead of us. She was the most beautiful thing I ever saw, and blonde. I wonder if Ginny ever seduced her. If I ever go to Rochester I'm going to find out, if it's humanly possible. Your girl in New York, is she a blonde?"

"No," I said. "Dark brown hair."

"It'd be funny if she fell into Ginny's clutches."

"It'd be funnier still if this Ginny wore a Tuxedo," I said.

"Ginny would never do that. She wasn't chic, but she was probably the only girl in my four years at Wellesley that I never saw wearing saddle-straps. Always high heels, to get that extra height."

"Did she ever go out with boys?"

"Go out with them, yes. Her brother was at Harvard, and she

used to go out with friends of his. One of them had a big old Rolls-Royce touring car and they'd drive out and get Ginny and a girl named Dot Rivkin, from Philadelphia. Ginny couldn't stand her, but Dot was very much on the make for Ginny's brother. Actually I had the feeling that all their dates were arranged by their families. Dot had dates with other Jewish boys, but Ginny's brother was the prize. Actually, Dot was seeing a lot of a terrible creature named Gallagher, from Holy Cross."

"They're all terrible creatures at Holy Cross, and Boston College and Fordham, and Georgetown."

"No, I knew a terribly attractive boy that went to Georgetown. He was from New Orleans."

"But he wasn't Irish?" I said.

"No. Catholic, but not Irish," she said. "Oh—I get it. You're pulling my leg."

"Not pulling it. Just giving it a nice feel."

"Well, don't. Let's get dressed and tomorrow night we'll be in New York and I won't care what you do," she said. "What's the most you ever did it in one night?"

"Three times," I said.

"Tomorrow night we'll do it three times," she said. "Four, if you're up to it."

"How about two tonight and two tomorrow night?"

"No. I'd really like to get out of here," she said. "We've accomplished something tonight. Tomorrow we'll accomplish something else. You may have a hard time getting rid of me. I might break my promise to leave."

"I'll forgive you," I said. I kissed her and squeezed her breasts, and her smile came back. But she broke away and retired to dress.

It was agreed that she would come to my apartment on Bank Street at six o'clock the next evening. Accordingly, at five o'clock I was home, had my bed made, filled the ice bucket, rinsed out the tub, saw to it that there were Camels, which she smoked, and enough bath towels. I thought of everything except the possibility that she would not show up, and at half-past seven I was still more worried than annoyed. It never occurred to me that she had not come to New York. I had taken the morning train that got me to the city shortly before noon, eaten some lunch at Penn Station, and spent the rest of the afternoon in and out of my apartment, preparing for her visit. I had even sent my other girl a telegram from Philadelphia, saying I was detained there for a couple of days, just in case she had one of her impulses to drop in without warning. Therefore when my telephone rang at eight-thirty I knew it was Isabel. "Where are you? I've been worried about you," I said.

"I'm home, in Gibbsville," she said.

"What happened?" I said.

"I don't really know," she said.

"Will you be here tomorrow? You could take the sleeper," I said.

"I thought of that," she said.

"Is there somebody there, that you can't talk?"

"No, the family are out to dinner," she said. "It's nothing against you. I loved it—what we accomplished last night. But I've been thinking all day, what we accomplished last night was the end, the completion of everything we had before. It isn't going to be the beginning of something else. Because I don't like what it would be the beginning of. You have girls in New York, and I don't want to become your out-of-town tourist that comes to New York with hot pants, expecting to be laid and sent back to the provinces. I know the type and I could turn into just that."

"If you were here now I could convince you otherwise," I said.

"If I were there now I could convince myself," she said.

"There's more to this than you're telling me," I said.

"Oh, there's a lot more," she said. "You know a great deal more about me than you knew the day before yesterday, but I didn't give you the whole story by any means. Darling, I know that selfishly it would be a great mistake for me to see you now. I loved last night, all of it, and it isn't one of those things of hating yourself in the morning. Far from it. I went for a long ride this morning and I kept thinking how nice it had been to have you between my legs instead

of just a horse. I'm having such thoughts now, but not uncontrolla-
bly."

"Is your horse by any chance a mare?" I said.

"I could slap you for that," she said. "A complete lack of respect
for my confidences. I think it's time for me to hang up before you
say something else nasty."

"All right. I don't see that we're getting anywhere, or that we ever
will."

"Darling, I'm afraid you're right," she said. "We were never
going to get anywhere."

"If you should ever decide to change your mind, I have a carton
of Camels here that really belong to you. I have no use for them."

"See? We can't stay cross at each other," she said. "Maybe that's
our trouble. No anger, no jealousy, and certainly no love. If you
move from there will you let me know your new address?"

"Why, sure. Whatever it was we had last night, I'll go on liking
it."

"Just don't count on it," she said. "Goodnight, and I'm sorry."
She hung up, and I went over to a Coffee Pot on Sixth Avenue and
had some bacon and eggs and French fries. They could not have
given me planked steak even if I had ordered it.

Fate now proceeded to deal me several harsh blows—an awfully
fancy way of saying that I lost two jobs and could not sell anything
to any magazine on earth. I could not even get a job as a rewrite man
on City News, and as I had never saved any money, the only cash I
had was what I could borrow. My credit was still good at a few
speakeasies, but I owed three months' rent on the Bank Street apartment. I tried doing my own laundry, but the ironing of shirts was
never one of my skills. My friend in the advertising business chose
this period to resume her companionate marriage with her husband
and to dun me for $150 she had lent me. She had no chance of get-
ting $150 out of me, but by dunning me she effectively removed her-
self from among my candidates for an occasional small touch. There

were so many millions of men and women who were no better off than I was that the people who had jobs or a little money of their own built up a resistance to hard-luck stories. I had three friends who were good for five-dollar or ten-dollar touches, if I spread them over several weeks. A press agent of my acquaintance, who could not write a simple declarative sentence, would pay me twenty-five dollars for writing a piece about one of his clients—if the piece got printed in the Sunday *Trib* or *Times*. The pieces, however, appeared under his byline, not mine, and I was unable to set up a press agency of my own. I ate, and smoked, on a dollar a day: fifteen cents for a pack of cigarettes, and eighty-five cents for food on days when I did not have to spend a couple of nickels in the subway. During this financial tribulation—perhaps because I was undernourished and my vitality was low—I was easily able to adjust to the abruptness of Isabel Barley's departure from my life. That was how I thought of it, when I thought of it: that she had rather ungracefully gone out of my life, as disappointing as a coitus interruptus, which, of course, it was. I had the problem of subsisting on a dollar a day, and the more fundamental problem of finding the dollar. Therefore the kind of love I had for Isabel was a luxury that cost me nothing and gave me little pleasure, but still a luxury, comparable at that stage to the desire to own a fine car that I had driven only once. When you are reduced to the condition where you must measure the cost of a pack of cigarettes against a breakfast of coffee and toast, nearly everything is a luxury. And though you may not realize it at the time, the things that are happening to your pride and your self-respect have an effect that lasts long after the ordeal is over.

My ordeal ended—my luck changed—in grand style: I was notified that my share of a maiden aunt's bequests to her nieces and nephews amounted to $667; I sold a piece to *The Saturday Evening Post* for $400; and I got a $75 a week job in the publicity department of a movie company. I paid up my back rent, made my peace with the telephone company, and gave the speakeasy people something on account. Then I had a party that lasted from Friday night to Monday morning, in the course of which I telephoned Isabel. What

I said to her I do not know, but I invited her to come to New York and join the party. She did not come, and I forgot all about inviting her until a week or so later she telephoned me, saying she was in New York and would like to see me. Her tone was not that of a woman who wished to be seduced as quickly as possible, nor was her manner when she appeared at my door. "Are we alone?" she said.

"Of course. Why?" I said.

"The way your party sounded, it could have gone on for a week," she said.

"It very nearly did," I said.

"A real orgy?" she said.

"What time was it when I phoned you?" I said.

"About two o'clock Sunday morning," she said.

I nodded. "By that time it had reached the orgy stage," I said.

"That's why I came to see you," she said.

"Want me to arrange an orgy for you?"

"That's not very funny," she said. "And it's just what I want to talk about. Your call upset me. In the first place, I'd gone to bed and my father answered the phone. *He* was annoyed. Mother was annoyed. Naturally I was annoyed. They'd gone to bed but they were still awake. I wasn't. I was asleep, and apparently you told them it was an emergency. But what really upset me most of all was your thinking about me at that particular time, as if you were sure I'd fit into a party like that. It's months since I've heard from you, and you break the silence by asking me to join you in a wild party. Why? I've never been on that kind of a party, and if you don't know that, you should."

"There wasn't much sense to my call, I'll admit," I said.

"No sense at all. And I've been worrying ever since that that's what you think of me. The things I've told you about myself have led you to some very wrong conclusions, and I want to correct them. I'm first of all *not* an orgy girl. The very thought of a third person horrifies me. How many times have I kept you from kissing me because I was afraid someone would see us. You never saw me kissing another boy."

"No, not really," I said.

"Then why would you want me at a party like that?"

"It doesn't seem to have been a very good idea," I said.

"Was it a very bad party? I mean—degenerate?"

"Be specific," I said.

"Were there girls doing things to girls, in front of everybody?"

"Yes," I said.

"I thought so. That's what made you think of me," she said. "Isn't that the truth?"

"I suppose it crossed my mind," I said.

"Because I told you about a girl I knew in college, you now think that that's the way I am."

"No, I don't," I said.

"And you have a lady friend that is that way," she said.

"She's no longer my lady friend. She's gone back to her husband. A lot of things have happened to me. I had a very bad time financially, was absolutely flat broke and actually didn't have enough to eat. My lady friend, as you call her, went back to her husband. And so forth and so on. The party last week was to celebrate my change of luck. I got a little money, and I got a new job. The party started Friday night and kept on going, not always with the same people. Put ten or a dozen people in this room and a lot of booze, away go the inhibitions. And this is Greenwich Village, don't forget. This is where a lot of people come to lose their inhibitions. If one girl takes her clothes off, the others do or leave. In this case, most of them stayed."

"I'd be absolutely horrified," she said.

"Well, you never get really plastered."

"No, and I hope I never do," she said.

"You'd better not," I said.

"There, you see? You think I'm vulnerable," she said. "I want you to stop thinking that."

"Oh, you didn't come all the way to New York to tell me that, Isabel. What the hell is really on your mind?"

"Do you want to know?"

"Of course I want to know," I said.

"I came to New York to have one last fling," she said.

"With me, I hope," I said.

"Yes."

"And then what?"

"Then I'm going to get married."

"Anyone in particular?" I said.

"Yes. Samuel Turner," she said.

"It's all decided?" I said. "You're going to marry him and live in Turnersville?"

"Yes."

"You're waiting for me to show surprise, or make some sarcastic comments."

"You are taking it differently than I thought you would," she said.

"The fact of the matter is, I'm not sure whether to believe you or not. Just tell me why you're marrying him."

"Because he asked me to. He's over twice my age, and ugly, and I know he hasn't told me all the truth about himself. There are a lot of objections to marrying him, but he knew them as well as I did and even so he said I *ought* to marry him."

"I can see what there's in it for him, but not for you," I said. "You've been to bed with him, of course, so whatever he does, you like."

"Yes, we don't have to go into that," she said.

"All right. Probably make a good case history for Havelock Ellis, but who wouldn't?"

"Who wouldn't, indeed? *I* would, whether I marry Sam or not. Red Young was so full of complexes that you could write a whole book about him. And what about you and your orgies?"

"What about them? Shall we have one for your last fling?"

"No," she said. "My last fling is because we love each other. In our own way. You love me just as much as I love you, and I want you to always love me. And me to love you. I don't know what I'm getting into by marrying Sam, but I want us to love each other."

"For God's sake, Isabel, you sound like somebody that's going into prison and wants to have one friend on the outside. If that's the case you'd better take more time."

"I don't want to take any more time. I want to get started on my new life."

"You're frightened. You're terrified," I said.

"Of failure, not of anything he'd do to me," she said. "I was frightened of Red, too, and almost had a failure. But things got better until he was killed. Not everybody thought it would be a good idea to marry Red, you know. My father loathed him, could hardly be civil to him."

"Your father's going to love the idea of your marrying Sam Turner," I said. "Just make sure you're not marrying him because everybody's against it."

"Are you against it?"

"The quick answer is yes. But I wonder. You've had one conventional marriage, *with* an unconventional ending, it's true. But a big wedding and in-laws in a strange town and so forth. And you're not a conventional girl. I don't say I'm for it, but maybe you ought to give it a try. I know this—I'd hate to be married to you if you didn't give it a try. You'd be forever thinking of Sam Turner as the man who could have made you happy."

"I don't think any man or woman will ever make me happy," she said. "I don't depend on people that much. Sex, yes. But I can go without that, too. Then I want it, and get it, but I'll never be dependent on anyone for it. You'll always oblige, won't you?"

"Yes, I think I probably will," I said.

"Just to help a girl out," she said. "A favor among friends. *Between* friends, I should say."

"I wouldn't want to see you hanging around the Navy Yard," I said.

"That's what I mean. Just to be obliging. Like now, I want to have my last fling, so I come to you," she said. "No, darling, I'm not counting on anyone to make me happy. You and I like each other enough to call it quote love unquote, and Samuel Turner wants me for reasons of his own. Otherwise, I've gone through my whole life without caring much what happened to me or anyone else. It horrified me when Red was killed, but if he had died of pneumonia or appendicitis, I'd have got over it more quickly." She paused. "This afternoon I saw a man standing outside Penn Station, selling apples. I wanted to hit him! 'You big crybaby,' I felt like saying. 'You're not trying to sell apples. You want people to give you a dollar for an apple instead of buying them two for a nickel at a fruit stand.' They're all over New York, those people, and I think they're disgusting. I really can't stand people that have no guts. I'd have made a terrible mother."

"You may be one yet," I said.

"Not if I can help it," she said. "I don't like children and they don't like me."

"What if Sam wants you to perpetuate the Turner line?"

"He doesn't want children, either. They're afraid of him. When Sam dies I'll still be comparatively young, in my forties, and I'll marry again. I expect to keep my figure, which I wouldn't be able to do if I had a lot of children. My mother has *almost* as good a figure as I expect to have at her age. She had two, but she didn't nurse us. I'm very proud of my bosoms. Women notice them as much as men. I . . ." She caught herself.

"You what?"

"Nothing. I wasn't going to say any more."

"Yes you were, and you know you were," I said.

"All right. I was merely going to say that I have a long life to live, and a woman *being* a woman owes it to herself to keep her looks, her figure. A man can look like Samuel Turner, or Red Young, for that matter. But if a woman is lucky enough to have good looks, she'd better hold on to them as long as she can."

"Well, why not?" I said. "The birth rate's high enough. I'd much rather you'd let me gnaw at your bosom than some unappreciative kid. I care a hell of a lot more about what goes into your snatch than what comes out of it."

"The soul of a poet," she said. "Is my snatch what I think it is?"

"It is."

"Well, I prefer that to some of the words I've heard. Why snatch, I wonder? Does it snatch at you?"

"Let's see," I said. We made love with great care, as though engaged in a contest in which the object was to end in a tie. It did so, and we lay beside each other and silently considered the experience. "Another accomplishment," she said.

"I was thinking the same thing," I said.

"Maybe it's all we have, but we have that," she said. "I don't think it *is* all we have. It couldn't be and be so perfect."

"Oh, it couldn't be all we have. We just don't want to sign anything."

"Is that our trouble?"

"We don't want to sign away anything," I said.

"That's better," she said. "You're never going to give up anything, and neither am I. You're not enough for me, and I'm not enough for you."

"Except at the time," I said.

"Except at the time," she said.

She decided that she did not want to go out for dinner, and she scrambled some eggs and made a large quantity of toast. Her overnight bag stood unopened on the floor, and she put on one of my shirts. "Why do some men's shirts go on over the head and others not?"

"Because in my case, Brooks Brothers don't make me pay cash. I couldn't afford to buy a shirt at Macy's."

"I thought you were rich again," she said.

"I am—for me. Last week for about six hours I had over a thousand dollars. Most of it's gone, but my credit's good again. And I hope you notice I never hocked your cigarette lighter. Jesus, that reminds me I have to go up to Simpson's and redeem my father's watch. I have a Vacheron that's been in and out of hock but it's still mine. My last remaining connection with the days of opulence. The chain's gone, but I've held on to the watch. Not sentiment. Superstition. My good studs, that my uncle gave me when I was born. My coonskin coat. A pair of gold cufflinks that belonged to my grandfather. All gone. But if I ever lose that watch, I have some feeling that I'll never be in the chips again."

"You've always made a joke of money."

"I have? To hide the tears, I guess. I hate not having money."

"We always used to think your family were rich. When I wanted a pony, and you had *two,* I thought your family were much better off than we were."

"But you found out—and so did we," I said. "The hard way."

"Do you know that Red was worth over a half a million, of his own?"

"How would I know that? I hope you get it. I have a feeling you'll need it, in Turnersville."

"Yes, they're finally going to let me have it. Daddy got fed up with their stalling and hired a lawyer for me. A new Bedford lawyer. Why do you say I'll need it? I'm not sure I like that."

"I'm not implying that Sam Turner's marrying you for your money," I said. "All I meant was that you'll want someone besides old Gussie in that house. And a car. And a saddle horse. The money will come in very handy."

"Yes, I could do wonders with that house, brightening it up a little. The things are there, but Samuel only uses a few rooms. I hope I can persuade him to put in an elevator, one of those stairway things. Then we could use the whole house. Will you come and visit us?"

"I'll come for dinner, but I wouldn't spend the night there. Do you think I could sleep in that house while you were in bed with Sam?"

"I'll ask Mary Stauffer to be our other house guest. She'll take your mind off me."

"Mary and I, chaperoned by you and Sam. That's a prospect that pleases."

"I wasn't serious," she said.

"I think you were," I said.

"Not really. Samuel doesn't like Mary."

"He wouldn't like me either, if he could see you now," I said.

"But he can't see me now," she said. "I suppose I ought to start thinking about going to my hotel."

"Forget the hotel. Stay here."

"Well, that's what I'd rather do, but . . ."

"If it's going to be your last fling, at least we ought to sleep together."

"Don't have any doubt about it. It *is* my last fling," she said.

"You sure?" I said.

"As sure as I can be about anything about myself," she said.

"If it's a fling—do you want me to get another girl? I know one. She'll come over and do anything you want. She's without a doubt the most perverted girl I've ever known, and she looks like a dairy maid. Like a toothpaste ad. Big blue eyes, big white teeth."

"Why does my fling have to be with another girl? Why couldn't it be with another man?"

"Because I wouldn't like that," I said.

"Then it's your fling, not mine," she said. "Aren't I enough for you?"

"I was thinking that I might not be enough for you," I said.

"A fling doesn't have to be an orgy," she said. "Maybe in a year or two Turnersville will get to me and I'll be ready for anything. But you're enough for me now."

"Thanks," I said.

"Do you realize that it isn't even midnight?" she said.

"Do you want to go out?"

"No. Do you?"

"No," I said.

"What time do you have to be up in the morning?" she said.

"If I'm in the office by ten I'm usually ahead of my boss."

"Then I can get your breakfast. I never sleep that late. Do you ever get to bed before midnight? Somehow I don't think of you as."

"No, I guess I don't," I said.

"Will you be able to sleep if we go to bed now?"

"I probably could, but I don't expect to," I said.

"I mean—a little later."

"A little later I'll sleep the sleep of the just. The just-laid."

"You're as afraid of sentiment as I am," she said.

"If not more so," I said. "You're doing a very sentimental thing by marrying Sam Turner, no matter how you explain it. I could never do that."

"Could you marry me?"

"Not any more. A few years ago I could have, but not any more. I couldn't marry anybody now, not any of the girls I used to know at home. You're all so young, and rather innocent. At least that's the way I think of you. The girls I see now, we don't lose any time getting into bed. The odd thing, of course, is that most of the girls I see now are the same as you and all the other girls back home, transplanted to New York. The same schools, the same respectable families. But here they're making up for lost time, and so am I. A girl I know told me that she was horrified to discover that in her first year here she'd slept with five boys. She told me that as soon as it got to ten she was going to go back to Ohio and settle down. But it got to ten and she's still here in the Village. So you see what you're avoiding."

"I'll have slept with ten men before I'm through. I've only got four to go, actually."

"Have you got them all picked out?" I said.

"No, but I could name four that wouldn't have the slightest trouble. Three, now that Julian English is dead. I could never understand why he didn't fall madly in love with me. Don't say it was because he was in love with Caroline."

"That's what I *was* going to say," I said.

"That's what everybody says. But if he was so much in love with her, why did he kill himself?"

"Because the roof fell in, and part of it was the fear of losing her."

"I'm sorry, but I don't believe that," she said. "If she hadn't been so possessive he would have had lots of girls, me among them, and we'd have made life a lot more interesting than that prissy little wife of his."

"Prissy?"

"Yes, she was prissy. One of those prissy Bryn Mawr types. I've never heard a man say a single word against her, and very few girls. But she sucked the life out of him."

"A nice way to die."

"The spirit, the independence. She made him into something he was never meant to be. A carbon-copy of his father and my father and all those men at the Gibbsville Club. She reminds me of my mother-in-law—and of my mother, for that matter. I hate good capital-G women." She stood up and pulled my shirt over her head. "Aren't you glad I'm not Caroline English?"

Well, I was.

In the morning she was up and dressed and gave me a cup of coffee at half-past eight. I was charmed by the novelty of our simulated domesticity: the non-wife getting breakfast for the non-husband while the non-husband was shaving and hurrying to take his place in the world of business. "Makes me think of New Bedford," said Isabel.

"I was thinking the same thing," I said.

"Who are you having lunch with?"

"Joan Blondell."

"The movie star?"

"Rosebud Blondell, otherwise known as Joan. We're having lunch with a movie critic named Harriette Underhill. An interview. I won't have to open my mouth except to put food in it. Underhill is about a hundred and fifty years old, very fragile. But Blondell is full of vitality and people like her. Who are you having lunch with?"

"A girl I went to college with. First I have to check in at the hotel, change my clothes, and try to get a hair appointment."

"Are you having dinner with me?" I said.

"No."

"You're not seeing me again?"

"Afraid not."

"Then this is goodbye forever?" I said.

"Goodbye forever," she said. "As Isabel Young. As Isabel Turner, probably not."

We got a taxi on Seventh Avenue and she dropped me at Forty-fourth and Broadway, not far from my office. At ten o'clock in the morning, in Times Square, with the taxi-meter clicking away and a girl who is anxious to make an appointment with a hairdresser, you do not try to create a romantic atmosphere. I kissed her lightly and said, "I'll be at my office from three o'clock on, in case you want me."

"Thanks," she said.

As much as a courtesy as anything else I gave her breast a gentle squeeze, but as a courtesy it was wasted on her. In fact, she did not like it. "Will you tell the driver, the Hotel Barclay? Forty-eighth and Lexington, please?" The cab headed east and even before it had crossed Times Square I could tell by the set of her head and shoulders that she was already rid of me and on her way to whatever was next. But she owed me nothing; she had recompensed me for a night's lodging.

During the next two or three years I went back to Gibbsville two or three times, never for more than forty-eight hours at a time. I not only did not see Isabel; I did not hear a mention of her name. You do not vanish so completely unless you want to and your friends permit you to. Another girl in our crowd married a boy in our crowd and they lived in a poor section of town and stayed away from their old friends for obvious reasons. But Isabel was not poor; she did not have poverty and pride as an excuse for going into hiding. The coal business was shot to hell, everybody said, but a few independent operators were getting control of what was left of it, and Isabel's father was one of them. Duncan Barley, they said, was richer now than he had ever been. Perhaps it was because of his increased wealth that my friends refrained from reckless criticism of his daughter. I discovered that criticism was being made, but my visits had been so brief that there was only time to bring me up to date on the friends whom I would be seeing on a given visit. When I got some new information on Isabel Barley Young Turner it was not from one of our old crowd, and it was after Isabel and Samuel Turner had been married about five years.

I had a friend whom I had known in parochial school, an amiable boy named Horse McGrath, whose father was a perennial holder of minor political offices. The McGraths were white-collar people whose four children were all given music lessons, and Horse McGrath, who got his nickname from his size, learned to play violin and piano before he was ten years old. He might have gone on to better things in serious music (according to my mother, who was a serious musician), but he took to jazz because he was too big to engage in such a sissy occupation as classical music. He played tackle on four varsity high school football teams (so big he made the varsity in freshman year), and had seven or eight offers of football scholarships on the college level. He chose Bucknell because the high school coach was a Bucknell man and Bucknell was coeducational, Protestant, and not too far away from home. He left college in the middle of junior year, fed up with football and unable to remain without the football scholarship. He immediately began getting jobs with dance orchestras in East-Central Pennsylvania and briefly had a band of his own that was popular among the country clubs, but he was too easygoing to go out after bookings and his band fell apart. The limit of his ambition was ownership of a large second-hand car—Marmons, Cunninghams, and Lincolns were irresistible to him—and two hundred dollars in his pocket. He had a remarkable memory for tunes. Someone would say, "I'll stump you, Horse. Play 'I Got a Bimbo Down on a Bamboo Isle,'" and he would play it and follow it with "Stack o' Lee Blues" and "Lady of the Evening," just to mix them up. He was not an orthodox jazz musician; he liked to play the tunes. His improvisations reflected his classical training, and he could always make a living by playing in cocktail lounges of hotels. At his specialty he was as good as anyone I ever heard, but at the time of which I write he had not yet got beyond Philadelphia. In Philadelphia he had a local following which was not of sufficient size to keep him in big cars, and between jobs he would go back to Gibbsville and take what he could get.

He was there when I went back for the funeral of a doctor friend of my father's, a non-relation whom I called Uncle Henry. I was staying two nights, and on the first night I wound up at three o'clock in the morning, having pie and coffee at the Greek's. I was sitting at the counter and someone whispered in my ear, "You want to hear 'Lonely Acres'?" Without turning my head I said, "Horse McGrath!"

We hugged each other and he sat beside me. "I kind of thought you'd be in town for Doc Stapleton," he said.

"Yes, we all called him Uncle Henry," I said. "Speaking of 'Lonely Acres,' I don't think I've heard it since the last time I heard you play it."

"I don't think I've played it since then," he said.

"Well, where's the nearest piano?"

"At this hour? Jesus, I don't know. No trouble finding a piano, but letting me play."

"Where are you working?"

"I'm not. Nothing regular. Pick up a few bob Saturdays and Sundays, at the joints. I'm waiting to hear from a guy in Atlantic City, opening up a deadfall down there the week before Easter. There's nothing around here any more. Everything is Muzak, juke boxes. No flesh and blood."

"Well, they get plenty of flesh and blood when they get you," I said.

"Listen, you got another chin on the way there," he said. "You don't look as if you'd been giving the fleshpots the go-by."

"No."

"You've been to Hollywood. Is there anything for me out there?"

"Fresh air and sunshine," I said. "And a lot of what they call San Quentin quail."

"Young gash? There's some of that here, too, if you know how to go after it. Like walking from here to the corner."

"Or in your case, just sitting at the piano," I said.

"Yes, and I don't think it's the music that attracts them. They seem to think I have something special to offer. They all want to see if I'm built in proportion, and then they let out a scream."

"I'm surprised you haven't landed in jail," I said.

"I did. For reckless driving."

"You still go for the big cars?"

"Didn't you see what I have outside?"

"That Duesenberg? That's yours?"

"Who the hell else would own a thing like that? My old man won't let me leave it in front of the house. Say, speaking of big cars, didn't Isabel Barley use to be a girl friend of yours?"

"Used to be."

"Have you seen what she's driving around in?"

"I haven't seen her in five years."

"Well, you knew she married that gimp Turner, down in Turnersville?"

"I knew that," I said.

"She comes to town in about a 1925 Ford station wagon."

"I thought you said a big car," I said.

"The opposite. This is a Model T, with the wooden body and side curtains. But she has it all varnished and painted so it looks brand new. Here I am with forty-two dollars in my kick and driving a Duesenberg, and she drives a Model T. But her heap has class—and so has she, in her peculiar way. Did she turn dike or something?"

"I don't know. I haven't seen her. Five years."

"I remember her at those club dances and seeing her riding around in that Chrysler she used to have. I used to say to myself, if I could have just a little bit of that, I'd die happy. The fairest pussy in all the land, as far as I was concerned. But she married that little gimp and what the hell ever happened to her? She was in town yesterday, wearing a pair of those—begins with a j. Hindu riding pants."

"Jodhpurs."

"Right. A man's shirt and tie. You know, you can't miss me on the street, and she said 'Hello, Horse,' and I said 'Hello, Isabel,' but it was like two guys saying hello. 'Hello, Horse.' I bet if she knew my name was Preston she wouldn't have talked to me. She just wanted to say, 'Horse,' in a baritone, a good octave below Middle C."

"Was Turner with her?" I said.

"In the front seat, but didn't get out. He was all bundled up with a woolen scarf around his neck, and you couldn't call yesterday cold. He doesn't know me, but I know him from my old man pointing him out to me. Turner of Turnersville. The old man being in politics, he has to know everybody. The Silvers of Silver Creek. The Bucks of Buck Run. Why would a dame like that bury herself in a dump like Turnersville, with an old gimp old enough to be her father? I heard she was a little cracked after her first husband got burned to death. But I saw her after that and she didn't look cracked to me. She comes to town about once a week, I guess. That's about as often as I happen to see her. Maybe you ought to investigate, and tell her you know a big fat piano player that could learn to care for her. And take care of her. I'm a very understanding type of fellow about those things, tell her."

"Anything else you want me to tell her?"

"No, I guess not. Have Tux, will travel, can read or fake. But you never see her with anybody, only him. You'd think a dame like that would be with her own age. But no, I heard some story—this is a couple of years ago—about some friends of hers, yours and hers, that crowd—they were tying on a load down at that hotel in Turnersville and they decided to go call on her. She wouldn't let them in. She said she didn't want to see them, then or ever. That got around. Now why did that get around? There was some reason why—oh yeah. Now I remember. I got the story from my sister, and she never knew Isabel or Isabel her. But the society crowd used to go to that hotel in Turnersville before Repeal, and then after Repeal people like my sister and her friends went there too. They never had any music or anything, but they gave you a pretty good meal, Pennsylvania Dutch cooking, and it was cheap. And I guess for a few bucks you could rent a bed. They didn't have a piano so I never went there. But according to Madge, my sister Madge, the night Isabel's friends decided to go visiting her, the next day the hotel was closed down.

Tight as a drum. Put up the shutters, took down all the signs, and the Dutchman that ran the joint was ordered to leave. The place was owned by Isabel. Not by her husband, but by Isabel. And she closed it down. And it's still closed, three years later. All boarded up, nobody living there. How do you like that, eh?"

"Well, it certainly arouses my curiosity," I said.

"Come on, we'll go down and have a look at it," he said.

"We wouldn't be able to see anything now. We probably wouldn't be able to see anything in daylight."

"What the hell? I'll give you a ride in my beautiful car. You don't go to bed early, any more than I do, and it's only four or five miles."

"I have a funeral to go to tomorrow," I said.

"Protestant, though. Afternoon, isn't it?"

"Yes, that's right. I guess I don't have to get up so damn early," I said.

Daylight was still a couple of hours away, but if we had not taken the old mountain road we would not have needed our headlights. The moonlight, however, was not sufficient to get us through the thickly wooded road that I had so often covered on horseback and that Horse McGrath had never been on before. "I think you'd better let me drive. I know this road," I said.

"Why, sure," said Horse. "On the way back we'll take the state road and I'll let her out."

Like so many others of our age he had had no occasion to use the mountain road. "Kind of spooky," he said. "I'd hate like hell to get stuck here. If you got in an accident you might be here for days. Who uses this road?"

"Nobody, any more," I said. "It's really a shame to take a good car like this on it. But that explains why Isabel has an old Ford. A Model T'll make it as long as you don't fight the steering gear."

"That may be why she has that old crate, but I don't think so. I think she just wants to be different. She's telling the whole God damn world to go to hell. Imagine closing up a money-making saloon to keep visitors away? It would have made more sense to buy a dog, an Airedale or a Boxer or one of those. But if you have the

money, I guess you do what you please with it. I hear water. I didn't
know there was a river back here."

"Indian Creek," I said. "Probably was a river a thousand years
ago. Some places you can walk across it with hip boots, but other
places you run into pools eight feet deep. Over a man's head. Down
there to your right was where the powder mill used to be."

"Was that the one that blew up and killed everybody? I heard my
old man tell about that. The father and son had some kind of a fight
and one or the other blew up the whole works."

"Now *I* never knew *that*," I said.

"I'm not positive, but I can remember the old man saying something to that effect. They never found out the cause of the explosion,
but there was talk around that the owner and his son weren't getting
along. That was probably when my old man was a deputy sheriff,
before they had the state cops."

"I never knew any of this," I said.

"If you want me to, I'll ask my old man about it. He has a memory for everything like that. You know the old man. He's spent over
forty years in that court house, and what he doesn't know—testimony that isn't made public. Who's the father of who. When you
were reporting for the paper didn't you ever hear them say, 'Ask
Leo McGrath'?"

"Yes, as a matter of fact I did," I said.

"He can tell you every lawyer and every witness in every big case
they ever tried. That comes in very handy, you know. As far as the
old man's concerned, it's better than a pension. The party wants to
put a little pressure on somebody, they go to the old man and say,
'Leo, So-and-so is giving us trouble,' and the old man'll think a minute and say, 'Well, that fellow's brother-in-law was up for bastardy
back in 1905 and he had to pay the support of the child for seventeen years.' It saves a lot of going through the county records when
all you have to do is ask my old man. I'll ask him about the powder
mill. He's an old fart, but when you get him talking about some of
our upper-crust families it's as good as a mystery story. I know one
family won't go to the ten o'clock Mass because that's when my old

man takes up the collection and he knows the inside of how they got rich. I got my good memory from him, only mine's for old tunes and his is for ancient peccadilloes. Legal blackmail, you might call it."

We were in Turnersville, and it was even smaller than I remembered it; smaller, more deserted. We moved very slowly toward the old hotel, and I understood why the village seemed more deserted: I had never been in Turnersville when there was neither human activity on the street nor light pouring out from the hotel. Not a light of any kind shone in the village. We stopped in front of the hotel. "Do you want to get out?" said Horse.

"Nothing to see, but we might as well," I said.

"Might as well empty the bladder," said Horse.

I shut off the engine and put out the lights, and we got out. He went around to the side of the hotel where once had been the carriage shed and now stood a wild growth of grass and weed. He sprinkled his urine over the grass and chanted softly, "*Asperges me.*" He laughed. "Maybe she'll have us arrested for trespissing," he said. "Forgive us our trespisses, Isabel."

I laughed.

He looked up toward Samuel Turner's house and with his penis in his hand said, "Come on, Isabel. Last chance before I put it away for the night. No? Okay. You don't know what you're missing."

The hotel, unpainted and boarded up, posted with No Trespassing signs, was a very dull monument to some good times, and I got back in the car. Horse sat in the driver's seat and started the engine. The throbbing and then the roar as he raced the engine broke the world's silence, and almost immediately I saw a light go on in the Turner house, on the floor above the room where we had sat after Samuel Turner's dinner party. I did not know why, but I had a feeling that we had been observed ever since we stopped in front of the hotel. Other lights now went on in the lower stories and on the upper and lower porch.

"Get going," I said.

We headed for the Fair Grounds road, which took us past the Turner house. As we reached the end of the Turners' fence the upstairs porch door opened and Samuel Turner appeared and fired two shots from a shotgun. "Jesus!" said Horse, and put on speed.

"He wasn't trying to hit us," I said. I looked back and saw Isabel standing beside him in the doorway. I looked back once again and the house was in complete darkness.

"We're not welcome," said Horse. "That's the first time I've ever been under fire."

"Scaring us away," I said. "If he'd wanted to hit us he could have."

"He got his point across," said Horse.

"Does she know your car?"

"I don't know," said Horse. "I know hers, but that doesn't mean she'd know mine. They all know it in town, but I doubt if she does."

"I think she had a good look at us before she turned the lights on."

"Why do you think that?"

"Thought transference. Vibrations," I said. "Mental telepathy."

"Oh, you did lay her? I wasn't sure she could be had in those days. Think what I missed. I hope you got in bed with her. That's bed-pussy, not just cuthering in the back of the car. I could cry, to think of her going back to bed now with that ugly little gimp. But I don't want it that much that I'd care to be a clay pigeon. I'm big and strong but not very brave. I had a coach once, he used to say to me, 'Horse, all I ask you to do is get in their way. Let the ends go in and smear the plays. You don't have the right disposition for that.' I loved him for that. I fight better sitting down. You know, I never learned to box."

"You didn't have to," I said.

"That's right. The average guy, I can knock him down just pushing him. And if I want to keep him down, I just sit on him. The only time I ever got really mad was one dirty son of a bitch at Colgate—awh, the hell with him. Want to get laid or you want to go home?"

"Home. I got laid earlier this evening."

"I thought as much," said Horse. "You arrived at the Greek's with the nooky shift. Two o'clock on I call that the nooky shift. One o'clock is the pool-player shift. Two o'clock, nooky. Four o'clock, poker-player shift. Five o'clock, I call that the getting-shot-at-for-nothing shift. I had a little nooky myself earlier this evening. A very interesting little lady with a husband works in the post office. They have an apartment behind Williamson's drug store. She went to the early movie with a lady friend, so she could tell her husband the whole plot, and I went and had a lemon phosphate at the soda fountain to explain my presence in the neighborhood. Got the nod from her as she was going by the drug store, and five minutes later we were wrapped in fond embrace. All started when she wrote me a little note a couple of months ago and handed it to me while I was sitting in my car. She's new in town. About thirty years of age, not a dame you'd be attracted to at first glance. Married to Eddie Minzer. Did you ever know Eddie Minzer? Fellow with glasses and a big Adam's apple? Been working in the post office ever since I can remember, and he only got married about two-three years ago. Very active in the Ku Klux Klan and such."

"Yes, I know Eddie. He has a brother a letter carrier," I said.

"Right. Well, Eddie married this little lady from over Allentown way, a former schoolteacher. Kind of docile-looking. Dresses very quietly, and a shade on the skinny side. But I want to tell you something, mister, she has it all figured out. All figured out. She's got her application in for a regular teaching job, and when that goes through she's going to buy a house. That'll be bye-bye to me but she knows I'm waiting to hear from the joint in Atlantic City. But she'll find someone else. Eddie's not enough for her. No one man ever was, she told me. But Eddie has a government job, and she'll be teaching school, so if she doesn't get caught cheating on Eddie, between the two of them she's set for life. Can't have kids, so it'll all be hers. I said to her one night, half kidding, I said why didn't she make Eddie take out a lot of insurance and figure some way to knock him off. Just as calmly as if she was drinking a glass of water she said she'd thought about it, but she'd have to wait at least another ten years because she understood the insurance companies get suspicious when a couple were only married a short time and one of them cools. She thought maybe in ten years Eddie might get sick and die of natural causes. He'll be around fifty then, and she can stick it out for ten years. You wouldn't think to look at her that this quiet, docile-looking woman had such thoughts. But I knew she wasn't joking when she handed me that note. All it said was 'Apartment 2-D, 15 East Fairview, 9:15 P.M.' I didn't know her name, and all she said was 'You won't be sorry.' Why me? Well, she told me that night, she wanted plenty of man. She got it. I tell you something else. She scares the hell out of me."

"What can she do to you?"

"Well, she could shoot me. She's so positive she has everything under control, all figured out. But there's only one thing I learned from all the broads and all the nice girls and hookers and every kind of woman you can imagine, and that is, they're all crazy. They're all, each and every one of them, to some extent crazy. Sooner or later it has to come out in some manner, shape, or form. You've got to learn to expect the opposite. The hot piece of tail will suddenly go virgin on you. The virgin will hide in a bus and gang-fuck a whole orchestra. I saw that happen. A kid took on nine guys down near Hagerstown, Maryland. She wasn't a virgin, but she was only six-teen years of age, and came from a very respectable family. This wife of Eddie Minzer's, sure she can buy a house and say bye-bye to me and take on some other guy. But in the back of my mind is some night I'll be working in Atlantic City and I look up and there she is. That happened plenty of times. God damn it, they follow musicians. Some inconspicuous tenor sax player, with glasses an inch thick and a pecker an inch long—but there's always some broad leaving her husband and kids on account of him. You ask some of the colored boys about the propositions they get. Oh, it's cruel. And they don't know anything about the music. Play 'Beale Street' and they think it's a fancy arrangement of 'St. Louis Blues.' 'Listen to that man play St. Looey Blues!' She could shoot me. I guess by the law of averages one of them will. By the law of averages, one of them took a shot at me tonight."

"Except that it wasn't a woman and you weren't being shot at."

"It's still the law of averages. By the law of averages it doesn't have to be a woman that shoots me, and it doesn't even have to be the husband of a woman I laid. I'm only figuring that when you get your score up in the hundreds, which mine is, the law of averages is going to catch up with you, somehow. I only ever had one clap, never had the syph, never got beaten up, never been shot."

"I'm beginning to think you *are* afraid," I said.

"Well, I stopped going to confession four-five years ago, but once in a while I get a guilty conscience. That'll make you afraid, if you let it. Dames are so easy for me, you know. Not just bragging, but they are. Half the time it's the dame that makes the first move, not me. Therefore I ought to be able to blame them half the time. But why kid myself? A lot of guys go through life laying only one or two women. I'll bet my old man never laid anybody but my mother. But I don't have that strength of character. My senior year in high school I got offers from Villanova, Fordham, Mount St. Mary's, Duquesne, and Niagara. All Catholic schools. What did I pick? A Protestant co-ed school. You'd never guess why."

"Of course I would."

"I'm kidding," said Horse. "I never went a week without a piece of tail, the whole time I was at Lewisburg."

"Needless to say, you never got bored with it," I said.

"Never. I didn't even get a chance to get bored with a particular dame."

"Next question," I said. "Did you ever fall in love with any of them?"

"You mean enough to want to marry one?"

"Not necessarily. Just to fall in love, what people mean by falling in love."

"Well, I never did, but I can think of two that I came close. One is Eddie Minzer's wife. That skinny, quiet broad affects me differently than anyone else. It isn't love, but she does have some kind of an effect on me. The only other one—her husband just took a shot at us."

"Isabel, huh?"

"From the time she was around seventeen years of age. No, I guess she was older than that. Isn't she a couple of years older than we are?"

"Two or three," I said.

"She used to say hello if she saw me in the street, but I never said three words to her. Some of those other snotnoses didn't speak to me, but Isabel always said hello. Then when I began playing those private-party dates at the country club, I caught her a couple times looking at me. She wasn't on the make or anything, but I'd catch her looking at me. I don't think she even knew she was looking at me. I have a confession to make. I knew I was never going to be invited to your fucking country club. But I was good enough to make Phi Gam at Bucknell, so I wrote her a letter and invited her to the junior prom. Her old man was a Phi Gam at Lehigh, so she'd know about it. Boy, I sweated over that letter. I didn't want it to be too fresh, but I also didn't want her to think I was kissing her ass—not that I wouldn't. Well, you know what happened to that letter. I tore it up. The funny thing was, for a long time after that I was kind of sore at her, although I hadn't sent the letter. 'Who the hell are you, high-hatting me?' I used to say. Laughable. Just as sore as if I'd sent the fucking letter and she turned me down."

"Why do you think you could be in love with her, aside from her looks and her shape?"

"There you go again about love, and I can't answer you. But I state it as if it was a fact, that Isabel Barley wanted me to put my thing in her, whether she knew it or not. And *I* knew that if I ever did, she was one girl I'd want to go back to the rest of my life."

I said nothing.

"Why do you clam up? Does that make you sore?" said Horse.

"Hell, no," I said. "It's exactly what I feel about her."

He laughed. "Let's go back and shoot it out with the gimp?"

I laughed. "One funeral is enough, this trip," I said.

"Fix it up for me with Isabel, and I'll get you privileges with Eddie Minzer's wife," said Horse.

"You call that an even swap?"

668 ♦ JOHN O'HARA

"No, I don't. I really don't," said Horse.

He let me out at my house and I went to bed, rather too tired to permit my thoughts to dwell on Isabel and Samuel Turner.

The First Presbyterian Church was within five minutes' walking distance of our house, and I got there the next afternoon at a quarter of two. My mother, an extraordinarily healthy woman, had caught a cold and decided that her coughing would detract more from the funeral than her presence would add, so I went alone. I timed my arrival at the church so that I would not have to have much sidewalk conversation with the other mourners. I shook hands with four or five people and was about to enter the church when I heard the silly sound of a Model T horn, insistently repeated and disregardful of the fairly solemn occasion. I turned and saw Isabel in her station wagon, and she was blowing the horn to attract my attention.

She double-parked the station wagon halfway up the next block and came rapidly toward me. She gave me a perfunctory kiss and took me by the arm. "Escort me, please," she said. "I have a lot of things to talk to you about, after the service."

"Jesus, you're a bossy son of a bitch," I said.

"Ah, but you're so charming it doesn't really matter," she said, and did not speak again until the service was over and she guided me to her station wagon. She would not halt for conversation with anyone, and no one tried very hard to engage her. She was wearing a grey sharkskin suit and a darker grey silk shirtwaist and a black beret. I felt very conspicuous sitting with her in the front seat of her station wagon, as indeed I might well have. She had become a strikingly handsome woman in five years; and while I had not become a strikingly handsome man, it was nonetheless true that I was a returned native and there were old friends and acquaintances who would have liked to say hello. Instead, I was being taken over, if not overwhelmed, by a strikingly handsome, thoroughly disliked renegade in an outmoded vehicle on a solemn occasion. She lit a cigarette.

"I'd just as soon get out of here," I said.

"Give me a chance to light my cigarette," she said, then put the car in low gear.

"Where are we going?" I said.

"Oh—anywhere, nowhere," she said. She took her right hand off the steering wheel and patted my knee. "Nice to see you, you old crank."

"Nice to see you," I said. "You've lost all your baby fat."

"I never knew I had any," she said. "Or is that your way of saying I now have a jaw-line?"

"I guess that's what I mean," I said. "What were the things you had to talk about?"

"They fall into two categories," she said. "I thought you'd be interested in me. Undoubtedly you've been given full reports on me, but I'd like to give you the straight goods. That's one category. The other is, what were you and Horse McGrath doing in Turnersville at four o'clock this morning?"

"Getting shot at by a couple of maniacs," I said.

"Everywhere the eye can see there are no-trespassing signs," she said. "You may not know it, but we now own every bit of property in Turnersville. Turnersville is really Turnersville. There's not a stick or stone that isn't ours."

"What for?" I said. "It couldn't have cost you much, but it seems like a foolish way to spend your money."

"That's your opinion, but it gives us the right to put no-trespassing on the whole village, should we so desire. Guess who's chief burgess of Turnersville?"

"The lord of the manor, Samuel Turner."

"*Mrs.* Samuel Turner. Me. Samuel is constable, but I'm chief burgess. Without a dissenting vote, and that's the way it's going to be as long as Samuel or I live."

"Whose idea was this?" I said.

"I daresay it was originally suggested by Samuel, but I fell in with it with great enthusiasm."

"And a couple of hundred thousand bucks."

"Actually a great deal less than that. A little over seventy-five thousand. There isn't a house in the village worth over twenty-five hundred, and the land is practically worthless. My mother is so jealous. She wants my father to buy a village for her."

"Doesn't she know that he owns several villages in the county?"

"That's the Company, and they're only ugly little coal-mining patches. She'd like something rural, and change the name to Barleyville. What were you doing in Turnersville last night?"

"Taking a piss. Trespissing, as Horse said."

"No," she said. "Who suggested coming to Turnersville? And why? Were you intoxicated?"

"We weren't intoxicated, and it was Horse that suggested it. He has a very firm conviction that you want him to put his thing in you."

"Oh he has, has he? I suppose you told him that you'd had your thing in me?"

"Yes, I did," I said.

"Why did you have to do that?"

"I'm sorry now that I said anything, but I don't see that it's going to make any difference in anyone's life. You've undoubtedly told Sam about us, what there is to tell."

"Yes, he knows. I wasn't going to tell him, but I did. I told him everything, everybody that had ever touched me, that I had ever touched, and some that I had never touched but would have, given the opportunity."

"Then you can't blame me too much for a little boasting. That's what you were doing. Boasting. It's not called boasting when a woman does it, but that's what it is. If a woman is entitled to secrecy, so is a man. And what about Sam? Did he make a full confession of all his pre-marital experiences?"

"Yes."

"At your insistence?"

"At my request. I was curious to know how he'd got along all those years. I'm always curious about that where a man is concerned. Men are so—excitable, so easily stimulated—I'm always astonished at how few women the average man gets to go to bed with."

"How are you and Sam in that department?"

"Satisfactory," she said.

"Oh, come on, Isabel."

"If you think I'm going to tell you any more than that, you're crazy."

"Have you been faithful to him?"

"No."

"Does he know you haven't?"

"Heavens, no."

"I thought you were going to pay me a visit from time to time. I'm pretty annoyed at you."

"I couldn't have, with you. There were certain people that I wasn't to see again, and it would have been almost impossible for me to see you without his checking up in some way or other. I was never to see you, I was never to see Ginny, and there was someone else that I'd never actually done anything with."

"Who was that?"

"Promise not to tell him?"

"I promise."

"Horse McGrath," she said.

"You're kidding," I said.

She shook her head. "I don't think I ever said two words to Horse McGrath. But I used to have the most fantastic dreams about him."

"And of course you told Sam about these dreams?"

"Yes, some of them," she said. "Some of them were too complicated to tell. And some that I said were dreams weren't dreams at all. That is, I wasn't asleep when I dreamed them. I remember one night at a dance at the club. He was playing in the orchestra and I found myself staring at him. I couldn't stop staring, even when he caught me. That's why he thinks I have a frustration for him."

"A pretty good reason," I said.

"But he shouldn't go on thinking that. That was a long time ago."

"He would have stopped thinking it except that he has fantasies about you. In other words, you two are made for each other."

"You don't really think that," she said.

"Why not?"

"Well, since you put it that way—why not? But I assure you nothing will ever come of it," she said.

"What would Sam do if you got rid of your frustration?"

"It isn't a question of what he'd do," she said. "What would *I* do? I'd soon get another one, wouldn't I? So it's much more sensible to go on having my fantasies about Horse McGrath, an overgrown stallion. He's so big that the whole idea is exaggerated and becomes comedy. Besides, physically we probably couldn't manage. I mean he's probably so big in that way."

"Oh, no. You'd manage. Plenty of other women have and do," I said. "But don't kid yourself that he's only an overgrown stallion. He's a very talented musician. One of the best."

"That coming from you is a great compliment. He is good?"

"One of the very best. Musicians know it."

"Oh, I see. One of those people that play at jam sessions."

"No. Don't try to talk musicians' slang, Isabel. You only reveal your abysmal ignorance. Horse McGrath isn't a jam session musician. He wouldn't be welcome in a jam session. But jam session musicians—some of them—like to listen to Horse. He makes his living playing in cocktail lounges, entertaining people that like old tunes, because he has an astonishing memory. But ninety-five percent of the people that go to hear him haven't the faintest idea of the stuff that goes on *inside* his playing. They follow the melody, and that's all most of them want. But musicians and a few people like me appreciate the subtle stuff he puts in. It's a very special art."

"Why isn't he better known?"

"I just told you. It's a very special art. Not all musicians like him. Some of them say he plays slop, that he plays like a pansy. It's a funny thing about music, how it can bring out the worst in people. I've known little guys that Horse could decapitate with one blow of his right hand, get so mad at his playing that they want to pick a fight with him. They take it as a personal insult that he can sneak in a little Debussy or Brahms where you'd least expect it. He has a wonderful sense of humor, musically as well as every other way. I think he's a great guy, that's all."

She was silent, but I could see that she was pleased, and I thought I knew why. "I knew there was something else there," she said.

"No you didn't, but you're glad to be told there is," I said. "Now you don't have to be quite so ashamed of those fantasies."

"All right," she said. "But let me point out that I had the fantasies long before I was *told* there was something else there."

"All right," I said. "Getting back to Sam, how come you've got me in this beautiful old jalopy if you're not supposed to see me?"

"There was an exception made today," she said. "This is part of a plot to find out what you two were doing in Turnersville. I told Samuel that you were probably in town just for Dr. Stapleton's funeral, and I could accidentally bump into you there. Otherwise, I said, you'd be going back to New York and we'd *never* find out."

"So he gave his consent to this chance meeting?" I said.

"Of course."

"Are you *afraid* of him?" I said.

"Most of the time, no," she said. "But he is someone to be afraid of. Who isn't? You just got finished telling me about those little musicians that want to attack Horse. And I once saw my mother strike my father with a gardening spade."

"Why?"

"I don't know. Something he said. I was too far away to hear what he said, but whatever it was, she tried to bash his head in. No love tap. They don't know to this day that I saw them, but from the time I was nine years old I ceased to believe in marital love. She wanted to kill him, and there was just no pretending otherwise. For at least five years I used to think what terrible hypocrites parents were. I know now that that was part of their sex life. He often teased her till she'd storm out of the room, and then he'd excuse himself and follow her upstairs. Curtain. But that one time she wanted to kill him, not make love. Although who's to say how much difference there is? Samuel could murder me, under certain conditions. I have every reason to think—that he could."

"That's not what you were going to say," I said.

"What else was I going to say?"

"I don't know, but you finished pretty lamely," I said.

We were now in Collieryville, mining country that was only seven or eight miles from Turnersville but on the other side of Gibbsville and literally almost never visited by inhabitants of the farming country around Turnersville. "What are we doing here? You going to pick up a ton of coal?" I said.

"Heresy. We have an oil burner," she said.

"By the way, did you ever put in that elevator?"

"Oh, the first year I was married," she said. "I've done wonders to the house."

"I noticed that you're occupying the third floor. I saw the lights go on, just before you let go with the artillery."

"It's all right to joke about that now. It wasn't so funny at four o'clock this morning. He could have taken a rifle instead of a puny little four-ten. He didn't want to take the four-ten. I gave it to him."

"Thank you very much," I said.

"He said he was only going to frighten you, but I didn't trust him with a rifle. We use the four-tens as snake guns, when we go for hikes. I won't go into the woods without one. I killed a four-button rattler behind our barn last summer. At least I've gotten so I can shoot them when I see them. At first I couldn't do anything but scream."

"How else has this guy changed you, Isabel?"

"Mostly for the better. He really has. I didn't want New Bedford, Massachusetts, all over again, and I was positive that I didn't want the grubby kind of life you were living in Greenwich Village. I probably could have gotten a job in New York and waited around till I could snatch some bored husband from his equally bored wife. But that would have been New Bedford again, even if we lived in Mount Kisco or Cedarhurst. No. Not for me, wherever it was. I was very disturbed by sex. I couldn't be sure whether it was me, or the fact that because I was pretty I attracted people sexually and therefore their approach to me always started on that basis. The first night I ever met Samuel he horrified me with a sexual approach. Do you remember that?"

"Of course."

"So I deliberately had a sexual adventure with him, to see whether this degenerate—which is what I thought he was—was what I wanted. I also had an affair with a Lesbian. A real shocker, that was. A friend of Mother's, a woman you know. Married and all the rest of it. Don't ever ask me who it was, because I might tell you and you really wouldn't like it if you knew. She's been fighting it all her life, and she attacked me because I'd somehow led her to believe that I wanted her to. If that's the way I affected people, the safest thing to do was to retire to Turnersville, where I could do the least harm. And that's what I've done."

"I think you exaggerate your fatal charm. Especially in the case of the older woman. I think she's a God damn liar. But go on about Sam."

"Well, we didn't even go away on a wedding trip. We stayed in Turnersville. Travel is all hardship for Samuel. He can get through the woods very well, but crossing streets and climbing stairs—not to mention the psychological thing of having crowds of people looking at him. So we didn't go away."

"And you changed your mind about his being a degenerate."

"There was nothing I did with him that I hadn't done with someone else. And don't forget, *I* graduated from Position One quite some time ago. I still like it best, though, by the way."

"We must try it sometime," I said.

"Don't change the subject."

"Hell, you're the one that changed the subject," I said.

"Sorry."

"So you married Sam, and had a riot of sex. Then what?"

"The riot was spaced out over quite a while. He's no young man of twenty-one. What happened was that first I began to go over the house from top to bottom, every square inch of it, and see what I thought could be done with what we had, the house itself and the furniture. He had some beautiful things that had been stored away since his mother died. And a lot of wonderful stuff packed away in the hayloft. Furniture. Glassware. China. Boxes full of books. We had all the time in the world, so the two of us together made a complete catalog of every piece of furniture, every piece of glassware, every cup and saucer, and every book. We were very methodical about it. Ten to twelve every morning, two to five every afternoon, Monday through Friday. Saturday and Sunday we went for walks. It took us fifteen months to complete the catalog. It would have taken a lot less but a great deal of conversation went on with practically every piece of furniture. Family history kind of thing. Incidentally, I learned a few things about your mother's family that you probably don't know yourself."

"Very likely," I said.

"Came across the bill your father sent Samuel when he had his accident. All sorts of things like that. It was an education in itself, a wonderful way to find out about one's husband's family. And doing something useful at the same time. We gave a lot of old papers to the Historical Society, but we kept just about everything else. Then our next move was to go through the house room by room, changing things around, you know. Deciding on what should be redecorated and what shouldn't, and of course things like a Frigidaire and the oil burner, the elevator, an enormous radio. A new well."

"And so you got used to living with your husband."

"I got to know him. And of course to know myself somewhat better. I found out that if I had something to do, and someone to encourage me in it, by keeping busy I didn't sit around waiting for something to happen. I used up some of my restlessness in working on the house and the yard. I knew a little about gardening from my mother, and I'm learning more."

"Do you sleep with Sam? I mean in the same bed?"

"Not even in the same room. He's too self-conscious about his leg. It wouldn't bother me, but it does him."

We had come to a fork in the road to the west of Collieryville, and she turned off the main highway and drove along a dirt road that ended in a hundred yards in a picnic grove. The rough tables and benches and a small bandstand were permanent fixtures, but there were no indications of recent human visits. "Remember this place?" she said.

"Sure," I said. "The water tasted of sulphur. We always used to have to bring gallons of lemonade. Nobody wanted to drink out of the spring."

She stopped the car and turned off the engine, lay back and extended her arms and legs in a great stretch. Then she put her arms around me and kissed me on the mouth, and I kissed her. "I'm glad you came to Turnersville last night," she said, and put her hand between my legs. "I didn't like it when you were in town a year ago and never made any effort to see me."

"I didn't think it made the slightest difference to you," I said.

"The point is, it didn't seem to make the slightest difference to you. I don't want to lose you entirely. I need someone like you, and there really isn't anyone quite like you. For me."

"No, and there's no one like you for me, either," I said.

"Let me unbutton a few things here. I'm very accessible, but there are a few things in the way. My bra and panties are all I have on underneath. We're going to have to rough it a little bit. I'm ready this very instant, but let's look at each other. I always like it when you look at me. When we're really ready I'll lie on a picnic table."

"Do you think that would be wise?"

"Maybe not, but it'll be more satisfactory. I don't want you slipping out once you're in," she said. In a few minutes she said, "The time has come." She got out of the car and lay on the table, with her shirtwaist open and her skirt rolled up, and she led me inside her. It was very quick, but it was immensely pleasurable.

"Back to nature," she said. She sat up on the table and buttoned her shirtwaist. "Aren't you pleased with me? I've never failed to accommodate you. This took some planning, too, I want you to know."

"Did it?"

"Yes indeed it did," she said. "I hadn't intended to go to Dr. Stapleton's funeral, but then I thought, 'It's the only way I'll see my old lover.' And of course I couldn't go in jodhpurs, which I usually wear in town. And if I'd worn jodhpurs, we'd have had quite a problem. I could accommodate you, all right, but I wanted this, not a substitute."

"Is that what I am? Your old lover?"

"Yes, aren't you?"

"Yes, I guess that's what I am," I said.

"You're not old enough to object to being called old," she said. "What would you rather I called you?"

"Your permanent, sporadic lover," I said.

"All right. You're my permanent, sporadic lover. And what does that make me?"

"It makes you—oh—the Isabel half of the team of Isabel and Jim, sporadic, permanent lovers."

"I guess that's pretty good," she said. " 'Who did you see today?' 'Oh, I saw my permanent, sporadic lover, and I screwed him on a picnic table. And he screwed me on a picnic table. And go away from me, you ugly little man.' I don't mean that last part."

"The hell you don't," I said.

"No, I really don't," she said. "But I would mean it if once in a while I didn't have someone else. Just once in a while someone that I can have passion with without compassion. I spent the first year of my marriage convincing him that I didn't feel com-passion and building up his self-esteem. Now he believes it, so I feel free to go with another man once in a while."

"Would you care to tell me who the other man is?"

"Never the same one twice, and only four altogether. Five, with you, today. There was a resident at the hospital, when I went there for some x-rays. A plain case of seduction on my part, and I left the next day. A lawyer from New Bedford, that my father had hired. A very dull man, but a man. That's two. The third was a boy I'd known in college, who came through town on business and looked me up. He wanted to stay around, till I convinced him that he was going to get both of us shot. The fourth was a man that came to inquire about some old furniture he heard we wanted to sell. I thought he was a fairy, and so did Samuel. And he probably was. But the minute we were alone in the barn he made a terrific pass at me. He not only caught me completely by surprise but he knew that I was in heat, although I wasn't particularly conscious of it myself. I offered absolutely no resistance. I obediently got down on the floor and lifted up my dress and let him go ahead. I sent him away without taking him back to the house. I told Samuel he was a bargain-hunter and wouldn't pay more than five dollars for the best things we had. I said he infuriated me with his low offers, which I'm sure explained to Samuel why I was unusually not my usual self. Actually the man was a—a—uh—sexual athlete. He could have kept me there all morning. I hope he never comes back, because if he does, I'm very likely to do the same thing again. And those are the four. Not a lover among them. Anyway, not a sporadic, permanent lover."

"You'd better be careful," I said. "Especially with those double-gaited fags."

"How well I know it," she said. "They're dangerous. I've read about them. But the most dangerous thing about them, or anybody, is the way I seem to send out messages, 'Here I am, here it is.' If I can't control that—Horse McGrath knew it."

"Don't be too upset about it," I said. "I think every woman sends out those messages at various times, usually without being aware of it. And fortunately, most of the time the messages vanish into thin air."

"I know you're trying to keep me on the paths of righteousness, but I'm always going to stray. Probably because I never got on the paths of righteousness of my own accord. Or rather because they were never *my* paths. I'm married to a man that your mother and my mother would call a degenerate, and that *I* called a degenerate because I'd heard it from them. But I stopped calling him a degenerate because he was only a pervert, and a pervert in ways that I'd experienced before I ever slept with him. Get away from Position

One and you're a pervert, and you really are. So that makes you a pervert and me a pervert. As I get older, the only thing I see wrong in having an affair with Ginny and Mrs. XYZ is that I'd rather have it with a man. That's perverted, perverting yourself. On the other hand, Mrs. XYZ is most perverted when she sleeps with her husband, because she'd much rather be in bed with me. And it's perverted when a pansy gets me down on the floor of the barn and screws me, not like a man but like a machine. I'm a good-looking woman and I seem to have hotter pants than most women, and what I've been trying to do, married to Samuel and self-exiled to Turnersville, is work out a philosophy that's going to be best for *me*."

"Well, I guess you have," I said.

She shook her head. "It's not good enough."

"What the hell, you're not Plato," I said.

"But why shouldn't I be? He was an old fairy and I'm heterosexual, therefore I should be better equipped to be a philosopher than he was."

"Well, keep working at it and you may go down in history as Isabel."

"I'll certainly go down," she said. "I wish I could make up for all the reading I skipped—that Samuel *has* read. Then I'd like to write down all my thoughts, all of them, and go back and read them over again and see what they amount to. If I put down all my thoughts for say five years, when I read them over again I'd discover that I did have a philosophy. Then I'd boil that down, simplify it, and I'd start a colony, a cult, right here in Turnersville. I'd get rid of these morons that live here now and invite a group of serious thinkers like myself, to study Isabelism."

"You had a serious thought and now you're kidding it," I said.

"I have to kid it. It's too big for me."

"You could make a start, the start you invented. Write down your thoughts for five years. You spent fifteen months cataloging the stuff in your God damn house. Why not be just as methodical with your philosophy? Two hours in the morning for reading, two in the afternoon for writing your thoughts. And go for a hike on Saturday and Sunday. Maybe you wouldn't arrive at a major philosophy, but you *could* hit on some philosophical beliefs that would form the basis of a cult. Isabelism, if that's what you want to call it. Christ Almighty, the closest they ever came to a cult in Turnersville was the Ku Klux Klan."

"Oh, stop talking like a Catholic," she said. "A lot of worthwhile people belonged to the Klan when it first started. My grandfather, my great-grandfather. Not this trash. They're not the real Klan."

"Well, dog my cats, honey. If you don't talk like you' mammy. I swear."

"If you're not careful I won't invite you to join my cult."

"Oh, was I going to be invited?" I said.

"As sporadic, permanent lover you'd have a cottage at the other end of the village."

"Wouldn't I be moved up like the horses in Hobson's Choice?"

She put her head on my shoulder. "You're sweet, do you know it?"

I put my arm around her. We were sitting now in the front seat of the station wagon. "I love you," I said.

"With fingers crossed," she said.

"Yes, but I said it," I said.

"I love you, too," she said. "I'll never let you go. I promise you that when you get married and have a nice wife and five attractive children, you can always be my sporadic, permanent lover. Then you won't have to go to some whore that won't appreciate you, and your wife will think you're faithful and true. Do you think you could ever be faithful and true to anybody?"

"The odds are very much against it, going on past performance," I said.

"Good. Then you wouldn't make *me* feel like a whore. We'll just be sporadic, permanent lovers, and not bother about our husbands and wives. Have you still got your father's watch?"

"What you really mean is, have I still got the lighter? Yes. I even took it to Dunhill and had the thing on top fixed. The cap that goes over the wick."

"You're a sweet old thing," she said. "You always have been."

"You're a nice kid," I said.

"I really am," she said. "That's what I really am, is a nice kid. But you're the only one that knows it. And you knew it when I *was* a nice kid."

"I guess I follow that," I said.

"You do. You follow it. I wish we never had to leave here. I wish we could just sit here like this and never leave this car. Put your hand in my shirtwaist. Inside. Hold my breast. That's right. Now I wish we could just stay this way and never move. Just stay this way till we die."

"And we say we don't love each other," I said.

"We love each other. It's those damn outsiders. That miner on his way home from work. Do you see him?"

"Yes," I said.

"He hasn't seen us yet, but when he does, we'll stop loving each other. Poor miner. Poor us. You'd better take your hand out of there now, I think he's seen us," she said. "If you don't mind, I'm going to drop you at Twenty-third Street and you can take the bus from there."

"Why? We've been seen together leaving the church," I said.

"We've been together too long. In fact, we've been together just long enough to do what we've done, and that's what I don't want them to know. You know. *Them?*"

"All right," I said.

She reached out to turn the car key, but midway she put her arms around my neck and kissed me. "Oh, Jim," she said.

"Cut it out or you're going to make me cry," I said.

"You're sweet," she said. She straightened up, patted her beret, smoothed down the collar of her shirtwaist. "Isabel Turner," she said. "Housewife and slut. Very good on picnic tables."

I laughed. The words were so contradictory to the blue-stocking character that she had returned to. She could have been on her way to judge a dog show or preside at a meeting of the Women's Republican Committee.

She laughed. "I almost wish that poor miner had seen me on the table. It would have made his day," she said.

"It made mine," I said.

"As I said earlier, you *are* so charming," she said.

The world that I lived in at that stage of my life was not very different from the preceding Greenwich Village stage. Some of the inhabitants were the same. But now we had some money, ate and drank better, dressed better, and had worked our way out of total obscurity. The stagestruck little girls, who would do anything to get a walk-on in any Broadway play, advanced to speaking parts and the selectivity that came with their burgeoning self-confidence. The writing young men like myself could give up the drudgery of newspaper jobs and press agentry and working on small magazines that were distributed free in hotels. Nobody, or practically nobody, had yet achieved the kind of security that some of us got later, when our names were bright in lights or large on the jackets of books because the public was willing to pay money to see us or read us. We were known, but not famous; we were celebrities in the Algonquin lobby but not in the lobby of the Sterling Hotel in Wilkes-Barre. We were still scratching, but we did not have to scratch so hard and so much. We had had some recognition and we could enjoy not only the recognition but the work for which we had more time. I think now that that was the stage at which we all had the most fun—and of course we were still young. To see an ingenue arrive ten but not twenty minutes late for a luncheon appointment with her agent, putting on a breathless act that could have been written for Nell Gwynne, was to see the next great Juliet, and if not the next great Juliet, the next great Roxie Hart. And if not the next great Roxie Hart, maybe the future chairman of the entertainment committee of the Cincinnati Junior League. And the quiet young man in tweed jacket and flannel slacks, having lunch with *his* agent, was going to knock Ernest Hemingway out of the box, and if not Ernest Hemingway, Louis Bromfield, and if not Louis Bromfield he was certainly going to enjoy tenure as a professor of Creative Writing at the University of Wisconsin, or hang himself in a shack on Martha's Vineyard.

When I went back to New York after Dr. Stapleton's funeral I believed that Isabel Turner, for all the hazards of casual, impulsive adulteries, had arrived at a modus vivendi that was right for her. She was now past thirty, and it was not so much the good or bad that happened to you on one day that characterized your life as the effect of years undivided into days. Isabel knew that; it was her idea to write down her thoughts over a long period before attempting to make a recapitulation. Thus she could be excited and frightened by an adventure with a bisexual, but as against one such dramatic episode there were dozens and hundreds of days of her own special routine. I judged the value of her way of life not by its disturbances and disruptions but by her willingness to continue the program of existence that she, with Sam Turner, had been following. It was right for her, or she would have stopped it.

She made it easy for me to stop worrying about her. A man thinks kindly of a woman who shares passion with him and does not obligate him to responsibilities. But to some degree he reverts to the fundamentals of the mating instinct and cannot entirely enjoy the pleasure unless he can fight for or buy things for or be nice to the woman. There was an element of this in my sad selfishness toward Isabel, that I called my inability, *our* inability, to fall in love. I did not want to be in love with her; I did not want the responsibility of her; but I was going against a fundamental of the mating instinct and I was paying for it. There were no girls in New York who made me as sad as Isabel as we were leaving the picnic ground—but there were a lot of girls in New York. The safety that lay in numbers was, in this case, an instinct for self-protection that was in conflict with my affection for Isabel. Instinctively I always knew that I had to get away from her. I would always want to go back, but I must always go away.

I went about my business, dividing my energies between the flesh-pots and the typewriter so that I neglected neither. One night I dropped in at a bar where a girl I knew was singing, and before I had checked my hat I heard a cadenza that could be invented by only one man in the world. I sneaked up behind him and whispered, " 'Lonely Acres.' "

Without turning around he said, "Number 40 in the old book. I was wondering if you'd be in. The girl said she knew you."

"The girl being Frances?" I said.

"That's the name. She's not bad. She's not *good,* but she's not bad."

"When did you start here?" I said.

"Monday," said Horse. "If I triple the take at the bar they're keeping me another week, so drink up."

"You don't sound like your old ebullient self," I said. "What's got you down?"

"My girl died," he said.

"Who? Anybody I know?"

"Remember Eddie Minzer's wife I told you about?"

"Sure. She died?"

"She had a stroke. I didn't think people her age had strokes, but she did. Some kind of a tumor in the brain. Or a hemorrhage or some God damn thing. I couldn't exactly go and ask Eddie for the details, being's how I wasn't supposed to know her. There was just a little thing in the paper."

"Where were you? Atlantic City?"

"I didn't go. The job was offered me, but at the last minute I honestly couldn't tear myself away. From her. I think she had a premonition. It got pretty bad there, or pretty good. Or pretty bad. Maybe I had a premonition. Whichever way it was, a couple days before I was supposed to go to the Shore, I knew I couldn't. This mousy little broad had got to me. On Eddie's night off I used to walk up and down Fairview Street, torturing myself. I sold my car and got twelve hundred for it. Then she lent me five hundred of her own dough so I wouldn't have to take a job with a band. I was with her every night except Eddie's nights off. The reason why I'm sure she had some kind of premonition, every time I'd say something about leaving Eddie she'd change the subject. She always used to leave messages for me at the Greek's, when it would be safe to come to the apartment. Two straight nights, no message. The third day, the thing in the paper. Jesus, I never had anything hit me that hard. I put the arm on my old lady for a couple C-notes, and the guy that runs this joint used to know me from Philly, so he gave me a job. But I'm not doing so good. The playing is very tired."

"You tired are better than anyone else full of tea," I said.

"Thanks, but I know better."

"You hit a cadenza a minute ago," I began.

"Oh, I still have ten fingers. But when I sit down I don't *love* to play. You'd hear the difference in five minutes. Are you good for a bite? Five hundred bucks?"

"You caught me at just the right moment."

"I'd like to finish out the week here and go home," he said.

"I'll write you a cheque right now, but what the hell are you going to do back there? You're in New York now, Horse, finally. This is a good spot to work in. It's a great hangout for the radio and advertising crowd and the guys that sign people for recording dates."

"I know that. The girl pointed them out to me. Frances."

"Then it doesn't make any sense to go back home. This is that break they're always talking about."

"Maybe it is, but it came at the wrong time for me."

"And I can't see how you'll be helping yourself to go back to where she was."

"You're right, I'm wrong. But I have it figured out that if I go back there and stay awhile, I'll finally get it through my skull that she's gone and she's not coming back. You know, if I walk past the apartment often enough and so on. I know for a fact she's dead. It was in the papers and all. They had a funeral for her. The United Evangelical Church. I could name you the pallbearers. The undertaker. It's a screwy thing to say, but she died without my permission. I guess that means she broke it off without my permission. She walked out on me, and with me it's always the other way. So maybe what I want to do, underneath, is go back there and stand under her window and yell at her. 'You didn't walk out on me! I would have

walked out on you!' The mousy little broad, with the dark shadows
under her eyes."

"All right," I said.

He went back to Gibbsville, and I had a letter from him in which
he told me that he was following in the family tradition, "public service or maybe you'd call it robbing the taxpayer." His father had got
him a "temporary" appointment as a sheriff's deputy, which had to
be called temporary so that the politicians would not scream. "I get
the same pay as a regular deputy but it comes out of special funds
and does not go on the regular payroll. Billy Williams went on as a
temporary five years ago and has been on ever since." He inclosed
twenty-five dollars cash and said it would be the first of twenty such
payments. He said not a word about the mousy little broad with the
dark shadows under her eyes.

For five months the payments arrived punctually, with notes that
got shorter by the month. Then he sent me a bank cheque for $375,
and a letter.

Maybe you are wondering why suddenly I can come up with
the balance of what I owe you. Well, not because the county
gave me a raise in pay, or I got a more lucrative job. I am still
on the "temporary" payroll for $2200 a year divided by 12, but
on the side I am fronting for a brand new spot that opened up
just outside of town where the old Mountain View Hotel used
to be. They tried to do business with your friend Isabel Barley
and take a lease on the Farmers Hotel in Turnersville but she
told them to go to hell, through her lawyer. She refused to talk
to them, although they were ready to make a good offer. The
joint is owned by a fellow named Peter Stump, who made a
bundle operating the Colonial Inn outside of Reading. He is
branching out with new places near Allentown and Lancaster.
The idea is that he saves money by buying for all four places,
which he can do because they are pretty close together but do
not have to be in competition with one another. He has different names for all of them so that they seem to be separate but

he is the head man. He has a great set-up at the Colonial. Were you ever there? He took me there to show me how he liked things run. The Colonial gets a big play over weekends. A three-piece combo (piano, trumpet, drums). I put away a steak as good as any I ever sunk the fangs in. I looked around for the hookers but he did not have any. He had a private room with a can which he will let a regular use but no girls at the bar. He is a smart Dutchman and I guess he has outside backing but maybe he doesn't need it. He gets all the Jews that do not belong to the country club, also the goyim that care for good food and booze. He spent a lot of money making the Mountain View look the way it probably looked 50 or 100 years ago. He pays me a straight $100 a week, with a big raise if the place catches on inside of a year. I am supposed to be the genial host, greet the customers and play request numbers. He is putting in the same size combo for dancing. The prices are too high for the grocery clerks and the high school kids but we get a lot of doctors and lawyers and young business men. We figure to break even up to Friday night and get ahead Saturdays and Sundays. I never see the books, so I do not know how close we come but he is not complaining so far. Have my eye on a foreign car but will tell you about it when I get it.

Another friend to stop worrying about, although in his case I was as taken aback by his recovery as I had been surprised by his misery. There could be no doubting the sincerity of Horse McGrath's unhappiness upon the death of Mrs. Minzer. He had never pretended to any emotional involvement with anyone else. I began to see that I had got into a bad habit for a writer: I was attributing to people a capacity for long-lasting emotions that were impossible for them to sustain. I would happen to catch a man in great sadness, and I would expect him to remain sad a year later. I was right about Isabel: going against conventions, she had evolved a fairly rigid convention of her own, and I was compelled to see how a rigid unconventionality such as Isabel's might be as restrictive as life inside the conventions that she and I had been brought up in, that she had abandoned, that notwithstanding my protests I had not escaped from. My reaction to Horse McGrath's incapability of sustaining grief told me how much of a conformist I really was. It was a humbling if not a humiliating discovery, and it might mean that as a man and as an artist I would have to start all over again, either returning wholeheartedly to the old standards or, like Isabel, creating a new set of my own. Of my own and for myself. Lazily I had told myself that my fear of the Lord had introduced me to wisdom; but what business did an artist have in the acceptance of a wisdom based on fear, and a fear based on an indoctrination in a faith that began to vanish as soon as I was able to question it? Perhaps the only true wisdom was doubt, and I could now begin to acquire wisdom by doubting the instinct for understanding human beings that in my complacency I attributed to wisdom. Two human beings whom I knew as well as I knew anyone had lately shown me how wrong I could be. During this period of panic I wondered whether it would not be safer to be wrong and stick to it than to take the chance of being right and turn out often wrong. But I had a quiet religion of my own that I called art, and one dependable instinct that told me that in art safety had no place. This tenet of my secret religion made me happy, and when it did not make me happy it at least saved my reason. I was not a tragedy until I yielded to despair; Horse McGrath and Isabel were not tragic until I should call them so. And no one was funny until he made me laugh. The funniest man in Pennsylvania at that moment was Peter Stump, who was going to go broke with a scheme to make money.

Of that—Peter Stump's failure in business—I was so sure that I wondered why I cared enough about it to have a conviction. I had scarcely given him a thought since my visit to the Colonial Inn with Isabel, half a dozen years earlier. He had only come back into my thoughts by way of Horse McGrath's letter. And yet he made a vivid reappearance. I could see him (and hear him) in conversation with Horse, Horse in conversation with him. The coal region Irishmen and the Berks County Pennsylvania Dutchmen were natural enemies, but once in a while there would be an exception to this tradition of hostility (my father's three most intimate friends had been Pennsylvania Dutchmen, two of them Masons). I could only guess at the immediate reasons for a friendly relationship between Horse McGrath and Peter Stump—a mutual fondness for food and drink was the obvious one—but when in my mind's eye I saw them together in the Colonial bar, in my mind's ear I could hear them talking about Isabel. She always intruded in these imagined conversations, so much so that pretty soon I very nearly believed that they constituted some sort of threesome. The presence of Isabel in the threesome was, of course, the reason why I had a conviction about Peter Stump's eventual business failure. She could pass in and out of my life even when I was not consciously thinking of her, when I was so sub-conscious of her that I had to analyze an imagined disaster to realize that I was wishing the disaster on a man who had if any only the slightest contact with her. Perhaps what I refused to call love was a sentimental obsession, and it was proper and accurate to refuse to call it love. I loved the idea of love in those days, and I was very strict about admitting unworthy emotions into the category. It did not disturb me that I might be prudish or hypocritical in my standards. I was certainly not going to torture myself with regrets for faults that only I would know about. If I was prudish and hypocritical, and admitted it to myself, I had satisfied the requirements of my religion, my art. I was to mine own self true—and by God, or by Art, to almost no one or nothing else.

It is not to be inferred or imagined that I brooded much about Art or God or Isabel or prudishness or hypocrisy. I was a brooder by nature, but by second nature I was a toper, and the brooding that often sent me to the bottle lasted only long enough for the whiskey to reach my brain, whereupon it took other forms, such as violence or sex or euphoria or the enjoyment of music. The brooding therefore had less damaging effect than it might have had on me otherwise. Whatever shallowness this indicated, it was indicated only to me, and no one else was entitled to an explanation or an apology. I was working conscientiously, and I was having a good time. I gave money to the needy, such as unemployed newspaper men and girls who had to have abortions, and most of it I spent in places where food and drink were served, from Third Street to 133rd Street. I would have been embarrassed to speak to anyone, anyone at all, about my work as art; too many people I knew and had known spoke about their art while having accomplished no work, and the few I knew who had achieved art were even reluctant to speak about their work. Besides, no one had yet invited me to discuss my work in artistic terms. I was glad enough when anyone said I was good, since there were already those who would not go that far.

These reflections on my intellectual processes are set down in this chronicle because I have made myself a character in them. Isabel had married a young business man, who was killed; she had married an older man who was a cripple; she had had half a dozen affairs with other men and at least one girl, and unless I was very much mistaken, she was now about to satisfy her curiosity about Horse McGrath; and her one constant if sporadic lover was I. Of course the probability did not escape me that she retained me as lover because of the sporadic nature of our affair, which gave the relationship the nature of several affairs. We had come from adolescence all the way into our thirties, with time lapses that had had significant effects upon each of us. Whatever it was that made us return to each other regardless of the distractions of others in between, the continuing relationship was unique to her and to me. The physical pleasures we shared were surely stimulated by our separations, but not only by the separations. Always some of the old Isabel was gone and aging had created something new, and for her this must also have been true of me. And yet we had, as it were, a joint personal history, exclusive of all others, which minimized the strangeness whenever we were reunited. I was a character in these chronicles because of my relative importance to Isabel, the heroine.

I do not know the circumstances which advanced her relationship with Horse McGrath. They would not be difficult to supply. The geographical fact that the Mountain View Hotel was only about three miles from Turnersville undoubtedly had something to do with their getting together. Whatever the circumstances, I was at work in my apartment in New York one day; the street doorbell rang, I clicked the lock, and when I opened the door of my foyer, the massive figure of Horse McGrath was standing in the hall. "For Christ's sake," I said.

He was grinning. "Look what I got here for you," he said, and stepped aside to let Isabel come into my line of vision.

"For me?" I said. "A likely story."

"She made me bring her here. I didn't care for the idea," he said.

"Well, *you* say something, Isabel," I said.

"I made him bring me here," she said. She put her arms around my neck and kissed me.

"Cut! *Cut!*" said Horse.

"Go home boy," I said, still holding her about the waist.

"Not before you give me a drink," he said.

"Oh, all right," I said.

At this moment I could not be sure, positively sure, of the extent of their relationship. And now that she was within sight and touch I hoped that he had not got very far. But as soon as I closed the door behind them my hopes vanished. "Isn't he wonderful?" she said.

"No," I said.

Defiantly, defensively, she went to him and leaned against him, rubbing her bosom against his belly. "He is so, wonderful," she said.

"What did you come here for? To borrow my bed?" I said.

"Maybe," she said.

Horse had the good manners to be slightly embarrassed. "No, we had lunch up the street and we decided since we were in the neighborhood we'd pay you a call."

"Well, the booze is over there. Help yourselves. I'm temporarily on the wagon, working."

Horse poured out a couple of Scotches-and-water, very strong. Isabel took off her hat and tossed it on a chair. She was wearing an expensive, unmasculine suit, and feminine pumps. "Have you stopped dressing like a dike, or is this just New York?"

"I knew you'd notice," she said. "I told Preston you would."

"Preston?" I said. "Is that for serious, or are you kidding?"

"I refuse to call him by that nickname. I consider it slightly obscene," she said.

"It is, if your mind happens to be working that way," I said.

"Well, I guess that's the way my mind works—which shouldn't be any news to you. Don't be difficult. Preston knows I've been your girl, but he didn't act up when I suggested coming here. So don't you act up or we'll leave."

"So you finally got together," I said.

"Yes, and stop looking at us as though you were imagining us in bed together," she said.

"That's exactly what I was imagining," I said. "Do you get on top, Isabel?"

"Sometimes," she said. "We'll show you, if that's what you want."

"No thanks," I said.

"You don't really think I would, do you?" she said.

"Yes, I really think you would," I said.

"Well, maybe I would, if you weren't so disagreeable."

"Would you take on the two of us?"

"If Preston didn't mind, I would. Why not?"

"Would you mind, Preston?" I said.

"Sure I would. She's my girl now," said Horse.

"I don't think Preston understands you very well, Isabel," I said.

"He doesn't have to," she said. "Whatever he wants to do, I'll do. Whatever he doesn't want me to do, I won't do. At least on this trip."

"Do you go on many trips together?" I said.

"No, this is our first," she said.

"Well, then you don't want to spoil it," I said.

"Listen, pal, I don't know who you're ribbing. Me, or her. Or the two of us. But I'm not having any fun. If I knew you were going to start needling us I never would have come here. I happen to be stuck on her, you see?" Horse leaned forward, slowly turning the glass in his hand.

"Oh," I said.

"She doesn't have to be stuck on me. I'm stuck on her. I've always been stuck on her. You know that, better than she does."

"Well, I've been kind of stuck on her myself," I said.

"Not the same way I am," said Horse. "You come and go—"

"That's putting it exactly right," I said.

"Lay off. I mean it. I'm jealous of you, pal. And I was never jealous of anyone else before. That's a new sensation for me, and I don't know how to handle it. Frankly, I'm shaking inside." He pointed a finger at me. "You know something? Right now I hate you."

"Well, I don't want to tangle with you, Horse. Before you take the first poke at me, maybe you'd better leave."

"That's what I was thinking," he said. "There wouldn't be much left of you."

I happened at that moment to catch a glimpse of Isabel's expression. She was terrified—not for me, but for herself. She was seeing for the first time the dormant danger of a big, easygoing man. I knew it was what she was thinking, because I was thinking the same thing, and I was terrified. He was half a head taller and a hundred pounds heavier than I.

"Finish your drink," I said. "I have work to do."

"I don't want to finish it," he said. He placed the glass carefully on the table, and as I watched him I tried to figure out my chance of snatching the poker from the fireplace before he could attack. He got to his feet and I moved casually toward the fireplace. "Come on, Isabel. Let's powder out." I was now standing within inches of the poker.

"Maybe she doesn't want to go with you," I said.

"Maybe she doesn't," he said. "Do you?"

"Of course I do," she said.

"See? She does," said Horse. He was so pleased with his triumph that I now knew she was in no danger from him. The bad moment had passed. He put his arm around her shoulder and gave her a quick hug, and they left without again speaking to me. But I knew—and I hoped that Isabel knew—that only a single bad moment had passed. The danger remained, and would never again be quite so dormant.

Every once in a while I would wonder how she was going to get rid of him when the time came to get rid of him, a time that was bound to come. In his present state of mind Horse McGrath was not likely to be amenable to the regulations that Isabel, the wife of Sam Turner, would impose. Isabel, on the other hand, was not likely to be accommodating to Horse's demands if they involved too great a risk to her marriage. By this time I was convinced that her marriage to Sam was institutionalized in her mind. Sam Turner was sixty or close to it, and though I had not seen him in recent years, I imagined him to be a man who approached old age with all its crotchets and no vestiges of youth. In whatever manner he entertained Isabel sexually, I was convinced that she preferred marriage with him to a more abundant sexual life without him. Above all I was convinced that her affair with Horse McGrath was episodic experience, in a category with her experiment or experiments in Lesbianism. But it would not be so easy to banish Horse McGrath. In a few minutes in my apartment I had seen for myself how enormously she had affected him. The easygoing man had turned mean, and she had seen it too.

It was probably two, perhaps three, months after their visit to my apartment that she wrote to me.

Sporadic Love—Can you—and will you—do me a great favor? I *must* talk to you very soon. Even today would not be too soon. I cannot come to N. Y. and do not want you to come to Gibbsville. The farthest away I can go is Reading, which is where I hope you can meet me. Could you possibly meet me at the Berkshire at 12 noon Friday? If so, please make a reservation there & *I* will telephone *them* to see if you have reserved a room. Do not telephone me in any case. Please!!!

The note was unsigned, postmarked Gibbsville and sent special delivery. I, of course, did as she wished. At five minutes past noon the telephone rang in my room at the Berkshire and she told me to meet her at a garage around the corner. She was standing in the office when I got there. "Where are the plans of the fortifications?" I said.

"You were dear to come," she said. "We can sit in my car. I can't even have lunch with you."

Her old station wagon was parked in a gloomy corner of the garage. "The last time we sat in this old heap——" I began.

"The picnic table," she said. "I have only a little time. I'm supposed to be doing the marketing in Gibbsville."

"All right, I won't interrupt," I said.

"It's Mr. McGrath. I had no idea what I was starting there. I don't think he did either. At first it was like nothing I'd ever known but just what I expected. Oh, dear. My wildest dreams come true. I used to *walk* to meet him, a place just off the mountain road. Nobody could see us from the road. The birds chattered, and we could hear the creek gurgling, but no human beings—if you could call us human. Three or four times a week I'd go there, and if he didn't appear I was like a crazy woman. Then he wanted to go away, and we did go to New York that time, and then he wanted me to leave Samuel and marry him. That was where the trouble began. I was not to sleep with Samuel any more. I was not to let Samuel see me naked. And so on. And I made the great mistake of telling him about you and me on the picnic table and one or two other deviations. He called me a degenerate, a pervert, and I said of course I was, which made him even more furious. Oh, Lord, what I got myself in for. He decided that *he* was going to tell Samuel if I wouldn't. And I said that if he did, he would get me killed and himself killed. And then he told me something that I thought no one else knew but me." She stopped. "Obviously I trust you," she went on. "But this is something I have to have your most solemn promise never to repeat. Never even repeat it to me."

"I promise," I said.

"You remember hearing about the explosion at the powder mill, before you were born?"

"Yes."

"It was set off by Samuel Turner. He did it with a rifle. He fired it into a small building where they kept the nitroglycerin, a laboratory. And nine people were killed."

"Why did he do it?" I said.

"It wasn't revenge, it wasn't jealousy, it wasn't any reason except that he had the gun in his hand and he had an uncontrollable impulse."

"And he hated the world," I said.

She nodded. "Yes. He did that instead of killing your father. Deep down he knew he couldn't blame your father for his leg. If he was going to blame your father, first he had to blame himself for getting tight. But that didn't keep him from hating the world. It was revenge, in a way, but not against the people he killed. It was practically impersonal. He's told me over and over again, he had absolutely nothing against any of those people."

"That makes it all right, of course," I said.

"It almost would, except that he lied," she said. "He's been lying to himself and lying to me, all these years. The day before I wrote to you to ask you to come here, Preston McGrath told me that his father knew the true story. The Longs, the family that owned the mill, had a daughter that Samuel Turner tried to rape. They hushed it up as much as they could. No arrests or anything like that. But the upper-class families knew about it, and Samuel Turner was ostracized. Never invited anywhere to anything. Completely and absolutely ostracized."

"So he had two things to be sore about. That, and his leg." I said.

"But he's only ever admitted to his leg," she said. "Mr. McGrath, the elder, knows all the dirt about every family in Lantenengo County, going back fifty years or more. And he remembers how they tried to pin that dreadful thing on Samuel Turner. They got dynamite experts from the mines to investigate, and apparently they could tell that the explosion was set off one way and not another."

"They can, sometimes," I said.

"But proving that it was set off by a bullet from a gun, and then proving that the gun was fired by Samuel Turner—that was something else again. That part of Samuel's career was really kept secret. But it isn't as much of a secret as it was three days ago. I know it now, and you know it, and Preston McGrath knows it."

"That's a lot of people," I said. "What do you want me to do?"

"I want you to tell *me* what to do," she said.

"Oh, boy," I said. "The only thing I can think of is for you and Sam Turner to get the hell out of here till Horse McGrath cools down."

"But how can I persuade Samuel to get the hell out of here without telling him why? I have to admit having an affair with Preston, and I have to admit that he and his father know about the explosion."

"Well, what will Sam do if you tell him you've been having this affair?"

She considered. "At just this time, I think he might kill me, kill Preston, and then kill himself. I say that because of certain—certain —uh—physical and emotional changes he's undergoing."

"You mean sexual," I said.

"Of course I mean sexual, but emotional tied to the sexual."

"You mean he can't get it up."

"I mean *I* can't get it up *for* him," she said. "And he's begun to blame me. Under those conditions the last thing I want to do is tell him I've been screwing a Percheron stallion, which is just about what I've been doing."

"Well, why don't you go away with your stallion?"

"Because I'm afraid of him."

"Then isn't it a question of which you're more afraid of?"

"Not entirely. I'd like to keep the stallion for what I get from him, but in every other way I'm happier with Samuel."

"And yet you know that you can't have both," I said.

"For Christ's sake help me! Don't keep telling me things I already told myself, a hundred times."

"I have to think out loud to help you," I said.

"I wish you were the answer, but you're not," she said.

"Yes, we always get around to that, somehow or other," I said.

"McGrath hates you," she said.

"Yes, I'm sorry about that. I don't like him much any more, either."

"And you shouldn't because you're the only person he really knows among my various lovers, sporadic or otherwise. Consequently, you bear the brunt of all my misdeeds. In fact, it was you that got me off in the wrong direction, according to him."

"Oh? How did I do that?"

"Well, you were the first boy that I did some things with."

"But not the first to deprive you of your virginity."

"No, but he thinks the other things were worse. More immoral. He says you ruined my morals, corrupted me."

"That ain't the way I remember it," I said.

"Me either, but I'm only telling you what he believes. Am I bad? He's been making me sort of half reconsider my moral standards."

"Oh, it's time to get rid of him," I said.

"Yes, but how?" she said.

"If he cared more about money you could buy him off, but he's always been pretty decent about that. There *is* a *way*. At least I think it might work."

"Oh, you lovely man! If we weren't in a public garage I'd show you my appreciation."

"Take your lecherous hand off my fly till I tell you my idea. It probably won't work at all. But it might. And only a well brought up Catholic would figure this one out. Have you ever seen his father?"

"No, what would I be doing in the Court House?"

"His father is a fairly unattractive old guy. Pure white hair, false teeth, wears a wristwatch *and* a watch-chain with a big Knights of Columbus charm. He spits a lot. Takes a lot of time bringing up an oyster and rolls it around in his mouth before letting go of it. He walks all the way to the curbstone with it, I will give him that, but sometimes his aim is bad and the oyster lands on the toe of his shoe. By and large, all in all, I would say that McGrath *père* would have had a very slim chance of making the Porcellian."

"I wish you'd get to the point," she said.

"This *is* the point. I'm telling you what kind of man you are going to have to see."

"I'm going to have to see him?"

"If you go through with my scheme," I said. "Horse doesn't like his father very much, but they are pretty close. There's admiration in the way he speaks of his father. Now my suggestion is that you go up to the Court House and ask to see old McGrath on a private matter. Make sure you emphasize that it's a private matter. You'll get to see him right away. He hasn't got very much to do. Tell him who you are, and watch how he puts on a poker face. Then as if in a burst of confidence tell him that you've fallen in love with Preston and are thinking of divorcing your husband to marry his boy."

"Oh, come *on!*" she said.

"Shut up. You then tell the old bastard that the one thing that worries you is how the McGrath family are going to feel about their pride and joy's marrying a divorced woman. And for good measure you can throw in the remark that you won't mind if Horse remains a Catholic, *although—although—*of course you couldn't possibly turn Catholic yourself."

"How shall I be dressed? In my most demure, housewife costume?"

"God, no!" I said. "The most bull-diking outfit you own. A suit with pants, if you have one. And maybe drop a cigarette on the floor and say, 'Oh, shit!' You're not trying to make this guy like you. You want to form the worst possible impression. He'll be polite, all right. But the minute you leave his office he'll be on the phone to Horse and asking him what the hell's going on with him and that Turner dame. The point isn't so much what kind of an impression you make on the old man. That's of minor importance. The important part of this scheme is the effect it will have on Horse. He'll ask himself what the hell's got into you, going to his father with all that crap about marrying a divorced woman and the Catholic stuff and so on. I know Horse McGrath, I've known him all my life, and he's never had a high opinion of domesticity. The only thing he liked about marriage was the convenience of having it there when you felt horny. Actually, you know, Horse McGrath would much rather play the piano than sit and talk to a woman the way I've often sat and talked with you. All his life girls and women have wanted to find out what he's like in the hay, just like you."

"There he's wonderful," she said. "I thought he might be too big for me, but he wasn't. I was ready."

"Now every other man will be too small for you," I said.

"Goodness, don't say that. Besides, it isn't true. I could be exactly your size in a matter of minutes, if we had the time. But unfortunately we *haven't* the time. I'm supposed to be doing the marketing, thirty-five miles away. So let's get back to this scheme of yours. McGrath *fils* is opposed to domesticity, but he has asked me to marry him. Repeatedly. Insistently. Angrily. Is it your theory that he'll see me as some kind of a shrew, a busybody?"

"You're catching on," I said. "This will give him his first glimpse of you with clothes on, so to speak."

She looked at her wristwatch. "Is this the best scheme you can think of?"

"Yes, and I couldn't think of a better one no matter how long we stayed," I said. "To get rid of Horse McGrath you have to make yourself unattractive, and you won't be able to do that physically. All you can do is make him realize that being married to you would be sheer hell. And by the time his father gets through putting the knock on you, you're not going to seem so glamorous. One other thing, Isabel."

"What?"

"If the scheme works, and Horse begins to lose interest, you have to stop seeing him."

"I was wondering about that," she said. "There will be times, you know . . ."

"Oh, I know," I said.

She looked at her watch again. "I have to go. I can't go very fast in this lovely old thing. And I have to leave you without any satisfaction at all. This'll be the second consecutive time I've seen you and we haven't done anything. If that man washing the car would only look the other way—but I don't think he's going to."

"Never mind," I said. "The next time I see you we'll make up for these last two times."

"Whenever that will be," she said. "Now you have to go. I don't want anyone from Gibbsville to see us together."

"I want to ask you something," I said.

"What?" she said.

"What are you going to do when Sam Turner dies?"

"I haven't been able to face that possibility. I know you think he's wicked. But a *good* man would never have been able to—to be a restraining influence on me. And God knows what I'd be without that. No, I haven't faced that possibility."

"Well, get yourself out of the present jam," I said.

"You care what happens to me, don't you?" she said.

"Very much," I said.

"No one else does, you know," she said. "Not anyone."

She kissed the back of my hand and gave me a gentle shove, and I did not see her or hear from her again for a whole year. True, I went to Hollywood for part of that year, and to France and England for another part of it; but neither by letter nor by telephone did she make any effort to communicate with me, and no one in Gibbsville gave me any information that would serve as a report on the success or failure of my scheme to get rid of Horse McGrath. My ties with Gibbsville were atrophying; my mother moved to New York, and I no longer felt compelled to represent the family at funerals and weddings. Then one day I was having a drink with a publisher friend of mine in the Little Bar of the Ritz-Carlton, and Isabel came in and I heard her ask Charley if Mrs. Trumbull was there. "No, but I'm here," I said, and got up to speak to her. She was startled, and not at all pleased to see me.

"I thought you always went to 21," she said. There was a moment's awkwardness while I leaned forward to kiss her and she kept me away by extending her hand.

"Well, I'll go there right away if it'll make you feel any better," I said, and went back to my table.

"I would say that you got the brush-off," said the publisher. "Who is she? She's a good-looking dame."

"Well, fuck her—and I have," I said.

New York probably has a lot of Trumbulls, but I was not surprised when the Mrs. Trumbull who came to met Isabel turned out to be Bobbie Trumbull, a woman whom I had been observing for years at opening nights and fashionable restaurants, always in the company of women who wore Valentina dresses and of youngish men with drawn faces who stared appraisingly at each other's shirt studs. There was a Mr. Trumbull, who was usually described as a Wall Street banker, but it was always Mrs. Trumbull and not Mr. and Mrs. Trumbull who got her name in the papers as sponsor or co-chairman of ballets and art exhibitions and fund-raisings by ailurophiles. I had once seen her described as dramatically beautiful, which I took to be a photographer's tribute to her use of eye-shadow and her flat chest and long thin neck. She was driven around in a long thin Chrysler town car by a long thin chauffeur. She touched cheeks with Isabel and I heard her order a vermouth cassis and a martini for Isabel. I heard no more, but presently she leaned forward and stared at me, and I stuck my tongue out at her. She kept staring a little longer and then waved her fingers—not her hand, her fingers—at my companion. Then she got up and came to our table.

"Hello, Bobbie," said my companion.

"I wanted to ask your friend—why did you do that to me?"

"Do what?" I said.

"You stuck your tongue out at me," she said. "Why?"

"You must be imagining things," I said.

"You stuck your tongue out at me—and I don't mind telling you, I couldn't *finish* your last book."

"Well, what *was* the last book you finished, Madam?" I said. "Now don't go back too far."

"Oh, balls," she said. "Balls, balls, balls."

"Cock to you, lady," I said. "Go back to your table and stop making a nuisance of yourself, or I'll ask Charley to throw you out. For soliciting."

She went back to her table but did not sit down. She and Isabel left immediately.

"Well, now I see where you get your reputation for real Irish charm," said my companion.

"Oh, you ought to catch me when I'm really turning it on," I said. "That was nothing."

"You can say that again," he said.

"All right, if you want me to, but it'll get monotonous," I said. "Who does that scrawny dike think she is?"

"She's got your girl, that's all I know," he said.

"Yes, I guess so," I said.

"Who is the girl? Is she from Gibbstown?"

"Gibbs*ville,* you stupid son of a bitch," I said. "You'd get it straight if I'd let you publish me."

"That's why I like to have lunch with you, because I don't publish you. No complaining about royalties and advertising. Who is your friend?"

"The most amoral woman I know," I said. The words were out before I knew what I was saying.

"She's in good company now," he said. "I could tell you a few things about Bobbie Trumbull that would curl your hair. I've known her since we were kids together. Always used to want to wrestle. 'I can put you down,' she'd say. She never could, but it gave her a good chance to grab hold of your pecker. It was boys then. The girls came later. That chump she's married to, Trumbull, I've never been able to figure him. But anybody that'd stay married to her as long as he has must have some angle."

"Maybe he just likes to watch," I said.

"It must be something like that. You never hear of him getting involved, but she has her girl friends stay at their house for weeks at a time, and if he doesn't know what's going on he ought to be put away somewhere. Anyone as smart as he is about money *must* know *something* about people."

"Well, I don't know anything about money, but I pride myself in knowing a lot about people," I said.

"Sure. But you were surprised by that brush-off from your friend."

"You're damn right I was. By the brush-off. But nothing really surprises me about Isabel. Not any more. I've known her most of my life, too. She's the only woman I ever knew that has just what she has, whatever it is, for me. Part of the time she doesn't exist, I never think of her. But she gets away with things that if it were any other woman, I'd say the hell with her. Today would be a good day to say the hell with her, but that's not going to happen."

"I can see that, all right," he said. "But I'll tell you this much, my friend. Bobbie took a girl away from me one time, six or seven years ago, and I never got her back. It's a kind of seduction, or corruption, that you or I don't know anything about. The seduction I can understand. A woman has had it with a man, so she decides to try it with another woman. Kicks. But when Bobbie gets through with a woman she's corrupted her, psychologically. There's a theory I remember about a mare that's been bred to a jack mule. The mare is never any good again for a horse. I don't know how much truth there is in that, but I've seen it happen when Bobbie goes to work on a woman. My girl broke it off with me, divorced her husband, and became a card-carrying Lez. She admits it. Men are ugly. Men are ill-formed. Selfish. Cruel. Weak. Women of the world, unite! That kind of stuff."

"I don't think it'll work with my girl," I said. "She doesn't think men are ill-formed."

"Maybe not. But Bobbie will give a guy a great piece of tail just to get at his wife. She's done that more than once. As I say, she and I grew up together and in that respect we're old friends. But I consider her the most evil woman in New York. Even the fairies don't like her. They're afraid of her. You know you see these fairies around New York, all banded together, and you forget that they didn't start out as a group. They got together usually when they were in their twenties, but before that they were sons and brothers and so on, and in spite of their homosexuality they usually had a sister or a mother that they are or were very fond of. And they try to protect them from women like Bobbie. One of my authors is a fairy, and he had a sister that Bobbie went to work on with the result that the sister broke her engagement to a nice, proper young man, and she's now a drunken mess. This guy cries when he talks about her. He hates Bobbie Trumbull—like the devil hates holy water, to use one of your Irish similes."

"As long as there's anyone around with a good stiff prick, Isabel is safe," I said.

"Let's hope so," he said. "I'm a very tolerant man, but I'm against the Lesboes' taking over. And they're getting stronger all the time. Is that our fault, do you suppose?"

"It probably is, to some extent," I said. "But maybe not in Seattle."

"Why Seattle?"

"Oh, I always think of Seattle as a nice American city where men are men and women are women, all riding to work in Chris-Crafts and free of complications. I've never been there, and I think I'll stay away and keep my illusions."

"My Seattle is Detroit. I've never met a Lesbo in Detroit. It's really a man's town. But so is London, and there are plenty of them there, God knows."

"I wonder how it is in Boys' Town, Nebraska," I said.

"Well, I never saw the movie, so I don't know," he said.

We finished our lunch without my yielding to the wish to ask my companion for Bobbie Trumbull's telephone number. I wanted to see Isabel so that I could inflict some punishment on her. But I did not see her, and after an indeterminable length of time the abscess produced by our encounter went away without breaking. It is a handy metaphor and true: the irritation went away, but only with a gradual lessening of its effects on my nervous system, and while it was still bothering me, suppurating inside me, something was happening to my feelings for Isabel. One day, months after the encounter, I discovered that I could think of her, respond to the name Isabel in print, with no desire to see her, talk to her, touch her. For fifteen years whenever I saw the name Isabel in type it meant her alone. Many times I would be about to pass quickly over the women's pages or the theatrical or obituary pages of the newspaper, and on an impulse I would go on reading until I saw the name Isabel. It would be Isabel Somebody, a debutante; or Isabel Somebody, an actress; or Isabel Somebody, who had died; and it did not matter except that the name Isabel, buried in a paragraph that I had not intended to read, had had an irresistible pull. Similarly I had always had the same impulse when my own name was in print. Once, for instance, I had turned the pages of a newspaper to the real estate news, which I never read, and come upon a brief account of the demolition of a seedy hotel where I had had a room. My name was mentioned as a former resident. Thousands of times I had read that newspaper without ever turning to the real estate news, and the one day I turned to it, my name was there. This phenomenon, too esoteric to comprehend, was even more remarkable in the case of the name Isabel, without her true last name, but I had never satisfactorily explained to myself the real nature of my feelings for her either. "Loving without love" was no more satisfactory than "love without loving." But now that all feeling seemed to have vanished I seemed to be having an easier time with finding a reason for its disappearance. In the simplest terms, I had lost out to a Lesbian; in somewhat less simple terms, I had lost out to Lesbianism. In rather more complicated terms, the Lesbian thing had happened to Isabel so thoroughly and completely that it had created a protective resistance to me and what I stood for, as demonstrated by her hostility on our last encounter, and her attitude was my warning to stay away. And so I did, at no cost to my pride or my way of life.

Or so I believed.

Then one day about two years after our small scene in the Little Bar of the Ritz-Carlton, I went there again. It was not unusual for me to go there; I had continued to be a fairly regular patron regard-

less of the unpleasantness caused by Isabel and Bobbie Trumbull. I
hoped that if the associative memory would make anyone stay away
from the Little Bar it would be Bobbie Trumbull and she did. I had
seen her from a cool distance at the theater and a few parties in the
interval, but we had not spoken or even nodded to each other, even
when it was practically unavoidable. On the day of which I speak I
was sitting with a fellow named Charley Ellis, a Wall Street friend of
mine, who saw me and whom I saw because we liked to see how the
other half lived. The other Charley, the bartender, said to me, "Say,
somebody phoned and asked if you were here or were you expected.
I told them you usually came in around twelve-thirty, days you were
coming. No message. No name."

"It was probably Louis B. Mayer," I said.

"She didn't sound like Louis B. Mayer," said the bartender.

"Could have been Sam Goldwyn. He has a high-pitched voice," I
said.

"I'd know the difference," said the bartender.

"Well, I'm sure it was somebody that wanted to enrich my life," I
said. "People are always trying to make me happy, improve my lot."

"I can't imagine why," said Ellis.

"That's the side of people you don't know about," I said.

Ellis ordered a double martini, and I ordered a Scotch-on-the-
rocks, and we chatted. The Little Bar was a small room that probably had once been an unprofitable storage space. It had a service bar
against the north wall, banquettes against the east and south walls,
and at the south end of the room was a sort of niche, separated from
the rest of the room by partitions. You could see through the partitions, which were fashioned of thin wooden poles, and I never understood why, in such a small room, they bothered to have the
niche, but it was there, and did not seclude its occupants from the
rest of the room. Ellis and I were sitting at a table in the niche, and I
saw a lone woman appear at the entrance to the room. The bartender, who was also the only waiter, spoke to her. It was contrary
to policy to allow unaccompanied women to drink there, and I
could guess that the bartender was keeping her out. But then he

nodded and looked in my direction, and for the first time I recognized Isabel. She came straight to my table.

Now there was none of the girl left; she was all mature woman; her suit looked as if it had been made by one of the Wetherills, I could not even describe her Windsor tie and Eton collar as feminine, since they were what I had had to wear as a ten-year-old in dancing school. She was hatless, and her hair was cut short over the ears. She now had the head and face of an effeminate boy, and in the few steps she took to reach us I could see that she had developed a slight roll in her gait. "Hullo," she said, not hello. "Do you mind if I crash?"

"Not a bit. This is Mr. Ellis, Mrs. Turner."

"I think I met Mrs. Turner a long time ago," said Ellis.

"Oh? Where was that?" said Isabel.

"I think you were at Wellesley when I was at Harvard," he said.

"How nice of you to remember," she said. "You sure it was me?"

"Pretty darn sure," said Ellis. "Wasn't your name Isabel—Isabel—Barley?"

"Yes it was," she said. "I must apologize for my bad memory."

"Well, it was a long time ago," said Ellis.

She turned to me. "How are you? I called up to see if you were by any chance going to be here."

"I'm fine, thanks. What'll you have to drink?"

"Vermouth cassis, please," she said.

I gave the order, and Ellis got up. "I'll run along. You two will have things to talk about."

"What about lunch?" I said.

"Some other time," said Ellis. "Goodbye, Mrs. Turner." For Ellis this was extraordinarily bad manners.

"He's pissed off because I wouldn't play," she said. "He practically told you that I slept with him."

"Did you?"

"Once," she said. "And I wasn't going to have him leer at me through lunch."

"He doesn't leer. He's quite a nice guy, and I did have a lunch date with him."

"Well, would you rather eat alone?"

"No."

"You probably would, but you have a lot of curiosity," she said.

"That's putting it correctly," I said. "As Ellis said, we have a lot to talk about, but are we going to talk about it?"

"I'll bring you up to date on me, as much as I have to. I'm in a bit of a jam, and the last time I got advice from you it was golden. You're very smart about some things. You got rid of McGrath for me, or I did by following your advice."

"How is your charming and attractive husband?" I said.

"Not very well. Not well at all, in fact. He fell down the stairs and broke his hip."

"Why? Couldn't he wait for the elevator?" I said.

"Something like that," she said. "He's in the Gibbsville Hospital now, convalescing from an operation, but it's going to be a long siege. They did that pin operation, you know? It wasn't too successful. Obviously you haven't been keeping up with the home-town news."

"No, I haven't," I said.

"Then you haven't heard about me," she said. "Or have you?"

"Not a damn thing about you or from you. What have you gone and done now?"

"You haven't heard from McGrath?" she said.

"No."

"I don't know why I ordered this damned thing when I wanted a martini. Get me a double martini, will you please?"

I reordered for her, and she puttered with cigarettes while the drink was on its way. "Did you lose your lighter?" she said.

"No, I still have it somewhere," I said.

She drank half the martini in one gulp. "McGrath tried to blackmail me."

"You know, I don't believe that," I said.

"There are other forms of blackmail besides money, if that's what you mean. He'd get inebriated and want to sleep with me, and I fi-

nally had to go away for a while. It was while I was away that Samuel broke his hip. But at least while I was gone McGrath began to
make some sense, and when I went back to Turnersville he left town.
Someone said he was playing the piano in a low dive in Atlantic
City. He lost his job at the Mountain View."

"With some help from you?"

"Possibly a little," she said. "Stump always liked me, and he put
two and two together."

"With some help from you?"

"Yes," she said. "But the place wasn't doing very well with
McGrath anyway."

"And somewhere along the line you became friends with Mrs.
Trumbull," I said.

"There's no doubt about it. The two facts are related," she said.
"After my experience with McGrath I was really fed up with men,
and seeing poor Samuel on his bed of pain—I don't know. It seemed
to me that men were either selfish or fragile, or both. Bobbie Trumbull was really a life-saver to me."

"What flavor?" I said.

"What? Oh. One of your feeble witticisms. Yes, I'm a Lesbian.
I'm convinced now that I always was. Looking back to boarding-
school and college, I'm convinced that the necking and the other
things I did with boys were only because I didn't want to give in to
the other. I was really more genuinely attracted to girls, and they to
me."

"Isn't it funny, I don't remember it that way at all," I said.

"Why should you, when I didn't even know it myself? But it was a
tremendously helpful experience to be able to talk to Bobbie. She
knew me better than I ever knew myself. The first time she saw me I
was trying on some dresses here in New York and she told me that
she'd studied me for the better part of an hour before she finally
came up and introduced herself, with that strange Oriental beauty
of hers. She said she had her car outside and could she give me a lift?
I could have walked, from Saks to the Barclay, but I said I was going

to see what they had at Bergdorf's. Instead of that I accepted her invitation to go to her house and have tea with her, and she made me feel I was doing her a great favor by staying for dinner."

"Which you were," I said.

"Oh, you're wrong. There was nothing then," she said. "She showed me her house, her pictures, and of course it always turns out that we had friends in common. One in particular."

"Let me guess. Was it the girl that had the big house up the Hudson?"

"Yes, as a matter of fact, it was," she said.

"And where was Mr. Trumbull during this house tour?"

"In London, I think. London or Paris," she said.

"When did the seduction take place?" I said.

"Well, I stayed there that night, and the next day I had my things sent up from the hotel. I stayed two more days. She gave me a whirl. I think I must have met every celebrity in New York."

"Did you meet Babe Ruth?" I said.

"*Not* people like *that,*" she said.

"I'd stake my life on it," I said. "And then you went back to Turnersville, a new woman, so to speak."

"A new woman is right," she said. "I didn't expect you to be quite so corny. Babe Ruth, for heaven's sake. I didn't expect you to give me your sanctimonious approval, but I thought you might be more sophisticated. Babe Ruth! You really dislike me now, don't you?"

"What makes you say that?" I said.

She put her hand on her chest. "There's nothing in here, for you or for me. There used to be, but it's gone."

"Yes, I guess it has," I said.

"I could still give you a very pleasant afternoon, and I suppose I'd enjoy it too, with you. You were always—I never put you in the same category with the others. You and I learned together, pretty much, and if I'd been brighter I might have realized that if I couldn't love you, I couldn't love anybody. And if you'd been brighter you might have guessed what I really was. You had some instinct about it. I remember you used to try me out, to find out whether I was willing to have a *parti à trois*. A *parti à trois* with the third person, another girl, not another man. So you at least had *some* instinctive understanding of the real me."

"I can't take bows for that, Isabel," I said. "I just wanted to get you in bed with another girl. That was what I call my orgy period."

"That's why I expected you to be more sophisticated about me now. Can I have another martini?"

"Certainly. Are we going to eat lunch, or drink it?"

"Either way. I need the second mart to tell you about my troubles," she said.

She had another drink and we ordered some food, to be served in the grill. We said nothing of moment until the captain came in from the grill to tell us our luncheon was served. "This place has great style," she said, as we were seated.

"All it needs is a piano, violin, and cello," I said.

I had ordered whitebait and oyster crabs and a small bottle of wine. I was not much of a wine man, but I wanted to divert Isabel from a third double martini. "They look like something by Salvador Dali, those eyes," she said.

"Spread the sauce over them and dig in," I said.

She obeyed; ate a couple of forkfuls, had a sip of the wine, and held on to the stem of her glass. "Do you remember some people at home named Luder?"

"Harvey Luder? Yes. He works for your father, doesn't he?"

"He's vice-president of Daddy's company," she said. "He's come up in the world since you've been away. Daddy has a lot of confidence in him and he'd probably be the next president of the company if it weren't for *her*. Harvey's wife, Lillian. I don't see what difference it makes, what the wife of a coal company president is like, but apparently it does. Daddy is in other things, too, and he'd like to turn over some of his work to Harvey. But the thing that makes him hesitate is Lillian. Nobody can stand her. She's noisy, common, flirtatious, and a bad drinker. In a way, she's the secret of Harvey's success, so far. She's so awful that he spends all his time at the office, to get away from her."

"I remember her. She is pretty awful," I said.

"The worst," said Isabel. "Well, they have a daughter Elissa, an adorable child, just turned sixteen. She's in high school. She should be in boarding-school, but she has two older brothers at college and they can't send her away till one of the boys graduates. Finances. Harvey never had any money till a few years ago, and he's gone into debt to buy stock in Daddy's company. In addition to what Daddy has given him in the form of bonuses. I have to tell you all this to give you the background."

"Take your time," I said. I went on eating while listening to her, not looking at her but watching her fingers revolving the stem of her glass.

"From here on it gets harder to tell you, you've been so un-friendly," she said.

"Are you sure you want to tell me? This might be just the place to stop," I said.

"I don't *want* to tell anybody, but you're still the only person I can go to."

"Go ahead, then," I said.

"The daughter, Elissa Luder, got a crush on me about a year or so ago, and began writing me letters. At first they were unsigned, but then she wrote me a long one, identifying herself and admitting that she had written the other letters. I've never been to the Luders' house and I'd never had any conversation with the child. It was all from a distance. But she wanted to come and see me, and she called up on the telephone and asked if she could come down on her bike the next Saturday afternoon, and I said yes. That's a pretty long ride on a bike, and practically all uphill on the way home. The first day she came, I insisted on putting her and her bike in my car and driving her home. She was a fascinating child, but I really had no inten-tion of letting her come again. But when I dropped her at her house she pleaded with me to let her come again the next Saturday, and I gave in. That was my big mistake. The next week she arrived on her bike and we went for a walk in the woods and she put her arms around me and kissed me. It was what I was trying to avoid. Actu-

ally she began necking me, like a boy, and as I was already excited
by her, we made love to each other. Oh, dear. She telephoned me
every day, and every Saturday she came to my house. We were
madly in love."

"And where was Mr. Turner during this idyll?"

"Oh, I'm coming to that. He was surprisingly innocent about it,
amused by my having a fifteen-year-old admirer who came to see me
once a week. He thought nothing of it, really, and he left us alone.
But one afternoon she came to the house and it started to rain, so we
couldn't go for our walk. Samuel was in his study and we went upstairs and got undressed and were in bed together when he appeared."

"What did he actually see?" I said.

"The two of us bare naked with our arms around each other. We
hadn't been there very long. 'That's a pretty sight,' he said, and sat
on the edge of the bed and began making passes at Elissa. She was
terrified, but she didn't stop him. And I didn't want to stop him,
because I knew if I did he'd go out of his mind. I'm not going to tell
you the whole thing, but I got him to screw me with her lying there.
Once he'd had his orgasm she was safe. He goes right to sleep, and
he did then. I expected the child to be terrified or jealous or something, but instead of that she took pity on me. This was what I had
to put up with and so on. Poor dear Isabel. She had never seen intercourse, and had never had it herself.

"Well, for the first time he knew that about me, that I was having
an affair with a fifteen-year-old girl. Did he disapprove? Far from it.
From then on he wouldn't go to bed with me unless Elissa was there,
and when I explained that to her, she was acquiescent. In fact, she
rather got to like it, because it seemed to give her a stronger hold
over me."

"How?"

"Don't you see? My husband wouldn't have intercourse with me
unless she was there, but if he didn't have intercourse he made life
miserable for me."

"Ah, yes, I do see," I said.

"What it amounted to was that I was dependent on her," she said. "She wasn't jealous of Samuel, and she needn't have been. Because I was mad about her and she knew it. And then when he broke his hip she knew that I was happy because I didn't have to make love to anyone but her. And she to me."

"Then the roof fell in," I said.

"Yes."

"How?" I said.

"Her mother had begun to get suspicious a while back, and finally took to listening in on our telephone calls. Elissa spoke to me in very endearing terms sometimes. How she could hardly wait for Saturday and we could be in each other's arms. And so on. And last Friday she browbeat Elissa and forced the whole thing out of her. Including the business about Samuel. The incredible thing is that she went to the Gibbsville Hospital and in his weakened condition made him admit his participation. Then, of course, she came to see me, and you'll never guess what she wanted."

"Your father's business," I said.

"Just about. First I was to give her the money to send Elissa to boarding-school. I was never to see Elissa again. Then I was to transfer my stock in my father's company to her husband. Then I was to go to Harvey Luder and tell him the whole story. Next I was to give a large party for her and Harvey, to show Gibbsville and my father that the Luders had my full support. And finally, I was to sign a paper, the like of which you can't imagine. A confession that I had seduced and corrupted her daughter. Well, there was no use denying anything. The small point that Elissa made the first pass at me wasn't worth arguing about, in view of the fact that I probably would have made advances before we got back from our first walk in the woods. As to the money for boarding-school, I was willing to do that. I know just what's going to happen. The child will go away to school and be sent home in six months, and have a hard time getting into another school. She'll never be anything but what she is. A confirmed Lesbian. And I didn't do that. I helped, but she hasn't the slightest interest in boys and never will have. Anyway, I told Lillian

to come back and see me on Saturday. She warned me that if I tried
to pull a fast one on her, she'd go straight to a lawyer and there'd be
the biggest stink Gibbsville's had in a hundred years. This was Lillian's big chance, you know, and she's not going to let it pass. I said
I didn't think it would be very good for Harvey's reputation in
Gibbsville or the coal business. But she said she wasn't worried
about that. I'd have too much sense to let it get that far. And as of
the moment, she's right."

"Then what do you want my advice for?" I said.

"Well—everything," she said.

"My advice to you is to get a damn good lawyer. Go see Arthur
McHenry."

"I can't. He's my father's lawyer."

"Once you start shelling out to Lillian Luder, it'll be the old
story," I said. "That's the easiest kind of easy money. On the other
hand, what else is there for you to do? On still another hand, suppose you give her everything she asks—what's to keep her from getting drunk some night and spilling the whole can of beans? There's
only one thing I can think of, and curiously enough, the idea came
from Lillian herself."

"What did I miss?" she said.

"She wants you to go to Harvey Luder and tell him the whole
story. Okay. Do that. Tell him the whole God damn thing and let
him handle Lillian. I think that's your only out. Harvey is a decent
man. He's so decent that I feel sorry for him, with that wife and kid
and you, all three of you screwing up his life. But the penalty for
being a decent man is that people like you do screw up his life."

"I sometimes think of you as a decent man," she said.

"Don't make that mistake," I said. "I'm giving you this advice
because in the long run it'll be better for Harvey and for your father,
another decent man although a bit of a horse's ass."

"I guess my father is a horse's ass," she said. "But I guess he's
decent too."

"And suppose you get out of this one, Isabel. What do you plan
next?"

"Well, I'll try to keep out of trouble, naturally. Samuel will be in the hospital for at least another six weeks, and when he gets home I'll have to take care of him. That'll keep me busy. But you surely don't expect me to say I'm going to change my ways."

"No," I said. "Will you have some dessert?"

. . . That was thirty years ago. I went to see her last month in Turnersville, not having seen her in the intervening years. "My good old friend," she said. "How nice to see you again." She had put on five or maybe ten pounds and had done something to her hair that made it iron grey. There were a great many lines in her cheeks, which could have been but were not disguised by makeup, and on her upper lip a row of tiny perpendicular lines that could have been hidden by lipstick but were not. She was wearing a grey flannel skirt and a blue cashmere slip-on, with a paisley scarf that she knotted on the side of her neck. She patted my belly. "That's not good, you know. You ought to do something about that," she said. "Well, have a seat. I was thinking just before you came, the first time I was ever inside this house, you brought me."

"I well remember," I said. "I remember being shot at from this house."

"Oh, my," she said. "You and a boy named McGraw."

"McGrath, but that's close enough."

"Oh, I remember him, but I didn't remember his name. You're going to have tea in a few minutes, but would you like a drink first?"

"No, I quit, over ten years ago," I said.

"So did I! Are you AA?" she said.

"No, I just don't drink any more."

"I'll have a sherry, if I have a guest that won't drink alone. But that doesn't use up much sherry—I have so few guests. Well, now tell me all about yourself."

"Well, I was born in 1905—"

"Oh, you haven't lost your sense of humor. Some of it you used to waste in sarcasm, but most of the time it was delightful." She paused. "My sporadic lover. I've been trying to think of the exact phrase you used to use. Sporadic. And we certainly were that. But it's nice to know that we, us, took those trips together into the world of passion. That's what they were—little trips together. Even if we didn't stay very long, they were nice trips. At least I remember them that way, and I hope you do. You have no regrets, have you?"

"Not a bit," I said.

"Nor I," she said. "I can see seventy just around the corner. I'm that much closer to it than you are. And I've lived a very full life. Very little I've missed. The same is true of you, isn't it? With the difference that you're still living it up, as they say nowadays, with your books and your travels and your family life and so on. Whereas I'm quite content to live the way I do, here in this old house, taking my walks when the weather permits, reading everything I can lay my hands on, and amusing myself with my perfectly dreadful imitations of Emily Dickinson."

"You're writing poetry?" I said.

"Incessantly!" she said. "I've never sent anything away to be published. One or two I think might have had a chance as, uh, you know, those little fillers you see in the magazines. But I never wanted to play favorites with my poems. The others that were left behind—I'd feel differently toward them, as if they were my retarded children."

"Isabel, you amaze me," I said. "But then you always have."

"Because I write poetry? But why? I think poetry, I feel it, so why not write it? You've been in one or two of my poems, because I felt poetry with you, long ago. You'd never recognize yourself, but you're there. Well, here's tea! Elissa, you're so very prompt. I don't think you two have ever actually met. Jim, this is Elissa Luder. I know you knew her father and mother."

"How do you do," she said. She put the tea things down and shook hands with me, then sat in a chair between Isabel's and mine. She was, by my quick calculation, in her late forties; very slender, dressed in frontier pants and an army officer's shirt with shoulder straps, but she also wore a brightly beaded Indian belt and a crowded gold charm bracelet and a scarf that matched Isabel's. She had the appearance of a woman who was used to being liked and wanted to be liked some more, and I liked her. I liked her very much. She had very blonde hair, too blonde to be natural, cut almost in a page-boy bob but not quite so long. As I took in the fit of her shirt over her bosom and the pants over her hips I caught Isabel watching me, knowing that I was approving, and proud of her possession. And Elissa was her possession; there was no doubt about that. "Isn't she pretty, my Elissa?" said Isabel. She reached over and touched Elissa on the knee.

"*I* think so," I said.

The girl, the woman, smiled at Isabel but not at me. I had a quick suspicion that she had been so prompt with the tea so that I would not stay long, but I was not offended. This was what the Lesbians themselves called a marriage, and it was love. Isabel poured the tea, Elissa handed me my cup and served the sandwiches, and the conversation degenerated into their questions and my answers about movie and television personalities. It was fascinating how they, so far removed from the world and its gossip, happened so often to ask me about homosexuals, some of whom were so covert that only the well informed in show business knew about their sex life. They chose one in particular, a durable and popular comedienne, about whom there never had been any scandal of any kind. "What's she like?" said Elissa.

I was tempted to say, "She's just like you two. She has a friend," but though I could have said it to Isabel if we had been alone, I could not say it with Elissa there. "She's lovely," I said. "And she's a very good musician. Piano. Still takes lessons from somebody very good."

Then it was time to go and Isabel walked down to my car with me, down the porch steps and as far as the gate. She was silent on the way down, until we reached the gate. "It has worked out very well, Jim," she said.

"Be glad about it, don't be solemn," I said.

"I am solemn. I thought I'd get through today without telling you, but you were so nice to come, having despised me all these years."

"I got over that," I said.

"I'm glad you did," she said. She rested the palms of her hands on the sharp paling of the fence. "The thing I have to tell you, that I can't tell her—I had a biopsy. And I'm riddled with it. Oh, Jim. What's going to happen to her? She's been with me, in this house, over twenty years. I know what I could do about myself, but that would be even worse. She'd think she had let me down in some way or other, and blame herself. So I'm going to the hospital, and let them pretend there's something they can do, when I know there isn't. And when I die she'll be able to say it was better for me to die than to go on in pain. But what happens to someone like her? I almost wish you were free, and younger. I saw you looking at her. Maybe you could have taken care of her and she of you. But you can't, and no one can. She gave up absolutely everything to come with me."

"Well, how much time have any of us got left, Isabel? If loneliness or pain becomes unbearable, whose business is it if we shorten the time?"

"She may do that," she said. "She's said she would, if anything ever happened to me. If anything ever happened to me! Everything has happened to me." She reached in my breast pocket and took out my handkerchief, and blew her nose, dabbed her eyes, and put the handkerchief in her skirt pocket. "I owe you a handkerchief, as I owe you so much else. Just three or four tears, Jim, and I can go back now." She took my hand in a tight, strong grasp and kissed me. "If she's watching, it won't do her any harm to see me kiss you. You and I had a few trips and some poetry together."

"Yes," I said.

"I'm not going to ask you to come again," she said. "In fact, I'm going to ask you not to come again. I've arranged to be cremated.

Ghastly, isn't it, such talk? When you think of me, think of me on a picnic table."

"All right," I said. "I often do."

"That was the day you made up 'sporadic lover,' " she said.

"It was indeed," I said.

"Goodbye, Jim," she said.

"Goodbye, Isabel," I said.

A NOTE ON THE TYPE

The principal text of this Modern Library edition
was set in a digitized version of Times Roman,
a typeface that dates from about 1690 and was cut by Nicholas Kis,
a Hungarian working in Amsterdam. The original matrices have
survived and are held by the Stempel foundry in Germany.
Hermann Zapf redesigned some of the weights and sizes for Stempel,
basing his revisions on the original design.